Margaret Yorke lives in ⟨...⟩ ⟨...⟩air-
man of the Crime Writ⟨...⟩ ⟨...⟩ing
contribution to the genre ⟨...⟩ the
1999 CWA Cartier Diam⟨...⟩

GUILTY SECRETS

A Margaret Yorke Trilogy

No Medals for the Major

Serious Intent

A Question of Belief

timewarner
paperbacks

A *Time Warner* Paperback

First published in this omnibus edition by Time Warner Paperbacks in 2004

Guilty Secrets: A Margaret Yorke Omnibus copyright © Margaret Yorke 2004
No Medals for the Major copyright © Margaret Yorke 1974
Serious Intent copyright © Margaret Yorke 1995
A Question of Belief copyright © Margaret Yorke 1996

A CIP catalogue record for this book is available
from the British Library

ISBN 0 7515 3553 2

Printed and bound in Great Britain by
Mackays of Chatham Ltd, Chatham, Kent

Time Warner Paperbacks
An imprint of
Time Warner Books UK
Brettenham House
Lancaster Place
London WC2E 7EN

www.TimeWarnerBooks.co.uk

No Medals for the Major

PART ONE

I

MAJOR JOHNSON closed the front door of his bungalow and tested the lock. He paused on the porch and surveyed with pride the small, shaven front lawn with its fringe of antirrhinums. Over his head hung a wooden sign bearing the single word *Tobruk* carved in poker-work; a faint smell of varnish came from it, for the major had just given it a fresh coat.

The day was warm and humid, and the sun shone down on the major as he strode forth into the village street. He stepped out with a light tread, for he was going to Fleckington, and his mind dwelt fondly on the charms of Miss Mainwaring, the town's librarian, whom he planned to invite to lunch with him at The Feathers.

Though today feeling young in heart, Major Johnson was in fact fifty-eight years old, a short man, stockily built, with wisps of grey hair around a bald dome and a neatly trimmed moustache. At the close of his military career he had come to live in Wiveldown, where property was cheaper than in areas nearer cities or the coast. He had bought the bungalow with his gratuity and his savings, and had spent happy months doing it up, profiting from all he had learned about home maintenance on his army resettlement course.

He had met Miss Mainwaring when, ignorant of what to plant in the garden round his new home, he had gone in search of helpful books; she had led him past horticulture to other pleasures, and a book about Java and the memoirs of a general were due to be returned today. Not much of a reader until he retired, he now made constant forays into new worlds, and the

7

chief delight of this fresh interest was discussing what he had read with Miss Mainwaring afterwards.

'Not got your car today, then, Major Johnson?' asked a woman as he boarded the bus behind her.

It was Deirdre Flint, one of the sisters who ran the post office, taking time off to go to market, for Thursday was market day in Fleckington.

'It's having a new gear-box fitted. I'm fetching it this morning,' Major Johnson said. He found Mrs Flint, with her jet-black hair and aggressive bosom, alarming in the post office, but out here among other travellers she did not seem so formidable. 'Lovely morning, isn't it?' he added.

'It'll rain by night-time, mark my words,' said Mrs Flint.

'My runner beans need rain,' said Major Johnson. He waited for Mrs Flint to stow herself and her baskets in one seat, and took another across the gangway so that they might converse without physical proximity.

'Farmers don't,' said someone sitting in front of Mrs Flint, who now leaned forward to talk to this other acquaintance.

Major Johnson sat back, relieved to be spared a dialogue with Mrs Flint throughout the journey, but pleased with their small interchange; he was beginning to mingle.

Seated high in the bus, the outlook was different from when he drove to town in his dark green Morris 1300. He had a good view of the village as they passed the last cottages and a gaunt Victorian villa, *The Hollies*, set back at the end of a long drive, behind a wilderness of shrubs. Then there were fields for some miles before they reached the outskirts of Fleckington.

It had begun in the library, but Major Johnson's friendship with Miss Mainwaring was not confined to the realm of books, for they had met at cookery classes all last winter. When he saw a notice about them in the library, he had consulted her about his suitability as a pupil. A bachelor, he had lived in barracks as a young man, and after he was commissioned in the mess, so that beyond simple fry-ups and opening tins, he was no great cook. Miss Mainwaring had reassured him. She would be at the classes too and would shepherd him along. Thus encouraged, he enrolled, and was not the only man to do so; the class included a widowed schoolmaster, a man whose wife was in a wheelchair, and an enthusiastic schoolboy.

The tutor, Mrs Fellowes, a large woman with a commanding manner, placed Major Johnson and Miss Mainwaring at adjoining tables, and so their acquaintance grew from week to week until summer came and the course ended.

With the bungalow painted, the garden tamed, and some finer elements of cooking mastered, Major Johnson had time on his hands and realised that he was lonely. So, slowly, he made his decision: there was still time to marry. Older people did it every day.

It was to Miss Mainwaring, of course, that he planned, after a careful campaign, to offer his hand. She seemed kind; and though not pretty, she had a pleasant face; her curly brown hair was only lightly flecked with grey, and above all, she was small. Beside her, Major Johnson forgot that so was he. Now that youth was past, she would not look for ardour in a suitor, and he would proceed slowly, in order not to alarm her. Companionship was what he sought, no more; most of the time he successfully banished thoughts of wrapping his arms around Miss Mainwaring's neat form.

Once, as a young man, he had been in love, but the girl had married another man, and though he had always hoped to find someone else, it had not happened. He had moved about the world so much that there never seemed to be time, and then, somehow, the years ran out. The other officers in the mess grew younger and younger; they called him Uncle Fred and invented a giddy past for him. When he heard about their conquests he knew he could not compete. He sank gradually into his bachelor role, useful at dinner parties and even sometimes baby-sitting. Now all that was gone, and he was adrift in an unfamiliar society.

At first, after he retired, he planned to get some sort of job, but the only suitable one he could find was that of time-keeper in a paint factory in Fleckington. After he had straightened up the bungalow he worked there for some months, but he made no

9

real friends. He decided to leave and seek something with more human contact; then came the cookery lessons, and this summer he had spent five afternoons a week selling admission tickets at Chorlbury Manor, a local stately home. Miss Mainwaring had found him this job, for Admiral Bruce, the curator of the Manor, had asked her if she knew of anyone, so she was, in a sense, already his guardian angel.

Thus, with hope in his heart, he embarked upon his courtship.

II

Miss Celia Mainwaring had lived in Fleckington ever since her mother was widowed during the war. They were comfortable together. Celia did not bother much about housekeeping, for her mother's health was excellent until she died of a heart attack soon after Major Johnson came to Wiveldown. For years both ladies were members of an amateur orchestra, the mother playing the cello and the daughter the violin. Miss Mainwaring belonged to the dramatic society, and to a group dedicated to preserving the beauties of rural England, and she was captain of Fleckington's Ladies' Tennis Six. She did not enjoy sitting idly about, nor did she like to hear of anyone else just whiling time away, hence her interest in getting Major Johnson settled with his gardening and cooking; she had done the same for others in the past, though usually guiding men more towards woodwork than *haute cuisine*. She kept abreast of what was currently being published during library hours.

Her sister had been the pretty one; she had married young and now had four children to whom Celia was a rather bossy aunt. No one had ever asked her to marry them, nor did she expect that anyone ever would now. She seldom thought about it, for she was much too occupied.

She ran the library with the help of several part-time assistants whom she also saw out of office hours since some of their other interests overlapped. She was welcome in her friends' homes, for she was no threat to matrimonial safety and was always helpful in a crisis. She and her mother had entertained a lot, the mother cooking, and Celia laying the table, arranging the flowers and whipping the cream. Now, single-handed, Celia found she lacked expertise and so she took the cooking lessons. Each winter, in any case, she followed two courses, one academically slanted such as German or the History of Art, the other recreational like the cooking; in this way she had learned to dressmake, model in clay, identify birds, and speak smatterings of several languages.

When Major Johnson, accepting from her Sir Arthur Grimble's *A Pattern of Islands*, invited her to lunch she was taken aback. Each time he left the library she forgot about him till they met again. She hesitated, something she rarely did, while the major hovered anxiously before her desk, holding up the queue of other readers waiting to change their books.

'Thank you. That would be nice,' she said, and pointed out to her friend Mavis later that it would have been difficult to refuse since she went to The Feathers nearly every day in any case.

Major Johnson had timed his visit to the library for a quarter to one, so that he could be there when it closed for lunch and thus escort her down the road. He read *Country Life* while he waited for her, then walked proudly at her side on the kerb edge of the pavement. The Feathers was busy, but the major, though small, had commanded men, even though they were mostly military clerks and not fighting troops. He found a corner table in the crowded bar, bought two sherries, and gave their order all with a minimum of fuss and a maximum of efficiency. Miss Mainwaring was quite impressed.

'There's Mrs Fellowes,' she said, when he sat down. 'Over there, near the window.'

'Oh yes,' said Major Johnson. Mrs Fellowes, the cookery tutor, had seen them and gave a slight wave in their direction. 'She lives in Wiveldown,' he added.

'Yes,' said Miss Mainwaring.

'Where I live,' Major Johnson said.

11

'Oh – do you?'

Why be cast down because she had forgotten? He thought of all the postcards she had sent him, telling him that certain books were waiting for him.

A flash of recollection came to Celia.

'Ah yes – *Tobruk*. That's the name of your house, isn't it? Were you there?'

'Yes,' he admitted, and was rewarded by the way Miss Mainwaring's blue eyes widened.

'What an experience,' she said.

Major Johnson did not tell her that his job had been not to fight, but to find supplies for those who did. He hoped she would not ask him about the siege; he might have to reveal the true nature of his role.

'I enjoy my job at Chorlbury Manor, the one you found for me,' he volunteered, to change the subject. 'I'd like to be a guide, if I could learn enough about the house to do it properly.'

'Why not?' asked Miss Mainwaring.

'Mrs Fellowes is a guide there. Did you know?'

Miss Mainwaring did.

'She's most capable. She's very good at answering difficult questions.'

'She's used to that. She teaches at the comprehensive school, part-time,' said Miss Mainwaring.

'Oh!'

Time flew. Major Johnson had rehearsed in advance some topics for discussion so that conversation would flow smoothly. He described his garden and suggested she might care to see it one day. She disclosed that she was going to Italy soon for her annual holiday. This dismayed the major, for it meant a delay in his programme, but he rallied. He had been stationed in Italy after the war and gave her tips on what to see. Miss Mainwaring had been to Italy six times already. She scarcely listened.

'I'll see you again before you go,' he said to her, resolving if need be to sit up half the night finishing the books she'd given him today.

She refused his offer to escort her back to the library. He

thought of asking her out for a drive in his car over the weekend, if he could find a time to suit her when he was not on duty up at Chorlbury Manor, but then he dismissed the idea. It would be rushing things. There would be other opportunities later.

He drove home whistling happily, and did not notice the tall figure of Mrs Fellowes waiting at the bus stop. Some way further on, however, he met a small girl standing by the roadside, thumbing a lift.

Major Johnson frowned. Small girls, and big ones too, should not thumb lifts from strangers. He slowed down. Only when the child was sitting beside him in the car and had said she wanted to go to Wiveldown did he realise who she was. Her name was Mary Forman, and her father worked in the paint factory where Major Johnson had been employed himself. Her mother had a job in a shop in Fleckington.

'You shouldn't be hitch-hiking, Mary,' Major Johnson reproved her. 'Isn't the bus due soon?'

'Yes. I'm meant to be on it,' Mary said. 'But lots of people from Wiveldown go to market and I knew I'd get a lift today. Then I can save the fare.'

'I hope you wouldn't go in a car with anyone you didn't know,' said Major Johnson.

She did not answer, busy picking at a sticking plaster on her knee.

'Will anyone be at home? Aren't your parents both at work?' He realised that she was adrift on a weekday because the schools were on holiday.

'I'm going to see my gran. She lives in Wiveldown too,' said Mary.

'Show me where her house is, and I'll drop you,' said the major.

III

Roger Brewis and Tom West loafed along an alley-way between a row of stalls in Leckington's market. It was

13

mid-afternoon, and the hot, late summer air was heavy with the threat of thunder. Scraps of paper and withered vegetable leaves littered the ground; babies in prams, some of them fractious and whining, blocked the aisles while their mothers gossiped or examined the goods and their brothers and sisters scuffled about in the dust.

The two boys wore skin-tight jeans into which their thin hips and legs seemed to have been poured, and despite the heat, leather jackets. Roger's was adorned with various symbols; Tom's was undecorated. Both wore their hair to their shoulders; Roger's was straight and lank, Tom's a mass of corkscrew curls which stood out like a halo round his pale face. They had spent a couple of hours earlier in the day going round the pubs in the centre of the town and drinking a pint of beer in each, and they had eaten, between them, a single packet of crisps. As they lurched along, Roger eyed the young women with their children and made loud remarks about them. Tom listened to him vaguely, his mind almost a blank; he felt sleepy.

They were both out of work. Tom had worked at a local garage, on the pumps, hoping to become a mechanic one day. The garage had been closed under a road-widening scheme and the owner had moved away from the district to open up elsewhere with his compensation money. Tom, meanwhile, was drawing his unemployment benefit and enjoying a rest. Roger had never had a steady job since he left school; two weeks here and three there was as much as he could manage. He'd sold small goods in an electrical store until the manager caught him stealing the stock; then he'd done a stint with a builder which had set him up financially for a time. He'd tried a milk round, but the early rising didn't really suit him.

They passed a vegetable stall. The stallholder was busy serving a crowd of women who were clustered round picking up apples, inspecting cauliflowers, and feeling plums for ripeness. Roger adroitly filched a small bunch of bananas from the front of the display and slipped them into an inside pocket in his jacket. He sauntered on, and when some yards past the stall

14

started to fall about with laughter. Tom followed, slightly aghast but admiring. When they were well out of range, Roger shared his spoils and they ambled on, eating the bananas.

'Your turn next,' Roger said. 'I fancy some shoes. Them boots with studs round. Let's nick a pair.'

'We can't. We'd get caught,' Tom protested.

Roger had stopped at a footwear stall. Boots and shoes, men's, women's and children's, were arranged on a long trestle under an awning. Baskets of job lots, plimsolls and sandals, stood in front of the stall.

'That pair there.' Roger pointed. Some bright tan boots with studs over the instep had caught his fancy. 'Them's my size, nines. I'll chat up dad here, while you nick them. Meet you in the gents.'

He advanced to the edge of the trestle and leaned against it. The stallholder was showing cut-price sandals to a woman hung about with little children; a persistent toddler kept delving into the display basket as if it were a bran tub and coming up with assorted trophies. Out of the corner of his eye the trader had noticed the two boys, and he watched warily in seconds snatched from attending to the woman as Roger picked up a pair of canvas shoes and began to examine them.

Tom, with a sinking heart, looked at the boots. If he didn't do it, Roger would think him chicken, and he'd be right. It was just a lark, really, he reasoned. The boots weren't all that dear; Roger could pay for them if they were caught, since he'd cleaned up well on the building site and could always get taken on there again, for all he didn't fancy the work.

Someone would be sure to see, if he took them. There were so many people about, busybody women, if the stallholder himself didn't catch him in the act. Still, he could run. By the time they'd called the fuzz he'd be away. He glanced round. All the shoppers were intent on fighting their way through the narrow spaces between the stalls or spotting the best buys; they weren't looking at him. But the boots were bulky; he couldn't hide them.

At the far end of the stall Roger had picked up a lightweight

15

shoe of the kind a clerk might wear. He ran his hand along its sole and peered inside it at the lining.

'Be with you in a minute, lad,' said the stallholder, handing his woman customer yet another sandal. 'Not your style, that, hardly,' he added to Roger.

'Take your time, dad. I'm not pushed,' Roger said. He leaned more heavily against the counter and over went several opened boxes of shoes on to the ground, spilling their contents. With an exclamation, Roger dived after them. 'Sorry, dad – clumsy, that's my trouble,' he gabbled, picking them up with every appearance of wanting to restore order.

Tom had seized his chance. He grabbed the boots and darted down another aisle to the rear of the shoe stall. Then he strolled along, holding them openly, so that they looked like an innocent purchase. He idled on, pausing to look at other things that caught his eye, one ear cocked listening for sounds of pursuit, but all was well. At the end of the gangway he put on speed and turned towards the public lavatories in a corner of the square. He pattered quickly down the steps and bolted himself into a cubicle until Roger should arrive. He felt slightly sick, yet elated. Beyond the odd apple or banana or a packet of sweets, he'd never stolen anything before.

IV

Mary Forman spent an hour with her grandmother in her council bungalow at the end of Welbeck Crescent and then she went home. The house, which was at the other end of the estate, was empty, since her parents were both still at work. She took the key from beneath a brick in the coal shed, unlocked the back door and let herself in, as she did after school every day. The house was very neat; it was well furnished, and in the kitchen there was a big refrigerator and a washing machine. A set of children's encyclopaedias on which Mary's mother was still paying the instalments filled a shelf in the living-room and there was an upright piano, for Mary was having music lessons. Mrs Forman was ambitious for her only child.

Mary sat at the piano and practised her scales a few times. Then she played two pieces she was learning. That would do for today. After that she went into the kitchen, poured herself out a glass of milk, opened a tin and took out three angel cakes, and then sat at the table to eat her small feast. She cleared up tidily after she had finished, for her mother had trained her to be neat. Then she went upstairs to change into her Brownie uniform. She and her friend Heather Smith were going to be tested for their Brownies' Writers' Badges at five o'clock.

The plaster on her knee needed replacing. A smear of blood had trickled down her leg from underneath it; all her picking at it must have re-opened the small wound. She went to the bathroom where the plasters were kept and carried out this repair. Then she fetched her school satchel, which contained her work to be examined, went downstairs, let herself out of the house, locked the door and put the key back in the coal shed.

Heather lived in a bungalow not far away. Wiveldown had been subjected to a good deal of in-filling development, and there was a close of eight new bungalows at the end of Church Street, one of which belonged to the Smiths. The arrangement was that Mary would call for Heather and they would walk together across the village to the cottage where Miss Evadne Price, who was to test them, lived. She was a retired schoolmistress who now wrote historical romances and was thus doubly equipped for the job.

Heather's mother came to the door at Mary's ring, full of concern because Heather had been sick that afternoon and was not fit to go.

'Never mind. I'll go by myself,' said Mary.

'It's something she ate, I think – or this hot weather,' said Mrs Smith. She wondered for a moment if Mary ought to go alone and then dismissed her doubts. Miss Price lived in the village after all, and Mary was so sensible; she was used, too, to being on her own. There she stood, neat as a new pin, her round pink face shining with health, the embodiment of the perfect Brownie.

'I tried to ring up Mrs Jenkins, but there was no answer,' Mrs Smith worried on. Mrs Jenkins was the Brown Owl who ran the Brownie pack and had made the appointment for the children with Miss Price. Twice Mrs Smith had been up to the call-box in the square trying to reach her.

'She's away. She's gone to Spain for a holiday,' said Mary. 'I hope Heather will be better soon,' she added. 'Now I'd better go.'

She walked off. The road wound round past the church, and she trod in sober fashion for in her Brownie uniform she felt old and important. She passed Major Johnson's bungalow; it looked deserted and the garage was closed but she heard a strange sound as she went by: the major was playing his trombone and the deep notes echoed into the outside world though all the windows were shut. Mary marched on. She jumped when a sudden rustling and then furious barking came from behind a privet hedge outside another house; a collie dog leaped at the gate, clawing the ironwork and making a frantic noise. Mary's heart thumped with fright as she hurried by, and a stern voice called the dog to order.

Soon she reached the square, where the road forked left for Fleckington and right for Chorlbury and the north. There was some traffic here. Her mother would be on the bus which arrived just before six but her father would be late, for on Thursdays in the summer he went straight from the factory to a house where he did odd-job gardening twice a week, and then on to a meeting of the Fleckington Caged Birds' Society. The Formans, between them, brought in a fair income, but their outgoings were heavy with their various hire-purchase commitments.

Duckett's Stores in the square closed on market days, but the post office was open. Mary had the money saved from her bus fare earlier, so she went in and bought some sweets. She did not like the two Mrs Flints, who were both sisters and sisters-in-law, having married a pair of brothers, but the post

18

office was a useful place since it sold sweets as well as stamps, and also supplied the newspapers. The lino on the floor was always dirty, and the air seemed fusty. Mary did not know why she disliked the two Mrs Flints; they both wore crumpled clothes which looked as if they slept in them, and the ancient spaniel they owned had usually shed hairs upon them. Marilyn Flint was alone today since her sister was still at market; she looked stale, somehow, thought Mary, wrinkling her nose fastidiously as she went out again into the cleaner air of the square.

She put the sweets into her satchel to eat later. Beyond the square the road looped and a footpath between some buildings offered a short cut to the Leckington road where Miss Price lived. Mary took it, passing between two iron posts which were there to prevent bicycles being ridden this way. There were some tall white daisies growing in the rough grass at the side of the path, and Mary thought a bunch of them would make a nice present for Miss Price. As she moved about picking them, something caught her attention, an object lying in the grass; it was a shabby leather purse.

She picked it up. You took purses to the police, she knew, but there wasn't a policeman in the village now. Still, Dad or Mum would take it in to Leckington in the morning. She put it in her satchel.

V

After dropping Mary outside her grandmother's door, Major Johnson drove home, put his car away, and pottered round the garden snipping the odd dead head off the roses. There was not a weed to be seen; he had mowed the day before and the lawn was striped in neat swaths from the marks of the blades as though it had been swept. The air was heavy with the ominous stillness that precedes thunder and the sun was hidden now behind livid clouds. Soon he went indoors and took out the accounts of the Wiveldown Horticultural Society, of which he was the treasurer. He had taken on this task willingly, for he had plenty of spare time and he hoped it might be a way of being drawn into the life of the community. But he still felt a stranger, even though he was on nodding terms with many people. He did not play bridge, so he was excluded from the group who did, which included the Philpots next door. He went to church regularly, not from religious conviction but from habit begun when he joined the army as a band boy after his mother and father were killed in a railway accident. His only relative was an uncle who was a sergeant in a county regiment; it seemed the best solution at the time and he never questioned it, soon learning to play the bugle, and later the trombone. When the war came he transferred to the quarter-master's department where his meticulous sense of order had an outlet. He was quartermaster sergeant at the end of the war, and, remaining in the service, was commissioned soon afterwards.

Wiveldown's vicar was one of the bridge players. He was a scholarly widower round whom the ladies of the parish fluttered like solicitous doves. He was tall and looked distinguished, with white hair and a beaked nose; he should have been a bishop, thought Major Johnson, conscious every Sunday of his own small size beside the other man. The vicar had marked him down as someone likely to be useful, and with ready goodwill Major Johnson had run the tombola at the village fête and helped to trim the hedges round the churchyard, but he would not be drawn into the choir nor become a sidesman.

It was strange, he thought as he put away the accounts, now satisfactorily balanced, how you could live in a place for months and know many people by name, yet get close to no one. Still, it had always been like that for him, though he had never before had time to notice it. He looked around his sitting-room with its two armchairs upholstered in speckled hairy tweed; something was lacking here, but he did not know what it could be. Perhaps it was simply company.

Over the mantelpiece hung his bugle, which he polished twice every week. He kept his trombone in its case in his bedroom, and sometimes he got it out to play a few bars, when he thought there was no one near enough to hear him. Mrs Philpot was out a lot, at golf or bridge, and most afternoons Cathy Blunt from the other side, whose garden ran at right angles to his, went out with her new baby for a walk. Major Johnson intended to ask Miss Mainwaring if a trombone would be useful in Fleckington's amateur orchestra. He knew she played in it for he had seen her violin case in the library, and asked her. His wind was not as good as it had been, but he could still blow, and he had been commended often for his sense of timing.

He played a small part of a Gilbert and Sullivan overture, which had been a popular piece in his regiment's repertoire all those years ago; the notes scored for the trombone were not the most melodious, and to Mary Forman passing by, the sounds were like the braying of a donkey; but Major Johnson imagined himself back on the parade ground, stepping out with a light heart amid his fellow musicians.

He did not play for long. He wiped his mouth, his lips smarting a little because he played so seldom, and put the instrument away. He would have a bath and then go up to The Grapes. There were two pubs in the village, The Grapes and The Rising Sun, and Major Johnson had tried them both. The Grapes, besides being nearer, had a slightly older and less trendy clientele than The Rising Sun. He walked up there most evenings for a pint, and sometimes there was someone willing to chat in the bar.

As he soaped himself in the bath he heard a distant rumble of thunder, and when he opened the front door half an hour later the first huge drops of rain had begun to fall. Should he go? He would get soaked. Yet the evening would be long if he stayed at home. He had a television set, but he really only liked the football; plays and documentaries did not appeal to him and he seldom saw humour in the comedy shows. Mostly he read in the evenings.

He would get the car out and drive to The Grapes, even though it was only a few hundred yards away.

21

He backed it out, turned, and drove off through what was suddenly a deluge. Great gobbets of rain bounced up from the tarmac and thudded on the bonnet; already the gutters were full as torrents of water raced towards the drains. As he neared the pub he saw a figure scurrying along the road. It was a tall woman in a light jacket with a scarf tied over her head. She rushed into the pub ahead of him and stood gasping in the lobby. It was Mrs Fellowes.

'What a storm, Mrs Fellowes,' he exclaimed, following her inside.

'Oh – Major Johnson – yes – isn't it awful? I just came in here for shelter, I'm afraid.'

'You're soaked through,' he said, peering up at her. She had taken off her scarf and her grey hair hung damply round her face. 'Come along in and let me get you a drink.'

'Oh – you're very kind. Thank you,' she said.

He helped her off with her wet jacket and they went through into the bar. Nobody else was there; the evening was so bad that none of the regulars had turned out. A young girl with long, dark hair, wearing a purple dress that reached to her ankles, appeared from a side door and slipped behind the bar to serve them.

'Oh – Mrs Fellowes, it's you!' she said, sounding surprised.

'Hullo, Penny. So you're home. I thought you were off to Greece or somewhere,' said Mrs Fellowes.

'I go on Saturday – camping,' said the girl. She had a pale face and huge dark eyes. Major Johnson thought she looked half starved.

'This is Penny Hurst,' Mrs Fellowes told him. 'Major Johnson lives in the bungalow where the Boyds used to live, Penny. I don't think you've met, have you?'

They hadn't, but Major Johnson knew that the Hursts, who ran The Grapes, had a daughter at university.

'What can I get you?' Penny asked, leaning on the counter. Her hair fell forward, meeting under her chin. It must be a hazard when she pulled the beer, Major Johnson thought, imagining it dangling in the tankards. He persuaded Mrs

Fellowes to accept a whisky, since she'd got so wet, and had the same himself. Penny served them and then left, bidding them shout when they were ready for another. Mrs Fellowes smiled at her retreating back but Major Johnson was nonplussed at this abrupt treatment.

'She's packing, I expect,' said Mrs Fellowes. 'Though I suppose she'll only take a toothbrush and a bikini.'

'I'm not very used to young people, I'm afraid,' said the major, although it wasn't strictly true. He was accustomed to young men, but he soon disciplined them if they needed it. The girl had looked grubby, as well as famished, and there was no excuse for grime.

'She's a clever child,' said Mrs Fellowes. 'She's reading physics.'

'She looks as if she could do with a good meal,' said Major Johnson.

'That hungry look seems fashionable just now.' Mrs Fellowes sipped her drink. 'This is good,' she said. 'I don't come in here very often. That's why Penny looked surprised to see me. I've just had tea with Cathy Blunt, your neighbour.' Cathy had told her about presents of runner beans and lettuces offered over the hedge by the major.

Major Johnson knew the Blunts only slightly. The large, fair young man worked in insurance in Fleckington, and the new baby's reedy wail was a fresh sound in the neighbourhood. He rather liked hearing it; it was company, of a sort.

'You must let me drive you home,' he said. 'It's still raining hard. But have another drink first. Do you think your young friend will come if we call?'

'It would be kind of you to drive me,' Mrs Fellowes said. 'I was stupid to come out without a raincoat – at least I had a jacket. But you must have the second drink with me. I've got some whisky at home. Shall we go?'

The thought of summoning Penny Hurst from the inner fastness of the pub did not fill Major Johnson with enthusiasm.

'Very well,' he agreed.

Mrs Fellowes had finished her drink. She stood up.

While they were seated, Major Johnson had forgotten how tall she was, but now she loomed above him. She must weigh twelve stone, he thought. She was like a rather pleasant female sergeant-major, with her bright, intelligent eyes behind her glasses, and her fresh, healthy complexion.

He held her jacket while she slid her arms into it, and, standing on his toes, managed to hoist it part of the way up towards her shoulders. She shrugged it on, used to this difficulty.

She took up a great deal of room in the front of his car, and her grey flannel skirt billowed over the hand brake. Major Johnson felt quite awkward groping for it.

'Sorry,' she said, drawing back, quite unperturbed.

Her house was in Lammas Lane on the edge of the village; the lane wound round past it into open country and there were no other buildings near it. It was thatched, set back from the road up a bank, with a wooden fence and wicket gate, and a tall yew hedge behind the fence.

'We'll have to run for it,' said Mrs Fellowes as Major Johnson stopped the car, pulling it in as close to the side as he could. She hurried ahead of him, and had opened the front door by the time he got there. The rain was still spilling down, and a distant clap of thunder echoed. Major Johnson sped up the path past bent and dripping hollyhocks and entered the cottage.

VI

Roger put the stolen boots on in the lavatory, much to Tom's relief, and ditched his shabby canvas shoes. Next, he combed his lank hair and preened himself in the spotted mirror. Tom's curly mop was too tangled to submit to combing; he left it alone and leaned against the wall, waiting until Roger was satisfied with his own appearance. Then they emerged into the outer world.

Roger headed away from the market towards the shops, and Tom loped along beside him. They went through the swing doors of the big supermarket, where Roger picked up a wire basket. He walked slowly round posturing in front of the shelves and saying in a falsetto voice, 'Oh my, what have we here? Savoury snacks for dad's tea – how tempting,' and licking his lips. Tom was embarrassed by this exhibition until he saw a few smiles on the faces of ordinary shoppers. Roger put two small pork pies in his basket as they went round.

There was an off-licence in the store. Here, Roger once again surveyed the shelves. There was the usual range of wine, varying from bulk-bought plonk to a few vintage bottles, and a full complement of spirits. A number of customers were studying the display pensively, like readers in a library. Roger put a bottle of cheap red wine into his basket and then, with a movement which even Tom, who was agonisedly waiting for it, almost missed, slid a bottle of sherry into the big inside pocket of his jacket. Taking his time, he wandered on and added a swiss roll to what was in his basket. Then he gave the basket to Tom to take through the check-out and strolled on ahead of him, waiting among the discarded trolleys beyond the tills and whistling under his breath.

Tom had just enough money to pay for what was in the basket. He could have done without the wine and with bigger pork pies.

'What did you want to do that for?' he remonstrated when they were well away from the shop.

'Got it for my old gran, didn't I?' said Roger with a wink. 'It's easy. Them things is just asking to get nicked. It was whisky I was after, but there were two old bags standing in the way.'

'What're we going to do now, then?' Tom asked. He wanted to go home, but his mother would only look at him reproachfully and ask what he'd done about getting another job, and when his father got in he would lecture him too. And the house was so small. His two sisters would soon be back from work filling the place with their giggles and chatter.

'Going to have a bit of nosh,' said Roger. He was striding along, fast for him, since his usual speed was a fatigued amble.

They walked past the end of the market and down an alley where some of the stallholders parked their trucks. A few pick-ups and a number of lorries were drawn up by the kerb. There was no one about.

'Come on. Let's nip up here,' said Roger, and he shinned over the tailboard of a truck that had a canvas flap at the rear.

Tom followed. At least they were hidden from view inside the truck. It smelt of vegetables. There were some empty sacks on the floor.

'Make yourself comfortable. We've got a right palace here,' said Roger, doubling some sacks up under his thin buttocks. He produced a large knife from his pocket. It had a corkscrew among its numerous fitments and to Tom's eyes looked suspiciously new. More loot, he supposed. But with it, Roger dealt efficiently with the cork from the wine. He swallowed several mouthfuls and then passed the bottle to Tom. 'Here,' he said, 'have a bit.'

They stayed in the truck eating the pork pies and the swiss roll, and drinking the wine. Tom felt better after the food and some of his earlier sense of elation returned.

'Time to go,' said Roger, with one of his snap decisions. 'We'll find a couple of birds now.'

The shops and offices would soon be closing, and there would be girls in the streets, hurrying home or waiting for buses. It was a good idea. Flushed with wine, Tom quite fancied a bird. But they'd left it too late. Voices echoed from outside the truck. A sack of something was tossed through the canvas curtain. It smelt as if it was full of rotted cabbage stalks, and it landed almost on top of the boys as they retreated towards the driver's cab. Roger gripped Tom's arm. The truck rocked as someone got into the driver's seat and they heard the engine start. With several jerks the truck moved off.

The boys could have climbed out before it gathered speed, but they were taken by surprise and did not think fast enough. Before long they were travelling through the middle of the town.

Roger began to shake with suppressed mirth.

'What a giggle,' he whispered. 'Wonder where we're going?'

26

In fact they drove for ten miles. Then the truck bumped over a rough track and finally stopped. The engine was switched off and the driver got out. Now they'd be caught. Tom told himself that they would be found guilty only of a minor offence, a prank, and if the man was decent he might let them off without calling the police. He wouldn't know about the stolen sherry or the boots. His heart thudded painfully against his ribs as he waited for discovery.

But there was total silence. No one came to the back of the truck. After a time they looked out. The truck was parked in a large barn among bales of hay stacked up to the rafters. The doors stood open, and outside rain was spilling down from the sky as though some giant waterfall was dropping from the heavens.

VII

Miss Price's cottage had very small lattice windows peering out at the world from under its thick thatch, and inside it was very dark. Mary had never been there before. Miss Price was old, but she rode about the village and for miles around on an ancient, upright bicycle, wearing in winter a flowing black cloak. The younger children thought she was a witch, but she had no cat, only a budgerigar which warbled now from its cage in a corner of the living-room. Mary looked round with interest. The walls and ceiling were criss-crossed with beams, and the room was full of heavy old furniture. At one end of it was a loom, for Miss Price wove her own tweed and had made the fabric of the sweeping full skirt she wore now in the manner of one of her heroines. The table at which she wrote her books, in longhand using plain pen and ink, stood in the middle of the room. Two reference books were open on it, and a pile of manuscript covered in neat writing was stacked under a piece of pink blotting paper with a model of Edinburgh Castle on top of it acting as a paper-weight.

It was all most unlike Mary's house in Welbeck Crescent, and Miss Price was not at all like either Mary's mother or her grandmother.

'I taught your mother at Leckington Secondary Modern School not so long after the war,' Miss Price remembered. 'Is she still working in the ironmonger's?'

'No. She's at Moffat's now, in the millinery department,' Mary said.

'Hm. Able girl. Should have got herself some training,' grunted Miss Price. 'Selling hats, is she? No one wears them now, do they?'

'She does the knitwear too,' Mary offered. Miss Price was rather alarming. She wore her white hair in a plait pinned round her head, and her eyes were dark and seemed to see right through you.

'Knitwear, indeed. Jumpers and cardigans, Mary. Jumpers and cardigans. All these euphemisms – terrible. Millinery and knitwear – it's disgraceful. Say what you mean, my dear, in clear language, and you won't go wrong. Now, what have you got to show me?'

Timidly, Mary produced the poem and the story she had written. Part of the test had to be conducted under the examiner's eye, and while Miss Price read these efforts, putting on a pair of steel-rimmed glasses to do so, she wrote a letter to an imaginary aunt. When all this was done Miss Price, who had mellowed while she looked at Mary's work, pointed out some spelling errors and a split infinitive. There was no serious fault to be found, however, and the Brownie badge was safely won. Miss Price wrote out the certificate which Brown Owl would present at the next meeting. Then she gave Mary a glass of milk and a piece of sponge cake, and showed her how the loom worked. Mary was allowed to weave several rows of the black and yellow fabric that was threaded up. She was fascinated by how the various strands were raised and lowered by the treadles. Because of her interest, Miss Price said she would invite all the Brownies up another day to see it, and Mary left.

She walked down the road, still feeling important in her

uniform, but lighthearted now, secure in her achievement. When she had gone a little way she opened her satchel to get out the sweets. There was the purse. It was quite bulgy. Whoever it belonged to must be worried if it was full of money.

She opened it. There were a great many coins – about two pounds – and a few notes tucked into the flap. There was also a pension book. Mary took it out and read the name. It belonged to Mrs Ellen Pollock, of *The Hollies*, Wiveldown. That was old Mrs Pollock who lived in the last house in the village along the Leckington road. She lived alone with her cat, and her garden was a wild jungle. The village children told frightened tales about her; she was sometimes seen shuffling along, bent almost double, on her way to the post office. Mary had once opened the door for her and been thanked in a high, clear voice and rewarded with a smile of extraordinary sweetness and a mild glance from faded blue eyes.

Mary was not afraid of her, even if she was a hermit. She would take the purse back to her. It wouldn't take long.

She turned about and set off, hopping along now, her fair hair flopping on her shoulders. She did not notice how black the sky had grown, but the first rumble of thunder sounded as she opened Mrs Pollock's gate. The drive was full of grass and creeping weed. Tall shrubs loomed on either side, and the scent of old-fashioned roses filled the air with a heavy fragrance. Mary sniffed it as she walked along.

The rain began as she reached the front door. It was painted black, and the paint was peeling from it. The knocker was too high for Mary to reach. She flapped the letter box, but it did not make much noise. Then she noticed a knob beside the door; it was an old-fashioned bell-pull, something Mary had never seen before, but she caught hold of it and tugged, and immediately a jangle echoed from within the house. After a long time she heard scuffling sounds from the other side.

'Who's there?' called a voice.

'I'm Mary Forman. I've found your purse,' piped Mary. Raindrops were plopping now on her head and making marks as big as pennies on the step she stood on.

29

She heard the rasp of a bolt being drawn and the door of the house opened a little way. Two blue eyes, not mild now, but wary, regarded her. The little old lady was not much taller than Mary was herself. She was very wrinkled, and she smelt rather, a bit like the ladies in the post office yet differently. She was not at all alarming.

'Mary Forman, eh? So that's your name. I remember you,' said Mrs Pollock.

'Your purse,' said Mary, holding it out. 'It is yours, isn't it? I found it on the path by the square.'

'That's mine all right. Come along in, child,' said Mrs Pollock, opening the door wider.

Mary had not meant to go into the house, but it was raining now in earnest and there was a sudden louder clap of thunder while she hesitated. It made her jump, and she skipped across the threshold. Mrs Pollock laughed. At least, Mary supposed that the cackling sound was laughter.

'Don't like thunder, do you? Well, never mind. It'll pass. I'll be glad of company while the storm lasts,' said the old woman.

'I opened your purse to see whose it was,' said Mary. She handed it to Mrs Pollock. 'I saw your pension book. I didn't touch anything except to read the address on the book.'

'What a good thing you found it, a nice little girl like you and not some good-for-nothing lout,' said Mrs Pollock. 'Though I don't suppose all those long-haired lads are wicked either,' she added in a mumble to herself. She looked inside the purse. 'Everything's there. You're a good girl.' She took out a fifty-pence piece. 'You shall have this as a reward.'

'Oh no,' protested Mary. 'Please keep it.'

She tried to press the coin back into Mrs Pollock's skinny hand. The old lady was obviously very poor and couldn't spare it. Her clothes were dirty and ragged and the house was in a shocking state. The lino in the hall where they were standing was worn into holes and the wallpaper was faded and stained. All the furniture was smothered in dust.

'You take it,' Mrs Pollock said. She popped it into a pocket of Mary's dress and patted her. 'Now, come along into the kitchen. We'll be warm there. You can't go home till the storm is over.'

She put the purse into a drawer in the heavy carved sideboard in the hall and hobbled off towards the back of the house. Mary followed. They went through a door and along a flagged passage into the kitchen. This was a much nicer part of the house. There was a Rayburn stove in front of which slept the tabby cat. Red and white checked curtains, rather grubby but still bright, hung at the windows, and there was a big deal table. Two dilapidated wicker chairs with patchwork cushions stood on either side of the range. Mary wondered how such a bent old lady managed to fill it; she knew that no one came to the house to help her. She had lived like a recluse for years and would let no one in, not even the vicar or the meals-on-wheels ladies. Mr Duckett, from the stores, who ran a delivery service, dropped her a regular order once a week; she left a box for it on the step, and the money for the previous week's purchase, but she never spoke to him.

'Let's have a cup of tea,' said Mrs Pollock.

Mary was still full of the milk and cake she had had with Miss Price, but it would have been rude to refuse.

'I'll make it,' she said, and bustled about doing so while her hostess sat back in her wicker chair, knobbled hands plucking at her skirt, directing operations in her oddly high voice. Outside the storm grew loud and frightening, but the two sat snug. Mrs Pollock wanted to know all about the Brownies, and what Mary thought of school. It seemed that she remembered Mary's father from when he was a boy; he had always lived in the village, but she did not know Mary's mother. They had a most interesting talk, and Mrs Pollock told Mary what things had been like when she was a girl. She remembered quite clearly the day that Queen Victoria had died. All this passed the time most agreeably while the thunder rumbled overhead and the rain poured down. It streamed against the windows and rushed out of the gutters in great jets.

'This is a solid house,' said Mrs Pollock. 'Men knew how to

31

build in those days – not like the dolls' houses they build now.'

Mary supposed the old lady would think her home a doll's house. It certainly was tiny compared with Mrs Pollock's, but she preferred it. This house was gloomy; it smelt damp; and all the furniture was huge and ugly. Mrs Pollock took her into the room she called the parlour and showed her faded photographs of Mr Pollock in his soldier's uniform. He wasn't really old enough to fight in the Boer War, Mary learned, but he had lied about his age and been accepted. Mary had never heard of the Boer War till now. He and Mrs Pollock had come to live in this house fifty years ago. Mary wasn't quite sure how long Mr Pollock had been dead, but it was obviously a very long time, and the pictures of Mrs Pollock's son and his wife showed what looked to Mary an old man and woman. They lived in Australia and had a sheep farm, and four sons, all married with still more children. It was rather confusing, and Mrs Pollock herself seemed muddled about who was who. They'd wanted her to go out to Australia to live with them, but she'd refused.

'I'm too old to move,' she said. 'I manage.'

They went back to the kitchen and Mrs Pollock settled down in her chair again while Mary washed up the tea things. It was still raining, but the thunder had faded into the distance. When she had put away the cups and saucers and the chipped brown teapot Mary saw that Mrs Pollock had fallen asleep. She sat there, her head resting on the back of the chair, wispy grey hair framing her wrinkled face, her mouth a little open, breathing heavily.

Mary felt she ought to go. Her parents might wonder where she was – well, her mother might. Dad wouldn't be home. She had no idea of the time and there wasn't a clock to be seen. But it would be rude to go without saying goodbye, and it was still raining quite hard. Probably her mother would think she had stayed with Miss Price till the storm ended. What a funny day she had had, visiting these two old ladies in their two different sorts of houses. She did not realise that Mrs Pollock was almost twenty years older than Miss Price.

There was a row of books on the dresser. Mary went over to

32

look at them. One was *David Copperfield*. She took it down and began to read it. It was a long book and the print was small, but she skipped the first part and soon found it absorbing in an odd, slow way. There were pictures in it, too. It was only gradually that she realised there was something wrong in the room. She lifted her head. Mrs Pollock's breathing had stopped and there was silence.

The old woman looked just the same. Her mouth was still open and her hands were still folded on her lap.

'Mrs Pollock!' Mary said in a shaky voice, and then again more loudly, 'Mrs Pollock!'

The cat stirred. It got to its feet slowly, then stretched and crossed to its mistress. It pawed at her skirt and then mewed. The plaintive sound was eerie in the still room. Mary's heart began to race. She approached the old lady. 'Mrs Pollock?' she said again. There was no answer.

She's ill, thought Mary.

She must get the doctor. She was a capable child, and though she was frightened she did not panic immediately. There was a rug on an upright chair in a corner of the room, and she picked it up to cover the old lady's knees so that she would catch no chill while Mary went for help. As she tried to tuck it round the skinny form, Mrs Pollock's hands fell from her lap and swung limply at her sides. Her head sagged against the chair and her mouth fell further open.

Mary did not wait. She ran to the hall, wrenched open the door and raced down the drive as fast as her terrified legs would carry her.

Behind her the door of the house swung to again and shut.

VIII

While the storm was raging overhead, Roger and Tom sheltered in the barn. They had no idea where they were, but it was warm and dry in their refuge. The climbed up the hay bales and found a hollow where they would be hidden from anyone entering the barn.

'We're right enough here,' Roger said. 'No hurry to get away.'

'How'll we know where we are?' Tom asked, but he did not really mind about that. They were safe from being caught in possession of stolen goods, and no one would ever know they had been in the truck. They could easily creep out from here later on.

'We'll follow the track. It'll go to a road somewhere. Must do,' Roger said. 'Pity we never got them birds.'

Tom thought it was lucky. Girls would have giggled and squealed and they'd have been discovered.

Roger was opening the bottle of sherry.

'Come on. Have a swig,' he said.

They finished it before the storm was over. Roger had the lion's share, but Tom drank a great deal of it and his head felt very swimmy. He kept wanting to giggle and his legs felt weak. Roger seemed unaffected by all that he had drunk so Tom kept quiet about the effect it had on him. After a time the thunder faded away and the rain slacked off. Roger thought it was time to go.

They looked out of the barn door and saw that they were in a farm yard. Rain dripped from the eaves of every building and there were puddles on the ground. A tractor was parked against one wall, but there was no one in sight. Nervously at first, but then with increasing confidence, they passed the sheds and went under an arch that marked the end of the yard.

'We're in luck. The farmhouse must be up the other way,' said Roger. They stood under the arch looking at the track which stretched away ahead of them, its ridge still firm though twin rivers of water filled the ruts on either side. There was a door under the archway and Roger opened it. It revealed a shed which housed farming implements – there were a harrow and some rakes and a small trailer. There were also two bicycles, one gleaming new machine with upright handle-bars, chopper type, and a smaller ordinary one.

'Phew, what luck,' said Roger. He grabbed the taller bicycle and wheeled it out. 'It's O.K. No one's about,' he said, and pedalled off.

Tom would rather have chanced it on his feet, but he did not want to be left behind. He took the other one and followed. It was much too small for him, and his knees stuck out as he tried to keep them clear of the handle-bars. Roger was rapidly vanishing into the distance. The track ran through a field and ended in a gateway leading into a tarmac lane; Roger had turned to the left and Tom went after him. The going was easier on the hard surface of the lane. It was still raining, but not hard; thunder rumbled in the distance.

'This is great,' said Roger, leaning back, hands high in front of him.

'Great,' echoed Tom, saving a skid.

They rode for about three miles, meeting no one, and then their lane joined a bigger road. A finger post pointed back the way they had come. It said: *Mordwell Village Only*. Neither of them knew where Mordwell was.

'Must be a crummy place,' said Roger.

They pedalled on. A car came up behind them and blew its horn; Tom braked and wobbled into position behind Roger as it passed them, spattering up water and drenching their legs. Roger shook his fist as it disappeared.

After ten minutes more riding they could see a thirty-mile-an-hour traffic sign ahead.

'We're getting somewhere now,' said Roger. 'Must be houses there. We'd better ditch the bikes. We'll hitch a ride.'

Tom was thankful to fall in with this idea. They stopped at the next gateway. It was securely locked with a padlock and chain but they lifted the bicycles over it, wheeled them a little way into the field along the hedge and laid them down in the long grass at the side of it. It was a field used for grazing cattle, though it was now being rested, but the two town boys did not realise this. They were simply thankful to meet no cattle face to face.

Once they were back in the road again they walked on towards the traffic signs. Nothing passed them. This was not a

35

much-used road. Their legs in the thin jeans were soaked but their thick jackets had kept their bodies dry. Roger's hair hung down in rat's tails round his head; Tom's curls stood out in a wild fuzz.

Near the thirty-limit sign was another which gave the village's name: *Wiveldown*.

'Ever been here before?' asked Roger.

'Yes,' said Tom. 'Came here with the football team.'

Before he met Roger he had played for Leckington Colts.

'I haven't. Dead and alive, isn't it?'

Tom had thought it rather a pretty, peaceful little place but he said nothing. They walked on. The rain had come on harder again and they hunched their shoulders against it. They passed a few cottages which showed no sign of life and then they came to a fork in the road. Neither knew which way to turn for Leckington, and there was no signpost, so Roger tossed a coin and they took the left fork.

'What a deserted place,' said Tom as they plodded on. He remembered a village square, a church, at least one pub and some shops. He'd certainly never been down these by-ways. His head no longer felt swimmy, but he had a remote feeling, as though all this was happening to someone else.

They did not notice the car until they were almost upon it. It was drawn well into the side of the road on the grass verge, bonnet towards them.

'Wonder if it's locked,' said Roger. 'We might sit in the dry for a bit.'

'I can open it, even if it is,' boasted Tom. 'I've got a bit of wire.' He had not worked in a garage for nothing.

'Right, then. Let's try it,' said Roger.

But they did not have to force it; it wasn't locked.

They sat inside, their breath steaming up the windows, while the rain fell steadily.

'Could you drive this crate?' Roger asked after a while.

'Course I could,' said Tom. 'I can drive anything.'

'There isn't no key. Could you start it?'

'Course,' said Tom again.

36

'Well, get on with it, then. We'll drive it home and leave it in the car park.'

'Oh no!' Tom said, but then the idea began to appeal to him. The bloke shouldn't have left it like this, just asking to be nicked. And he was sick of being second fiddle to Roger. Here was something he could do and Roger couldn't.

He pulled a lock under the dash to open the bonnet, then got out into the teeming rain, raised the lid and fiddled with the engine. Roger looked impressed when soon it was running. Tom adjusted the choke with an important air. When he'd said that he could drive he'd been exaggerating. Sometimes while minding the pumps he'd moved the occasional car around the forecourt, but he'd never been on the open road. However, he found first gear and with only a few jerks crawled off down the lane.

'We've got to turn,' he said.

He drove back to the junction where they had tossed for their route, managed to reverse into the other road, and swung round with some panache. As they moved forward again Roger leaned across and tooted the horn.

'What d'you want to do that for?' demanded Tom. Like many another man behind the wheel of a car, he now felt a great sense of power. He speeded up and changed gear. The wipers, which had been left on and so worked automatically when the engine was started, scraped back and forth distractingly in front of him and the rain fell down in blinding sheets. He turned his head to look at Roger.

'Look out – ' Roger cried, leaning forward.

Tom barely heard him. He was only half aware of a blur in front of him before there was a heavy thud. The car went on, thumping over something.

'For Christ's sake stop!' screamed Roger.

At last Tom found the brake and stopped the car. Roger was out in a flash but Tom could not move at first. Then his limbs unfroze and he followed. Roger had run back the way they had come, and Tom found him standing over the body of a little girl lying in the road. One hand was turned palm upwards to the sky, and as they watched the fingers slowly uncurled and then were still.

'You ran right over her,' Roger said.

'I never saw her,' Tom whimpered. He began to tremble. 'A doctor! We must get a doctor!'

Roger looked down at the child.

'Ain't you never seen a dead rabbit?' he asked. 'A doctor won't help this kid.'

'Oh no!' wailed Tom. 'I never saw her,' he said again. 'Where'd she come from?'

'Must have been walking in the road,' said Roger.

'It wasn't my fault,' Tom cried and began to sob.

Roger slapped him sharply across the face.

'Maybe not, but no one's going to believe you,' he said. 'We've got to get out of here. Cut out that snivelling.' He walked back to the car and tried the boot. It was unlocked. Roger returned to the child, picked up her limp body and carried it back to the car, where he laid it, none too gently, in the boot, beside a petrol tin and a bag of tools. He closed the lid.

'Now, get that car turned round and put it back where you found it,' he said. 'Quick, before someone comes along.'

Still sobbing, Tom climbed back into the car. Somehow he managed to start it. He went up the road and found a place to turn. When he came back, grinding along in first gear, Roger had disappeared.

PART TWO

I

On Friday morning the air was fresh and sweet after the storm, and the sky was streaked with clouds which gradually dispersed as the sun rose. The day began for most people in Wiveldown in the normal way. Two milkmen made rounds in the village, one at half-past six and his rival at ten. Major Johnson patronised the early one; he seldom slept later than six, so he got up then and made tea, which he drank in his dressing-gown before he washed and shaved. He was always astir before anyone else in the road. Soon after seven a few cars would pass, driven by men on their way to various factories, and later a tractor might clatter by. The newspapers were unreliable at the moment because of the school holidays; in term-time they were delivered by a boy before the school day began.

Major Johnson could set his watch by the timetables of his neighbours. Derek Blunt left for his insurance office in Leckington at a quarter to nine. A new part of routine was Cathy Blunt's morning trip down her garden soon after nine to put out her washing; a row of white nappies would flutter like bunting from her line, visible to Major Johnson from his patio.

On the other side of the major lived the Philpots. The land where his house and the Blunts' were had originally been theirs, but they had sold it for development. Mr Philpot was a butcher; he owned more land on the far side of the village and kept cattle and sheep there before they were slaughtered. Cathy was glad he did not fatten them where she could see them; she told Major Johnson when they were talking over the fence one day that she did not fancy buying chops from beasts she'd seen on the hoof.

Mr Philpot had a shop in Leckington and others in two large villages in the county; he was often in The Grapes in the evening when the major went there and was friendly over a pint, but he was usually in the midst of his friends while the major sat quietly in a corner taking small part in the conversation, for what did he know of beef and farming?

Mr Philpot left home at ten to nine most days, but earlier on market days. Mrs Philpot played golf and went off early on Tuesdays and Thursdays to the golf club. Friday was her day for shopping and she stayed in Leckington for lunch. She played bridge too, and in fact was seldom at home during the day. Major Johnson did not know if they had any children; they must be adult now, if so. Perhaps there were grandchildren, but he had not heard of any. Mrs Philpot with her bright chestnut hair didn't look very grandmotherly, but appearances were deceptive. Mrs Fellowes, now, was different. He could easily imagine her as a grandmother, with her grey hair and generous curves, but her only daughter, now working as a secretary in Vancouver, was not married. She had a son working in London in television; he was married but he had no children.

They'd had a very pleasant evening. Major Johnson had been able to admire from the window her garden, which was full of roses, michaelmas daisies and dahlias. She grew soft fruit to sell: raspberries and strawberries, and currants. In the end he'd stayed to supper. She'd produced delicious chilled watercress soup, left from some party she'd had the day before, and had made a fluffy omelette, filling it with chicken.

'What would you have had at home?' she'd asked him, as they ate this meal in her kitchen. She'd spread a checked cloth on the round table, and drawn the blinds to shut out the weather. They'd eaten by candlelight.

'Oh –' Major Johnson looked sheepish. 'Egg and bacon, probably.'

'Did the lessons help?'

'Oh yes. I can give a dinner party now,' said Major Johnson. But he hadn't yet. However, in the autumn he would do it. He would ask the Philpots, and, naturally, Miss Mainwaring. He might even include Mrs Fellowes and the vicar, if he felt bold enough to cope with six.

They talked about Chorlbury Manor, where Mrs Fellowes had been a guide for years. She knew Admiral Bruce, the curator, and his wife quite well. Mrs Bruce had started a garden centre which operated in the walled garden and was a great success.

'She's used to organising naval wives, she needed something to do,' said Mrs Fellowes.

'The admiral was lucky to find a job like that,' said Major Johnson. 'I wish I could do the same, but then I'm not an admiral. All I could find were clerking jobs.' He told her about his stint in the paint factory.

'What did you do in the army?' asked Mrs Fellowes.

He told her the whole story, from his enlistment in the band as a boy, covering the time at Tobruk where his contribution was not glorious, but necessary, and the months afterwards when he had been in charge of prisoners in Italy. After the war he had been to the Far East, and to Germany; he had finished his career in Aldershot. He hid no unglamorous facts from her; she heard it all.

'How well you've done. You must be proud,' she said.

He looked astonished.

'I've nothing to show for it. No medals. No high rank.'

'But you started as a boy – all alone. I think it's splendid,' said Mrs Fellowes warmly. 'And your trombone. Do you play it still?'

'Only if I'm sure the Philpots and the Blunts can't hear me. It would annoy them,' he said.

'You ought to join the orchestra,' she said, putting his ambition into words. 'Celia Mainwaring will know about it.'

So her name was Celia. He had not known what the C stood for, and had guessed Cynthia, Cecily, and Charlotte, but never Celia.

'She does so much,' said Mrs Fellowes. 'At Christmas the amateur dramatic society will be doing *The Mikado* – they do a

Gilbert and Sullivan every year, much better than a pantomime. Sometimes Celia acts, and sometimes she plays in the
orchestra. She's so good at both, she needs to be cut in two.'

Major Johnson was sure that this was so.

'Do you perform?' he asked.

'I help with costumes,' Mrs Fellowes said. 'It's difficult for
me to get into the town at night – I've no car and the buses
aren't good. And I can't act or sing. I'm much too big. I'd be
well cast as Katisha if I'd got the voice.'

'I've never done any acting,' said Major Johnson, who was
uncertain if he understood the allusion. Wasn't Katisha the
woman who had a caricature of a face? 'It must be difficult,
living out here without a car,' he added.

'My daughter thinks I should move to a town. London for
choice. But I love this village. I've lived here for so long. And
I love this cottage too.'

'Don't you drive at all?'

'Oh, heavens, yes. I ran a car until fairly recently. But it's
such an expense, I sold it. Sometimes I hire one, for holidays.
I keep my licence up. I bicycle a lot,' she said.

Major Johnson had seen her pedalling along, a bulky figure
dressed in slacks.

'How do you get to Chorlbury?' he asked.

'Madge Fazackerley takes me.'

Another guide. He knew her by sight.

'She's a great friend of Olive Philpot's. They play golf and
bridge together,' said Mrs Fellowes. 'Bill Fazackerley farms the
land between here and Mordwell.'

Major Johnson knew nothing of who owned what beyond the
limits of the village. Mrs Fellowes told him about the changes
she had seen since she came to live in Wiveldown. The village
was no longer, as she put it, truly rural; now it was becoming
a dormitory for the nearby towns where industry was developing.

Major Johnson did not leave until eleven o'clock, so swiftly
fled the time, but it was of Miss Mainwaring that he thought as
he composed himself for slumber, not his hostess of the evening.

When Mary had not come home by seven o'clock on Thursday evening, her mother did not worry. It was raining hard; Mary must be sheltering from the storm either at Miss Price's house, or with her friend Heather Smith. She often spent the evening with the Smiths. The storm lasted for a long time, and before it ended Mrs Forman had to go out herself to a meeting of the Wives' Club. She left some ham and salad ready for Mary's supper and a note telling her to go straight to bed. Joe would not be back till late from his Caged Birds' Society meeting, but Mary was used to being left. She was eleven now, and a sensible child.

It was after half-past ten when Mrs Forman got back to find Mary's supper untouched and her room empty. For a moment she could not take in what this meant; then she began to wonder frantically what had happened. The Smiths would never have kept her for the night without sending a message, but they would know what time the girls had returned from seeing Miss Price. She rushed round to their bungalow.

They had gone to bed. Ted Smith came to the door in his trousers with his shirt off.

'It's Jean Forman,' he called to his wife. 'Seen Mary?'

Betty Smith came into the hall wearing a flowered dressing-gown.

'Come in, Jean, do – it's still raining, isn't it?' she said. 'Isn't Mary home, then?'

'No. I thought she must be waiting with you till the storm finished. I've been at the Wives' Club. I thought you'd be there too.'

'No, I couldn't go. Our Heather's been sick. She couldn't go with Mary this afternoon.'

'Mary didn't come back here, then?'

'No, love. Oh – you mean she hasn't been home at all?'

Both women stared at each other.

'I did wonder if she ought to go alone – but Miss Price lives right in the village and it was daylight – she'd have been back in an hour or so. Perhaps she took shelter there. Ted'll pop up and see,' said Betty. 'You come along in, Jean.'

Ted had disappeared during this interlude and he returned now, wearing a sweater. He carried a torch.

'I heard. I'll go there right away, Jean. You stay here.'

'I'd best go home. She might come back,' said Mrs Forman. 'Isn't Joe there?'

'It's his night for the caged birds. He won't be back for a bit.' And then he'll be full of beer, Jean thought.

'You'd better go, then. But she'll be safe and sound at Miss Price's, you'll see. I expect she's staying there because of the storm.'

No one mentioned the fact that there had been a lull earlier.

'Miss Price would never have kept her without sending a message. She's on the phone.'

'Yes, but you aren't. And maybe the lines have been affected by the lightning,' said Ted, on a flash of inspiration. He was sure that something serious had happened, but Jean dissolving into hysterics would help no one. 'We'll soon find out. I'll get up there now, and I'll come straight round to your place after – with Mary, likely enough.' Mentally, he crossed his fingers.

The women watched while he put on his raincoat and his wellington boots and then started up the road. When his bulky presence had left them they felt curiously forlorn.

'I'll be going, then,' said Jean Forman bleakly.

'Yes, love. I'd come with you, but I can't leave Heather.'

'No – of course not. It'll be all right,' said Jean.

'Of course it will. What could happen to her here in Wiveldown, where she knows everybody, pretty nearly?' Betty Smith said stoutly.

Jean repeated this reassuring statement to herself as she walked home. She had left the lights on, but no one was there. Joe came in ten minutes later. She heard the car, but she did not go to meet him.

As she had expected, he smelt strongly of alcohol and took a minute or two to grasp what she told him when he came into the house.

'We must get the police,' she said. 'Go and telephone them, Joe.'

'We must wait till Ted gets back,' Joe said. 'He'll have found Mary up at Miss Price's, you'll see. I'll take the car and go up after him.'

'No, don't. You shouldn't be driving, you're full of beer.' Jean said. 'You'll make things worse. I'll put the kettle on. You need some coffee.'

She was white-faced with shock. Joe watched her mutely while she made two strong cups of instant coffee, and tried to pull his errant wits together while he drank his. They sat in silence, waiting for Ted.

Miss Price had gone to bed and was reading a book on spiritualism when she heard him banging at her door. She thought he was some malefactor, and took a good deal of persuading before she would open it, but at last he convinced her that he was in fact Ted Smith, foreman at Walter's, the paint factory in Leckington. She opened the door and was revealed to him in a man's woollen dressing-gown with her grey hair in a long plait over one shoulder. Her glasses were on and she still held her book, with a finger between the pages marking her place.

'What do you want at this time of night, young man?' she demanded.

'I'm looking for Mary Forman. She's missing from home. Did she come for her Brownie test today?'

'Of course she did. Right on time. And a very nice, polite child she is too,' said Miss Price. 'Did you say she never went home?'

Ted repeated the facts.

'She left here at six. No later,' said Miss Price. 'You'd better ring up the police. Come in. The phone's on the window here.'

'Her parents must do it. She may have turned up,' said Ted. 'You'll let me know at once if she's safe?'

'Certainly.'

Ted left her standing there framed in the lighted doorway, a bulky, imposing figure. She turned slowly back into the house and closed the door. Then she sat down in the chair beside the hearth to wait until the police came, for come they would, she knew. Presently the habit of a lifetime reasserted itself and she began to read again.

Ted hurried back towards the centre of the village. As he walked at top speed down Church Street towards the turning for Welbeck Crescent where the Formans lived, a car passed him. It was a dark car, black or some similar colour, a Morris or Austin 1300. It drove on, its tail-lights dwindling into the distance. Then he saw it turn to the right, somewhere near where Mr Philpot the butcher and his wife lived in their large, mock-Georgian house.

III

Two uniformed policemen in a Panda car arrived at the Formans' house six minutes after Joe's telephone call. They were brisk but kind, and their expressions were grave as they listened to Jean's account of Mary's movements, as far as they were known. One of them then went out to the car, and the other asked some more questions.

'Has she any other friends where she might have gone for the night?'

'She's plenty of friends, but she's never stayed away for the night except at the Smiths' or her granny's,' said Jean.

'Her granny? Where's that?'

Joe explained that his mother lived at the other end of the estate in a council bungalow.

'Mary'd never stay there without leaving a message,' he said.

'Maybe your mother sent someone down with a message and it didn't arrive – some other child, perhaps,' said the constable. 'We'll soon find out.'

At this possibility both Jean and Joe brightened. They supplied a list of the names of her friends, and explained about Mrs Jenkins, the Brown Owl, to whom ordinarily Mary might have gone after the test to report on her success.

'On holiday, is she? And Mary knew it?' The young policeman made a note.

'Had she anything on her to show who she was?' he asked. 'Her name on her clothes?'

'She'd her satchel with her. It's not in her room. She'd have her work in that for Miss Price to see. Why – ?'

'If she's not at her grandmother's, we'll be trying the hospitals in case there's been an accident, Mrs Forman,' he said.

The second policeman now returned.

'Chief Inspector Coward's on his way over,' he told the Formans. 'He'll be here directly. We'll be off now to follow up these addresses.'

The two constables went away. Joe accompanied them to their car, and when he came back his face was grim. He was completely sober now.

'We never should have left her on her own, a little girl like that,' he said.

'It's serious? The bobbies think it's bad?' Jean asked. Both of them knew now that Mary was not with her grandmother; it could not be so simple.

'They do. I told you it wasn't right to leave her,' Joe said. 'You should have stayed at home.' His mind was full of horrifying images of what might have happened to his child.

'Well, I'll be off,' said Ted, acutely embarrassed by this exchange. 'Don't want Betty starting to worry.'

'Oh – right, Ted. And thanks,' said Joe.

Jean took no notice as Ted left the room. Her eyes were fixed on Joe.

'You're glad enough to have the things my money buys,' she said. 'Besides, I want Mary to have a chance. I never had nice things when I was her age.'

'She'd be right enough on what I get,' said Joe. 'I bring a decent packet home, good enough for most. You could have got a job here in Wiveldown, if you'd a mind, cleaning and that. They'd have let you take Mary along in the holidays.'

But Jean Forman was far above domestic work.

It was into this charged atmosphere that Detective Chief Inspector Coward and Detective Sergeant Davis arrived. The air between husband and wife was so tense that they felt it the moment they entered the house.

'Any news?' asked Joe.

'Not yet, Mr Forman,' said the chief inspector. He was a burly middle-aged man, and he had daughters of his own. 'There's no report of any road accident involving a child in this vicinity this evening, and she isn't in Leckington hospital. We're making enquiries further away. Would she accept a ride in a car with a stranger, do you think?'

'She's been told over and over not to,' said Jean.

'Some of these men can be very persuasive,' said the chief inspector. 'I'm sorry to alarm you, but we must bear in mind this possibility.'

'Of course,' said Joe. 'It's what I thought of straight away.'

The older man gave him a sympathetic look. A swift glance round the Formans' living-room had shown him a lot: a new three-piece suite, bought on the never-never for sure; a potted hydrangea; framed prints on the wall which were the same as a series his wife had sent for from a glossy magazine; the mock sheepskin rug on the hearth; and the vase of dried flowers in the grate. This was an ambitious mother. He nodded to the sergeant, who went out.

'Mary was on her own, I believe, this afternoon?' asked Coward.

'She was used to it,' said Jean defensively. 'I'm home by six. Sometimes she goes to a friend or to her granny's. On schooldays she has homework, and then there are her piano lessons.'

'Oh – learning the piano, is she?'

'Yes. She likes it. She's a good girl, Inspector.'

'I'm sure she is,' answered Coward. 'Now then, she went to Miss Price at five o'clock.' He went over Mary's movements

48

again. 'Miss Price says she was punctual, and left just before six. You were home soon after that, Mrs Forman?'

'Yes. The bus was on time. But it was raining hard. I got soaked coming from the square. I thought Mary would be at the Smiths' waiting till it stopped, so I didn't worry. She and Heather Smith were to have gone to Miss Price together.'

'Yes. So I understand,' said the chief inspector. 'You went out again yourself later on?'

'Yes. I had my tea; then it was time for the Wives' Club. I'm on the committee now,' Jean said.

'And you were out too, Mr Forman?'

'The caged birds,' explained Joe. Because of the rain he hadn't been able to put in his usual gardening spell; he'd had an extra few pints instead.

'I see. Well, if we don't find her as a result of the enquiries we're making tonight, we'll start a full-scale search at first light,' said the chief inspector. 'We can't do a lot while it's dark, as I'm sure you'll understand.'

At this point the sergeant returned, and shook his head when Coward glanced at him.

'Hm. She's not at her grandmother's, nor, as far as we can say, at any friend's in the village but there are still calls to be made. Now, have you a photograph of Mary?'

Mrs Forman could find only an old snap taken at the seaside a year ago with some other children.

'I see. Pity it's not more recent. But I expect a good many people in the village know her,' said the chief inspector. Wiveldown was still small enough for most of the inhabitants to recognise each other by sight, if not by name.

'I'm going to look for her,' Joe suddenly burst out. 'I can't sit here all night waiting. We ought to be searching, not talking.'

'We are searching,' said Coward. 'You won't do a bit of good going out now. You'd much better try to get some rest. You won't find anything while it's dark.'

'I might,' said Joe obstinately. 'I can't sit here and do

nothing. I know the fields and paths around. She might have gone off looking for blackberries on her way home.'

They could not dissuade him.

'We'll send a policewoman out to stay with you,' Chief Inspector Coward said to Jean.

'No – I'll be all right,' Jean said.

Her husband looked at her hard.

'You'll stay here,' he said. 'No going round next door, or that. Mary might come home.'

'I'll stay,' said Jean.

'Your mother's on her way, Mr Forman,' said Detective Sergeant Davis. 'She'll be here in five minutes.'

IV

After drinking his early morning cup of tea, Major Johnson opened the front door and stood on the porch inhaling deeply. The air smelt fresh, cleared by the storm which seemed to have moved completely away. On the other side of the road, and some way further down, he could see a police car parked outside the vicarage, and while he watched a policeman came out of the gates and walked up the path of the cottage next door. Almost at once the vicar's shabby old Ford Prefect, twelve years old, emerged and went off up the road, with the vicar crouched over the wheel and his white hair a nimbus about his head. A burglary, thought the major.

He returned indoors and had just spread a good lather all over his chin before he began shaving when his front door bell rang.

A policeman stood on the step.

'Good morning, sir. I'm sorry to disturb you so early but there's a child gone missing in the village and we're enquiring at every house to check her movements. Your name, sir, please?' said the constable.

Major Johnson supplied it. He dabbed the soapsuds off his chin.

50

'Who's missing?' he asked. 'I don't know many of the children by name.'

'It's an eleven-year-old girl, Mary Forman.' The constable produced a blown-up print of Mary's photograph made from the group her mother had found, but Major Johnson did not look at it.

'I know Mary Forman,' he said. 'I gave her a lift back from Leckington in my car yesterday. She was hitch-hiking. I scolded her for it.'

'What time was this, sir?' asked the constable.

'About two o'clock,' said Major Johnson.

'I see, sir. Perhaps I might come in a minute while I get the facts?'

'Certainly, constable,' said Major Johnson. He led the way into his sitting-room.

'Take a seat, constable,' said the major.

The constable sat down on an upright chair, his notebook open, and Major Johnson took one of the armchairs.

'Now, sir, exactly where did you pick Mary up?'

Major Johnson described his journey and how he had dropped Mary outside her grandmother's bungalow.

'I see, sir. And how did you know her name? Did she tell you?'

'No. Mary is one of the few children I do know. I was time-keeper at Walter's, where her father works, for some months. I've seen him with Mary about the place. What's happened to her?'

'We don't know, sir. She was last seen at six o'clock on the other side of the village.'

'I went up to The Grapes at about six-thirty – perhaps a little later. I often do in the evening. I didn't see Mary, though.' The major cudgelled his memory. 'No, there was no child about. It was raining then – there was a heavy storm. Perhaps she went to shelter somewhere?'

'That's what we must hope,' said the constable. 'Thank you, sir.'

'I hope you find her soon,' said Major Johnson. 'She was a very nice little girl.'

He showed the policeman out. His face felt tight from the dried soap on his chin, and he went back to the bathroom to spread a fresh lather over his beard.

Before getting back into the car, the alert constable made a note of the major's last remark.

V

The vicar went immediately round to the Formans' house as soon as the police left him. They were not churchgoers, but they were part of his flock and he must offer comfort if he could.

The Reverend Cedric Wilson was interested in early English madrigals, and it was a disappointment to him that no one in his parish, not even clever, devout Miss Price, shared this enthusiasm. He was also a keen ornithologist, and not unlike an eagle in appearance himself with his beaked nose and fine brow. He took an interest in the Brownies and had shown them his wildfowl slides, and he knew each child individually.

He found Jean Forman and her mother-in-law in the kitchen, with a pot of cold tea on the table between them and two untouched cups poured out. Both women were haggard; Jean had been crying and her face was blotched with tear stains.

Her face fell when she saw who the caller was.

'Oh – vicar – I thought it might be – ' she did not finish.

'I've just heard the news, Mrs Forman. You must be very anxious. But we must pray that Mary will be found safe and sound.'

'Would you like to come in? We're having some tea.'

Mrs Forman senior had braced up, rinsed out the teapot and put the kettle on again the moment the visitor arrived.

'Do you mind the kitchen?' Jean asked, offering him a chair.

The vicar's mind seldom dwelt on such mundane matters, but even he noticed how well equipped the Formans' kitchen was, not only compared with his own, which his sister when she came to stay called prehistoric, but compared with others he drank tea in on his rounds. Bright yellow cupboards lined the walls; black and white tiles covered the floor. The stainless steel sink gleamed.

The vicar knew Mrs Forman senior better than her daughter-in-law. She was a dressmaker, and his sister, every time she visited him, brought lengths of material for her to make up. He turned to her.

'I'm so sorry about this,' he said. 'The police told me Mary was with you during the afternoon.'

'Yes – for an hour. Then she went home to get ready for her Brownie test,' said Mrs Forman. She went through what Mary had done, as far as they knew it. 'Joe was out all night, searching. Of course he found nothing. The police have got men out now, in the fields, and dogs.'

'They'll find her. Perhaps she sheltered somewhere – in a shed, for instance – and fell asleep.'

'Joe knocked up every house between here and Miss Price's in the night,' said Jean. 'No one saw her after six o'clock. She bought some sweets at the post office just before five.'

'They might not have seen her pass on her way back,' said Mrs Forman. 'They'd have been closed by then.'

'Where's Joe now?' asked the vicar.

'Out with the police,' said Jean.

'He's had no rest, not a bite to eat, only some tea,' said his mother.

'I expect he feels he's helping, by joining the search,' said the Reverend Wilson.

'He blames me for going out,' said Jean, and began to weep again. She found a handkerchief in the sleeve of her dress and dabbed at her eyes.

'And do you blame yourself?' the vicar asked her, sitting down at the table. He accepted a cup of tea from the older woman with some relief; he had rushed out from the vicarage without any breakfast and his stomach had uttered a warning rumble; such an awkward noise at an emotional moment.

'I'd not have gone with her to Miss Price's, even if I'd been

53

at home,' said Jean. 'She was old enough to go alone. She was eleven.' Jean was using the past tense.

'She *is* eleven, Jean,' said Mrs Forman firmly. 'And that's old enough to go about the village by herself. But when she wasn't back at six, you should have looked for her, or waited here, and not gone out yourself.'

'Oh dear,' thought the vicar. 'Here's a coil.' Aloud he said, 'Now, let's not apportion blame today, when all we are concerned about is that Mary should be found, safe and well.'

He was still there, trying to restore domestic harmony, when Chief Inspector Coward arrived and told them that Mary had hitch-hiked back from Leckington the previous afternoon.

'Did she tell you she'd done that?' he asked the child's grandmother.

'No. I thought she'd come on the bus,' said Mrs Forman. 'Did she miss it?'

'No. Major Johnson came back before the bus. She told him she wanted to save the fare,' said the chief inspector.

'Now I come to think of it, she was early. She couldn't have come on the bus. I never noticed at the time,' said Mrs Forman.

'Well, it doesn't matter now. But it means that if she hitched a lift from Leckington, she might have gone in someone else's car.'

'Not a stranger's,' Jean insisted. 'She'd have recognised the major.'

'Mrs Forman, strangers can be plausible,' said the chief inspector. 'Unfortunately there was so much rain in the night that there's not much hope of picking up any scent of her. But we'll find something soon.'

I hope, he added, under his breath.

VI

There were two policemen in the car that stopped at Mrs Pollock's house. Mary had not shut the gate when she rushed out, and it swung on its hinge, creaking. They walked up the overgrown drive and rang the bell. When there was no reply they rang it a second time. Then they walked round to the back door. A cat-flap was let into it, and while they stood there a tabby cat pushed through it and sped past them into the bushes. There was a rinsed, empty milk bottle on the step. They didn't know that Mrs Pollock took a fresh pint only on alternate days.

'Owner away,' said one constable. 'The kid couldn't have come here, anyway. It's in the wrong direction altogether.'

His colleague peered in at the kitchen window. Everything looked orderly. The dishcloth, neatly draped over the sink, was just as Mary had left it. Mrs Pollock, dead in her chair, was invisible from where he stood.

The two policemen went away.

VII

Tom got out of the car, stumbled down the road and was sick into the ditch. He stood there, heaving and trembling, for some minutes, and all the time the rain poured down. That little kid. He saw the small hand slowly uncurling in his mind's eye. Where could she have sprung from? She must have moved right in front of the car when he turned to speak to Roger. Perhaps she was thumbing a lift.

What was he to do now?

He stood, irresolute, in the lane. Then he began to walk back the way he and Roger had come earlier. Where the road forked, he would take the other turn, no matter where it led. He couldn't think where Roger had vanished to, either. He needed him, to be told what to do. Roger led all their enterprises. But it was Roger's fault that this had happened. If he hadn't taken up Roger's challenge and stolen those boots in the market he wouldn't be here now, and that kid would still be alive. He began to sob, still half-drunk and very shocked, as he walked along, tears mingling with the rain on his face. His wiry hair got wetter and wetter and his soaked jeans clung to his legs.

That kid would be missed soon. The police would be out looking for her. And what about the geezer whose car that was? They'd be certain to catch up with him, and it would be all the harder for him if he'd hidden what he'd done.

But he walked on. After a long time he came to another village, really just a hamlet, a cluster of cottages and a farmhouse near a cross-roads. Because of the rain the sky was dark now, though it was only nine o'clock. Tom was quite surprised to find his wristwatch still working. He stood at the cross-roads wondering which way to go, and as he hesitated a bus came along. He made up his mind and hailed it. He must get out of the rain.

There were only a few passengers. Tom bought a ticket to Leckington and went right to the back of the bus, where he sat huddled and shivering as it moved off. It was warm and dry, and his relief at being out of the storm was immense, but he couldn't stop shaking. The bus went into Wiveldown, and he shrank further back into his seat when it stopped in the square, his face turned away from the window. Two middle-aged women got on and sat a few seats in front of Tom. They had been spending the day in the village and carried polythene bags full of flowers and vegetables they had been given to take home. They never stopped talking throughout the journey.

Leckington was the end of the run. Everyone got out except Tom, in whom all thought had ceased. The driver-conductor roused him.

'Well, lad, all change here. We don't go any further,' he called genially.

Tom jerked into life.

'Oh – thanks,' he said and got out quickly.

'Goodnight, lad. Best get home and into some dry things,' said the driver, who recognised Tom as being a local boy but could put no name to him.

'I will. Ta,' said Tom.

56

But he couldn't go home, not yet. They'd all be about and they'd see that something was up. He went to Bert's Café and bought a cup of tea and a cake with the last of his money. Maybe he'd feel better with something inside him. He looked round anxiously in case Roger was in here too, but there was no sign of him.

The tea was hot and sweet and he gulped it down, but he gagged on the cake and couldn't swallow it. Two girls he knew came and sat at his table. Normally he would have chatted them up, but tonight he barely noticed them.

'Some folks is a bit too big for their boots, not saying can I buy you a coffee,' said one girl to her friend.

'It's a different story on Friday nights, flashing his money around and that,' said the other. 'But I forgot – he lost his job. Maybe we'll have to pay for him if we aren't careful.'

They continued to talk at him in this way. Tom heard some of the words but the sense washed over him. He got up and left the café without speaking to them.

'Looked awful, didn't he?' said one, when he had gone. 'Proper ill, and soaking wet.'

'Been out without his umbrella,' said the second, tittering.

They did not have to sit alone at their table for long. Soon two other boys came to join them. They forgot about Tom.

The tea had stopped him shivering, but he began again as soon as he went out into the street. He couldn't go home yet. His mum and dad would still be up. His dad would want to know whether he'd been along to the labour, and if they'd sent him after a job. His mother would look solemn about his wet clothes and start to fuss. His sisters would be watching television or giggling together if they weren't out with their boy-friends. If he went straight up to his room he'd just lie on his bed and see that kid again. Fair hair, she had. She had on a Brownie dress. His sisters had been Brownies, centuries ago.

He walked the streets till after midnight, when he knew his parents would be in bed and asleep. Then he went home and let himself in quietly by the back door.

VIII

Although he told Tom that Mary must have been walking in the road, Roger was not sure that this was so. He had been looking ahead when he blew the horn and there was no sign of her; and she must have heard them coming. When Tom went off to turn the car he saw a gap in the hedge at the side of the road; there was a stile there, and a sign which pointed to a public footpath. He was over in a flash and loping across the field beyond.

Mary, in fact, once clear of Mrs Pollock's house, had taken a short cut across the fields; the road looped round in a semicircle but the other way cut several hundred yards from the journey home. In spite of the rain, Mary had known the way. Roger had no such local knowledge; he missed the second stile and came to a gate. It was securely wired up, so he climbed it and crossed the next field. There were some heifers in it; they looked at him, puffed and snorted, and came to investigate the intruder, one of them lowing loudly. Roger ran as fast as he could away from them, and they set off in lumbering, interested, harmless pursuit. He got across the next gate and leaned against it, panting, while they blew at him from their side, disappointed at being foiled in these friendly overtures.

Warily, he set off again; however, there were no livestock in this field. But there was a shed.

It offered shelter, for the rain was pouring down. Roger went into it and stood huddled in a corner waiting for the storm to pass and trying to think straight. Putting the child in the boot of the car had been an instinctive action with him, a bid for time, but she'd be found soon, and that git Tom would crack. Well, it had nothing to do with him. Tom had driven the car and his prints would be on the wheel. But Roger's would be in the car too. He didn't want any part of a murder rap, and that's what it would be, for sure.

He must get away, out of the district, to London, or maybe to the north. He'd make for the motorway and hitch a lorry.

He'd still got a pound or two, and with luck he'd nick a bit more somewhere on the way. But he mustn't risk running into Tom again.

He waited till it was nearly dark and then he struck off once more over the fields, glad to leave the shed which smelt of cow-dung. He'd lost all sense of direction, but he met no more cattle, and at last he reached a road.

He had trudged along it for only a hundred yards when he heard a car behind him and saw its lights approaching. He raised his thumb, and the car stopped. It was driven by a plump young man with a fair moustache.

'I'm going to Bletchford. Any good?' he asked.

'It's on my way,' said Roger. 'Thanks.'

IX

Chief Inspector Coward's men, searching the fields for Mary, found two abandoned bicycles early on Friday morning. They were not missed from the farm until two hours later, when their loss was reported at once.

The sergeant at the desk in Leckington police station took the details down over the telephone. The matter did not seem to be connected with Mary's disappearance, and every available constable was out searching for her; the theft of two bicycles, though tiresome, did not at that moment seem an urgent matter, but Superintendent Harris heard about it as he passed the desk on his way out to the temporary police headquarters in the school in Wiveldown. When he got out there and discovered that the bicycles had been found he thought there might be some link; one was quite a small machine. Detective Sergeant Davis and a constable were sent to Mordwell right away to see the farmer, Mr Bryant.

Mordwell had not so far been included in the house-to-house search for Mary because it was six miles from where she lived, but as no trace of her had yet been found the range would have to be extended. Already the first reporters had arrived, and soon appeals would be made in the press, on radio and television.

Mr Bryant grew vegetables on a large scale; he had contracts with a canning factory for peas and beans, and he owned five greengrocery shops. When he had a glut of produce, he sold the surplus off in the market, and this Thursday he had had several hundred cabbages and marrows to dispose of which would rot if left.

'Quick work, sergeant, finding the bikes so soon,' he said.

'I'm afraid you can't have them back just yet,' said Sergeant Davis. 'We want to look for prints on them.'

'Oh, why bother? You say they aren't damaged. Let's forget it this time. I'm sure you've enough to do. Probably just some kid's prank.'

'I expect so, sir. I hope you're right,' said the sergeant. 'But there's a child missing in Wiveldown, an eleven-year-old girl. There could be a connection. We'll let you have them back as soon as possible.'

'Good. My boys want to go off fishing – they're on holiday now, bike for miles, they do.'

'It'll be a day or two, sir,' said the sergeant.

'Hum. What do you think has happened to the child?'

'Can't say, yet, sir. So far we haven't found a sign of her.'

'Sounds bad, eh?'

'Yes. But we must hope she's safe. Children sometimes turn up after several days, having hidden in barns and so forth.'

'I've got a barn. Do you want to have a look at it?' asked Bryant. 'It's a long walk, though, from Wiveldown.'

'I would like to see it, yes. Is that where you kept the cycles?'

'No – they were in another shed with the tractor. It's out, in fact, I left it in the yard, but it was raining cats and dogs when I got back from market yesterday and I didn't bother to put it away.'

He led the two policemen to the barn. The truck was there, just as he had left it. Sergeant Davis put out a hand to stop Bryant from walking up to it.

'Just a minute, sir,' he said, looking down at the ground.

60

The tyre marks of the truck showed clearly in the dust, and there, sharply defined near the entrance to the barn, was a footprint.

'Not yours, Mr Bryant,' said the sergeant, looking down at the farmer's huge foot. 'One of your men, perhaps. Anyone been in here since you got back from market?'

'No. I've got two men who work for me, but they haven't been up here today.'

The constable had disappeared further into the barn and was poking about at the back, near the stacks of hay. He came forward. In his hand, held gingerly in a handkerchief between finger and thumb, was an empty bottle of Bristol Cream Sherry.

X

Miss Price rose as usual at half-past six. She had slept only intermittently since the police had called the night before; they had checked her account of Mary's visit and then left. Miss Price had tried to convince herself that Mary must have wandered into someone's garden shed seeking shelter from the storm and got locked in, but it seemed unlikely. The rain did not begin till after she had gone; the walk home should have taken only ten or fifteen minutes – even if she dawdled along and picked some more flowers she could not have taken more than half-an-hour. Miss Price had shown the policemen the daisies Mary had brought for her; she had put them in a pottery jug on the window-sill, where they stood now, bright and glowing.

Outside the house sunlight shone on the rain-soaked grass and all the flowers in the garden hung wet heads. Miss Price went round her garden talking aloud, as she often did.

'What can have happened to Mary?' she asked the holly-hocks. Then she fed the budgerigar and asked him too. After that she made a pot of tea and drank two cups, and ate three digestive biscuits. By then it was half-past seven: still too early to visit the Formans, she supposed. Her habitual early rising meant a lot of hanging about waiting for the rest of the world to wake up and start the day.

She recited aloud the first twenty stanzas of how, according to Lord Macaulay, Horatius held the bridge. Then she wheeled out her bicycle. Though she was nearly seventy she still rode round the district for miles on her old-fashioned machine. She kept it well maintained, and until recently had mended all her own punctures, but lately the young man next door had been doing this for her. He had seen her once with her bucket of water finding the hole in the tube; intrigued, he'd watched over the fence and asked to be taught how to do it, so that he need not take his own small boy's cycle to the garage. Silently marvelling that a generation could grow up so helpless, Miss Price had taught him what to do. Since he had so much time to make up, and needed to keep his hand in, she gave him her own repairs now.

She rode off, dressed in a baggy skirt and thick stockings. A few cars taking people to work passed her, and she saw the square was active; a police van was outside the school, and two police cars were parked beside it. Several people stood some distance from them, staring. She pedalled past The Grapes, where all the curtains were still drawn; the Hursts kept late hours, and she felt tolerant towards them, knowing they must be washing up far into the night, although in her opinion people who lay in bed on summer mornings missed the best of the day.

She turned into Welbeck Crescent and met the vicar's car coming towards her. He stopped when he saw her, and she dismounted from her machine. The vicar realised where she was going.

'Is there any news?' she asked him.

'Not yet.'

He told her how Mary had hitched a lift from Major Johnson.

'It means she might go in someone else's car,' he said.

'Oh, do you think so? Wouldn't she go only with someone she knew?' Miss Price shared the same optimistic view of Mary's likely conduct as her mother.

'No one she knew would be likely to offer her a lift out of the village,' pointed out the vicar reasonably enough. 'Alternatively, even one's acquaintances may unfortunately go beserk.'

'You really think something terrible may have happened?'

'Don't you?' the vicar asked.

'I find it hard to explain why she wasn't home soon after leaving me, certainly,' said Miss Price. 'And she couldn't have had an accident in the village without anyone knowing. But we must hope there's another explanation.'

'I'm glad you're going there,' said the vicar. 'Joe's just come back. He's been up all night searching for the child and out with the police this morning. He's blaming Jean for not staying at home.'

'And he's quite right, though she can't be held wholly responsible for this,' said Miss Price. 'Jean always had a lot of silly ideas, even as a child. She was bright – I taught her, you know—but her values were all wrong. She was lucky to marry Joe. He's a good, kind man, but not ambitious enough for her. I'll get on up there, vicar.'

With that, she mounted her bicycle again and pedalled off. The vicar had forgotten that she had known Jean Forman from childhood. She would take this tragedy, if it proved to be one, as a personal disaster, but she might put some of her own forth-right spirit into Jean Forman. Miss Price had, as a girl, played hockey for Somerset, and she was still equal to a battle.

At the Formans' house, Joe was having a bath and his mother was cooking him bacon and eggs. Jean was industriously vacuum-ing the living-room. Miss Price marched straight in upon her.

'Well, Jean,' she said. 'Switch that thing off and sit down. You won't bring Mary back by polishing.'

'I can't sit still,' said Jean, but she obeyed.

'Very likely not. But you can try, while we talk. Now, has Mary any special places where she likes to go? Secret haunts? Children do.'

'Not that I know of.' Jean looked surprised. 'Why?'

'She was alone a lot. She didn't always stay here waiting for you in the empty house, I'm sure. I met her once up at the old chalk-pit when I was out for a ramble.'

63

Miss Price made constant long-distance rambles on foot or by bicycle, devising the plots of her books, and was a well-known local sight on this account.

'The old chalk pit?'

'Yes. On the Chorlbury road. I told the police I'd seen her there. They're searching it.'

'I didn't know she'd ever been there,' said Jean.

'She said her father took her once. This time she was alone. She remembered it as a nice place, full of wild flowers – that's why she'd gone back there. I brought her back to the village with me,' said Miss Price. 'I made her promise not to go there alone again without telling someone. She'd keep her word, I think.'

'Yes, she would,' Jean said. 'She was – is – very obedient.'

But she'd gone for a ride in the major's car.

'So I wondered if there were any other spots she might go to, like the chalk-pit,' Miss Price pursued. 'But if there were, you wouldn't know about them, would you?'

Jean shook her head.

'I don't think you know her at all,' said Miss Price. 'You're out of the house so much, when you're at home you must be too busy to talk to your family. When do you do your housework? I must say, you keep the place immaculate. Mind you, I'm not against you working, Jean. I'm in favour of it. But not if your family suffers. You could have found a part-time job, or something in the village. Mrs Hurst at The Grapes is always short-handed.'

'Domestic work,' said Jean.

'You meet people in a pub,' said Miss Price.

Jean stiffened and looked at her. Miss Price was regarding her steadily with the same intense gaze that had caught her cheating as a child.

'I suppose you were at the Wives' Club last night. It can be checked. But the meetings end well before ten, I know – usually nine-thirty. I've talked at them. I wonder where you went on the way home. You didn't miss Mary till nearly eleven o'clock.'

Miss Price stood up and looked down at Jean, who had not answered.

'You were always a muddled thinker, Jean. I sincerely pray that Mary will be found. It's much too soon to give up hope. But sort your priorities out, my dear.'

She swept regally from the house, and as she rode off down the road the sound of the vacuum cleaner could be heard again, through the open window.

Bicycles travel silently, and one summer evening not so long ago when Miss Price was returning from visiting a friend she had seen Jean Forman in a grey car that was parked in a gateway. The man with her had lighted a cigarette, illuminating both their faces, as Miss Price rode noiselessly past.

Superintendent Harris and Chief Inspector Coward were conferring together outside the temporary police headquarters in the school when Miss Price passed on her way home. She stopped to ask for news, explaining who she was.

'Ah yes – the last person to see Mary, as far as we know,' said the superintendent. He was a tall man with clearly marked black eyebrows and a strong face. Miss Price took to him at once. If it was possible to find Mary alive, or alternatively if anyone had harmed her and must be brought to book, this man would see that it was done. 'We've found nothing yet,' he told her.

'You've searched the chalk-pit?'

'Some men with a dog are up there now.'

But none of them really thought that Mary had gone all that way in a thunderstorm. Not voluntarily.

When Miss Price had gone, Superintendent Harris said:

'This report of a pair of boots stolen from a market-stall yesterday – get on to it. There might be a link with the bicycles, though it seems a long shot. Abducting little girls isn't usually in the line of tearaway youths, but we'd better make sure, one way or the other. I don't like the smell of this case at all.'

XI

Major Johnson went out to pick runner beans at the bottom of his garden. He had a good crop of them, and they were just at their peak; he could not eat them all himself. They twined luxuriantly round the tall poles, orange flowers high up the stems and clusters of slender beans among the leaves. He stripped off all that were ripe and then stepped over to the hedge which divided him from the Blunts. Cathy should soon be pegging out her washing. By standing on an upturned tub the major could look over the top and call to her.

Cathy was there. He could see her corn-coloured hair and blue dress.

'Mrs Blunt,' he called.

'Oh – Major Johnson!' Cathy always called him the Cheshire Cat because his face usually appeared grinning above her suddenly, like this. They seldom met in more conventional situations. 'Hullo!'

'Would you like some beans?'

'Yes, please.'

'I've picked a lot. Got your basket?'

Cathy always stood on a garden seat which the Blunts had on the further side of the hedge and held up a basket to receive the bounty from next door.

'No – I'll get it – or why don't you come round?' It was ridiculous that the old boy had never been inside their house; she'd kept saying to Derek that they must ask him in, and Derek had agreed, but what with the baby arriving and one thing and the other, they had never done it. And this morning she felt upset; the police, arriving just after she had fed her baby, with such a distressing reason for their call, had disturbed her. It would be nice to talk to someone. Miss Amanda Blunt was only six weeks old and not yet very chatty. 'Come round and have some coffee,' she invited.

'Oh, thank you. That's most kind,' said Major Johnson. He was delighted.

He dismounted from his perch, rubbed his hand over his wisps of hair to flatten them, and walked round promptly, feeling a little shy but very pleased. He liked the Blunts but felt awkward if they met; they were so very young. And Cathy had been so conspicuously pregnant that he'd felt embar-

66

rassed; a friendship over the hedge was about their limit, he'd accepted.

'The police must have come to you too, I suppose,' said Cathy as she carried the cups on to the paved terrace outside the sitting-room.

'Yes, they did. I gave Mary a lift back from Leckington yesterday,' said the major, and told the tale again.

'I don't know her,' Cathy said. 'But it's awful. You hear of such dreadful things these days. They could happen even in Wiveldown.' She gazed anxiously at the pram, parked in the shade, where Amanda lay peacefully sleeping. Major Johnson had duly admired her before he sat down, though very little of her – a minute ear and the top of a small head covered in golden fluff – was visible from under her wraps. What threats lay in store for her daughter, Cathy thought worriedly.

'Mary must be safe,' said the major. 'She was so near home. I'm sure she'll soon be found.'

'I wonder if Ruth Fellowes met her,' said Cathy. 'She came to tea – she left not long before the storm began, she must have got caught in it. Do you know Ruth?'

'Yes, indeed,' said the major, and was about to tell her that he had taken Mrs Fellowes home the night before when he changed his mind. He had left her house rather late; she was a lady living alone, and Major Johnson was an old-fashioned man who had lived abroad a lot and not kept pace with contemporary life in Britain. Though it was impossible to imagine Mrs Fellowes in compromising circumstances, people's tongues were long and he did not wish to cause her any embarrassment. So he kept silent.

'Why is your house called Tobruk, Major Johnson?' Cathy asked him, biting into a ginger biscuit.

He looked at her, amazed. Could she be so young that she didn't know?

He told her.

XII

Ruth Fellowes was still asleep when the police knocked at her door. She looked out of the window to see who was below, then hastily pulled on her dressing-gown and dabbed at her springy grey hair with a brush before hurrying down.

She knew Mary. Just as Miss Price tested the Brownies for literacy, so did she for their cooking and hostess badges. Mary had already earned both.

'How dreadful,' she said. 'I didn't see her last night – I was out in the village at about half-past six. I went to see Mrs Blunt in Church Street, and I was walking back when the storm broke, so I went into The Grapes, for shelter. I had a drink too,' she added.

'I see.' The constable wrote it down. 'We'll just take a look round your garden, madam, if you don't mind. Have you a shed?'

She had.

'By all means, constable,' she said. 'But Miss Price lives on the other side of the village. How could Mary have wandered this way?'

'It doesn't seem likely that she did, but we must check everywhere,' said the policemen.

'Of course,' said Ruth.

Their search was soon over. When they had gone she dressed and had breakfast, then walked down to the post office for her newspaper. Because her cottage was in an isolated position no delivery boy could be found to go there, so she and the few other people who lived in that lane had to fetch their own.

She scarcely noticed the clear, sparkling weather for she was so shocked about Mary's disappearance. There had been no sign of her about when she had been with Major Johnson in his car, but anyone would take shelter in such a torrential downpour.

It had been a pleasant evening and she had enjoyed Major Johnson's company. Like many large women, Ruth was inwardly rather timid and she had spent most of her adult life acquiring a manner to match her bulk. Her husband had known how she felt, but he was large too. She guessed that Major Johnson had the same problem in reverse; he must be sensitive about being so small. But he was not in the least aggressive, as many small men were. She had admired his tenacity at the cookery classes, for he made valiant efforts to keep up with the other pupils who all started off with more basic knowledge than he had. Celia Mainwaring had laughed about him. 'One of my protégés,' she had said, and wondered what subject he should pursue next. He had talked so naturally last night about his army life, and then, when a huge spider had sauntered across the sitting-room floor, he had risen, gathered it up in one square, capable hand, and put it out of the window.

'I don't expect you like them,' he said. 'Most ladies don't. But I never kill them – not in this country, anyway. Some people think it's unlucky.'

Ruth, who quite liked spiders, melted into her chair feeling about five feet two inches tall, and as warm as if she had swallowed a double brandy. He was a kind, unassuming man, and he was lonely. She resolved that he should bring her back from Chorlbury Manor in future, instead of boring Madge Fazackerley.

The two Mrs Flints, Deirdre and Marilyn, who ran the post office and sold the papers, were forty and forty-two years old, and both weighed over eleven stone. The two brothers they had married managed a haulage contractor's business while their childless wives gossiped away the day, not with their customers but with each other, occasionally interrupting their chat to pay pensions or sell stamps. As they never tired of explaining, they sold the newspapers just to oblige, since no one else in the village would take it on. While they talked together, the two Mrs Flints knitted. Vast sweaters in elaborate lacy patterns poured from their needles, and woe betide the customer who expected to be served in the middle of a row.

But today the knitting still lay furled in its plastic bags beside each lady. The two plump faces, thickly plastered with pan cake make-up and with carmine lips beneath helmets of stiff black hair, gazed avidly out over the counter, the two huge busts leaned on the rounded arms while their owners surmised what fate had befallen Mary.

Like Mary, Ruth Fellowes was not fond of these two, but she said her usual cheerful 'Good morning', to them both.

'I'll take my paper, shall I?' she said, and went to help herself from the pile of *Daily Telegraphs*.

'I'll get it for you, Mrs Fellowes.' The slightly fatter Mrs Flint came round from behind the counter and, with dampened thumb, sorted through the pile till she came to the one with Mrs Fellowes' name on it.

'Oh – thank you.' This was unaccustomed attention.

'Terrible about little Mary Forman, isn't it?' said Mrs Flint the larger.

'Has she been found?' asked Ruth.

'Not yet – but it's obvious, isn't it? I mean to say – '

'What's obvious?' asked Ruth in a voice like steel.

'Stands to reason,' said the second Mrs Flint.

'What does?' asked Ruth ominously.

'She'll have been murdered of course, poor little mite, and her in here only last evening buying some sweets.'

'I hope you're wrong, Mrs Flint,' said Ruth. 'She's probably wandered off somewhere and will turn up perfectly safely.'

At this point another customer arrived: Major Johnson, in smart grey flannels and navy blazer.

'Ah, good morning, Mrs Fellowes.' His smile was tempered with reserve, for all Wiveldown must be grave today. He nodded to the Mesdames Flint. 'May I take my paper?'

'We've no boy today, major,' said Deirdre Flint. She plucked out Major Johnson's *Daily Mail*. 'We were just saying, isn't it sad about Mary?'

'She's been found?' asked the major.

'No,' said Ruth. 'There isn't any news.'

'But we all know what will have happened,' said Marilyn.

'Some maniac, it must be. These wicked men.' She shuddered greedily.

'I don't think we should assume the worst yet, Mrs Flint,' said the major firmly. 'Think how such talk would distress her family. There must still be hope that she's safe.'

'I quite agree, Major Johnson,' said Ruth. 'It's very worrying, but it's too soon yet to fear the worst.'

'It's always the same in these cases,' said Deirdre. 'Several days pass, and then the kiddies' bodies turn up, marked by dreadful wounds.'

'Mrs Flint, you must not talk like that,' said the major. 'Only a few weeks ago a missing child was found asleep and unharmed in a wood, somewhere in Hampshire. There must be other children in the village, Mary's friends, who could be needlessly upset if they knew that older people feared for Mary's life, not to mention her parents.'

'I quite agree with you, Major Johnson,' said Ruth. 'We must all hope that Mary will be found unharmed in the next few hours.' She stalked out of the post office on these words, followed by the major, and the two Mrs Flints looked at one another and shrugged.

'Well, I don't know! Some people,' said one.

'A little too big for our boots today, aren't we?' said the other.

Outside the post office Ruth Fellowes turned to Frederick Johnson, looking down at him with a solemn expression.

'I'm glad you said that. Those two are like the *tricoteuses* by the guillotine,' she said. 'They give me the creeps. But I'm horribly afraid they may be right about Mary.'

'So am I,' said Major Johnson. The two of them looked across the square to where a police car was parked; beside it, two men in plain clothes were talking to a uniformed sergeant in the road, and another policeman, radio squawking, came up on his motor-cycle as they watched. 'Mrs Flint and her sister are like the ghouls who go to accidents and goggle at the victims. Not the nicest people in the village.'

'No,' said Ruth.

71

'That was a very pleasant evening,' said the major. 'Thank you so much for your hospitality.'

'You must come again,' said Ruth.

'I'd like to,' said the major. 'Well, I must be off.' He smiled at her again and turned away.

Ruth smiled too. She was still smiling when she reached her own house.

XIII

Surprisingly, once his shivering ceased, Tom slept; but when morning came and the bustle of his father and sisters getting ready for work began, he pulled the bedclothes up over his head, curled himself into a foetal bundle, and remained there, motionless, until successive bangs of the back door announced their departure. The house then echoed to the clatter of his mother, down in the kitchen, and the syphoning sound of the water system refilling.

He got up, flung on a pair of jeans and a sweater, and his plimsolls which were still damp, and rushed out of the house. His mother heard him, but she was too late to catch him. She went up to his room and sighed over the disorder she found there: the sheets and blankets were dragged off the bed and pulled on to the floor, and under them was a pile of discarded clothes. She picked them up; they were soaking wet, and had made the sheets damp too. She took them down to wash.

Until the garage closed and he lost his job, Tom had always been such a good boy; he was quiet and gentle, not at all like his noisy sisters, and she hoped he was set for a good career in the motor trade. Now he idled about from day to day and she never knew who he mixed with. His sisters said he went to that rough Bert's Café, which they wouldn't be seen dead in; all the town's yobbos went there, and it was not the sort of place Mrs West thought her son should frequent. She had lain awake last night, worrying, until she heard him come in. He was seldom out so late, and he had never gone off like this in the morning without a word, and without a bite to eat.

Tom, who had found some odd coins in his dry jeans, bought a *Daily Mirror*, expecting to see in enormous headlines, CHILD'S BODY FOUND IN BOOT OF CAR, but the main story was an alleged case of bribery in the police, and though he scanned the paper thoroughly there was nothing about a missing child in it. Next, he went to where Roger lived in a terraced house on the edge of the town. Roger's mother was a thin, drawn widow, always exhausted, who worked as a cleaner; she was afraid of Roger, who treated her almost as badly as his father had done. She had already left for work when Tom arrived, and there was no sign of Roger; the house was empty.

Leckington was always busy on Fridays, but that day there were several police cars among the traffic; one went through the town with its light flashing and its siren sounding. Tom heard two women with shopping bags on their arms speculating about the cause of the activity. While he listened a third woman came and told them that a child was missing somewhere in the district.

'Murdered, most like,' said the woman, and Tom felt sick to his stomach.

He wandered about for a while, without an aim, and then he walked up and down outside the police station wondering whether to go in and tell them what had happened. It was an accident. He hadn't meant any harm to the kid, he never saw her. But whose was the car? It wasn't one he recognised from his days at the garage. Maybe it came from far away. It would look bad for the poor bugger whose car it was when the child was found.

After walking about for a couple of hours in a confused state, Tom went up to the labour exchange where he was told of a job as a loader and cleaner at the paint factory. Not his style at all, he'd have said the day before. But now he set off to apply for it, determined to get it, no matter how dull the work and whatever the wage.

73

XIV

Major Johnson turned on the radio for the one o'clock news while he ate a quick snack before going to Chorlbury Manor for his afternoon's duty. After the political news there was an announcement about the missing child and she was described.

The Manor opened at two o'clock and Admiral Bruce liked all the staff to be there in plenty of time. Major Johnson was often the first to arrive. His route lay past the square, and today a small crowd had collected outside the school. As he drove out of the village he saw a group of policemen in rubber boots, twenty or more, coming towards him. Several were leading dogs. Some men with cameras, newspapermen he supposed, were among them. What a terrible business.

He reached the Manor and parked in the courtyard reserved for the staff. Then he walked round to the forecourt. Admiral Bruce was already there, pacing up and down as if on the quarter-deck. He hailed the major.

'Ah – Major Johnson. If you're not in a hurry this evening I'd be most grateful if you'd spare a few minutes after we close. I want to consult you,' he said.

'Certainly, admiral,' said Major Johnson.

'Splendid,' said the admiral, sketching a gesture in the air with his hand.

Major Johnson fought the desire which always attacked him when in the presence of the admiral to come to attention and salute. The admiral looked benign and his own conscience was clear; he was not being summoned to any parade of defaulters. He went into the house and began to prepare for the afternoon's intake of visitors. He liked this time, with the vast house hushed and expectant; the air of spacious repose was soothing. The major would have liked to live there when the house was at the height of its splendour, with servants scurrying round bringing comfort to the magnificently dressed occupants. But then, in those days, he would have been a servant, the major had to remind himself, at the very best a senior groom. At least now he was able to experience a little vicarious gracious living, seated in the linenfold-panelled hall at his ancient oak table, selling the tickets.

Fridays were always busy; today there were several coach-loads of Americans and a party of Danes, and a women's outing whose members were all a little too old to enjoy the stairs and the long passages, but who collapsed with delight over their special tea served in the orangery. But the day came to an end eventually and when the last visitor had gone and the house had been searched and locked, Ruth Fellowes came into the hall. Major Johnson was checking his day's takings, which were above average.

'The admiral wants to see me,' the major told her. 'Some matter he wants to discuss. Excuse me.'

He left her, looking pleased and important, and Ruth sighed. Madge Fazackerley it must be, after all.

Major Johnson found the admiral in his office with whisky and soda beside him on a tray. He poured out a drink for the major and bade him sit down, then came straight to the point. The Manor was becoming more popular every year and new attractions were constantly being added. He needed help with administration, especially the book-keeping.

'You'd be just the man for it, Major Johnson,' said the admiral. 'I want a man for this job – we've enough women about the place as it is. You'd be my deputy, my number one, you might say.' He wondered if the other would appreciate this naval allusion. Then he went on to name a salary.

The major could hardly believe his luck. The job would be almost full-time and very well paid. In the winter, when the house was closed, there were its maintenance and repairs to be dealt with. It would be interesting, worthwhile work of the kind he excelled at.

'Think it over,' said the admiral.

But the major needed no time to reflect.

'I'll be proud to accept,' he declared.

His one thought as he drove home was to wonder how soon he would be able to tell Miss Mainwaring this news. The money, too, would make a great difference to how he lived; small luxuries would be everyday matters now, not rare extravagances. He wove a daydream in which he took her to dine at The Lamb and she said to him, over champagne, 'It's only what you deserve, Frederick, after your lifetime of experience'.

XV

That evening Major Johnson went up to The Grapes for his usual pint. He felt buoyant. At last he was adapting to civilian life and finding a niche. He had a job; he was on friendly terms with his young neighbours; he had a plan for the future. For a short while he forgot all about Mary, but he found the familiar bar at the pub full of strangers and was reminded at once of the tragedy. The press was here in force.

It was good for trade. Mr and Mrs Hurst were serving pints without pause.

Major Johnson fought his way through the mob to the bar counter and ordered his usual.

'Ah, major. Good evening,' said Mr Hurst.

'You're busy,' said Major Johnson. He, greeted personally, belonged in this pub, unlike all these strangers who would be gone for ever as soon as the excitement died down. He was warmed by the thought.

'Yes. One person's misfortune is another's good luck,' said Mr Hurst.

'Still no news?'

'Not a bit, I believe. Dreadful, isn't it? Most of the men in the village are turning out with the police tomorrow to go over the ground again.'

The landlord turned from him to attend to somebody else, and Major Johnson was buttonholed by a brisk man with a large moustache.

'Live here, do you?' he asked abruptly.

'I do,' answered Major Johnson.

'Did you know Mary Forman?'

'I do know Mary,' said the major.

'Seen her lately?'

'Yesterday afternoon,' said the major.

'Know the family?'

Major Johnson knew Joe from his days at the paint factory; he had heard about his wife's aspirations, but he did not propose to gratify the reporter's curiosity.

'Telling your readers a lot of tittle-tattle about the family won't help to find Mary, will it?' he said tartly. 'Print her picture, ask anyone who saw her yesterday to come forward – that's what you should do. But spare the family's feelings.'

'Well said, Major Johnson,' said a feminine voice. Penny Hurst had appeared in the bar. She still wore her drab long dress, but now she carried a rucksack and was with a pale young man wearing an orange shirt. 'Goodbye.' She drifted away, her companion following behind her, and Major Johnson remembered that she was going camping in Greece. What unsuitable clothes for life under canvas, he thought.

'Who's that?' asked the reporter.

'My daughter,' said Mr Hurst.

The reporter hurried out after the couple and there were noisy sounds of argument from the road. Finally there came the roar of a car's exhaust and the reporter returned, grinning.

'Camera shy, your daughter,' he told the landlord.

'Why do you want her photograph, for heaven's sake?' asked Mr Hurst.

'Human interest. Writing up the village for the Sundays,' said the reporter.

The certainty that Mary had met some terrible fate was with them all. They were like vultures, the newspapermen, waiting for the kill, thought the major. Doubtless they'd been hounding the wretched Formans all day. He finished his pint, his earlier elation gone.

After he left, the reporter who had talked to him, and who had heard Penny address him, made a careful note of his name. He did not take kindly to snubs.

XVI

Saturday's newspapers had the news about Mary's disappearance on the front pages, and they all carried an enlargement of the indifferent snapshot her mother had produced. Some had shots of the council house in Welbeck Crescent. DISTRAUGHT MOTHER, said one, with a picture of Jean. FATHER SEARCHES ALL NIGHT, said another.

Over her orange juice, grape nuts and coffee, Celia Mainwaring read *The Guardian's* precise account of the situation. She could not remember coming across either the child or her parents in the library; probably they did not read, or used the mobile van. She drank a second cup of coffee and then departed for the library wearing a new biscuit-coloured linen skirt and pale shirt, with a row of silver bangles on her wrist.

Saturday mornings were always busy, for the library closed at twelve and did not open again until Tuesday morning; there were dozens of customers changing their books for the weekend and Celia was late in closing. She hurried home with not much time to spare before she must be at the tennis club for a match in the afternoon, and found on her doorstep a large blue hydrangea in a pot. It was wrapped in florist's paper and a card in a neat, crabbed hand said: *With kind regards, Frederick Johnson. P.S. I have some good news to tell you.*

For a moment Miss Mainwaring wondered who Frederick Johnson was; then the major's round, always rather anxious-looking face swam into her mind's eye. She began to rock with laughter. What on earth could he want to tell her? That he'd been elected to the parish council?

In a lull at the match, during which Leckington Ladies made a bold stand against their opponents from across the county, she sat sunning her sturdy legs and told Mavis Combe, her partner, what had happened.

'Made a conquest, have you? What's he like?' Mavis enquired.

'Oh – tedious, and knee-high to a grasshopper,' Celia said. 'Silly old fool.'

'Watch out for fireworks,' Mavis said, giggling.

Tom West read the newspaper headline over his father's shoulder at breakfast. Now that he had a job he was trying to behave normally at home. He had watched television the night before and seen pictures of the search for Mary, and of her parents and her grandmother. So the child was still undiscovered. What could have happened to the car? Maybe the owner had found the kid, panicked, and dumped her somewhere miles away. It's what he would have done. When his father put the paper down he picked it up, trying to look casual. *My daughter wouldn't accept a lift from a stranger, sobs thirty-five-year-old heartbroken mother,* he read. There was a picture of Miss Price on her bicycle with the caption: *Well-known novelist the last to see Mary – is she alive?*

'It's terrible what the papers do,' said Tom's mother. 'That poor woman.'

'Must have been done in,' said one of Tom's sisters. 'Poor kid – some loony must have got her, I s'pose, like you was always warning us, mum.'

'Poor little sod,' said Tom, and burst out of the room. They heard him rush upstairs and a few minutes later came the sound of the lavatory flushing.

'What's with him?' asked the second sister.

'Leave him alone, you two,' said their mother.

Later, Tom went to Roger's house again. Mrs Brewis was there on her own. She had not seen Roger since Thursday morning, nor heard a word from him, but that was nothing new. He often vanished for weeks at a time and then reappeared just as suddenly, sometimes with a wad of money but more often broke.

Roger himself was in Birmingham when he read the paper. He had hitch-hiked there in three stages and spent last night in a hostel. So the kid hadn't been found yet. That was a lucky break. But he'd better get further away. He'd find a job for a week or two to put him in funds, and he'd look for some new mates. By then the trouble would all have died down. He must just hope that creep Tom West would keep his mouth shut.

79

Major Johnson had to walk to the post office once more for his *Daily Mail*. He collected the Blunts' *Daily Telegraph* and the *Express* for the Philpots, and said shortly to the Mrs Flints that he hoped the paper boy would soon be back.

One of the papers had a picture of the elder Mrs Flint on its middle page. *Sold sweets to missing child*, ran the text, and an interview with Deirdre was printed below. Marilyn was put out because she had not been featured and determined that when Mary was found her views would be given full publicity. Both ladies had intended to show this report to the major, since it was not in his paper, but when they saw the glint in his blue eyes they changed their minds.

'Looked ever so fierce, he did,' they said to one another, and repeated it to anyone who would listen in the days that followed.

XVII

Major Johnson had sent the hydrangea on a sudden impulse, inspired by seeing some flowers delivered to Cathy Blunt next door. It was her birthday, she told him later over the fence.

When was Miss Mainwaring's, he wondered.

But he need not wait for a special occasion to send her some; why not do it now? Taking her out to lunch had marked the start of his special campaign; flowers would consolidate the position gained by the first manœuvre. He drove into Leckington, arranged it all, finding Miss Mainwaring's address in the telephone directory, and drove back home in a state of euphoria. Then he took Cathy round a bunch of small early chrysanthemums, pink ones from his garden; the Blunts' garden was in the process of reorganisation, and Derek was out, stripped to the waist, guiding a rotavator over the ground among his apple trees.

The police were still active in the square as the major drove by on his way to the Manor that afternoon; patrol cars had been out during the morning asking through loudspeakers for anyone who had seen Mary on Thursday to come forward.

Several of the lady guides were arriving as the major drew up in his car. He saw Mrs Fellowes with Mrs Fazackerley get out of a green mini and go into the house ahead of him.

Admiral Bruce waylaid him as he walked across the forecourt.

. 'Ah – Johnson. I'm arranging for someone else to take over your job in the vestibule from Monday week. Shall we say that you'll start in your new post then? Splendid.'

The major felt like answering 'Ay, ay, sir,' he felt so jaunty, but he restrained himself and replied with a calm affirmative. He strode into the house wondering if the rest of the staff knew of his appointment, but no one mentioned it. He hummed a military march under his breath as he arranged his desk, and one of the lady guides said, 'My, major, you are in good spirits today.'

'Indeed I am, indeed I am,' agreed the major.

He was tireless that afternoon, remaining cheerful as the hordes of visitors trooped in and the guides all began to wilt. He directed the hungry towards the orangery and tea with unflagging patience; he counted heads with zeal and accuracy. When he got home that evening he still felt full of energy and decided to wash the car. He left it parked on the gravel outside the bungalow, changed into working trousers and rubber boots, and began to roll the hose out.

From next door the sound of Derek's rotavator ceased. As the major fixed the connection to the tap, the young man appeared in the gateway.

'You haven't a drop of petrol, have you, Major Johnson?' he asked. 'I've run right out – I do want to finish this stretch tonight. This is when one curses because there's no pump in the village.'

'I've some in the garage,' the major said. 'Not much – just enough to fill up my mower once more. That won't last you long. But I've a gallon in the car. I always carry a spare can in the boot. You never know when you'll need it.'

He took the car keys out of his pocket and went round to the back of his car. Bending down, he put the key in the lock.

'That's funny. It isn't locked,' he said, half to himself.

He raised the lid.

Mary was found.

PART THREE

I

DEREK WENT up to the square in his own car to tell the police. It seemed more direct than telephoning to Leckington. They closed the boot of the car before he left, and the major spent the short interval until he returned disconnecting the hose and putting it away again.

Two constables arrived with Derek, and a few minutes later Detective Chief Inspector Coward and Detective Sergeant Davis joined them. They did not take Mary away for some time. First they rigged up tarpaulins to hide the scene from the road; then a police photographer and the doctor came. The press followed, and very quickly a small crowd of spectators gathered on the pavement. Several policemen stood outside the major's bungalow keeping them away.

Chief Inspector Coward went to tell the Formans and to prepare them for the fact that they would have to identify Mary formally, later on. She was removed after an hour, a tiny form on a stretcher covered with a blanket, and a policeman drove Major Johnson's car away to be examined.

Superintendent Harris interviewed Major Johnson himself.

The major could hardly take in what had happened.

'How could she have got there?' he kept saying. 'Why wasn't the boot locked? I always lock it.'

'It wasn't locked? You're sure?' demanded the superintendent.

'Quite sure,' said the major.

'Mr Blunt?' The superintendent turned to Derek.

'I'm not certain – Major Johnson said something about it

being unlocked but I didn't notice, I'm afraid,' said Derek, whose face was as white as the major's. He had been sick in the major's bathroom after they had found Mary. The sight of the child lying there, whey-faced, was one he would never forget. The major had seen many dreadful sights in his life, so he did not vomit, but he felt distinctly queasy.

'You've used the car today?'

'Yes,' said the major. God, how long had he been driving round with that pathetic child lying there? 'I went to Leckington this morning, and to Chorlbury Manor this afternoon – I work there.'

'Your car was here on Thursday night? In the garage?'

'Yes. I used it to go to The Grapes that evening – I usually walk up there at about half-past six or so. There was a thunderstorm that day, so I took the car.'

'I see. And you put it away when you got home?'

'Yes, I did.'

'How long were you in The Grapes?'

'Not long. Twenty minutes, perhaps.'

'And you lock your garage at night, Major Johnson?'

'Always.'

'You locked it on Thursday in spite of the storm?'

It had stopped raining when he got home that night. He remembered standing on the gravel drive sniffing the damp air as he turned the key.

'I know I did,' said the major. 'I'd just collected the car from being serviced and having a new gearbox fitted that morning. Perhaps the garage didn't lock the boot after checking the spare tyre. I'd have probably noticed it sooner if it hadn't been for the storm.'

'You collected it before you gave Mary that lift?'

'Yes – it was ready about half-past eleven. I had lunch in Leckington, at The Feathers.' There was no need to mention Miss Mainwaring; why involve others? The police would soon find out how poor Mary got into his car. 'Could she have opened the boot and climbed in?' he wondered aloud. 'The lid might have dropped shut on her – there wouldn't be much air.'

84

'I don't think so, sir. There were various bruises on the body. It looks as if she was dead when she was put into your car.'

'Oh dear,' said Major Johnson.

'Yes. A bad business.'

'The poor Formans,' said the major. 'Who could have done it?'

'Done what, Major Johnson?'

'Why, killed her, of course.'

'You think she was murdered?'

'Surely it's the only explanation?' The Mrs Flints were right after all. 'One of these – these child murderers, I suppose, killed her and hid her in my car. But how – when – I just don't understand.'

'We'll know more when the doctor's examined Mary properly,' said Superintendent Harris.

'If you've finished with me, I'll go home,' said Derek. 'It's Cathy's birthday. We've got a baby-sitter coming. We were going out.' He looked at the older men. 'I couldn't eat a thing.'

'You'd better try,' advised the superintendent. 'You don't want your wife brooding too, do you? You'll feel better soon.'

Derek went away.

'Still wet behind the ears,' said Chief Inspector Coward, who had returned from his mission to the Formans while Superintendent Harris was talking to the major. 'Some of our lads have seen worse than that long before they're his age.'

'If you think of anything else – something that might throw light on how anyone could have got at your car – you'll let us know at once, of course,' said the superintendent.

'Certainly,' said Major Johnson.

'And you're not planning to go away, are you?'

'Of course not. I'll be here if you should want me.' What an odd remark.

'We'll want to talk to you when we've examined the car.'

'I shan't be going anywhere,' the major said.

The policeman went away and Major Johnson poured himself a stiff drink. Could someone have put the child's body in his car while it was parked at Chorlbury Manor? It was the only thing he could think of. Once the staff were all in, the courtyard where they parked was deserted. He finished his drink and poured himself another. Then he realised that he had not eaten since midday, so he scrambled some eggs. He was sitting down at the kitchen table, on the point of eating them, when the doorbell rang.

Two men stood on the step. As the major opened the door a flashlight went off in his face. They were reporters, and one of them was the man with a moustache whom he had spoken to in The Grapes the night before.

Major Johnson was very angry.

'Go away,' he said fiercely, and slammed the door,

They rang continuously for some minutes but he did not answer. After a while he heard their footsteps on the gravel. He did not finish his supper.

II

Cathy Blunt was awake early, feeding her baby. She had tried not to disturb Derek, sliding out of bed with as little upheaval as she could manage. Derek gave a grunt and rolled over. She looked down at him, smiling indulgently as she sometimes smiled at Amanda; his hair was tousled and his beard showed dark on his jaw-line. For a while she forgot the terrible discovery of the night before, but when she had finished with the baby and tucked her back into her cot she looked out of the window over the garden, and there, across the dividing hedge, was Major Johnson hoeing his cabbages. At six o'clock in the morning.

Derek put out an arm and gathered her to him as she got back into bed.

'He's out there already,' she said.

'Hmmmm – who is?' mumbled Derek, still almost asleep.

'The Cheshire Cat. In his garden. I suppose he couldn't sleep. Poor old boy.'

'Hum. Yes.' Derek, though very shocked at first, had managed to banish the nightmare to the back of his mind.

'He couldn't have had anything to do with it,' said Cathy.

'Good God, no. He'd scarcely have opened the boot like that if he'd known the kid was there. He had as much of a shock as I did.'

'But how did she get in there?' Cathy persisted. 'Oh, poor Mrs Forman.' And Cathy knew with startling clarity that she, herself, would never live a totally unworried life again, now that she had a little daughter of her own.

'Some crazy maniac,' said Derek. 'Let's forget it now, Cathy. Go to sleep.' He kissed her ear, getting a mouthful of long fair hair as he did so.

But Cathy lay awake, thinking of the child and her parents, and of the odd, repressed man next door who had become so incongruously mixed up with the tragedy.

Later, when they were having breakfast in their sunny kitchen, she said, 'Derek, let's ask Major Johnson to lunch. We've got a chicken – there's plenty of food.'

'Oh, not today, Cathy.'

'Why not? He shouldn't be alone, poor man. He must be feeling awful,' Cathy said.

'No, Cathy. We'll ask him later, when this has all blown over.' Derek finished up his cornflakes. 'I don't want you mixed up in this business, it's bad enough already.'

'Bad enough for the Formans, yes, and the major,' Cathy said.

'I was there, remember, when Mary was found. That's quite enough involvement for us,' said Derek.

Cathy looked at him and her eyes widened.

'You're afraid of being mixed up with a scandal,' she accused. 'Derek, how could you?'

'It isn't good for business,' Derek said.

'But you've just said Major Johnson couldn't possibly have had anything to do with Mary's death. What harm can it do, asking him to lunch?'

'It connects us with him. It might be bad tactics, if it got about,' said Derek. He was on the brink of promotion in his firm, and he did not want to risk blemishing his image.

'Oh, Derek, how can you think like that? When he's been so kind to us!'

'He's rather an odd chap. There's something a bit strange about him,' Derek said. There must be, or how had the body got into the car? Bodies just didn't get into people's cars. Seeking to justify his attitude, Derek suddenly thought with an icy feeling that the major might be suffering from amnesia. He could have killed the child and forgotten all about it. He said so.

'I don't believe it,' Cathy said. Her cheeks were flushed and her eyes were bright with anger. 'He's a nice, shy, harmless old man, and someone's played this terrible trick on him. I'm ashamed of you for thinking like that.'

But the more Derek thought about it, the more sense the idea made. The old man might easily have found out from Mary that she was due at Miss Price's on Thursday evening. He could have waylaid her there. She would have got into his car without a murmur.

'He's not coming to lunch, Cathy, and you're not to talk to him,' Derek said. 'I forbid it.'

Cathy's heart was thumping hard and she felt slightly sick: who was this hostile stranger sitting facing her?

'I shall do as I please,' she said. She was beginning to tremble. 'He's always been sweet to me, and he has lovely old-fashioned good manners.' She got up, went out of the back door, and walked straight down the garden to the bench. She climbed up on it and looked over the hedge.

'Hullo, Major Johnson. Good morning,' she called. 'Isn't it a lovely day?'

And Major Johnson, jolted back from his dark thoughts to the present, looked up from thinning out the lettuces, which was what he was doing now, to her pink, glowing face framed with long fair hair. She looked like an angel appearing over the fence.

'Can you spare some parsley?' Cathy asked.

He gave her some.

But Cathy did not ask him to lunch.

III

The news that Mary had been found dead was given on the radio at nine o'clock, and Miss Mainwaring heard it as she started her leisurely Sunday. Because the Formans were a local family, Leckington had taken the child's disappearance closely to heart, and even Miss Mainwaring felt a personal concern. She looked in her *Observer* for more details before turning to the book reviews, and found a paragraph which disclosed where the body had been found.

Miss Mainwaring's gaze flew to her hydrangea. She was not a nervous woman, but she shuddered. It was some minutes before she felt able to resume her toast and marmalade.

One of Tom's sisters told him the news. She was in her dressing-gown, reading the *News of the World*, with her hair in rollers and cream on her face while Mrs West exclaimed in resigned dismay at her failure to conform to orderly breakfast habits.

'They've found that kid. In some bloke's car, she was,' said Brenda West. 'Look, there's his photo.' And there was a picture of the startled Major Johnson at his front door. 'Rotten bastard,' added Brenda.

'Why rotten bastard?' growled Tom.

'Well, he done her in, didn't he? Must have,' said Brenda.

'Does it say so?' Tom demanded. He snatched the paper from her and read the headlines.

MISSING CHILD FOUND IN MAJOR'S MORRIS, they ran, and the text went on to describe with fair accuracy the circumstances. No details, it added, had yet been released about the cause of death.

'It doesn't say he touched her,' said Tom. He read on, his lips forming the words silently. Then he repeated them aloud.

89

Major Johnson, a bachelor, said he did not know how the child's body had got into his car.

'Course he said that,' Brenda exclaimed. 'He's not going to admit it, is he?'

'If he killed her, he wouldn't have left her in his car,' said Tom. 'He'd have dumped her.' As they had dumped the bikes.

' 'Spect he was going to, only they found her first,' said Brenda.

'Give your father the paper and get out of my way,' said Mrs West, coming to the table with the teapot.

On Sundays in Wiveldown, since the post office was closed, the papers were collected from a shed in the garden of the senior Flints. The brothers took it in turn, Sunday by Sunday, to fetch them from Leckington and put them out on an old deal table. Whichever brother was then in charge sat there exchanging gossip with his customers as they straggled in. If he got bored, he went away, leaving a tin for the money.

On that Sunday there was no shortage of subject matter, and the village came early for its papers. Most of the papers carried picture's of the major's bungalow, and one showed his car being driven away.

The major was among the first callers. As his firm footsteps sounded on the path the small group clustered round the door of the shed fell silent and stared at him.

'Good morning,' said the major in his clipped voice, and stepped into the shed.

'*Sunday Telegraph*, please,' he said.

Silently the elder Flint folded it and gave it to him. The major always brought the exact price with him; he handed it over and strode off. No other words were said, but when he had gone, the voices broke out.

'Well! Did you see that?'

'Fancy walking in like that, as if nothing had happened!'

'As bold as brass – '

He heard it, as he was meant to, and he squared his shoulders, walking on with his usual firm tread. He must expect this for a time; soon the police would discover how Mary had got into his car and things would return to normal.

He walked down the road, back to *Tobruk*, and saw his neighbour Mr Philpot approaching. Major Johnson prepared to greet the other man; Mr Philpot, with great ostentation, crossed the road to the other side and ignored him as they passed.

Mrs Fellowes did not collect her papers until quite late that morning, and when she did the shed was unattended. She had heard the police sirens the evening before and had realised there must be some development in the hunt for Mary, but unlike most of the village she did not know where the child had been found, only what she had heard on the radio news. She walked all the way home before she opened her *Sunday Express* and saw on the front page a picture of Major Johnson's bungalow.

When she rang him up, he had already left for church.

Major Johnson went to church every Sunday morning, so today was no exception. He wore his best grey worsted suit and sat in his usual pew. When he came in, those already in the church nudged each other and stared at him; those who arrived later also stared.

The Reverend Wilson looked round at his flock and saw Major Johnson sitting there. He had assessed the major as a man whose code was Kiplingesque; now he wondered. He took as his text: *Whoso shall offend one of these little ones* and led prayers for Mary and the comfort of her parents, who, being Baptists, were similarly petitioned for in that sister establishment up the road. At the end of the service he stood in the doorway to greet the congregation filing by. He shook Major Johnson's hand firmly when his turn came, and looked hard at his face with his vague blue eyes. The major returned his stare steadily. The vicar was the only person in church that morning who looked at the major and did not turn away.

When the major reached his bungalow a flock of small boys was gathered outside it. At the sight of the major they scattered, but not without a flow of language obscene at any age, but shattering at theirs.

IV

A pair of brand new, bright tan boots with a row of ornamental studs across the instep stood on Chief Inspector Coward's desk. He sat before them, staring at them pensively, and Detective Sergeant Davis leaned against a filing cabinet, also in an attitude of meditation.

'A pair of boots like these were nicked from Leckington market last Thursday afternoon,' mused the inspector. 'Two yobbos made a rumpus at the stall, and one of them took the boots while the other chatted up the stallholder.'

'That's right,' agreed Sergeant Davis. He was tired. He had been up most of the night, and so had the inspector, but he felt wrung out, whereas the inspector seemed to be rejuvenated by the extra adrenalin coursing round his system.

'Hm. Well, get out with these to Mordwell, see how they match up. The size may be different, but we should be able to get a pair the same size as the footprint, though it won't be evidence. Anyway, we're not looking for a sex maniac. That'll be some comfort to the parents.' If anything could be. 'I'll go and see them. And I'll call on Major Johnson while I'm there.'

'Do you think he had anything to do with it?'

'No, but it may be hard to substantiate that. Someone else dumped the child in his car, I'm certain. If the fingerprints on those stolen bikes match up with any on his car, we'll have something to go on.'

'And the sherry bottle.'

'Right.'

'It may be difficult to isolate any prints on the car,' said the sergeant. 'The lab boys say it's smothered in them – the garage mechanics and the major himself, probably.'

'There may be something on the boot. The major opened it, so his may be the only ones to show. We'll have to see.'

'They might not have taken well, on a wet surface,' said the sergeant.

'We may get something, if they were at all greasy. No one rubbed the car down. Well, let's get going.'

They separated on their various errands. Detective Sergeant Davis went to Mordwell where he made visual comparisons of the printmarks in the barn with similar ones caused by the boots he took with him, and he sent for a man from the forensic department to make a cast of the one they had found. It had already been photographed. All this took some time.

Chief Inspector Coward found Joe Forman down at the bottom of his garden, where he kept his birds. Even they were silent this morning, not a coo came from a pigeon, not a tweet from a canary. There was no sign of Jean. The Inspector had noticed that all the curtains were drawn in the upstairs windows as he approached the house. At least there were no reporters outside.

'Well, Mr Forman, what sort of night have you had? Rough, eh?' There was really no need to ask, but the conversation had to start somehow.

Joe Forman nodded.

'Been out walking,' he said. 'I didn't go to bed. Jean's asleep now. The doctor gave her something.'

'You should try to get some rest, you know,' said the inspector.

'Would you be able to, in my place?' asked Joe. He looked at the inspector and his manner altered. 'I doubt you've had more than a couple of hours yourself,' he said.

'I'm a father too, Mr Forman,' said Coward. 'This is a bad business, but you can put your mind at rest on one point. She wasn't murdered by any pervert. We've had the preliminary report from the doctor – his full, official one will be through later today – but there was no sexual interference. It looks as if she was killed by a car – she had a head wound, and internal injuries.' He paused. 'The doctor said she died instantaneously – she wouldn't have known about it.'

Joe Forman let out a breath.

'I'd been thinking it must be the major,' he said. 'Though he seemed all right. Used to work up at Walter's. Quiet, though, for an army man. And not married, of course.'

'Is it a crime to stay single?' asked the inspector.

' 'Tisn't natural, is it?' said Joe. 'Makes you wonder.'

The inspector sighed.

'Maybe she wouldn't have him, Mr Forman,' he suggested. 'May not have favoured the roving life.'

'I hadn't thought of that,' admitted Joe.

'He'd have been looked after in the army, in the mess.'

'Hm.' Joe looked abashed. 'I'd been planning to go down there – do him over, maybe.'

'I'd thought you might.' Luckily he had discouraged Major Johnson from calling to offer his condolences.

'He could have done it, though, even so. Run her over, I mean.' Joe's colour rose again.

'Mm. But he's a careful man, the major. Not likely, would you say? Suppose someone borrowed his car?'

'But when?'

'Ah – that's the difficulty. It was locked in its garage all Thursday night, as far as we can tell. But maybe someone dumped Mary in it when it was parked, say at Chorlbury Manor? Someone who'd run over her in their own car.' The doctor had been vague, so far, about the time of death. The car had been standing out in brilliant sunshine at the Manor; it had been hot in the boot.

'If that's it, how will you ever find him?' Joe asked despairingly.

'We'll do everything we can, Mr Forman. Something may turn up,' said the inspector.

'If I could meet the bastard – ' Joe clenched his big fists.

'Yes, well – ' Chief Inspector Coward turned away. 'We'll find him, if it's possible.'

He got back into his car and drove down to Church Street. The front gate of the major's bungalow was closed, but a group of women, some with prams, stood on the opposite pavement staring at the place and muttering together. Some clutched toddlers by the hand.

In a few succinct words the chief inspector suggested that they would be better employed cooking the Sunday dinner. None of them were churchgoers on their way home; they had simply come to gape.

94

He spent fifteen minutes with the major checking on where the car had been since Mary disappeared. It had been outside The Grapes for twenty minutes or so, which was long enough for someone passing to stop, open the boot and dump the child, but at the risk of being seen, though few people were out during the storm. Mary's legs were splashed and her sandals caked with mud; her hair was matted and her clothes were damp, though some of the wet had dried off while she had been shut in the car.

'If only I'd looked in the boot before,' the major said. 'Those poor people, the Formans – they'd have known sooner. And you'd have been able to start your search for whoever is responsible earlier, Inspector.'

He looked haggard. Even the neat little clipped moustache seemed to droop.

'But it was lucky I opened it when I did,' the major went on. 'If young Blunt hadn't wanted the petrol I might not have looked in there for several days.'

The policeman knew that the effect of the heat on Mary's body would have made the major wonder what was in his boot before much more time had passed, but he did not say so.

'You may have a little unpleasantness for a day or two, till we get a lead on who may be to blame,' he said. 'There were several women outside just now, and the newspapers haven't helped. Let me know if there's any trouble, and I'll put a man outside.'

'They would think you'd got it in for me, Inspector, if you did that,' said the major wryly.

Chief Inspector Coward went up to The Grapes when he left the major. Both bars were full and the Hursts were busy serving customers who had come from outside the village just to see where the tragedy had happened.

'Major Forman was in here on Thursday evening, I suppose?' asked the chief inspector. 'He comes in most nights, I believe.'

'He does – but not on Thursday. At least, I didn't serve him. I'll see if my wife did,' said Mr Hurst. He went to ask her, returning at once to say that she had not done so.

'But Penny may have – she's our daughter. She was looking after things on Thursday evening early. We went out for the day and didn't get back till after opening time.'

'May I see her, then?'

'Sorry – she isn't here. She's gone off abroad on a camping holiday.'

'She didn't mention serving the major?'

'No. She didn't say that anyone had been in at all. We had our regulars in later, but it was quiet that night because of the weather.'

'Hm. Would she have mentioned Major Johnson, if she'd served him?'

'I don't know. Probably not. But who can tell? She's wrapped up in her own affairs and might have forgotten him. He's not particularly memorable, is he?'

Neither was Crippen.

Chief Inspector Coward went away deep in thought. Every instinct he possessed told him that the major was innocent of all blame, but if there was any connection between the stolen boots, the bicycles, and the major's car, the sooner it was found the better.

V

After she had finished her breakfast, Celia Mainwaring went out into the town to buy a paper which carried a fuller account of how Mary's body had been found than the brief paragraph in the *Observer*. When she saw how some of the newspapers, for want of any other titillating scoop, had exploited the story, she bought several.

After she had read them all and studied the various photographs of Mary, her parents, and the major, not to mention the shots of his bungalow, she looked across at the blue hydrangea. She could not keep it. What had been merely a joke was now a matter for horror. She went to the telephone and rang up Mavis Combe.

Mavis had read the news, like everyone else, but she had not connected Major Johnson with Celia's admirer.

'Of course you can't keep it,' she agreed at once. 'But what can you do with it? Give it to the hospital?'

Celia had not thought about an appropriate means of disposal, but now she knew what must be done.

'I'll give it back to him. I should never have had that lunch with him. He took it as encouragement, obviously.'

'You and your lame dogs, Celia. You'll get yourself into a jam with them one day.'

'It looks as if I've done it now.'

'Not really. I'll take you out there and we'll get rid of it,' said Mavis.

'What – ring the door-bell and hand it to him?'

'Better dump it on the step. We don't want to be clobbered too,' said Mavis, who was five foot eight and had been a physical training instructress before she married.

'No,' Celia agreed.

'I suppose he forgot what he'd done – amnesia – that must be why he left the body in the car,' said Mavis, who had read the case in detail.

'Could be. It's all very nasty. He must be to blame in some way – no smoke without fire and all that,' said Celia. 'Anyway, I don't want to be mixed up with it.' She and Mummy had always kept clear of any unpleasantness.

'We'll go this afternoon,' said Mavis. 'I tell you what, you come over to lunch – Don's got a friend coming but there's plenty. Roast pork. We'll leave the hydrangea in the car and go over when the men have gone out. I'll get Don to fetch you.'

Don was a mild little man who worked in the Midland Bank and as a hobby did brass-rubbing. This took him off for hours at weekends; it was an interest Mavis did not share. They had no children. Donald's friend was a fellow brass-rubber; they were going to Gloucester that afternoon in pursuit of more rubbings for their collections.

They talked about the death of Mary Forman over lunch.

'Major Johnson doesn't seem to have done anything criminal,' said Donald. 'Just owned the car the body was dumped in. It could have happened to anyone. I think you should keep the hydrangea.'

'I can't. I should never have accepted it in the first place,' said Celia. 'I ought to have rung up the shop and made them take it back. There are things one just mustn't do.'

Donald went into the kitchen with a stack of dirty plates and stood there muttering.

'What's that you said, Don?' asked Mavis.

'I said, "The fellow's not likely to rape you," ' Donald repeated, and stood grinning in the kitchen as he put the cutlery to soak before bringing in the gooseberry tart.

'Donald!' cried Mavis. 'You are awful! Take no notice, Celia.'

Donald's friend, however, looked at him with new respect as he brought in the pudding. Old Donald might give that cow of a wife of his hell yet.

VI

Major Johnson looked in the fridge at the chump chop he had bought for his Sunday lunch and felt it was all too much trouble. But he was due at Chorlbury Manor at two o'clock so he must eat something. Without a car, he would have to walk as the buses did not go that way, and he must allow at least half an hour for the journey. If he was lucky someone might bring him back.

He settled for bread and cheese and an apple.

It was hot when he started out at twenty minutes past one, and the thundery, close feeling that had been in the air on Thursday had returned. A lot of cars were parked outside The Grapes. The major walked past and turned to the right. The police had left the school. But in the square, a group of boys with bicycles had gathered. Major Johnson walked by with his

98

eyes fixed straight ahead; he did not recognise any of them, so they might not know him, either. But one did. Next minute, like a swoop of swallows they sped up to him, swerved very close to him as he marched along on the footpath, and rang their bells loudly.

Major Johnson strode on, and the boys circled round, approaching as close as they could. Then they stopped ringing their bells and began to hiss at him through their teeth, not uttering a word. His heart thumped painfully. If they were young soldiers he would be able to quell them at once, but they were not; they were a pack of idle youths with no discipline except that of the mob, and a misconception in their hearts. He wondered what to do. Suddenly, as they swooped round in the road for the sixth time, he stopped abruptly, turned round and glared at them. Anger had made his face go red, but though he was small he was still a figure of authority.

'Stop that!' he bawled at them, and in their surprise two of the boys jammed on their brakes. The front wheels of their bicycles clashed and the riders came off. The other boys had to swerve away to avoid piling up on top of them. While they sorted themselves out, Major Johnson walked on. He calculated that they might lose interest in him when he passed the village boundary, but before this theory was tested a police car came towards them from the Chorlbury direction. Major Johnson heard it slow up after it had passed him, but he did not look round.

He had no more adventures on the way, but by the time he reached the Manor gates he felt very tired. I am getting on a bit, after all, he told himself. Several cars passed him as he trudged up the long drive, bringing the rest of the staff. They slowed when they drew level with him, then went on without stopping. He was puzzled; perhaps everyone thought that as he was so near he might as well end his journey on foot.

But before he reached the forecourt he saw the admiral coming towards him. He wore a dark suit, and for a moment the major thought he was in his naval uniform.

'Ah, Johnson, mm,' said the admiral. 'Just a minute, my dear chap, if you don't mind.' He turned off up a pathway among shrub roses and bushes of spiraea, where it was shady and midges circled in the air. 'I tried to get you on the telephone, but there was no answer.'

'I left early. I had to walk. My car – my car's out of action for a day or two,' said the major.

'Ah yes. Of course. Exactly,' said the admiral. He hunted about for the words to express what he had to say. Damn it, the fellow looked hot, tired, harmless, and what was more, to his experienced eye, utterly reliable. But you never could tell, and he didn't want all the guides walking out, as most of them had threatened to do if the major went on duty. He'd had to deal with some tricky situations in his service life, but never one like this.

'The fact is,' he said, plunging in, 'just till this unfortunate business has blown over, I think it would be wise if you stayed away from the Manor. I'm sure the police will have things sorted out in a day or two, but meanwhile, I'm sure you understand.

The major laughed shortly.

'I understand,' he said. 'And this affects the new job too. You won't want to go ahead with that, as things are.'

'Not just at present, my dear chap. Good of you to see it that way,' said the admiral. It was all going off more smoothly than he could have hoped. 'You hadn't mentioned it to anyone, had you? The new appointment, I mean.'

'No. Not to a soul,' said the major.

'Splendid – splendid. Well, I'll get back – I'm standing in for you, today, as it happens,' he said. 'Follow this path down, why don't you? It comes out lower down the drive. No need to go up to the house.'

No need for you to be seen beside me, you mean, thought the major.

'You'll let me know, admiral, if you want me again,' he said in a steady voice.

'When we need you, not if, Johnson,' said the admiral, quite gentle in his relief, and he walked away.

VII

Tom West spent Sunday morning getting in his mother's way. One of his sisters went off on the back of her boy-friend's motor-bike for the day, and the other spread out a length of material all over the living-room floor and proceeded to cut out a dress. Mr West, who was a lorry driver employed by a local cement works, went to his allotment, where he grew prize chysanthe-mums. Tom mooched about, following his mother round the house picking things up and putting them down again, without talking. Finally, exasperated, Mrs West snapped at him.

'Tom, what's eating you? You've got the fidgets properly – sit still, for goodness' sake, or do something useful.'

In the end she settled him down with the potatoes to peel for dinner, while she made a plum pie.

'I'm glad you've got that job,' she said, thumping the pastry on the board with a floury fist before she rolled it out. 'It'll lead on to a better, never fear. Doesn't do to sit about. You were right unlucky, losing that other. You'll get back to the mechanics by and by. P'raps you could go to the tech., evenings.'

'P'raps.' He might at that, if he could ever forget the sight of Mary Forman lying in the road with blood in her mouth. At the moment he felt as if he never wanted to get into a car again. He scratched away at the potatoes. They came from his father's allotment, and though they were large, they still scraped well. His great shock of hair hid his face from his mother's eye.

'You were out in that storm, Thursday,' she said, accusingly. 'Your clothes were soaked. It'll be a wonder if you've not caught a chill.'

'I haven't,' Tom said. He sniffed as if to contradict this, and ran the back of his hand across his nose.

'Use a handkerchief, if you please,' reproved his mother. 'Where were you, then?'

'Where was I when?'

'On Thursday, in that thunderstorm.'

'Oh, out,' said Tom vaguely.

'I know that. Who were you with? You weren't alone.'

'Why d'you ask?' Tom stiffened and turned to face her, the knife still in his hand. 'Someone been asking?'

'No. Why should they?' But it was his mother's turn to look wary. 'I wondered, that's all.'

'I was with a feller you don't know and a couple of birds,' said Tom. He turned back to the sink and dug savagely at an eye in a rather gnarled potato. His mother arranged her sheet of rolled pastry over the pie dish and pressed it down before fluting it expertly all round the edge. She sighed. She knew when Tom was lying.

Tom did not eat much dinner. Afterwards, his sister, her cutting-out done, set the sewing-machine up on the kitchen table. Mrs West took a deck-chair out into the small patch of garden, and Mr West settled down with the paper in the living-room. Soon he would be asleep. Tom slouched out of the house. He had no clear plan in his mind, and without really thinking what he was doing he took the Wiveldown road out of the town.

VIII

A police car took Joe and Jean Forman to the mortuary. Mary looked like a wax doll. There was no visible trace of injury on her; a strand of her fair hair nad been arranged to cover the bruise on her forehead, and her limbs had been straightened. The contusions on her body and the sutures of the pathologist were all concealed from her parents. Joe stood looking at her with tears pouring down his coarse red cheeks; Jean, who had insisted on coming too, was dry-eyed. Detective Sergeant Davis drove them home afterwards and told them enquiries were proceeding in the normal way.

'You mean, you haven't a clue,' said Joe bitterly.

'I wouldn't say that, Mr Forman,' said the sergeant.

By now a thumbprint found on one of the stolen bicycles had been proved to match another on the passenger's door of Major Johnson's car. The stallholder who had lost the boots had given a fair description of the youth who had turned the trestle over, though not such a clear one of his companion. Both were long-haired and dressed in jeans and leather jackets, but the one who upset the boxes of shoes had been a big lad, with large scarred hands and bitten nails, which the stallholder had noticed as they delved about retrieving the scattered goods. However, these attributes were common to a great many youths in Leckington and everywhere else, so finding the right ones would mean quite a search. The police were starting at the homes of known trouble-makers; something might turn up from this.

However, it was no good telling the Formans any of these facts yet; they were all straws in the wind at the moment. He did his best to console them, and then drove down towards *Tobruk*.

Church Street was deserted. It was hot and sultry again, and a Sunday stupor seemed to have descended on the inhabitants of Wiveldown. The police search parties had gone from the area and the visible upheaval connected with Mary's death had disappeared. At the moment there was nothing to stare at.

Major Johnson did not come to the door immediately the sergeant rang the bell. He was about to press it a second time when there came sounds from inside the bungalow and the front door was opened. Major Johnson stood there looking angry; his face was red and his wispy hair was askew.

'Well?' he barked, before he recognised his caller. 'Oh – sergeant – I'm sorry, I was just changing,' he said. 'I went up to Chorlbury Manor as usual today and they sent me home. I'm pitch, it seems. Not to be approached for fear of defilement.'

'I'm very sorry to hear that, sir,' said the sergeant, stepping into the house as the major stood back to let him in. 'Folk are strange when these things happen. You soon find out your friends.'

103

'You're right, sergeant,' said the major grimly.

'People forget, very quickly,' said the sergeant.

'Maybe. But I shan't,' said Major Johnson. 'Well, what can I do for you, sergeant? More fingerprints? Or samples of blood?'

'No, sir. Nothing like that. Just, if you wouldn't mind, the clothes you were wearing on Thursday when you gave Mary a lift.'

Major Johnson looked at him for a long moment.

'Very well, sergeant,' he said heavily. 'You'd better come along and take your pick.'

He led the other man through the hall and into his bedroom. The sergeant looked around, poker-faced; he had surprises every day and he had one now. He might have been in an army barrack, or even a prison cell. A narrow divan bed stood against one wall; it was covered with a chocolate-coloured woven spread. There was linoleum on the floor and one small, black mat beside the bed. A white-painted chest in one corner had a small shaving mirror standing on it, and the major's hair-brush with a comb neatly stuck into the bristles. There was also a large clothes brush. A single upright chair stood below the window. Beside the major's bed was a plain white table with a gardening encyclopaedia on it, and a lamp with a white plastic shade and a wooden base. There were no pictures; no concessions to comfort. A fitted cupboard was built into a recess, and this the major opened, to reveal his clothes neatly hanging, with his shoes side by side below.

Major Johnson took out a tweed jacket and sorted through several pairs of trousers.

'I had on grey flannels. These, I think,' he said.

'Shoes?' asked Sergeant Davis.

'This pair. The ones I'm wearing.'

'Shirt?'

'Washed,' said the major crisply. 'I wash my shirt every night and hang it in the bathroom to dry. And my socks the same. I have a few better shirts which I send to the laundry along with sheets and towels.'

104

'You don't go to the launderette, then?'

'I do not,' said the major austerely. He had thought of it, but could not face the mob inside, even though he saw that many of the patrons were male. He had been far too long insulated from this sort of enterprise. He sat on the bed, unlaced his shoes and took them off. The sergeant, who felt embarrassed because the major was somehow displaying enormous dignity throughout the encounter, bent and picked them up. They were warm from the major's feet.

'I was about to change my shoes in any case,' the major said. He had worn his best grey worsted suit to go to the Manor; now he was dressed in twill trousers and a sports shirt, with a cravat at the neck. He looked neat, if heated, and could never have been mistaken for anything other than a retired soldier. He took a pair of navy-blue canvas shoes from the cupboard and put them on, tying the laces firmly.

'Anything else, sergeant?' he asked, before closing the cupboard.

'No, sir. That will be all, thank you,' said Davis. He put the garments into various polythene bags he had brought with him, and then packed them in a leather holdall. 'We'll let you have them back as soon as we can.'

The major led him to the front door and opened it. Both men looked down in surprise. There, on the step, was a large blue hydrangea in a pot.

IX

'He went quite pale. Looked awful – he was flushed and over-heated-looking when I got there.'

Detective Sergeant Davis was sitting in the chief inspector's office describing his visit to *Tobruk*.

'Did he explain?' asked Chief Inspector Coward.

'Didn't want to. I dragged it out of him. Seems he'd sent it to a lady, and she didn't want it. There was a note with it.

He read it and crumpled it up. Went scarlet in the face again.'

'Bad for the arteries.'

'Mm.'

'Who was she?'

'He wouldn't say. Very chivalrous, the major.'

'You didn't see this female?'

'No. I hadn't heard a car, either, while I was there. The major's bedroom is at the back – overlooks the garden. Grim, it is, too.' He described it.

'Poor Major Johnson. He lacks a woman's tender touch, obviously,' said the inspector. 'Maybe the hydrangea was an attempt to secure it. Shouldn't be too hard to trace her – get on to the florists. Can't be all that many pot plants bought at this time of year. With luck there'll be a record of the major as purchaser. She may be a Wiveldown lady – hence you hearing no car. She might have come on foot.'

'Conspicuous, eh? Carrying a plant.'

'Mean way to act,' said the inspector. 'Now, let's get round to see some of our bad lads. Find out where they all were on Thursday.'

'Before we do that, sir, there's one other thing I noticed after I'd left the major,' said Davis. 'May not mean much, but I've a hunch it could.'

X

The newspapers had wrung the last possible drop of human interest out of Welbeck Crescent and its residents while Mary was still missing. Now, until her funeral could give that angle a fillip, they were concentrating on the police enquiries. So when Joe and Jean Forman returned from their trip to the mortuary on Sunday afternoon there were no reporters round their gate. After Sergeant Davis had gone, Joe said he was going to see Ted Smith.

'You be all right?' he asked his wife.

She nodded.

'I'll be off then.'

Joe left her. He could not think of a word to say to her nor any comfort that he might give her. Their tragedy should have drawn them together, he felt obscurely, but instead it seemed as though what had been a small crack between them had turned into a vast gulf. As for himself, he had to turn somewhere in this nightmare; a cup of tea and a chat with Ted and Betty might help.

Jean went up to her bedroom when he had gone and sat in front of her mirror. A pale, drawn face looked back at her. What would happen now? What was the point of anything? She gazed round the pretty room with its white fitments picked out in gilt paint. Joe had done them for her. She had made the padded headboard for the bed herself, following the instructions in a magazine. It was a room anyone would be proud of, not just a housewife on a council estate.

Automatically she brushed her hair, fair like Mary's but helped with a brightening rinse, and put new lipstick on. Then, at last, she went into Mary's room. It was very tidy. Her mother-in-law had been in and put away the clothes Mary had left out after changing into her Brownie uniform. Dully, Jean looked round. A stuffed bear wearing a gingham dress and apron lay on the bed; there was a row of china animals on the window-sill. Mary's yellow dressing-gown hung on the door. The furniture in here was painted apricot colour, and a white acrilan rug lay on the patterned carpet beside the bed. It was a charming room for a little girl. Jean stared at it. Then she went to the cupboard, opened it, and looked inside. Mary's dresses hung there, fresh and crisp. She gazed round the room once more. Something was wrong, not accounted for, but she could not think what it was.

She went downstairs again and into the kitchen, where she put the kettle on for want of any other occupation. She felt completely numb, as if she were dead herself.

When a tap came at the back door she jumped.

The handle turned and it opened slowly.

'Who is it?' she called out sharply.

'It's only me, Jean,' said a man's voice, and the door opened fully.

'I saw Joe leave, so I came round,' he said. 'There, love.'

He put his arms out to her, and the woman who had been able to get no comfort from her husband collapsed into this other embrace and wept.

After a long time Tony Miller said, 'I'd better go. Someone may have seen me come in, or Joe may come back.'

Jean said, 'It doesn't really matter now, does it? The point's gone. It was Mary, really.'

Tony stared at her.

'You mean you'd leave Joe now?'

'Why not?' said Jean.

Tony looked at her face, blotched with tears; she no longer had the ability of a young girl to weep without looking ugly. Did he want her after all? He'd tried to persuade her, often enough, but wasn't part of the excitement the feeling that she'd never really leave her family – that she would always be just out of reach?

'You can't decide anything now, while you're so upset,' he told her. 'There's plenty of time. I'll still be around.'

But would he? He'd have to make his mind up quick.

When he had gone, Jean wondered for a while if she would leave Joe and go off with Tony. He was young – too young, maybe; vigorous, and on their stolen Wednesday afternoons in the back of his car, very exciting; but she was five years older. He was doing well, it was true; he earned much more than Joe already and he was ambitious; he would go far. But in a year or two he might tire of her and want someone younger.

She sat there turning it all over in her mind and reaching no conclusion. Then she realised what had worried her in Mary's room. The police had not mentioned finding her satchel, yet she had taken it with her, the day she disappeared.

108

'How's Jean taking it?' asked Ted.

'Seems kind of stunned,' said Joe. 'Hasn't said much at all.' How could he say that Jean and he had not been able to communicate? 'She looked so pitiful, Ted, did Mary. Sort of shrunken, like a little doll.'

'Pity you had to see her.'

'I had to, Ted. I couldn't have believed it, without.'

'Heather's pretty upset,' said Ted. 'Betty's taken her black-berrying – not that they're really ripe yet – but to keep her busy, like. If they'd been together on Thursday it wouldn't have happened.'

'Might have been both of them, not just Mary,' said Joe. 'You can't tell.'

'Those chaps – those madmen who lure little girls – they don't usually try it when there's two,' said Ted. He lit his pipe and puffed at it slowly. It was a good thing Joe had come down; he'd something to tell him, and it was better said when Jean couldn't hear it.

'It may not have happened like that,' said Joe. 'She may not have been lured. They think she was run over.'

'Yes – but not here – out of the village. She must have been taken away first.' Of course she'd been enticed away; it was the only explanation, but Ted knew if it were Heather, he wouldn't be able to accept it either, he'd reject the thought. No punishment was too bad for a man who hurt a little kid; it was all very well to say such criminals were sick: what about the victim?

'She'd know Major Johnson. Wouldn't think of him as a stranger,' said Ted.

'Of course she knew him. He gave her a lift that afternoon.'

'Maybe he arranged to meet her again, later. Perhaps he said he'd pick her up after she'd been to Miss Price.'

Joe stared.

'Why should he?'

'Bit odd, maybe. Taken with her, very likely. Anyone would

be.' Ted didn't want to be too blunt, all at once. 'Solitary sort of individual, isn't he? Doesn't have any friends. Says very little if you meet him in the pub.'

'I've always got on with him,' Joe said. 'He was liked at Walter's.'

'That's another thing. Why did he leave there? Too grand, was he, for factory work? Better up at the Manor with the admiral and the lady guides?'

'He only sells tickets at the door,' said Joe. 'Jean and I took Mary along there a while back, and he spoke to us real nice.'

'And why wouldn't he? You'd got your pretty little girl with you and he wanted to be friendly.'

'What are you trying to say, Ted?' Joe asked. 'I don't get your meaning.'

'I'm saying that I don't think Major Johnson has told the police al¹ he did on Thursday,' said Ted. 'I think he met Mary in the evening and took her for a drive.'

'But it said in the papers he was in The Grapes.'

'I know. Who told them that, though? The major, that's my guess. The Hursts don't remember seeing him that night. I asked them,' Ted said. 'In any case he'd have had time to kill Mary and put her in the boot, and go in for a beer afterwards.'

Joe shivered.

'Or he may have dumped her somewhere, and fetched her later.'

'But why? Why should he want to hurt her.'

'Because he's kinky – a nut. That's why.'

'But she was run over, they say.'

'Yes,' said Ted. 'Very likely. Afterwards.' Ted knocked his pipe out on the hearth, making a nasty mess of tobacco bits. Jean would hate a thing like that, thought Joe, irrelevantly. 'I saw the major's car, later on Thursday night, Joe. When I was walking back from Miss Price's after looking for Mary, it passed me. A dark green Morris 1300, it is.' The whole of Britain knew that, and the registration number. 'I checked today that no one else living down his end of Church Street has a car like that. Philpot, the butcher, in the big house, has a Jaguar and his

110

wife has a mini, and that young couple have got a Triumph Herald – one with a soft top.'

'But, Ted,' Joe insisted. 'She wasn't interfered with. The police wouldn't say that if it wasn't true.'

'Might have looked, though,' said Ted. 'We'll let the police find out, eh? I'll ring them, shall I?'

Joe was silent, and Ted waited patiently. Of course he'd resist the truth; who wouldn't?

'Very well, Ted. Yes, ring them,' said Joe at last.

XII

Major Johnson stared at the hydrangea. It was on the table in his sitting-room, where he had put it after the sergeant had gone. He sat in one of his twin armchairs and he felt completely stunned. He was tired after his long walk to and from the Manor. When he drew near to the village on his return he had made a detour to avoid the square, in case the boys with their bicycles were still there, but he had felt this to be an act of cowardice. He was completely innocent of any implication in the death of Mary, so he had nothing to fear. His clothes had been taken because the police must eliminate all possibilities, so that was not a matter for concern. But he had never before felt at first hand the effect of rumour. His army career had followed a prescribed path; there had always been the next duty to carry out, the next promotion to deserve, finally the respect due to his seniority, until at last the gulf in age between him and the other officers of similar and even senior rank had been too much to ignore. He had done well, he knew, rising from band-boy to major; he had served his country loyally in many lands, not in the forefront of the battle, but in just as vital a way, behind the scenes. Now he deserved peace, at least. He had not foreseen the loneliness retirement would bring, and now, just as it seemed that he would conquer even that, this tragedy had happened.

111

He had not told the police about his visit to Mrs Fellowes' house because it was not connected in any way with Mary's disappearance, in his view. It was the same reasoning that made him refuse to divulge the name of the lady to whom he had given the hydrangea. There was no justification for involving either of them in this sorry business. Mary could not have been anywhere near Mrs Fellowes' house on Thursday evening; Miss Price lived on the other side of the village. She must have been put in his car while it was at the Manor, and it was sheer chance that it was his car which was used, not someone else's.

His fault lay in leaving the boot unlocked.

If he had still been in the army there would have been a colonel, and after him a brigadier, to go to now with this load of worry. However much younger than him they were, they would be duty-bound to help him. As things were, there was no one. He thought of the vicar, and dismissed him at once; he was kind, true, but vague; and Sunday was his busy day. He'd got at least one more service to take. No, time would be the remedy; in time the real culprit would be found.

He faced what the return of the hydrangea meant. Miss Mainwaring had read the Sunday papers and she shared the reaction of the women who had watched him walk back from church, and the louts on their bicycles with their hissing. And those women at the Manor, the cultured grey-haired ladies with their rigid vowels, they were no different. Even the admiral was the same.

He would sweat it out. In a few days the truth, whatever it was, would be known, and these same people who had shunned him would forget. But he would not. How could he?

He stood up and looked at his bugle, brightly shining above the mantelpiece. Then he turned round, picked up the hydrangea and marched with it out into the garden where he hurled it from him across the lawn. The pot hit a stone in the rockery and was smashed; the plant lay on the grass surrounded by the scattered peat in which its roots had lain.

A moment before, Cathy Blunt had come down her own garden path with a large slice of home-made coffee cake on a plate. She meant to stand on the bench and call to Major Johnson, if he were in sight. Derek was out, fetching the petrol he had intended to borrow the day before, so she'd seized her chance. He'd have to go at least to Leckington to find a pump open on Sunday. She had been horrified at what the papers said, and more, what they implied, when as far as she could see the major was simply the victim of circumstance. But now, standing on the bench, she saw him fling the plant across the lawn and then stand, staring at the wreckage, hands on hips and grey wispy hair on end.

What sane man would do a thing like that, she asked herself, feeling slightly sick. She clambered quietly down and took her piece of cake back to the house.

XIII

By the time Chorlbury Manor closed at half-past five, Ruth Fellowes had spent a wretched afternoon. She had been in one of the cars which had slowed at the sight of Major Johnson and then sped past him in the drive.

'What a nerve – fancy showing his face here,' Madge Fazackerley had said.

'What? What on earth do you mean?' Ruth was genuinely bewildered. 'Do stop for him, Madge.'

'He must have killed that child,' said Madge.

'What – ' Ruth was incredulous.

'Of course, he did. It's obvious.'

'It's not at all.' Ruth was almost speechless.

'Ruth, be your age. How did the body get into his car if he wasn't involved?'

'I should think that's proof that he wasn't,' Ruth snapped, recovering. 'You'd hardly open the boot of a car in front of witnesses if you'd put a body in it.'

'Amnesia,' Madge said. 'He did it in a fit of insanity and forgot about it.' She stopped the car with a squeal of brakes and backed into the spot the major usually chose. 'We're damned lucky he didn't pick one of us, but I suppose his tastes must run to little girls.' With that she got out of the car.

Ruth did too, more slowly because it was a very small car and she was folded up to fit into it.

'Major Johnson is a thoroughly nice man, Madge. He wouldn't hurt anyone, much less a child. You must stop talking like that,' she said.

'I shall refuse to stay if he comes on duty,' was all Madge answered.

Ruth soon found that this was the view of almost all the guides. She saw the admiral walk down to intercept the major, and then return alone. Later, they were so busy that she suspected some of the visitors had come to the house merely to see the major; several people asked where he was, and some pressmen called to take shots of him at his post. Tomorrow's headlines were tailor-made by his absence, Ruth thought bitterly.

After the house closed the guides had their first chance to discuss the drama, and they proceeded to tear his character to shreds.

'Always thought him odd – far too quiet,' said one.

'These lone men – very sinister,' said another.

Ruth exploded with anger.

'It's no crime not to marry – why should he, if he doesn't want to? He must have had plenty of chances.'

'And why didn't he take them, then?'

'Because he didn't want to end up in a prison perhaps, like some of you,' said Ruth, her temper snapping. 'Suppose this had happened to one of your husbands, or sons? It could have, just as easily as it has to Major Johnson? What would you say then?' She glared at them. For once her height was an asset. Silly bitches; she pitied their husbands.

'But our husbands and sons don't pick up little girls, Ruth,' said Madge.

'If they see them hitch-hiking, and they know who they are, I'm sure they do, for fear the child really does get picked

114

up by someone who might harm her,' Ruth said. 'Madge, are you taking me home? I'm in a hurry.'

Madge shrugged at the others. If Ruth was going to get in a state she was better removed. She went out to her car, and the other guides followed her and Ruth. Admiral Bruce watched them go; he had heard the excited female voices and Ruth's spirited defence of Major Johnson but had basely stayed out of the argument. The Manor closed on Mondays; with luck the whole thing would be sorted out by Tuesday, when it re-opened.

Ruth could not bring herself to speak to Madge throughout the journey back to Wiveldown; when they reached the village she asked to be dropped in the square, where she got out of the car with a curt word of thanks. She had not been so angry for years.

When Madge drove off she walked rapidly towards Church Street and hurried down it to the major's bungalow. Derek Blunt in his Triumph Herald passed her and waved. At least the major had pleasant neighbours, thought Ruth; the Philpots were reasonable people, too.

A youth was sauntering down the road ahead of her, eating crisps from a bag. He was tall and thin, dressed in shabby jeans, and with a great bush of curly hair that stood out round his head in a fuzz. He walked slowly, looking at the houses as he passed, and then he paused opposite *Tobruk* and stood staring at it. As Ruth drew nearer he became aware of her and turned away, walking off at a faster pace than before. Ruth did not recognise him. She opened Major Johnson's gate, walked up the short gravel drive, and rang the bell.

There was no answer.

She rang a second time. He must have got back hours ago. Had he walked all the way? It was a long walk on a hot day. She peered in at the front window but could see no one in the sitting-room.

Ruth walked round the side of the house and into the garden. Across the lawn, beyond the vegetable beds, Major Johnson was standing over a bonfire. Ruth went towards him. He had not seen her. With half her mind she noticed how very neat the garden was; the lawn was closely mown and there seemed to be not a single weed, but just at the edge of the grass, where the rockery began, there were a few bits of peat or potting soil spoiling the general neatness, and a fragment of broken flower-pot. Ruth picked it up.

The bonfire was not going well. There were hedge trimmings on it, and something blue: what looked like a large hydrangea in its prime. Major Johnson was stabbing at it fiercely with a fork and there was a reek of paraffin in the air.

She did not want to startle him.

'Major Johnson,' she called.

She had to call his name a second time before he turned and looked at her. His face had a wild, ravaged look, and his sparse hair was bedraggled. Sweat poured off his forehead.

Ruth was not a particularly imaginative woman, but she was fifty-five years old and she had seen a lot of life. Even so, today's reaction at the Manor had astounded her. If so-called cultured women, many of whom had led relatively sheltered lives, could behave in such a way, so could other people. Major Johnson had, no doubt, discovered this.

'You look very tired,' she said. She was too shy to call him by his first name, though she knew it from the newspapers. 'This is awful for you. Do leave the fire and come indoors. Let me make you some tea, or have you any brandy?'

He hesitated, and she took the fork from him, as she would have with a child. Then, silently, he let her lead him back towards the bungalow.

XIV

None of the Sunday motorists who passed Tom stopped at the appeal of his upturned thumb and he walked all the way to Wiveldown. He did not know where Major Johnson lived, but he could find the bungalow; the village wasn't large. There might even, he thought in a wilder moment, be a cordon of police all round. In the square a group of boys were wheeling and swooping about on bicycles; they were like a flock of birds, communicating by some means of thought transference; suddenly they coalesced and shot off down a side turning. When they had gone, Tom mooched over to the post office and stared in the window. Among fly-blown notices about pensions and television licences there lurked a few faded sweet cartons; it was a drab and dingy exhibition. He ambled on and gazed at tins of peaches and pears in the grocer's window. If he asked where Major Johnson lived he would draw attention to himself.

He would walk all round the village. In that way he would, eventually, come upon the place – what was it called, an odd name, some old battle – *Tobruk*, that was it.

He spent the afternoon wandering about. Wiveldown's cricket club had cancelled their match because all the men had been out searching for Mary; instead of the small crowd usually to be found on their field at weekends there were just five small boys who had set up a wicket at the side of the pitch and were playing a game amongst themselves. A woman with a basset hound on a lead was walking round the edge. It was hot and close; most folk were at home, sleeping off the Sunday lunch or working in their gardens; few had gone out in the car for the day, for the village still felt stunned by what had happened and had withdrawn behind its ramparts.

Tom found himself in the road where the accident had happened. He forced himself to saunter nonchalantly past where the car had been parked, casting a glance at the cottage standing high above the road. This was not the major's house. The tarmac surface of the road had melted slightly in the sun and was tacky under his feet; there was no trace of Thursday's accident. The air felt heavy; he could hear bees humming about and smell a heady smell, the scent of flowers in Ruth's garden where roses hung above the road. He could see now where Mary had come from; there was a gap in the hedge filled by a stile. Tom climbed over it and wandered across the field. It took him some time to find his way out, for he would not go through the next one which was full of cattle, but after circling about

117

and climbing various gates and fences he came to another road. It was, he saw, the Leckington road, which he had walked along some time before. On the far side there was a wooden gate, the paint on it chipped and green with mould, and beyond it a mass of shrubs. He could make out a house beyond them; it looked deserted. The major did not live in that one.

He walked back into the village again and turned right in the square. The boys with their bicycles were back, standing astride the machines, talking in a stationary group. As he walked along a solitary policeman in a car drove towards him. The man was not in uniform but the car had a sign and a blue lamp over the windscreen, neither operating. Tom stared straight past it and the driver ignored him. Tom went on, and soon came to a turning on the left with a sign saying *Welbeck Crescent*. Trim semi-detached houses stretched away on either side of it; Tom's feet turned up that way without his mind ordering them. Number Thirty-three was halfway up on the left. The curtains were pulled across the lower windows and there were blinds drawn upstairs. Marigolds and dahlias blazed in the garden, far too gaudy for a house of death. The grandmother lived in this street too, but Tom couldn't remember where. In some of the gardens, children were playing. Normally, the bigger ones played on the wide grass verges or even in the road, but today only the teenagers were outside their own bounds. A group of girls whispered together across the road from Number Thirty-Three. They kept glancing at the Formans' house. Two women talked over a hedge. Several men were washing their cars. It looked peaceful, but Tom felt menace in the air. He came to the end of the Crescent at last and found himself back in the other road.

He saw a close of bungalows opposite to him, and walked round that, peering at all the names above the doors or on the gateposts, but none was called *Tobruk*. Suddenly, when he was almost at the church, he came upon another bungalow; it crouched, squat, between a large brick-built house covered in virginia creeper, and a smaller, white-painted one which was set back from the road at the end of an approach drive. Over the bungalow's door hung a sign with the name *Tobruk* upon it. Tom's heart thumped so hard that he could not look properly at the place now that he had found it. He hurried on to the church at the end of the road and went into a shady corner of the churchyard, under a yew, to decide his next action. An old man in a cassock with white hair and a beaked nose came out of the church while he stood there biting his nails. Tom panicked. He vaulted over the low stone wall and cowered in the grass on the far side, but the Reverend Wilson had not seen him.

After a while Tom pulled himself together and went back up the road. There was no one in sight now. As he drew level with the major's bungalow a maroon Triumph Herald with the hood down came out of the drive beside it and turned up towards the square.

The major's bungalow looked tranquil. There was no policeman to be seen, much less a cordon of them. The garage doors were closed and so were all the windows at the front. Maybe the major was out. Tom walked on. It had been silly to come. He couldn't expect to meet Major Johnson face to face, and that was what he really wanted, to see what sort of a geezer he was.

He went back to the cricket field and sat on the ground for a bit, watching the kids. They took no notice of him. He'd bought some crisps and a Bounty Bar on his way out of Leckington, and he ate the chocolate while he sat there. Then he got up and wandered back again down Church Street, eating the crisps. Still there was no sign of life at the major's bungalow. Tom glanced over his shoulder and saw a woman coming down the road towards him. She was tall and grey-haired, walking fast. He went on towards the church again, and when he glanced round once more the woman had vanished.

XV

As he drove away with the major's clothes, Detective Sergeant Davis saw Tom West walking down the road. He did not know the boy, although his face was vaguely familiar. Some instinct, the one that regarded checking the major's clothes as a mere formality, prompted him to stop alongside the boys with their bicycles clustered in the square. They all made as if to ride away at once but he called out sharply.

'Wait a minute, there.'

'We ain't causing no obstruction,' said one lad aggressively.

'I didn't say you were,' said the sergeant mildly. 'Name, please.'

The boy glowered, but eventually gave his name. The sergeant asked the others their names, round the group, and sulkily they answered. He wrote nothing down.

'Two bicycles were stolen from a farm near here last Thursday and dumped down Lammas Lane. Know anything about it, any of you?'

'No. We all got bikes, ain't we? What we go nicking them for, then?' said one boy.

A reasonable answer.

'That a mate of yours just went down Church Street?' asked the sergeant.

'Never seen him before.'

'Not a Wiveldown boy, then?'

Heads were shaken all round.

'Don't live here,' said a small, tow-haired boy with freckles.

'Right, then.'

The sergeant left them to their cycling. There was a lot to be said for the village bobby, he thought ruefully. He'd been one himself, once, and had known every family in his area and its potential for good or ill. The boys were speaking the truth about the stranger in their midst; if he had been a village boy they would have denied seeing him at all.

As he drove into Leckington and passed the boarded-up garage property, soon to be demolished, where Tom had worked, recollection came to him. That was where he had seen the boy in the past.

Chief Inspector Coward listened in silence to the sergeant's report of this chance meeting.

'Just a hunch, eh?' he said when it was over.

'The boy was alone. He had a great mop of curly hair. So did one of the lads involved in lifting those boots in the market. He doesn't belong in Wiveldown so why was he there?'

'Visiting his auntie.'

'Maybe.'

'Hm. Well, put someone to finding out who he is, and when you've done that we'll get on out after some of our other friends.'

He was still waiting for Sergeant Davis to return from arranging this when Ted Smith telephoned and told him about seeing Major Johnson's car late on Thursday night.

XVI

Major Johnson, letting himself be shepherded into the bungalow by Mrs Fellowes, felt like a small boy in the clutch of a firm schoolmistress. He surrendered briefly to her authority, but once they were inside his own sitting-room self-consciousness returned. As Ruth took in the austere room, Major Johnson felt the obligations of a host crowd in upon him. Neither had spoken since Ruth's one sentence in the garden.

'Mrs Fellowes – '

'Some brandy. You need some.'

Both spoke together, but it was Ruth who continued. She saw that the major, who had been very red in the face, was now pale; she went on in the commanding manner which she had cultivated so hard over the years that now it was second nature.

'Sit down. Tell me where you keep the brandy.' He must have some.

'In there.'

He pointed to a carved mahogany sideboard. She found the bottle and a glass and poured him a stiff tot. He gulped it down and his colour began to return.

'Don't talk,' Ruth instructed. She refilled his glass, and then sat down facing him. The hairy upholstery of the rather uncomfortable chair prickled her legs through her tights.

Major Johnson sat in obedient silence, alternately sipping the brandy and breathing gustily. He studied his shoes, the canvas ones he had put on under the sergeant's gaze. They were covered in dust from the bonfire. He had taken off his cravat and his shirt was open at the neck. Wisps of wiry grey hair were visible. I'm not respectable, he thought dully, but he could not muster the strength to put matters right. After a bit he spoke.

'I'm sorry – how rude – you must excuse – '

Ruth cut him short.

'I saw what happened at the Manor. I couldn't get here any sooner. It was disgraceful,' she said.

The major grimaced.

'People believe what they want to believe. The papers only told the truth. My car was used. How, I don't know.'

'Have the police any idea who did it?' Ruth asked. 'They can't let this happen to you.'

'They've taken away my clothes for some form of test,' said Major Johnson. 'They must eliminate me, I suppose, before they look for someone else.'

'Could someone have taken the car without your knowledge?'

'I don't think so. I always lock it, even in the garage, here.'

But on that one day he hadn't checked that the boot was locked, when he brought the car back from Leckington. When he took Mrs Fellowes home in the thunderstorm, had he locked the car? He couldn't remember doing so. But it had been just where he'd left it, outside her house, when he went home. He rubbed a hand across his forehead, leaving a smear of ash.

'Inspector Coward will get to the bottom of it. I'm sure he doesn't think I'm to blame,' said the major.

Maybe, but you'll be crucified first, thought Ruth.

'I wonder how long it will take him?' she said.

'The laboratory work all takes time. It's not twenty-four hours, after all, since the child was found. I expect it will all be sorted out in time for the inquest.' Major Johnson was beginning to feel better. 'Won't you have a drink, Mrs Fellowes? You see, I'm quite myself again now. You prescribed excellent medicine.' He managed a smile.

Ruth, who had seen that the interior of the sideboard contained a good assortment of bottles, asked for a gin and tonic. He would be bound to keep her company by having another drink himself, and a mild alcoholic haze was, she felt, his best defence against despair.

'You'd like some ice,' he said, pouring her drink. 'I'll have a quick wash, if you'll forgive me, and then get it.'

'You wash – I'll find the ice,' said Ruth, standing up.

'Oh – how kind – ' he said. He looked a little put out, but Ruth, towering over him, smiled in her firm, cooking-class manner and he did not argue.

She went into the kitchen, which was very small but spick and span. In the refrigerator she saw one chump chop, half a pound of margarine with a small piece missing from one end, a half-full milk bottle, four eggs and two tomatoes. She took out the ice tray, and opened a cupboard seeking a bowl. She found the shelves sparsely loaded with a tea service such as might be bought at a knockdown price in a bargain department, and some dinner plates which did not match. She put the ice in the sugar bowl. Impelled partly by curiosity and partly by compassion, she opened a couple of drawers in the sink fitment. There was a full set of stainless steel cutlery which looked as if it had never been used. One knife, fork, and spoon were set apart in a separate section of a fitted drawer, apparently for daily use.

She closed the cupboard and the drawers, filled the ice tray with water and replaced it. A washing-up mop and a dish-cloth were tidily stowed at the side of the sink, the cloth on a hook and the mop between two small clips. It was all so neat, and it was utterly bleak.

She had time to take in the full austerity of the major's sitting-room before he returned. She saw the bugle, gleaming, over the tiled mantelpiece, the square of drab, sand-coloured carpet, the single picture, a print of Windsor Castle. There were no books, no ornaments, not even a cushion except the upholstered seats of the two armchairs. At least there was a television set.

At this point in her appraisal of the room, Major Johnson returned. He wore a clean shirt and his regimental tie. A triangle of spotless handkerchief protruded from his blazer pocket and his precious strands of hair were neatly flattened. He looked his normal self, but in her mind's eye Ruth still saw the sweating, angry man stoking the bonfire.

XVII

Mrs Brewis had her hair in rollers and was watching television on Sunday afternoon when the police called. She knew at once that the firm knock on the door meant trouble; useless to pretend to be out, for they would have seen the flickering screen through the window. She shuffled into the hall in shabby bedroom slippers; her varicose veins ached.

She knew Chief Inspector Coward.

'Well?' she demanded truculently, but her heart sank. What had Roger been up to now? He'd disappeared, and that was proof enough that he'd something to run away from. It must be serious, as the inspector was here himself.

"Evening, Mrs Brewis. Mind if we come in?" said the inspector. 'This is Detective Sergeant Davis. You haven't met each other before.'

This tea-party treatment did not suit Mrs Brewis. She glared at the two men as she grudgingly opened the door wide and stood back. Better to have them in than the neighbours gaping while they stood on the step. As it was, their car was outside for everyone to see. She led the way into the living-room and turned the sound down on the television. There was a smell of boiled cabbage in the air, and a tap could be heard dripping in the kitchen.

'Your boy home, Mrs Brewis?' asked the inspector. He

could tell from the atmosphere that there was no one else in the house. 'We'd like a word with him.'

'He's out just now,' said Mrs Brewis.

'When do you expect him back? Will he be long?'

'Don't know, do I? Can't tell with boys. Depends.'

'Where's he gone, then? Out with his mates? Let's see, who's he running round with now? Young Jeff Cardew's gone down for a couple of years, hasn't he? Left your boy a bit lonely, hasn't it?'

'Roger's not been in no trouble for a long time,' said Mrs Brewis.

'Glad to hear it,' said the inspector.

He got up and went over to the doorway that led into the kitchen while Sergeant Davis took up the questioning.

'Been in work this week, has he?'

'Casual like,' said Mrs Brewis. They could not prove otherwise. 'Odd days.'

'Where was that, then? Down on the building? Done a bit of labouring, hasn't he?'

'Odd jobs, he's been at,' said Mrs Brewis.

'Got his card stamped, has he? Hope he's given you a few quid, then. Tough, your life, isn't it?' said Coward, from the doorway. 'You still cleaning at the bank?'

'No. I got a job at the supermarket. Better money. And I do part-time at the laundry, too.' She recovered some spirit and added, 'You want to keep up to date.'

'Ah. That's good. Because you need a bit, don't you, with Roger not bringing any in?'

'Who said he wasn't bringing none in?'

'He's not been home for some time, has he?' Coward remarked, coming away from the kitchen. Mrs Brewis was not houseproud, and he could see on the drainer, upside down, one cup, one saucer, and a dinner plate. 'Where is he, then?'

'I don't know. I told you.'

'When did you last see him? Now, come on, Mrs Brewis. I can ask next door, you know. Some of your neighbours will know when he was at home. Wouldn't you rather tell me yourself? They'll be nosey enough as it is.'

'He's not done wrong. I'm sure he hasn't,' Mrs Brewis blustered, but her defiance was giving way to fright, and her voice shook slightly.

'When did you last see him?' repeated the inspector patiently.

'Thursday morning. He was here Thursday morning.'

'I see. And when did he leave? Went to work, did he?'

'No, not Thursday. He went out about eleven. Didn't say where he was going.'

'You weren't at work yourself?'

'I was back. Have to be at the shop at seven-thirty. It opens at half-eight. I go down to the laundry after dinner.'

'Hm. Two lads caused an upset in the market on Thursday. Turned a stall over and nicked a pair of boots. Your Roger didn't come home on Thursday with a new pair of boots?'

'Never saw him.'

The inspector nodded at Sergeant Davis, who got up and left the room. They heard his feet heavily ascending the stairs.

'What size feet has your Roger? Eights? Nines? Big chap, isn't he?'

'He takes nines.' Useless to hide it; there'd be some old sneakers or something of Roger's upstairs. 'You've got no warrant,' she added.

'Don't need one, when you're being so helpful,' said the inspector. 'He's left home, has he?'

She shrugged.

'He's done it before,' she said. 'He'll be back.' And then, recovering some of her fire, 'why do you have to pick on Roger? You don't know as it was him in the market.'

'No, but it could have been, from the description. It's his style, too.'

'Huh – what's a description?' she said scornfully.

'Two bicycles were pinched later, down at Mordwell. They were ditched near Wiveldown.'

'Wiveldown? That's where that kid – ' Mrs Brewis did not end the sentence.

'Yes. That's where Mary Forman lived.'

126

Mrs Brewis said nothing.

'Roger's left home before to escape trouble,' said Coward. It was a statement not requiring an answer. The boy had been mixed up with a gang who had done several breaking and entering jobs, and disappeared, two years before. They'd been found in Brighton.

'He's not a vicious boy,' said Mrs Brewis in a faint voice.

'No?' said the inspector. He looked up as the sergeant returned. 'Well, that's all for the present. Send him round to see me, if he comes back, won't you?'

She could not speak, and she made no attempt to go with the two men to the door.

'Well?' said the inspector when they were back in their car.

'Pair of sneakers upstairs. Couldn't see the size so I took them.' He patted his pocket. 'And a pair of winkle-pickers – very old – out of date now. Not good for size-matching. She was scared, all right. Worn out, too.'

'She's had a bad time of it. The boy's father was inside more than he was out. Nothing violent – mostly petty thieving. Then he got in with a mob who pulled a bank job. One of them had a gun. Her old man got five years and when he came out he left her flat – and the boy. We'll put out a call for him.'

'And Major Johnson?'

'It's odd about Thursday night. I wonder where he was?' mused the inspector. 'I still don't think he's got anything to do with this, but we'll have to ask him. Perhaps he was tucked up in bed with whoever he gave the hydrangea to. He seems anxious to hide her identity.' It seemed unlikely, somehow. 'We'll talk to him tomorrow. We'll have the full report on the car by then. He won't run away.'

'No, poor bastard,' said Sergeant Davis. He thought complacently of his own comfortable semi-detached house on the outskirts of Leckington, and his plump, pretty wife. With luck he'd be home before dark.

XVIII

Ruth was constantly being cast by life in the role of authority to whom others turned in time of crisis, so it was second nature to her now to take command. Therefore, when she and Major Johnson had had their drinks, she asked him what he had eaten for lunch. Very little, seemed to be the answer.

She could cook that chop for him, but would he eat it if she did?

'Have you any tins of meat?' she asked him.

'No. Why?' He looked surprised. 'I shop from day to day. It makes for a little routine, don't you see?'

She did: a framework for his empty day.

'You must have something now – I'll just run round to Cathy Blunt and see what I can borrow. You go down your garden and dig up some potatoes and pick some beans. I'll cook a meal for both of us. I only had a snatched lunch today.' It was true. She had been so upset at the newspaper accounts of how Mary had been found that she had not bothered to cook anything.

'Oh no – ' he began, but she interrupted.

'I've known Cathy for years. She's sure to have something. I'll repay her in kind. And I'm hungry, even if you aren't. I won't listen to any protests.' She stood by the door. 'Now, have you a basket? Something to put the vegetables in? You can help by slicing the beans.'

She saw him start meekly on his way down the garden and then she went next door. The roar of the rotavator filled the air as Derek churned the soil. Ruth opened the front door and let herself in, calling to Cathy, whom she thought would be busy with the baby now.

In fact Cathy was just ready to put Amanda down in her cot; she came to the top of the stairs holding the small bundle against her.

'Ruth! Is something wrong?' She came quickly down the stairs.

128

'It's Major Johnson,' said Ruth, and saw a guarded look come over Cathy's face. 'You know him – you said you'd always found him a pleasant neighbour.'

'I've always thought him a dear old boy,' Cathy said, and then wondered if that was tactful, since he and Ruth must be much of an age. 'But now –'

'You don't think he had anything to do with this business, surely, Cathy? You've got more sense.'

'I didn't – but – ' Cathy hesitated, and then came out with the story of the hydrangea.

'Would Major Johnson be likely to buy himself a pot plant for the house?' Ruth demanded. 'Use your brains, my dear. Have you been inside that house? It's about as comfortable as a prison cell. He tried to give the plant to someone and they sent it back.' For the major, realising he must explain his odd behaviour, had admitted as much.

'Oh dear,' said Cathy. 'How awful!' She looked at Ruth in dismay. 'And I'm no better,' she added, and confessed about the coffee cake. 'Derek doesn't want me to talk to him,' she finished.

'Well, you must decide what to do about that yourself,' said Ruth. 'What you can do now is lend me a tin of something – stewed steak for choice, or mince.' She explained her intentions.

'Oh, Ruth, you are good,' said Cathy.

'I'm not. I'm bossy and interfering,' said Ruth. 'But I can't go home and leave him like that, miserable and unfed. I'm good at feeding people. It's what I'm trained to do.'

'I've got some mince – there may be something better, I'll look,' said Cathy. 'Hold Amanda while I do. Do you want anything else? Rice or something?'

'No – he's got potatoes, and bread.' Ruth had looked in the bread bin.

Cathy handed the baby over and went into the kitchen. Ruth followed, holding the child against her sensible courtelle shoulder.

'Imagine what other people are capable of, Cathy, if even you, a normal kind-hearted girl, could think as you did,' she

129

said. 'He's having a terrible time.' She told Cathy what had happened at the Manor.

'Here's some steak. It's not bad,' said Cathy. 'I'll keep an eye on him over the fence, Ruth – chat him up. I'll be friendly – give him my love or something, poor old boy. I feel rather ashamed.'

Ruth hurried back to the bungalow. She had been longer than she expected because of her talk with Cathy so Major Johnson should have finished his errand in the garden. She found him standing on the front step talking to a youth in jeans with a shock of curly hair. The boy turned as she approached, said something to the major, and hurried past her.

'Who was that?' asked Ruth.

'I've no idea. One of the village boys, I suppose. He wanted me to find him some sort of job for an hour or two – washing the car, he said.' The major laughed, a mirthless bray.

'What an odd time to call. So late,' said Ruth. She had seen a boy in the road earlier; it must be the same one.

'He seemed a nice lad. Very polite. Doesn't do to judge by appearances, does it?'

PART FOUR

I

CHIEF INSPECTOR COWARD always got a great sense of satisfaction when he had accumulated enough facts to draw in a net. When a case was unresolved his mind kept coming back to it and fretting over what was known; if he was convinced of how a crime had been committed but lacked evidence to prove it, he experienced a sense of personal failure.

He sat in his office on Monday morning with the reports of the Forman case spread out around him and listened to the latest information, as related by Detective Sergeant Davis.

'Shall I go and see this Miss Mainwaring?' asked the sergeant at the conclusion. Only one of Leckington's three florists had delivered a blue hydrangea at the weekend; an assistant remembered it was ordered by a small elderly man with a moustache, who had given no name.

'I don't think so. Not just now. We'll go and see the major. He's got to tell us a few things we haven't found out for ourselves.' He picked a paper up from his desk. 'Here's the report on the car. See what you think about that.'

'Right, sir.'

'Traced that boy yet? The pump attendant?'

'Got a constable on to it now, sir. Should have something soon.'

'Hm. Seen the papers?'

'Yes. Done us well, haven't they?'

Most of the morning papers carried a photograph of Roger Brewis taken two years before when he went to Borstal for six months. In it, his hair was cut short. *Wanted for questioning in*

131

connection with mystery death of child, said one paper, and went on to reveal that the police believed Roger Brewis might have been in Wiveldown when Mary died.

'Someone may bother to tell us they've seen him,' said the Inspector.

Detective Sergeant Davis went back to his own desk with the report on the car. There were traces of Mary's blood on the gear lever, but nothing on the bumper or the tyres. However, it had rained so hard the night she was killed, and the major had driven so much since then, that any signs might have disappeared. There was some distinctive mud in the boot, and on the child's sandals, but none that matched in the interior of the car. There were numerous unidentified fingerprints besides the major's, and other details.

They were on their way to Wiveldown when a call came through from headquarters. One of the two milkmen who served the village of Wiveldown and who did not come on Sundays, had called at a house named *The Hollies* and found the pint he delivered on Saturday still on the step. He'd rung and knocked, but got no answer from the householder, a Mrs Pollock. It seemed he seldom saw her, but there were usually signs of life such as a tea towel on the line when he arrived. A Panda car was on its way.

'We'll go too,' said Chief Inspector Coward.

They left the car in the road outside *The Hollies* and walked up the overgrown path. The weeds were lush after the storm, and under the trees the air smelled dank. There was still thunder about, and it had rained again in the night.

'What a place,' said Davis. 'Looks uninhabited.'

As they approached the front door a tabby cat bolted round the side of the house and shot between the inspector's legs. No one answered when they rang; the doors were all locked and the windows fast. There was a cat-flap in the back door. The unclaimed pint of milk stood in a box on the back step with a slate on top of the bottle to protect it from the birds.

In the end Sergeant Davis broke open the kitchen window and climbed through on to the draining board. He saw Mary's satchel hanging on a chair beside the table before he saw the old lady.

Chief Inspector Coward left Sergeant Davis to wait for the doctor and some more men and went himself into the village to find out what he could.

The post office was the obvious place to call, and as the milkman had telephoned from the box outside it, the two Mrs Flints were eagerly waiting for the next development. They were peering from their windows, their knitting in their hands but the needles still. When the police car stopped they were stabbed into the balls of wool, one tangerine, one lime, and both ladies came round from behind the counter.

'Poor Mrs Pollock. She's dead, of course,' said the elder Mrs Flint.

'I'm afraid so,' said Chief Inspector Coward.

'Oh dear, we'll all be murdered in our beds next,' said Deirdre Flint with relish.

'Who mentioned murder?' asked the inspector.

'Well, first little innocent Mary, and now this – '

'As far as I know, no one has said anything about murder at all,' said Coward. He stepped into the post office. 'There will be an inquest on Mary tomorrow, and that will determine the cause of her death. Mrs Pollock probably died of old age – heart, I should think.' The fact of Mary's satchel being in the house must be kept undisclosed at present. 'Did she come into the village at all?'

'Not often – led a life like a proper hermit,' said Marilyn Flint. 'Wouldn't have anyone to the house. Even Mr Duckett – he's the grocer – just put her order down on the step.'

'She'd come in for her pension now and then,' said Deirdre. 'About once a month. And she'd send off a letter to Australia at the same time.'

'Australia, eh?'

'That's where her family is.'

'I suppose you don't happen to have noticed the address?' asked the inspector innocently. It was doubtless engraved on their hearts.

133

'Well, funny you should ask,' said Marilyn. 'I did, as a matter of fact. Her writing was a bit shaky, see, and I'd print it out again sometimes, to make sure it arrived. She always wrote to just the son – Dennis Pollock's his name. I'll write it down for you. In Queensland, it is.' She bustled away back behind the counter, massive buttocks wagging under the yellow crimplene. Chief Inspector Coward repressed a shudder; it was hard to stay impartial.

'When did Mrs Pollock last come in to draw her pension?' he asked.

'Oh – a few days back – let's see, which day was it? Thursday, that's right, and next day Mary'd disappeared.'

'It was quite a walk for her.'

'There's a path from the square goes along to the main road. It's shorter. She always came that way.'

The path had been well combed during the search for Mary. And had no one called at *The Hollies* then? Someone was in for trouble.

'Thank you, Mrs Flint,' said Coward.

'Oh, not at all, inspector. Any time.' Marilyn bared her gums at him and saw him to the door, and when he had gone two customers who had not liked to enter while he was inside hastened to find out why he had come.

The doctor had arrived at *The Hollies* when he got back there, and agreed that the old lady's death looked at first glance as if it was natural.

'Find anything else besides the satchel connected with Mary?'

'No, but we're only just starting,' said Sergeant Davis. 'There are some letters in the sideboard in the hall, from Australia. Oh, and the old lady's purse, with some money in it, and her pension book.'

'Check the lot for prints. And Mary's satchel too. We can't be sure she brought it here herself. Now I'll get down to the major.'

Major Johnson was cleaning the windows of the bungalow, using a small pair of folding steps to give him the extra inches he needed. When the car stopped outside his gate and Chief

Inspector Coward got out, he got slowly down from the steps and laid his leather across the top of the bucket.

'Good morning, sir. I'd like a word, if you don't mind,' said Coward.

'Come in, inspector,' said Major Johnson. He led the way into the sitting-room and sat down silently, indicating the other easy chair to the policeman.

'No more trouble with sightseers, I hope, major,' said the inspector genially. The major looked a wreck, as if he had not slept for a week. He was as neatly turned out as ever, but his face was haggard and the policeman saw that his hands were shaking. He clasped them in front of him in an effort to steady them.

'I had some horrible letters,' said Major Johnson. 'Dozens of them. I haven't read them all. They were – vile.'

'That happens, sir, I'm afraid.'

'The papers said nothing that wasn't true. It was what they implied – useless to sue,' said the major. 'It was just the way it was slanted.'

'Very unpleasant, sir. The sooner we get to the bottom of it, the better.'

'What about that boy? The one mentioned in the paper today, Roger Brewis. Do you think he had anything to do with it?'

'We aren't sure, sir. We think he was concerned in the theft of some bicycles we found dumped near here. There may be a link.' It was too soon to tell the major that Roger's prints were in his car. 'Now, sir, information has come to me that you were out late on Thursday night. Your car was seen turning in at your gate sometime after eleven o'clock. That doesn't tally with what you told us.'

'I didn't specify a time, did I?' asked the major.

'You went to The Grapes, left about six forty-five, and put your car straight in the garage, I think you said. I'd better tell you that neither Mr or Mrs Hurst remembers serving you that night.'

'But – ' Major Johnson passed a hand across his forehead.

He had a headache, at least he supposed that was what the pain in his head was; it was unlike anything he'd experienced before. 'The daughter – it was the daughter served – the daughter, it was,' he said confusedly. 'She'll tell you.' And so would Mrs Fellowes if she were asked, but she had gone to Tenby today to stay with a friend, she must have left by now. Anyway, why should she be drawn into this sordid affair?

'She's gone on holiday, the girl. Pity neither of the parents saw you.'

'Yes. I suppose it is.'

'You went somewhere else after that, didn't you, Major Johnson?' Suddenly the inspector's voice had grown stern. 'Did you, or did you not, return home at about eleven o'clock?'

'I did,' said the major in a dull voice.

'Where had you been?'

'Dining with a friend.'

'And who was that?'

'A lady,' said the major. 'I prefer not to give her name.'

'Would that be Miss Celia Mainwaring?' asked the inspector, and saw Major Johnson go even paler than before.

'No – certainly not,' he snapped. 'Keep her out of it. She has nothing to do with any of this.' How had they discovered he knew Miss Mainwaring?

'The other lady's name, sir, then.'

'I don't see why I should tell you, inspector. Look at what's happened to me, because of this unfortunate affair. My name and reputation bandied about in the papers. Do you wonder that I want to protect my friends?'

'Major Johnson, I must point out to you that you could make a lot of trouble for yourself by keeping silent,' said the inspector. 'If you say where you were, and the lady confirms it, we shall know you weren't in the village when Mary was killed.' Could the old boy really be having a giddy sex life on the side, Coward wondered. It didn't seem likely, but he'd had bigger surprises before.

'It was just a friend, and I didn't run Mary over on the way,' said Major Johnson. He tried to speak calmly but he felt thoroughly mulish by now. Let the police damn well find out who'd killed the child; he knew he hadn't done it. British justice and the British police were supposed to be so wonderful – let them show a bit of initiative now.

'We found a trace of blood in your car from the little girl,' said Coward. 'And there was a hair on your jacket we identified as hers.'

'I gave her a lift in the afternoon. You know that. She had a plaster on her leg – a sticking-plaster thing. Maybe the blood came from there.'

There had been an elastoplast strip on Mary's knee when she was found.

'And the hair?'

Major Johnson shrugged.

'I suppose children do lose hairs like older people. She'd longish hair. If one got caught on the seat it might have transferred itself on to my coat.'

'Major Johnson, you could have run the child over and put her in the boot yourself,' said Coward.

'Are you accusing me?'

'Not yet. I'm just saying that on the facts we've got it could have happened.'

'At least you're not implying that I murdered her,' said the major.

'Mary was run over. She had a blow on the head and internal injuries. The car must have passed right over her body.'

'Why don't you tell the papers that?'

'They'll know in good time.'

The major was silent.

'You've no more to tell me?'

'Nothing that is the least relevant.'

'You're being very foolish, Major Johnson. You're withholding evidence that might help us to find the person responsible. And it's in your own interests to prove that you weren't that person.'

'I'm not going to tell you where I was that night, Chief Inspector.'

137

'Well, then, perhaps you'll tell me how long you spent with this lady?' Coward decided to try another tack.

'Oh – three hours – a bit more, perhaps.'

'So someone could have put the child's body in the car during that time without your knowledge?'

'Yes – yes, I suppose so,' the major agreed. 'But it seems very unlikely.'

'Why?'

There was no answer.

'You mean the car was parked outside the lady's house?'

Still no answer.

'I wish you would tell me, sir,' said Coward. He knew that this thrust was the right one.

'Well, I won't,' said the major. 'You can damn well find out for yourself, if it's so important.'

After the inspector had gone, Major Johnson sat without moving for some time. Why had he been so stubborn? It was silly, really. Mrs Fellowes would be the first to rebuke him. But the police couldn't seriously think he had anything to do with Mary's death. Someone knocking her down with another car and passing Ruth's cottage that night could have switched her body across but it was most unlikely to have happened then. Hardly any traffic went that way. No, the transfer must have happened some other time and Chorlbury Manor was the likeliest place. It was random chance that had chosen his car. He would keep that kindly woman out of all this.

She'd made them a delicious meal, the night before, out of the steak. He'd go up to Duckett's himself, later today, to replace it. Mrs Fellowes had said she couldn't do this herself for a day or two as she had this long-standing arrangement to stay with a friend in Wales. She wouldn't let him see her home. He was tired, and she was quite used to walking about the village. She was much too old and ugly and enormous to fear attack, she said, and laughed.

He felt forlorn when she had gone, but it had not occurred to him to contradict her description of herself.

As he sat in his chair reviewing the chain of events he

remembered something. While he and and Mrs Fellowes had been so comfortably enjoying their evening in her cottage on Thursday, there had been a sound from outside. A car horn had hooted, one sharp, short blast.

II

Tony Miller sat in his bedroom at The Rising Sun reading the *Daily Mirror*. On the front page was a picture of Roger Brewis and a paragraph asking anyone who had seen him to communicate with the police. Believed to have been in the tragedy village, said the paper.

Last Thursday night, after the Wives' Club meeting, Jean Forman had slipped away promptly and hurried up the street to where Tony's car was parked in an unlit patch. He'd whipped her away, out of the village, to a quiet spot for a bit of a cuddle. There wasn't time for much, before Joe got back, but any week now Tony'd grown confident she'd ditch the club and spend the whole evening with him. It would be weeks before Joe found out she wasn't with the other women – if he ever did. They'd be able to keep it up till one or other of them tired of it. But there was something about Jean that was different from women he'd been mixed up with before; that was why he hung around in spite of her prevarication, and why he'd gone to see her after reading about the kid. A terrible thing, that. But not his fault, nor Jean's.

And now there was this picture of the youth.

After leaving Jean near the turning to Welbeck Crescent but not close enough to be observed by nosey neighbours, Tony had gone on to Bletchford, where he knew a widow always glad to see him. He'd met a lad hitching, and had picked him up. He'd left him at an all-night transport café where he'd be sure to get another lift.

Tony did not want to get mixed up with the police. He'd just been home for the weekend; his wife spent the whole week counting the days till Friday when he got back from his week's

139

selling, and the weekend lamenting that Monday must come so soon. The life suited Tony; home comforts every weekend and freedom while he travelled in his area. There was no lack of company, but until Jean he'd never felt tempted to become deeply involved. She'd no idea, naturally, that he was married. They'd met when he went into the shop where she worked, with his samples; he was new to the district then. He'd seen her later, walking away from the shop on Wednesday, early closing day, and he'd stopped to talk to her. They'd ended up having a bite together in a pub. So it had all begun; she was restless, tied to a dull, unambitious man whose efforts did not meet her aspirations, ripe for an adventure. The prospect of spending the rest of her life in Welbeck Crescent was at this moment filling her with despair; she wanted more than that for Mary and herself. Tony was seriously wondering if he would offer to give it to her.

Now this.

He'd have to tell the police about Roger. The boy had seemed just a normal, loutish youth; they'd told crude jokes to one another as they drove along. He'd not seemed vicious. But if he'd been mixed up with poor little Mary's death, that altered things. Not that Tony had met Mary. Jean hadn't allowed it, for she was bringing the kid up primly. But he'd seen her in the distance. He'd no kids, himself.

He'd not ring up, though; they'd hear him from the back. He didn't want the landlord knowing all about it. He'd call round at the police station.

He felt better having made the decision. Once this was done with he'd pull out his hooks and find another base for working this territory. Give him time to think a bit, and Jean a chance to get over what had happened.

III

Joe had gone to work that morning. He couldn't stop at home; he'd nothing to say to Jean, and there was nothing he could do for Mary, not ever, any more. He felt better when he got to the factory. His mates were surprised to see him, but once they'd got over the first embarrassment their sympathy was comforting. Many of them knew Mary, who'd been to works social occasions with him. As he carried out his duties Joe began to feel some sort of life returning to him; but how he'd get through to Jean, well, that was another thing.

He'd left her going through Mary's clothes. She'd asked the police where Mary's satchel was, and they'd said it hadn't been found. They were going to look for it; finding it might throw some light on what had happened. Now she was parcelling up bundles of sweaters and dresses to give to charity. It seemed as if she wanted to blot out Mary utterly, already.

He'd tried, during the night as she lay in bed with her back to him, to talk to her. He'd wanted to say that they could have another child one day, when all this was behind them. She was only thirty-five, after all. But she wouldn't listen and she'd drawn away from him as if his touch was poison. She'd get over it, he told himself. She wasn't going to the shop. With Mary dead her prime motive for work had gone; now there were no piano lessons to pay for, no need to go on putting money away for the bicycle Mary would have had on her birthday; no hurry for the next instalment on the lounge suite. She didn't seem to mind being left alone, in fact she appeared eager for him to leave.

Nothing had happened as a consequence of Ted telling the police that he had seen the major's car late on Thursday. Joe didn't like it; he didn't think the major was a bad bloke. But Ted might be right. You couldn't tell. More would come out at the inquest, probably. That was what Inspector Coward said.

Meanwhile the days must be got through. And the nights.

IV

The paper boy was back. Major Johnson found his *Daily Express* stuck into the gate. He was relieved to be spared the

141

mascaraed stares of the Mesdames Flint. He took it in and read all about Roger Brewis on the front page. It made him feel better.

Soon he would go up to Duckett's to buy the replacement tin of steak for Cathy, but it was too early yet to call on her. He cleaned the bungalow from one end to the other, putting polish on his bedroom lino with a rag tied round a mop as he had done when he was a young soldier. He rubbed it up the same way. Then he got his laundry ready; the man called on Tuesdays. Routine, that was the thing; if you stuck to that you couldn't go far wrong. He'd clean the windows, then walk up to the shop. He wouldn't go to Leckington today. Maybe he'd have his car back by tomorrow, but if not, he might go in by bus. Or would the inquest be held then? He would have to go to that, presumably. He'd like to confront Miss Mainwaring in the library. If he didn't do it quickly, he never would.

A black lump seemed to fill his chest when he thought of Miss Mainwaring. She, who had seemed so clever and good, was no better than the anonymous letter writers in her condemnation of him. Even when the real offender had been brought to justice he would never be able to forget her action.

He was thinking like this, rubbing away with the leather at the windows, when Chief Inspector Coward called.

It was some time after the inspector had gone before he could return to his task. Surely the police couldn't seriously think he'd had anything to do with it? Only a madman, having committed such a crime, would keep the body and then expose it in front of a witness. But surely only someone insane would kill a little girl?

But she hadn't been murdered.

Or had she, and her body been put on the ground and run over, as a blind?

That was a new thought, and the major didn't care for it. Wouldn't the police know? Scientific tests would show it, wouldn't they?

And what had the inspector meant when, as a parting remark, he had said, 'Remember what you said to the constable.

142

Very significant, that. "Mary *was* a nice little girl," you said. Not "Mary *is* a nice little girl." As if you knew her to be dead.'

'But good heavens – ' Major Johnson had blustered. 'Anyone might say that, in those circumstances.'

'Well, you did, didn't you?' the inspector had said, and departed.

How could those lads who'd stolen the bicycles be involved? Maybe they'd seen something. The car that had hooted while he was with Mrs Fellowes – whose was that? But Mary couldn't have been killed in Lammas Lane – she'd no reason to be there. It wasn't on her way home from Miss Price. And no one had taken his car; it was exactly where he had left it when he came out of Ruth's house.

But had it been locked? He couldn't be sure. He always did lock it; routine again; but he had failed to check that the boot was locked so his efficiency must have been slipping.

His brain reeled from sleeplessness and going round in circles. He'd finished the windows. He'd go up the village now, buy the meat, and take it round to Cathy.

Monday was never peak morning in Duckett's Stores. Most housewives were busy with their washing and cleaning up their homes after the weekend. Mr Duckett was alone in his shop when Major Johnson entered. He greeted the major in the normal way and they conducted their transactions calmly. Major Johnson bought two tins of steak, one to have as a spare himself, and a few other items. He still did not feel like cooking, but he had promised Mrs Fellowes to eat properly, so he bought some fish fingers too. As he was paying, a woman came into the shop.

"Morning, Mr Duckett,' she said, and stood rigid in a corner of the shop by the deep freeze, as far away from Major Johnson as she could put herself.

"Morning, Mrs Brown,' said Mr Duckett, accepting the major's money.

'Heard about Mrs Pollock, have you? Deirdre Flint just mentioned it. Awful, isn't it? There'll be a third, sure to be. Who next?'

'Very sad about Mrs Pollock, yes,' said Mr Duckett. 'But she was nearly ninety. Liable to go at any time, I reckon.'

'Took her groceries up there, didn't you?'

'Aye. But I hardly ever saw her. She left the money for me, and a list.'

'She came to the post office for her pension. In there Thursday, she was. Same as Mary. Whoever killed that poor child may have lured her to her death too.' Mrs Brown cast a baleful look at Major Johnson as she said this.

Mr Duckett was counting out the major's change.

'She wasn't killed, was she, Mrs Brown?' he said, looking for a halfpenny piece at the back of the till. 'No one's said that. Old age, you'll find. There you are, major.'

'Thank you, Mr Duckett.'

'Thank you, sir.' Poor bastard, he looked a wreck this morning, thought Mr Duckett, who was keeping an open mind. He'd always found the major very pleasant.

'Well, the nerve!' exclaimed Mrs Brown as the shop door fell to behind the major. 'Fancy coming out as bold as brass.'

Mr Duckett did not answer. He had no intention of gossiping about his customers.

'What can I get you, Mrs Brown?' he asked.

'Half of butter, please – New Zealand. And a pound of granulated,' said Mrs Brown, to be going on with. 'That man, I mean! Major Johnson. After what he's done! You'd think he wouldn't show his face. When are the police going to arrest him? That's what I'd like to know.'

'We don't know that he did anything, Mrs Brown,' said Mr Duckett. 'And the next thing?'

'A bag of flour – self-raising. And some Daz. He must have done it. Stands to reason. And walking about without a care, planning the next if you ask me.'

'It's all circumstantial, Mrs Brown,' said Mr Duckett. 'Just his car was concerned. That's all we know.'

'No smoke without a fire is what I always say,' said Mrs Brown.

Another woman entered the shop then and she turned to her. 'Don't you, Lily?' she enquired.

'Don't I what, love?'

Mrs Brown put forth her theory, and between her statements Mr Duckett got her somehow through her list of needs. Major Johnson might be as innocent of any crime as little Mary was herself, he thought, yet these women would never be convinced.

Major Johnson walked back down the street in a particularly upright, soldierly manner, his back a ramrod. He kept his eyes fixed to the front, but he met no one except the vicar, who had heard about Mrs Pollock and was on his way to *The Hollies*, not that it would do the old lady any good. The Reverend Wilson drove past the major without stopping; he must talk to the man sometime soon, he reminded himself, but there was no hurry. He had seen the headlines in the Sunday papers, but he had not read them yet in detail; he saved them until Monday afternoons.

Cathy felt so guilty because of the bad thoughts she had allowed herself to have about the major that she greeted him almost too effusively when he offered her the tin of steak across the hedge. Poor Cheshire Cat, his grin was rather weak this morning. She invited him round to admire Derek's rotavating. A devastated area lay before them where once there had been long grass laced with tall white daisies.

'He got too keen and swept away my annual bed,' said Cathy. 'I'd got it as a temporary thing, until we'd laid some flower-beds out properly, like yours.'

'You'd quite a show, hadn't you? Larkspur and marigolds. I've admired them over the hedge,' said Major Johnson.

Cathy made him stay to coffee. He did look awful, pale and with dark sleepless marks under his eyes.

'You must come to dinner soon,' she said. 'We'll have a celebration. Derek's going to be promoted.'

'Ah – splendid.'

'I'll ask Ruth too.'

'Ruth?'

145

'You know Ruth. Ruth Fellowes.' Surely he knew her name; they'd mentioned her before.

But the major had forgotten it.

V

Tony Miller had a long session at Leckington police station. Detective Sergeant Davis was still at *The Hollies* investigating Mrs Pollock's last hours when he got there, and Chief Inspector Coward was with Major Johnson; in their absence the sergeant who took his statement was punctilious, checking times and everything else to the last detail. He typed up Tony's statement, got him to read and sign it, and was about to let him go when the inspector came back.

He took Tony straight into his office and went through it all again. No one was interested in why he was going to Bletchford, so his widow's name was not disclosed, which was just as well in case Jean, or even his wife, heard about her. He was sure the boy was the one in the photograph, and when asked to describe him and his clothes, mentioned the boots he was wearing. He had noticed them particularly because they were very muddy; they also looked new.

'Cleaned your car out yet?' asked the chief inspector.

'No, I haven't – very slack of me,' Tony said, looking surprised.

'Good. Let's have a look at it, then. Outside, is it?'

'Yes. In your yard. I thought I'd be safe there from getting a ticket,' said Tony with a grin.

Chief Inspector Coward hustled him down the stairs and into the yard where the grey Ford Capri was parked.

'This it?'

'Yes.' Tony unlocked the driver's door and leaned across to open the passenger's. He kept a lot of samples in the car and was meticulous about locking it up. 'It is in a mess. I usually wash it on a Sunday, but I was back home with the wife, and that.' He grinned again, man to man, at Coward.

146

'I'm very glad you didn't clean it,' Coward said. He was peering down at the floor in front of the passenger's seat, his bulky body wedged in the doorway. 'There's quite a bit of mud here. I'd like you to leave your car with me for a couple of hours. It's very important to trace that boy and prove he was in Wiveldown. We'll need to test this mud, and there may be some other things.'

'Yes, I see that. He didn't do poor little Mary in, did he?'

'We don't know what happened yet,' said Coward.

'I thought it must be that old man – the one with the car,' said Tony.

'Anyone been in your car since you picked the boy up?' asked Coward, not commenting on this remark.

'I took the wife down to the local on Sunday. Just a mile or so.'

'Ah – handed her in, did you? Opened the door for her, I mean?'

Tony thought.

'Yes, I did,' he agreed, and laughed. 'How d'you know? I've been married five years.'

'You're away from home a lot. Courting habits sometimes last when that's the case,' said Coward. 'Means she won't have superimposed her prints over the boy's. We may find something.'

'Keep the car as long as you like,' said Tony. He reached over to lift a case off the rear seat. 'I can make a few calls in Leckington, so I won't be wasting my time.'

'Right. Thanks, Mr Miller,' said Coward. 'We must hope whoever picked the boy up after you did will come forward too. But we'll find him, anyway.'

When Tony left the chief inspector was busy with a pair of tweezers and a plastic bag picking up grains of dried mud from the floor of the car. Tony couldn't see how the mud would help, but if it would collar whoever bashed that poor kid of Jean's, then good luck to the inspector. He walked off filled with mixed emotions; the whole thing might blow up and his involvement with Jean be discovered. Well, it couldn't be helped.

147

Shaking his head, he took his bag into the Star and Garter. He was parched.

VI

Constable Forrest, new to the force, had tracked down Tom West. It had taken him all the morning and part of the afternoon, but he'd done it, and the report of his endeavours, neatly typed, rested on Chief Inspector Coward's desk alongside one from the lab. that confirmed mud found on Mary's sandals and in the boot of Major Johnson's car as identical with that in Tony Miller's Capri. And Tony, when he fetched the car, had agreed that the boots Roger was wearing were the same as a pair in the chief inspector's office. Rather unusual ones, heavy for the time of year, Tony had thought when he saw them, but these lads had to follow the latest trends.

Chief Inspector Coward gave thanks for an observant and positive witness. He asked Tony not to leave the district without letting him know, and they parted.

Mary's prints had been found on Mrs Pollock's purse; no one else's, except the old lady's. Mary's fingerprints had also been found in various places at *The Hollies*.

'So now we can guess where Mary went after she left Miss Price,' said Coward. 'Mrs Pollock must have dropped her purse on her way home after collecting her pension. Mary found it and took it back.'

'And found the old lady dead?' asked Detective Sergeant Davis.

'No – she couldn't have got into the house. She obviously spent some time there – the purse was put away, her satchel was slung on the chair. The old lady must have died while the child was there. She got scared and ran off.'

'And a passing motorist knocked her down?'

'That's about it.'

'Hm. Those Flint women said she'd only a little money when

she bought the sweets. But there was a fifty pence piece in her pocket when she was found.'

'A reward from the old lady, perhaps.'

'Could be.' Sergeant David cogitated. 'Major Johnson?' he asked at last. 'It looks black for him, doesn't it?'

'Only for want of other evidence,' said Coward. 'I think he's a good man, in the old-fashioned sense – always lived by a strict code. An honourable man. There are a few still around. Those boys were mixed up in it somehow, I'm certain. Brewis's prints were all over the car.'

'The major seems to fancy the ladies,' said Davis mildly.

'I don't think he knows how to fancy them,' said the chief inspector. 'Or how to pick them. That one at the library must be a hard case. Do you know her?'

'I've seen her about. Nothing to look at – mousy, rather. My wife knows her – she plays in the orchestra and so does Phyllis. Bit conceited, Miss Mainwaring, Phyllis says, but with reason. Very capable – good in the library, good at the violin, and good at tennis.'

'Hm. What about human relations?'

'Likes sorting people out – telling them what to do,' said Davis. 'Or so Phyllis says.'

'Sexy?'

'Phyl wouldn't know. Want me to find out from somebody else? Someone at the tennis club? Or shall I call on her and find out for myself?'

Tension was slackening. Both men knew they were going to crack this case, and soon.

'We'll see – it may be a good idea,' said Coward. 'About the other lady – the mysterious one. How do we know it is somebody else? Major Johnson denied that it was Miss Mainwaring but he seems to have this notion that the age of chivalry is not dead.'

'She sent the plant back. Wouldn't he have told us after that, if she was the one?'

'I wonder.' The chief inspector thought for a few seconds, twiddling his biro. Then he decided. 'Let's ask the fair Celia

149

herself. We know of no other women in the major's life. If it wasn't Celia, she may know who her rival was.'

'I'm to go myself?'

'Yes. We need a man of experience for this mission,' said Coward, grinning. 'Now, about Tom West. Young Forrest's done a good job on this one.' He tapped the report. 'Couldn't find the garage owners – they've moved away – so he tried the bank. Went round all the banks asking who used to pay the money in and do the books. Some woman working part-time. She knew Tom's name and remembered his address, from his insurance card. Forrest very sensibly didn't go barging in on top of the family, just checked they did all live at the address given – mother, father, son and two daughters. Very much respected as a family. Son's been out of work for weeks, idling about. Forrest happened to be passing Bert's Cafe on his search, so he went in and asked if Roger Brewis had been seen there lately, such as on Thursday last. He wasn't, but Tom West was, late in the evening. He was soaked through. Couple of girls were there when Forrest was asking, and they remembered. Must be the right night, because of the storm. Seems they tried to chat him up and got a dusty answer. They also said they'd seen him with Brewis at other times.'

'Forrest seems to be a promising lad,' said Davis.

'Yes. Better watch him. Too much zeal can lead to trouble,' said the chief inspector. 'Now, who was responsible for calling at *The Hollies* in the search for Mary and passed it up?'

'I've dealt with that, sir,' said Davis, and named the offending constables.

'Hm. Thought it was unnecessary to proceed further, did they? When every house and hovel in the village was to be investigated? Who were they to decide what was necessary or not?'

'Yes, sir. Exactly, sir. I told them all that,' said Davis.

'Threw it at them, did you?'

'I did, sir.'

'Want me to leave it, then?'

'Reckon I did enough,' said the sergeant.

'All right, Dick. Lucky for them I'm so busy, or they'd wish they'd never been born.' The chief inspector put his biro down and pushed his chair back. We'll go and talk to Mrs West and the enigmatic *belle dame sans merci*. Miss Mainwaring, I mean.'

'What, both of us?' Davis was grinning. The inspector only called him Dick when he felt benign and things were going well. 'I thought you wanted me to go alone.'

'I've changed my mind,' said Coward. 'That man must be in hell, though most of it's of his own causing. We'd better get our skates on. Come on. Let's go and see the lady. Now.'

VII

Roger Brewis had run out of money. He'd moved on from the hostel and spent last night sleeping rough. He'd have to do something – get some cash somehow, and then find a gang who'd let him in. It should be easy enough if he could flash the money around. On Sunday night he started prowling, looking for somewhere to break in.

As dusk was falling he wandered into a residential area on the outskirts of Liverpool. The houses were trim and expensive, most of them screened from the road by high hedges or elaborate fencing. There would be things worth taking here, if he could find an unlocked window or an open door: jewellery for sure, and with luck, cash. He circled round the deserted streets noting the lights that came on in downstairs windows as the daylight failed. The folk inside would be having their supper, settling down to the telly. He came to a house where no lights showed, opened the gate and went up the short drive and round to the back.

The top half of a window was open. Roger was able to swing himself up and reach inside to open the lower half. He climbed through, and was in a cloakroom.

He had no torch but he'd got a box of matches. By their light he groped his way upstairs to the main bedroom where he found without very much trouble a couple of rings, a watch, and a brooch. He went downstairs again and into the various rooms on the ground floor. Here he was careful not to let his flickering match shine anywhere near the uncurtained windows. There were several ornaments and figurines about the place but they were bulky to carry away and might break. However, in a desk in a book-lined room that smelled of leather and cigars he found twenty pounds in banknotes.

He felt better after that and made off quickly before his luck ran out.

Half a mile away, after several false tries, he found a house with an open door. There were some more rings there and a travelling clock. In a mug in the kitchen he found some money; not much, two pounds and a few odd pence, but it all helped. There was a pork pie and some milk in the fridge in this house, and he had a quick snack there. He took a silver cigarette-lighter, too, which he found on the sitting-room mantelpiece; it would be better for lighting his way around than the matches and he could flog it later. This was money for old rope. He'd invest in a torch for the future.

There were quite a number of houses where the people were out or away, and most were securely locked, but Roger found a third with a window open. He took a transistor radio from there; it fitted into his inner pocket. In the main bedroom a woman's handbag lay on the bed; there was a purse inside containing her generous housekeeping allowance. Roger strode away from the area with jaunty steps. Folk were stupid. He'd find some mug who'd buy the rings, and the other things; meanwhile he'd enough in hard cash to last quite a time and to flaunt about while he found some new mates.

VIII

Mrs Forman senior looked at her daughter-in-law.

'It's true then, Jean?'

Jean stared back at her, plucking nervously at the fabric of her blue cotton skirt. She shouldn't be wearing such a bright colour, she supposed, but she'd nothing black.

'It was Eileen Brown told me,' said Mrs Forman, pressing on doggedly. 'She's fond of minding everyone else's business, as you well know. So I told her it was rubbish and to watch her tongue. But I'd to find out the truth for myself. Seems she's seen you getting into this car of a Thursday after the club meetings and driving off. The young fellow that lodges at The Rising Sun, she said it is.'

Jean said nothing.

'Joe doesn't know?' The older woman's voice was not quite steady as she asked this.

'No – he hasn't a notion. He thinks I'm – I was – perfectly happy,' Jean said in a bitter voice.

'And why weren't you, with a good man and a nice home? Oh, Joe's no film star, I know that, but he's solid and decent, and that's worth more than all your glamour.'

'Joe's a good man,' Jean agreed.

'You'll not let him find out. He couldn't stand it – the shame – not on top of this other,' Mrs Forman stated. 'Young women get ideas. It'd have come to nothing. You'll not be going on with it.'

'Mrs Brown will tell him,' Jean said. She didn't care what happened. She felt utterly numb, as though nothing would ever move her again.

'I'll see to Eileen Brown,' said Mrs Forman grimly. 'You needn't fear she'll spread a tale like that abroad. I haven't known her for thirty years for nothing.' She got up. The two women had been sitting stiffly in armchairs in the sitting-room. 'I had to speak,' Mrs Forman went on. 'I'd only brood on this, else. Now's the time to clear the air. I'll never mention it again.' She paused, resting her hand lightly on Jean's shoulder. 'It made no difference to poor little Mary,' she added. 'Don't be thinking that.' At the door she turned. 'The inquest's tomorrow?'

'Yes. At the school. Eleven o'clock.'

'I'll see to dinner then. I'll make a pie. You'll both be needing something hot, after. Come round to my place when it's over.'

'You'll be there, won't you?' Jean asked.

'Oh yes. They may want to ask about Mary coming to see me that afternoon. We'll sit together, Jean,' Mrs Forman said. 'There'll be no talk.'

IX

The library did not open on Mondays. This suited Celia Mainwaring. She was usually out most of the weekend, with various friends or playing tennis, which went on throughout the year since the Leckington Club had three quick-drying hard courts. So on Mondays she did odd jobs at home – not much cleaning, for a woman came in three times a week to deal with that – but she went to the launderette and she had a shampoo and set at three o'clock every week. After that she had tea at The Hazel Nut, where she always found at least one acquaintance.

She was about to set forth for her hair appointment when Chief Inspector Coward and Detective Sergeant Davis rang her bell.

'Miss Celia Mainwaring?' Coward eyed her with interest when she opened the door. She was small, about five foot three inches tall, and quite curvy, but at first glance she seemed to him to be totally without the elusive quality he and the sergeant had been discussing.

Celia knew at once that they were policemen.

'Yes?' she said in a frosty voice.

'I am Chief Inspector Coward and this is Detective Sergeant Davis. We'd just like a word or two with you, if we might come in for a moment. We won't keep you long.'

What could they want? She would have to admit them. Celia led the way into her sitting-room and sat down in a Victorian button-back chair, upholstered in turquoise velvet.

154

'Sit down, inspector – sergeant – ' Celia said, drawing her pleated grey skirt down over her knees. Coward saw Davis wink at him slightly as they lowered themselves on to a knoll-type settee covered in yellow damask.

'What a charming room,' said Coward, looking about him.

It was. Celia's mother had had excellent taste and had been left a modest but adequate income when her husband was killed during the war. She had come to Leckington then, as it was an area away from likely bombing targets, and had found this small house in a quiet cul-de-sac. A doll's house, she'd called it.

'I'm glad you think so,' said Celia. She looked at her watch pointedly. 'Now, what can I do for you, Inspector? I have an appointment in ten minutes' time.'

Coward decided to go straight to the point.

'You are acquainted, I believe, with Major Frederick Johnson, of *Tobruk*, Wiveldown,' he said.

Miss Mainwaring stiffened.

'He comes to the library,' she said.

'Ah – a business relationship?' said Coward.

'That is all,' said Celia.

'Yet I understand he sent you a gift?'

'He had the effrontery to send me a potted plant. I returned it,' said Celia coldly.

'Oh, why? Wasn't it, perhaps, an expression of gratitude?'

'For what?'

'Services given,' said the chief inspector, and Sergeant Davis took out his handkerchief to mop at his nose.

'My acquaintance with Major Johnson was strictly limited to library hours,' said Miss Mainwaring firmly.

'But you'd been helpful to him at the library? Taken trouble to find him particular books?'

'No more than any other subscriber,' said Celia. 'I enjoy my work and try to do it conscientiously.'

'And don't some of your readers appreciate it, and give you occasional tokens of esteem?'

'At Christmas, occasionally.' There had been some homemade fudge once, she remembered; no more. 'Not flowers – from male readers,' she said in a voice charged with outrage.

'Well, then – I take it you did not invite Major Johnson to a meal here with you on Thursday evening?'

'Certainly not! Why? Does he say that I did?'

'No – not at all. But we believe he dined with a lady that night and we don't know who. You have no idea, I suppose?'

'I do not,' said Celia. 'And now, if you'll excuse me – '

'Just a moment, Miss Mainwaring. Why wouldn't you keep the plant?'

'I have no wish to be mixed up with that man,' she said.

'But why? Has he ever insulted you? Or made an improper suggestion to you?'

'No, not at all. I wouldn't permit such a thing,' said Celia.

'You lunched with him last Thursday.'

For a fraction of time Celia's poise wavered.

'I could hardly avoid it, without making a scene. He waited for me at the library and almost insisted. He seemed friendless so I took pity on him.'

'I see. You know of no other women friends he might have?'

'No. But I am not his keeper. Oh – ' she hesitated.

'Yes?'

'He sells tickets at Chorlbury Manor sometimes. Mrs Fellowes – Ruth Fellowes – she lives in Wiveldown too – they are acquainted with one another. But hardly friends, I imagine. Mrs Fellowes gives cooking lessons and Major Johnson attended a course last winter.'

'Ah yes. Her address, please?'

Celia supplied it.

'And now I must go,' she said.

They drove her to the hairdresser's, since they had made her late. She bustled into the shop without a backward glance. How right she had been to return the flowers; the very fact that the police were enquiring about Major Johnson showed how undesirable a character he must be.

'None,' said Davis, shaking his head as they watched her walk into the shop. 'All the equipment, but none of the magic.'

'Odd, isn't it?' remarked Coward. 'A worthy woman, too, in the world's eye as well as her own. But clearly a perpetual virgin.'

X

Like Roger's mother, Mrs West knew Chief Inspector Coward by sight, but she had never spoken to him. She felt slightly sick when he asked for Tom.

'He hasn't been working lately, I believe,' said Coward.

'He's got a job now, down at Walter's, the paint factory. Started today,' she said quickly.

'Ah.'

'He's not in trouble, is he?' she asked, unable to conceal her anxiety. 'He's always been a good boy – never been in trouble.' She clasped her hands together.

'We're not sure, Mrs West. That's what we have to find out,' said the chief inspector. 'Do you know what he was doing last Thursday?'

'That was the day there was that bad thunderstorm. No, I don't know where he was.'

'You remember it was the day of the storm. Now, why?'

'Well, you do remember things, don't you? And besides –' she stopped.

'Well?'

'Tom got soaked through,' she said lamely. 'But anyone would, out in that lot.'

'You've washed his clothes, of course?' Mrs West had been ironing when they called, and a neat pile of clean washing was stacked on the kitchen table.

'Yes.' She gestured at the heap of laundry. Some faded jeans could be seen.

'What about his shoes?'

'He had a pair of plimsolls on. Those rubber things. He's got them on today.'

'What time did he come home on Thursday, after the storm?'

'Not all that late. Midnight, maybe,' said Mrs West.

'Or later?'

'Could have been. I didn't look at the time.'

No, thought the policeman, but you listened for him. You were anxious.

'I see. And who are his friends now, Mrs West?'

'I don't know. He used to go to the youth club. They'd tell you. But he hasn't been there lately. He'll go again now he's in work.'

'Did he know a boy called Roger Brewis?'

'I don't know,' said Mrs West again, but her face went pale. 'That's the boy you're looking for. Oh, Tom wouldn't know him.' Now she looked really frightened.

'Leckington's not a big town. They're of an age. Probably they do know each other, Mrs West.'

'Yes, but not to be friendly. He wouldn't be mixed up in anything, would Tom.' But he'd been in a terrible state of nerves these past few days. If he'd seen Roger – no, it wasn't thinkable.

'Brewis has disappeared. Your Tom might be able to help us find him – that's all,' said Coward. 'I'll see him some other time and find out where he was on Thursday. Thank you, Mrs West.'

He went back to join Detective Sergeant Davis, who had waited in the car in case Tom, if at home, had tried to get away from the house. As the sergeant slid the car into gear and moved off down the road, the chief inspector sighed.

'This is when I hate our job, Dick. What a nice, respectable woman.'

'We don't know that young West was involved.'

'No – but he was seen with Brewis in the market. And there are all those dabs in the car. Some may be his.' In a way he hoped so, for the major's sake.

'Are we going to the paint works now?'

'No. We'll wait for the boy. Or rather, you will. Take young Forrest with you, let him meet his prey. Bring the boy in and

158

treat him gently. And get a print – the cup of tea method, for choice.'

'Let him go, then?'

'Unless he asks to stay, yes, this time.'

XI

While Sergeant Davis and Constable Forrest made their plans to meet Tom West on his way home from work, Chief Inspector Coward went out to Wiveldown again. He found Ruth Fellowes' cottage and soon discovered that she was out, so he took an exploratory prowl round her garden. The road below was invisible and he could not see even the roof of his car, which he had left close to the side of the road. Thoughtfully, he walked back to it.

The stolen bicycles had been found not far from here. He drove to the spot and stood in the road meditating. Then he got back into his car and drove slowly back towards Ruth's cottage. In all this time nothing had passed that way.

He parked once more outside Ruth's gate and walked slowly along towards the village. There were hedges on both sides of the road, cleanly cut-and-laid the year before but sprouting strongly now; a mechanical cutter would trim them next time. Less than a hundred yards beyond the cottage he saw a gap in the hedge filled by a stile. Beyond was a field with some cattle in it.

Coward climbed the stile and walked some distance over the field. In places it was still damp and the mud stuck to his shoes.

He went back to the police station and pored over a map, plotting Mary's possible movements when she left *The Hollies*, while a constable went down to the laboratory with a generous supply of mud from the Wiveldown field.

159

Mrs Eileen Brown was having a cup of tea with her friend Cassie Castle.

'And there he stood, right in Mr Duckett's shop as large as life, and he'd do you or me in next, as like as not,' she said. 'I can tell you, it made my flesh creep. He shouldn't be let out, that's what,' she added, with a delighted shudder.

'You think he did it, then?' Mrs Castle did not form her opinions with the same haste as her friend.

'Who else?' demanded Mrs Brown. 'He was going to bury poor little Mary in his garden, by dead of night, but it was too wet on Thursday, and on Friday it was full moon. Someone might have seen.'

'Oh, Eileen, I don't know. He never did it, surely.'

'Who else?' Mrs Brown asked for the second time. 'I've always thought him a strange one. Them eyes. They kind of look through you.'

Mrs Castle was not sure if she had ever seen the major. She had certainly not gazed into his eyes.

'And living alone like that. It's not natural,' Mrs Brown went on.

'Folk do. The vicar. And Mr Bellings.'

Mr Bellings was a widower, like the vicar, and he lived near Mrs Forman senior in a council bungalow.

'They were both married. Poor Bertha.'

'Yes.'

Both ladies were silent for some seconds in tribute to bad-tempered Bertha Bellings, long deceased, whose bereaved husband was now one of the happiest members of the Darby and Joan club, where ladies outnumbered gentleman by four to one. He was invited out to Sunday dinner regularly by the various widowed ladies whom he met there, and his life was a great deal pleasanter now than it had been when Bertha kept at him for making marks on all her floors, and made him wear a collar and tie on Sundays.

'The children, Cassie. We must think of all the children,'

Eileen said. 'Your grandchildren. My grandchildren. What about them, with that monster free among us? I've told our Ivy not to let them out until he's put away.' Ivy was Mrs Brown's daughter, mother of three tough little boys all rather like their grandmother.

Cassie's grandchildren were still in their prams, so she felt unaffected at the moment. The two women had lived in the district for their whole lives; their fathers had worked on the land, and they had married local men who had begun their working lives as farm labourers, but now Eileen's husband worked for a haulage firm, and Cassie's drove a van for the local water board.

'Let's go down there, Cassie, and tell him what we think of him,' said Eileen.

'What – Major Johnson? You mean talk to him?'

'Well – let's see if he's there. If he sees how we feel, maybe he'll give himself up.'

'Oh, I don't know, Eileen.'

'He wouldn't meet my eye, in Duckett's shop,' insisted Eileen, who had kept hers so averted from the major's contaminating gaze that he could not have done so if he tried. 'If he'd been innocent, he would of.'

'Well, I'm not sure.'

'You're scared,' taunted Eileen.

'No – no, I'm not.' Eileen was always so impetuous. 'We could walk down and have a look, at least. There'd be no harm in that,' Cassie allowed.

'Right, then,' said Eileen promptly. As they walked down the path she picked up two or three stones, each nearly the size of a golf ball, and put them in the pocket of her shapeless cardigan. Cassie, alarmed, pretended not to see.

They started down the road. On the way they met some friends, and their ranks swelled when Eileen explained where they were going.

'Just to have a look,' Cassie kept insisting. 'Not to talk to him.'

By the time they reached the church there were ten of them,

all middle-aged, some uncertain why they'd come but all convinced by now that the major couldn't be 'quite right'.

The bungalow looked peaceful in the evening light, with the sinking sun casting a rosy glow above the major's garage. Shadows stretched across his front lawn.

'That's where she was,' said Mrs Brown. 'Poor Mary, stiff and cold in that garridge. All those hours, there she lay.' She was quoting from the press.

A woman gave a sob.

'While Jean and Joe were hunting high and low for her,' Eileen went on, not quite accurately, since Jean had never left the house.

'And all our men.'

That was true. Almost every able-bodied man had joined the search parties.

'Murderer,' hissed Eileen Brown, and one of the other women repeated it.

They began to chant.

'Murderer! Murderer! Give yourself up! Come out and give yourself up!'

From inside the bungalow came an odd, deep booming sound. It was the major's trombone.

XIII

Cathy and Derek were having a row when the mournful sound of the major's trombone came wafting to them over the garden.

When Derek got home from work, Cathy told him that she meant to invite the major to supper the next evening, after the inquest.

'I forbid you to do it. We don't want people to think we're friends with a man like that,' said Derek.

'Why not? I am friends with him,' said Cathy defiantly. 'He's a nice, harmless old man.'

'He's mixed up in this terrible business. It could ditch my chances of promotion if I'm involved too,' said Derek.

'Well, you are involved already. You were there when Mary was found.'

'That was just an accident,' said Derek.

'You'll have to go to the inquest, won't you? You can't dodge that,' Cathy said. 'You can't seriously think the major had anything to do with it, Derek.'

'I don't know what to think. People just don't go round with bodies in the boots of their cars,' said Derek. 'Until the police have sorted it all out I'm not having anything to do with Major Johnson, and neither are you. In fact, even if there is some sort of explanation that absolves him, I'm not sure – anyway, we don't know how it will go.'

'What do you mean?' Cathy asked him.

'I don't like solitary old men who make a habit of talking to little children – boys or girls,' said Derek. He suddenly looked so obstinate that Cathy's heart sank. Where was the kind man she thought she had married?

'You're condemning him before any court has done it,' she said in a very quiet voice.

'I don't think it's healthy,' Derek insisted.

'And what if the vicar talks to little boys or girls? Is he a pervert too? Is there no relationship that isn't suspect?'

'Oh, of course there is. Don't twist my words,' said Derek angrily.

'And don't you try to twist my mind,' said Cathy, just as violently. 'I shall ask him here tomorrow night.'

'And if you do, I shall refuse to have him in the house,' said Derek.

They stared at each other, both suddenly terrified by the enormous chasm that had opened up between them. Into the silence that fell came the notes of the trombone.

'Whatever's that?' cried Derek, thankful for the diversion.

Cathy was bewildered at first, but then she realised what it was.

'Major Johnson played in a military band when he was young. It's his trombone, I expect,' she said.

'I've never heard it before,' said Derek.

'No. He only plays when everyone's out,' said Cathy. 'He told me so.'

'I wonder why he's playing it now,' said Derek.

The windows of their house were open and the sound had drifted through. He walked out on to the flagged terrace and listened. Cathy followed. She was trembling, but she knew she must stick to her views or she would betray herself as well as the major.

They heard the bass notes, slow and ponderous. Then the noise altered, and another sound, less hesitant, came to them. It was the chant of voices.

They could not make out what was being said. The trombone had ceased, and Derek began to walk towards his gate, trying to catch what the voices shouted.

'Murderer! Murderer!' he heard, and Cathy, following, heard it too.

'Give yourself up! Give yourself up! Murderer!' came the cry, as Derek went into the road.

The women were standing on the pavement outside the major's bungalow, shaking their fists and shouting. Cathy and Derek looked at one another in horror, and as Derek stood there hesitating, the first stone was thrown, shattering the glass in the major's front door.

'Go and ring the police, quick. I'll stop them,' Derek said, striding forward.

Cathy paused long enough to see him raise an arm to shield his face from another stone as he moved into the group; then she fled back into her own house.

XIV

Tom did not know that Joe Forman worked at the paint factory. He was sweeping out the yard under the direction of an elderly man whose job it was to keep the stores and surrounding area tidy, when two men walked past.

'That's Joe Forman. Chap whose little girl got killed last week,' said Tom's superior.

'What? Who? Where?' Tom started and stared at the men.

'Him on the left. Poor bugger,' said the old man. 'Nice little kiddie, she was. Used to come on the works outings and to social club parties sometimes. Bad business, that. Papers seem to think that Major Johnson was responsible. He worked here too, once.'

Tom was gazing at Joe's retreating back. All he saw was a stocky shape in overalls, with dark hair and a small balding patch.

'Oh! Did he?' Tom said.

Ten minutes later, Joe, alone, returned through the yard, and Tom saw his face: pale, rather lined. Not a young man any more.

' 'Morning, Bill,' he said to Tom's boss, and Bill went to talk to him. While they conversed quietly together Tom swept his way industriously out of earshot. He had caught Mary's name being mentioned. It wasn't just her death for which he was to blame, but also for the grief of this man who was not unlike Tom's own father. The full extent of the horror of his act at last began to register.

He worked zealously throughout the day, for by heaving heavy boxes around and leaping to the bidding of Bill, he was able to thrust it all out of his mind for a time, but the end of the day came at last when he had to stop this activity.

'You and me'll get along, young Tom, I can tell,' said Bill approvingly, thumping him on the back. 'Quite a worker, you are. See you tomorrow, lad.'

Tom nodded and managed a smile.

He walked home thinking of Joe Forman, and thinking too about Major Johnson, who had done nothing wrong but who had become, like Mary, a sort of victim. Bit of an old fogey, he'd seemed, but he'd listened to Tom's request for work very civilly.

It was all Roger's fault. He'd been behind the whole thing – the stealing of the boots, the drinking, the lot.

But Tom had driven the car.

Of course they wouldn't clobber the major for it. The fuzz would know he hadn't done it. The thing was to play it cool and in the end it'd all blow over. Roger would keep away, that was for sure, and good riddance too. All he, Tom, must do was keep his nerve.

He was thinking along these lines when he turned into his own street and saw the police car. It began to move slowly towards him as he approached. He kept his eyes fixed on the road ahead and tried to ignore it, but it was hopeless; he kept glancing at it. And he hadn't the heart to run; what would be the point?

I won't admit a thing, he vowed. They can't make me. He kept telling himself this as he allowed Detective Sergeant Davis and Constable Forrest to take him off to police headquarters.

XV

Derek had witnessed mob violence when he was a student, but he had never before seen middle-aged women lose control and he was revolted. Until he saw their faces contorted with hysteria he had to some extent sympathised with the viewpoint of these women, but this conduct was primitive. He sought for a face he recognised, and saw one: Mrs Castle, who for a time had helped behind the bar at The Rising Sun.

'Mrs Castle,' he thundered. 'Stop that at once,' and at the same time he grabbed the arm of the woman nearest to him and pulled her back from Major Johnson's fence.

Cassie, who had stifled her earlier doubts and was shouting as loudly as anyone, hesitated and took a backward step; the woman Derek had seized fell silent from sheer surprise. Derek elbowed his way past them and reached the gate, which Mrs Brown had been about to open. He interposed his own body between it and her.

'Go back to your homes immediately,' he commanded.

166

The chanting dribbled to a halt, and the women gaped at him; then they looked at each other, some of them seeking guidance but others feeling sheepish. Derek tried to think of a telling remark to make but failed. Attack was the best method of defence, so he rounded on Mrs Brown.

'You threw that stone. You'll be liable for damages,' he snarled at her. 'What's your name?'

Mrs Brown did not answer. She was trying to summon up her reserves for a counter-attack.

'Never mind. I won't forget you. You'll pay all right, I'll see to that,' he said. 'And you'll be prosecuted too, if I have my way.' He glared round at them all. 'The lot of you will,' he threatened.

At this even Eileen Brown's belligerence faltered. Cassie pulled at her arm.

'We'd better go,' she said. 'Come on, Eileen. We've had our say.'

They began to disperse, shuffling off down the road, some looking rather abashed but a few still angry.

'Who's he think he is?' demanded Eileen Brown. 'Have the law on us, indeed? The law should do its own job, that's what.' She continued to mutter, but she moved away.

When he saw that they were really going, Derek went up the path to the door of the bungalow. He put his hand through the broken glass and opened it. Major Johnson was sitting in the living-room with his head bowed forward, his face in his hands, staring at the floor. The trombone lay at his feet.

The two constables in their Panda car who came in response to Cathy's telephone call met the little band of no-longer-militant women moving away up the road, and they found Derek still staring at the major, who had not moved nor spoken since he entered the bungalow.

PART FIVE

I

THE NEWSPAPERS were quick to exploit this new turn of events. There was a dearth of political drama that week, and they were featuring the Forman case in detail since they had space to fill. An alert reporter saw the Panda car hurrying out to Wiveldown and soon discovered what had happened.

Ruth's hostess, in Tenby, read the news to her at breakfast.

'I see the villagers where you live have been taking the law into their own hands,' she remarked. 'That man must be mixed up in it somehow, in spite of what you say.' For they had already discussed the tragedy, though Ruth had not been very forthcoming about it.

'Of course he isn't. He wouldn't hurt a fly – unless it threatened Queen or country,' Ruth said.

'Where was he, then, on Thursday night?' Ruth's friend demanded.

'What? Here – let me look!' Ruth snatched the paper from the other woman and learned from it that Major Johnson's car had been seen returning late on the night of the incident, when he had alleged he was at home. 'Oh no! Oh, how could he be so foolish!' Ruth exclaimed, half to herself. 'I must ring up the police at once,' she told her friend.

Detective Chief Inspector Coward arrived at *Tobruk* soon after half-past nine on Tuesday morning. Major Johnson was wearing a dark suit and a black tie, in readiness for the inquest. He was pale, and all the lines on his face sagged downwards; in two days he had aged ten years. A pile of letters, not all of them opened, lay on the table in his sitting-room, and the telephone was off the hook.

'Hm – more letters, I see,' said Coward. 'And you've had phone calls, too, have you?'

'Yes.'

Major Johnson had slept very little during the night. A police guard had remained outside the bungalow, and there had been no more trouble from the village, but it had taken him some time to think of leaving the telephone receiver off.

'Well, your worries are over now,' Coward said. He felt expansive. 'I should burn that lot.' He waved his hand at the letters. 'We've got it wrapped up now. But you should have telephoned, yesterday, when those women came round. You could have had protection sooner.'

Major Johnson laughed shortly.

'British justice,' he said. 'Mob law.'

'People behave strangely at these times,' said Coward. 'That Mrs Brown, the ringleader – termagant type.' He was pleased with the word, and said it again. 'A termagant. Do you want to bring a case against her? You'd be within your rights.'

'What good would it do?' asked Major Johnson. 'The harm's been done. But you know what happened, do you?' He'd almost stopped caring by this time.

'We do. We've got the two boys concerned – the pair who stole the bicycles. Roger Brewis was picked up in Liverpool yesterday. He'd been trying to sell stolen property. He'd broken into several houses on Sunday night – left fingerprints all over the place – there's no doubt about his identity. He's on his way back here now, to be charged.'

'With what?'

'Stealing a bicycle and a pair of boots to start with. Another boy actually drove your car, but we believe Brewis was the ring-leader. Tom West's the other lad. He was the one who killed Mary Forman.'

'She was killed with my car?'

'Young West admitted everything last night, when he heard Brewis had been caught. They saw your car in Lammas Lane

170

on Thursday night and took it to get home, having ditched the two bicycles they'd stolen earlier. They'd made a day of it – pinched some drink and lain up in a barn at Mordwell knocking it back. West knew how to start a car without the key – bragged about it – he'd worked at a garage, though only on the pumps. They'd gone a hundred yards or so when Mary suddenly appeared in front of them – she came through a gap in the fence – there's a stile there. They never saw her. You'd think she'd have heard them, but she'd had a fright – she may have run out in front of the car intending to stop it.' He told Major Johnson about Mrs Pollock. 'When the boys found Mary was dead they put her in the boot of your car and took it back to where they'd found it. Brewis disappeared and left young West to face the music on his own. He came to see you on Sunday. Curious to know what you were like. Troubled with his conscience.'

'What? That boy with all the hair?' The one he'd thought a civil lad.

'That's right. He met Joe Forman, too – brought it all home to him. He'd have given himself up pretty soon if we hadn't got on to him – couldn't have stood it.'

Major Johnson was silent.

'What will happen to him?' he asked.

'Probably have to face a manslaughter charge,' said Coward. 'And of course driving without a licence and all that.'

'Prison, then?'

'Certainly. There's all the thieving too.'

'And the other boy? You say it was all his fault?'

'Yes – but he wasn't driving the car. He's got a record, though, and a lot to answer for up in Liverpool.'

'Young West doesn't seem very good at choosing his friends,' said the major slowly. 'He's a victim of circumstance, like me.'

'You'd have saved yourself – and us – a good deal of trouble if you'd told us where you were on Thursday night,' pointed out the chief inspector.

'You seem to have discovered anyway.'

171

'West told us where the car was. And Mrs Fellowes telephoned just before I left the station this morning. She'd read about the women molesting you and all that.'

Molesting. So that was what it was.

'Why didn't you tell us about her, Major?'

'I saw no reason why she should be involved,' said Major Johnson austerely. 'I knew the child's death was not of my direct doing, and that you'd find out the truth eventually.'

'Yes – but at what a cost,' said Coward. In a way the man was ridiculous, yet somehow this attitude impressed.

'It was my fault that Mary died,' said Major Johnson. 'I was to blame.'

'You weren't, Major.'

'I couldn't have locked my car. I am always most particular about locking it, but that night it was raining hard and I must have been careless. The boys wouldn't have taken it if it had been locked.'

'They might have. Young West would have opened it. He'd have boasted to Brewis that he could and been forced to prove it, to save his face.'

'Then it would have taken longer, and Mary would have escaped, perhaps,' said Major Johnson. He shook his head. 'Those poor people, the Formans. Perhaps Mary did try to get a lift. I told her that afternoon that she shouldn't hitch-hike. She said she was doing it to save her bus fare.'

'Mrs Fellowes was on the two o'clock bus that day. She said you passed her while she was waiting at the stop. Why didn't you pick her up too?'

The major looked surprised.

'I never noticed her. We're just acquaintances, you know, that's all, but she's been kind. I gave her a lift home that night because of the storm, and she invited me to supper.'

'So she said.' Poor old fool, thought Coward, fantasising about the proud librarian when all the time there was this widow on his doorstep; she'd been very concerned about him on the telephone and said she was coming home at once. Coward decided not to impart this piece of news. 'Well, there's a neat report for the coroner – everything cut and dried, with no loose ends,' he said.

'I'm to attend the inquest?'

'Yes, please. Just a formality – you may not be called.'

'And Mrs Pollock?'

'Oh – that's a separate matter. No problems there.'

Except for his negligent constables.

II

The inquest did not take long. The school was packed, and the silent spectators heard a verdict of accidental death returned. They trooped out of the building talking in hushed voices, some still very shocked by what had happened, but a few with blunted sensibilities feeling a sense of anti-climax. There was no lurid murder after all.

The vicar drove the Formans home and went in with them to talk about the funeral, which could now be planned. Miss Price walked along the road, wheeling her bicycle, talking to Joe's mother. Derek hurried back to his office, and everyone else dispersed in various directions. No one gave a thought to Major Johnson.

He went home and wrote two letters. One he put on his sitting-room mantelpiece, underneath his gleaming bugle, the other he took immediately to the letter-box on the corner near the vicarage. He met no one on this excursion.

His telephone was still off the hook and he did not put it back. Cathy had been trying to get through to him with her invitation for the evening but had got no reply, so she intended to call in later in the day.

To his surprise, Major Johnson felt hungry, so he cooked some of the food he had bought at Duckett's the day before. Then he sat at his window watching until Cathy went past wheeling the pram. On Tuesday afternoons he knew she took the baby to the clinic and would be out for an hour or so.

When she had gone by he went out into the garden and walked around it. He had achieved something in claiming it back from the wilderness it had been, but it was not enough to comfort him now. His integrity had been questioned and found wanting, and he saw no end to loneliness ahead. He was of use to no one any longer.

Inspector Coward would get his letter in the morning. It was unfortunate that he would cause more trouble, but his affairs were all in order. He hoped the rough will he had made would be valid; his possessions would be scant compensation to the Formans for the loss of Mary, but if they sold the bungalow they would raise enough to start up some small business of their own, in another area, perhaps.

There was no one within earshot. On Tuesdays Mrs Philpot played golf in the morning and bridge in the afternoons, so she was not at home, and her husband would be at his butcher's shop.

Major Johnson went back into the bungalow. He took the bugle down from the wall and gave it a rub on the sleeve of his jacket. Then he opened his desk and took out his service revolver. In the same drawer was his row of medals, just service ones, no special awards for valour or for duty done. He gave them a glance and closed the drawer again.

He thought for a moment as he sat down in his armchair of his companions in the army; of the sense of comradeship; the heat and dust of the desert; the calmer, postwar life. There were tasks for every day.

Then, holding his bugle tightly in his left hand, with his other hand he raised the revolver to his head and shot himself.

Serious Intent

1

STEVE HAD ALWAYS stolen from old Tom, though Mark didn't realise it until he had been going to the house for several weeks.

'We give him our time, don't we?' Steve had said, when at last Mark, understanding, had protested. 'That's worth money.'

Steve's stepmother, Ivy, cleaned for Tom, and the boys – just Steve at first, but later Mark as well – often went round after school because she was anxious about the old man.

Steve overcharged Tom for shopping done, rendering falsified accounts scribbled on scraps of paper, never challenged, and accepted a pound, sometimes more, for his trouble.

So Steve was doing it on purpose, not making genuine mistakes. As the two boys walked back to Ivy's house together, Mark accepted some crisps, bought with Tom's money, and quite soon he got used to what was going on.

He liked visiting Tom's house, and sometimes he went there alone.

Tom couldn't walk far. His shuffling gait would carry him from room to room, and he managed the stairs very slowly, clinging to the handrail specially installed, making just one trip each way every day. Steve often helped him go upstairs to bed, patting him gently, urging him on with encouraging words. At fourteen, Steve was a big boy, bigger than Tom, who had shrunk down almost to Mark's level.

Mark didn't like watching Tom edge himself along: not when he remembered that Tom had been a pilot in the war and had won medals. Mark had seen them. It seemed all wrong that he could barely move unaided. But Steve was always gentle with him; there was no bullying, though Steve was tough when they were playing with other boys in the park, and he wasn't always kind. Mark had seen him elbow an elderly woman with a laden shopping basket off the pavement in front of oncoming traffic, and he had done other things Mark knew were bad. He'd pushed a boy who annoyed him from his bike, then ridden off, laughing, on the bike, which he'd later abandoned, leaving it with a buckled wheel and a lacerated tyre. He'd smashed a car's windscreen because he said the driver had shown no respect at a crossroads: that time, he watched the driver park, lock his car and leave it, before carrying out his action.

'He's got to be punished,' Steve had said.

Mark didn't like it when Steve was in one of his angry, vengeful moods, and he thought charging old Tom more for shopping than the real price was disrespectful, but he did not want to lose his role as Steve's assistant, so he kept quiet. Steve ran through people, Mark knew. Boys formerly his friends gave him up when he flew into a rage or 'borrowed' their possessions once too often.

Tom said that without the two boys' help he might not be able to go on living at The Willows, and Ivy thought Tom was good for Steve. She worried about him. He wasn't doing well at school, and often she had no idea how he spent his time. At least she knew where he was when he went to Tom's.

Tom's money seemed to flow in regularly. Steve didn't know how it came. Perhaps the bank sent it by post. Steve had offered to collect Tom's pension from the Post Office.

'Wouldn't it help?' he'd suggested. 'My mum gets loads for other people,' he invented. He always called Ivy his mum;

it saved explaining that after his mother died, Ivy and his dad had got married, and then they had a daughter, Kylie, who was now seven. Ivy already had a daughter of her own, called Sharon. Eighteen months ago, Steve's dad was killed in an accident. That was sad, and Steve did not like to think about it. Kylie had been in a terrible way at the time, and so had Ivy, but they were all right now, and so was he.

Tom hadn't accepted Steve's offer. He'd said it was all under control and the pension money went straight to the bank.

He'd got stocks and shares, too, Steve knew. Once, when Tom was dozing, he'd looked through some drawers in his desk, but he couldn't pry when Mark was around; the kid had too many scruples.

'Maybe he'll leave all his stuff to us, we're so good to him,' Steve had said one day when the boys had collected a video to watch with the old man.

Tom's tastes and Steve's didn't coincide and much of what they watched was too tame for Steve, though it appealed to Mark. They'd had some comic films like *Crocodile Dundee* and *A Fish Called Wanda*, and they'd all laughed at those, even Steve, as they ate fish and chips bought from the van which parked in the market square three times a week.

It was nice, Mark thought, sitting in front of the television with the plates of food – Tom wouldn't let them eat it from the wrappings even though it meant they had to wash up later. Steve did well on those nights because Ivy gave him the money for his and Mark's meal when she did not feed them at home, and Steve also claimed it from Tom.

In the soft light from the gas fire – one which looked like coal – the flickering television screen, and a standard lamp switched on in the corner, the room was peaceful, the atmosphere easy. Mark would imagine that Tom was his grandfather. He liked the old man's pink face and fine white hair, and his crooked smile. Mark would pretend that he lived here all the time, and his mother too, so that it didn't matter that she was out so much. She had to work hard to keep them both and to pay Ivy for looking after him out of school hours – it came to a lot in the holidays. If his mother had to be away all night, which happened when there were conferences and big functions at the hotel where she worked, he spent the night at Ivy's, but soon he would be old enough to stay at home by himself and save money. He planned to suggest it next time his mother seemed depressed when doing her accounts.

Ivy had looked after him for a long time, even before Steve's father died. Mark had liked Joe, who had played football with the boys and promised that they'd all go camping when Mark and Kylie were older. Mark missed Joe a lot, but he didn't like to say so in case it made Ivy sad. She'd cheered up when Sharon had her baby, Adam, who was four months old now. The baby, like Mark, had no dad, but nor had Steve now, and Mark didn't know what had happened to Sharon's. Perhaps he was dead, too. It was all right not to have a dad; lots of people hadn't, or shared someone else's, but Mark would have liked one.

His mother had told him that she had wanted him so much that although she wasn't married, she had decided to bring him up on her own. He wasn't quite sure what the alternative was, and at the time was not curious about his father, but he was now, only she wouldn't answer questions about him.

'I wanted you. You're mine and I love you,' she would say, and she did, he knew. She gave him lovely hugs and she bought him toys. He had a computer and a Scalextric car layout, and at weekends, if she wasn't at work, they were happy together, but he wished he had more of a family. Steve had a gran, though she lived in Wales and he didn't see her much; Kylie and Sharon had cousins who visited and with whom they sometimes stayed; but Mark had no one except his mother.

Mark liked going round to Ivy's after school, even though at ten, he was old enough, now, to go straight home. After his next birthday his mum would let him; he could cook things in the microwave and put on the telly. He could still visit Tom, too, as long as he was back before mum. But he'd miss Ivy's meals. At weekends their food was brilliant; she made shepherd's pies and tasty stews, and sticky brown gingerbread which Mark loved. Mark didn't mind the small children she sometimes looked after, as she had him when he was young, but Steve found them a pain. Mark quite liked Sharon's baby, which did little more than sleep and cry at present, or hang like a limpet on Sharon's large, pale breast, a sight which fascinated Mark and yet embarrassed him.

'Such huge tits she's got now,' Steve would say, and laugh. He liked staring at her, and Sharon would get cross and tell him to piss off, and then Ivy would ask her to watch her language.

She was really quite strict: much stricter than Mark's mother.

The boys knew they must watch what they said in front of Tom. It wasn't too hard; there was no need for strong words at The Willows. Tom always had time to hear what they had to say and he never failed to ask if they had done their homework. Sometimes they brought it with them. Mark didn't have very much at the moment, and Steve skimped his so that they could settle down to playing cards or watching telly. Tom had recorded a number of old films which they put on when there was no programme that appealed. One of the old man's favourites was *The Dam Busters*, and Mark liked *The Great Escape*. Tom had been a bomber pilot in the war, and he was shot down over Hamburg. He had spent the rest of the war as a prisoner, but he hadn't managed to escape, though he'd tried several times before giving up and settling down to study for some exams, which had been a wise thing to do, he told them both. It meant he had done well in later life.

He must have, to have bought a big house like The Willows. Ivy said it was worth a tidy penny, and if Tom had to go into a home, selling the house would pay for years of care.

She and Sharon thought it was ever so sad that Tom had no family, and so did Mark. But there must have been someone once: a boy. There was that room upstairs with the posters of aeroplanes, and all the children's books, which Tom encouraged the two boys to borrow. Steve wasn't interested, but Mark was.

Perhaps the boy was dead. Mark didn't like to ask.

Tom suspected that Steve was stealing from him, but the amounts were not large and he could stand the loss. However, he felt that Steve should not be allowed to succeed with his pilfering; getting away with small thefts might lead him on to larger ones and he could end up in serious trouble.

He ought to tackle the boy, bring the stealing to a halt. There was Mark, too; Tom hoped Mark was not a party to the deceit. He was so young, his cheeks round and smooth, his brown eyes trusting. Tom knew that Mark loved coming to the house. He had discovered the books upstairs and, if he did not like what was on the television, or if Tom and Steve were playing poker – which they sometimes did, for matches, and Tom usually won – he would sit curled up in a big armchair, rapt in the adventures of Biggles or William, or even the Famous Five. Tom played chess with Mark. Steve would leave them together while he went to fetch the fish and chips, and occasionally he would slip out without saying where he was going. Tom tried not to wonder what he was up to then; he hoped the boy wasn't turning his talents elsewhere, looking for more scams. Wordsworth Road was so quiet; there were other secluded houses, which might not be securely locked up, within a few hundred yards.

If he challenged Steve, the results might be costly. He would lose his errand-boy and Mark wouldn't be allowed to come on his own to visit. Or would he? Children were independent at an early age now and he was a capable lad.

Tom compromised. He began to check the money handed out and the change received, and told Steve he'd need receipts in future.

'But why? Don't you trust me?' Steve asked, his thin, fair skin flushing over his cheekbones, the pupils enlarging in his pale blue eyes.

'I need to work out my budget,' Tom replied. 'My funds are limited.'

It was close enough to the truth.

'I'll shop around a bit. Get marked down stuff,' Steve volunteered, and for a week or two he brought back receipts from various tills, though he still filched from Tom's purse.

Tom couldn't maintain strict vigilance. He was too frail and it was too much of a strain. He'd rather have the boys happy and dishonest than lose them altogether.

Then the man came.

He called on a Saturday afternoon. Steve and Mark had been watching *Grandstand* on television. They had given Tom his lunch, and he had dozed off, as he often did after eating, when the doorbell rang.

Steve answered it, and saw a stocky man with grey hair, dressed in jeans and a fawn anorak, carrying a holdall.

'Who are you?' the man asked him, stepping forward so that his nose was a few inches from Steve's. He smelled of beer.

'Who's asking?' Steve responded, standing firmly in the doorway. He wished he'd put the chain up, but the only people who'd ever called were the do-gooders, like the vicar and the health visitor, and once some Jehovah's Witnesses. There'd been no one showing disrespect before.

The man pushed past Steve, one hand thrusting him against the doorpost as he strode by. Steve, who was tall for his age and well built, was not used to being defied and he was startled when the man marched on into the sitting-room, where Mark had abandoned the ice hockey match on the screen and was reading.

'What's happening here?' the man demanded. 'Are you running a kid's home now?' He spoke in an angry voice, and as he moved across to Tom's chair and stood over him, for a moment Mark thought he was going to hit the old man while he slept. Then Tom opened his eyes.

'Eh? Eh? What – who——?' he muttered, blinking, trying to focus on the newcomer.

'Wake up,' said the man. 'It's me, Alan, come to see his dad.'

Tom gaped at him, his head tilted back. He'd gone a funny colour, sort of bluey-white and blotchy. Mark stared at them both. The man had brought fear with him into the house.

But Steve had rallied.

'What right have you to shove me around?' he demanded, squaring up to the intruder, bravely, Mark decided. 'And how do I know Tom is your dad?'

Like Mark, Steve was frightened, but he had recognised a bully. If the man proved to be a villain, he and Mark could run out of the house fast, and get help, then be heroes. If, however, he was Tom's son, a whole new situation existed. Had Tom sent for him because of Steve's cheating over money? He drew breath, preparing to defend himself, getting ready to counter-attack.

Tom had now turned red, an alarming purply shade.

'It's all right, Steve,' he said, and to the man, 'You never let me know you were coming. Should you be here at all?'

'Of course, as you're not well,' the man replied. 'I've only just heard about your illness.'

'You should have warned me,' Tom said.

'I thought you'd enjoy the surprise,' said the man. His manner had grown quieter. 'Who are these kids?'

'They're my friends,' said Tom. 'They do my shopping and keep me company. Steve and Mark.'

'You can go now, kids,' the man told them. 'And there's no need to mention my visit.' He tapped his nose with his finger. 'It's no one else's business.'

Steve thought that made sense. Mark never talked about Tom anyway.

2

RICHARD GARDNER WAS travelling back to Haverscot from his office, which was south of the river, a large anonymous building where corporate insurance was handled. His working hours were calmer than his time at home, and he was wondering what sort of reception he would receive that evening. Sometimes Verity was out at evening classes; she was studying a form of meditation this term, seeking tranquillity. She left the boys alone if he was not back when it was time for her to leave; she said that they were old enough. Justin was thirteen and Terry was eleven; they were her children by an earlier marriage.

If Verity were at home when he returned, she might greet him with moist, sticky kisses, twining skinny arms around his neck; or she might remain silent, dishing up a meal that was nearly inedible – burnt or almost raw, or part of some new diet fad she had decided they should follow.

'For your good, Dickie,' she would say when the menu was bean sprouts or tofu, or both, and she would burst into tears if he shuffled the unpalatable food round his plate, planning to abandon it and look for bread and cheese when she had gone to bed.

On other evenings, she would greet him with a tempest of tears and accuse him of having a mistress, deceiving her, and of planning to turn her and her children into the street.

Until recently, this had been a baseless charge; now, though, there was Caroline, hard-headed and shrewd, a colleague with better career prospects than Richard, and not the marrying type, as she had told him when their casual friendship metamorphosed into an affair.

Once, Richard had hoped to be the conventional father in a happy family with two or three children, a comfortable house in the country, and a pretty, affectionate wife who would be content to give up whatever work she had been doing to stay at home looking after all of them – perhaps resuming a career when the children were no longer small. But it hadn't worked out that way.

Like many of his contemporaries, Richard, at university, had made the most of the new sexual freedom of the Sixties until, disastrously, his girlfriend, Karen, had declared that she was pregnant.

Neither had considered an abortion, recently made legal, nor adoption. They had been a couple; they would marry. The wedding had been an affair of white satin and tulle with a marquee on Karen's parents' lawn in Hertfordshire; she had been princess for a day, while everyone decided that it was an occasion for rejoicing.

Anna was a fine, healthy baby, much loved by them both, and for several years it seemed that success would follow this shaky start, but Richard, working hard, hoping to climb his professional ladder, was, said Karen, dull, and she hated life in London. They moved out to the country; she began to ride and go to agricultural shows where she met the man whom Richard, to hide his hurt, called 'The Jolly Farmer', and who had several hundred acres and a farmhouse in Somerset.

When Anna was six her parents separated, and after their divorce Karen married her farmer and had three more children.

During the years that followed, he had tried to keep contact with Anna, whom he maintained financially with willing generosity. At first he drove down to Somerset every other weekend; gradually, though, as the little girl's life developed with new friends and then her two half-brothers and her half-sister, Richard saw how his visits were beginning to affect her, to interrupt her social life and to cause her problems of loyalty. She was fond of her stepfather, who had provided her with a life which she enjoyed. Richard's visits grew less frequent and were tailored to suit her diary. For a while he took her on holiday each summer to a hotel catering for children, suggesting she should bring a friend, and this worked for several years; it was Richard who could no longer bear the strain of getting to know her again every year. The holidays had stopped when she was thirteen.

She was twenty-six now, and working as assistant purser on a cruise ship. Richard saw her when she had shore leave, but that was seldom; if she came to stay, the pleasant, confident, pretty girl was a stranger: it was easy to believe they were not related at all.

Richard had hoped that he and Verity would have children of their own but this did not happen and now, as her depressions, interspersed with elation, grew more frequent, he was thankful. He believed that heredity had more effect on character than upbringing and environment. Musicians bred musicians, and actors' children went into the theatre, not simply because they were surrounded by music and drama from infancy; the talent lay in their genes. In Verity's elder son, Justin, he saw the same mood swings and sudden bursts of temper, and it alarmed him.

Verity's moods were getting worse and were less predictable. Richard had devised various ruses to avoid spending too much time with her: he had a workshop in the garden where he carved figures and animals. He'd given Verity a swan; once, he'd thought she looked like one, with her long neck and her way of pointing her head upwards. She'd knocked it off the shelf where she kept it, and its neck had broken. Richard had taken it away to mend, but had left it in two pieces in a drawer where he kept some of his tools.

Leaving the train at Haverscot, he saw a thin, pale young woman whom he had often noticed on the train. She always read intently, never looking up from her book, and Richard wondered who she was and what she did. Tonight, in driving rain, she hurried from the station while he went to fetch his car. She looked malnourished: was she a starving student? Richard reminded himself not to get interested in anyone who might be a lame duck. Verity had been one when he met her, stranded with a puncture by the roadside with her two small boys. He had changed the wheel for her, pumped up the flat spare, and followed her home to Reading to make sure she arrived safely. She had seemed so forlorn and helpless, standing there with the wheelbrace in her hands as she ineffectually sought a means to jack up the car, tears rolling down her face.

At first she had said that she was a widow, but he soon discovered that her husband had left her and the boys, and gone to work abroad. The boys had told him; they remembered their father. Richard could have been on the brink of bigamy, he thought later, but soon after he met her there was a divorce because her husband had wanted to remarry.

She had lied about that, and she had lied about her name. She had been christened Vera, after an aunt, but had elected to be known as Verity: no great sin, perhaps, but an embellishment. She was good at disguising the truth.

These days, people did not set such store by marriage. This saved trouble if things went wrong: there were fewer legal hurdles to negotiate. If he hadn't married Verity, he could have left her when her accusations and her tantrums became so extreme, but he had wanted to provide security for her and to build a family, and had bought a large, solid house in which to do so. Merrifields was a solid Edwardian structure, set in a quiet road not far from the church, its acre of garden running down to a field which bordered the river, where willows grew along the bank. Richard was still improving the garden, creating leafy corners, and bowers where climbing roses sprawled; this, like his woodwork, was a solace to his troubled soul as he pruned and sprayed, clipped and weeded, prising out every errant interloper.

Verity had said she wished to grow salads and vegetables on which to feed them all, but two rows of lettuces which quickly ran to seed the first summer were the limit of her achievement; Richard, though, now cultivated a productive kitchen garden and had joined the local horticultural society. Verity, meanwhile, had turned an upstairs room into a studio and there she covered canvases with tortured landscapes in heavy greens and purples, always tempestuous in composition. She had told him that she had planned to be a designer before she had the boys; he never fully understood what had prevented her, for she was in her late twenties when Justin was born. For her, marrying Richard was an upward move. He soon learned that she had debts and was threatened with eviction. She had told him this when he arrived one evening to find her swallowing pills, washing them down with gin. He'd called an ambulance.

She'd been expecting him. It was not a serious attempt at suicide, but, temporarily bewitched, he had felt enormous pity for her. He had stayed overnight, looking after the boys while she was in hospital, had taken them with him to bring her home next day, and was ensnared. For a few brief months he felt all-powerful, necessary to them all.

After their wedding, Verity declared that the boys must assume Richard's surname and think of him as their father. They all went on the honeymoon to Corsica, though her parents had suggested that the children should stay with them. At five and seven, they were too old to accept him easily and they began to idealise their real father, although they never heard from him and he made no contribution to their upkeep. The boys had managed to forget the noisy arguments they had so often heard, and their mother's tears. Now, though, when she lapsed into fits of weeping, they were convinced that she was crying for their father.

Richard took each day as it came, training himself to live within small frameworks: the office, and his colleagues there; his home with its tensions which he shed each morning like a jacket, and resumed again at night. He began to work longer hours quite regularly, partly to delay his return and partly to make the evenings when he went to Caroline's flat less conspicuous. Then, as winter approached, he joined a choir which met on Thursdays at eight o'clock to practise for a Christmas concert. At Easter they would do *Elijah*.

Verity had no singing voice nor any sense of music. She did not encourage her sons to learn an instrument, though Richard thought they should at least have the opportunity. Neither progressed beyond the recorder at school, but when Justin sat down at Richard's piano, he was able to play by ear tunes he had heard on the radio or in television jingles. Richard was impressed by this rare gift and wanted to nourish the boy's innate ability, but Justin rejected all such help. Any idea produced by Richard was anathema to him and he became increasingly rebellious as he grew older. Maybe it was natural, Richard would think wearily. Justin resented what Richard had tried to do for him: useless to expect gratitude; that was an uncomfortable emotion.

What would have happened to them all if he had not rescued them? Would someone else have come along? Perhaps. Verity had had an appealing bruised air about her when they met and, like Richard, she had been rejected. Coming together had seemed, at the time, healing for them both. Now, Verity simply looked angry when she was not weeping. She accused him of burying her in the country and stifling her talent, but he never saw her attempt any design work, although that could be done anywhere, as he pointed out. She spent long hours painting her sombre pictures; Richard thought they represented the torment in her soul and were some sort of safety valve; at least while she was painting conflict, she wasn't setting fire to things or creating mayhem.

Once, she had set his books alight, his collection of Everyman classics and his reference works. She had done it one Sunday and he had smelled the smoke and put it out before the fire had spread to the curtains or the furniture in his study. His books were badly damaged, however, and some of them were ruined.

He'd had smoke alarms installed everywhere afterwards, and put fire extinguishers on the landings.

She hadn't repeated that, but she'd wreaked other forms of havoc — scraping marks on his desk, a valuable one inherited from his father and worth a lot of money, and she had smashed a Meissen figure he had bought at a sale when, before meeting her, he had had an affair with a woman who was a collector, but they had broken up before he could give it to her. Once, when Richard was playing the piano, Verity had come in with a kettle of boiling water and poured it over his hands. He'd reacted quickly, knocking the kettle from her grasp and moving away, so that although he had been painfully scalded, he had saved the piano keys from serious damage and himself from worse injury. While he did so, water had spilled over Verity's flowing cotton skirt and thin, bare legs, so that she was also hurt.

She'd cried then and, for once, had said that she was sorry and she didn't know what made her do it. Richard believed her remorse was genuine as he led her upstairs, sponged her legs with cool water and made her change her skirt. She wanted to make love then: she often did, after such scenes, but this time Richard's own scalded, blistering hands demanded his attention and he would not be won round.

Bandaged awkwardly, he gave in later.

It was soon after this that his affair with Caroline began. To be with her was so restful. They had always got on well at work; she was capable and assertive but never needed to challenge Richard, whom she liked and saw as no threat of any kind. He often wondered how they had ever become so intimate. She sometimes gave him a lift to Paddington, which was near where she lived, and occasionally she asked him in for a drink. He always accepted, because to do so meant he won a domestic reprieve by catching a later train. It was pleasant in her large, ground-floor flat. Her sitting-room had pale gold curtains and two huge sofas covered in cream brocade; her bedroom, he discovered later, was a peaceful place with mushroom-pink curtains and calm seascapes on the walls. Making love with her was not a fight; it was, he began to understand, a mutually rewarding encounter; unalarming and enriching rather than exciting. He did not pine for her between their interludes together, but he often thought about her.

Caroline had been hurrying off this weekend, going down to the country, she said, visiting friends, not telling him who they were. He felt mild curiosity; he would have liked to have gone with her, he thought: spent a casual weekend, free from stress. Instead, he had to face Verity and the boys.

As he drove through the town in the heavy rain, he saw the pale girl hurrying along, a small umbrella over her head. Where was she going? Where did she live? He slowed the car: if he offered her a lift, would she cry 'rape' and flee? Probably, he decided, sighing; it would be folly to try. Current fears had put an end to such kindness among strangers.

He had had such high hopes when he bought Merrifields. There was space for them all – a room each for the boys, and a playroom where they had their toys at first, and now a computer and their own television, a retrograde step, he felt, but taken in the interests of avoiding discord. Justin had a compact disc player in his room. Terry was so far content with the simple stereo system which they used in their playroom. Richard, in his workshop, could escape the noise and, because the house was old and solid, built by a prosperous Edwardian tradesman, his study was almost soundproof. It would all have been much more difficult if they were forced to live in a cramped box attached to a row of similar boxes on each side. No wonder murder was done when people were forced to live like battery hens, denied personal space.

Verity had recently given up cooking, which was an improvement on earlier days, Richard thought. She shredded vegetables and grated cheese for the boys, who were not satisfied with such fare. When Richard came home they demanded pizzas from the shop that delivered or to go down to the fish and chip van which came three times a week to the square. Richard thought growing boys needed plenty of protein and fruit, and at weekends he roasted meat or made thick, nourishing stews and steamed puddings which they loved. They were often punctual for these meals and had been known to praise them.

This evening there was peace. Verity was in her studio; she discouraged interruption. The boys were in their playroom watching television. Richard decided to assume that every-one had eaten and made himself an omelette. There was lettuce in the fridge, and he found a tomato, slightly squashed, on the floor where somebody had dropped it and left it to rest in peace. There was cheese, and he thawed some frozen bread in the microwave; Richard had invested in time-saving equipment.

Verity appeared just as he had finished eating, and made a scene because he had not gone up to her studio to say that he was back.

'You've made it clear that you don't like being disturbed when you're working,' he replied.

'I could have been dead for all you cared,' she raged, and he thought, yes, you could.

Richard had never allowed himself to think like that before. He made a business of putting the plate and cutlery he had used in the dishwasher, and wiping down the sink while he fought to put himself into a more charitable frame of mind, but as he did so, Verity sprang at him and began clawing at his neck and shoulders, screaming that she hated him.

He swung round quickly, which wrong-footed her and she stumbled against the table, catching her hip on a corner. That hurt, and she doubled over. Richard left the room, not shutting the door on her, not leaving her completely cut off from an audience.

What was the matter with her? Why could she not enjoy her life, her security, her children? She often said that all she wanted was to be happy, yet she was the one who made happiness impossible.

It couldn't go on, but if they broke up, what would happen to her and to those boys? Wouldn't all three of them be doomed?

Justin and Terry were in their playroom – or their personal room as Verity had taken to calling it, since they were too old now to have a playroom.

'Why not the den?' Richard had suggested mildly, and she had answered that it made them sound like wild animals.

She was as defensive as a lioness in relation to her young, he thought, but did not fault that, although in his view she was over-indulgent with them, set no store by consideration for others – him, for instance – and was no stickler for truth. But, though hostile to him, the boys were not too trouble-some: they were rude and noisy sometimes, but what boy wasn't? He did not think they were bad boys.

Now, he went into their room. If she followed, she might restrain her behaviour in front of them. Perhaps it was a craven action but he would do a lot to cut short one of Verity's fits of histrionics.

'What are you watching?' he asked, and sat down in a spare chair beside Justin who was glued to some game show.

Verity came into the room behind him and stood in the doorway with tears rolling down her face. She sobbed audibly. Her husband and her sons kept their faces turned to the television screen until she crossed the room and switched it off. She stood glowering at them.

'None of you cares,' she told them, quivering, her thin hands clasped across the black knitted tunic she wore over a purple polo sweater. 'I spend all day slaving here to keep the house decent and none of you gives me a word of thanks for all I do.'

At least she was not swearing at them, which often happened. But her sons ought not to see her in this state. A swift memory of Richard's controlled parents came to him: one must keep up the façade of behaving well, even if the world was crashing round one's ears.

He rose to his feet and took her by the elbow.

'Come along, Verity,' he said. 'You're tired. I'll take you upstairs.'

He led her away, and she permitted it: she had got his attention now, and once upstairs, he helped her take off her clothes, bundling her into bed, touching her as little as he could. He felt no desire for that thin body with the prominent ribcage, the small drooping breasts, but she was vulnerable and he still pitied her. He fetched a glass of water and a valium tablet; their own doctor rarely prescribed tranquillisers but during his absence she had persuaded a locum, an older man, to do so and she had been able to get more. Richard, unaware that this was not straightforward, blessed the pills because they brought peace — tranquillity, their very purpose, albeit intermittently.

She went to sleep. The storm was over for the evening. Tomorrow was another day.

3

ON SUNDAY TERRY had a guest to lunch. Richard had roasted a leg of lamb – it would last, cold, for a day or two, giving him and the boys something to eat even if Verity preferred to toy with bean shoots and lettuce.

'There's enough for Mark, isn't there, Cat?' asked Terry.

They wouldn't call him Dad, or by his name, and Justin had bestowed this nickname on him after a visit years ago to a pantomime when at first he'd called him Whittington. Richard had regarded it as a sign of acceptance, but when the name was switched to Cat, uttered in a sneering tone, he realised that he was wrong. However, Justin knew his limits: he was offhand, graceless, but not overtly rude to Richard, testing him sometimes, trying to see how far he could go without incurring open wrath but not quite overstepping what Richard would tolerate.

'You're not my dad,' he sometimes said, when told to tidy up his possessions, put his bike away, or finish his homework.

'I pay the bills,' Richard had started saying several months ago. On the whole, both of them avoided conflict. Terry, so far, was less difficult, but he could flare up into sudden rages. The brothers were very much alike, both dark, with heavy eyebrows and almost black eyes. Justin's hair was longer than Richard thought it should be, but Terry had a bristle cut, each hair standing up about an inch, like a mop.

They seldom brought friends home, so Richard was pleased when Terry said that Mark Conway was coming over with a new computer game he'd got. The two boys had spent a contented morning before coming into the kitchen. Beside Terry, Mark was short and stocky, and his brown hair fell in a true pudding bowl cut around his chubby face.

'You'd better ring your parents to ask if you may stay,' said Richard.

'There's only Mum, and she's away,' said Mark. 'It's OK.' Then, seeing Richard's expression, he added, 'It's just for the day. She's on a course. She's got a mega important job. Ivy knows I'm here.'

'Who's Ivy?'

Mark explained about her.

Steve had made the plan, because he did not want to be stuck with Mark as he wanted to go off with some friends in a car. They'd run into Terry in the park the day before and Steve had proposed that Mark should take his computer game over to show Terry. The idea had caught hold, and Steve was highly delighted with himself.

Mark hadn't minded. Terry was all right, and afterwards he could go round to The Willows and see Tom. He wondered if the angry man would still be there, Tom's son.

Justin had loafed off somewhere and he was late for lunch, but he did turn up. Richard's cooking made the effort of coming home worthwhile. Verity was still in bed, and, cravenly, Richard sent Terry up with a bowl of soup, a warm roll and two bananas, some of which she might decide to consume. He returned without the tray. Even martyrs needed food.

Mark did not know when he had eaten a more delicious meal. It knocked spots off even Ivy's stews and pies. The pudding had a kind of meringue on top and was all lemony underneath. Mark had never had it before.

Richard was pleased when he accepted a second helping. It was nice to be appreciated.

'You ought to run a hotel,' Mark told him. He was unsure of Richard's name: he wasn't Terry or Justin's father so it might not be the same, and he couldn't really be called Cat. As uttered by Justin, it hadn't sounded respectful. Mark was interested in respect because Steve was always on about it. 'My Mum works in a hotel,' he added.

'Which one?' asked Richard, thinking it might be The Red Lion or one of Haverscot's several pubs.

'The Golden Accord. It's on the way to Swindon,' Mark replied.

Richard knew it. He and Verity had even spent a night there once, when the boys were visiting their grandparents.

'It's a very good hotel,' he said truthfully.

The weather improved after lunch, and Richard decided that the boys should play outside, but first they must help clear away and load the dishwasher.

'Ivy could do with one of those,' Mark said. 'She's got a big family.'

'I expect she could,' said Richard. 'Now, why don't you take your football out, Terry, and kick it around?'

'It's too wet in the garden,' Terry said. 'Can we go to the park?'

Before agreeing, Richard made sure that Mark, who was younger than Terry, was allowed there unsupervised. It was true that recent rain had flooded the river below the garden and made his lawn very soggy; they'd damage it if they played out there for long. The park was on higher ground, though much of its turf was sour and dog-fouled. Children had to be independent and streetwise these days. At Mark's age, Richard had already been a pupil for two years at a boarding-school housed in a mansion amid twenty acres of grounds, some of them woodland, where there was freedom to play both organised games and the other kind. Contrary to popular belief about such places, he had not been abused, nor bullied, but during his first weeks he had felt utterly forsaken, unable to understand why he had been sent away from home. He had concluded that this withdrawal of love, as it had seemed to him, had made him the more anxious to seek it in his adult life. He had certainly been eager to give affection, liable to fall seriously in love rather than indulge in passing fancies.

You had your whole childhood in which to grow used to your family; even so, there were quarrels and misunderstandings. Yet people frequently chose a partner with whom they intended to share the greater part of their life on a very brief acquaintance. It worked sometimes; there were couples who fell in love and married within weeks, and remained content after forty or more years together.

It was pointless to think like this; it made him feel too sad. He blamed himself for being bad husband material, although he had tried, both times, to be reliable and kind. He was dull, he supposed; that was the main problem. He wanted a quiet life, absence of strife even if romance had withered away. He still didn't know where he had failed Karen; her farmer, also, seemed rather dull, but perhaps she liked the country existence he provided. Verity, he now understood, could not deal with life except through confrontation; she was like a panther, poised ready to pounce, except when she had swallowed a pill and lapsed into an exhausted torpor.

'Is your mother coming home tonight, Mark?' he asked.

'Oh yes,' said Mark airily. 'She won't be late.'

'You must go back before it gets dark,' Richard said. 'I don't want either of you out there then. Understood, Terry?'

Terry nodded. He had suggested the park because he had wanted to demonstrate to Mark how he could manipulate his stepfather; in fact, there was plenty to do in the garden here; Cat had built a tree house, quite a high one up a large beech tree, and he would have liked to show that to Mark, but it would do for another time.

The two boys set off together. Mark skipped along. It had been a good day so far, and it would end with a visit to Tom.

He said nothing to Terry about the old man, and the visitor who had turned out to be Tom's son. His visits to The

Willows were a secret. Terry's stepfather was nice, but so inquisitive. Mum had said it was rude to ask questions, yet adults always did it — wanting to know what you'd done at school, where you were going, who with and such, and had you done your homework. Even Mum did that. In the park, they'd be on their own.

Rare calm settled on Merrifields when the boys had gone out. Verity was still in her room, but might not remain there if she had revived and felt like creating fresh drama. Richard snatched some time with the Sunday paper; then he went out to his workshop, where he was carving a figure from a piece of old yew he had found in the churchyard. It had seemed to him that there was a gnarled old man with grizzled hair and a beard trapped inside the timber, waiting for release. He always worked like this with his wood sculptures, seeking form within the branch or log he had picked up either in the garden or when walking in the countryside. He worked slowly, enjoying the sensation of the wood beneath his fingers, watching the gradual realisation of his original idea.

He had given Caroline a pale, galloping horse he had made from a length of ash; she had exclaimed with pleasure, surprised that such power of observation, even artistry, could exist within what seemed to be a grey, conventional exterior. She didn't ask him what his wife thought about his skill; she was not interested in his family life.

Failing light reminded him of the time. He glanced towards the house and saw that it was in darkness, apart from Verity's studio window. So she was up and slopping paint about; that was something. Perhaps it would relieve her anger. But it looked as though the boys had not returned. The playroom showed no light.

Of course, when you were out of doors at dusk, you did not realise how dark it was until you went inside. They'd be home soon. He locked his shed and walked slowly up the garden towards the house.

Half an hour later, when there was still no sign of the

boys, Richard, with a feeling of responsibility for Mark, if not his stepsons, set off towards the park to look for them. He'd probably meet Terry; Mark, who had disclosed at lunch that he lived in Grasmere Street, would be on his way home. He'd no idea where Justin was.

He reached the park without encountering the two younger boys or Justin. There were various figures running about in the gloaming. A few children were still on the swings with two young fathers watching them. A tall woman walked a dog around the perimeter, a Dalmatian which gleamed in the dusk. He could not see Terry or Mark among the boys scuffling together in mock combat; no one was kicking a football.

Perhaps Terry had gone home with Mark. Richard thought of going to see, but he did not know which was his house in Grasmere Street. Conway – that was the boy's surname; during lunch they'd joked about the castle because Mark had not heard of it and Richard had treated them all to a brief discourse on the subject of thirteenth-century fortifications.

He did not hurry back. Terry might catch him up, or perhaps had taken the path through the churchyard and across the fields, though with the water flowing fast so far beyond the river, that was not a good idea.

Not for the first time, Richard wished that he could have afforded to send Verity's boys away to boarding-school. It might have given their marriage more of a chance, and the unemotional, steady framework might have benefited Justin and Terry. Richard, thinking like this, disregarded the memory of his own isolation when he was sent away; he had grown used to the life and had settled down. So would they, and for those months of their absence, he would cease to feel like an intruder in his own house.

He sighed. Not long now till Monday morning. He wondered if Caroline had had a good weekend; perhaps they could meet on Monday evening, for a drink and a chat, if nothing else; a touch of kindness, just to keep him going.

*

Mark could not get rid of Terry. They had kicked the ball about for a while, and then some bigger boys had come and snatched it from them, kicking it themselves with so much force and strength that the smaller boys had no chance of retrieving it. Terry, whose ball it was, began to snivel, and in the end the older boys, having succeeded in upsetting him, grew bored with their teasing and kicked it out of sight, over the railings and into the road where it bounced off the windscreen of a passing Renault, causing the driver to swerve and crash into a stationary car. He missed a slowly-pedalling cyclist by two inches.

Brakes screamed, horns blew, and the bigger boys disappeared in the opposite direction. Terry and Mark were still standing on the rough grass, no great distance from the fence, when the irate Renault driver and the owner of the parked car, who had rushed out of his own house at the sound of the disturbance, appeared in the park. One of them carried the offending football.

Terry turned to flee, but Mark stood his ground.

'It wasn't us,' he said staunchly when the two angry men drew near. 'It was our ball but those other boys took it.'

He gestured in the direction of the far entrance to the park.

Tears on Terry's face were signs of guilt. The two motorists were not eager to accept Mark's explanation and one of them had raised his arm, ready to burst into a torrent of speech if not to rain blows on the nearest boy, when a voice came from behind him. The speaker was an elderly woman with a checked tweed hat worn low down over her eyebrows, and wearing a Burberry raincoat. She was accompanied by a golden cocker spaniel on a lead.

'It wasn't these two boys,' she said. 'I saw it all. There were three of them, all much bigger than these boys. I should think they were fourteen or fifteen.'

'Is that so?' The angrier of the two men was still glowering.

'They were teasing these two, snatching their ball,' said

the woman. 'I don't suppose they thought about the consequences when they pitched it into the road.'

'Maybe not,' said the calmer man, only marginally placated. 'Well, we must take your word for it. Would you give us your name and address as a witness? For the insurance.'

'I'll write it down for you if you have some paper and a pencil,' said the woman.

The man produced a gold ball-point and a card on which she wrote, resting it against the fence to get some purchase. Then he asked the boys for their names.

'That's not necessary,' said the woman firmly. 'The older boys, yes, if known, but not this pair.'

The second man agreed.

'No one was hurt,' he said. 'It could have been worse.' He turned to the other man. 'Let's sort out the details in my house. It must have shaken you up. I wasn't in my car when it happened.' He began walking back towards the road, and the second man followed.

Terry, still sniffing, was standing beside the old woman. Mark glanced at him and then trotted after the men.

'Please, could Terry have his ball back?' he asked.

'Oh, I suppose so,' said the angrier man, who was holding it. He threw it to Mark, quite viciously, but Mark caught it.

'Thanks,' he said, and added, 'I'm sorry.'

'Don't push your luck,' said the man ungraciously. 'You and your friend get off home, and don't bother the lady.'

Mark hurried back to Terry, who was being told by their saviour to blow his nose and brace up.

'You know those boys, don't you?' she asked Mark.

'They go to the upper school,' said Mark cautiously.

He did know them; one was a friend of Steve's.

'Hm. Well, if someone had been hurt, you'd have had to tell the police all about it and there would have been a great deal of trouble,' she said.

'It wasn't our fault,' said Terry. 'You said so,' he added.

'No, it wasn't,' she agreed. 'And those boys were very

thoughtless. Let it be a lesson to you two. Think about the consequences of your actions.' She'd used that word to the men. Mark had heard her. He knew what consequences were; he'd played the game with old Tom and Steve and he'd enjoyed it, but Steve found it boring. He was no good at thinking of the names, and kept writing down football players and Madonna, or Sylvester Stallone. Even Tom and Mark tired of them.

'Get on home, then,' the woman instructed. 'Terry, isn't it? And what's your name?' She peered at Mark, eyes screwed up under the brim of her hat. He thought she was very ugly.

'Mark,' he answered. 'Come on, Terry, let's get going,' and he ran off, stopping a few yards away to call back, 'Thanks, missus.' He'd heard Steve call a woman 'missus' when he'd wanted to wheedle money, allegedly for fireworks, from her. Steve had said it was respectful, and certainly the woman had paid up. Mark didn't know what Steve had used the money for: it wasn't for fireworks.

Terry trailed after him. With his tears dried and the ball returned, his fear had turned to anger.

'Sod them,' he muttered, kicking at the grass as he followed Mark through the gate by the road through which the two enraged motorists had entered the park.

'That's right. Don't let it get to you,' Mark advised. He was feeling calm and powerful. He had taken charge of Terry and had managed to get the ball back. Thanks to that old woman, they'd escaped being blamed for something not their fault. What if the police had been called? It might have been the death of Terry's mum, who seemed to be rather ill as she hadn't appeared for lunch and had been given only soup and fruit.

There was no point in telling Terry this, and besides, he was in a hurry to visit Tom.

'I'm going,' he said. 'Thanks for lunch.'

They parted at the corner of Grasmere Street and Mark walked down it, as if returning home, allowing time for

Terry to disappear before retracing his steps to cross into Wordsworth Road.

Terry slouched off, not looking back, but he did not go home. He remembered where the boy who had kicked the ball lived. He was called Greg Black; Justin knew him. Holding the ball under one arm, Terry walked to the square and along the High Street, turning into the more densely populated part of the old market town until he reached the street where, in a neat semi-detached house separated from the pavement by a small patch of grass and a parking spot occupied by a dark red Maestro, Greg's sister was now upstairs, doing her homework.

The houses on the far side of the road were terraced, and on one step stood an empty milk bottle. Terry picked it up, crossed over and flung it hard at the downstairs window, which shattered in a satisfying manner.

On a dank Sunday, there were few people about, but one family returning from an outing saw the boy running away, still holding his football. There were shouts and yells, but Terry ran fast, disappearing down an alley before anyone could catch up with him.

MARIGOLD DARWIN PULLED her tweed hat down more securely over her thick eyebrows and trudged resolutely round the circumference of the park, her spaniel, Sinbad, obedient at her heels. He was a well trained, mature dog she had found at the Battersea Dogs' home, after her retirement earlier in the year. Naturally, no one there knew his history, but he had not been neglected. She had been lucky to find him: deciding to acquire a dog had been part of her programme, but she had not wanted a neurotic beast, nor one given to snapping and whining; she would not have had the patience to deal with temperament.

Walking, she reflected on the incident with the boys. Youngsters had to learn to stick up for themselves, and the bigger boys had been teasing, not bullying; there was a distinction, but where did it lie? It had always been a difficult question, and one that had affected her throughout most of her youth.

She was plain now, and had not been an attractive child – sallow, with heavy eyebrows from a very young age. Given pretty names by her optimistic parents – her second name was Angela – she grew up with her initials spelling MAD, and with neither name appropriate to her looks, so that nothing would be gained by shedding the Marigold and opting for Angela.

No man had ever loved Marigold Darwin. At the children's parties she had reluctantly attended, boys had sometimes been dared to kiss her. Afterwards, they said 'ugh' and went off giggling, the forfeit paid.

In adult life, she had compensated by achievement, doing well at school, getting a good second-class degree at Oxford. Her college, even now, did not accept men, and she had felt safe there, working hard, singing with the Bach Choir as her one recreation. She had a fine contralto voice and hoped, in Haverscot, that there might be a choir which she could join. She had climbed the civil service ladder within the Treasury, working on calculations and analyses, always with figures, undisturbed by personal problems, conflicts and alliances experienced by her colleagues. Avoidance of pain was her aim and on the whole she had been successful. She was efficient and undemanding, determined but unemotional, not a leader. No one felt threatened by Marigold Darwin, and no one needed her as a friend.

She was the only child of her disappointed parents, who had done what they could for her in terms of education and care. Her pretty mother and reasonably good-looking father were proud of her academic prowess.

While at the Treasury, she went home each weekend to her parents, who offered her a refuge and a reason to avoid making independent plans. Later, as they grew frail together, they in turn depended on their daughter. She shopped for them and filled their freezer, and organised help for them during the week. When they died, within three months of one another, she truly mourned them both.

Her inheritance enabled her to move from her modest flat in Pimlico to a small house just off the Fulham Road, which, despite the recession, she had recently sold at a good price. In Haverscot, she was renting a bungalow while seeking a place to buy. For some years she had been able to afford expensive holidays with a cultural aspect, and had been to music festivals in several cities, and on art appreciation tours. Alert and interested, she kept detailed diaries of her travels, with the relevant costs, and wondered if, one day, she might turn them into a book, but she feared she lacked narrative skill. She read biographies and travel books for pleasure: never fiction. Dreaming, in her youth, had brought disillusionment; it was safer to stick to fact.

In London, lectures and concerts had attracted her, seldom the theatre or the cinema; inspecting other people's lives made her uncomfortable. Lectures and concerts would be available to her still, and she would continue to travel; Australia would be a goal, as she could spend more time away now, making longer tours possible. There would be plenty to do in the years ahead; she must not become a recluse, and Sinbad would help her combat such a tendency. She must find some good kennels where he would be happy; he was not to become a tie.

She might get a car. She had driven as a girl, and during her parents' lifetime, but had not needed to in London and was out of practice. Owning one would increase her range, and Sinbad's, though Haverscot was well served by public transport. She would have to take lessons to ensure that she was still competent.

She had come to Haverscot because she had once lived there. Since then, the town had expanded, with an industrial area to the east, and housing estates all round the perimeter. The centre, near the town hall and the market square, was little altered, but old shops had become parts of chains and there were parking problems. She had formed a plan to buy Merrifields, which had been her childhood home. In those days, she had wandered about on the banks of the river wondering why she had no friends, blaming her piggy eyes and ugly face. During the war, she had been despatched to boarding-school while her father was in the army and her mother worked for the Red Cross. By then she had already learned that keeping to herself was a way of avoiding persecution. Now, at sixty, she had the habit of self-preservation and enough money to cushion isolation.

Merrifields was not for sale. A local estate agent approached the owner, saying he had a client who might be interested in buying the place, but there had been no response. She had walked past, both along the road and by the river, stepping through the meadows, looking up at it. Places known in childhood always seem small when revisited in later years, and she remembered Merrifields as a mansion; seen now, it was still large, its gables visible above the hedge, a huge willow and a beech tree in the garden. She suddenly had a memory of the gardener planting a beech tree; was this the one? There was a structure in its upper branches, bare now of leaves: a tree house, she realised. There were no willows in the garden in her day.

Her parents had sold the house soon after the war and moved to Woking. They had lived there until they died.

Mr Phipps, the agent, alert and keen in his sharp suit, with his mobile telephone, worked on commission. He suggested that Merrifields, even if it had been on the market, was perhaps too big for one lady, but he did not waste time showing her inappropriate properties, however desirable, on estates; she wanted a 'residence'. There were several old houses with beams and with cracked walls that needed repairing on his books, and he showed her some of them, but she took a practical line about the work that would have to be done, and the expense, not to mention the time that it would take, and turned them down. She did not want to pay rent longer than she must, though her capital was earning enough interest to cover the cost. Her present lease, however, ran out at the end of the year.

Those two boys, the weepy one and his sturdier friend, must learn, as she had done, to hide emotion: to reveal neither pleasure, lest its source disappear, nor fear.

She had felt anger when she saw them provoked by the bigger boys, and that was rare for her. Luckily, she had been able to avert injustice.

One of the men had said he was glad she had prevented them from blaming the innocent pair.

'But for your testimony, I'd have dragged them both off

to the police station,' he had declared.

Miss Darwin knew that he had meant it.

When she reached home, Miss Darwin wrote down a concise account of the incident. Her evidence might be needed if the men claimed from their insurance companies, and time always blunted accurate recollection. She typed it up neatly and filed it, sighing because she had none of her own furniture around her and her papers were in boxes stacked against the living-room wall. The contents of her London house were in store; she might need more furniture when she moved, because she would have larger rooms and increased space all round. Some would think her foolish proposing to expand at an age when most people wanted smaller homes, but she longed to return to her roots, to the comfort and security she had known as a child. She sought, too, to establish her status in the town as it had been defined by the level she had reached in her career.

That evening she decided to go to church. This was not because of any religious conviction; she had long ago shed the beliefs which had carried her through adolescence in expectation of divine revelation. Disappointed by no such experience at her confirmation – and amazed by the weight of the Bishop's hand on her head – she had continued to expect some ray of enlightenment to justify her acceptance of unkindness, because the meek were destined to be blessed, only gradually abandoning this philosophy. Now she knew that it was the tough who survived.

She was restless. The episode in the park had troubled her but she did not understand why; it was, after all, of no great importance; no one had been hurt nor suffered injustice. Perhaps it was the boys: the intent, chubby one and his unhappy friend. She seldom spoke to children and was not used to their ways.

Once, she had wished for children in a vague, undefined way; they looked sweet and were affectionate. She hid her mild yearning, suppressed because confessing to it, even to

herself, admitted weakness, and now she had almost forgotten it. As a diversion, church would do; she had not been
there since she returned to the town, and there would have
been changes. She put on a long camel coat and a felt hat and
set forth.

The outside structure of the fourteenth-century church
looked as if it had recently been repaired; there were patches
of paler stone over some windows, discernible when you
walked past in daylight, as she had done more than once in
recent weeks. Inside, she found that the wooden pews had
been replaced by pale oak chairs. They were more comfortable, she allowed, remembering how she had slipped and
slithered on the old shiny seats. The big brass eagle lectern
was the same: behind its spread wings her father had
sometimes read the lesson. Closing her eyes, she could
imagine his sonorous voice, reading without drama but
clearly, so that every syllable was audible throughout the
building. Such was not the case now, she reflected, listening
to the current vicar intoning the prayers and to the man who,
this evening, declaimed a section from the latest translation
of the Bible. In her head, she recited the Authorised Version.
The hymns, however, were traditional, and she enjoyed
singing them. A middle-aged man some seats away from her
seemed to do the same.

She walked back to the bungalow past Merrifields, and
saw a police car standing in the drive.

Tom's house was warm, almost stifling. He'd got the heating
on high and his gas fire was alight.

Steve wasn't there. Mark was glad of that; he'd thought
Steve might have dropped in on the way home. He liked
being on his own with Tom, who had been pleased to see
him. He'd been thinking about getting himself some
supper. Now, Mark could open a tin of soup, cut bread for
both of them and find the cheese.

It was easy to pretend that Tom was his grandfather when
Steve wasn't there, but now Tom's son had turned up and

Mark didn't want to imagine that man as his father.

'He's gone, then,' he said. 'Your son.'

'Uh huh,' said Tom. 'Yes.'

'How long did he stay?'

'Not long.'

'Where does he live?'

'He's on the move at present,' Tom replied.

He'd given Alan money, which was what he had come for, and he'd left at once, a great relief to Tom who, seeing the bag he carried, had feared a prolonged visit.

'Is he coming back?' asked Mark.

'I don't know. Not for a while,' said Tom.

Alan was on rehabilitation leave from prison. With money in his pocket, he had gone away to spend it while the authorities thought he was at an approved address.

Mark was relieved to hear that the man would not be interrupting their evening. Neither he nor Tom had seemed pleased to see one another, which was puzzling. Why had the man come, if he didn't like Tom? But then, sons did go to see their fathers, didn't they? If they had fathers.

After their supper, they played chess. Mark could sometimes beat Tom, who had taught him how to play. Both of them enjoyed their game and it was half-past eight before Tom noticed the time and told Mark he must go home.

'Your mother will be getting anxious,' he said.

'She'll think I'm with Ivy, if she's back,' said Mark calmly. 'But I think she'll still be out.'

She was. He let himself in, had his bath – he was grubby after the park – put his dirty clothes in the machine and turned it on. Then he found clean ones for the morning – Mum had done the ironing before she left – and went to bed. He hadn't brushed his teeth, and after a fierce struggle with his conscience – Mum might ask whether he'd done them if she came back before he went to sleep – got out of bed and scrubbed them hard. Then, clutching his squishy green Kermit, he pulled the duvet over him. He tried hard to stay awake, listening for her key, but in three minutes he was asleep.

*

Tom worried about Mark, after he had gone. The boy was left alone a lot, but what was the mother to do? She was the sole provider and her job demanded that she work a shift system. In his day, mothers stayed at home, at least until the children were older than Mark was, but widows had always had problems. He remembered coming home from school to the smell of baking, tea ready, a fire lit, and a welcome. In turn, he and Dorothy, his wife, had provided a secure background for Alan.

These days, people seemed to have babies to gratify a whim, or because other people thought they ought to reproduce. Tom wondered if they looked beyond the cot and toddler stage to the child like Mark, who needed a framework to his life. Mark, at least, did not have to share his mother with three or four children by different fathers, none of whom took responsibility for them. According to the press and television, there were men who went around scattering their seed at random. Tom thought the Bible had something to say about that sort of conduct.

Despite their care, he and Dorothy had failed with Alan. He had not done well at school, becoming lazy and insolent as he entered his teens and began playing truant. When he was fifteen, he had been caught stealing and since then he had been arrested several times, finally on a charge of murdering his wife. It had been too much for Dorothy. She knew that he was guilty and after he was convicted she had slowly sunk into what the doctor called a clinical depression, and, eventually, had dwindled away and died.

That was six years ago, and Tom had been alone ever since. Most of the time he had been working as a consultant to the firm of accountants where he had been a partner until his retirement. Before his stroke he had been active and had enjoyed gardening, though with less enthusiasm because there was now no Dorothy with whom to share its results. He had been on the town council, and had become interested in local history. When it was clear that he was going to recover, he thought, wearily, 'What for?' but did not complain aloud.

Alan's visit had seriously upset Tom, who had persuaded himself that they would never meet again. He was trouble – always had been, and always would be. That poor girl, his wife: Tom had met her only once, at the wedding. She was still so young, and doomed, he had known then, but he had thought to misery, not death. Memories of Alan's childhood flickered into Tom's mind and would not be banished. He was glad when young Mark arrived to impose his own sturdy reality over such unwelcome images.

Mark was independent and self-reliant – just as well, as his mother seemed to be absent more often than not. Sometimes, when he came alone, Mark talked about her, wishing she didn't have to work so hard to keep them both. Tom had asked about his father, and Mark had said she wouldn't talk about him, and that perhaps they had parted because of Mark.

'How could that be?' Tom was horrified.

'Well, maybe he didn't like me. Didn't want me, maybe,' Mark had answered, speaking nonchalantly, dealing out the cards, for they were going to play rummy.

'He can't have not liked you if he never saw you,' Tom had said, wondering who would not be proud of such a fine little chap. 'Maybe he didn't know you were on the way,' he suggested.

Mark hadn't thought of that. It consoled him.

'Maybe he'll come and see Mum one day, and have a surprise,' he remarked.

'Maybe,' said Tom, picking up his cards.

MARK'S MOTHER, SUSAN Conway, arrived home at half-past nine. The house was silent, but a lamp burned in the living-room; it was operated by a timer, switching itself on automatically, so that Mark did not return to a dark house.

Susan could hear the washing-machine churning away. Mark was a good boy, putting his dirty clothes in it. She thought quickly about what he had been wearing: was his sweat-shirt red? Would there be pink pants in the final result? It was too late now to alter that; they'd bleach, she decided. She tiptoed upstairs. His door was ajar; he always left it like that if she was out, and by the light from the landing she saw that he was fast asleep, smooth, round cheeks, long lashes like frills. Kermit's world-weary face peered out above an arm. She crept away and went downstairs again. She was lucky that he had such an equable temperament. They managed well; it was easier since she had been promoted, and he was getting older. Her career had taken a slide when he was born.

Before that, she was personal assistant to the manager of an independent London hotel. Earlier, she had worked in various offices improving her administrative skills until a love affair with a colleague ended when he married someone else. She took herself and her damaged heart away on a trip to India before looking for another position.

She had met Mark's father while he was at a conference in the hotel. She knew that he was married, but as their affair developed, he convinced her that it was only a matter of time before he parted from his wife; then they would marry. Their meetings were frequent, but they never lived together.

Her illusions were shattered when one day his wife arrived at the hotel where he was attending a business lunch. Susan witnessed their meeting in the foyer. He was obviously startled, but he embraced his wife with warmth and walked off with her, both of them eagerly talking to one another. Their evident closeness was unmistakeable: or was it all an act?

Susan never knew what had brought his wife to the hotel. Had she become suspicious and traced him there? Or was there some important family news she needed to impart? Time passed, and she did not hear from him. When she telephoned his office he would not speak to her, and his firm's next meetings were not held at that hotel.

She contemplated confronting him, demanding an explanation, making a scene. She knew where he lived and could have embarrassed him by challenging his marriage. Half intending to do so, she drove to the Kent village and saw his pleasant house, set in a large garden with a pony looking over a nearby gate. Various scenarios ran through her mind but she banished them all; there was such a thing as pride.

Hers had been seriously wounded. She saw, now, that it, more than her heart, had been damaged, also, by her first rejection; he had never intended to leave his wife at all and once again she had been deceived.

Susan's career was a consolation, but soon she discovered that she was pregnant. She had been a little careless about taking the Pill, playing a sort of Russian roulette, reasoning that if it failed, he would have to marry her. In any case, she was thirty-three; time was passing and she had always wanted children. Otherwise, why get married? Now, hurt and bitter, she resolved not to tell him about the baby. She would exclude him from its life, bring it up single-handed. She could earn a good living for them both. There was no need to go cap in hand to him and thus give him some claim to the child.

In those first, decisive weeks, she thought it would be easy, but time proved her wrong.

At work, she said nothing about her pregnancy, planning to carry on as normal for as long as possible, then take maternity leave and return when she had arranged child care. She had barely begun investigating child minders and the possibility of shared nannies when problems began. She became quite unwell, her blood pressure fluctuated and rest was advised.

She gave up her job but was able to find a part-time temporary post, lower down the hierarchical ladder, in a country hotel, part of a chain, where the manager was a friend of her former employer. It was close to Haverscot, and she moved there, to a rented flat, for the last weeks of her pregnancy.

The financial loss was severe, but she had some savings, and her rent was far less than for her London flat. However, she had to stop work a month before Mark was born and she did not return until he was six months old, depending, meanwhile, on state benefit.

The hotel was not obliged to re-engage her because she had been only a temporary staff member, but a position was found for her as a wages clerk. No more senior opening was available at the time, and the manager was doubtful about her reliability, now that there was a baby to consider. If the child were ill, she would stay away, he reasoned. But by this time she had discovered a reliable child-minder with whom Mark was happy. Now her aim was to make good the lost months and climb back up the ladder. She was capable of reaching top management level, but she must be willing to go on courses and to consider moves to other hotels within the group.

The Golden Accord, where she was working at present, was some distance away, but she was now an assistant manager. She had remained in Haverscot because it represented continuity for Mark and she had discovered Ivy; Mark was too old now for his original child-minder. There might be other moves, a manager's post with a flat in the hotel, one day; it would be soon enough, then, to uproot Mark.

Susan had had no lover since Mark's birth. She trusted no one now and had lost all desire to marry. Her life was too busy to leave her time for a new affair, and one-night stands had never appealed to her. She had a son; the two of them were fine on their own and she owed no one anything.

Susan had no family of her own. Her father had died when she was twelve, and her mother not long before Susan met Mark's father. She had no brothers or sisters, and both her parents had been only children so there were no cousins. Mark lacked the advantages of uncles and grandparents, but he showed no sign of missing these attachments which many children had. His life was simple, uncluttered by complex step-relationships like those of Ivy's son, Steve. Mark would sometimes talk about evenings spent with Steve. Susan had no idea that some of the videos they watched were viewed, not in Ivy's house, but at The Willows. She liked to hear of games of chess and rummy, and she had seen the books Mark brought home – good, old-fashioned stories such as she had read herself. It surprised her that Ivy had this stock: she didn't remember noticing shelves of books when she went to the house. Maybe they were Sharon's. She'd asked Mark if Steve read much, and it seemed that he didn't. He was very keen on cars, Mark said, and could tell you the engine capacity and acceleration rate of almost every make. Mark then proceeded to tell Susan how rapidly various cars reached speed from standstill.

He was enthusiastic when he talked, his eyes shining, his thick straight hair falling over his brows. He did not look remotely like his father, about whom Susan, now, seldom thought. Her life was disciplined. At the hotel, she had learned to adopt a casual, friendly manner towards the men she worked with, or who were guests. The occasional come-on was warded off almost before it became one. Some of the staff thought she had a lover; she let them carry on with this assumption: it was a sort of protection.

When a police officer rang her doorbell soon after she had come home that Sunday night, she was startled, opening the door to him on a chain, regarding him in the brightness of the security light outside the door. Behind him, she discerned the outline of a woman officer.

They asked if they could come into the house.

Susan was not unused to the police. They had to be called in at the hotel occasionally, when there were thefts or incidents of drunkenness, and they came as a matter of routine at other times.

'What is it?' she asked, admitting them.

If Mark had not been safely upstairs, she would have feared that he had had an accident. But it was Mark about whom they were asking. Had she a son, Mark, who was a friend of Terry Gardner?

Susan had heard Mark mention Terry.

'Yes,' she said. 'Why do you want to know?'

'Were they together today?'

'They may have been, for some of the time,' said Susan. 'But Mark spent the day with the woman who looks after him when I'm at work.' She must be careful; Ivy was no longer registered as a child-minder, and Susan did not want to get her into trouble.

'You were working today?'

'Yes.'

'Where do you work?'

She told them.

'Is Mark at home now?'

'Yes. He's asleep upstairs,' said Susan.

'It could have been another boy who was seen with Terry in the park this afternoon,' said the male officer. 'He's gone missing – Terry Gardner. He was seen alone around five-thirty, so the boy with him earlier had left him by that time. Your son, Mark, had his lunch at the Gardners' house today.'

'Did he?' Susan was surprised. She'd imagined him settling down to one of Ivy's steak and kidney pies.

'You didn't know?'

'No. I suppose he arranged it with Ivy – Mrs Burton,' Susan said. 'That would be quite in order, if he was invited.' Ivy would not let him accept an inappropriate invitation.

'The Gardners live near the church, at Merrifields,' said the woman officer. 'But you'd know that, seeing that the boys are friends.'

Susan didn't. All she knew about Terry was that Mark had mentioned him as being keen on football, and owning a small snooker table. She knew where Merrifields was, however; she and Mark, walking in the meadows above the river, had looked speculatively and with admiration at the large houses ranged along the ridge, and Mark had said that though they were grand and had big gardens, he liked their small house in Grasmere Street. Susan had bought it as soon as she was able to afford a mortgage; now it represented negative equity because of the fall in value, but they had no need of anything bigger; it suited them.

'Could we speak to Mark, please, Mrs Conway?' said the woman officer.

'Oh, but he's asleep. I told you. Must I wake him?' Susan asked.

'I'm afraid so. He may know where Terry's gone,' the woman officer replied.

'I do hope nothing's happened to him,' said Susan, but what she really meant was, oh God, if someone's hurt Terry, it could so easily have been Mark – the kind of thought she never allowed herself to entertain.

A tousled Mark, gently roused and put into his red dressing-gown, was brought downstairs. He clutched Kermit under one arm. While they waited, the two police officers noticed the neat, well-kept room, the small sofa and single armchair covered in grey-blue leather, the sensible fawn carpet, the deeper blue curtains, a few framed flower prints on the walls, a bookcase holding a mixed collection of paperbacks and some hardback novels. There was no neglect here. Forming this thought, WPC Dixon heard the washing-machine start its spin-dry cycle with a noisy whirr just like her own machine. Susan, coming home late, had, she assumed, put the wash on; clearly, she was no slouch.

Mark, sleepy and bewildered, agreed that he had seen Terry that day, which the police already seemed to know. He did not mention lunch at Merrifields because his mother had not known that he was going there.

'We played football in the park this afternoon,' he said. This must be about the two motorists and the damage to their cars. They'd gone to the police, complaining, in spite of the old lady. 'We left before it began to get dark,' he added quickly. 'As we'd been told.'

'Separately?'

'Yes,' said Mark, yawning. He wanted to go back to sleep but it was nice sitting on the sofa with his mother, who had lit the gas fire so that it was warm and cosy.

'Terry was going straight home?'

'Yes. His mum gets really cross if he's out after dark,' said Mark, who did not suffer from this problem with Ivy, as long as she knew he was at Tom's.

'And you came home too?'

He had, but not at once, so to agree did not mean that he had lied.

'Yes,' said Mark. He was puzzled. Why weren't they asking about the damaged cars? 'That is, to Ivy's, where I go when Mum's on late,' he amended. This part wasn't true.

'Terry didn't get home, Mark,' said WPC Dixon. 'Do you know where he might have gone instead? Some other friend's, perhaps?'

Mark didn't.

The officers went away without discovering that Mark had been unaccounted for until nearly nine o'clock, and no one, except Tom Morton, knew that he had been at The Willows.

*

Neither of the police officers who visited Susan lived in Haverscot, which came under the Radbury division of the local force and whose small police station was not manned at night. Several others, though, were from the area and one was the community officer who worked with the various schools. He knew many of the children well, and most of them by sight. His two colleagues lacked this advantage as they started on the hunt for Terry.

He had been seen running off after the incident with the milk bottle, the white globe of the football he was clutching making him stand out, but he could have been any boy of eleven or twelve years old. When Greg Black came home, however, after spending the evening with his companions from the park, and saw the damaged window, he guessed at once who was responsible. His father, who had been visiting friends, had found Greg's sister Mandy very upset after hearing the glass crash inwards. She and Greg had an older brother with some rough friends whom Mandy didn't like. She thought it might have been one of them, but Greg had no hesitation in naming Terry as the likely miscreant. Who else would have been carrying a football through the streets, and was under-sized?

'Kid was cheeky in the park. I told him off,' he said.

What if Terry gave his version of the episode? Greg would deny it, say Terry was inventing it to cover up his own misdeeds. It would be Greg's word against his, and Greg backed himself. Besides, the kid would only get a caution. It would give him a fright and teach him a lesson.

An officer went round to Merrifields, hot on the heels of one who had been there taking details because Terry had failed to come home that night.

It was easy, now, to see why he had not returned. He'd done something stupid and was afraid of trouble. At least he was not likely to have been abducted, and he might be found quite soon. The police took an optimistic line with the distraught mother and reassured Richard that, when found,

Terry would get off fairly lightly over the broken window.

'If he is the boy who did it,' said the constable who had called to question Terry.

'Bit of a coincidence if he didn't,' Richard said.

He had been annoyed, rather than anxious, at Terry's disobedience. The boy had been told to come back before dark, but he might have gone to visit a friend. Thinking he might be at Mark's house, Richard had looked up Conway in the telephone book; there were several listed, some with Haverscot addresses. Hadn't Mark said he lived in Grasmere Street? There was an entry, S.J. Conway, at number 38.

He had rung the number, but there was no reply. This implied that the boys were still together. Perhaps they were with the woman who looked after Mark. Yes, that was it, and she'd send Terry home. Meanwhile, his mother had not missed him. She had got up during the afternoon and was in her studio. A Joan Baez tape was playing. Richard left her undisturbed. To have her in a hysterical state of anxiety would not bring Terry home. Very likely he would soon return.

Justin, at least, was back, virtuously doing homework in his room.

Richard had decided to go to Evensong. He did this sometimes, because it was peaceful in the church and he enjoyed singing hymns and psalms. He left a note in the kitchen stating where he was going, exchanged his waxed jacket for a raincoat, and set off.

In church, he sat in the same row of chairs as a grim-looking elderly woman with a maroon felt hat set vertically across her forehead; small boot-button eyes gave him a quick inspection. Richard left some empty seats between them. During the first hymn, he heard her sing: her voice was pure and low, beautiful in tone. She, for her part, noticed his confident baritone. As they sang *Amen* and resumed their seats, preparing to lean forward in a devout posture, they exchanged glances. Marigold Darwin almost smiled; Richard did.

After the service, he had not gone straight home, deciding to take the longer route around the town, thinking he might meet Terry. In fact, he was postponing having to confront whatever situation had arisen in his absence. He was sure the two boys were still together and suspected no more trouble than their simple disobedience.

Meanwhile, Verity had come downstairs, found him out and Terry missing, and Justin with no knowledge of where Terry was.

Verity was angry because Richard was not there and she needed an audience for an emotional scene. Now she had two triggers: his desertion, and Terry's absence.

She asked Justin if he knew where Terry was. He was not the target of her wrath and her manner was still controlled, her voice calm, but Justin saw the gleam in her eye and knew trouble loomed.

'Guess he's still with that little kid. It's early, Mum. I wouldn't worry,' he said. He'd finished his homework and wanted to watch a video a friend had lent him. If Mum started to carry on, he would be thwarted.

'Richard's gone out,' she said, adding, 'to church,' in a tone appropriate for a destination of utter depravity.

'Well?' Justin saw no harm in church as long as he was not expected to attend.

'When Terry's missing,' Verity said.

'He's not missing. He's just late,' said Justin. 'Cool down, Mum.' He remembered Richard telling the small boys to be home before dark, but did not mention this to his mother. She'd blow a fuse anyway when Cat returned, and another when Terry turned up. 'What's for supper?' he decided to ask, and provoked a tirade about how could he think of food when his brother might be lying murdered in a ditch.

'Not Terry,' Justin said, laughing at her. 'He can take care of himself.'

'But you don't know who's out there — perverts — sadists—' Verity began, and soon she was well away, weeping first, a tragic figure. Next, she'd start drinking and the rage would follow. Justin sighed, resigned. Perhaps some food would distract her.

'Let's get something to eat, Mum,' he said. 'There's plenty of the lamb we had at lunch. I'll put some potatoes in the microwave. Terry will be back before they're ready, you'll see, and he'll be starving.' He spoke reassuringly, like a nurse, and took her arm, leading her out of the room.

His tactics briefly worked. She stayed reasonably calm and went with him to the kitchen where she sat at the table while he gave two fair-sized potatoes a token wash, punctured their skins and put them on the turntable, pressing the timer for ten minutes. He thought they would take longer, but by then Terry or Cat, or both, might have come home.

'You're a good boy, Justin,' his mother told him. 'At least you haven't run out on me. You won't, will you?'

Justin hated talk like this. She'd get soppy and emotional.

'Course not,' he said gruffly, going to the fridge to find the lamb. It wasn't quite his choice of supper; he'd rather have a pizza or some chips, but it needed little preparation and he knew his mother had had nothing much to eat that day. If she was going in for a drinking session, she ought to have some food to mop it up. This was one of Cat's precepts which Justin supported. If she started to moan about not killing little lambs, refusing to eat it, he'd put a hunk of cheese on her potato. Sometimes she forgot her vegetarian principles, and she ate fish, which he thought was inconsistent. Surely fish had souls and feelings, if sheep and pigs did?

But Verity couldn't sit there idly at the table. She got up abruptly and left the room, returning with a glass half full of either gin or vodka; they both looked the same. Justin's heart sank. He hoped Cat would be back before she was fully launched into what must surely develop.

It didn't take her long to get maudlin, and in that mood she telephoned the police. She was still emotional, not yet angry, when they came to the house. They presented a touching sight, the weeping mother with the mane of tinted wild hair, and her attentive son, who had thrust her glass of alcohol, which she'd refilled after telephoning, into the fridge where the police would not see it. She'd need it later, after they had gone. Justin knew there was no point in pouring it away for she could always fill it up again. Justin liked taking care of her, but he found it difficult. If it wasn't for the money Cat provided, they'd be better off without him. Justin had never liked seeing them together in that big bed. When he and Terry were smaller, they'd clambered in with Cat and Mum on Sunday mornings. Cat usually got up almost immediately and the two boys were left, smug and gleeful, alone in warm intimacy with their mother.

Cat arrived while the police were there, and Verity at once turned on him, demanding to know why he had gone out when Terry wasn't home. Why wasn't he searching the streets for him?

Richard managed to make the police officer understand that he had gone to the park trying to find Terry and had walked round the town looking for him before going to church. Verity, winding herself up from woe to wrath, rounded on him for this but one of the police officers, quite a young man, managed to calm her down, saying 'Now then, Mrs Gardner, we won't get any nearer to finding Terry if we argue, will we?' in a soothing voice.

Richard said that the boys had been told to come home before darkness fell, but that he thought Terry must be with his friend Mark.

'I rang what I thought was Mark's mother's number,' he said. 'There was no reply, so I decided he must have gone to the family who look after him when his mother's working. I'm afraid I don't know who they are. Shall I try the number again now?' he suggested, and as the police officer approved, he went off to do so.

There was still no answer.

'Perhaps it's the wrong number, but I thought Mark said he lived in Grasmere Street,' said Richard.

'We'll try some other Conways,' said the policeman. 'But

I'm sure Terry's safe. He's just lost account of time. It's easy at that age.'

Richard was hoping that Terry had not led Mark into mischief. He thought about the floodwater in the fields below the garden; that could be tempting to a boy. But they had been intent on playing football.

'Perhaps someone saw them in the park?' he suggested.

'Most likely,' said the policeman, not adding that it would be difficult to find such a person now, when those who might have been about would have gone home.

At that point in their discussions, the second pair of officers, seeking the vandal, arrived. Immediate concern for Terry's safety disappeared as the reason for his absence became clear.

'That other boy, Mark, must have led him into doing it,' said Verity. 'Terry's a good boy.'

While they were talking, Justin had quietly left the room and gone upstairs, taking refuge in a bath, his radio on. Luckily it wasn't the community officer who had called, and the two police officers had not got in touch with him; when they did, the next day, they learned that Justin was one of several boys suspected of spraying graffiti on hoardings and who had been seen loitering near cars in the station yard, though none had been actually caught in the act of breaking into one.

The police went off at last, and Verity, who had maintained some control until then, turned on Richard with a torrent of abuse. She flew at him, her fingers aiming for his eyes. Richard caught her wrists and flung her away from him. One of these days, she'd fall against a cupboard, hit her head, be hurt and accuse him of attacking her.

'I'm going out,' he said. 'I'll look for Terry.'

He put his waxed jacket on again and found his cap and a torch.

I'm driven from my own home, he told himself, striding off into the night. There must be something about him that provoked this hostility – not that Karen, rejecting him, had been exactly hostile. But Verity and her sons despised him. He was used to Justin's veiled enmity and expected trouble from him; if the police had called to question him, Richard would not have been surprised, and there had been warnings from school, where his performance was disappointing.

What could he do? Was he to turn away from Verity and her problems? Reject them all? If he did, what would become of her and the boys? A divorce would be difficult and expensive. But not impossible. The thought of escaping from his present situation seemed very attractive as he contemplated it, walking along in the now heavy rain.

And there was Caroline.

6

RICHARD WALKED ROUND the churchyard, shining his torch among the tombstones and the sombre evergreens which grew near the walls. This was the sort of place where a child might hide; there was cover. It was very wet, however; if Terry were here, he would be so cold. Silly boy! What had made him want to throw a bottle at a window? And why that window? Why that house? The police hadn't been too clear about why he was suspected of being the guilty vandal.

They might have searched here already. They were making door-to-door enquiries, they said, and they would trace Mark Conway, unless he, too, had disappeared. There was not much that they could do tonight, however, though facts about the missing boy would be broadcast on the local radio station. People might look in sheds and outhouses.

Richard toured the park, trying the doors of the cricket pavilion and the scout hut, but both were securely locked and no windows had been broken to admit a fugitive.

Terry couldn't have run away. He'd had no money on him, as far as was known. He was avoiding retribution.

Eventually, Richard's peregrinations took him along Clement Lane, out of which led Bevan Road and so he reached the end of Grasmere Street. He walked down its length, and passed the house, Number 38, where S. Conway lived. A police car was parked outside it.

So this was the right address. He contemplated calling in; the mother must be very anxious. But the police were there: they'd deal with her, fetch a neighbour in, someone who knew her. There was nothing he could do. He'd better get on home, face whatever situation had arisen in his absence.

Deciding thus, Richard nevertheless walked back by way of the street where Terry, allegedly, had broken a window. He saw the afflicted dwelling, where boards had been nailed across the broken pane. Was it impossible to get a glazier out to make an emergency repair on a Sunday night? The houses among which this one stood were solid, well-built and mostly semi-detached, with short driveways in which cars were parked. On the opposite side of the road, much of the Victorian terraced row had been modernised. Glancing across, Richard saw empty milk bottles on several steps; people here still patronised the roundsman. Verity had stopped, saying it was cheaper to buy in bulk from the supermarket, but the result of this was that they were always running out because she forgot to get it or was too wrapped up in her painting to go shopping.

Cold and very wet when he reached home, Richard shed his coat and cap and went in search of Verity, who was in the drawing-room, a leatherbound album on her knee, looking at photographs of the two boys when they were very young. She was not crying now but was crooning under her breath; her face was red and blotchy, and Justin, looking terrified, was sitting beside her, trying to give comfort.

'He's dead. I know he is,' she said, when Richard appeared. 'Justin and I have been planning the funeral. What hymns to have. The flowers.' She turned her distraught face up to Richard and sudden colour flooded it. 'And where have you been when I needed you?' she hissed at him. 'Not here, by my side. Oh no! Out you go, seeing some fancy woman while my Terry lies dead and mutilated. Church, indeed! What an excuse! And lasting all this time, the service? You must think I was born yesterday.'

In seconds, she had summoned up energy which Richard was amazed she still possessed, considering that she had drunk a vast quantity of gin. Richard picked up the bottle, which stood on the coffee table in front of her. It was empty. A glass smeared with lipstick and greasy fingermarks was on the floor near her feet. He rescued it, wondering if she had been swallowing pills as well as alcohol.

Verity had wound herself up again.

'And now you're going to hit me! I knew you would. See, Justin – he's got the weapon ready – he'll hit me with that bottle,' she cried. She was standing now, jutting her hips forward at him, her small, sagging breasts loose beneath her sweater, which was spotted with stains.

Before he could reply, she flew at him, scratching his face while he was powerless, glass in one hand and bottle in the other, to prevent her.

'Mum, don't,' said Justin, ineffectively. 'Mum, give him a chance.' He caught her arm, but Verity threw it off as if he had no more strength than a baby.

Richard dropped the bottle and the glass and seized her upper arms.

'Stop it, Verity,' he said. He shook her, not hard, longing to slap her but aware that she scarcely knew what she was saying. 'Terry's missing. He'll be found. What use will you be to him in this state? Pull yourself together.'

She was beyond doing that. Suddenly, mercifully, she swayed where she stood, rolled up her eyes and passed out. Richard caught her as she fell. He laid her on the sofa.

Justin looked at him and shrugged.

'She never drank before she married you,' he said, and slouched out of the room.

Richard picked up the bottle and the glass again, and took them out to the kitchen. Then he went upstairs and fetched a duvet, which he spread over Verity. After that, he made another trip to get a towel, which he put beneath her face. He turned her on her side, to prevent her choking if she vomited.

He could do no more. He went upstairs to bed where, in unaccustomed solitude, knowing that Verity would not be capable of another outburst for several hours at least, he read for a while. Lately, on the train, he had been reading Trollope, and he had just begun *The Small House at Allington*. It was a soothing read, and, not a witty man himself, he appreciated humour in others.

The whole household was asleep when Terry, cold and exhausted, unaware that he was the subject of a major police operation which was focused on his safety, not his punishment, got out of Richard's car in which he had been hiding until the fuss died down, and let himself quietly into the house, using the emergency key, which was kept in a tin on a high shelf in the garage among jars holding paintbrushes and cans of paint.

He went up to his room, undressed, and climbed into bed, pulling his duvet, which was covered with vivid prints of dinosaurs, over him, and was soon asleep.

Richard woke up in the small hours. Going to bed alone, knowing he was safe from persecution, had been such a treat. Usually he tried to time things so that Verity was already in bed or had embarked on a studio session of either painting or drink, or both, so that he could feign sleep when she came to bed, but often she would wake him, seeking an audience for whatever was her current mood. Now, roused by a feeling of unease, he remembered that she had passed out downstairs and he had left her on the sofa. Was she all right?

Part of him did not care a jot; however, habit and prudence told him he must find out.

He got out of bed, shrugged his arms into his green towelling robe and went quietly downstairs, anxious not to wake Justin, who had had a bad time with his mother the previous evening. If it was heartless to go to bed while Terry was missing, it was also sensible, Richard told himself: wakeful vigil would not bring the boy home. A long day lay ahead, for sure. He had appointments at the office, but could he, in conscience, abandon Verity in order to keep them? Perhaps he could get a friend to keep her company, he thought, padding down the stairs. But had she any friends? There had been a few, from time to time, but, one by one, they dropped her, worn out by her moods.

She was just as he had left her, snoring a little now, her mouth half open, not attractive and not even pitiful, just a squalid sight. He tipped her further over on to her side; she did not stir.

Once he had loved her, or thought he did. Once he had loved Karen, his first wife — and still did, in a sense, or, nostalgically, the idea he had of her.

He glanced at Verity's flushed face, streaked with sweat and tears. She looked ugly, yet a few years ago he had found her pallor — she was seldom pale now — and deepset eyes, which looked as though they would soon brim with tears, appealing. He had longed to make her smile, but all too often she had wept and wailed. He had never seen her truly happy.

I've failed her hopelessly, he thought, treading up the stairs again. I've failed to give her what she needed. It did not occur to him that Verity's inability to experience pleasure was nourished by her desire to make others suffer.

On the landing, he paused at Terry's door, then opened it, his head full of unanswerable questions about the boy's state of mind. Light shafted into the room and he could see the bed, the rumpled duvet, and, incredibly, the dark hair above it. Blinking, sure that he must be imagining it, Richard went into the room and laid a hand on the firm outline in the bed.

It was no mirage. Terry was back.

Richard did not wake him to demand an explanation. That would mean dealing with what must follow — telling Verity and informing the police. Apart from patrols keeping an eye out for him, there would be no real search until daylight. It would be time enough to discover that Terry had returned in the morning. Richard went back to bed.

*

At six o'clock, his normal time, Richard woke again. It was still dark outside. He stretched, remembering that he was alone: there was no risk of accidentally touching Verity. Every night he set the alarm, but every morning he woke before it buzzed at him, always determined that Verity should not be disturbed.

He remembered childhood breakfasts – those before he went away to school, and later, in the holidays. His mother laid the table every evening after dinner. Cereal, marmalade and honey would be on the table with the blue and white striped Cornish crockery; butter would appear next morning, and she would fry or scramble eggs, cook bacon and tomatoes, or sausages; perhaps there would be fried potatoes. No one worried about cholesterol then, and, he thought, people were much happier. Every day his father went to the office – on the train, just as Richard did now – with a good hot meal inside him. Now, Richard would have two Weetabix with milk and a mug of Gold Blend, while the boys swallowed fruit juice and whatever cereal was their current favourite. That had to last them until their midday meal at school, which might be good and nourishing, but might, according to their choice, be neither.

If Verity had put eggs and bacon before him, Richard knew he would consume them and would not be pining for coffee as soon as he reached the office, nor ready for his lunchtime sandwich long before one o'clock. There had been a time when he went to a pub in his lunch hour, and drank a pint of beer, which staved off his hunger, but he had begun to put on weight and, with Verity already drinking too much, he saw danger ahead. He had cut out drinking except with Caroline, and an occasional half pint in the evening at the station if he reached it with enough time before his train.

There were other men who did this, some knocking back double gins or whisky. He saw familiar faces at the bar and would nod to them, perhaps exchange small talk with a few regulars. He wondered if any of them were eager to get home. He saw men buying flowers from the station shop; were these peace offerings or spontaneous tributes? Who could tell? He'd bought flowers too, often enough, hoping to win Verity round from sulks to smiles. It was the same motivation that led him to buy her expensive presents: a brooch, a ring, even an exercise bicycle when she decided, rightly, that she was unfit. She soon abandoned it. He used it now.

Belatedly, he had understood that you could not buy love, but gifts had brought him brief spells of peace.

Now, as he sat up in bed, the events of the previous night came shatteringly back to him. He checked quickly that Verity was not beside him. Reassured, he sighed with relief; much of his pleasure, these days, came from absence of strife, not from any positive experience. Now there was time to shower, shave and dress before he need face her, and time to telephone the police from the bedroom extension before they resumed the search for Terry.

He went into the bathroom, and afterwards looked into the boy's room: for all he knew, Terry had done another flit, though he had seemed, like his mother, to be out for the count.

He was still asleep, one hand now exposed, very grubby, hanging over the side of the bed. A scruffy teddy bear lay on the floor, no doubt pushed out during the night. He was still a vulnerable little boy, thought Richard, and the victim of his genetic inheritance. Richard had formed a picture of his absent father as a violent brute; it had occurred to him only recently that this might not be an accurate portrait of his predecessor and that the two boys' temperaments could have been handed to them by their mother.

He returned to his room, closed the door, dressed, and then rang the police to report the runaway's safe return.

An officer would be round to hear what Terry had to say for himself.

'Don't hurry,' Richard said. 'He's still asleep, and so's his mother. They need their rest.'

He won time, but not much. During the interval before the police arrived, he remembered the other boy, Mark. Was he still missing, or had he, also, sneaked home to bed?

The police were gentle with Terry.

He was asleep when they arrived, but Richard had roused Verity, led her upstairs, and made her have a shower to sober up and regain some control before they came. During this, she managed to take in the fact that Terry was safe. She made a lot of noise, wailing and swearing as the water hit her, and Justin woke up. He hated her exhibitionism and hysteria, but he blamed Richard for them and wove a fantasy in which he saved her by becoming the protégé of a rich patron — sex indeterminate in the dream — sometimes a Michael Jackson figure and sometimes a woman not unlike the Queen, grey-haired and gracious. He had once seen her when she opened a hospital wing near his school before they came to Haverscot and he, with other children, stood in the street waving a flag. Lately, these dreams were fading; he was too old for fairy tales and had begun to think more in terms of becoming a pop singer and making a million, or of major theft. He knew boys who stole successfully. If you took cars, you could sell them for a bomb. Before now, he'd nicked bars of chocolate, magazines, and even audio cassettes without being caught.

The discord at home frightened him. Though he did not want to acknowledge it, he could remember shouting matches between his parents, blows exchanged, his father as well as his mother being bruised and even cut about the face and arms. When he was younger, he had simply thought her unlucky in her choice of husbands; now, he was beginning to recognise, though he did not accept it, Richard's patience, but he still blamed his stepfather for provoking scenes.

He got dressed quickly and went downstairs, where he found there were no Coco-Pops, so he had to have Rice Krispies, Terry's favourite. He took his plate into the playroom and turned on the television, volume up. *The Big*

Breakfast programme drowned out other noise and he was still watching it when the police officers rang the front doorbell.

Meanwhile, Richard had instructed Terry to get washed and dressed. Verity had put on black leggings and a long black sweater. She brushed her damp, unkempt hair which in certain lights glinted like metal from the rinse she used. She styled it so that it fell over her face, peering out between the frizzy strands in the little-girl-lost mode which Richard knew so well. He sighed. Early in their acquaintance it had deceived him, and it might deceive the police, too. Perhaps that would be just as well. He wondered if they would smell alcohol on her breath; she had brushed her teeth with mint-flavoured toothpaste.

The interview had best be conducted in the drawing-room. Richard had tidied it, plumped up the cushions and drawn the curtains while Verity and Terry were dressing. He opened the windows briefly, letting in a blast of cold, damp winter air. From the playroom came the sound of Justin's television programme: well, that meant he would keep out of the way, thought Richard grimly.

After a good night's sleep, Terry had almost forgotten his adventures of the previous day and thought a mere scolding from Richard for being late would be his only punishment; in fact, Richard had said nothing to him beyond ordering him to wash and dress. But when he was told to go into the drawing-room and saw two uniformed police officers, one male and one female, already in the room, with his mother, he turned to flee. Richard, however, stood behind him, barring the doorway.

He looked towards his mother. She would save him and protect him. But she was sitting on the sofa, hiding behind her hair as she dabbed at her eyes with a pink tissue. He thought of running to her, flinging himself against her, wanting to be hugged, as had happened when he was small and she was in a receptive mood; these days, you could never be sure how she would respond, so he did not try it. He glanced at the police officers, both of whom were standing up. Neither smiled at him.

Verity was so used to casting herself in the role of victim that she could not, now, make any effort to imagine what he was feeling. She let her tears brim over.

'Oh, Terry, how could you do this to me? You are a wicked, wicked boy,' she sobbed.

'He's safe, Mrs Gardner, that's the main thing,' said Sergeant Dixon, the woman officer. 'Sit down, Terry.'

Terry gave her another quick inspection. She was the enemy, of course, but she had spoken quietly and didn't seem too cross. The policeman with her was the one who came to talk to them at school, warning them about strangers offering lifts in cars, and drugs, and all that stuff. He was all right, Terry had grudgingly to admit.

'Now, Terry,' said PC Withers. 'Can you tell me where you were at about half-past five yesterday afternoon?'

'Out,' said Terry, looking at the ground.

'Out where?'

'I'd been in the park. I had permission,' Terry said, his tone now aggrieved.

'Did you come straight home?'

'Er—' Terry hesitated. He remembered the feel of the milk bottle in his hand and the satisfying crash of glass as it hit the window. They couldn't know that it was him. Could they?

'Did you come home by way of Greenham Road?' asked Sergeant Dixon.

'I might have,' Terry said.

'Do you know anything about a broken window at number forty-seven, Greenham Road?'

Terry did not answer.

'A boy was seen there, Terry, running away, with a football,' said Withers.

'It might have been another boy,' said Verity.

'It might have been,' Withers agreed. 'Was it, Terry? You'd been in the park earlier, with your football, hadn't you?'

'What's wrong with that?' asked Terry. 'He said I could go.' Saying this, he glared at his stepfather.

'You were told to be back before dark,' said Richard.

'Now, Terry, someone thinks it was you who broke that window,' Withers said. 'OK, you were late going home, but Greenham Road isn't on your way back from the park. Why did you go there?'

Did the police know about the broken windscreen and the other damaged car? Were they to be blamed for that? The old woman had said they hadn't done it but what if those two men had told a different story? Terry felt trapped.

'I can go that way if I like,' he said.

'Yes, of course you can, but you mustn't break windows,' Withers said.

'It's you says I did it, not me,' said Terry.

'Why didn't you come straight home, Terry?' asked Sergeant Dixon.

'I went to see a friend,' said Terry promptly.

'What friend?'

'Mark,' said Terry promptly.

'Mark Conway?' Sergeant Dixon needed to be clear.

'He doesn't live in that direction, and he says you parted in the park,' said Withers.

'He's lying,' came the instant answer.

'So everyone's lying except you, eh?'

'Must be.' Terry yawned.

'When did you come home? You weren't here when everyone else went to bed,' said Sergeant Dixon.

'Later,' said Terry, forced to speak the truth at last.

'Didn't you know your parents would be worried? It was dark and you were meant to be in before dark? What were you doing?'

'I was frightened,' Terry muttered.

'What of?'

'They'd be angry. He'd be angry.' Terry glowered at Richard, but his lower lip quivered. Justin had it in for Richard, but he'd been decent enough to Terry.

'Why? Because you were late?'

'Yes.'

'But why were you late? Wasn't it because you'd broken the window and were afraid of being found out?'

Terry did not answer.

'Where did you go before coming home?'

Now Terry could be pleased with himself, because they hadn't caught him out.

'I hid in the tree house and then in Cat's car,' he said smugly. 'I came over the fence,' he added. 'Justin and me sometimes do.' It was Justin who had banged strong nails into the fence posts so that it was possible to clamber over the tall fence in both directions. Terry had hidden in the churchyard first, but it had been cold and wet out there, and he'd begun to imagine ghosts. There'd been a service going on, with quite nice singing, a bit of which he could hear, and he'd realised people would soon be leaving. They might find him there, like that boy in that film when the convict caught him. Cat had made them watch it. He said it was a classic. It hadn't been too bad, in parts, but he'd thought the mad old woman stupid. While he was in the tree he'd heard cars coming and going, and knew that he was being hunted; only when all was quiet had he got into the car. Luckily, Cat hadn't locked it, nor the garage, though usually he did.

'Cat?' queried Sergeant Dixon, though she understood who was meant.

'The boys call me that,' said Richard, adding, as if it gave the reason, 'I'm their stepfather.'

'I see,' said the sergeant.

'Greg took my ball,' said Terry at last. 'In the park. Mark will tell you.'

Mark hadn't mentioned it.

'So that made you angry, did it?' Withers asked.

'Yeah. He'd no right. He kicked it in the road,' said Terry. Let Greg talk himself out of what happened after that; he'd think the men had shopped him. Maybe they had.

'Did he?' asked Withers.

'Yeah – and it caused a crash,' said Terry, speaking now with animation. 'It hit a car and the driver hit another car. The drivers blamed us. Me and Mark. But some old woman said it wasn't us. All I wanted was my ball back,' he ended, looking righteous.

'But you got it back.' It was a statement.

'Yeah.'

'Where is it now?'

'In my room.' During his adventures, he hadn't forgotten it. He'd clutched it all the time, even as he threw the bottle, and had tossed it over the fence before he climbed it himself. It had rolled only a short distance into the wet, tussocky grass under the trees, and was easily retrieved.

'You wanted to get at Greg for taking it, didn't you?' said Withers.

Terry did not answer. He stared at the floor. There was a dull mark on the carpet, a wine stain. Terry knew well enough what had caused it: Mum at the bottle again.

'Breaking the window meant aggravation for Greg's parents,' Withers was saying. 'They hadn't been tormenting you. Why should they be made to suffer because their lad had been getting at you?'

Terry shrugged.

'It was there,' he said.

'What was?'

'The milk bottle.'

'So it was easy?'

'Yeah.'

What would he have done if there hadn't been a bottle handy? All the adults wondered, even Verity, and none knew the answer. Maybe he would have been content to mutter curses but he might have found another missile. Round the corner from the house there was a skip containing rubble; if he had been able to climb up and reach into it – and probably he could – Terry might have found a brick.

But he'd admitted his offence, if not in so many words.

That was the big hurdle passed.

'I'll make good the broken window, Terry. I'll pay for the repairs, I mean,' said Richard. 'That will make Greg's parents feel less angry about it. But you mustn't do anything like that, ever again.' Through his head ran the notion of docking Terry's pocket money until the job was paid for, but he banished it because of the fuss Verity would make. The same idea was going through the minds of the two police officers but neither uttered it.

Terry was eyeing Richard from under his lashes: at that moment he looked so like his mother that Richard felt a pang; she had beguiled him when she wore that expression but now she enchanted him no longer, and her cheeks were not soft and smooth, like Terry's, but gaunt.

He made a decision. The boy must not get away with it.

'You'll work it off,' he said. 'I'll deduct whatever it costs from your pocket money, and you can do some jobs about the place. Wash the car. Do some weeding.' The ground would be too wet for weeding for a couple of months, he thought, but the threat could hang over Terry.

Verity needed some attention now. She would save challenging Richard over the punishment until later; meanwhile, she burst into renewed weeping and moaning.

'How could you do this, you naughty boy?' she wailed. 'You've disgraced me.'

'Now, come along, Mrs Gardner. It's not the end of the world,' said Sergeant Dixon. 'Let's go into the kitchen and make some tea.' Despite her rank, there were still moments when it was wise to adopt the stereotyped female role, and if the mother was out of the room, Withers and the boy's stepfather could give Terry a proper ticking-off.

They did so, with Withers arranging to show Terry the police cells in Haverscot the following Saturday. It wasn't an offer: he had to be there, and he could bring his brother, if he liked, and his friend Mark Conway. Once the boys saw where suspects were put while being held for questioning, they might be anxious to avoid qualifying. There was always the nearest prison, too; a visit there might be arranged, said Withers.

'I trust I'll be able to persuade Mr and Mrs Black not to press charges,' he added.

As the two police officers left the house, Withers remarked, 'I wonder who the old woman was who sorted it with the motorists.'

The matter need not be pursued. Once Greg Black's parents had been persuaded to be merciful, the incident could be considered closed.

They would be cooperative. Their own elder boy was no angel; the daughter, though, was a nice girl and quite clever.

7

MARK, ROUSED DURING Sunday night to recount his earlier movements, understood that Terry was in trouble for not going straight home after they parted, but was sure no harm had come to him. The police asked about other friends to whose houses Terry might have gone, but Mark could suggest no names, nor did he know of any secret hiding-places where Terry might be taking refuge. He had decided not to mention the two angry men and the damaged cars; lots of things were better kept to oneself, and telling wouldn't find Terry. He'd be all right; he could look after himself.

The police had not stayed long, and Mark, back in bed, had soon dropped off to sleep again.

His mother had the next day off, and there was time to chat over breakfast. He liked it when she was there when he left; however, she did not humiliate him by escorting him to school on these rare mornings.

While he was buttering his toast, Sergeant Dixon, the woman officer who had called during the night, telephoned to say that Terry had been found, safe and sound. He had come home.

'Just in case you and Mark were worrying,' she told Susan.

Susan thanked her. The police had a bad name for

68

following up actions of that kind; they did not always let victims of crime know when the perpetrators had been traced, or even brought to trial, much less the result. Here, at least, some consideration had been displayed – and by a woman officer, noted Susan. Neither she nor Mark knew about Terry's vandalism.

'He probably was with some other friend,' said Susan, after telling Mark the news. 'Does he ever come back here with you?'

Terry hadn't. Mark never brought friends home, whether or not his mother was there.

'No,' he said.

'It's all right, if you want to bring a friend in,' she said. She'd told him this before. 'I trust you about who you invite.'

She'd always trusted Mark; it was the only way.

'I'm usually with Steve,' he said, to reassure her.

That morning, Terry arrived late for school.

'The police were round at my house last night asking for you,' Mark told him. 'Where were you?'

'My mum thought I'd run away or been kidnapped,' Terry said. 'She acts mad sometimes,' he added. 'I didn't go straight home. Why should I? I thought it would be cool to scare them.'

This explanation had just occurred to him. He didn't think Mark would admire his window-breaking deed, particularly as he had been found out. If you were going to do that sort of thing, you shouldn't get caught. He wouldn't tell Mark about the invitation to accompany him to the police station at the weekend. In Terry's case, the visit was mandatory; Mark might guess that there was more to it than simply going missing for a few hours. The idea that he had caused a commotion was quite satisfying; Terry felt no shame. His mum had been in a right state but that was nothing unusual. He knew his escapade had not earned her approval, but he had won her attention.

'That's silly,' Mark responded. He had no desire to scare

his mother: quite the contrary. Terry was peculiar, sometimes.

Richard was nearly three hours late reaching his office that morning.

Verity had wanted to keep Terry back from school.

'What? And pamper him?' Richard had said. 'Reward him for his behaviour? Terry, get your coat. I'll drop you off.'

Justin had sloped away at his usual time, anxious to escape from the heavily charged atmosphere in the house. He'd overheard some of the discussion between the police and Terry, and had formed a more or less accurate impression of what his brother had been doing. He'd get the details later. Stupid prat! He needed a few hints on not getting caught.

Justin's friend Bruce had lifted a car from the station yard on Saturday afternoon, in broad daylight. They'd not taken it far, as it was their first effort. Bruce hadn't a lot of experience at driving, and he'd rammed a lamp-post when they were trying to turn in Norfolk Road. They'd left the car there, hurrying away, laughing and laughing, on a real high. They'd go further, next time.

They hadn't hurt themselves; they'd been in reverse gear at the time. They didn't look to see how much damage had been done to the car. It was insured, after all.

Justin hadn't been there to hear his mother tell Richard that he'd no right to give orders to Terry.

'He's my child,' she'd said.

Richard had not bothered to answer this remark.

'Come along, Terry. You're lucky you're not down at the police station facing charges,' he said, ignoring her.

Terry knew this was true. He thought about defying Richard, since his mother was clearly in a mood to spoil him, but if he stayed at home, she'd cry all over him and he'd miss football. He went to fetch his coat.

Richard had telephoned the school to say that Terry would be late; he'd been delayed because his mother wasn't well. The explanation was accepted. He marched the boy out to the car and dumped him at the door of the school, waiting until he had disappeared inside. Then he drove on to the station.

Sitting in the train – less crowded than usual because he was so much later than his normal time – Richard read the paper and mused on the working day ahead. Much would be routine and he had already missed an important meeting scheduled for ten o'clock. He had telephoned earlier, using the same, virtually true excuse he had given the school: his wife was unwell. He had used it before, when she had lightly slashed her wrists and bled all over the bed. He had bound her wounds, changed the bed linen and left her in her studio. If she chose to hurt herself while he was absent, that was her affair.

'Think of the boys,' he had admonished, when leaving. 'Don't punish them.'

She had told him that hers was the temperament of an artist: how could a philistine like him be expected to understand its nuances? But he might at least consider her needs, she would declare. Richard, however, was tired of trying to anticipate her behaviour; after some of her wilder extravagances, a mere hangover was trivial and could sometimes be ignored. If Verity intended to swamp her system with alcohol, he could not prevent her, nor could he keep searching every cupboard to find her supply.

He'd failed her, and he'd failed her sons, he thought, settled in the train, staring at the crossword. If he had been able to meet her emotional demands, to tune in to her moods, she would not need to drink and make scenes. She was a troubled soul, as her paintings demonstrated. Were they any good? He did not care for her dark, dramatic daubs, where occasionally a tiny, shrinking figure lurked in the foreground. Did they represent her own fears and forebodings? Some had been hung at local exhibitions. If she could produce enough to have her own show, maybe a critic would commend her work, make it fashionable, and thus give her a sense of achievement.

After a while, sitting in the peace of the warm train, he
dozed.

At work, he was busy, catching up on what had happened
at the meeting and making decisions as to future policy. The
day passed without a telephone call from Verity, which was
a relief. He almost managed not to think about her: time
enough to discover her state of mind when he reached home.

He went into Caroline's office at four o'clock.

'You look awful,' she told him bluntly. 'Had a rough
weekend?'

'You could say so,' he admitted.

'What's the matter?'

'One of the kids has been in a spot of bother,' he said.
'How about you? Did you enjoy wherever it was you went
to?'

'The weather was foul,' said Caroline. 'But it was pleasant,
yes.' She did not tell him any more.

'What about this evening?' he dared to suggest. 'I needn't
hurry home.'

'Sorry, Richard. I've got a date,' said Caroline.

'Oh!' For a moment he felt as if she had kicked him in the
ribs. A date! But why not? She was a free agent.

'Lucky guy,' he said lightly.

'Isn't he?' she replied, smiling.

Disappointed and depressed, Richard whiled away half an
hour in the station bar, letting one train leave without him,
postponing the inevitable moment when he must return.

It was raining when he reached Haverscot station. He'd
missed the thin young woman; she always travelled earlier.
Would he ever pluck the courage up to offer her a lift? She
might turn round and accuse him of assault. He mused on
all the dangers threatening a modern man as he walked back
to his car. There, he found one tyre was flat, and, in pouring
rain, he had to change it, discovering that it had been slashed
with a knife.

The car park, on the outskirts of the town, was not
supervised, and the station was not manned after one o'clock.

Vehicles had been stolen from it; regular travellers kept pressing for more staff or, at least, patrols, so far unsuccessfully. Richard sometimes thought of walking, but it was too far for convenience, and if he took that step, it implied one car would do for the family, and what would happen then? Verity would appropriate it, and, on one of her bad days, might smash it up. Perhaps he'd get a bike, he thought, wiping his hands on some tissues which, luckily, were in the boot.

By the time he reached home, he was soaking wet and in a far from good mood. He found Verity clean and tidy, in black velvet trousers and scarlet tunic, sober — or so it seemed. She and the boys had eaten, as he was so late, but his meal was waiting. It was mixed grill — chops and sausages, mushrooms, tomatoes and peas, with chips. She turned on the microwave to heat it through and mistimed it, but Richard rescued it before it turned into concrete. It was very nearly palatable, an accomplishment for Verity, and this indicated that she had made some effort. He ate it, chewing the hard meat, the peas like bits of shot.

He told her about the car. Justin heard him and smiled. While Verity was busy in the kitchen, he'd taken his bike out of the garage and cycled to the station. His rear lamp was feeble and his front light did not work at all, so that he was a danger to himself and others, but he made the journey safely. A train was just arriving, so he stood apart, beside the fence, waiting till the passengers had gone walking off with umbrellas up or driving away in their cars. Richard was never as early as this.

He did the deed when it was quiet, wanting to slash all the tyres, but the sound of another train approaching on the up line made him scurry off.

Never mind. He'd done it once and he would do it again if Cat went on upsetting his mother. He was to blame for everything that kept going wrong.

Verity had planned gratitude; she realised that Terry was lucky not to be in deep trouble and she meant to make amends, although the bullying boys were really responsible for what had happened. Now and then, she had rushes of emotion when she recognised Richard's patience and the security he had provided for them all, but more often she longed to spark a reaction from him. The boys' father, in the end, had hit her when she lashed out at him, and then had left her, but Richard never struck her, even when she hurt him. She wanted to provoke him to violence; then she would have reason to complain. Occasionally, she grew frightened, for what if he decided he had had enough and left her? She'd get money from him – a lot, probably – but she couldn't manage on her own. She'd discovered this, before they met. Other brief relationships had been just that, but Richard was a good man, and in her calmer moments, Verity acknowledged it to herself. So, tonight, to be on the safe side, she meant to win him round again. She'd always been able to do it, with soft words and gestures, and reconciliation was an erotic stimulus.

But not tonight. Richard turned away from her in bed.

'I'm very tired, Verity,' he said. 'It's been a bad day. Good night.'

He heard her crying softly. She didn't scream or yell, just wept. Feeling guilty, Richard drew the duvet around his ears and, exhausted, fell into merciful, healing sleep.

Early in the morning, drawing close, she woke him, thin arms twining round him. This time, sighing, Richard responded, thus securing temporary peace.

8

IT WAS STEVE who found the old man dead.

A few days after the strange man who was Tom's son called, Ivy asked him to go and check on Tom who had, she said, looked poorly that morning. She had cleaned round and prepared some lunch for him, but he had been very quiet, not even asking about Sharon and the baby, nor joking with her about Bingo which she played on Wednesday nights, her evening out while Sharon stayed at home. But Tom hadn't looked near death.

Steve and Mark arrived at The Willows at around seven o'clock. Steve had had a lot of homework that could not be avoided, and Mark had wanted to finish one of the books about The Secret Seven which he'd borrowed on his last visit; then he could exchange it for another. He'd gone all through the Famous Fives and was well into the other series now. He liked them. The children's lives were comfortable and secure; they had mothers and fathers and a dog and lived in nice houses where money did not seem to be a problem. It was the same with the William books; he enjoyed those, too, and wished he had a friend like William who thought of exciting schemes. William got into trouble, but it was by accident; he wasn't really bad.

Mark was having doubts about Terry. His stepfather had come to see Mum about him disappearing. He'd wanted to explain and to apologise, because she must have found the visit from the police upsetting.

'Mark was no help to the police. He went back to the child-minder after leaving the park,' Susan had told him, which wasn't true, and Mark felt very guilty about this part of the story.

'What about the boys who took Terry's football?' Richard had asked Mark. 'Who were they?'

'Greg Black was one,' said Mark. 'They were all older.'

'What's this about the football?' Susan had heard only that they'd been playing football, not about losing one.

Richard related what had happened, as far as he understood it, and asked for Mark's confirmation.

'There was the old lady,' he said.

'What old lady?' asked Susan.

'I don't know her name,' said Mark.

'Evidently she got the boys off the hook as far as the motorists were concerned,' said Richard. He filled in the gaps for Susan.

'You didn't mention her when the police were here,' Susan said to Mark.

'No one asked me,' Mark pointed out. 'They just wondered if I knew where Terry'd gone, and I didn't.'

'No – it's all right, Mark,' Richard reassured him. 'That was why they came to see you. We didn't know anything about the other boys and the football till Terry told us the next day. It wouldn't have made any difference to finding him sooner if we'd known. It was why he ran off,' he added, to Susan. 'He broke a window at the Blacks' house.'

'I see,' said Susan. 'Oh dear!'

'Yes – well, it's regrettable, but there we are,' said Richard. 'Terry's got off lightly this time.'

Susan was thinking of Mark.

'It was lucky the old lady was there,' she said. 'The motorists might have caused a lot of trouble, otherwise.'

'It was,' Mark agreed. 'She had a dog,' he added. 'Sinbad, that's his name. I heard her call him.'

'That's a good name for a dog,' said Richard.

'Wasn't he a sailor?' Susan said.

'Well, Rover's a common name for a dog,' said Richard. 'It's the same sort of thing.'

For some reason, mystifying to Mark, his mother and Mr Gardner — he knew, now, that this was his name — began to laugh. In the end Mr Gardner stayed for a glass of wine and some cheese biscuits, and Mark was allowed a Coca-Cola.

'Come and play with Terry any time,' Richard told Mark, as he left, and added to Susan, 'Terry and his brother Justin are my stepsons.'

Now why did he tell me that, she wondered, after he had gone. Perhaps he didn't want to own to having a vandal son. She wouldn't have liked it, either.

It was the next evening that was so terrible.

Ivy had been baking and she gave the boys some homemade biscuits to take to Tom. On the way, they ate one each. Steve unlocked the front door of The Willows and went into the sitting-room while Mark hurried upstairs to return the book and choose another, which he would put in the hall to take when he left. The books were kept in the room that must have been where Tom's son slept when he was young. It was strange that his boy's things were still there, now that Alan was so old and didn't live with Tom. Mark wasn't curious enough to wonder where Alan lived now.

He'd been diverted from The Secret Seven books by some others he'd noticed earlier, about four children who went sailing, when he heard Steve shout.

'Mark! Come down,' he called. 'Something's wrong with Tom.'

Clutching *Swallows and Amazons*, Mark came leaping down the shallow staircase. It turned back on itself, with a little landing, and he always jumped the last four steps to the bottom. It was his aim to miss five, then six, then seven steps until he could leap the whole flight.

Steve, ashen-faced, was in the hall.

'He's asleep,' he said. 'He won't wake up. I think he's dead.'

Steve had had a shock. He had entered the room, seen Tom apparently asleep in his big armchair, and had taken the opportunity to look in the old man's wallet, which was in the dresser drawer. He'd taken out five pounds and put it in his pocket, replacing the wallet and sliding the drawer shut very quietly, then turned.

'Evening, Tom. Mum's sent you these biscuits,' he'd said, in a bright voice.

Tom didn't answer. It was not unusual for him to drop off to sleep, but as a rule he could soon be roused.

Steve switched on the television and turned up the volume. There was a football match later; it might be a bit too late for Mark to stay and watch it, but he could be sent off home on his own.

After a while, something about Tom's stillness impinged on Steve's consciousness and he felt uneasy. He went over to inspect the old man, watching his chest, which was covered by a Fair Isle sweater. He wore a checked shirt beneath it, the collar points protruding. Ivy saw to his washing and was paid well for doing it.

There seemed to be no movement in Tom's chest. Steve touched his hand, which lay on his lap above the light rug tucked round his wasted, feeble legs. The hand was icy cold. Steve snatched his away.

His first instinct was to flee the house, leaving this for someone else to deal with, but he wasn't alone with the corpse: Mark was here. A faint sense of responsibility for the younger boy stirred in Steve; he mustn't panic. Mark must be impressed.

He adopted a slight swagger as Mark arrived beside him.

'I expect he is just asleep, really,' he explained to Mark. 'Only he won't wake up.'

'Maybe he's had another stroke,' Mark said, sensibly. He'd heard Ivy and Sharon talking about the possibility. Old Tom would be all right if he didn't have another, Ivy had told her daughter, and he might improve a lot, as his speech was normal and he had regained so much movement. Mark didn't know what a stroke was. Was it like a fit? Did you froth and foam? He felt a pang of sorrow because Tom wasn't well, but he was interested, too, and marched confidently past Steve into the sitting-room.

When he saw Tom, he knew. You couldn't look more dead than that if you had bullet wounds all over you, he thought, seeing the waxy pallor, the total stillness. Unlike Steve, he wasn't frightened, but he was shocked and felt very sad. Tears prickled in his eyes.

'He is dead,' he said, and he, too, touched the old man's hand, but he left his own small, warm paw upon it. In that moment, not fully acknowledged until years later, Mark's desire to be a doctor was conceived.

'We'd better get someone,' he said. 'You go. Or ring up. I'll stay with him.'

He had no urge to leave. Death was normal, but it was so sad and he thought he might cry properly quite soon. He didn't want Steve to see him.

'Perhaps we should ring the police? Dial 999?' said Steve.

'They can't help him,' Mark answered. 'Ring your mum. She'll know what to do.'

Steve, in crisis, didn't resent being given orders by the younger boy. He meekly obeyed, picking up the cordless telephone which Tom had found so useful.

His mother did not panic. Sharon was at home and could look after Kylie and Adam.

'I'll come straight down,' she said. 'You boys go into another room and shut the door.'

She rang the doctor, who arrived at Tom's house only a few minutes after she did. Tom had, he thought, suffered another, lesser stroke, followed by a heart attack. His death was not wholly unexpected and, in the end, had come in a merciful manner.

Before he and Steve's mother dealt with what must be done, he praised the boys for using common sense and suggested that they both go home.

Ivy picked up the bag of biscuits.

'He won't need these now,' she said, handing them to Steve. 'You two might like to eat some on your way home.'

The sitting-room door was closed. Old Tom was in there, with the doctor. Mark wanted to say goodbye to him. He saw the door-key on the hall chest, where Steve had left it when they entered the house. *Swallows and Amazons* was beside it. Mark picked the key up and slid it under the book, which he tucked inside his jacket. Ivy wasn't looking.

He'd come back later, maybe tomorrow, and say goodbye properly. He'd keep the book until he'd read it.

He ate a biscuit as he walked along the road with Steve. It tasted good.

Mark returned to The Willows the next evening.

As his mother knew nothing about his visits to Tom, he did not mention the old man's death at breakfast. She had waved him off to school; her shift began later in the morning.

After tea at Ivy's, he told her that his mother would be home early, and left.

He didn't like telling lies. Steve did it all the time, and Ivy always believed him; he said it saved aggravation, but Mark didn't feel right about it. It was not the same as having secrets, like his visits to Tom. Perhaps tonight's excuse to Ivy wasn't quite a lie, because he was only going to Tom's house to say goodbye. Then he would go home.

Steve, glad not to be lumbered with Mark, who could be a drag, went to see a friend, an older boy; with Tom gone, he'd need to find another source of income. He'd be lucky if he hit on anything as easy. The two boys left together, and parted at the end of the road. Steve headed off towards the town and Mark slipped away, down Wordsworth Road, to The Willows. It wasn't far; he liked walking alone through the dim streets and he took no notice of the rain. He knew his hair was getting wet, but his anorak was new and water ran off the poplin.

The house was in darkness. Mark hadn't thought of that but of course Tom, being dead, wouldn't notice. It was difficult to find the lock and insert the key; he twiddled about but eventually succeeded and, once inside, turned on the hall light. That was better.

Mark kicked his shoes off. The boys always did that when entering any house, trained to do so by Ivy who did not want them walking mud round her place or anyone else's. Then he went into the sitting-room. Tom would be there, surely? He'd be sitting in his chair, his rug over his knees, just as they had left him.

But he wasn't. The room was unnaturally still, and very tidy, the cushions plumped up, the carpet vacuumed. Ivy had cleared up after the undertaker's men. She had not missed the key which Mark had taken because it was a spare, kept for Steve's use.

She'd had another key cut for him because once Tom's key, passing between the two of them, had been mislaid and that had been very inconvenient.

Mark felt anxious. Where could Tom be? Perhaps they had taken him up to bed. Yes, that would be it; he'd seen films with dead people lying in their beds, just as if they were asleep, sometimes with flowers all round them. Mark should have brought him some. Never mind, he would tomorrow, though there were none out in the garden at home; he'd have to buy them.

He went upstairs and entered the big bedroom, but it was empty, the bed neat, the coverlet stretched taut. He looked beneath it; there were no sheets or pillow slips and the blankets were all folded up. Ivy had taken the linen home to wash.

Tears sprang to Mark's eyes. Now he really understood that Tom had gone and wouldn't be returning.

Standing there, he had a little cry, scrubbing his eyes with his none-too-clean hands. Then, reluctant to leave, he wandered slowly through the house, settling at last in the sitting-room, where he drew the curtains. It was nice and warm; no one had turned the heating off. He switched on the television to watch the quiz show he'd often seen with Tom, who wouldn't mind, Mark knew. For a while he was able to pretend that the old man was there, that nothing had changed, but when the programme ended he felt a deep, heavy ache inside his chest because there was no Tom to talk to about what had happened on the screen and suggest the next occupation for the evening.

He would have to go home.

Leaving the house, he remembered the curtains. He'd better draw them back, leave them as they'd been when he arrived.

He'd come again. He knew he would.

The next afternoon, after school, Mark went to the shop in Haverscot where they cut keys for you while you waited. He'd been there with his mother when she got him one for their house, and a spare to hide in a secret place outside in case anyone got locked out. Only he knew about the spot — and Mum, of course. He wondered what it would cost. He'd taken along two pounds and hoped it would be enough. He didn't get the flowers. As Tom had gone, there'd be no point, and he couldn't have afforded both them and the key. Flowers were expensive.

He was late reaching Ivy's house, but she didn't fuss.

'I had to see Mrs Williams about my maths,' he said, the lie tripping as easily off his tongue as if it had been Steve speaking.

'No trouble, I hope,' said Ivy, helping him to baked potato and mince, which was spiced with chilli. He liked Ivy's mince; she often gave it to them with various accompaniments such as pasta, beans, or even bread.

'Oh no,' said Mark smoothly. 'Just something I didn't understand.'

He'd put the borrowed key back on its hook and that was lucky, because Steve decided that they'd go to The Willows that night. He'd assumed Ivy had replaced it after clearing up the house, and she, if she thought about it, supposed that Steve had done so.

'I'd like to have a look around,' said Steve. 'Might pick up a few useful bits. Tom won't want nothing now. Besides, we can watch telly.'

Mark knew that Tom wouldn't object to them visiting the house and watching television, but the old man wouldn't want them poking round and prying. He knew what Steve had in mind: stealing. Well, he needn't join in that bit.

They went in together and Steve drew the curtains before putting on the lights.

'Don't want folk getting curious, do we?' he said, but the house, separated from the road by a short drive with trees and shrubs at either side, was not overlooked, and it was in such a quiet road that their presence was unlikely to attract attention.

It was clever of Steve to think of that, thought Mark, who had drawn them for his own security the day before, not from fear of being seen.

Steve lit the fire and Mark settled down beside it, watching television, while Steve went prowling round the house. After some time he came running down the stairs, excited.

'Look what I found, Mark,' he cried.

He was carrying a bundle of old newspaper cuttings, yellow and fading, in a plastic folder.

'These were in that room with Tom's son's stuff in it,' he said. 'In the desk. They tell all about him – that guy Alan. He's in prison. He must have escaped. That's why Tom wasn't very pleased to see him.'

Mark stared. He didn't understand.

'Go on. Read it for yourself,' said Steve, regretting that he had so poor an audience for this revelation. He pulled out a sheet of newsprint and shoved it at Mark, who took it and began to read.

It was a tabloid, more than eight years old, and it reported how Alan Morton, aged thirty-five, had been sentenced for the murder of his wife, June, after he suspected her of having an affair with a local farmer. Alan had shot her with a four-ten shotgun.

'He was on the run,' said Steve, excited. 'I wonder where he's hiding out?'

9

MARIGOLD DARWIN WAS not aware that a Haverscot boy had been briefly missing. She did not listen to local radio, but she watched nature programmes and discussions on television, and, on wet afternoons, of which there had been many lately, occasional schools broadcasts, which were often interesting.

Because her furniture and most of her possessions were in store, she could not occupy herself with the art work she had developed as a hobby; on a weekend course she had learned découpage, led into it by a fascination with marquetry in furniture. Decorating plain boxes and tins with detailed cut-out designs from paper, then varnishing them until the ornamentation looked solid, was a possible way of emulating this intricate work. It had become an absorbing occupation, one to which she could flee when no other activity attracted her. Meanwhile, since renting the bungalow, she had learned of a road development scheme which would affect the area. A planned bypass implied later inclusion in a motorway extension and there were meetings to discuss the consequences. Marigold had attended one and concluded that working for the protest lobby might exercise her administrative skills productively; she need not be impartial now. But organising her future life must wait until she found a house, and her failure to do so was depressing. Not that she acknowledged such a state: Marigold's temperament was equable; she knew no highs or lows.

Walking in the park with Sinbad, after the incident of the boys, she would see youngsters kicking balls about and thought she recognised the two smaller lads on one occasion. She couldn't be sure; children of a similar size looked so alike unless they had red hair or some other distinguishing feature.

She did not need a social life, but it was not wise to pass too much time in isolation. Marigold had no close friends; there had been acquaintances, occasional shared activities with colleagues, but intimacy with anyone was outside her experience. Even her parents, though never unkind and often generous, had been remote and undemonstrative. She had no childhood memories of revealed affection.

As the days shortened and Christmas approached, so did the end of her lease. She was due to surrender the bungalow early in the new year and if she had not yet found a house, she would have to rent something else, or move into a hotel, which would be difficult with Sinbad. She was on the books of every agent in Radbury, six miles away, and bigger than Haverscot, and daily she received details of available houses within a radius of twenty-five miles, but she wanted to be in Haverscot.

Mr Phipps was in despair because she was so difficult to please, and then, through a solicitor friend, he heard that The Willows was coming on the market very soon, an executors' sale. Mr Morton, who had lived there for many years, had died, and his heir was a niece who lived in Canada. She wanted the house and its contents sold; speedy possession could be arranged. The solicitor, who was one of the executors, told Brian Phipps that he could take his potential buyer to see the house at once.

Mr Phipps telephoned Miss Darwin. Time and money would be saved if she could be persuaded to buy without the house going on the market, which was too uncertain at the moment, and at this time of year, to warrant the risk of an auction.

Miss Darwin showed some interest when he said that the house was in Wordsworth Road, not far from Merrifields. It had a similar outlook over the now water-logged meadows leading to the river.

'Those houses are all built on a ridge, as you know,' he reminded her. 'The water never gets beyond their gardens.'

She did know. As a child, she had had a canoe, not to be used when the river was up, but once she had taken it out on the still floodwater, and several times, when it froze, she had skated on the flooded fields. It was so safe. If the ice broke, you went through only on to grass. She hadn't skated very well, but she had enjoyed it, and so had many other inhabitants of Haverscot, young and old.

She remembered The Willows. When she was a child, two sisters had lived there, retired teachers. They were keen gardeners; each year they held a party — tea and sandwiches amid beds of lupins and delphiniums, and there were climbing roses. She had gone there with her mother and had hidden from the crowd of guests beneath the concealing tresses of a large willow on the lawn. So close to the river, such trees thrived; there were three of them, she thought; had they survived? If not, one could grow more, very quickly; they were not like oaks, taking generations to reach any size.

Mr Phipps drew up outside the bungalow. His car, provided by the firm, was a Volvo Estate, large enough to cope with the For Sale signs which he sometimes had to carry and erect. It also had room for the three small Phipps children and their mother, who in her spare time made curtains and chaircovers at home. She meant to have her own interior decorating business as soon as all three of them were at school.

He told Miss Darwin about the sudden death of Mr Morton and the niece in Canada.

'He died in the house,' he added. It was best to tell her

now, so that if she had any objections on that score, they were declared at once. She was sure to discover, later, what had happened. Most people seemed to die in hospital; it was tidier. Mr Phipps, who had moved to Radbury from Essex six years ago, knew that there was a son who had inherited nothing. He was some sort of bad hat, Mr Phipps had gathered, but he did not know any more than that. There was no need to mention him.

'Lucky man,' was Miss Darwin's observation. 'Had he been ill long?'

'No. I think it was quite sudden,' Mr Phipps replied.

'Lucky again,' said Miss Darwin.

She had almost made up her mind to buy the house before she even entered it. It had been built in the 1920s, of brick, plastered over and painted cream. The proportions were pleasing to the eye, and it looked solid.

'It's got a damp course. Houses built after 1924 had to have them,' Mr Phipps told her. 'So it's not like your really old places, which can have problems.' He was trying to sell such a millstone at the moment, and had shown it to her, glossing over the snag of crumbling beams.

Mr Phipps turned in at The Willows' gate. The drive was short, but the house was set far enough back from the road to be secluded. He wondered if she would think it too well protected from the passing gaze. Crime prevention theories suggested that a screen of trees and shrubs invited burglars, but all the houses in Wordsworth Road were similarly shrouded. If she bought it, once everything was signed, he might suggest installing an alarm: one lady on her own would thus feel safer. But she didn't look the nervous sort; indeed, he found her formidable.

The house was warm, its heating still turned on, to protect the pipes. As they entered, Marigold had the odd feeling that invisible arms reached out to welcome her. At any moment a smiling woman in a pinafore would greet them and offer coffee. She gave herself a shake; fanciful notions of that kind were not permitted.

Mr Phipps showed her round. There were four bedrooms. One was small and had been used as a study; there were a desk and filing cabinets, shelves of reference books.

'Mr Morton was recording local history. He left all his books and papers relating to that to Radbury Museum,' Mr Phipps told her. 'They're collecting them next week.'

He led Marigold into the largest bedroom, which over-looked the meadows at the back of the house; it had the same view as Merrifields but was closer to the church. Marigold looked out and saw several swans swimming on the grey flood water. Her heart, seldom disturbed, beat a little faster.

She knew she was going to make an offer for the house, but she let Mr Phipps describe its merits and display his skills. However, she did not want to risk losing it to another customer by dissembling. He had indicated a price; she proposed another as soon as he returned her to the bungalow and Sinbad's welcome.

'I'll have to contact the executors,' he said. 'They'll need to consult the beneficiary.'

'Of course.' Marigold would pay the asking price, if necessary. 'You know how I'm placed, Mr Phipps. I should like to move in as soon as it can be arranged.' Surely the beneficiary would view with favour the swift settling of the estate?

She knew she should have the place surveyed. The house might have many flaws – dry rot, a faulty roof – all sorts of problems which an inspection would detect, but she would risk it. Let the worst be discovered when she had painters in to decorate. Mr Morton – or perhaps it was his late wife's taste – had done the house throughout in neutral tones, and Marigold thought that it would be improved by using more definite colours.

Mr Phipps was wondering whether to press one of his wife's business cards into her hand but decided that could wait until contracts were exchanged; however, perhaps he should refer, now, to the black sheep son.

'There was a son,' he said. 'Estranged, I don't know why. Hence, he didn't inherit.'

'I see,' said Marigold. 'That room upstairs was his. The posters. All those books.'

'Exactly. Everything is to be sold,' said Mr Phipps. 'I shall be arranging it with the executors.' There were good local auctioneers, some of whom dealt with whole libraries; unfortunately there wasn't enough to merit a marquee on the lawn; besides, that was too water-logged at present. Luckily Miss Darwin had been content to stand on the terrace outside the sitting-room and look down at the shaggy lawn and the three willow trees while he pointed out the large garden shed.

By that evening, her offer had been accepted. The niece was perfectly content when told the buyer's money was waiting and was not dependent on a survey. She had last seen her uncle some years before Alan's arrest, when she had been the London correspondent of a Canadian newspaper. Her mother, Tom's sister, had married a Canadian soldier during the war and they had always kept in touch. Despite Alan's disastrous history, the bequest had amazed her. She had flown over for the funeral, made the necessary legal arrangements, and flown back again within a week.

In matter-of-fact tones, Marigold told Sinbad that soon he would have a splendid garden in which to prance about and bury his bones. She thought of the roses she would like to grow; she had been to La Roseraie de L'Hay, outside Paris, two summers ago and had been dazzled by the collection. What was in The Willows' garden now, she wondered: all she had been able to discern from the terrace were bedraggled brambly shoots twined round wooden arches, and some withered flowers in a border. She would have to discover what lay buried under the cold earth, whether there were daffodils and snowdrops.

Suddenly there was a future. With that decided, Marigold poured herself a celebratory glass of sherry and as she sipped it, she experienced an unfamiliar sensation, a sort of internal glow.

Though she could not name it, it was happiness.

She had another drink, and then a third. As she prepared her meal, she began to sing.

'I'm just a little tipsy, Sinbad,' she declared, aloud. 'Well, never mind. Who cares?' and, pouring herself a refill, she danced a little jig, while Sinbad, stubby tail wagging to and fro approvingly, looked on.

Steve had asked his stepmother what would happen to The Willows.

'I'm sure I don't know,' Ivy had replied. 'I don't know what happened to his son. Tom never mentioned him, but they'd kept all that stuff of his. His mother wouldn't part with it, and after she died, Tom hadn't the heart.' She'd thought it such a pity all those books lay there unused, when they could be sold to bring in money for the local playgroup. 'Maybe they fell out,' she said.

'Are you sure he didn't do the old man in?' Steve asked.

'Of course he didn't. What a thing to say,' said Ivy.

'Well, he did kill his wife, didn't he?' said Steve.

But Ivy didn't know that. She had lived in Haverscot only since she married Joe.

'Where do you get these ideas?' she exclaimed. 'I think the son's dead. He must be, or he'd have been at the funeral.'

Steve didn't show her the newspaper cuttings.

'Why didn't you?' Mark asked. He found it scary. An escaped murderer had come to old Tom's house, and he, Mark, had met him.

'She'd have ticked me off for poking around,' Steve said.

He'd put the papers away in his room. Mark thought that was stealing, although with Tom dead, they couldn't be of use to anyone, not like the books and other things. Where was the murderer now? No one seemed to be looking for him. He must have been recaptured.

'If we see him again, we'd better tell the police,' he said.

'We'll do that,' Steve agreed. 'There might be a reward.'

Mark knew the son hadn't killed old Tom. There was no blood, and Tom had looked so calm.

He went on going to The Willows. It was easy. He told
Ivy that his mother would be home early, and simply left her
place when it suited him.

He did not visit The Willows every night, only when he
needed a new book. Then he would stay and watch television
for a while. Mark could pretend Tom was there. His hat and
raincoat hung in the cloakroom, and there were still biscuits
and drinking chocolate in the kitchen. Sometimes Mark
helped himself, always washing up and putting things away.

Ivy had said that the house might be sold. When that was
to happen, a board went up outside, and Mark never saw one
at The Willows. Perhaps it would stay empty. If the son was
still on the run, he wouldn't move in because the police
would be sure to catch him; Mark was certain he was back
behind bars, if he had escaped, but Steve might have been
wrong about that. People were let out, even if they'd done
dreadful things; he'd heard Sharon and Ivy talking about it.

'Free to do it again,' he'd heard Ivy say, about a man who'd
done something awful to a woman. When Mark asked what
had happened, they'd been vague.

Steve sometimes did get things wrong. Mark had gone off
him, rather; apart from taking money from Tom, he now
went round with a group of boys among whom was Greg
Black. Ivy thought he was at the youth club, but he never
went there. Mark, however, copied Steve's methods and
sometimes told Ivy he was going to see Terry Gardner and
would go home from there. Such an explanation was
acceptable to Ivy; Susan would approve of that friendship
and it was so close: no journey through the middle of town,
where the rough element hung out, was involved.

Soon Sharon would be going back to work and Ivy would
look after Adam. She had more time, now that she was no
longer needed at The Willows.

Ivy paid no attention to Steve's remarks about Tom
Morton's son. He'd been reading too many horror books or
watching alarming videos. She knew he spent time with
Greg Black and a boy called Bruce, but she could not stand

over him all the time, watching where he went and what he did; she and Joe had taught him right from wrong; what more could they do? He'd grow out of his interest in morbid matters. While he was at Tom's, he'd been safe from such influences, but those days were past. She missed the old man. The solicitor had sent her a cheque in settlement of her wages, with a bonus, and that was good; she bought new duvet covers for Steve and Kylie, and Sharon gave her a perm. Sharon had been apprenticed to a hairdresser before she had the baby.

With her new hair-do, Ivy felt ready for the next few rounds life had to offer her. She was growing used to widowhood: it was more respectable, she had found, than being divorced, as she was before; people were surprised and sorry when they heard about it. There was plenty to do each day; she had children to collect from school most days, and there was Mark; other children were left with her occasionally. Tom had paid well for what she did for him but she could find other cleaning jobs if things got tight. At the moment, they were managing.

Sharon's baby's father sometimes came around; he was unemployed and living with another girl who was pregnant by him. Sharon was still fond of him; Ivy feared she might be fond enough to get herself pregnant again. It was all very well for him; he was sure of a welcome from either girl.

'It's no example for Kylie or Steve,' said Ivy, after one such visit.

'He's got every right. He's the father,' Sharon had replied.

'But he doesn't have any of the responsibility, or the expense,' said Ivy.

Jason had brought a soft cuddly rabbit for Adam, but no money. There was nothing to stop him going round giving girls babies all over the country and living off each woman in turn. He was a nice enough young chap who wouldn't hurt a fly, Ivy thought, but what use would he be in any trouble? And what chance had Sharon, now, of finding a man who would be, one like Joe? Though it was true she already had Sharon when they met: that thought consoled Ivy in her bleaker moments, but she had been married to Sharon's father.

She hoped Jason would stay with his new girlfriend and not want to come and live with them.

WHEN ALAN MORTON went to The Willows, he had been on leave from prison.

He was supposed to be spending the weekend at an approved hostel, but he had never meant to stick to that plan. From the time when he had first been taken on shopping trips to town as a preliminary to his release on licence, he had been preparing for his freedom.

He should never have been given life. It was a case of manslaughter due to provocation, for June had been unfaithful to him. She had been having an affair with Phil Wickens, her childhood sweetheart, whom Alan had cut out when he had decided to make a play for June — largely because he wanted to get the better of Phil, who was a farmer. It hadn't been too difficult; he'd simply swept her off her feet, pursuing her with gifts of flowers and boxes of chocolates, and persuading her to have dinner with him at various local restaurants during a long summer when Phil was working all hours bringing in the harvest.

They had met at a young farmers' dance. Alan, at the time, was the manager of a hardware store in the small market town of Billerton, and part of its business was concerned with spares for farm machinery, paint and other such goods. The event was held in the Town Hall; Phil Wickens, not a customer of Alan's store, was a guest, and June was his partner.

95

Alan had already met her across the counter of the building society where he had his mortgage; he had bought a house on the outskirts of the town and had been living there with a woman who had left him a few weeks before the dance. They had not been together long; none of Alan's relationships lasted, and he had one divorce behind him.

He had been invited to the dance to partner the visiting sister of a customer; they'd had dinner first, at The King's Head in the town square. The customer, a market gardener, had been a generous host but Alan had bought drinks all round and liqueurs later; he had an expansive manner and a booming voice, impossible to overlook. The sister did not take to him and, at the dance, shed him for a quiet man she found standing by the bar. Alan, adrift, asked various women whom he knew by sight to dance with him and was sometimes accepted; then he noticed June, who recognised him and smiled pleasantly. Alan swept her on to the floor as he, later, swept her off her feet by his pursuit.

How meek she'd been, how sweet, smiling and attractive in her understated way, with soft blonde hair and large blue eyes. Even at that first meeting he had wanted to make her cringe and appeal to him for mercy, as he had his wife. He had had that wish, but she had left him, shown her bruises to a doctor and had obtained a divorce as soon as they had been apart for long enough.

At least she hadn't wanted any money.

June left him to dance with Phil Wickens, and Alan realised that they were well acquainted; after the dance, glass in hand, he tagged on to their conversation and, persistent, bought them drinks. Phil was civil; he had not known who Alan was until June introduced them, and he did not want his company, but it was a jolly, social evening and he would not stoop to rudeness. Alan managed to have another dance with June. He was quiet and polite. He knew how to act when he wanted something, and sometimes he regretted the rage that surged within him when the meekness that had at first attracted him began to disgust him.

He waylaid June outside the building society when she was going home, and several times in her lunch hour, inviting her to eat with him in Billerton's new wine bar. In the end his sheer persistence prevailed.

He took it slowly as the summer – hot and dry that year – wore on. June, disappointed because she saw so little of Phil while he was busy at the farm, fell in with Alan's plans to meet, and during that time he never overstepped the mark. He was physically a short, stocky man and she did not feel intimidated, though she sometimes wished he would be less aggressive with waiters and car park attendants. But he spent money on her and he let her know that he admired her. Eventually, one warm July night, he succeeded in seducing her, not forcing himself upon her violently but leading her along with practised technique and alcohol. They were in his house, after an evening at an inn by the river. To his amazement, he discovered that she was a virgin – almost an extinct species, he believed. To June, this step, once taken, was momentous and it heralded her brief infatuation with Alan.

Meanwhile Phil, who had always meant to marry her when his future at the farm was secure – his father ran it now – did not realise what was happening. Her engagement to Alan took him by surprise.

June herself was being whirled along on a tide of flattery and sexual excitement, but she thought being married to Alan would be wonderful. He was attentive and seemed devoted to her; he owned his small, pleasant house and he had a good job, with plans, he disclosed, for running his own business in the future, though of what variety she did not learn.

On her honeymoon, she discovered what her predecessor had also learned from harsh experience: Alan was a bully whose gentleness had been a fake. He liked to hurt people, and he was insanely jealous. He took to dropping in to the building society at odd hours and if he saw her smiling at a

male customer he would attack her, verbally at first and then
with blows, as soon as both of them were in the house – she
never thought of it as home.

Pride stopped her from telling anyone, at first. Several of
her friends had warned against the marriage, telling her that
she didn't know Alan well enough, pointing out that Phil
adored her.

'He's never said so,' June had protested. 'He never has
time for us to meet.'

June's mother and father were disappointed in the match.
They and Phil's parents had always hoped the pair would
marry. For all of them, the wedding had been an occasion for
wearing a brave face, but June was radiant. Later, though,
things changed, and June's mother told Phil's mother that
she thought the marriage was a disaster. June was looking
pale and exhausted, and if the couple went to functions in
the town – as they did – Alan never left her side and would
glower if she spoke to any other man.

Phil's parents gave a party in the New Year. They asked
the Mortons, Alan and June, and at the party Alan saw June
talking to Phil. In fact they were discussing the prospects for
the new lambs, now beginning to arrive, and Phil had to
leave the party to attend to some of them. June went to fetch
her coat and followed him, and there, in the lambing shed,
she confessed her plight.

Alan saw them leave the house together. He did not kill her
then, but he had noticed where the guns were kept, locked in a
cupboard in the farm office. He'd have to find the cartridges; it
shouldn't be too hard. He went back two days later, when the
house was empty, the men out on the land and Phil's mother at
a meeting of the women's branch of the British Legion. Alan
had known that the house would not be locked; as people were
in and out all day, farmers often left their houses open. Even the
collie dog was away in the fields, and it was easy for him to
break into the gun cupboard and steal a shotgun. After a
search, he found a box of cartridges in a desk drawer. Then he
went home and sat waiting for June.

Brooding in the quiet house, dusk falling outside, Alan thought about her faithlessness, convincing himself that he had been betrayed, and excited by the thought of vengeance.

Sitting in the darkness, in his big armchair, its back towards the door, he heard her key in the lock and saw the lights come on. She hung her coat up in the hall, then went straight into the kitchen; that would be right, she'd got his meal to cook and would have bought food in her lunch hour or on the way home.

Alan, in stockinged feet, moved into the kitchen behind her. He called her name, stringing it together with shouted obscenities – 'Bitch, harlot,' and many more. She turned, terrified, and he shot her in the chest. As she sank to her knees, blood gurgling in her throat, he moved towards her and put the second shot into her head.

There was a lot of blood. He hadn't expected there to be so much. He wrapped her up in bin liners, tying the head and feet, and the waist. It was a good thing he hadn't done it in the living-room; it would have messed the carpet up, and left evidence. As it was, if she were found, he meant suspicion to fall on Phil, her jilted lover.

Late at night, he put her body in his car and drove off into the countryside, where he dropped her in a ditch a few miles from the Wickenses' farm. Early the next morning, snow fell for several hours and it did not thaw for weeks; the snow plough was out on the roads and this caused heaps of piled-up snow to linger at the roadsides long after the main fall had gone.

Alan told the building society that June had not been feeling well and had gone away for a holiday. He said nothing to her parents, carrying on his normal routine but now forced to cater for himself and deal with his own washing.

The Wickenses reported the theft of the shotgun and a box of ammunition. No one had seen Alan enter or leave the farm; he had left his car in the lane outside and had slipped in quietly on foot. If anyone had come along, he had a story planned about wondering if they wanted to take advantage of a bulk order of wood preservative that he could offer at a bargain rate; when you were the manager of a business, there were always lines that you could push, and you could be absent from the premises without anyone's permission.

The kitchen took some time to clean, but as no one suspected trouble, he did it at his leisure, washing the walls and floor with soapy water more than once.

After a time June's parents wondered why they had not heard from her. She was out, he told them, every time they telephoned, but after two weeks they rang the building society, hoping to catch her there, and learned that she was, allegedly, away. The society was not happy about this long sudden absence, and June's father went to see Alan.

He was ready. He looked downcast and said that they had had a row. June had packed a bag and flounced out of the house, saying she was leaving him.

'I thought she'd run off with that Phil Wickens,' Alan said, managing to look distraught rather than aggrieved. 'I knew they were having an affair. That was why we quarrelled.'

June's father could not believe that part of the story, but if June had walked out of her marriage, why had she not contacted her parents? Where was she living? Had she any money?

'Her clothes?' he asked.

They'd gone, said Alan. He had packed them up and taken them to a charity shop, not in Billerton but across the county. He'd thrown away her toilet things. There had been time to see to everything, even to concealing the gun and ammunition. He might need them again.

Her father had insisted on calling the police. At that time, he suspected suicide, though if that was June's intention, why had she packed up all her clothes? Why hadn't she come to them, her parents? Was she ashamed of having failed in her hasty marriage?

She was found when a man walking with his dog along the high road where the snow had melted heard excited barking, and saw his pet scuffling in the ditch where Alan had dumped her body.

Alan acted the part of the grieving widower to perfection. The cold had preserved June's corpse and she was instantly recognisable when he was asked to identify her; her head wound had not obscured her features. There was no doubt that it was murder, and he was the prime suspect, but there was no immediate evidence to link him with the crime, and the gun could not be found.

Alan had, at first, planned to leave it with the body, so that Phil Wickens would be linked with the killing. Then he changed his mind. He had travelled south and buried it beneath the ground in the garden shed at his parents' home in Haverscot, more than a hundred miles from Billerton. Alan interred it there at night, when his parents were in bed; he did not enter the house at all, so that they had no knowledge of his visit.

Because her body was so well preserved, the forensic pathologist found on it evidence of serious bruising. Some contusions had occurred shortly before death; others, yellowing, were healing. There were signs of a rib cracked not so long ago. Colleagues at the building society declared that, since her marriage, June had become jumpy — nervy, said one girl — and another had noticed bruises on her neck which could not be hidden by her uniform shirt. No one had liked to ask about them.

Phil Wickens was given a good grilling. He admitted that he had been devastated when June married Alan, particularly after such a short acquaintance, but if she had seemed happy he would have made the best of it and been pleased for her; however, instead of blooming, she had begun to wither. That was how he expressed it to the Detective Inspector interviewing him. Alan, at any social gathering, prevented her from speaking to other men, coming up and almost forcibly removing her, he said, and less than a week before she disappeared, she had told him that Alan had forbidden her to speak to him.

'For your own sake, you'd better not come near me, even at work. Go to another desk,' she'd warned, and he had said it was ridiculous, they'd known each other all their lives.

'It'll get easier in time,' she'd said. 'He'll learn to trust me.'

In the lambing shed, Phil had urged her to leave Alan. The marriage was a mistake. She could admit that and divorce him. But June had said she must keep trying.

'I still love him,' she had declared.

'Do you?' Phil had been incredulous.

'Yes,' she had answered. 'This is all my fault, you see, Phil. I don't come up to his expectations.'

'You come up to mine. More than,' Phil had gritted out. 'I'd look after you.'

The inspector had seen it all before.

'"Love is blind",' he quoted. 'Its victims don't want to see what's obvious to other people. She was making excuses for him, and for herself. She'd made a big investment in him, hadn't she, throwing you over for him?'

'We'd got no official understanding,' Phil said, reddening. 'I didn't move fast enough, I suppose. We'd plenty of time, I thought.' He was still only twenty-three. June had been not quite twenty-one when she was killed.

At this stage in the investigation, the police had discovered that Alan had been married before and that he had twice been charged with rape. Both times he had been acquitted, alleging that the women had consented. Each had known him slightly; each had been cross-examined in such a way as to imply that they were morally lax. By law, his identity had been concealed. Had she known about these incidents, June might have found Alan less appealing. His first wife, now happily remarried and with a baby son, was traced; she described him as a sadist.

'He liked the rough stuff, seemingly,' said Detective Inspector Rutherford.

This time, after the wedding, Alan had insured June's life. Rutherford thought June had been doomed from the day she made her vows. The police were sure that Alan was their man but evidence was scarce. The Crown Prosecution Service and, later, the jury, must be certain of his guilt.

They had the bruises. These could be explained away by excuses that she had fallen, had been clumsy, even though work colleagues would testify to her altered manner and the marks that they had noticed.

Alan's house was examined minutely. His clothes were taken away for testing. Without the weapon, proof that the gun stolen from the Wickenses had been used could not be found, and in any case ballistic proof from shotguns was notoriously difficult to establish.

It was the string with which he had tied the bundle containing June's dead body that secured Alan's conviction. One of his assistants had seen him take such a ball from stock a few days before June disappeared. He'd watched to see if Alan paid for it, but he hadn't. Typical, the assistant said, and who would get the blame when stocks didn't balance up? The ball of twine was found in a cupboard in Alan's kitchen; it had been cut with scissors, and the frayed end matched the twine tying up the bin bags. In a drawer in the kitchen were the scissors used, and a wisp, extremely small, had attached itself to the hinge between the blades. Taken alone, this was not conclusive; the fragments could have come from an identical ball, but added to the evidence, admitted by the accused, of discord between the pair, and the fact that Alan had no alibi for the evening of the day when June was last seen, it was enough.

He could not plead manslaughter. Theft of the gun proved intent to kill. The insurance policy was further confirmation.

Alan had been found guilty, but though the mandatory sentence for murder is life imprisonment, most killers are let out on licence after nine or ten years. His mother had visited him at first, making the journey alone when, after a while,

Tom stopped going. Then she, too, had ended her lonely pilgrimages, but she never got rid of his possessions. To the end of her life, she would go into his room and try to recapture the image of the little boy whom she had loved. What had gone wrong? Why had his life turned out so badly? It was only after the murder trial that she and Tom learned the nature of his earlier brushes with the courts and the fact that he had been accused of rape. Dorothy recalled a puppy he had had; it would not obey him, running off, not coming when he called it. Tom had found it with its head bashed in. Alan had denied killing the animal, but his mother had never been convinced that he was innocent for there had been other episodes: butterflies pulled to bits while still alive, toads cut in half. She knew he had a cruel streak, a tendency to violence.

After her death, Tom had not had the will to get rid of Alan's things, though he wanted to turn his back on him, just as if he, too, had died.

But Alan wasn't dead. He had killed one woman and assaulted others — for he had: Tom knew he had carried out the rapes, and there was his cruel treatment of his first wife. One day he would be released from prison and what would happen then? He might kill again. After he came to The Willows, in the presence of Steve and Mark, Tom's physical decline was rapid.

Alan had come to collect the gun. He had plans to use it after his imminent release. With it, he could rob a bank. With money, he could leave the country. Why stay where he had a criminal record? He'd start a business overseas: he'd prosper, making up for all the time he'd lost.

His scheme backfired, however. He had intended to enter the house armed with the gun, use it to terrify the sick old man, and hide it under the floorboards in his room or in the attic, ready for collection later. However, he'd reckoned without the flood water. Years ago, Tom, to defeat the annual winter sogginess of the garden, had had a flagged path laid leading to the shed. That was not a problem, but inside the shed, where the gun, well greased and wrapped in plastic sheeting, together with the box of cartridges, securely sealed in several protective layers, was buried at least three feet deep, there was now a solid concrete path between the benches.

Digging them out would be a major task. He'd need to break the concrete up. The job would have to wait until a later visit. This time, once the boys had gone, he'd had to be content with frightening the feeble old man enough to get some money from him.

He'd had a night out with the cash, but there hadn't been a lot: less than three hundred pounds, some of it in a drawer in the sitting-room, the rest upstairs, an emergency fund, the old man had said, in a bedroom cupboard.

'If I tell you where it is, will you go?' old Tom had gasped.

'Sure,' said Alan. 'But I'll be back.'

As he left the house, Tom's words had echoed in his head.

'You're responsible for your own actions. Everyone is. When they let you out, remember that,' he said.

'I'm out now,' Alan had jeered. He'd said that he was on official leave.

Tom hadn't been certain that this was the truth. Alan might have absconded from some rehabilitation expedition, and if so, the police would soon be round.

'Don't go hurting other people,' Tom had implored. 'Not again.' There'd been so many: those wretched girls, and his mother.

He was too tired, too shocked by Alan's appearance and his conduct to do more than make this small appeal. Tom suspected nothing about the concealed gun; Alan knew he hadn't found it, or he would have mentioned it. He'd get it on his next leave. By then the water would have receded, or if it hadn't, he would dig the gun out as soon as his release came through; that wasn't too far off now. If necessary, he'd tie the old man up to stop him interfering.

Tom's sudden death surprised Alan; he had realised that the old man was very weak but had thought him merely convalescent. Now he was angry. What right had the old fool to die before he, Alan, had finished with him, wreaked revenge? Forgotten were the rescues of the past, the debts paid, the job found; instead, scoldings and punishments were remembered. Alan did not want to think about his mother's tears, her attempts to mediate between them, to minimise or excuse his transgressions. Finally, even she had deserted him, thanks, Alan convinced himself, to the old man's influence.

There would be compensations, though: he'd get all the money, and the house, in nice time for his release. He was the only heir. Alan made no attempt to attend the funeral, although he would almost certainly have been permitted to attend. Nowadays, his face was unfamiliar in the area, and it was better left that way. He didn't even send a wreath.

It was some weeks before he learned that he had not been left a penny in the old man's will.

11

MARK HADN'T THOUGHT much about Christmas yet. Until last year, despite evidence to the contrary, he had managed to convince himself that Father Christmas came down the narrow chimney of their small house, past the gas fire, and plodded silently upstairs to fill his stocking.

For the last three years he'd stayed awake for hours, suspicious about the contents of small parcels his mother had brought home and not unwrapped, taking them mysteriously to her room. He'd thought of searching for them, but it seemed that they were private: he had secrets; she might have some too, and he respected that.

This year, Ivy and Sharon were conspiring. Kylie had written a letter asking for roller blades for herself and a toy garage for baby Adam; she was sure he'd soon be old enough to play with one.

'Have you written your letter, Mark?' Kylie asked him, and when he said no, she pressed him to do it.

Blushing, Mark scribbled something on a pad, folded it and sent it up Ivy's chimney, where a coal fire burned in the grate.

'What did you ask for?' Sharon asked. She liked Mark, who was intrigued by Adam and would hang over him, making him smile and even crooning to him, promising to read to him when he was older.

'If I tell, I won't get it,' Mark replied. His wish was impossible to grant; he wanted a family.

He was often at Ivy's with the younger ones, now. He knew that since Tom's death, Steve had been with other boys hanging around cars, looking for any that might be unlocked so that they could steal things. This made Mark uneasy. He didn't think Steve would really steal – but then, he'd thieved from Tom; Mark knew that. Perhaps he'd got a taste for it. He once came home with a camera which he said he'd bought for Ivy; it was going cheap, he'd explained, since everyone knew he couldn't have afforded it at the proper price. He said it was her Christmas present, early. Mark knew that he had stolen it.

Mark didn't want to be a big boy yet. It was enough to be considered old enough to be at home alone. He had no wish to go out in a gang with Steve and his friends.

'Send the kid home,' Bruce had said to Steve, who had once taken Mark along, largely at Ivy's insistence; she thought his place was with the boys, not with her and the girls. Adam didn't count yet. But Mark had thankfully returned and played cards with Kylie till it was nearly time for his mother to return.

She would be on duty over Christmas. The hotel ran special breaks to attract people who wanted to escape from one thing or another: their families, the chores, even solitude. Festive programmes were arranged, and activities for children. Mark was going with her; he could join in some of the junior treats. He'd spent occasional weekend nights there recently, since her promotion; the head chef had a son much his age and they got on well. Mark liked these excursions; sometimes he sat quietly in the office where his mother worked. She knew he wouldn't interrupt her; he would read quietly or play patience, which he'd learned from Tom. Later, his mother would take some leave and spend time with him. They'd swim, maybe go to the cinema, or skate. They might visit a castle or a museum. Susan always devoted herself to enjoying these days, sharing his pleasure and trying to increase it. He was never wild or naughty, and he was enthusiastic about everything they did together. He was doing well at school and was good company. Much of the credit must be due to Ivy, Susan thought; she'd been so lucky to find her and Joe, whose sudden death was tragic. Susan had thought his influence so good for Mark; he was a solid, decent man who had run the booking office at the station.

His death must have hit Steve hard; now he had no natural parent. In the past, Susan had sometimes taken Steve on trips with her and Mark, but the age gap was becoming more pronounced with Steve in his teens. Perhaps some other boy might be invited, though she had reservations about Terry as a suitable friend, after his disappearance. What had really happened then?

Susan was too busy with the present to think much about the future, apart from doing all she could for Mark. A good education was essential, and the comprehensive school in Haverscot had such an excellent reputation that it was a reason for staying in the area. She had turned down the offer of a job in London; she didn't want to go back there. If she were to take promotion elsewhere, she would have to be sure that Mark's schooling would not receive a setback.

She did not want to marry. In the hotel, she saw couples of all kinds: some were happy, maybe celebrating; others were enjoying one-night stands, or not enjoying them. Many guests were there on business, and if they whiled away some hours with casual partners, it was not her concern. Her work was stimulating and had become more demanding; she often had to sort out problems with the staff, and she wanted to keep her own life simple; she had had enough emotion in it to last a lifetime.

Things would be different when Mark grew up and left home, but she would face that when it happened; meanwhile, there was Christmas. When the hotel festivities were over, perhaps she would take Kylie and Ivy to the pantomime; it would do Ivy good. Sharon was tied down with Adam.

Where would Sharon be without her mother's support? She was little more than a schoolgirl, herself. Susan, much older when she was pregnant, trained and with a good job, had found things difficult enough. It was lucky that Ivy was so fond of babies and small children; Sharon would have more, unless Ivy could coax her in the direction of some effective contraception, and even then, things could go wrong.

Stepfathers could be assets: Joe had been to Sharon and clearly Richard Gardner was a pleasant sort of man; it hadn't stopped the boy Terry from freaking out, however. At least he'd reappeared with no damage to himself. There were no easy answers, Susan knew.

Richard was dreading Christmas, that period of enforced confinement amid one's family. He could spend time in his workshop – but that would be seen as selfish, shutting himself away, not joining in the daily round with three people who were, he now admitted, not really his family at all: no blood tie linked them. He didn't even like them very much.

The confession, albeit made only to himself, was shocking; didn't he love them? You could love people even when you didn't like them: love was visceral, but it could be killed. His love for Verity had died, but not his sense of obligation to take care of her, since she was so bad at doing this for herself.

The two boys were increasingly distancing themselves from him. He recognised in Justin real hostility, though there was tolerance, still, from Terry. What should they do about a holiday next year? Christmas was the time for planning one, and in the past he had taken them and Verity to various seaside places in France, from Brittany to Bordeaux; they had rented gîtes in isolation and in the grounds of châteaux. He had dug sandcastles, played beach cricket, financed wind-surfing and even sampled it himself. While this went on, Verity painted, substituting clouds and darkness for what were sunny landscapes. Often she destroyed her work when it was done, lapsing into hysteria and self-denigration. Then he would feel pity for her, would put his arms around her, smooth her tousled mane of hair, and try to calm her.

Later, he would find the wine bottles. Even now he did not always connect cause and effect. She still swallowed pills, those calming capsules which her own doctor was now prescribing.

Perhaps next summer they could find an activity holiday, where the boys could spend the day occupied with sports or pastimes – go-karting, he thought, or maybe sailing: yes, that would be an idea; he could learn to sail, too, if he found somewhere with adult and junior courses, so that they would be separated. Verity would not want to sail; perhaps there would be a painters' group – not a class: she did not consider that she needed teaching – where she could meet like-minded folk, near the sailing school. Trying to find such a location would occupy him. He could make enquiries, scan advertisements, send for brochures.

Following his disappearance, Terry had been subdued for about a week. Richard had given him a real scolding after their visit to the police station, where Terry had been edgy, cracking unfunny jokes about locking up terrorists in the cells. The station sergeant had not found this amusing and had described the offence of wasting police time. Terry had been very lucky not to be charged with committing criminal damage, he pointed out.

Richard understood that some of Terry's behaviour had been due to nerves, but a little remorse would not have been out of place, and he said so.

'They couldn't do anything to me at my age,' Terry had scoffed.

'They could. You could receive an official caution and that would give you a record, so that next time you got into trouble it would count against you,' Richard said. Then he spoke more gently. 'There's not going to be a next time, Terry. I know those boys were teasing you and Mark, and

maybe if you'd punched them, it would have been understandable, though foolish, but to go breaking windows and
giving your mother all that worry is another thing. Aren't
you at all sorry for upsetting her?'

Terry was, though he could not bring himself to say so.

'I couldn't punch them. They were much bigger than me
and Mark, and there were three of them,' was the sulky
response.

As the Christmas break began, Richard thought about
this conversation. Had Terry learned his lesson? Would he
again react in an extreme way at the next attempt to tease
him? The other boy, Mark, was a nice little lad. His company
might be good for Terry. Richard wondered what Mark was
doing over Christmas, with his mother working in a hotel.
She was unlikely to have much time off; presumably the
child-minder took charge of him.

Anna, Richard's daughter, was at sea, aboard her cruise
ship, where there would be gala festivities for the passengers.
He hoped that she was happy; she seemed content enough,
on their rare meetings. Absent from her, though unwillingly,
he felt that he had let her down, however in the lottery of
life, she had not done badly. Her mother's second marriage
had turned out well, but another man had brought his
daughter up, successfully, while Richard was failing with a
different man's two sons.

There'd been no Christmas card from Anna. Probably
she'd posted one in Adelaide or Sydney and it would arrive
eventually. He had sent hers, in plenty of time, to the
shipping line's address for the week before Christmas. In it,
he told her that he had paid a cheque into her bank account
so that she could buy her own present; this was what he did
each year, and for her birthday. It was impersonal but
practical; she always wrote to tell him how she would spend
the money.

Where was young Mark's father? The boy hadn't mentioned him. Would he see his son during the holiday? Or was
he dead?

Verity, who had abandoned her meditation classes after Terry's escapade, had made mince pies. She was having one of her domestic effort spells, which was a good thing as long as it endured, keeping her busy in the kitchen. Richard had bought the turkey and a Christmas pudding, assisted by Terry who had offered to accompany him. This unusual helpfulness was, perhaps, a sign of contrition. They'd stocked up well, remembering fruit juice and Coca-Cola, and bumper packs of crisps as well as all the normal weekly things, enough to withstand a siege. It was a pity Verity's parents had refused to come for Christmas; last year, they'd promised to be there but two days beforehand they had telephoned, pleading incipient influenza. The previous year, during their visit, Verity had wept all through the Christmas lunch, eaten at three o'clock instead of the planned half-past one. By that time, her father had filled himself with whisky and her mother was attempting, in the kitchen, to retrieve disaster, for the sprouts had burned and the potatoes were not done. The turkey was cooked to shreds and dry. Verity had pronounced herself useless and burst into tears while Richard and his mother-in-law feigned jollity for the sake of the two boys. That was when Richard had finally understood the extent of his predicament. He could not walk away from Verity; his task and duty were to try to help her overcome her temperament and control it, instead of letting it rule her and wreck the lives of those surrounding her.

On Christmas afternoon she'd gone to bed, and her father had fallen asleep on the sofa.

'I used to wonder if it was in their genes, this drink thing,' Verity's mother had said, as she and Richard washed up. The boys were in their playroom, busy with their presents. 'Mind you, I do it, too, at times,' she confessed. 'If you can't beat them, join them. But it doesn't make Hugh wild, like Vera.' Her mother would not play the game of changing names. 'He just gets silly,' she declared. 'Her other husband couldn't cope, and I won't blame you if you can't, either.'

Richard liked his mother-in-law, a thin, scrawny-looking

woman with hair dyed to match her daughter's — or was the mimicry the other way? She had a sense of humour and was good with the two boys, asking them silly riddles and teaching them card tricks.

'She can't help it,' Richard had remarked.

'Yes, she can — we all have choices,' said Verity's mother.

Richard was too loyal to answer, but he knew that Verity believed all hurt was aimed at her: the boys were naughty simply to upset her, and Richard came home late simply in order that the meal should spoil. How had this all begun?

He'd hoped Verity's brisk, no-nonsense mother would be at Merrifields this year; her presence would be helpful. But it was not to be. Parcels had arrived from the couple; others had been sent. The conventions were observed.

Richard could escape to church. There were several services, carols one evening, midnight Mass, and matins on Christmas Day. He could take his pick or go to all of them: no one could legitimately complain.

He wondered what Caroline would be doing. She was spending Christmas with her parents, who lived in Cambridge, where her father had been a history don and her mother a geologist. He imagined that she would have an agreeable and intellectually stimulating time, perhaps visiting her brother, another don, and his family who lived just outside the city in a large house much swept, she said, by icy winds blowing straight from Siberia. Richard wished that he was with her. He imagined going there as her acknowledged lover. But amid those academic types, he would seem so dull, so slow-witted, he reflected.

A shriek from the kitchen brought him back to the present, and he hauled himself out of the deep, comfortable chair in his study where he had been successfully hiding while indulging in his melancholy thoughts. He hurried out. This time, the crisis was not major. Verity had burnt one lot of pies because she had gone upstairs to her studio, to do more work on a painting of a Christmas scene she had suddenly felt inspired to create: dark holly, berries dripping blood; a father, mother, infant and donkey all apparently half-buried under snow; Richard saw it later. Taking the blackened pies from the oven, she had also burnt her hand — not badly, but it was red and painful, and the pies were smoking.

Richard held her wounded fingers under running cold water. When she was able to stand unsupported, he threw away the pies and told her not to worry. Anticipating this disaster, he had bought two dozen at the baker's in the town the day before. They were in the freezer, with some other emergency stores.

Setting off for midnight Mass, he once again reflected on how lucky it was that his employment brought in a generous salary; Verity and her family needed every penny.

Verity was asleep when he came silently to bed. She was breathing heavily, and he caught the smell of alcohol. It seemed she had found ways to pay for all the bottles she consumed.

She was still asleep next morning when he went quietly downstairs to make some tea. The house was quiet, the day not yet begun, the boys not yet awake. He supposed Verity had carried out her role of filling the boys' stockings; she had bought presents for them. Probably she had filched money from the amount he gave her for them to buy drink; he couldn't deprive her of a certain amount of cash, though he had sought every means to limit or define what she spent.

He made the tea and drank a cup in peace, then poured one for her and took it to her.

She was just waking up.

'Oh, my head,' she groaned. How she suffered with her daily headache! She was a martyr to pain, she claimed, and Richard did not understand her frustrations; all she wanted was to paint, and, instead, she had to cook and clean. Conveniently, she forgot the cleaning women Richard had gladly paid for, who had come and gone because Verity was always finding fault with what they did, and even with their mere presence in the house.

Now she peered at him as he crossed the room with a cup and saucer in one hand, and a large, ungainly parcel in the other. He put the tea down on the table beside her and drew a small parcel from his pocket.

'Happy Christmas, dear,' he said brightly, bending down to kiss her, aiming at her forehead.

She turned her head away and he met a faceful of scratchy, tangled hair. However, she unwrapped the parcels, discovering in one a large azalea, and in the other a bottle of Chanel No. 5.

'Oh, Richard, you know I prefer Diorissima,' she said, though this was quite untrue. Last year Chanel had been what she desired. He could not win this contest, so he abandoned it.

'Don't hurry to get up,' was all he said, and left the room, taking the scent with him.

She would not be adopting her housewife role today, so he must do it. He didn't mind – he even liked it – and it was easier to know from the outset that this was his task rather than have to take it over in mid-operation. He'd plan the bird for half-past one and maybe they would eat it on time this year.

Then he remembered. He'd invited someone to share their turkey.

He must have been out of his mind! How could he have lost his wits to that extent! Too much Christmas spirit in the church porch: that was the trouble.

Some of his acquaintances from the choral society were among the congregation. He had sat next to a couple whom he knew slightly from this contact, and on his other side had been an elderly woman who seemed vaguely familiar. As they sang the hymns she revealed a lovely clear contralto voice, and he remembered that she had sat near him at evensong the night Terry disappeared. She was a forbidding-looking woman, with a felt hat pulled down over heavy greying brows, and wisps of iron-grey hair just showing round its edge. Last night she had not taken Communion, and nor had he; they'd exchanged a calm, unsmiling glance as the others in their row of chairs filed out, and each had looked about the building as the long procession of communicants wove back and forth to the altar.

After the service, he stood back to let her precede him down the path. There were little groups of people chatting as they made their way towards their houses or to their cars.

Richard exchanged greetings with those people whom he knew, and who were near him as he left the church, but they were few, and he soon caught up with the woman in the hat, as he now thought of her. She had a very efficient torch, which she shone to light her way down the flagged path.

'Yours is better than mine,' he said, indicating the weak beam coming from his own pocket torch.

'I expect you need a new battery,' she said. Her speaking voice was mellow, too.

'You're right,' he said.

'I like to carry this at night,' said Marigold Darwin. Her own torch was a considerable instrument; useful as a weapon, Richard thought. Was that what she meant? He remembered a shocking case a year or two ago, when an elderly woman had been attacked and raped walking home from church in some country town. Where was it? Was no one safe?

'Have you far to go?' he asked.

'To Shelley Drive,' she said.

'That's some distance. Have you a car?'

'I'm on foot,' she answered.

'Would you allow me to escort you?' Richard offered. 'Let me introduce myself. My name is Richard Gardner and I live at Merrifields. It's just along the road.'

'I know Merrifields,' said Miss Darwin. Her voice altered, deepening and growing stronger. 'I lived there as a child.'

'No! Did you?' Richard asked. By now they had fallen into step together.

'Yes,' said Marigold. 'I was so sad when we moved away.' She had never told that to another soul.

'It's a lovely house,' he said. 'And it has a lovely garden.'

They talked about it as they walked, the strong, icy wind cutting into them as they left the shelter of the yews around the churchyard. Marigold explained how she had rented her present bungalow while she was house-hunting, and about her acquisition of The Willows.

'You'll be a neighbour, then,' said Richard.

'Yes.' By now Marigold had learned that he was married with two stepsons, and an older daughter by an earlier marriage, and Richard had heard more about Marigold Darwin than people she had known for years. 'I suppose your family is quite excited about Christmas,' she said.

'I suppose so,' he replied. Then he remembered that she was new to Haverscot, and alone. 'What about you? Have you friends visiting you?'

'No,' she said, adding, 'Not this year.'

He had noticed that she referred to the family as singular; she was a pedant and he liked her for it.

'Why don't you join us for lunch?' he invited. 'You must come and see your old home, in any case. Why not tomorrow? No formality,' he added. 'Just us. Please do. I won't let you refuse.'

Marigold thought of the chicken she had bought. Sinbad was to share it with her. It would keep till Boxing Day; he could have his usual Chappie.

'I'd like that very much,' she said. 'Thank you.'

By this time they had reached her gate.

'One o'clock,' he said. 'See you then. Merry Christmas.'

'Merry Christmas,' she replied, as they parted, Richard making a gesture to remove his hat. A polite man, she thought, and sad.

Now why had she thought that?

She went into the house regretting her swift acceptance of his invitation. In daylight, she would have refused the meal but asked to see the house and garden another time. In daylight, she would not have told him of her grief at leaving Merrifields. In darkness, not looking at the other's face, one's defence was down.

Richard, walking back with long, swift strides, was also regretting his impulsiveness. What had made him do it?

It was the night, he thought; it was the night.

12

IN THE MORNING, Marigold resolved to excuse herself from keeping the engagement. She could plead a diplomatic cold. She woke early and made coffee and toast, listening to carols on the radio. Then she put on a recording of *The Messiah* and was so uplifted by it, by the blue sky outside and the sudden sunshine, that she felt more confident. Why not go round to Merrifields? She longed to see the house again, to walk round the garden and discover how much of it remained familiar. She would soon be the Gardners' neighbour and she must not be aloof, though she did not expect to be liked. She knew that people found her hideous, but as she grew older she had developed from being a gauche girl into a competent, impersonal administrator; efficiency and intellect could carry one through a professional life; procedures and protocol dictated action. By the end of her time at the Ministry, she had earned respect, if not affection, and early timidity had long been overcome.

She did not intend to be a complete recluse in Haverscot. Richard Gardner's invitation was kind, and at Christmas, when turkey and plum pudding were the fare, one extra meant nothing — another potato peeled, a few more sprouts prepared. In a family, it was simple. Marigold had been asked to families before; she was godmother to some colleagues' children, not because the parents prized her but because they knew she was reliable, and they pitied her without a family of her own; they were doing her a kindness. She had never yet forgotten a godchild's birthday or neglected one at Christmas; that was all the parents wanted from her, and the comforting knowledge that if anything were to happen to them – some fatal accident – she'd be there, a background figure of stability. Marigold had attended the weddings of her two eldest godchildren and learned, sadly, of one's later divorce; the second seemed to be happy, living in Notting Hill, a journalist married to a video editor. They never asked Marigold to visit them and she had stopped sending her goddaughter presents after providing a dinner service when she married. But she still sent cards, though none came back.

She had received some Christmas cards; they came from a few former colleagues, and one was from a widow met on holiday last year, when Marigold had been to the opera at Verona. Next year, the widow would exclude her from her list; this was what happened after such chance meetings. Marigold knew she had been included only because everyone in their group was exchanging addresses. A row of robins, sacred scenes and wintry landscapes was spaced out across the bright wood of the mantelpiece in her bungalow. Marigold looked round the room: it was so tasteless, with the tiled hearth, the lozenge-patterned carpet, the beige dralon-covered chairs. Merrifields must be a better place to spend the day than Fairways.

She went to matins: it would pass the time. After that, she took Sinbad for a walk.

When Richard rang to put her off, intending to use the excuse of his wife's indisposition, there was no answer. He tried again half an hour later: still no reply.

He gave up. Perhaps the presence of a guest would prompt Verity to produce some better manners; she used to try in front of other people, but he hadn't tested her for more than a year.

*

Marigold drew a deep breath as she walked through the gates of Merrifields. Well trimmed bushes bordered the drive, which curled round in front of the house. Today, the air was crisp with frost; if this continued, the flooded fields would freeze and there might be skating. To the left, trees bordered the property, many more than she remembered, or perhaps they had simply grown larger: no, some were young. They formed a barrier between Merrifields and the house next door. A boy and girl had lived there; they had taunted her across the wall and would not let her climb into their tree house when their mother invited her to tea. They'd hauled the rope-ladder up and left her below. She hadn't made a fuss, nor cried. She'd sniffed and found a tree at the end of their garden, which she'd climbed, and had remained in its branches until dusk, when the grown-ups had come searching for her. By then she was cold and stiff, but she was the victor, for the brother and sister had been punished for neglecting her. She'd forgotten all about it till this moment.

What had become of those two? She would never know.

The house, built of brick, bow windows in front, a garage round the back, was covered now with climbing plants: roses, she observed, approaching, and was that a wistaria? Berries on a cotoneaster glowed against one wall. She didn't remember such a covering; hadn't her father said that plants harboured insects, beetles and flies, which would invade the building if encouraged?

The front door was startlingly unaltered: solid oak, buttressed with iron studs and a heavy knocker, the letter slit narrow, no doubt causing problems for the postman now but in those days he used to ring. He came on Christmas Day, she recalled. Hadn't the milkman come, too? She couldn't be so sure of that.

Marigold had left Sinbad at home. He was a well-trained dog and would be content, after his walk, for several hours. She rang the bell.

There was some delay before it was answered and she almost turned away, wondering if she had, after all, misunderstood the invitation, reluctant to press it a second time. She had just stepped back, preparing for retreat, when the door opened and there stood Richard, looking harassed, wisps of greying brownish hair standing up round his head. He wore a shiny plastic apron decorated with a Snoopy motif, and a swift, artificial smile.

'Hallo! You came,' he cried, effusively. 'Welcome. Do come in.'

Marigold knew at once that he had repented the arrangement, but it was too late now for either of them to withdraw. She must exert herself to be a perfect, unassuming, helpful guest.

'So nice of you,' she murmured. 'Happy Christmas once again.'

'Indeed, indeed,' cried Richard, falsely merry.

He took her camel coat and laid it over a chair which stood against the wall. 'Perhaps I should hang it up?' he asked himself, aloud.

'No, no. It'll be splendid there,' she assured him. She was wearing a hat, this time one made of flecked tweed, not unlike his own, and now she removed it, laying it and a pair of brown leather gloves on top of her coat. Then, with short, stubby fingers, she briskly plumped up her wavy iron-grey hair.

Entering, she had set down a basket full of packages covered in Christmas wrappings. Now she picked it up.

'I brought you these,' she said, tentatively. 'Nothing exciting. So last-minute.'

'You shouldn't have bothered.' Richard had not thought of finding a present for her. There might have been a box of chocolates among their own presents; perhaps he could contrive to find one. Then he looked at what her basket held. 'Do I espy a bottle?' he cried, extracting a parcel shaped unmistakably. It might contain some non-alcoholic concoction – elderflower wine, for instance – he warned himself.

But it didn't. It was a bottle of a very good Chardonnay. How fortunate, because as he had stopped buying wine or spirits, he could not have produced anything with the meal, unless he tapped Verity's secret supplies, and he would not ask her where she had them hidden. He knew there was some sherry; he'd put a bottle in his study, in case of seasonal callers such as carol singers.

He took her into the drawing-room.

'I expect you feel a little strange,' he said. 'Coming back like this after so many years.'

'I don't know how I feel,' she said. 'Not yet.'

She looked around her. Near the window was a large fir tree, more than six feet tall, decorated with painted glass baubles, mainly red and silver. There was tinsel on it, and tiny starlike lights.

'How lovely,' she exclaimed. 'Our tree was always in the hall.'

It had seemed immense to her, reaching up to heaven, though it must have been about the same height as this one.

'Sherry?' he offered, adding, 'Verity will soon be down. She's changing.' Dressing, he meant. She'd not yet surfaced for the day.

'Thank you.' Marigold accepted the sherry, in a pretty glass – Georgian, she suspected, of some value. She had been thinking about the rooms the house contained in her day: drawing-room, dining-room, study, and a room the maids used as a sitting-room. There had been two maids, living in: amazing! One had been the cook. Upstairs, there had been six bedrooms and her father's dressing-room, and a single bathroom. Leading off the kitchen, in a sort of extra scullery, had been a bath, covered with a board by day, for the maids, who shared an attic bedroom. 'How many bathrooms have you got?' she asked abruptly.

Richard laughed.

'Three,' he said. 'One en suite, as they say. Four bedrooms on the first floor and two in the attic. The boys have those; they're both a good size.'

When they moved in, frequent guests had been expected, at least by Richard, but none came except, occasionally, his daughter Anna, and, still less often, Verity's parents.

'So many!' marvelled Marigold. If there were two attic rooms, why had Doris and Mabel, the housemaid, not had one each? She would never learn the answer.

'I expect you'd like to look around,' he said.

With Verity still upstairs, this was not the moment, and Marigold demurred.

'Another time,' she said, but he showed her the ground floor.

Here, the kitchen had been entirely re-done when Richard bought the house. Its design was modern but its wood fitments retained the older character of the house. In the centre was a vast table.

'It's got a heat-resistant top,' said Richard. 'I had it specially made. We eat in here most of the time.'

In Marigold's youth, Doris, the cook, had operated at a large scrubbed deal table: not so very different. Marigold had been allowed to put pastry leaves on pies and cut out circles for jam tarts.

Today, the dining-room table – mahogany, a good reproduction, Marigold decided – was laid for five people. Red candles rose from swags of holly and there were scarlet paper napkins set beside each place. Silver gleamed. Heavy cut-glass tumblers sparkled.

'How lovely it looks,' said Marigold.

'My wife's artistic,' Richard loyally declared, but it was he who had done all this. Verity, the night before, had painted large black streaks across her Christmas scene and turned it to the wall after Terry had said it looked too sad for Christmas. 'She paints,' Richard added.

He led his guest on, showing her his study.

'It was my father's study, too,' said Marigold. 'It's still dark.'

Even on this sunny day, the room was dim. Marigold remembered that in the summer, her father always had the light on when he was in the room. She entered it sometimes, to read to him. He wanted to be certain of her progress.

'Verity uses one of the bedrooms as her studio,' Richard said. 'It's much lighter. I've got a workshop in the garden.'

Marigold had noticed the large wooden hut as she walked up the drive.

'What do you make?' she asked.

'I do a bit of carving,' he replied, opening the playroom door.

The two boys were in there, one intent before a television screen, obsessed with his computer game. The other one was reading a book with a fearsome cover; he had a headset on, pumping rhythm into his head as he read. Neither glanced up. This room, Marigold recalled, had been the maids' sitting-room.

'Forgive them,' Richard said, leading her out again. 'They're deaf to the rest of the world. You'll meet them properly when we eat. Now, if you'll excuse me, I must just dish up the bird.'

Marigold did not offer to assist; the wife, Verity, would be doing that. She sat down in the drawing-room and closed her eyes, trying to refurnish it as it had been more than fifty years ago. The curtains – green now – had been a sort of coffee colour and the chairs and sofa had worn coats of flowered cretonne – yes, that was what it had been called. Wasn't it really printed linen? Blue, it had been, with large pink sprawling blooms like paeonies all over it, quite pleasant. There had been several casual tables here and there; ornaments had stood on some, and photographs on others. The room, in winter, had been extremely chilly unless there was a roaring fire, though there had been central heating, with a coke boiler in the cellar. Today, there was a log fire which looked much the same as she remembered, but the room was very warm; a more efficient heating system must have been installed when the house was renovated. She wondered which of the bedrooms had been turned into bathrooms; how luxurious it sounded.

She was still lost in the past when she heard a sound and opened her eyes. A thin woman had entered the room: a tragedy queen, she thought at once, observing Verity's haunted expression. She was dressed in peasant style, with a flowing skirt of some eastern printed cotton, and a long black sweater which clung to her meagre breasts and bony elbows. Dark hair, glinting with copper shades, tumbled abundantly about her shoulders, but it did not hide her scrawny neck and it emphasised her somewhat raddled – yes, that was the word – face. Her dark eyes were large and staring, slightly unfocused. She did not speak, but gazed down at Marigold, uncomprehending.

Marigold stood, levering herself out of her chair with powerful arms. A stocky figure in a burgundy-red woollen dress, she was a surprise to Verity, who expected to see an old, frail woman in her eighties, not this resolute-looking person who could clearly play two rounds of golf, straight off.

'Marigold Darwin,' said the visitor. 'Your husband most kindly invited me.' She extended a small, square hand.

Verity advanced and touched the outstretched fingers. Her own were icy, and felt fragile. Marigold did not clasp them.

Silence fell.

'I'm shortly moving to The Willows, just along the road,' said Marigold, at last. 'It's a delightful house – just as yours is, though much smaller of course. I lived here as a child. Did your husband mention that?' Why should he, she reflected, as soon as she had said the words.

'How nice,' said Verity vaguely, then, brightening, 'Ah – I see you've got some sherry. Where did Richard put it?'

'It's over there.' Marigold gestured towards the bottle which was on a table by the window.

There was no spare glass. Verity made an impatient sound, became more alert and hurried from the room, soon returning with one, which she filled, tossed the contents down her throat, filled again and swallowed half, topped it up once more and then sat down on the sofa, opposite the hearth. She spread herself across it, skirt fanning round lean thighs.

Marigold thought, not for the first time, that love was very strange. What had attracted this ill-assorted pair to one another? Or were opposites, like magnets, inexorably drawn together? Before another silence overwhelmed them both, she spoke again.

'A lovely day,' she said, in her low, rich voice.

'Is it?' asked Verity. 'I hadn't noticed.'

'Very cold.' Marigold persevered. 'Maybe it will snow.' It wouldn't; the sky was too clear. 'I expect your boys would enjoy that.'

'I daresay.' Verity had finished her sherry. She refilled her glass and, as an afterthought, waved the bottle enquiringly in Marigold's direction.

Marigold shook her head.

'No, thank you,' she said.

With the sherry, Verity was relaxing; her tense expression softened but her focus was now even less acute. She's had something already, Marigold decided, but was it drink? She felt a flicker of concern; that nice man, Richard, had a problem here.

At this point in her speculation, he appeared, smiling warmly and announcing that the meal was ready.

'Where are the boys?' asked Verity. Her voice was harsh, in contrast to her drowsy appearance.

'Waiting eagerly for nourishment,' said Richard. 'They've been helping me dish up.'

Hunger and greed had driven Justin and his brother to the kitchen, where they had hopped about in some excitement, not too sophisticated to be unmoved by the sight of a large turkey, roasted to a perfect golden brown. One had stirred the bread sauce; the other had drained the sprouts. There were carrots, too; some people – Richard among them – did not care for the traditional sprouts.

On the sideboard in the dining-room stood the bottle of wine which Marigold had brought. She wondered whether to ascribe this to his tact and then remembered that when they visited this room on their tour, she had noticed only tumblers at the place settings. Now, everyone had a wine glass.

'This is Justin and this is Terry,' Richard introduced, as the two boys waited by their chairs, Richard having sharply told them to stand up when they had already seated themselves, Terry brandishing his knife and fork around in anticipation. He replaced them, crookedly, as an old woman entered with his mother, and he knew immediately that she was the woman from the park. He'd seen her there a few times since that episode, always in her hat and with the dog. She recognised him, too: he saw it in her face but, to his amazement, she gave no sign that they had met before.

'Happy Christmas, Justin. Happy Christmas, Terry,' she said, her stern features creasing into what was, for her, a smile. She identified the smaller boy at once, but did his parents know about the incident in the park? He had done nothing wrong; the bigger boys were the miscreants. In her experience, it was best not to complicate matters so she did not mention their earlier encounter.

Somehow, Richard kept the talk going while they ate. There was quite a lot to do, what with serving everyone and passing round the vegetables and all the trimmings.

'Miss Darwin lived here years ago,' Richard told the boys, in between carving and seeing that Justin was handing round the gravy and bread sauce. Verity sat silent, and idle.

'Did you?' Terry looked at her directly.

'Yes. Until I was about your age. Then we moved away,' she said.

Terry was intrigued by her hair. It was so thick and curly, like a wig. Perhaps it was a wig.

'Did you have a tree house?' he tried out. 'Did people then?'

'I didn't, but the children next door did. I envied them,' said Marigold.

'Cat made us one,' said Terry.

'Cat?'

'The boys call me that,' said Richard. 'Because my name's

Richard – Dick Whittington, you know.'

'I see,' said Marigold. Somehow she did not think the name was intended as a compliment.

'Willy would have been better,' said Terry and began laughing wildly.

'That isn't funny, Terry,' said Richard. 'Mind your manners and pass Miss Darwin the cranberry sauce.'

Marigold had, after a second, understood the boy's remark. Why were the two of them hostile to their stepfather? Why was Verity so obviously miserable? Despite his apparent geniality, was Richard really a domestic tyrant? It was possible. Malevolence could lurk behind benign facades, despots could beam kindly upon children, the mild man next door could turn out to be a murderer or a rapist.

Verity contributed little to the conversation. Richard had given each boy what he preferred to drink – Coca-Cola – after offering them some wine.

'You're not too young to have a taste,' he told them, but they both declined.

Marigold noticed that he only half-filled Verity's glass while being generous to her and to himself. Verity drank hers rapidly, and when he did not top it up, she asked for more.

'In a minute,' he replied, and rising, filled all their tumblers with water.

She drinks, Marigold thought: she really does, and if I hadn't brought that bottle, it would have been a soft drink meal for all of them, though Richard might have been embarrassed by not offering wine to a guest.

'It's a very nice wine,' he told Marigold, topping up her glass and his and just covering the base of Verity's. 'Thank you. Miss Darwin brought it,' he told the company.

'And I'd like some more of it,' said Verity distinctly. 'Richard doesn't like me drinking,' she told Marigold.

'I got it at the wine merchant's in the town,' said Marigold, smoothly ignoring this observation. 'Where it is, there used to be a draper and haberdasher. The money went in small screw-top containers on an aerial pulley to a cashier, who put the change in it and sent it back by overhead wire. It used to fascinate me as a child.' She thought of purchases made from the Miss Morrises, who kept the shop: knicker elastic, lisle stockings, linen buttons for the dreadful liberty bodices.

'It must seem very different,' Richard said kindly.

They talked about the changes she had noticed while the boys ate without comment and Verity toyed with her food, abandoning the meat and barely eating any vegetables. Then Marigold, rather daringly, enquired if the boys liked football.

'Don't ask,' said Justin. 'Terry got himself into a fair old row in the park while playing, not so long ago.'

Marigold could see by Justin's expression that he had said this to cause trouble.

'We don't want to discuss rows on Christmas Day, do we, Justin?' Marigold replied.

She was surprised to see Terry, his mouth full of roast potato, gaze amazed at her and then almost grin. Was that gratitude because she had blocked his brother's attempt to reveal the incident, presumably not mentioned to their parents? She sent another diversionary remark on its way.

'Do you enjoy swimming?' she asked.

Yes, they did. They wanted Cat to instal a pool.

'Do you skate?' she asked, and learned that they had roller blades and skateboards, and went occasionally to the ice-rink.

She told them about the floods freezing in her youth and how she had skated in the fields. Richard fed her questions. The boys concentrated on their food and, when the pudding, which had flamed effectively while it was carried in, was being eaten, she questioned Verity about her painting, wanting to know which medium she preferred.

Verity ground out responses about oils and gouache. She spoke with such reluctance that Marigold wondered if it was her own presence which had provoked this sour mood. Had there been a fearful quarrel before she arrived? She began to fear this was the answer. Richard would regret his friendly act.

After lunch, the parcels she had brought were opened. There were sweets for the boys – nothing exciting, but she had some toffees left from those she had bought as an answer to Trick or Treat children over Hallowe'en, and had bagged them up in polythene and tied them with ribbon. There was a box of chocolates for Richard and Verity. It was her own Christmas indulgence; otherwise she would not have had a present. There was nobody to give her one, now that she had left the office and was not part of the ritual gift exchange between colleagues.

Then Richard astonished her by handing her a parcel. When she opened it, she found inside an expensive bottle of Chanel No. 5.

She did not see the look of pure hate which Verity directed at him.

'Oh, how lovely!' she exclaimed. 'Oh, thank you. I shall enjoy using this.' Her opinion of Verity did a turnaround; how generous of her to let this bottle be thus redirected.

'I think most women like that fragrance,' said Richard lightly.

'I do, certainly,' said Marigold, who, when younger, had sometimes sprayed herself with samples. Why shouldn't she enjoy it now, just a tiny dab to add glamour for herself alone?

He took her around the garden after that, and while they were out there, the boys appeared and began kicking Terry's football about. They were showing off, making a lot of noise, heading the ball to one another and toeing it as far as each was able.

Marigold admired their tree house.

'They don't use it much these days,' said Richard.

'How old are they?' asked Marigold, and he told her.

'Terry gave us an awful fright a few weeks ago,' he said. 'That's why Justin was needling him at lunch. He and another boy, Mark Conway — he's about a year younger than Terry — went to the park one Sunday and got into some scrap with a few older boys. It seems they took Terry's ball and kicked it into the road. It caused damage to some cars and the boys might have been in trouble with the police, but luckily there was a witness who had seen what happened. Terry flew into a rage afterwards and didn't come home. He was missing for hours. We had to call the police.'

'Oh dear,' said Marigold. She was horrified. 'What a fright you must have had.'

'Yes,' said Richard. He did not tell her about the broken window.

Briefly, Marigold considered confessing that she was the mystery witness, but if she did so, what explanation could she give for not admitting to recognising Terry earlier? She and the boy had already connived at a deception. It had better stay that way.

While they were outside, Verity was in the drawing-room, finishing the sherry. She stood at the window gazing out over the garden where the two boys romped, co-operatively for the moment, and where her husband, in his waxed jacket, was walking towards the end of the garden with that weird old woman in her camel coat and speckled hat. They were talking animatedly.

He never talked like that to her. There he was, turning to look down at Marigold, and laughing.

Richard, remembering Marigold's fine singing voice in church, had mentioned the choir of which he was a member and had asked her if she would like to join. They were giving a concert in the town hall the following Thursday. She should try to come.

Marigold promised to do her best, though her house move was taking place the following day.

'I'm so lucky that they're letting me move before completion,' she said. 'Everything's signed, of course, and the solicitor will hold the money. I'd be very glad to join the choir if I'm found suitable.'

Watching them, Verity felt her anger rising. It was ridiculous, she knew, to feel jealous of a woman old enough to be her mother and who looked like a suet pudding, but she was.

13

CHRISTMAS PASSED RELENTLESSLY in prison. In the new year, Alan Morton would be released on licence. To aid the process, he had been obliged to express remorse for killing June, when all he really felt was rage at his conviction. It wasn't fair for him to be punished when she was the offender, deceiving him with Phil. Alan had convinced himself that she had meant to leave him. While serving his sentence, he had been a model prisoner, determined to avoid any action which might hinder his return to life outside, but he had made plans for the future. First came vengeance; next, total freedom, which implied escaping from the country.

While his mother was alive, he had bled her with emotional blackmail, painting hopeless prospects for the time when he got out unless he had some money put away. She had opened a building society account for him and had regularly paid in as much as she could put aside from her housekeeping allowance and the savings she had made when, after he grew up, she had returned to work. Before her marriage, she had been a secretary; she had revived her skills and found a post with a firm making furniture, and there she had stayed until his arrest. After that, she lost all heart, and soon, in any case, she reached retirement age.

Each time she came to see him, she told him what the sum

now totalled, reminding him that he could adopt a new name easily; there was no need for any legal action. He could start again, wipe the slate clean and make amends in the years ahead. No one need find out about his past.

Her visits bored him, but he placated her with the assurances she sought and said he was following an educational programme, aiming at GCSEs in subjects which had eluded him at school. She chose to believe him, but it wasn't true, though he did make an effort to learn Spanish. He was going to live in Spain after his release – Spain, or South America. When he had retrieved the gun, he would kill Phil Wickens who had seduced his wife and so caused Alan's present plight; then he would rob a bank and with the proceeds go abroad. He had planned the bank raid with another man who would be freed soon after Alan; they'd met at the open prison where the last part of their sentences were being served.

It would have been so easy if the old man hadn't died. A visit, a quick trip to the garden after dark, then bingo. After that, if the old man turned his toes up, not to worry: Alan would be on his way and somehow his inheritance would follow him. He hadn't worked out yet how that could be arranged but there would be an answer. As he would not have been responsible for Tom's death, there would be no ban on his inheriting the estate, and though he might have left the country illegally, he would not be a wanted man because he would not be connected with the bank robbery. He and Mick would leave no traces.

Before his last leave expired, he had been to Billerton, spying out the land. He'd stolen a car to drive there, one he'd found parked in a street near the school. He'd learned a lot in prison, and how to steal cars was among his new accomplishments. He'd picked an old one; newer models weren't so easy to lift.

Phil Wickens was married. He had two children and was making a success of running the farm. No doubt his father had died. Well, learning his habits and picking him off with the shotgun would be easy. Or maybe he'd kill the wife and cripple Phil; that might be a better punishment. He'd have to catch them separately as he might need two shots for each of them. That would leave plenty of cartridges for the bank job. They'd saw the barrel off the gun for that; Mick knew more about guns than Alan and he'd regretted that it was not a more powerful weapon. Alan toyed with the idea of shooting him after the raid and going off with all the stolen money, but Mick knew about false passports and where to hide; he was more useful as an ally than a corpse. But perhaps all he needed was a visitor's passport, obtainable over the post office counter on production of some documents. The solicitor acting for his cousin had told him that the house was to be sold and that such papers were safely in his office. They could be collected at Alan's convenience. Soon, it would be most convenient.

How dared the old man leave it all to Penny! What a stab in the back that was, a blow to a man already down. And to think that she would sell the house! He could have settled there, become a respected member of the community, found a new wife, started a business, had the chance he needed to get his life organised. Plenty of people prospered after a spell inside.

Alan had spent hours brooding, turning it over in his mind, working up his anger.

He'd get the gun, whoever had bought the house. No one was going to stop him.

Mark had enjoyed Christmas. His mother and he had left home very early, arriving at The Golden Accord in time for breakfast. He'd already undone his stocking, and had given his mother some soap he'd chosen on Sharon's advice; it was a success and she was delighted. His present, which was waiting at the hotel so that he could ride it in the grounds, was a mountain bike. Peter, the chef's son, already had a good bike and they had ridden round together. The whole day was a festival. There had been a conjuror and there were games Mark and Peter and some other staff children had joined in. The new manager was more tolerant than the last; he said he wanted people to be happy. Mark rather liked him. His name was David and he'd given Mark and the resident staff's children presents. Mark's and Peter's were tool kits for their bikes, so he must have known that Mark would need one. The bike was exactly the right size.

Peter told Mark that David was sweet on his mum.

'P'raps they'll get married,' said Peter's older sister, Hazel. It was she, hearing her own mother talking, who had identified the situation. Mark was too young to work out that this accounted for his own presence in the hotel over Christmas, and the freedom he had been allowed.

Once or twice there had been men who had called at the house, given Mum flowers, all that stuff, but none had come more than two or three times. Mum didn't have a boyfriend, like, for instance, Sharon.

'We're all right, the two of us,' she'd often said.

He'd agreed with her, but occasionally he felt the burden of responsibility; Mum had no one else. Of course he would look after her when she got old and feeble, and he meant to work hard, get a good job and earn lots of money so that she could take things easy, but it would all depend on him. Some help might be a good idea. He thought about it a bit, in bed that night: it would mean David being with them all the time. Would he mind that? He didn't know. David seemed quite nice.

But Mum hadn't mentioned it at all; she was no different. He decided to forget about it, which was easy when they went home after the weekend. They'd gone to see *Scrooge*, just him and Mum and Kylie in the end; Ivy was too busy. He'd enjoyed it; it was a sad story with a happy ending when the horrid miser saw the error of his ways. They'd had several days together before his mother had to go on duty once again.

He'd finished *Swallows and Amazons*, which he'd taken from The Willows, and had exchanged it for *Coot Club*, which he must return; the house would still be empty so he could go on borrowing books. Ivy said she'd heard The Willows had been sold but she didn't know who had bought it.

'They won't be moving in yet,' she had said. 'These things take time.'

Ivy was worrying about Sharon. She had a new boyfriend, a young chap no older than herself, not working at the moment but intending to become a lorry driver. You had to have a special licence for that and Ivy thought you needed several years' driving experience before you could apply, which he hadn't had. He'd spent several nights in Sharon's room with her and the baby, which wasn't right. Ivy had spoken to Sharon who had lost her temper and said she was entitled to some fun and that Keith cared about her. Ivy thought he cared more for her own good cooking and for rent-free accommodation. The next thing would be another baby and a second absent father. Sharon was so careless. What if Keith and Adam's own father, Jason, coincided on a visit? Then the sparks would fly.

Ivy was too busy with the present to dwell on these difficult problems. Two of the children she used to meet from school had moved away, but she had a new toddler to take care of all day. He had to get accustomed to her, be made to feel safe and happy. Sharon's baby fitted in with him, but where was Sharon's help? She was often out now, alleging she was job-hunting. Maybe she was.

Young Mark scarcely seemed to need her, except for eating up his tea with gusto. Susan might save herself some money by cutting down the time he spent, officially, with her. She was working more conventional hours now, and spent fewer nights away from home. Most days, she was back by eight at the latest. The new manager and her promotion had made a difference to her timetable. Still, Mark could get into mischief if he was on his own, free to run wild, though even now he had a busy social life; after his tea he often went to various friends such as Terry Gardner.

For Justin and Terry, once the novelty of their presents had worn off, the holidays dragged. Their stepfather spent hours in his workshop, sculpting away at his wood, or reading in his study, emerging at intervals to see about food if their mother was not functioning. Unlike many offices, Richard's opened between Christmas and the New Year, to his relief. How her children spent their time then was up to Verity; she should make plans for them and take them out. She knew he would provide the cash.

Justin thought Terry's trick of running off that night had been stupid. There were other ways to harass people and cause them grief. You could make bogus telephone calls, pretending there were bombs in shops, or that you'd seen a thief in action, or you could light a fire, run away and come back to watch the firemen put it out: just a little fire, not one to cause a lot of damage. It would be a breeze.

When his mother had set Cat's books alight Justin had found it first frightening, then exciting. Cat had dealt with it quite quickly, but she must have been so cross with him to do a thing like that. It would have served Cat right to lose the lot. The older boys Justin had started to go around with in town got up to various tricks. They not only stole cars to drive for thrills, but lifted things from shops. Justin admired their daring.

Richard had been looking forward to seeing Caroline again. He hoped to spend a few hours in her flat one evening soon, not specifically to make love, though he'd be happy if things worked out like that. He simply wanted to be in a place where he felt easy, to enjoy domestic minutes free from wondering what the next crisis would be and how best to handle it.

Caroline told him she had enjoyed the Christmas break but soon disappointed him.

'I'm sorry, Richard – I'm busy every evening,' she declared, on the first day back.

People were, of course: it was the time for entertaining. Even he had his concert, hurrying home on an early train on

Thursday. Miss Darwin should be in the audience. She had written a prompt letter of thanks to Verity; her handwriting was small and angular, like that of a classical scholar. Perhaps she was a classical scholar. It had been delivered while they were out.

He worried that Verity might stage a drama to prevent him going to the concert; a wrist-slitting had stopped him on a previous occasion. This time, though, she had forgotten about his plans and he was able to come home, have a quick shower, shave and put on his dinner jacket without alarms, then make himself a sandwich. There was still plenty of ham left; he had bought a huge piece of cooked gammon which, with the remains of the turkey, should keep the household going till he shopped again.

Ready to leave, conscience made him look in at the studio. Rapt, Verity was busy painting. On her easel stood a canvas depicting willows bending in the wind and stormy clouds above troubled grey waters where a small boat tossed; in it, threatened by alarming waves, a female figure lay, Ophelia-like, her head thrown back, reeds clasped in her hand. What troubled thoughts had prompted this? How allegorical was it? When he first met Verity, some of her work had been garish in tone, gaudy colours used for clothes and buildings, and for landscapes, like tropical scenes; now everything was sombre. Perhaps this represented her change of mood from hope to despair. Was he responsible for that? Surely, at first, they had shared moments of joy? Now, they seemed to bring out the worst in one another; there were times when he felt like strangling her and he could understand the rage that led to violence. So far, he had always managed to walk away.

She did not look up when he entered the studio. Perhaps she really hadn't seen him. He left a Post-It note on the fridge to say where he had gone; then, banishing his gloomy thoughts, he set off to the concert. Tonight, he would think only of the music.

He saw Miss Darwin sitting in the audience. She had on the maroon dress she had worn on Christmas Day and her serious hair was regimented across her forehead, going into frizzy curls around her head. Was it a desperate perm, he wondered, or had nature dealt her this grizzled wire? He smiled at her as the overture began, the choir in echelon above the orchestra, which was composed of local amateurs and the best players from the school. She nodded in acknowledgement. After that, he forgot her.

Marigold enjoyed the concert. The singers were, she knew, heedless of everything except the music, voices blending, surrendering to the sound they were creating. It was a sort of rapture; she imagined sexual love might be like that. It was the only way in which she had ever let herself go, and even then, the mingled voices were under the rule of the conductor.

The crisp, cold weather had broken and it was wet again. She put up her umbrella as she left the town hall and set forth homewards. Tomorrow she was moving. The Willows was empty now, with everything removed except a few items which it had been agreed that she could buy, notably the contents of the garden shed; she would need a full set of gardening tools and these had looked to be in good condition. She was taking the existing curtains and carpets; changes could be made later. She was excited: she admitted it, just to herself.

Richard, driving slowly out of the market square where he had parked, saw her trudging along. That determined stride, the rather flat feet in low-heeled shoes, toes turned out, the sober raincoat and the plastic hood over her head under the umbrella which the gusting wind was catching, could belong to no one else.

He slowed down and offered her a lift.

'You are kind,' she said, accepting gratefully.

'Half a mile can be a long way on a night like this,' said Richard. 'Did you enjoy the concert?'

'Yes. It was glorious.'

He was surprised to hear her use such an extreme word;

moderation, he had sensed, was her mode.

'I'll let you know when rehearsals for the Easter concert begin,' he said. 'I'm sure they'll love to have you, if you want to join. Something to plan for, eh?'

'Yes,' she said again. 'I'd like to.'

'You move tomorrow, don't you? What weather for it. I hope it clears up by then.'

'At least they haven't got to load,' said Marigold. 'Everything's in store. I've only got a few things at the bungalow.'

'You'll soon get straight,' said Richard heartily. Had she anyone to help her? The removal men would do it all, he supposed.

'Can I offer you a nightcap?' she suggested, when they drew up at her gate. 'Though it's not too orderly inside,' she added.

He could not imagine this controlled woman being anything but organised. Probably there were some packed boxes waiting for the van.

'No thanks – I'd better get home,' he said. 'I'm going to the office tomorrow.'

'Perhaps you and your wife will come to sherry one Sunday at The Willows,' she said.

'Thank you. We'd like that,' said Richard, though Verity would not. She had had plenty to say after Christmas Day about his choice of guest: a boring old crone, had been her verdict. Even Terry had objected, hearing that description.

'She's all right,' he'd said. 'Rather hideous, though,' he conceded.

As she let herself into the bungalow, Marigold reflected that now, in her retirement, she had twice within a week been escorted home by a pleasant man. She could not remember this ever happening before in her adult life, not even by a colleague. Everyone had known that Maddie would get home safely; the old nickname coming from her initials had followed her into the civil service.

Well, she was not too old to enjoy this belated courtesy;

she appreciated Richard's kindness, which was not the patronising false solicitude displayed to older people by some brisk shop assistants. It could be that her time in Haverscot would be the best years of her life: she would be accepted as she was, a plain elderly woman with a good career behind her; she would not be competing in a world where she had never been a starter, the world of the good-looking and attractive.

The next afternoon, at The Willows, as she stood among her packing cases, a bouquet of spring flowers, sent by Interflora, was delivered. They were from Richard. No one — male or female — had ever sent her flowers before. And flowers, too: not a pot plant; she was overwhelmed.

Richard did not quite know why he'd done it.

Caroline was going away for the weekend and she left the office early. He had meant to send her flowers to welcome the New Year but as she was not at home, he had been foiled. Perhaps that was why he had chosen Miss Darwin as the recipient. Well, he was sure that she would like them; she had been a tactful guest on Christmas Day when the tensions in the house must have been apparent. She had not made a fuss of the boys but she had not ignored them, and her presence had prevented Verity from making a scene. The holidays were nearly over: soon the boys would be back at school and the country would tick into action once again. It was amazing how one managed to negotiate each obstacle as it came along, learning not to look too far ahead — unlike the world of insurance where anticipating disaster was part of the job.

In the train, he began to think about Caroline. It was more than a fortnight since his last visit to her flat. At the office they maintained a certain distance, not wanting their colleagues to divine their relationship, and that had not changed; she was friendly but cool. However, there was no special look for him when they were alone, which occasionally had been the case in the past, though only ever for an instant. The secret had, to him, been quite exciting.

She wanted it to end: he knew it, with a sense of desolation. She had met someone else and she had not summoned up the courage to tell him. Perhaps she never would. Perhaps she meant it just to fizzle out.

He'd let her go without a struggle. He had enough of that at home. He'd wish her happiness, if he heard she had a new partner. Perhaps she had met someone who wanted to marry her, a man free to do so, and to whom she could respond.

Would he have liked to be that person?

Sitting in the train, Richard admitted that he would. He loved her gently and sincerely: yes, he did, and he had lost her.

Further down the coach was the thin, dark young woman who travelled regularly on this line, the one who walked away from the station. He looked at her as she read her book. What was it? He could not tell. It was a hardback, perhaps from the library. He'd never met her there − he often called in on a Saturday.

He tried to think about her instead of Caroline or Verity. Where did she live? What did she do in London? He might get to know her, if he tried.

But he didn't want to: he didn't want a new entanglement, even if she could be persuaded to enter into one. Besides, she was so thin, like Verity. She might snap, like a twig.

He should be bringing flowers to Verity. Perhaps he'd get some in the morning; the shops were opening tomorrow.

Verity was in the kitchen when he reached home. A savoury smell came forth: she'd chopped up ham and turkey and made a spicy sauce; there was a pan of water boiling on the stove, ready to receive the pasta that was waiting to be cooked. She'd washed her hair and wore clean patterned leggings and a white sweater. She even had some scent on: not Chanel, of course. He caught a whiff of it as she came towards him, smiling grimly, lifting up her face to receive a kiss.

He brushed her cheek with his lips. So this was to be her role for the next few hours – or minutes. She was playing the devoted wife. Such intervals never lasted long. Was she sober?

He decided that she might have had one or two drinks, but no pills. That meant she would soon be manic, tearing round, wanting to rearrange the furniture or play charades or some other noisy game. Such ventures always ended in a scene.

'How was your day?' he tried, and heard that she had cleaned the house from top to bottom and remade all the beds with fresh linen.

'And the boys?' he asked, when she ran out of breath. He was longing for a drink. Perhaps he could slip out to the Red Lion after supper. Maybe he could copy her and start keeping a bottle in his workshop, which he always locked because of his tools; the boys might hurt themselves if they went in there and began messing about.

They'd been out all day, she said. She didn't know where. She supposed they'd been down to the river as they'd come home soaking wet.

Richard thought about their safety in the flooded fields. He wondered if they'd had any lunch. Well, they were her children, not his, if she chose to let them drown or starve. He wouldn't provoke her by suggesting she should have some idea of where they spent their time. They were here now; the beat of Justin's pop music was redounding dully in the background.

'Terry had that friend of his, Mark, over for the morning,' said Verity. 'They came in and got crisps for lunch. Then they went out again.'

'And Mark's gone home now?'

'I suppose so.' Verity shrugged.

Richard went off to the playroom where he spent some seconds trying to get the boys' attention and an answer to his question.

Mark had left at about five, they said. They'd been to the

river doing nothing much but splash about, all three wishing they had a canoe; that would have been brilliant today.

'It would have been dangerous,' said Richard, sounding like a killjoy to himself as he added, 'The water is flowing very fast; you could have been swept away or tipped over.'

'Well, we can swim,' said Justin. 'Anyway, why are you steamed up about it, Cat? We haven't got one.'

Richard thought he should check up on Mark. He dialled Susan Conway's number, and had an answerphone response. That was new: there had been no reply when he rang the night Terry was missing.

He gave his name and said that he hoped Mark had got back safely: he was simply checking.

Mark saw the light blinking when he returned and he listened to the message. It was therefore not revealed to Susan when she came back later.

Richard had been rather hoping that she would return his call, but she didn't. While he was telephoning, Verity had a few quick slurps from a bottle hidden behind cereal packets in the store-cupboard. This caused her to let the pasta boil too long and the sauce to catch. Even so, her husband and her sons found the meal much more palatable than was usual when she undertook the cooking.

Afterwards, they played Monopoly. The game became rowdy but even Verity seemed to enjoy it; perhaps they could find some contact after all, thought Richard, if only through these sorts of activities. His head began to ache, but he played on doggedly, doing his bit for the cause of domestic harmony.

When the boys had gone to bed, Verity accused him of being patronising.

'You weren't enjoying it. You looked bored to tears,' she said.

'I did enjoy it. I thought it was good that we were all getting on so well,' said Richard.

'You kept looking at your watch. You couldn't wait for it to be over.'

'It's a long game,' he said. Then, suddenly, he lost his temper. 'I've had a hard day at the office, I'm tired and I've got a thumping head, but I've done my best to be a good stepfather – a role model – that's what's thought so necessary today, isn't it? I might as well save myself the effort.'

He had been going to pack the game up and put it away, a small task he'd told the boys to do, only to have their mother countermand the instruction and tell them to hurry off to bed, she'd see to it. Now, he pushed the board away from him, leaving the scuffed piles of money on the table, walked out of the room and found his coat. Verity heard the front door bang behind him.

She burst into tears. She'd intended to be nice tonight, to be the good little wife and mother, not to quarrel. She'd played the boring game as well as she was able and hadn't lost her temper. The sherry she'd had before dinner had helped to calm her down and Richard hadn't made a fuss about the meal, though the boys had complained that it tasted burnt. She'd woven a fantasy in which she and Richard made rapturous love; surely it had once been like that between them? Yet again it had all gone wrong and he, this time, had been angry, at last reacting to the provocation she applied whenever she had the opportunity. She'd thought him like a piece of dough, impervious to needling; tonight, he'd proved otherwise, and the discovery unnerved her. Where was her safety now, if even Richard had a point at which he might explode?

She'd say that she was sorry. She'd done that before, when she'd gone too far and been frightened that she would lose him, and then what would happen to them? He had stroked and calmed her, then made love, silencing her tears with kisses. The last few times, however, he'd simply said 'I accept your apology,' and left the room.

This time, she'd really make him listen: she'd cry and even go down on her knees. He'd have to turn to her, after that.

But he didn't come back. She waited up for a long time, feeding the fire with logs, sitting by it, shivering. In the end she went to bed, where she swallowed several of her pills, recklessly, with no firm intent to harm herself beyond vaguely thinking, 'If I die, that'll show him.'

But she didn't die. She sank into a heavy sleep and did not hear Richard stumble in, late and rather drunk. He had been in The Red Lion until the bar closed.

14

MARK HAD HAD a good time with Terry. Later, he and Mum were returning to The Golden Accord for another weekend, with a New Year's Eve party and a big wedding on the Saturday. His mother was quite pleased for him to go to Merrifields that morning, after Terry telephoned to see if he was free. She let him ride his new bike round; David had brought it back for him in his Mitsubishi Space Wagon. Mum had been in a happy mood, but then she was nearly always cheerful, though often in a hurry. She didn't sit about in tears. Mark didn't associate tears with mothers; Ivy never cried, not even – or at least when he was there – after Joe died.

So when he saw Terry's mother crying, he was most surprised.

His own mother had made him promise not to join in any mad schemes Terry might be planning, and if it began to rain hard, he must come home, unless he sheltered in the house waiting for it to stop. In any case, as they had to leave at three o'clock, he must be back well before then.

'That's all right,' he said. 'I won't forget.' He had his watch, which Mum had given him for his birthday.

She hugged him. He was growing up so fast. He would never run off foolishly, like Terry.

The boys had climbed into the tree house to survey the

150

area from its branches. Terry did not tell Mark he had hidden there the night he ran away; he didn't want to hear Mark tell him he'd been stupid. From their high perch, the water-covered meadows looked inviting, like a lake.

'Let's go down there,' Terry suggested.

Mark agreed. He was wearing his rubber boots. This was not a silly scheme. Terry had his football with him; he seemed attached to it. Mark hadn't noticed that it had been in the tree house, lodged in a corner, when they clambered up. Terry threw it over the fence before crossing himself. There were strong nails to tread on to climb the solid structure.

'Cat doesn't know about these,' Terry said. 'He doesn't know we go across like this. He thinks the fence is strong enough to keep intruders out. Mum knows. She saw Justin banging them in. She goes over sometimes; she likes walking in the fields.'

Mark thought that Cat would find the nails one day. He didn't say so; it was handy to get across like this instead of walking down the road to the path near the church. The two boys kicked the ball about, aiming to send it near the water, and then Terry began throwing it in at the edge, to make a splash. It was a good game, and while Mark found bits of stick which he flung out to float with the tide, pretending they were boats on their way to join the Thames, Terry went on doing it until the ball dropped rather too far out, and he fell in when he collected it. He got drenched.

'Your mum'll kill you,' said Mark unsympathetically.

'We need a canoe,' said Terry. 'I'll ask Cat to give us one.'

That sounded good to Mark.

'Will he?' he enquired.

'Of course,' said Terry. 'I've only got to ask.' If Cat said no, he'd make a scene, like Mum and Justin did, and Cat would soon give in.

After his ducking, Terry decided he was too uncomfortable to stay longer in his sopping clothes, so they went back to the house. He left his boots and jacket in the rear lobby by the kitchen door. Mark put his boots there, too, and hung his jacket on a peg. Then they went into the kitchen, where Verity was sitting at the table, crying. She looked at them as they entered but she did not speak, not even commenting on Terry's dripping jeans and socks. Mark thought she had not noticed them; she simply went on crying.

'Oh, Mum,' said Terry. He did not ask her what was wrong but picked up a roll of paper towels, pushing it over to her, and tearing off a sheet which he thrust into her unresponsive hand. 'She does this,' he told Mark, turning away from her and heading for the store-cupboard. He left a trail of water as he crossed the floor. 'Come and help yourself,' he hospitably invited, opening the cupboard to reveal packs of crisps and canned soft drinks.

Mark did as he was bidden. He was hungry. Glancing at his watch, he saw that it was two o'clock. He'd have to go soon. There was just time to have a little meal. Laden with his selection, he followed Terry to the playroom. Wet footprints marked the polished floor on which were several handsome rugs.

'You're soaked,' Mark said. 'Hadn't you better change your jeans and socks?' He'd make such a mess if he didn't.

'I suppose,' said Terry. He put down his can of Tango and, carrying a pack of crisps, went upstairs eating them and leaving crumbs.

Mark settled on the sofa, eating his. He wondered briefly where Justin was. Out writing on walls with Greg Black or his friends, perhaps. Mark had seen him doing just that, with an aerosol near the scout hut. They'd written a lot of words which Mark knew were very rude; he understood what most of them meant. Ivy, hearing Steve use some of them, had got extremely cross and said that saying them was silly. Mark knew his mother wouldn't like to hear him say them, either.

Poor Mrs Gardner seemed so sad. What could be wrong? Perhaps she had a pain. He spared her quite a lot of sympathy before turning on the television to watch till Terry came downstairs again.

She was still in the kitchen, sobbing quietly into a wad of paper towelling, when he went past to get his boots and jacket before rescuing his bike from where he'd left it, leaning against the wall of Richard Gardner's workshop. She never noticed him pass by, and Mark decided she'd be most embarrassed if she knew he'd seen her crying. He crept out on tiptoe, almost silently.

Marigold was very busy in the house. The solicitors had employed a firm of cleaners to go through it after the contents were removed, and it was spotless, but she could see where the paintwork was flaking, and the walls were marked where pictures had hung and furniture had stood. The whole place must be redecorated, but meanwhile nothing was offensive to her, and she had slept soundly in her own bed, released from store, the mattress warmed through with an electric blanket.

Sinbad was enjoying the garden. He flapped about in the flood puddles and got very wet, the long feathery hair on his legs saturated. Marigold fussed over him and kept a special towel in the back porch to dry him.

She found some vases where the men had left them on the dining-room floor after unpacking their boxes, and arranged the amazing flowers in two of them. There were so many! Instantly the place seemed brighter, more her own. A glow of pleasure lifted her spirits, which, when she was in the bedroom where the children's books had been, had fallen. Empty, it looked so bleak, though bright patches marked the walls where posters had been fastened. It seemed the disinherited son had been interested in aviation; the posters had shown aircraft, she remembered. What had happened to him? Why was he disowned? Had he vanished?

If she were to disappear, who would notice?

The sudden thought made Marigold shudder. When she died, there would be none who mourned, no one to lament. Oh, a few old colleagues might put on a show of respect, if they knew, but who would tell them? Not her godchildren, who would wonder only what she had left them in her will. She had divided everything between them; what else should she do?

A charity, she thought, but what? One that aided children? Famine relief? Battered wives? A mixture of good causes? She'd think about it, after she was settled in.

Sinbad would miss her, and he needed feeding. She gave herself a shake, pushing away bleak thoughts as she had sought to do throughout her life: The main thing, now, was to look outwards, while getting the house organised. She must join in one or two local activities to give structure to her days: the choral society, as Richard Gardner had suggested, would be a start. There was probably a charity shop where she could be usefully occupied, she thought, depressed at the very notion. And she'd get back to her découpage: now she could unpack everything – the plain wooden boxes waiting to be embellished, the varnish, the glue, the small neat scissors. She'd use the dining-room as a working area; her large table, covered with a protective cloth, would make a perfect surface. She'd keep her desk there, too, for all her business papers and her files. She would eat in the kitchen which was large enough to hold a good-sized table and six chairs, but she did not expect to entertain. She could not see Verity Gardner coming willingly to lunch or dinner, and whom else would she ask?

On Sunday she would go to church, and if the Gardners were there, she'd invite them back to sherry. How many other people went to church, as she did, to punctuate their lives, with no particular belief to support? A good few, she guessed, including Richard, who would find peace there.

Why did she know he needed that? Marigold was not perceptive about other people and interacted with so few; at work, contact with her colleagues had been superficial, for which she blamed herself, knowing her brusque awkwardness did not endear her to them. Already, though, in Haverscot, she had sensed Richard's sadness. Why did his wife drink? Why had the silly small boy gone into hiding?

Why had he and she forged a secret bond between them? What was wrong with that family? Was it Richard's fault? Could he be a villain in disguise?

Surely not. He must be what he seemed — a decent, ordinary man, such as many she had met, on superficial terms, at work.

If there were any chance that they might come so soon, she must get the sitting-room in order. Spurred on, she plugged in the vacuum cleaner to sweep up behind the removers.

When everything was arranged as far as she could manage, and there was no more that she could do, silence fell at The Willows. Even Sinbad had gone to sleep in front of the gas fire. At the bungalow, there had been the distant buzz of traffic; even, when the wind was in the right direction, the sound of a train. Here, as she listened, she heard the rain begin again, a swishing sound, and the spattering it made on the flagged terrace beyond the windows. She knew a moment's desperation; then her gaze fell on the flowers. She would not give way to dread: instead, she would go out to dinner, have a meal at The Red Lion. During her weeks at the bungalow, she had been there several times. A good steak and some burgundy would set her up. She was used to dining out alone in unassuming places; it was one luxury she could afford and which had become easier to handle as she grew older. She did not need the restaurant staff to like her, merely to respect her.

Respect was lacking nowadays. She meant to command it, where possible, for herself.

She did not hurry over her meal, enjoying the steak, followed by an excellent crème brûlée. She sipped her wine and drank her coffee. The hotel was small; it had two stars, and she had stayed there while she found the bungalow, sleeping in a comfortable room with an uneven floor, a beamed ceiling and a small mullioned window overlooking the market square. She'd occupied a double bed — the hotel had only one small single room, without a bathroom of its own — and she'd wondered what it was like to have someone lying there beside you, touching. Years ago, when she was young, she'd expected the experience; she knew no one would fall in love with her, but she thought she might experience a flirtation or a holiday romance. Neither had ever come her way. Yet she could have loved someone. Children could have followed. She'd known none well, not even her godchildren in their youth.

Perhaps she would get to know Richard Gardner's stepsons, now that they were neighbours. But they didn't like him, calling him Cat in a tone that held no affection. She had been astounded by Terry's escapade; what had made him behave in such a way? The boys were not in any trouble; he should have gone straight home. What about the other boy? Children could be very naughty and act unpredictably; some were even wicked. Perhaps, by having none, she had been spared a lot of worry. Those two weren't Richard's own children: did that make a difference? Could you love the child simply because you loved its mother?

She paid her bill and rose to leave, passing the bar on her way out. Something made her glance inside. The room was busy, but not so crowded that she did not see Richard, who was standing by the counter, a brandy goblet in his hand. She paused. He was not talking to the people near him; indeed, he looked morose, almost desolate.

Marigold very nearly went to speak to him, to thank him for the flowers, but she held back. She wasn't good in crowded bars and there was something so dejected about his appearance that she felt he might not want anyone he knew to recognise his misery.

Though of course, as a long-time resident of Haverscot and member of the choral society, he must know others who were in the bar.

Perhaps he came here often in the evening, but she had never noticed him when she was staying at the inn.

15

MARIGOLD HAD NOT looked inside her garden shed since moving in to The Willows. Water lapped around it, a large pool in a hollow of the lawn around a bare weeping willow, the rest of the lawn soft and saturated. She liked the pool; birds fluttered on it; she had seen a wild duck and there were several moorhens, but keen gardeners might suggest that drains should be sunk under the turf. She would consider it, she thought, at last stepping down the garden to inspect the collection of tools which she had bought. She wore her wellingtons, ones with strong ridged soles in case the ground was slippery, and an old raincoat, with a rainproof hat. As she walked along the brick path which wound its way towards the bottom of the garden, she saw bulbs thrusting through the ground on either side: daffodil spikes, and the greener stems of grape hyacinths. Discovering what lay beneath the ground would be exhilarating, Marigold decided, still reluctant to admit excitement, though she had felt it several times in recent weeks.

Inside, the shed smelled damp and musty; the window glass was grimed and masked with cobwebs. It must all be cleaned up, but not now. At least the floor was solid concrete, dry under her feet, and the tools were tidily arranged, a spade and several forks in different sizes suspended by their handles, a besom brush upended in a corner, various rakes. The mower was an old Atco. Did it work? If not, she'd have to get a new one. She might have to pay a man to come and cut the grass; there was a lot of it and it would take more than an hour to do, she estimated. She'd often done the mowing for her parents and had enjoyed walking up and down behind the machine. Her parents' mower had been tricky to get started and temperamental when in action; doubtless modern ones were easier to operate. She need make no decision about what was best until the grass began to grow, perhaps in March.

Flower pots were stacked neatly on a bench, some old earthenware ones and newer ones made of plastic. Trowels and other implements were well cleaned; there were few signs of rust. She'd made a good purchase.

She closed the door and left. There was no bolt, but, not visible from the road, the shed would surely not attract a thief, and its contents were of small value. If she bought a new, expensive mower, though, perhaps she ought to lock it up. She'd heard no talk of local burglaries, but nobody was immune to predators.

Richard had not been in church on Sunday, so she had been unable to invite him and Verity back to sherry. She had written him a note of thanks for the flowers and posted it: cowardly, in a sense, since if she had delivered it, he would have received it promptly, but she did not want to risk meeting his prickly wife without warning. She'd ask them round another time.

Mr Phipps, the estate agent, had suggested a painter who could come and tackle the redecorating. Her own bedroom would be first, and she must decide what to do about that sad room where the children's books had been. For some reason she felt uncomfortable in there, as though an unhappy ghost lingered in the shadows. It was a fanciful idea: instead of speculating about the estranged son of Mr Morton, she should think of the happy spinster sisters who had lived here in her childhood. Even so, her thoughts kept returning to question-marks about the Mortons. How would the niece use her windfall? Had she been kind to her beneficent uncle? Had he been to visit her in Canada?

Marigold's own income was assured; her pension was a good one and, with some investments she had made, she had no financial worries. Thanks to her own inheritance, she had seen her capital increase; the London house had financed the purchase of The Willows. She had never known material insecurity and that gave her a form of confidence, but she had also had a successful career; if she had done less well, her pension would have been less generous. She was lucky; things that worried other people did not apply to her.

When she had seen the painter she felt optimistic. He could start almost at once; in winter, work fell off, and these days many people did their own decorating, especially indoors. They discussed colours and the order in which the rooms should be tackled. Marigold thought she would probably have the kitchen completely refitted but that could wait; she wanted to test its layout before deciding on a plan. As it was, the inoffensive cream worktops and pale green cupboards were, though showing signs of wear, pleasant enough. Her fridge from London fitted in to the slot where Mr Morton's smaller one had stood. It was relatively new, solid, with a freezer on the top which held enough emergency supplies for one person. If she grew soft fruit, perhaps she would need a larger one, but that was for the future.

'We'll be busy, Sinbad,' she said, when Mr Samson, the painter, had agreed a date to start. He would have a mate to help him, he had said, which reassured Marigold, for he was very small and thin, unlike his namesake.

She would have company, too: it might stimulate her. Since stopping work and having no particular timetable for her day, she had slowed up. Until a few months ago, she had risen early and tidied up her London house before leaving for the office. There, she had made decisions and written directives, all to a prescribed policy with which she did not necessarily agree but which was customary in her department; her mind was working actively. Now, visiting the supermarket was a major feature in her life, and choosing furnishing fabric rather special.

She still took Sinbad to the park, which was drier than the garden; besides, he needed more exercise than it provided. She knew several other dog-owners by sight, but was too inhibited to greet them unless they first spoke to her. Unaware that she appeared forbidding, with her hat drawn down over her brows and her face set in an expression which reflected not ill-humour, but determination, she seemed to discourage friendly greetings, and any tentative approach some walker might have made was stillborn because she never looked at those approaching. Marigold walked firmly onwards, eyes to the front, like a guardsman on parade.

She wrote inviting Richard and Verity to sherry on a Sunday in the middle of January, but received no reply. Richard had not even seen her letter, which Verity had left lying on the table in the drawing-room. Later, she had picked it up with a pile of magazines and it was sandwiched between them. Verity forgot about it.

Though she found it odd that they had not answered, Marigold prepared for them. She'd bought flowers to replace those Richard had sent her; she had provided tiny toasts spread with cheese or fishy mixes; she had cut thin squares of brown bread and butter and laid smoked salmon on them. No one came.

She thought of telephoning to see if there was a misunderstanding, but if it was their error, they might be embarrassed. If they'd simply forgotten, they'd remember later and would telephone. But they didn't.

She felt obscurely sad. Richard would not have been deliberately rude; she knew that. Verity, however, was unpredictable, at least to Marigold.

Three sherries cheered her up, and she began to sing while putting Sinbad's meal in his bowl. She ate most of the smoked salmon herself; the rest, she saved for supper.

*

Mark wanted to return *Coot Club* to The Willows and exchange it for another sailing adventure. He was sure Tom would want him to go on borrowing books. One evening, when Steve had gone into the town to meet his friends and so could not be curious about Mark's activities, he told Ivy he was going to see Terry, and set off.

Soon he was marching down The Willows drive, in pitch darkness. He'd forgotten his torch. Never mind. He'd find the door.

He fumbled about seeking the lock, and managed to insert the key. Once inside, he located the light switch and turned it on. He was surprised to find that things were different. There was a new carpet in the hall, and an unfamiliar table, a chair with a tapestry seat, other pictures on the walls. He examined one which showed a square-rigged ship in full sail; he liked the look of that.

Not apprehensive, simply intrigued, he went into the sitting-room. Sofa and matching chairs, covered in blue fabric, stood on Tom's carpet. The television was a small modern one. There was a CD player and he inspected that with interest. Steve had acquired enough money to buy one and Mark, though happy with his own ghetto-blaster, thought it great.

He touched nothing, walking carefully round the house in his socks. He had left his shoes by the front door, as he and Steve had always done. Finally, after a thorough inspection of the ground floor, he went up to the room where the books were kept.

It was completely empty. Even the curtains had gone and the window showed dark against the sky. Smeared, faded wallpaper was marked with squares where posters had hung. The bookshelves, which had been put up by Tom many years before, were in position, scratched and chipped, but bare.

Mark's heart began to thump. He couldn't exchange the book, which had been his plan, but he could replace *Coot Club*.

He laid it sideways on a shelf and then turned towards the door.

A figure stood framed in the doorway. It was a woman in an overcoat. She held a heavy torch in her hand. Miss Darwin had picked it up in the hall on her return from taking Sinbad to the vet. He had suddenly developed stomach trouble, writhing round in pain, and they had travelled to the surgery in a taxi. She had had to leave him there, for he might need an operation. They had left the house well before dark, and she had not expected to be long. Returning, she saw lights on in the house. She had let herself in with care, making no noise, and had almost fallen over a pair of sturdy black lace-up shoes, not very large, by the front door. She had expected to find several vandals in the house, small ones, breaking the place apart. Instead, she saw one boy, not five foot tall, staring at her, terrified.

Miss Darwin was the first to recover, and she recognised him.

'You're one of the boys from the park,' she said. 'You're a friend of Terry Gardner's. You're Mark.' At that moment she could not remember if she had ever heard his surname. He looked anything but menacing, standing by the bookcase, gazing up at her. 'What are you doing in my house?' she asked.

Mark had retreated towards the window as he realised who she was. She had on the same grim hat, pulled down, and the same coat. He saw the big, heavy torch she held. Her attitude was threatening, but when Miss Darwin saw his fear, she took a backward step.

Mark swallowed.

'I didn't know anyone was living here,' he said. 'I brought back a book old Tom – Mr Morton – lent me.' He gestured towards *Coot Club*, lonely on the shelf.

'Hm.' Miss Darwin crossed over, scrutinised the book and saw written inside, *Alan Morton, from his mother*, and the date, in 1958. 'Did you enjoy it?' she asked.

'Yes. I was going to borrow another,' Mark said, courage seeping back. This old woman wasn't a witch, though she looked so fierce; she had saved him and Terry in the park.

'I'm afraid you can't,' she was saying. 'As you see, all the books have gone and I've moved in. I live here now. How did you get in?'

'I had a key,' said Mark. 'I used to come and see Tom. Me and Steve did. Every night, mostly. We played chess and watched telly with him.'

'Who's Steve?'

'Steve Burton. Ivy's son. Well, not her real son. His dad died but he stayed on with Ivy. I go there after school till my Mum gets back from work.'

'Aren't you meant to be at Ivy's now?' queried Miss Darwin.

'I'm on my way to see Terry,' Mark said promptly, but it wasn't true, though he'd told Ivy that was where he was going. He had planned to stay at The Willows till it was time to go home.

'So late?'

'It's not that late,' said Mark. 'Six o'clock?' he hazarded.

Miss Darwin checked her watch.

'Nearly half past,' she said. 'You'd better come downstairs,' she added. 'Leave the book.'

She led the way, Mark following, watching the sturdy shoulders under the coat. In the hall, she took it off and crossed to hang it in the cloakroom. She removed her hat, not glancing at her hair in the mirror; she knew it would be orderly, compressed for hours beneath the hat. Then she returned to look at the small miscreant who was standing on the Indian carpet in the centre of the hall. He wore his school trousers, rather baggy, bought big to cater for his rapid growth. His socks were grey. Except for the slightly different clothes – instead of a blazer and shorts, Mark's trousers were long and he had on a navy anorak – he might have been William Brown incarnate.

'Have you read about William and his friends?' Miss Darwin asked. 'Henry was one, and Ginger,' she remembered.

'Oh yes. I borrowed them from Tom,' said Mark. 'They made me laugh.'

'They made me laugh, too,' Miss Darwin said, gravely.

She looked less alarming without her hat. She couldn't help being so ugly, he thought kindly; she was old.

'Would you like a drink?' she suggested. 'Milk? Or orange juice?' She could not send him off abruptly and she must decide how to deal with him. In his own eyes, he had not transgressed.

'Orange juice, please,' he said promptly.

'Take off your jacket,' Miss Darwin instructed. 'Hang it in the cloakroom. Then come into the kitchen. I'm sure you know your way around this house.' Better than I do, she reflected. Perhaps he had already helped himself from her stores, she thought, but saw at once that he had touched nothing. She took a carton of juice – she always had it for breakfast – from the fridge and poured some into a glass, then found a packet of chocolate biscuits. 'Would you like one of these?' she said.

'Yes, please,' said Mark, and added, 'Thanks.'

He'd stood his ground, Miss Darwin recollected, when the two motorists had been so angry. Terry had been about to flee, but Mark had denied their responsibility for what had happened.

'Terry will be expecting you. Perhaps you should ring him up and say you've been delayed,' she proposed.

'No – it's all right,' Mark assured her. 'I only said I might come round. It wasn't definite.'

'I see.' Miss Darwin did not think another hunt for a missing boy who had not really disappeared would be desirable. 'Very well. Come and sit down and tell me about the books you've read.'

She had arranged three chocolate biscuits on a plate, which she put, with the juice, on a tray, just like at Mum's hotel, thought Mark admiringly, used to drinking out of cans and tearing open packs of crisps; then she led the way to the sitting-room. Mark ate his biscuits very fast and neatly, careful not to drop crumbs on the floor, though some landed on the front of his grey school sweater. He noticed them and spiked them with a damp finger, then conveyed them to his mouth. He looked quite composed, setting his glass back on the tray which Miss Darwin had put on a coffee table in front of him.

'Where's your dog?' he asked her.

While he was drinking his juice and eating his biscuits, Miss Darwin had poured herself a stiff whisky, adding soda water. Bottles and glasses were in a cupboard built into a corner of the room. Tom had kept tapes and videos in there, and the games.

'He's at the vet's,' said Miss Darwin. 'He's not at all well, I'm afraid. He's probably got to have an operation. He'll be there a day or two.'

'Oh dear,' said Mark. 'That's sad. But he'll get better,' he assured her, bracingly.

Miss Darwin knew that this was far from certain.

'I hope so,' she said.

'When he is, I could come and see him,' Mark offered. 'I could take him for walks for you.'

'Thank you,' said Miss Darwin, taken aback but touched.

'I miss coming here,' Mark confided. 'It was so sad about Tom, but he looked quite peaceful.'

'You saw him?' Miss Darwin was astonished.

'Yes. Steve and me came in as usual, and he was in his chair, not moving, like asleep,' said Mark. He blinked, and Marigold, in some strange, visceral manner, knew that he had suffered a big loss and was grieving.

'And you've been coming in since then.' It was a statement.

'Not many times,' said Mark. 'But it's nice here. It still is,' he added politely.

'Do your parents know you come here?'

'There's only my mum. I haven't got a dad. I never have had one, not like Steve. His died, as I said,' Mark answered. 'Mum works at The Golden Accord. That's why I go to Ivy's.'

Miss Darwin had not heard of The Golden Accord. She imagined a pub, with his mother a barmaid.

'And where do you live?' she pursued.

'In Grasmere Street,' he said. 'Ivy's house isn't far from there. I see myself home at night now.'

'As you've changed your mind about going to see Terry, perhaps you should be thinking about doing that soon,' said Miss Darwin, though she was reluctant to part with her unusual guest.

'I needn't go yet,' said Mark, expansively. Tom had enjoyed his visits; this old lady might, too. But she wasn't a bit like a gran, he thought: not at all cuddly and spoiling, as they were meant to be. Some of his friends had them, but Mark rarely met one. 'Can you play cards?' he asked.

Miss Darwin had neither cards nor a chess set, nor anything Mark thought might provide her with a pastime. She was about to question him about his tastes in literature when he asked her about her activities in the dining-room.

'I saw you'd got some paste and stuff in there,' he said. 'What's it for?'

She showed him, and he was impressed, unstintingly admiring the small boxes she was decorating. She showed him how she grouped the neatly cut-out flowers, and explained that they needed several coats of varnish to harden it all off.

'Very nice,' he said, then, graciously, he took his leave.

She watched him go down the drive into the darkness. The nearest street lamp was twenty yards away. She thought he turned to wave to her before he vanished, and, not certain, she waved back.

She must have security lights put up, she decided: one at the front and another at the back. If he could get in so easily, so could a thief, who would not need a key.

He hadn't given his back to her. He could still get in. Did it matter? Perhaps she ought to change the locks. She'd think about it in the morning.

Marigold poured herself another drink; soon a warm glow of fleeting pleasure filled her, until her thoughts returned to Sinbad. She forgot about the key.

16

SINBAD DID NOT recover from his operation. Marigold
missed him and understood that by growing fond of
him, she had become vulnerable in a manner she had not
permitted herself for years. She would not get another dog;
at least, not yet.

Without him, she was freer. She could go to London for
the day; to leave him for so long would have been impossible.
She made several expeditions, enjoying them, though drenched one night when she returned in pouring rain. Surely
this was the wettest winter for very many years, she thought,
plodding flat-footedly towards home. Haverscot station was
on the very limits of the town; its booking office closed
around midday and there were no taxis on the spot; to get
one, you must telephone. She should pursue her plan of
buying a car and refreshing her ability to drive. There had
been a car in Mr Morton's garage, a well-kept Ford Escort;
he hadn't been able to drive it since his illness, she'd been
told. Like all his other possessions, it was sold.

She'd need something small, just a little box on wheels to
get about in. With one, she could visit stately homes and
study famous gardens. It must be in good condition, so that
it would not let her down.

She went to the Fabergé exhibition and to several
matinées, anonymous, a muted figure in the audience,

responding to the drama in a manner she had not enjoyed
before. The audience was the fourth wall of a room, peering
in. She had peered briefly through the fourth wall of life at
Merrifields, she thought one night when she noticed Richard
Gardner sitting further down the coach on her returning
train. He was reading, and did not notice her until they
climbed the steps to cross the bridge at Haverscot station.
She wondered what his book was, to insulate him from the
journey so successfully.

When he recognised her, he offered her a lift home and,
gratefully, she accepted. She told him not to take her to the
door; she would soon walk the short distance from Merrifields to her own house. However, he insisted.

'It's a foul night. You'll get soaked,' he said. She would
have, if he hadn't come along. He'd seen the thin young
woman, too, striding off, umbrella raised, wearing boots
today. She looked a bit like Verity had done when he first
met her: pale and anxious.

Miss Darwin, though, was very different, and a safer case
to transport in his car. She told him she had seen him in the
train, intently reading, and he said that he was catching up
with Trollope. She'd read none of the novels.

'I go more for biographies and travel,' she confessed.

'I was never one for the classics,' Richard answered. 'But
I like the gentle pace of these. People behave very badly but
on the whole everyone's so civil.'

He turned in at the gateway of The Willows, drawing up
outside her door. She had turned the porch light on before
she left that morning, but no light showed.

'Oh dear – the bulb must have gone,' she said. 'I knew it
would be dark when I got home, so I left it burning.'

'Have you got a spare? Let me change it for you,' Richard
offered.

'Oh – that's very kind of you,' said Marigold, who would
have needed to perch on steps to reach the socket. 'Yes. I
know I've got some bulbs.'

While he changed it, she told him she intended to have

security lights fitted, and he suggested an electrician she could use.

When the job was done, she offered him a drink, thinking he must be eager to get home and would certainly refuse, but he accepted a large whisky. She poured another for herself.

'I'm almost home. No breathalysing bobby will be waiting in the road,' he said, and sank back in a big armchair while Marigold lit the fire. 'Gas – how wonderful,' he said. 'No work or ashes.'

'It was already here. It's very convenient,' she said. 'But you don't get mysterious shapes and patterns in it, like you do with ordinary coal or logs.'

For someone who professed not to read fiction, this was an illuminating comment; she would enjoy it, if she tried it, Richard thought.

He had gulped down a large amount of his drink almost as soon as they were seated, facing one another. Marigold saw, with concern, that he looked dreadful. He was very pale, with dark patches underneath his eyes.

'I needed that,' he said, indicating his glass. 'Thanks.'

She remembered her sight of him in the bar at The Red Lion. Drink, she had learned, could alleviate despair, could bring a sense of ease and even joy. Until lately, she had never let herself experience this; only now, in her retirement, where there was no witness, had she discovered this pleasure, one which could be easily abused.

'A hard day?' she asked.

He nodded.

She waited in case he wanted to enlarge on this, but instead he seemed to give himself a shake and began talking about the choral society. He knew when it would meet again and said that he would take her.

He couldn't really want to do that, she reflected, looking at him, a middle-aged man, perhaps attractive – she did not really know about that – though, tonight, his face looked ravaged. Something terrible must have happened; perhaps his wife was leaving him, though would that be so awful, since their relationship was clearly, even to a stranger and one not well versed in such matters like herself, far from easy? Perhaps he was simply lonely.

So was she. Marigold had been lonely all her life but she had never admitted it to herself before. She rose, refilled his glass and her own, and went out to the kitchen, returning with some crisps in a small dish. She had bought them in case that boy, Mark, called again. Children lived on crisps, she had heard.

'A little blotting-paper,' she suggested. Her father used to use that phrase. 'For us both,' she added, offering them.

While she was out of the room, Richard's thoughts had left the present, returning to his interview with Caroline that lunchtime. She had asked him to meet her at an Italian restaurant they had been to before. She was looking very well, he saw; there was a glow about her and she was fuller in the face.

'I've got something to tell you,' she had said.

She was getting married: that was what it was, he felt certain, and he prepared himself to hear the news.

She insisted that they order their meal before she told him anything, then asked about Verity and the boys, trying, he bristlingly decided, to remind him of his own responsibilities before mentioning her plans. It was not until they were drinking their coffee that she made her announcement and then he was, literally, dumbfounded; he could not speak for quite two minutes, simply sitting there, incredulous.

'I want to tell you before it's all round the office,' she said. 'I'm pregnant. I'm not sure if you're the father, or another man I've been seeing for some time. He lives down in Wiltshire. He's married, too: a former boyfriend.' She'd paused to sip some of the house red wine, a Bardolino. He'd noticed that she drank very little of it, asking for some Perrier. 'I decided I wanted a child before it was too late. I don't want a husband, though,' she added. 'I was meeting the other man – let's call him X – from time to time, with this in mind, but nothing happened. He'd got some children, so I felt sure that he was fertile. Anyway, I decided to try someone else.' She was looking at him all the time she was talking, and Richard was staring at her, aghast.

'Me,' he managed to croak.

'Yes.' She smiled at him, a maternal smile, he recognised, with horror. 'I'm so fond of you. You're a nice man, and bright. Suitable,' she said. 'That makes it sound so cold and calculating, but we had some happy times together, didn't we?'

They had. He could not deny it, but it had been false, simply for a purpose: to acquire his acceptable genes.

'I don't know which of you is, in fact, the father,' she repeated, smiling still, a Judas smile. He had never heard of anything so cold-blooded. 'I don't want any money or support. I can take care of my own child.' She smiled again. 'A test could prove paternity, but who wants that? It's better to leave it vague, don't you think?'

'Are you going to tell this X?' Richard asked at last.

'Not specifically. We have mutual friends. He'll hear like that,' she said. 'Just as you would have, in the office, but I didn't want you to be alarmed.'

Richard was profoundly shocked. That was his chief emotion. His sperm had been hijacked. He'd been robbed.

'Won't this child need a father?' he managed to enquire.

'Oh no. There'll be men around. My brother, and my father's very fit. He'll have grandparents for quite a while, I hope,' Caroline said calmly. 'I'll get a really good nanny and send him or her to a first-class school.'

She could afford it. He knew that. The child would be well cared for, was wanted, and would probably be loved.

'Will it thank you for giving it no father and no siblings?'

'It might have siblings,' Caroline replied. 'There's time.'

'You'll have to find another sire, then. I'm not going to be used like this again,' said Richard. 'Maybe X will oblige, or you'll find someone else to play this game with. A younger man, perhaps.'

'Don't be bitter, Richard,' Caroline reproved him. 'It's not like you. Remember, I needn't have told you anything.'

'No,' he agreed. 'I suppose not.'

He finished his coffee, then, before she could do so – it had, after all, been her invitation – he secured the bill and paid it, tipping lavishly.

'I've upset you,' Caroline observed. She looked surprised. 'I thought you might feel flattered that I chose you.'

Richard managed not to say that she had exploited him; somehow, he succeeded in leaving the restaurant without losing his temper or his outward poise. He had a wretched afternoon, accomplishing almost nothing in his office, and, in the train, had found it impossible to concentrate upon his book, reading the same page over and over again, not absorbing anything.

People were going mad, he thought: young girls in poor areas got pregnant in order to obtain a flat and so leave home, or more practically, to have someone to love and to love them: a living doll. What emotional demands did single mothers make upon such children? When they turned from toddlers into ten-year-olds, some went out of control. Caroline would have expectations from her child: love and loyalty, maybe to excess.

Young Mark Conway's mother was alone. What was her story? She might be a widow. Whatever her situation, she was making a success of the boy, and she seemed pleasant. He suspected Mark's conception was not the result of feckless conduct.

Sitting in front of Marigold's gas fire, staring at the flames which, as she had said, made no new patterns, simply repeating their own formula, he felt an impulse to tell her what Caroline had done, but he refrained. She would not want to hear it, and anyway, what could she do? She might not even understand.

But she had news for him.

'I had a visitor a little while ago,' she said. 'Young Mark Conway, Terry's friend.' She did not say that he had entered the house uninvited. 'He came to return a book he'd borrowed from Mr Morton, the previous owner of this house.'

'Oh yes? What was the book?'

'A good one. *Coot Club*,' said Marigold. 'Arthur Ransome. I loved those books when I was young. Mr Morton had the whole set, it seems, and dozens of other children's books. Mark had been visiting him and borrowing them.'

Richard hid a smile. Here was someone who eschewed fiction, yet she had read it in her youth.

'What happened to them? The books, I mean,' asked Richard.

'They were sold, with all his other things,' said Marigold. 'If I'd known about the boy, perhaps I could have bought the children's books.'

'I wish Justin and Terry read Arthur Ransome,' Richard said. 'They barely read at all, and when they do, it's horror stories.'

'Did you know Mr Morton?'

'Not really. By sight, before he had his stroke. We said good morning, that kind of thing,' said Richard. 'He went to pieces after his wife died.'

They went on talking about Mr Morton and his sad decline, and the pathos of selling someone's possessions after their death, then moved to Marigold's plans for the garden.

Richard left at last, feeling much calmer, but Marigold knew that inside, he was screaming with pain.

She poured herself another drink, and after a while she put a disc on her new music system. Soon she forgot Richard, and even Sinbad faded from her mind.

17

THOUGH HE WAS desperate to retrieve the gun and store it safely, Alan did not visit Haverscot during his next leave. Instead, he found a flat in a part of Reading largely occupied by transients; an anonymous area where people came and went unchallenged as long as they paid their rent. He paid his for two months in advance, telling the landlord that his job involved travelling and he would be away a lot.

'No problem,' said the landlord, happy with the cash. His new lodger looked respectable enough, clean, with trimmed hair and wearing dark trousers and a corduroy jacket. Alan had always been a sharp dresser.

He spent the weekend in the flat enjoying sybaritic pleasures such as lying in a steaming bath, and sleeping late. On Saturday night he went out to dinner in an expensive restaurant, eyeing the other customers; in this place, many were middle-aged, enjoying what they ate and drank, living in the moment. Alan looked at the women, most of them well dressed, some overweight, some pretty, prepared, in his opinion, to lie and cheat to get what they wanted from their dupes, the men. He scorned them all, but later, in the bar, he picked one up, a smart tart who had a room not far away. He'd boast of that to Mick, when he went back, make a good story from their short encounter. He felt nothing for her:

that was not her function. Still, she was better-looking than some and he soon showed her who was in charge. Sex was not important to Alan; power was.

The flat was barely furnished, but it was adequately equipped for what he and Mick would need. There were two bedrooms, a tiny kitchen and a bathroom, and a sitting area. It was spacious after what he was used to. He could hide the gun here, once he'd got it out. He examined the floorboards; they could be prised up and it could lie there safely. So could the cash; he'd remove the rest from the building society as soon as he was out for good.

Alan stayed in bed for most of Sunday morning, but then he went out looking for a bank to rob, one that was well placed for leaving promptly, where a car could be left nearby. He marked down several, and disqualified others. Mick, he knew, had contacts, people who would make it easy for them to go abroad once the job was done. There was nothing for him here, in England: not now. He'd find it hard to get a worthwhile job with status, after what had happened, but if he'd inherited The Willows and the money, he could have started up a business of his own, gone straight. He had been unlucky; June had spoiled everything for him in Billerton. Alan conveniently forgot that until he went there, he had never stayed in one place long because an action of his own had always ended in some sort of trouble.

All women were traitors, even his mother. On her final visit to him in the prison, she had told him that he was not Tom's son. She was pregnant by another man when they were married, and Tom still didn't know the truth, but she could bear her secret no longer; after telling Alan, she was going to reveal the truth to Tom. He had been her childhood sweetheart and, while he was a prisoner of war, they had corresponded. Meanwhile, she had met someone else. Then Tom returned, just as she and the other man ended their transitory romance when she discovered that he was going out with another girl. Later, by chance, she and the man had met again and had spent their only night together; he had cajoled her, and she had given in, knowing at once that she had made a terrible mistake and that Tom was the man she really loved. They were married within a few weeks, and by then pregnant, she resolved that Tom should never know that he was not the father. In those days, abortion was illegal and difficult to arrange. Saying nothing was the easiest way out and anyway, perhaps she would miscarry; but she didn't, and on Alan's infant face she saw a likeness to his natural father. This recurred throughout the years that followed, but it was more a facial expression than a physical resemblance. Both of them, though, were selfish individuals; no one mattered other than themselves. That was why she had succumbed, that night; she could not say that she was raped, but she had been a most reluctant lover.

She had spent her whole life trying to make up to Tom for her deception. She'd hoped for other children, but none had come along, part of her punishment, she told herself. Tom, meanwhile, had never failed Alan, always there, trying to mitigate the consequences of his actions, always a good example of what a man should be.

She would not tell Alan who his real father was.

'I heard he'd died,' she said. 'We're all old now.'

After this revelation, Alan had brooded on his new knowledge, wondering if he had half-brothers and sisters, other relatives, curious about the man himself. Was he successful? Was he rich? Since his mother knew that he was dead, she would know the answers to the questions crowding in his mind. Alan mentally ran through his parents' circle of friends: was any of those men his father? Was there one in whom his mother showed interest? Did he look like any of them? He was not in the least like Tom, and now that was explained.

Dorothy Morton knew that Tom had blamed himself for Alan's failings. Now, at long last, she would release him from unnecessary guilt. If heredity had any bearing on the matter, Tom was not culpable.

After her confession, she gave up on life, eventually dying

more of despair than any precise illness, and then Tom changed his will. He owed Alan nothing, and it was a relief to know that he was not the father of a murderer, but was a tendency to kill inherent? Surely not, and surely upbringing could counteract a leaning towards violence? Every family had its black sheep; all that might be needed to trigger a latent impulse was a certain situation, and perhaps poor June provoked the worst in Alan, by default. Tom's sorrow was immense. Now he understood Dorothy's gentle fading through their life together; all the sparkle she had had when young had gradually disappeared, but she had loved the boy: there was no doubt of that.

Alan, in prison, concocted various stories which satisfactorily removed responsibility from himself for any misfortune, large or small, real or imaginary, that had occurred during his entire life. For want of another villain – he would not cast his mother in that role – his wrath was concentrated on Tom. Punishments were remembered: pocket money docked; chores enforced; his bicycle locked up, its use forbidden for a period. That was a favourite act of retribution, imposed because it curtailed Alan's freedom. By the time he reached The Willows in November, all Alan's old wounds were reopened, raw, and he was eager for revenge.

He supposed his mother had carried out her intention of telling Tom the truth. She might have chickened out; there had been no reaction, no angry letter or irate visit, simply silence from the pair of them, although his mother had continued paying money into his building society account. After she stopped coming to see him, he had no visitors; she had been his only one. He hadn't requested an official prison visitor; he did not need a stranger prying into his affairs. When, at last, he reached the open prison, with its rehabilitation programme, including shopping trips and work experience outside the premises, life expanded for him and he saw there was a future.

In spite of his mother's revelation, it never occurred to Alan that when Tom died, he would not inherit: after all, there was no other child. He'd barely known his cousin and it did not cross his mind that Tom might prefer her, a blood relation and without a criminal record, as his heir. If he'd known that there would be nothing for him after Tom's death, he might have killed him in November. But those two boys were in the house, those tiresome kids who seemed to have made themselves at home. They'd say that he'd been there. Of course, he could have killed them, too, but even Alan drew the line at killing children, and they had not annoyed him, personally; it was their mere presence that was the nuisance. Besides, a visit to an invalid parent plausibly explained his presence; a beaten-up or dead old man would end all chances of parole.

While the boys were in the house, he'd suppressed his rage, but after they left, he had watched the old man shrink back into his seat as Alan taunted him.

'I'm glad I'm not your son,' he'd sneered. It wasn't true. He'd been proud of the man he had thought was his father, boasted to his schoolmates about Tom's war record and had taken a genuine interest in aviation until, in adult life, he had rebelled.

'I'm glad, too,' Tom had answered. 'You've shamed me, and your mother.'

Alan had hit him then, hard, in the stomach, where bruising would be hidden, and the old man, winded, winced, but made no sound beyond a tiny groan. He'd surrendered his immediate funds without protest.

'You've destroyed everything you've touched, Alan,' he'd said, when he was able to speak. 'Yourself, as well as your mother and your poor, unhappy wife. What do a few pounds matter after that?'

Alan had not taken his credit card; using that could cause problems. It had taken Tom a few more weeks to die.

He'd go to The Willows when he got out. He had to find the gun, and make sure it worked. Mick had said the ammunition must be checked for damp.

'You could use a hair-dryer on it,' he'd suggested. Alan

didn't know if he was joking; you couldn't always tell with Mick.

While Alan was finishing his sentence, the days began to draw out: you always noticed this in January, said Ivy. She was worrying about Steve, who, as the weeks went on, was coming in too late at night.

He told her that he'd been with friends watching videos, or at the resurrected youth club. Sometimes these replies were true but Ivy was suspicious about a new pair of trainers he'd acquired, and a smart navy donkey jacket. How had he paid for them?

He said he'd bought them from a friend, that they were misfits, bad buys.

Then Sharon, who had a part-time job at the supermarket now, saw him pocketing cans of lager in the store. She did not tell her mother, but she tackled him.

'You were lucky not to get caught,' she told him. 'How do you think Mum would feel if she heard you were down at the nick?'

Like most thieves, Steve didn't expect to be caught, and he said so.

'If you go on with it, you will be, one day,' Sharon said. 'I'll have something to say about it, if you bring trouble on us. Your dad was good to us and Mum's treated you like her own son. What a way to act, after all that.'

'He shouldn't have died,' Steve muttered, scuffing the ground.'

'Well, he did. People do,' said Sharon. 'I don't think much of some of your friends,' she added. She had seen him with a group of tough-looking, slightly older boys, a few of whom she remembered from school, which she had left only two years ago herself.

'You should talk. Look at you – a kid with no father,' Steve retorted.

'Adam has got a father. He's an absent one, that's all,' said Sharon. 'No one thinks anything of that these days. Besides, he's got a good home, and so have you.'

Steve paid no attention to her advice. He had had an idea. The Willows' key still hung on Ivy's dresser; now that the place had been sold, there'd be stuff there to steal. There'd be money, probably, and a television and video. He could enter without breaking in, and take whatever he could carry. Greg Black's brother had a mate who sold things on at boot sales; he asked no questions about where they'd come from.

Steve asked his stepmother who had bought the place and Ivy said she'd heard it was a retired lady, Miss Darwin.

She'd be old, Steve decided. Perfect.

He'd never burgled a house before, but people did it all the time and got away with it. Once he'd offloaded the goods, he could brag about it; no one could pin it on him then. He dreamed about large sums of money: hundreds of pounds which he could spend on trips to London or to Birmingham, where there would be amusement arcades and clubs, bright lights and excitement. Steve was bored. He was lazy at school, scraping through his tests and sometimes playing truant, though not yet often enough to have been in big trouble. The group of boys he'd fallen in with couldn't wait to leave, despite an uncertain future. Though there were jobs in Haverscot, the town had suffered in the recession and factories on the perimeter had had to cut staff. However, there was work for those who really wanted it and did not expect to start out as managing director. Steve saw no point in working for peanuts when you could lift things for nothing, and either use or sell them. After all, he had no living expenses; Ivy fed and housed him, and clothed him too, though not in the style he'd choose himself, and some of what she bought for all of them came from jumble sales. He never thought that this would end when he left school: that it might be reasonable, then, to contribute to the household budget.

Steve took the key one Thursday night. He walked along the street in his new stolen trainers, and turned into Wordsworth Road, continuing past the first houses till he reached The Willows. It was so isolated, just asking to be done, he thought. If this went well – and it would – he could return, once there'd been time for the insurance to pay up so that the old lady could replace what he'd taken, and do it again. After all, she wouldn't lose; he might be doing her a favour as she'd get the latest models for her replacements, each time he visited.

He'd brought a holdall with him. Without wheels, he wouldn't be able to take away a television unless it was a portable. Steve didn't feel confident about lifting a car yet; he needed practice.

Turning in at The Willows' gate, sauntering up the drive, just as if he were about to call on old Tom, Steve had a sudden memory of his father and of Joe's wrath if he could see him now. Joe had never beaten him, but he would for this, Steve knew for certain. He felt a squirm of indecision but he shrugged it aside. His dad had left him, so he must do what he could to help himself, and thieving brought him things which Joe, if he'd been around, would have provided.

Was the old girl in? The place looked quiet, but there was a light showing in the hall. Old people went to bed early, so she'd be upstairs by now and he could move about below without disturbing her. Maybe she'd forgotten to turn out the light. He walked on, more confidently, and as he approached the front door a security light flooded him in sudden brilliance. He halted. Tom had had no lights like this.

He changed his plans, dumping his holdall under a nearby bush and striding firmly to the door. He would ring the bell, and if she answered, he would ask if she had any jobs for him – he'd come back and do them on Saturday, he'd say.

He rang the bell, but no one came. Marigold, now a regular member of Haverscot's Choral Society, was rehearsing for a performance of *Elijah*. Steve opened the door, and entered.

While he was there, Steve took a look around the house. Painters were working in the bedroom at the front; trestles and dustsheets were in position and the walls were bare, rubbed down. In Tom's old room, overlooking the garden and the river at the back, there were sea-green curtains patterned with tiny flowers, and the single bed was covered with a quilted matching spread. The room where all the books had been was now painted a warm primrose colour, and there were bright curtains at the window, printed with some sort of plant, each with its name below in funny writing. They were herbs, but Steve did not investigate that far. There was a table and a small, neat desk against one wall, and a chair. It was a sort of study, he supposed, not looking at a few books stacked neatly on the freshly painted shelves.

In what had been the dining-room, there was a large table covered with oilcloth and spread with heaps of vari-coloured paper, pots of glue and tins of varnish, and a row of wooden boxes, differing in size. On it, there was also a cylindrical tin; it looked like a waste paper basket and it had bits of mottled paper stuck to it. She was pasting paper on it, prettying it up; what a waste of time.

Then he saw a decorated box. It stood on a small table with some other objects Marigold had nearly finished. This one, hinged, was covered in flowers, matched and patched, darkly varnished; it looked like a sort of captured garden, Steve thought. It had a catch to hold it shut. It could be used for storing bits and pieces – costume jewellery, love letters, photographs. Ivy would love it.

When Marigold returned, her portable radio had gone; so had her new toaster, and the video. Steve had taken her jewellery; there wasn't much, just some things that had been her mother's. He hadn't touched the silver; he was still a small-time crook. She did not discover the burglary until the next morning when she could not make her breakfast toast.

She called the police, but the thief's mode of entry was not obvious. No window had been broken and no door was forced. She knew she had left nothing open, not even a fanlight; it was too cold for that. Then she remembered Mark, for whom she had equipped the haunted room and where he sometimes came to do his homework. She hadn't had the locks changed, and he still had a key; she'd never got it back from him.

Could he have taken the video? Was he big enough to carry it and the other things that had gone?

Perhaps he'd brought an accomplice with him: Terry?

18

THE POLICE SENT a detective round to dust for fingerprints. He made a mess of Marigold's clean surfaces, and,
as she expected, threw up a child's handprint here and there,
though not in her bedroom, from which the jewellery had
been taken. She did not mention whom she suspected. A
child had visited her, she said; adult prints might be those
of the two painters working in the house. The thief had not
ransacked the place; Steve had been a tidy pilferer when he
stole from Tom, and this time he had been restricted by what
he could carry away. There was no second set of child's prints
but Terry, taller than Mark, might have larger hands and his,
Marigold thought, could have been one of the unidentified
sets revealed. He would have known that she was out, with
his stepfather, at the choral practice. Mark knew there was
no dog to see them off – not that Sinbad would have deterred
a burglar; he was more likely to have welcomed an intruder
with a wagging tail and friendly licks.

All the stolen property could easily be sold, but Marigold
had marked the television and the video with the postcode
at her old address, using the recommended pen which would
show up the writing under ultra violet light. She had been
wearing, on her right hand, as she often did, her mother's
ruby and diamond engagement ring, and her pearl necklace,
but she was sorry to lose a gold locket which contained a lock

of her grandmother's blonde hair; such things were common in Edwardian times. There was a garnet brooch, too, and some other things. She hadn't photographed them. The police were not optimistic about her chances of regaining them.

She notified the insurance company immediately, but she took no steps to replace the larger items. If her suspicions were correct, she might recover them.

The thief had taken one of her decorated boxes. Mark, she remembered, had admired it.

Dealing with all this occupied her throughout Friday. In the evening, she telephoned Richard and asked him if he could spare the time to come and see her the next morning. It was important. When he arrived, she described the burglary and said that the police, so far, had no clues.

'But I've a suspect in mind,' she said. 'Young Mark. I didn't say so to the police because I hope to deal with it myself, perhaps with your aid.' She explained her theory, based on Mark's possession of a key.

'You think he had help,' said Richard, when he had heard her out.

'I don't think he could have carried all those things by himself,' she said. 'Do you?'

'Not really. You've got Terry in mind, haven't you? And you think we might find the things they took?'

'If it was those two boys, yes. Before they try to sell them,' she answered. 'I don't want to believe that they're the culprits, but I've good reason to suspect Mark.'

'Yes, you have,' he agreed. 'Terry gets plenty of pocket money. I know, because I provide it.' He pondered. 'Shall we go and see Mark's mother? If he confesses and Terry's involved, then we'll tackle him.'

Marigold understood that he wanted to approach the possible culprits in that order because he did not want a confrontation with Terry if he was not involved.

'Yes,' she said. 'I'm sorry about casting Terry as an accomplice but I don't know any other friends of Mark's.'

'No offence taken,' said Richard, who thought Terry, if he knew about Mark's key, could well have been the ring leader.

Together, they set out. The rain had eased off and the grey, dank day was raw. Richard had come by car as he was on his way to do the shopping. They drove round to Susan Conway's house and rang the bell, which was answered promptly.

'Yes?' Susan stared at the pair, the elderly woman with a felt hat pulled down above her sallow face, whom she had never seen before, and the tall, sad-looking man whom she recognised but could not identify. Susan met so many people in the course of her work that she found it difficult to place those she came across only rarely.

Richard saw her problem.

'Richard Gardner,' he reminded her. 'And this is Miss Darwin who lives at The Willows.'

'Yes?' Susan said again. She was busy cleaning the house and they were a tiresome interruption.

'The Willows,' Richard repeated. 'Where Mr Morton lived.'

'I don't know Mr Morton or The Willows,' Susan said, using professional calm to hide her impatience. She had remembered who Richard was: stepfather of the disappearing Terry.

'Mark knew him,' Richard said.

'Mark and he were friends,' said Marigold, intervening. 'I bought the house from Mr Morton's executors. He lent Mark books,' she added. '*Coot Club*, for example.'

'Oh!' Susan still looked puzzled, but here was a ray of light. 'I thought he borrowed them from Ivy – the woman who looks after him when I'm working,' she said. 'How did he get them from Mr Morton? How were they friends?' Then, facing the inevitable, for she must discover what had been going on, she stood aside. 'Won't you come in?' she said.

She was an attractive woman. Richard had thought so

when they met before. Her fair hair was cut short, almost like a boy's, and she had very blue eyes; he could see that she was irritated by their visit and had had a major surprise about Mark's activities. She led them into her sitting-room, which was functionally furnished; the chair and sofa looked like those often seen in a hotel bar, covered in soft grey-blue leather. Perhaps they came from a hotel supplier; maybe she got a discount through the trade.

They all sat down, and Susan, who wore narrow black trousers and a long pink sweater, leaned forward, looking intently at Miss Darwin.

'You said Mark knew a man called Mr Morton, who lent him books,' she said. 'I want to know about him. What sort of man was he?' All sorts of possibilities were passing through her mind.

'He was an elderly invalid who died just before Christmas,' said Miss Darwin. 'I never met him. He'd had a stroke. He was unable to walk far.'

'And?'

'He wasn't a child molester, Mrs Conway,' Richard said. He had followed the direction of her thoughts.

'Did Terry know him? Why are you both here?' asked Susan.

'Mark's been to see me, too,' Miss Darwin told her, adding, 'I've been pleased to make his acquaintance.'

Clearly, he hadn't told his mother about his visits. Miss Darwin did not want to get him into still more trouble than he might be in already; there had to be a reason for his secrecy.

'Where was he last night, Mrs Conway? Between eight and ten o'clock,' asked Richard.

'At Ivy's – Mrs Burton's,' Susan answered. 'I was on late duty and he stayed over. He does sometimes.' She coloured up suddenly. She had spent the night at The Golden Accord, with David; it was the third time this had happened, made possible by Ivy keeping Mark. Susan was not quite sure where this was leading her, but she had let herself stray into it. 'Why do you want to know?'

'Someone entered my house last night, while I was at a choral society rehearsal,' said Miss Darwin. 'They stole my video recorder, a portable radio, some jewellery, and other items.'

'Are you accusing Mark?' Susan's anger rose. 'How dare you!' she exclaimed. 'He'd never do anything like that.'

'He has friends you don't seem to know about, like Mr Morton,' said Miss Darwin. 'And he could enter the house. He has a key.'

'He wouldn't steal!' Susan was insistent, and still furiously indignant, but a doubt was entering her mind. How could she be certain? She knew so little about Mark's daily life, trusting him to Ivy, who could not watch him all the time. She'd agreed that he was old enough to play in the park and visit his friends, and come home alone. 'You think Terry did this with him,' she said, turning to Richard. 'That's why you're here.'

'He couldn't have carried everything himself,' said Richard. 'If it was Mark, he must have had some help.'

'Then it was Terry's idea,' said Susan. 'Mark would never plan such a thing – and Terry's been in trouble before.'

'That's true, but not for theft,' said Richard, admiring her spirited defence of her son. 'Why don't we ask Mark about it?' he suggested. 'Where is he now?'

'He's still at Ivy's,' Susan said, more calmly. She had been back only half an hour herself. 'I'm due to fetch him soon.'

'Suppose you do that straight away,' suggested Richard.

'I will,' said Susan. 'But what about the police? You must have reported the burglary. You said it took place on Thursday night. A whole day's gone by.'

'I have reported it,' Miss Darwin said. 'But I didn't mention Mark. I thought, if it was him, we might recover what was taken and no more need be said, as long as he is made to see the error of his ways.'

She did not want to believe that Mark was a thief. They'd grown so friendly and she looked forward to seeing him. He always rang the bell and waited to be admitted. Once or twice she'd asked him for his key and he had said that he'd forgotten it. She wasn't sure if this was true. She had bought some books she'd hoped he'd read, and she had taken him along to the library one evening, getting the librarian to enrol him. It seemed that no one else – not his mother, nor Ivy – had thought of doing this. Then she'd had the melancholy room re-done in a way that he might find appealing, equipping it with a table and chair so that if he wanted to, he could do his homework there. He'd used it several times and said that it was brilliant.

'I'm sure Mark's completely innocent,' said Susan. 'But we must get to the bottom of this now. I'll ring Ivy and tell her I'm coming round for him at once. Please wait here for us. I'll only be a few minutes.'

But Ivy said that Mark was out. He'd gone to Merrifields to see his friend Terry.

'We didn't see him when we were on our way here,' said Richard. 'We could have missed him, though, while I was picking you up, Miss Darwin.'

Inconsequentially, Marigold wondered if he would ever use her Christian name.

'It's possible,' she said. 'Shall we go and see?'

Verity had planned, that Saturday, to go to an exhibition of water colours at a gallery some twenty miles away. Nowadays she plotted to avoid Richard, either by shutting herself in her studio or by going out. His long, lugubrious face was a constant reproach, and for some weeks they had shared an unacknowledged conspiracy to escape from one another. He went to his choral society on Thursday nights and had just joined an amateur drama group which met on Tuesdays. Verity had taunted him about it.

'You'll make a fool of yourself. You can't act,' she said.

Richard thought he acted all the time. At work, he played the part of an efficient executive; at home, he adopted the role of benign parent and caring husband. Sometimes he wondered if he ever felt a genuine emotion or uttered a spontaneous word.

'I shan't be acting,' he informed her. 'I'm helping the stage manager.'

To his amazement, the stage manager proved to be the thin woman from the train, who was a solicitor with a city firm. She was getting married in September.

What if Verity, in one of her sudden fits of togetherness, offered her services as a scenery painter? But she didn't; since Christmas there had been no such lightning impulses.

She rarely went out at night, sometimes talking about joining another evening class but never doing so. Lately, she had often been in an alcoholic haze when he came home, and that was better than the belligerence which usually preceded that stage. For her own part, Verity could not bear to contemplate the plight that would have been hers and the boys' if Richard had not rescued them, and by inference, her debt to him. At that time, she had been popping pep pills as well as drinking; she was heavily in debt; the two boys lacked confidence and Terry had been bed-wetting. All that ended when she and Richard married. For months she had limited her drinking, and, in the euphoria of her new romance, had given up the pills. When this wore off, she turned to tranquillisers instead of winding herself up artificially; that happened now without a stimulant because Richard irritated her so much. He was too patient. He suffered all her provocation as she tested him to see how much he would take before he hit her, but he never did. The boys' father had not lasted any time at all.

Verity, in her calmer moments, knew that her conduct was indefensible, but she never blamed herself; it was all Richard's fault. He was so weak. He simply walked away when she was wound up for a quarrel.

That morning, she drank two cups of black coffee and ate a piece of dry toast, in her dressing-gown, then went upstairs to have a bath before the exhibition. She'd dress up, pull out all the stops, become the painter lady; maybe she'd meet people she knew and be encouraged to mount an exhibition of her own. That was her world, the world of art: if she hadn't saddled herself with a family, she could be having a successful career by now. She often thought like this, dreaming of the might-have-been. She lay in the bath, her hair pinned on top of her head, a few damp wisps trailing over her shoulders. Her body made islands in the foam: thin breasts, bony knees when she bent her legs. Her ribs, masked now, stood out against her white skin. Verity did not want to believe that she was unattractive; slenderness was desirable, wasn't it? But Richard didn't want her: not like that.

Tears of self-pity began to run down her cheeks as she lay there in the water, almost forgetting her plan for the day ahead, and then, breaking in upon her miserable wallowing, she heard voices.

Terry was talking, and there was another voice she did not recognise until she heard her son call his friend by name. It was Mark.

'We've got no dad, either,' Terry was saying. 'So what?'

'Don't you ever see him?'

'Not really. Not for years,' said Terry. 'But he will come back,' he added confidently, reassuring himself, not his auditor.

'And you've got him – Mr Gardner—' Mark persisted.

'Cat's his name,' said Terry.

'Him,' Mark repeated. 'He's like a dad.'

There was a rustling sound, paper tearing. The boys were eating crisps.

'He's not our dad,' said Terry. 'Our dad's an artist, like mum is.'

Verity, by this time, was lying motionless in the cooling water, listening intently. The voices, she realised, were being transmitted to her up the bath overflow pipe; the boys must be sitting near the outlet.

She had met the boys' father when they were both art students and he had gone on to become a graphic designer with a promising career, which he abandoned when he left her and went abroad. She did not know what he was doing now. It was so unfair that he had gone away and left them all; look what had become of them – her talent wasting, her sons dependent on an unfeeling man who loved none of them.

At this point in her thoughts she craved a drink, but the boys had resumed their conversation and she was compelled to listen.

'If your mum died, he'd look after you,' Mark was saying. 'Mr Gardner, I mean.'

'Well – yes,' Terry admitted, such a thought never having crossed his mind.

'And you've got a gran and granddad, haven't you?'

'Yes.'

They had two sets, in fact, though they never heard from the pair belonging to their father. There were some aunts and uncles too, also invisible.

'I haven't,' Mark said, cheerfully. 'Only my mum. I sometimes wonder what would happen if she got run over. Perhaps Ivy would look after me, like she does when Mum's away.'

'I expect so,' Terry said, not really interested. 'There's always the social,' he added. They'd come to see his mum once or twice before Cat came into their lives.

Mark didn't want to think about the social. They were all-powerful and could whisk you off without you having any choice. Dreadful things could happen to you in their care, he knew; he'd seen it on the telly, Ivy and Sharon clucking about it, while they thought that he was too intent upon his book to take in what was being said. Now and then, the dread of being left without his mother rose up like a nightmare in his mind. If that were to happen, there was no human soul responsible for him. He used to think that Tom would see that he was safe; more than once, when assailed by this rare panic, he'd mentally moved in to The Willows. But Tom had gone now; there was no safety net for him, unless Ivy took pity on him, but without Mum to pay for him, how could she afford to?

He seemed a long time answering. Verity wondered if the boys had moved away, and she sat up in the water, wringing out her sponge, ready to soap herself. Then she heard Richard's voice.

'Ah — Terry — Mark — there you are,' he said. 'I want a word with both of you. So does Miss Darwin. Come into the house.'

He sounded very stern. Richard was never angry, only annoyed, severe, reproving; these moods scarcely varied in degree.

Now what had the boys been doing?

Verity did not want to know. She sank down again, submerged her ears beneath the water and turned on the hot tap with her long, thin toes.

After a while, when all was silent, she stepped out of the bath and dried herself. Her hair had got quite wet and needed blowing dry. This took time.

She still had her own car, a small Fiat; Richard allowed her that and paid for it, including the petrol bill at a local garage.

Let him deal with this latest escapade, she thought, leaving the house quietly while voices droned on from behind the closed drawing-room door.

She did not ask herself where Justin was; sometimes it was better not to know, and it was not until hours later that she began to feel aggrieved because whatever had happened concerned one of her sons, and Richard had not thought fit to see that she was told.

19

MISS DARWIN BECAME certain, very early in the discussion, that Mark was not the thief. He hadn't understood, at first, what he was being accused of having done.

'You've been going to The Willows,' his mother had pitched in, before either Miss Darwin or Richard could open the bowling. She'd stated it as fact. She knew.

Mark, looking at Miss Darwin and Mr Gardner, saw them regarding him with very serious expressions on their faces. He was not afraid of either; in fact he liked both of them and was accustomed, now, to Miss Darwin's grim features. She could smile; he had seen her do so, especially when she'd had her glass of whisky. Besides, grown-ups were often hideous: children too, sometimes. He could name a few.

'You've still got a key, haven't you, Mark?' Miss Darwin intervened.

'It's on my ring,' he said, patting his waist. Beneath his anorak, he had a key-ring snapped to his belt. While he answered, he avoided looking at his mother. Mounds of explanations lay ahead. He knew that she was not just annoyed, but puzzled.

'Did you go into my house last night, Mark?' Miss Darwin pursued.

'No. I was at Ivy's. Me and Sharon played cards and then

I went to bed,' he said. He'd read in bed, a book borrowed from the library, by Terry Pratchett. It was good.

'What time was that?' asked Richard.

'Nine, about,' said Mark.

'What's all this about you going to The Willows?' Susan demanded. 'What's been going on?'

There was nothing for it. He'd got to speak up now. Mark took a deep breath.

'I used to go and see Mr Morton,' he said. His lip trembled. Why were they all so angry? His mother was furious, he could tell; he'd seldom seen her really cross, and though she was sometimes short with him when she was tired, she was never unfair.

'He lent you books,' his mother stated.

'Yes.' That wasn't wrong, surely?

'I thought Ivy lent you those,' his mother said.

'I never said so,' Mark replied.

'Why didn't you tell me about Mr Morton?'

'You might have stopped me going there, and I liked him,' answered Mark.

'He was an old man, and he was your friend,' said Miss Darwin. 'You told me that, Mark.' She turned to Susan. 'Mark had a book Mr Morton lent him just before he died. One by Arthur Ransome, wasn't it, Mark?' She looked at him, her gaze steady behind the dark-rimmed glasses which she did not always wear. Mark had worked out that she put them on when she was concentrating very hard, and when she did that work of hers, with the cut-out flowers and patterns.

'Yes,' he agreed, warily.

'Mark came to return the book, believing that the house was empty,' she told Susan. 'I was out at the time, but I returned while he was replacing it, and we made friends.' Miss Darwin spoke firmly; she had directed women like Susan in her working life. 'We'd met before, hadn't we, Mark? In the park when you and Terry were having trouble with some older boys.'

Mark nodded. 'Yes,' he muttered.

'I was living in a rented bungalow then, Mrs Conway,' said Miss Darwin. 'While I looked for a house.'

Now Richard was the startled listener. Miss Darwin had not, on Christmas Day, mentioned meeting the boys, and nor had Terry. She might not have recognised him, but surely he would not have forgotten her?

Susan remembered that it was from Terry's stepfather that she had heard of the old woman who had told the motorists that Mark and his friend were not responsible for damaging their cars. What else had he been doing that she didn't know about?

'You missed Mr Morton, didn't you, Mark? You were sad when he died,' said Miss Darwin, firmly leading her witness.

'Yes.'

'But you knew you should return his book.'

'Yes.' Mark spoke more confidently now.

'Miss Darwin's video and her portable radio and some other things were stolen last night, while she was out,' said Richard, thinking it was time they got to the point. 'You didn't take them, did you, Mark?'

Susan began to bridle but before she could defend her son, Mark answered for himself.

'No. How could you think so?' he said, on a wail, and the tears began to fall, though he tried hard to blink them away and did not sob.

Miss Darwin frowned at Richard.

'We didn't, Mark, but we needed to hear you say so,' she said. 'You see, you had a key, and whoever was the thief didn't break in. There was no sign of a forced entry.'

Mark knew then who was guilty. It was Steve.

'I shall change the locks,' said Miss Darwin. 'And you will still come and see me, if you want to, and if your mother says you may.'

She glanced across at Susan, who knew herself out-manoeuvred.

'Of course. It's kind of you,' she managed.

While all this was going on, Terry had sat there silently, but now it was his turn.

'So you knew nothing about this either, Terry,' Richard said.

'No.' Terry was completely mystified.

'I didn't think so,' Richard said, not altogether truthfully. Terry could have been an accomplice of whoever did it, if it was a youngster: one of Justin's dubious friends, for instance. But it could have been someone connected with the painters; he was unable to think of anyone else who would have been able to enter the house without leaving any signs of how it had been done. He had seen Miss Darwin lock up before she left; he'd even asked her if she'd checked all round, so used was he to Verity's slapdash ways. Miss Darwin wasn't careless; she would not have left any window insecurely latched. He hoped having an aura of suspicion, however fragile, directed at him would not make Terry disappear again. Mark was the one in possible hot water, for visiting without his mother's knowledge. He saw that she could not wait to pitch into him. He'd take them home; then she could get it over.

But Susan didn't give him the opportunity.

'We'll be going now,' she said, standing up. Then, turning to Miss Darwin, she added, 'Thank you for not mentioning Mark's name to the police.'

Richard stood up too, looking at her with some admiration. She was thin – not scraggy, like Verity, but slim; her expression was alert. She was a capable woman with a lot to manage, a strong person much the same age, he guessed, as Verity, though she looked younger. He wondered idly if she had some man in her life.

'I'll drive you back,' he said.

'No – please don't bother,' she said. 'It's not far, and it isn't raining.'

They let her go. Richard saw her to the door, Mark following behind her, head cast down. Terry seized his chance to escape, and when Richard returned to the drawing-room, Miss Darwin was alone.

'She can't wait to give that child the telling-off of his life,' she said.

'No,' Richard agreed. 'Poor kid.'

Mark still hadn't surrendered his key to The Willows, but his mother would soon take it from him; that was certain. There must be another one elsewhere, or someone with the skill to enter undetected: whatever the answer, Marigold knew she must call a locksmith in without delay. Mortice locks, she thought regretfully, like she'd had in London, with security catches on all the windows. She believed Mark's story, but he would have a nasty time when he reached home. His mother should have known about his visits to Mr Morton; they had been frequent, over quite a period of time: some months. Mrs Conway had been shaken by today's revelations, and was angry; there must be a way to smooth her down, make things easier for Mark. Marigold resolved to try.

Susan did not speak to Mark until they arrived home. She held him by the arm all the way, and he was frightened. He always tried so hard not to be a nuisance, and she knew she could trust him.

But this was exactly what Susan now accused him of betraying: her trust.

When they reached the house, she sat him down opposite her in the sitting-room and began.

'Now, Mark, what else have you been doing that I don't know about?' she asked. Ivy would have to answer some important questions, too, but Mark must first tell her everything.

'Nothing. Ivy knew I was at Mr Morton's,' Mark said, his face averted as he studied his sturdy shoes.

'Every time?'

'Yes.' Mark knew she hadn't known he was at The Willows after Mr Morton died, but that wasn't what his mother had asked. Until then, he and Steve had gone there with her blessing and often on her instructions. 'She looked after him,' he added.

'Looked after him?'

'Cleaned the house. Left meals for him. He couldn't hardly walk,' said Mark. 'Steve did shopping for him,' Mark went on. 'He couldn't, you see. He could only go out in a wheelchair. He was going to get one with an engine in the summer. They run on batteries like some milk vans.'

He hoped she wouldn't ask about the time when Mr Morton died; he knew she wouldn't like to hear that he and Steve were there. Susan, however, was calming down.

'Why didn't you tell me about him?' she persisted.

'I don't know.'

Because there wasn't time, she was thinking guiltily. She was always in a rush. She asked him about school and homework, gave him messages for Ivy, but seldom sat down and heard about his day.

'You were lucky Miss Darwin believed you about last night,' said Susan.

'I'm not a thief,' said Mark indignantly. 'She knows that.'

'Even so, if she'd told the police about you having a key, we'd have had them round again,' said Susan.

'I'd done nothing wrong then, either,' Mark protested.

Susan's head was ringing with propaganda about the children of single mothers being doomed to lives of crime. It did not have to be like that; she'd always said so. Look at widows' children; no one condemned them out of hand. Or did they? Anyway, they had had fathers, men they knew about, and some of whom, like murdered policemen, were heroes.

'I know, but if your friends want to do wrong things, you mustn't join in,' Susan warned.

'They don't,' said Mark. Steve did wrong things, but he wasn't exactly Mark's friend and it was nice not having to stick with him any more. 'I liked Mr Morton,' Mark affirmed. 'He was like a granddad might be, I thought.'

'Oh, Mark!' At this, Susan suddenly burst into tears,

rushed over to him and hugged him.

Mark felt most uncomfortable. Why was she crying, when he had done nothing wrong except have a secret? Was that so bad?

'Don't cry,' he implored, patting her anxiously.

Susan soon regained her self-control.

'Mark,' she said, now speaking firmly. 'You haven't got a grandfather because my parents are dead. You know that, don't you?'

'Yes,' he mumbled.

'Lots of children don't have grandparents,' she told him. 'But lots of children don't live in nice houses or have parents who can afford to buy them mountain bikes or computer games. Lots of people haven't got jobs, you know.'

'Yes,' Mark repeated miserably. 'I know that. It's all right, Mum. I just liked him being there,' he said.

He liked Miss Darwin, too, and she had said that he could use the room where the books had been. Something told him that he had better not repeat this to his mother. As he came to this conclusion, the telephone rang.

With a mutter of annoyance, Susan released him and went to answer it. He saw her expression of surprise, irritation, then a tiny thaw.

'Yes,' she kept on saying. 'Yes. Yes. Well – I don't know – no, I am free tomorrow. Thank you. Four o'clock.'

She replaced the receiver and turned to Mark.

'That was your new friend, Miss Darwin,' she said. 'She's invited us to tea tomorrow afternoon. I couldn't very well refuse.'

Tomorrow afternoon, thought Mark. That would give him time to see if Steve had done the robbery. That is, if his mother would let him go round to Ivy's.

She did. They went together. She meant to cross-examine Ivy about the licence she permitted Mark while he was in her care.

Ivy still saw Susan frequently, but not as often as when Mark had had to be escorted back and forth. Susan paid her weekly, and when Mark stayed overnight there were cooperative washing arrangements regarding his clothes. Ivy rendered an account which Susan checked against her own record of the hours Mark had spent with her, and the meals she had provided. They respected one another, got on well, and had never had a serious difference of opinion.

So when Susan arrived, wearing a frown and with Mark beside her looking thoroughly abashed, she sensed trouble.

Susan did not beat about the bush, following Ivy into the kitchen where Kylie was spooning a soggy mixture into the willing mouth of her nephew. Sharon was working at the supermarket.

'Mr Morton, Ivy,' Susan said. 'Who was he? Mark says you let him go visiting?'

'I did. He was a nice old man – very lonely after his wife died,' said Ivy. 'I cleaned for him and left him meals, but I was anxious about him at night. He'd had a stroke and could only walk with difficulty. Steve and Mark used to spend time with him. He taught them chess, and that. It was good for them to be with such a gentleman. Why?'

'Mark never told me he went there,' said Susan.

'Perhaps he thought you wouldn't be interested,' Ivy stated. 'There was nothing wrong, Susan. He was a good old man. The boys helped him – they kept him company and did shopping for him.'

'I'm not suggesting there was anything wrong,' said Susan. 'I just think I should have known about it.'

'You don't expect me to tell you every time they've gone to the park to play football, or Mark's been to see one of his friends, do you?' asked Ivy, drawing herself up and adopting a combative expression. 'I always know where he's going. Don't you trust me to look after him?'

'Of course I do, Ivy.' Susan had to retreat a fraction; she could not afford to lose Ivy's goodwill; where would she find someone to replace her?

'Mr Morton was a good influence,' said Ivy firmly. 'A man

in their lives, two fatherless boys.'

At this point, Adam began to wail because Kylie had allowed some of his pappy meal to go up his nose. Ivy, almost without seeming to move, wiped his nostrils clear, patted his back so that he ceased his cries, and spooned in another portion.

'Take Mark into the lounge, Kylie,' she said. 'Susan and I have to talk. We can do that and see to Adam.'

Mark and Kylie left the room at speed.

'Those two get on well,' Ivy said as they left. 'They do jigsaws together and play cards. Steve's gone a bit past Mark now, being that bit older.' She wouldn't tell Susan that she was anxious about Steve who, one night recently, had come back reeking of petrol. She'd caught a strong whiff of it from his discarded jeans. Next day she heard that a barn had been set alight some miles out of Haverscot. Challenged about his clothes, Steve said he'd helped a mate put juice in his car and they'd spilt some. Was it true? Ivy could not be certain. She knew that Steve missed his father; Joe would soon have found out the truth. When Steve was down at Tom's, she had never worried about what he was up to.

'Does Mark see much of Terry Gardner?' Susan asked.

'Quite a bit,' said Ivy, who was not altogether sure.

'Have you met his mother?'

'No. Some sort of artist, isn't she?' said Ivy.

'Terry ran off one night and hid. He was reported missing,' Susan said. 'The police came to us and woke Mark up, wondering if he knew where Terry might be. He didn't, of course.'

Ivy had not heard about this.

'Oh dear,' she said. 'Why did he do such a thing?'

Susan told her what she knew about the incident.

'Now Mark's visiting this Miss Darwin at The Willows,' she went on. 'She was burgled last night. She thought Mark might have done it because he had a key.'

Ivy's glance flew to the dresser hook from which hung a batch of keys. She went to check them, though she could already see the distinctive yellow label on Tom's, duly returned by Steve after his escapade. But how had Mark got hold of one? Perhaps the old man had given it to him.

'It wasn't Mark, of course,' Susan was saying. 'But it wasn't nice having him suspected and then not knowing about his visits there.'

'I can see that,' said Ivy. 'I should have told you, Susan, but I didn't realise Mark hadn't mentioned it.' By the same token, perhaps Susan should have reported Terry's disappearance, which was a significant event in the children's lives, but Ivy thought it wiser not to say so.

'Well — we've cleared things up now,' said Susan. She thought of seeking more assurances, but decided not to; until Mark was older, she needed Ivy. Unless she let things run on with David: part of her thought how easy it would be to give up the struggle to carry on alone; part of her wanted to remain independent.

Meanwhile, Kylie had shown Mark a pretty box that Steve had given Ivy. It was exactly like the one he had admired which Miss Darwin had decorated. He had known that his mother would love a box like that. If proof were needed that Steve had been the thief, here it was.

His mother, resolved to take more interest in how he spent his time, asked what he and Kylie had done while she and Ivy had their talk.

'Kylie showed me a box Steve gave Ivy,' he said. 'It was all covered with pictures of flowers, stuck on. This size.' He made a shape with his hands.

'How nice of him,' said Susan.

Mark could not say any more. He couldn't tell on Steve.

20

NONE OF HER guests wanted to have tea with Miss Darwin. Even Mark and Richard would have preferred a different occasion without their families, though both saw that attendance was unavoidable.

When Verity returned from the exhibition, she was animated, looking almost pretty; she had enjoyed herself and met several acquaintances who had asked how her work was going. Richard recognised the fey charm which had originally drawn him to her, her air of helplessness. He decided to tell her about the invitation before her mood changed, as, inevitably, it must.

'I won't go,' she said. 'Miss Darwin's your friend, not mine.'

'It's an opportunity to meet Mark's mother,' said Richard. 'Mark's Terry's friend. I think you ought to be there.'

'What was all that about this morning?' asked Verity. 'She was here then, wasn't she? Mark's mother?'

'Yes. Miss Darwin was burgled during the choral society's rehearsal,' said Richard. 'She knew Mark had often visited Mr Morton, who lived there before, and wondered if he knew who could have got into the house without forcing an entry.'

'You mean she wondered if Mark was the thief, because he might know how to get in,' said Verity bluntly.

'She thought it possible, but unlikely,' said Richard.

'And she decided Terry could have been his accomplice. Thanks very much,' said Verity. 'I'm certainly not going to tea if she suspects my son of stealing.'

'She doesn't. She never did,' said Richard. 'She wants to make friends with Susan Conway herself, and she thought you would like to meet her because of Terry.'

'Are the boys invited too?'

'Yes.' Richard thought the tea party was doomed in advance, but saw no way to prevent it from being held.

'Mark seemed a nice enough boy,' Verity conceded. 'What sort of person is his mother?'

If Richard replied that she was pretty, animated and smart, he would antagonise Verity, who would suspect him of a sexual interest in her; if he said she was plain, dowdy and dull, he would soon be proved a liar. How should he answer?

He shrugged.

'I hardly noticed,' he said. 'She was concerned about Mark and in a hurry to get him home and find out what he knew, if anything.' He was not going to say that he had met Susan before today; that would be committing kamikaze.

'Well, since you seem to have accepted without consulting me, I suppose I'll have to fall in with your plans,' Verity said. 'But it will be a waste of the afternoon.'

'You'd be doing Miss Darwin a favour,' Richard said. 'She's anxious to help young Mark. His mother's working hours make things difficult, as we already know, and she thinks it's good for him to come here.'

'I'm sure it is.' Verity briefly felt benevolent about exposing Mark to their large garden, tree house and other amenities.

'It turns out that she was the woman in the park who saw the boys being teased that time when Terry's football was snatched,' Richard told her. 'She saved them from a big problem then.'

'Oh,' said Verity.

He waited for her to ask why she had not been told this

before. Hadn't Miss Darwin recognised Terry on Christmas Day?

But Verity said nothing. She might think about it in the middle of the night and demand an explanation then; that would give him time to think of one. New spectacles required, he thought: that might pass.

He and Verity had not discussed Terry's brush with the law after it happened. There had been no obvious problems since then, and the boy had been chastened by his visit to the police station. He had friends they had not met, and so had Justin, but Mark appeared to be eminently suitable. It was clear that Miss Darwin thought well of him, and while she might not be used to children, she was shrewd and would see through cant.

Verity remained in a reasonable frame of mind for the rest of the day and Richard seized the chance to make an attempt at family unity. *Jurassic Park* was on at a local cinema; he suggested they should go, as the boys had wanted to see it since it first became a box-office success.

'Let's all go,' he dared to suggest, and when Verity agreed, his only worry was that all the seats would be sold.

But he was able to reserve four on the telephone, and Justin, though he said he'd meant to meet some friends, was persuaded to change his plans. They set off together, and for a few hours Richard imagined he might be able to salvage something of his marriage.

It was better than thinking about Caroline and her pregnancy.

Richard had been pretending that her condition had no relation to himself. A few people in the office had noticed it, though she wore loose jackets now and had made no mention of it.

Of course the father was the other man, the mystery begetter in Wiltshire, but after it was born, would either of them see the child? Would they have a chance to recognise their own son or daughter, maybe see a likeness which would

mean there was no need for scientific proof as to who had
scored? He wondered if the other man had been cast aside,
too, now that both of them had served their purpose – and
served was the operative word.

Wouldn't the child want to know who its father was?

What about young Mark? Did he see his father? Was
Susan a widow? He didn't seem to spend time with a
divorced father. Perhaps, like Verity's first husband, he had
run away from his responsibilities.

If this was his child, Richard did not want to run away
from it; he'd like to be involved. Indeed, he had fantasised
about marrying Caroline.

Why had she told him? Why not leave him in ignorance?
But of course, it was true that when he saw that she was
pregnant, he would have wondered if the child was his.

In the cinema, these thoughts, at intervals, obtruded.
Afterwards, they all went to a pizza bar nearby. The boys ate
hugely, while Verity nibbled at a tiny slice of the giant pizza
they had ordered. When they reached home, it was time for
all of them to go to bed.

Verity had drunk nothing since the gallery viewing
earlier. Richard managed to make love to her that night, but
it wasn't really love: more an act of pity.

On Sunday morning Steve stayed in bed till twelve. He often
did this at weekends, coming in late at night after an
evening with his friends. He always told Ivy he was with
Greg, or Bruce, or Kevin, and maybe he was, but not in any
of their houses, as she supposed, except when the parents had
gone out and the boys stayed in drinking beer and watching
videos.

He'd taken the stolen video recorder, the toaster and the
radio round to Greg's. Greg's older brother had given Steve
twenty-five pounds for them – peanuts, but Steve couldn't
have passed the stuff on himself: not yet. He wasn't in that
league, but he'd get there.

He'd try to sell the jewellery on his own, maybe in the

market next weekend. Some traders might not be too curious; he could say it was his mum's and she was sick and needed the money.

It was worth staying in for Sunday lunch. Ivy always cooked a roast and today it was pork, the crackling crisp, with apple sauce. All of them enjoyed it; even Adam had gravy and the mashed inside of a roast potato. Steve went out later; he left the jewellery in a drawer in his room. He might give a piece of it to Ivy, though he didn't think that it was quite her style; that locket thing, for instance, and the brooches. Were those red stones rubies? If so, they'd be worth a bomb.

He didn't know what his friends had lined up for that afternoon. The rain had stopped. They might go looking for some girls. Steve wasn't keen on wasting time with girls, but Greg and Kevin liked chatting them up, trying to impress them, and if that didn't work, then shocking them with insults. Steve wouldn't mind parading round with one, to earn respect; otherwise, he wasn't bothered. Respect mattered, though; he'd had it from being with his dad, who turned up at school meetings and at football matches when Steve was in the team. His dad looked good and didn't cheer too loudly: just enough to show he cared. Steve was never in the team now; he wasn't interested.

His mates were quite impressed by what he'd lifted from The Willows. Naturally, he didn't tell them where he'd got the stuff. He'd get some more, and soon, and make Greg's brother pay him better next time. Those big houses in Wordsworth Road were tempting; not much traffic went that way, as the road ended at the church, and they had big gardens offering concealment. There was that place where young Mark's friend lived, Merrifields: it was much bigger than The Willows and would have more loot. He'd really need some wheels to get stuff away from there. Perhaps he could use a wheelbarrow; if he pushed it briskly, it wouldn't take long to get the stuff to Ivy's and stash it in the garden. He wasn't keen on sharing anything, but young Mark might

help him get into Merrifields; he might even steal a key.
How could he get the kid to do it? He was an awkward little
bugger; he hadn't liked Steve's scams at Tom's. Scaring him
might do it; he could say he'd torch his bike or put worms
in his food.

As he ran through these possibilities in his mind, Steve
had an instant's vision of his father. Joe had been scrupulously honest. But he shouldn't have died. He'd left Steve on
his own.

Action was the way to banish these uncomfortable
thoughts. Steve thought he might take a look round
Merrifields this afternoon. Families went out on Sunday and
that guy at Merrifields might do the same. Steve would go
over the fields; then he wouldn't be noticed, lurking. He'd
climb the fence and approach the house across the garden.
He'd have a look around, size the place up, make a plan. He
could trap Mark into telling him about it – describing where
the bathroom window was, and so on, sorting out where it
would be easiest to enter if he failed to get the kid to find
a key.

A few nights ago, Steve had seen Greg and Kevin set light
to a barn stacked half-full with hay. He'd carried cans of
petrol for them, then stood back while Kevin lit the screwed-
up piece of paper he'd thrown into the soaked hay. Some
other, younger boys had watched before running off. It had
been a sight to see. Steve hadn't been too sure about the barn:
after all, cows ate hay and they might starve if their food
went up. But it was exciting, you couldn't deny that; all
those flames soaring into the dark sky. They'd got away in a
car Kevin had lifted to take them into the countryside, and
they'd dropped Steve on the outskirts of the town; once
they'd driven off, worried, he'd phoned the fire brigade from
a call box, then hurried home.

What would there be at Merrifields? Maybe a computer,
and cash. He'd found none at The Willows. There might be
a food processor. Ivy would find one very useful with all the
cooking she did. He'd like to get her one.

He ambled along the road. It was raw and damp. Some of the flood water had abated, but it could rain again at any minute. Almost automatically, he turned towards The Willows; it was on his route to the church and the field path which would lead him past the gardens of the houses above the river. He missed the quiet evenings at The Willows, the weekend afternoons spent in the warm, peaceful house, and he missed the easy pickings. Ripping Tom off had been a cinch, like stealing from a child, but he'd liked the old man and finding him dead like that had been a dreadful shock. The kid, Mark, had been so cool; funny, really.

As he walked towards the church, Steve saw, ahead of him, a blue Vauxhall which he recognised as belonging to Mark's mother. The brake lights came on as it slowed, then, indicator flashing, it turned in at The Willows. Why had she bothered to signal when there was no car in sight? Typical of a woman driver, decided Steve, who had no experience of being driven by one but who blotted up opinions expressed by others in his hearing. Several of his friends thought women slags, good for only one thing.

What was Susan Conway doing at The Willows? Was Mark with her? The old girl must have reported the burglary to the police. Steve walked on and peered up the drive. The air was dank and the lowering sky was black. He stepped between the gateposts and, hugging the sheltering shrubs, keeping to the sodden grass beside the drive, he went closer to the house. The porch light was on and he could see slivers of light between the drawn curtains and the downstairs windows. Steve slipped round to the back of the house and was there when he heard another car. arrive. Doors were banged, remarks exchanged, and when all was quiet he returned to the front to see if he could identify the new car.

It was the black Montego from Merrifields. He'd seen the man who owned it getting into it at the station when he'd been there with some other boys, including Justin Gardner, who had done brilliant patterns with spray paint on a wall. The kid was quite an artist. He'd had a few things to say about his stepfather; he didn't like the guy.

Steve stared at Richard's car. Why was he at The Willows? Was he alone? No sense of guilt about his thefts bothered Steve as he edged up to the sitting-room window and tried to peer through the chink in the curtains. He saw part of a head of tufty brown hair: that was Mark. He heard the boom of a male voice, then shriller sounds. A lot of people were in the house. Were all the Gardners there?

It seemed quite possible. If so, now was his chance to do Merrifields. Steve turned away. He'd best be quick. He'd brought no bag with him, but there would be one in the house if he could find it fast enough. There'd be the same sort of stuff as he'd taken from The Willows: a video, a radio, perhaps a camera, and the mixer. He forgot about the field approach he'd planned and ran back along the road.

Alan, peering through the window of the shed where the gun was buried, saw the figure of a youth flitting through the garden at The Willows. What was he up to? Nothing legal, that was certain.

It might be worth finding out.

Two days earlier, he had been released from prison and was living in his rented flat. He had hired a car, a Honda Civic, and had left it in Haverscot market square while he went on foot to The Willows. He wanted to discover if the house was still empty. Houses did not move much in the winter, he knew that, and there hadn't been a lot of time for a sale to have gone through. He'd seen no board outside, however, so, to be on the safe side, he hadn't walked straight up the drive but had come in over the fence from the field above the river, very early, just as it was getting light.

If his mother had kept her shameful secret, Tom would not have disinherited him. He'd be moving in there, now, himself, not planning a robbery to finance his future.

The dawn was grey: no sweeps of brilliance swept across the sky and the air was heavy with moisture. He'd seen lights come on in the house, and, keeping close to the shrubs along the boundary, he'd edged his way towards it. Then he'd noticed a figure at a window as the curtains were drawn back. He'd inched up to a point where he could look into the kitchen, and had seen an old woman moving to and fro. She'd made toast, bending to the cooker to extract it from below the grill, and he'd thought it odd that she had no automatic toaster.

Was this old woman the new owner? Was her husband still upstairs? Were there other people living in the house? Cautiously, he circled round the building, looking in at all the windows, leaping back when an automatic outside light, sensing him, came on. Nothing happened: if anyone had noticed, perhaps they thought a wandering cat or other animal had set it off.

He saw the new furnishings in the freshly decorated sitting-room, and the table covered with Marigold's art work in the dining-room. Then he returned to the kitchen. She was sitting at the table, her back towards the window which overlooked the sink. On the wall opposite was a large picture, a rural scene, sunny, a lot of blues and greens with red flowers in a meadow: a print of one of Monet's poppy paintings which Marigold had bought at Giverny. She liked looking at it during meals. He saw her pour some coffee from a cafetière; then she stretched an arm towards a jar of marmalade; there was butter on a dish. Alan's mouth watered. Before leaving the flat he had grabbed some bread, spreading it with Flora, and had drunk a mug of instant coffee, without milk as he'd forgotten to buy some when he went to the grocer's in the small shopping area around the corner. Despite his work experience, he was still uncomfortable in shops and public places, moving awkwardly and unable to utter more than curt words during transactions.

The kitchen had been altered. New wood fitments added warmth and colour to what had been pale cream and green. Alan considered breaking in and knocking out the old woman, still dawdling over breakfast. Then he could take his time over retrieving the gun and ammunition, and enjoy some food in the civilised surroundings which should, by rights, be his. But he couldn't be certain that she was alone in the house. It was so large for just one person. Once he'd got the gun, numbers wouldn't matter.

She stood up, pushing back her chair, and Alan quickly ducked away. Marigold glimpsed some movement, reflected in the glass covering her Monet print, but it was gone in an instant and she thought it was a trick of the eye. She ignored it.

She mustn't catch sight of him as he retraced his steps towards the shed. Alan made a circuit of the garden under cover of the bushes, avoiding open spaces and the lawn. Water still lay round the bases of the willows; he'd sometimes played with toy boats in these annual temporary ponds. His father – Tom – had helped him, fishing out a wreck that had sunk, causing him to burst into the frustrated crying of a child.

Dare he make a run for the shed? No other lights had come on in the house, and though it was lighter now outside, it was still overcast. He returned, hugging the wall, to the spot from which he'd overlooked the kitchen; the light was still on there, and, snatching a quick glance, he saw that the old bag was now standing at the table. She'd got flour out, and some bowls. She must be making a cake or pastry, just as his mother used to do in that very room. She'd be busy for some time, but if she took her bowls and spoons to the sink, she could look down the garden and might see him.

He went round the downstairs windows once again, but all the rooms were empty, with no lights burning. She had to be alone.

He reached the garage, and tried the door. It was unlocked, and when he opened it, he saw no car. The place was empty except for some old tea chests. *Miss M. Darwin*, he read on a label, and the address, *The Willows, Haverscot*.

That woman was Miss Darwin. He was right. There was no husband and no family.

It was dry in the garage, and warmer than outside. He

pulled the door to and stayed there, wondering what to do. He had no weapon to use against her if he burst into the house. There was nothing in the garage; it had been swept clean and the boxes had been unpacked; they were so light when he moved them that he knew he would not find anything in them with which to hit her. He had no qualms about using violence; anyone who got in Alan's way would not be tolerated.

If she saw him crossing the garden, she could call the police. On the other hand, she couldn't remain in the kitchen for ever. He hadn't noticed the time; how long had she been there, stirring up her mixture?

At this point in his thoughts, the church bells began to ring, making him jump. From so near, they were very loud. He remembered that his mother had gone to church every Sunday; it was possible that this woman might do the same. He pushed the door open a crack and peered through the gap. While the bells still rang, he saw her on the doorstep, in her coat and a dark hat, setting out. He breathed deeply. Now he could resume his plans, for she would be away at least an hour.

He didn't waste time on the house; the gun was what he wanted. Once he'd got that, he could control the woman, take the house over if he chose. He hurried back to the shed. There, below the concrete, lay his passport to freedom.

What sort of job had that man who was not his father done? He wouldn't have scrimped on things, but a workman might have. How deep was the concrete? Was there ballast underneath? He looked along the row of tools, seeking a sledgehammer, but he couldn't see one. Surely Tom would have had one? There was a pickaxe, and a heavy spade. He swung the pickaxe at the floor and succeeded only in sending up some chips of stone. Then he tried to prise it up at the side, but it was far too firmly grounded. Of course, these would be the woman's tools, not Tom's, he told himself; that was why there was no sledgehammer among them. Without one, since he couldn't risk the noise of a pneumatic drill, he'd never break it up.

He'd have to get one. He would go to Texas or B & Q, or another of the huge stores what were open at weekends. This was the phenomenon that had most struck Alan about changed conditions during his imprisonment: you could buy almost anything on Sundays.

As he left the shed, a sudden shower fell. He need not worry about the old woman seeing him when he walked out of her front gate; she'd be praying for sinners, saving her soul. She might need to do that, he thought grimly. She'd be back again, however, by the time he returned, but he was going to get the gun out. Using the hammer would make a noise. Maybe she'd put the television on and that would drown the sound.

Returning with the sledgehammer, he parked near the church, where there was plenty of space now that the service was over. Not wanting to be seen carrying his parcel by a casual walker, or by Miss M. Darwin from her window, he entered The Willows' garden by the field route once again. It was raining gently now, and he met no one. He'd taken time to have some food, stopping at a McDonald's he'd passed on his way back from the shopping mall. She'd be eating, too, by now, that old cow, he thought. He hated her for her intrusion into his mother's kitchen. He'd strike her down if she spotted him and came out, investigating.

He should have cut the phone. That would have been a wise precaution and he could have done it while she was in church. As he wasn't a burglar, he hadn't thought of it.

He aimed a blow with his new tool at the concrete, and it split at once, but, because he'd hit it gently, not right through. He sat there on the wheelbarrow, fuming, wondering if he should stack the sledgehammer against the wall with all the other tools and return tomorrow, watch to see when she went out – she'd go shopping; all women did – then take his opportunity.

He did not hear two cars drive up to the house, but, glancing out, he saw the lights come on downstairs and then curtains were drawn across the windows. He was just planning a voyage of inspection – if she had the television on loud enough, he might be able to work unheard – when he saw the youth, like a shadow, gliding past.

Alan shoved the sledgehammer back beside two spades, left the shed, and followed him.

21

MISS DARWIN'S TEA party began stickily.

She did not know what boys nowadays liked eating. Dim memories of dreaded childhood parties came to mind: there had been jellies, jam sandwiches, chocolate finger biscuits, sponge cake. She had a feeling that all this was out of date, but scones and a chocolate cake would be appropriate for the parents. She had taken trouble, rising early to do her baking before she left for church. Perhaps Marmite sandwiches for the boys? Or cheese? In the end, she made both, large ones, not dainty quarters like those her mother's cook had constructed. This was a chance to return the Gardners' Christmas hospitality, as well as a means of getting the two mothers together. She wanted the occasion to succeed, which meant that however difficult it was, Verity must be humoured.

It was to be drawing-room tea. If the boys had not met this before, it was time they were initiated. They could hand the plates of scones and sandwiches to the adults; it would occupy them between mouthfuls. Mark would certainly behave; the other boys were less predictable.

Dusk was falling as the time for their arrival drew near. She pulled the curtains across the darkening windows, seeing nothing in the garden, no hint of an intruder's presence.

Susan and Mark came first, which pleased Miss Darwin as

she was anxious to overcome Susan's understandable hostility at having Mark suspected of theft. She was wearing a long navy skirt and a hip-hugging pink sweater; her short fair hair shone, and she had on long silver earrings. Her expression was wary as Miss Darwin ushered her in, asking Mark to hang her coat, and his, in the cloakroom.

He seemed quite at home here, Susan thought resentfully, as he obeyed.

Miss Darwin was making comments on the weather as she led her guest into the sitting-room. Susan managed to respond; she was used to meeting strangers, and was used, also, to keeping a wall between herself and them, and she did so now, not wanting to get close to this rather formidable old woman who had somehow become involved with Mark.

The house, however, charmed her; it was so unlike her own, but as she had imagined she might live if she had married Mark's father. That thought flashed through her mind as she noticed the good, antique pieces which Marigold had inherited from her parents. Everything looked cherished and the place was comfortable. Her own house, she saw now, was strictly functional. No wonder Mark liked it here.

'Miss Darwin, will you show Mum your boxes before the others come?' he asked. He tugged at her elbow, not shy with her. He no longer noticed her appearance; like Tom's white hair and lameness, it was all just part of the person, and accepted.

'What boxes?' Susan asked. 'Do you collect them?'

'I decorate them,' Marigold replied. She led the way into the dining-room.

'Mum, you remember, I told you Steve gave Ivy a box,' Mark was saying as he followed them.

On the big table Susan saw a wastepaper basket, almost complete, ready for its final coat of varnish. There were several boxes in various stages of embellishment among Marigold's materials.

'I'm afraid my nicest box was stolen when the video and

radio went,' Marigold explained. 'None of the others are quite ready yet.'

As she spoke, she and Susan realised what Mark had just said. They were staring at one another, speechless, when the doorbell rang.

'There are the Gardners,' Miss Darwin remarked, reprieved from commenting, and went to let them in.

Through the murky dusk, Alan stalked the youth. When the rain stopped, mist rose, but there was no one about as he followed Steve down the road. He kept the boy in sight, and then, suddenly, his quarry vanished. Hurrying, Alan saw that he had disappeared at the entrance gates of Merrifields. He must have gone in there.

Hugging the side of the drive, Alan walked towards the house, from which exterior lights shone through the gloom. He lacked the knowledge Steve possessed: that one of the two cars outside The Willows was the owner's, and that most of the family, if not all of them, were out. Alan was wondering if this sly boy lived here: he had not been close enough to him to pick out details of his appearance; he was just a youth. There was plenty of cover in the drive; trees and shrubs dotted the shaggy grass, and he moved quietly from the shelter of one to another as he advanced.

The front of the house showed bland and undisturbed, a static light burning over the porch and a halogen one on the corner. That must have come on when its sensor detected the boy. Alan was impressed by these lights, which had become popular while he was inside. When trespassing at night, one must watch out for them.

He couldn't get near the front door of the house while that beam shone down. It would probably switch itself off in a few minutes; then, if he kept out of its range, he might get close enough to a window to look through. Why would a boy who lived in a place this size be skulking around The Willows, Alan asked himself: skulkers were rarely acting innocently.

The light remained on. It must be set to its maximum. In that case, he could use it to work his way round to the far side of the building. Staying at the rim of the lit area, Alan reached the rear of the house, where another light was on, and he could see the youth, almost floodlit, trying to open a window. Then he stooped and picked up a stone from the flowerbed near him, raising his arm, ready to throw it at the window.

Alan's immediate impulse was to stop him. Forcing an entry left traces of one's presence. When he stole the shotgun, he had opened the door and walked into the Wickenses' house without any hindrance. But this lad did not know that he was being watched. Alan decided that what followed might be interesting. He saw the youth apparently change his mind about flinging the stone; he moved on towards a French window, and cracked the stone quite gently against the glass near the catch, put his hand through the hole and opened the door. Alan, in the damp garden, nodded approvingly at this more prudent tactic, and, as the youth entered the house, prepared to follow. There might be benefits for him within, if he was lucky, even, possibly, a gun ready for the taking. Plenty of people legitimately owned shotguns.

Steve had tidily closed the French window behind him. Alan gave him a minute before opening it again and entering the house.

In a corner of the large room in which Alan now stood, the youth was on his knees disconnecting the video recorder beneath the television set, and he had a huge shock when he saw Alan's shoes beside him on the carpet. He looked up, and could not focus properly on whoever had caught him in the act because the man was behind a lit standard lamp.

'You don't live here, son,' Alan remarked mildly, pinning down Steve's wrist with one heavy foot.

'Who says?' was Steve's brave answer as he struggled to get free. This wasn't Mr Gardner.

'People don't often break the windows of their own

houses,' Alan said. He was wondering where the true
residents were: no one seemed to have noticed what was
going on, but he was poised for flight in case they appeared.
'They don't nick videos, either.' He raised his foot slightly.
'Get up,' he said. 'But watch it.'

As Steve stood, Alan seized his arm and twisted it behind
his back. He did not see what use he could make of this
captive, but an idea might come to him.

'Let me go,' said Steve, now whining. Held in such a grip,
his arm hurt.

'Not until you tell me what you're doing here,' said Alan.
'And I saw you trespassing at The Willows.'

'If you saw me there, you must have been trespassing too,'
said Steve, his spirits reviving at this revelation. 'And what
are you doing here?' he added.

'Following you, because you were acting suspiciously,'
said Alan.

But Steve had recognised him now. Incredulous, he stared
at Alan.

'You'd no business at The Willows,' he declared. 'Your
dad's dead and it's not your house.' He couldn't resist
adding, 'It was me and Mark that found your old man when
he snuffed it.'

Then Alan realised that this was one of the boys who were
being baby-sat by Tom on that November night.

'Who lives here?' he asked, and his voice took on a harsher
tone.

Steve was remembering about him now: Tom's son, the
murderer.

'They're out,' he said. 'They're having tea with the old bag
who's bought The Willows. That's why I knew the house
was empty.' He'd taken a chance: he couldn't be sure they
were all there. He'd welcome discovery now, held firmly as
he was by this man who scared him rigid.

'So you thought you'd see what you could find,' said Alan.
'Well, why not? Got an outlet, have you?'

'Course,' said Steve boldly, heart thudding with fear.

'Tell me who lives here,' Alan repeated, and Steve described the Gardners, adding that Justin sometimes hung out with him and his friends.

'Hm. And you're stealing from his dad?'

'It's his stepdad,' Steve replied. 'And I won't take anything that's Justin's. Or young Terry's,' he said, as an afterthought.

'Any guns here?' Alan asked.

'Not that I know of,' answered Steve. 'Why?'

'I just wondered,' Alan said. 'I'll take a look around while you help yourself.' He released Steve's arm.

He'd shot his wife, the paper had said. He was going to shoot someone else. Steve was quaking.

'That old woman lives there on her own, does she? At The Willows?' Alan asked, nonchalantly, moving towards the door.

'Yes,' said Steve, rubbing his arm. 'Why?'

'That's my business,' Alan answered. 'And by the way, you haven't seen me. Understood?'

Steve nodded vigorously.

'I won't say a word,' he promised.

'If you do, you'll be sorry,' Alan warned. 'You're stealing, remember.'

He sauntered out of the room and took a quick look round the rest of the ground floor. There was no gun cupboard. It would have to be the sledgehammer.

He let himself quietly out of the front door, leaving the boy, who wore no gloves, to get on with his thieving. Alan, his own hands warm inside new brown leather gloves, had left no prints.

He had no strong feelings about the Gardners' right to keep their property. Perhaps they should install a burglar alarm.

Leaving the boy to it, Alan began walking back towards The Willows. With the house occupied by the Gardner family and whoever the second car belonged to – he'd seen the

Vauxhall and the Montego when he was trailing the boy —
there should be enough noise and distraction going on to let
him reach the shed unnoticed.

That kid — Steve was his name, Alan remembered — was
local. Alan would recognise him if they met again and he'd
find him if he needed him. He was just a lad; he'd be at the
school, the one Alan had attended, though it had been a
grammar school then and was now a comprehensive. His
mother had crammed him hard to get him through his
eleven-plus exam. Alan wondered if the place had changed
much. In the town, some of the original shops remained,
such as the butcher's which had been handed on through
three generations. There was an antique dealer who had been
there for a long time. Alan did not want to meet anyone who
had known him previously, but he had altered since those
days: his hair was greying and he now wore a bushy
moustache. Even so, he did not intend to spend much time
in the more populated areas of the town.

After his warning, the boy wouldn't go shouting about his
presence, especially if he had the nerve to continue with his
burglary. Besides, the kid wouldn't know about his record.
All that must have been forgotten long ago. His parents —
or rather, his mother and the man Tom — had not been
besieged by the press because his trial was in the Midlands
and he was not living in Haverscot. Nowadays, the media
would have traced and hounded them, and might even, by
some means, have unearthed the truth about his parentage.

He must get that gun. Then he'd be in control.

How long would it take? An hour? Ten minutes? He'd
have to estimate at least an hour, he thought.

He'd better not risk it while the guests were there, but he
would have to deal with that old woman. He returned to his
car and turned it round, driving back to The Willows,
parking near its gate, ready for a quick getaway. He arrived
in time to see the two cars drive off, first the Montego and
then the small blue Vauxhall. He stayed in his car for quite
a while, sometimes running the engine to get the heater

going while he tried to work out how to incapacitate the old woman.

He was still there when the church bells began to ring and Miss Darwin emerged between the gates, bound for church again. Twice in one day? Alan couldn't believe his luck.

As soon as she was out of sight, he armed himself with the powerful torch he'd had the foresight to buy, and, his passage illuminated by it and by the exterior lights she'd left on, he hurried back across the garden to the shed.

After her guests had gone, Marigold had cleared away the tea things, loading the dishwasher and putting what was left of the cake and scones in tins. The remaining sandwiches would do for her supper. She covered them with foil and put them in the fridge.

What now? The house, which had come alive that afternoon, had become a silent place.

Going to church again was a sudden impulse. Normally, her solitude was no burden, and she had plenty to do, but this evening she was not in the mood for découpage or for reading. She felt restless. Stepping the short distance down the road and singing a few hymns would soothe her. Then she could cheer herself up with a couple of whiskies and finish the sandwiches. Since her set had been stolen, she couldn't settle down to television. *Mastermind* was back again, and she liked that, pitting her wits against those of the contestants. She often scored well in General Knowledge.

The afternoon had been a strain. The two mothers, edgy Mrs Gardner and the capable Mrs Conway — was she a widow? Mark still hadn't said a word to her about his father — had sat at either end of the sofa and had been spiky with one another.

'You work in a hotel, I believe,' Verity Gardner had begun.

'I'm the assistant manager. What do you do?' Mark's mother had replied.

Marigold, pouring tea and asking Mark to hand round plates, thought her tone acerbic.

'I'm a painter,' Mrs Gardner had answered. 'Or I would have been, if I'd had more time.'

'Come now, Verity,' Richard had intervened. 'You do yourself an injustice. Verity has had pictures in several exhibitions,' he told Susan.

'How clever of you,' Susan said, and her tone was warmer now. Marigold thought she might have imagined the earlier hostility.

'Milk?' she asked. 'Sugar?'

Richard passed the cups.

'We've had painting weekends at the hotel,' Susan said. 'Tutors come and hold classes for the guests. I'd love to be able to paint, but I can barely draw two straight lines.'

Verity unbent a little.

'It's possible to acquire a certain competence,' she conceded. 'With patience, and good tuition. But there's no substitute for talent.'

'Maybe I'll try it when I retire,' said Susan, who found it difficult to look further forward than the week ahead.

Mark and Terry were sitting in two tub chairs, each with a small table at his side, both eating heartily, following one sandwich with another, eyes on the chocolate cake. Marigold had iced it after church that morning. Justin had refused to come; he was going to see a friend, he said, and when asked which one, named Bruce. He might catch a bus and go to the cinema if he could think of nothing more exciting to do. He certainly wasn't going to some old lady's tea party.

Richard did not waste time expressing disapproval. Justin, as unpredictable as his mother, might have been rude if he had come with them. As it was, everyone else was, so far, being decorous in Miss Darwin's pleasant room.

Susan could not push from her mind the discovery that Steve might be the thief who had taken their hostess's video, radio, and the decorated box: Steve, her own son's companion, stepson of the trusted Ivy. All at once her arrangements for Mark had revealed major flaws; not only was he visiting people she had never heard of, but he was also spending time with Steve, who was dishonest. This must be faced and tackled before she went to work the following day. After leaving here, she would go straight round to Ivy's once again. She longed to leave at once, not waste precious minutes chatting idly to these people, but she made an effort to be friendly.

Richard tried to help. He mentioned two pictures which Verity had sold the year before, saying he was sorry to see them leave the house for the exhibition where they were bought.

'That wasn't what you said at the time,' snapped Verity. 'You said you were glad.'

'I said I was pleased about your success,' said Richard. 'You would have been disappointed if they had not been sold.'

She couldn't know that he had bought them, secretly, trying to boost her confidence. While she was out, he had hidden them in sacking in the loft. How else could he dispose of them without detection? He could not bring himself to burn them or give them to some charity shop.

He'd considered hanging them in his office, but he would not have been able to live with their gloomy purples and dull browns. There would have been comments from his colleagues, too, since by any standards the paintings were remarkable.

Susan was too experienced to express a wish to see Verity's work. She changed the subject.

'We have all sorts of courses at the hotel,' she said. 'It's a new venture, between conferences. We have a lot of them, and business visitors. Music is popular, too. We have concerts by good local amateurs.'

'Quintets? That sort of thing?' asked Richard helpfully, and Susan said that yes, they'd had quintets, and trios, but solo pianists were their most successful ventures.

'Richard plays the piano,' said Verity.

'Do you?' Susan asked. 'How nice to be able to do that. You are a clever family,' she managed, earning Marigold's approval by this positive remark.

'I'm not much good,' said Richard. 'But I enjoy it. Justin, Verity's other son who hasn't come today, plays well by ear.'

Marigold helped them knock this ball back and forth for a short rally, then asked Verity, who was beginning to look sulky, if the family planned a holiday this summer. The Sunday papers were full of enticing advertisements for sunny climes; doubtless Richard exported his difficult relations to some foreign spot.

'No,' said Verity.

'We've made no arrangements yet,' said Richard. 'Last year we went to Corfu.'

'Yes, and me and Justin got really sunburnt,' Terry said.

'Did you? That must have been painful,' Marigold replied. She peered into the teapot, which needed filling. 'I'll just go and fetch some more hot water,' she said. 'Mark, would you help me, please?'

Mark, who had been silently stuffing, got up, still chewing, and followed her.

'I'm glad to see you've got such a good appetite, Mark,' she said.

'We didn't have a big lunch,' Mark confided. 'Mum usually cooks something good on Sunday nights when she's in,' he added loyally, but cooking was not Susan's strong point. She had many of her meals at the hotel and had never bothered to acquire Ivy's expertise.

Miss Darwin boiled the kettle and topped up the teapot and the hot water jug. She showed Mark a key.

'I had the locks changed yesterday,' she said. 'But I want you to feel that you can come here, just as you used to, when you want to. I'm not going to give this to you but we'll keep it in a special hiding-place outside, where you can find it if you come here and I'm out. We'll choose a place next time you come.'

This might be a rash action on her part, but if she changed

her mind, she could have extra locks fitted to the doors and windows and end the arrangement.

'Thanks,' he said, beaming, and then added, 'Miss Darwin, I know who took your box. I'll get it back for you.'

'The box doesn't matter, Mark,' said Marigold. 'But the fact that it was stolen does. I think we both know who took it, don't we?' She should have thought of Steve earlier; of course he would have had access to his mother's key.

Mark nodded.

'There were things before,' he said, looking at the ground.

'You mean he stole from Mr Morton?'

'Not big things. Money, mostly,' Mark said.

'You weren't happy about that, were you?'

'No.' He shook his head.

'We'll talk about this another time,' said Marigold. 'Now we must go back to the others.'

Mark's mother had understood the situation; the miscreant boy's stepmother was her child-minder. She might intervene. In her place, Marigold would have gone straight round to see the woman. Probably she would do exactly that.

Marigold went to church resolved to postpone taking steps about it herself. Possibly the stolen property would be returned.

22

W HEN SHE LEFT The Willows, Susan's intention, as
  Marigold anticipated, had been to confront Ivy once
again, this time to demand that she challenge Steve about
the burglary, but, driving off, she decided that an hour or so's
delay would make little difference to the result. She must ask
Mark more about the box. Other things had been stolen, too;
he might have seen the video recorder or the radio in Steve's
room.

'We won't need much supper after such a big tea,' she
said, adding, 'I liked Miss Darwin.'

Susan was good at assessing people, or so she thought, but
now she was having doubts about Ivy, whom for years she
had trusted. Elderly ladies often came to The Golden Accord
for the cultural weekends, and Miss Darwin would have
fitted in among them. She would expect good service and,
having received it, would appreciate what was done for her.
She would be civil to the staff, but not ingratiating, and
would not respond well to any familiarity. She was, in fact,
a person to respect.

'I like her, too,' said Mark. He had resolved to keep the
matter of the new key a secret between himself and Miss
Darwin. He hoped his mother wouldn't raise the subject.

She parked the car – they had no garage but there was
hard standing outside the house – and they went indoors,

where after they had shed their coats, she asked him about the stolen box.

'You said Steve gave one just like it to Ivy. When was that?'

'Yesterday. At least, that's when I saw it,' Mark replied.

'Steve could have got into Miss Darwin's house, couldn't he? Ivy had a key.'

'Yes.' Mark nodded.

'Do you think the box came from The Willows?'

'I don't know,' said Mark.

'Stealing's wrong. It's a crime,' said Susan. 'People who do it and get caught can go to prison.'

'Will that happen to Steve?' asked Mark.

'So you do think he's the thief,' said Susan.

'He might say he'd bought the box.'

'If so, to prove it, he'd have a receipt, or at least the shop might remember selling it to him,' Susan said. 'What about the video, Mark, and the radio?'

Mark shrugged.

'He could have sold them,' he said.

'I must go and talk to Ivy about this,' said Susan. 'You understand that, don't you, Mark? It has to be sorted out, one way or the other.'

'Yeah.' Mark wanted Miss Darwin to get her things back, and he thought Steve deserved to be caught. 'Isn't Steve too young to go to prison?' he asked.

'He's not too young to get some sort of punishment,' said Susan. 'I'll go there now,' she added. 'You stay here. You can watch TV or put a video on. I won't be long.'

Mark was glad to stay behind. He did not want to witness Ivy's reaction to the news of Steve's crimes. When his mother had gone, he put on the tape of *The Secret Garden*, which Ivy had recorded for Sharon years ago. She had lent it to him. He liked the scene where Mary gave Colin a piece of her mind and he realised how selfish he was being. Perhaps that was what Steve needed: a piece of Ivy's mind.

*

Richard knew that Verity had not liked Susan Conway. As they drove away from The Willows, she made quite sure that he understood her views.

'What a waste of time,' she said. 'Miss Darwin's a boring old witch and that silly person, Mark's mother, made me sick, pouring on the oil all afternoon, buttering her up.'

'Miss Darwin wanted to return our hospitality, and she thought it would be useful if you met Susan Conway,' he replied austerely.

'So she's Susan, is she?' Verity had heard Richard use Susan's first name at The Willows.

'Well, of course she's Susan.' Richard answered, exasperated. 'Everyone uses first names these days.'

'Except Miss Darwin,' said Verity.

Marigold had begun formally, until Susan, won round because the old woman was clearly fond of Mark, asked to be called by her first name. No one, however, had been so casual with Miss Darwin, not even Richard, who had discovered her unlikely name when she joined the choir.

'She's of that generation,' he said, turning in at their gate. 'I wonder where Justin is,' he added, trying to divert Verity's grievance on to familiar ground.

'He'll come home when he's ready,' was her answer.

Sensing that his mother was spoiling for a fight, Terry disappeared as soon as they entered the house. He'd found the tea party boring, but most things involving adults were.

'It was rude of him not to have come with us,' Richard said, despite the fact that he had welcomed Justin's absence and proceeding to provoke inevitable conflict.

'Why should he? Miss Darwin is your friend. So's dear Susan,' Verity pursued. 'That's where you go when you're late home, I suppose. I should have guessed. Well, if she's your type, you're welcome to her — nasty, common little barmaid.'

Richard took a deep breath.

'I first met Susan Conway after Terry disappeared,' he said. 'This was only the second time I've seen her. Her son and yours are friends. That's all. Why do you have to invent plots and mysteries and jealousies, upsetting everyone?'

'I saw how you looked at her,' said Verity. 'As if—' she sought about for a metaphor. 'As if you could eat her up – lick cream from her navel,' she added wildly.

Richard had never licked anything from anybody's navel.

'I give up,' he said, turning away. He'd go out to his workshop. Chipping at some timber would relieve his feelings. He'd taken up carving not only as a hobby but as a means of letting out his anger.

'You stay here when I want to talk to you,' cried Verity as he moved towards the door. 'You humiliate me by your affairs with other women. That Susan's a tart – she's a whore, that's what she is, working on her back in that hotel. It's probably a brothel.'

Richard, stung at last, said, 'You're contemptible.' Where did these foul thoughts of hers originate? He raised his fist.

'Yes – hit me – go on,' Verity taunted him, thrusting out her pelvis. 'That's what you'd like to do, isn't it?'

Yes, he would. Richard glowered at her but he lowered his hand. So far, he had never lost control, and he did not mean to do so now. He turned his back and as he left the room, she picked up a china figure from a side table and flung it after him. It hit him on the shoulder, not his head, at which she had aimed, then fell to the ground, shattering into several fragments.

Pity, he thought, walking on into the night. That was the second piece of Meissen she had smashed. The security light came on as he walked across the garden to his workshop. The key was on a ring in his pocket, with his car keys. Tonight, on impulse, he locked himself inside, something he rarely did, and when, some minutes later, Verity came banging on the door, yelling at him and swearing, he made no response. She'd cool down eventually, perhaps get a drink if she could find some alcohol. Then she'd weep, but she never apologised for these scenes.

No wonder the boys' father had taken off, he thought, not for the first time.

He picked up a chisel and a mallet and began chipping at a block of wood held in the vice on his bench. He chipped and chipped, to no design, while outside in the garden, Verity shrieked and cursed. She'd give up in the end, and go away.

She did.

Justin had known his mother would fly into one of her rages either at The Willows or afterwards. He knew her so well because he was like that himself. Sometimes he was frightened by his own violent feelings, which he could not understand.

She got angry when Cat was calm and took no notice of her temper or her outrageous remarks. Justin knew they were outrageous, but she was driven to make them because of Cat's cool nature. At school, Justin would taunt other boys, trying to wind them up and start a row; if he failed, he longed to punch them, and sometimes he did, gratified by the reaction – either a fight, or tears. He was often in trouble because of this behaviour, but even at primary school, it had brought him to the attention of some older boys – Bruce and Greg in particular – and now they sometimes used him to watch their backs when they went thieving out of cars at the station or on shoplifting jaunts further afield. Steve Burton was also on the fringe of their gang and he had done a major job the other night, bringing in a VCR and a radio for Greg's brother to sell.

Justin was impressed. If he could do something like that, he'd earn respect from the older boys. Perhaps stealing a car would impress them, and it would be easier. Setting a fire would be easier still, and exciting.

He'd been there when they lit the barn. He'd gone to the station, vaguely planning another assault on Cat's Montego, and they'd turned up to steal a car. They'd taken him along and he'd seen Steve carry the petrol, heard the whoosh as the flames went up in a great roar, felt the thrill as the fire caught. They'd made a job of it, unlike Mum when she tried to burn Cat's books that time. Justin had been posted as the look-out; they'd taken him back to the station where he'd left his bike and dropped him there, then driven off. He didn't know what they'd done about the car; torched it, probably, after dropping Steve.

That afternoon, Cat had asked him where he was going.

'Out,' Justin had answered.

'You're expected at Miss Darwin's,' Cat had stated in that neutral tone which Justin found so irritating.

'I'm not coming. It'll be boring,' Justin said.

He'd seen Cat wondering whether to order him to go with them. If he did, Justin would defy him; he couldn't imagine calm Cat physically forcing him to obey. Anyway, it wouldn't be possible; Justin was five feet six now, and he could do some damage.

Cat had turned to Verity.

'Justin is refusing to come with us,' he had said, expecting her to say he must fall into line, but Justin knew she wouldn't.

'I don't see why he should,' she'd said, quite mildly for her. 'I don't want to, either,' she'd added. 'You're forcing me to go.'

'No one's forcing anyone,' said Cat. Justin had heard the note of strangled patience in his voice. One day, Mum would push him too far and he'd lose his cool. 'I just want you to allow Miss Darwin to bring you and Mark's mother together, since the boys are such friends.'

Were they, though? Justin thought Cat over-estimated the importance of the friendship but he knew Terry wasn't popular; he hadn't yet acquired the toughness needed for survival. Mark seemed to have it in his nature, and hanging out with him had helped Terry.

'It's a waste of an afternoon,' his mother had protested.

What else was she planning, Justin had wondered; did she mean to watch telly? Or get drunk? Or both? If she went out, it would keep her off the booze, at least.

'You go, Mum, for Terry's sake,' he said, avuncularly. 'Then you can feel good about it afterwards.' And take it out on Cat, he thought, sloping off before any further effort could be made to stop him.

He'd got no plans, but as he'd mentioned meeting Bruce, he went to find him, only to discover that he and two other boys were working on the wreck of an old car which one of them had bought for a few pounds. The parts could be cannibalised for other cars; they were dismembering the corpse and taking out the working vitals.

This bored Justin. He thought stealing cars was amusing but he saw no point in spending a cold, damp afternoon getting filthy. Besides, there was a limit to how many heads could bend over one engine. He was told to clean off the various parts assembled on the ground, but this important task soon palled.

'Got to go,' he said, and left them.

He could return to the empty house, which would be warm and where there was food and his computer, or he could watch a video. He'd seen some horrifying ones at Bruce's house; he hadn't liked them, they were too scary, though he'd laughed like the others at the gruesome bits. Maybe he'd go round to Steve's place first, see if Steve would like to come back with him. Steve was all right, but he lived with all those women – his stepmother and Sharon, and that little kid Kylie. Justin wasn't sure how they were all related. It was funny, really – none of them had the right fathers. Steve's was dead; Justin and Terry's had deserted them; Mark never mentioned his. Even Adam, Sharon's baby, had no dad at home. The men should get together, live in packs, thought Justin. The women didn't need them except to give them money and so they could get kids. Women seemed to like small kids, and the men needed the women for sex and to cook. Tribes: that was what was wanted, he decided, aiming for Ivy's house where he knew there would be rich cake, jam tarts and a welcome. He'd been there several times.

There were all those things, but no Steve.

'Come in, Justin. I daresay he won't be long,' said Ivy, who saw before her a boy who was cold and damp and had time to kill. 'How about a cup of tea and a bite to eat?'

Ivy did not hand out fizzy drinks in costly cans. At her house you had tea, or sometimes cocoa, or water, and now and then fruit juice when she'd been out shopping.

Justin accepted milky tea with sugar, and a piece of sticky gingerbread which Kylie had helped her mother make. It was delicious. When he'd finished this snack, and had warmed up, he played Snap with Kylie, who wasn't a bad little kid at all; rather cute, really, with her fair curly hair. Justin looked quite warm and rosy when, at last, he left the house.

'I'll tell Steve you called in,' said Ivy. 'Come any time, Justin. You're always welcome.' She liked to send a child away looking happier than when he arrived. These boys were all at sixes and sevens with themselves, no longer children but far from adult, full of conflicting feelings, hormones rattling around, and being pressed to conform to what their peers were doing. Steve worried her; he was so silent and secretive, going out at all hours. She was sure he missed Tom Morton; the old man had been a steadying influence after Joe's death.

She sighed. She loved Steve for his father's sake and would always care for him, but she wasn't sure about him. She hadn't liked that petrol smell the other night, but then, just as she was fearing he'd been mixed up in that business of the barn, he'd given her the lovely box.

He'd be all right. It would work out. He knew right from wrong.

Not long after Justin left, Susan Conway rang the bell.

Alan draped his jacket over a peg in the shed on which already hung a spade. His torch was balanced on the bench. He could have done with more light but there was no hurricane lamp among the tins and flowerpots, nor a candle end. Raising the sledgehammer, he smote the solid centre of the concrete path and, most satisfyingly, this time it cracked at once. It wouldn't take too long to break it up.

He was not in good condition, and it was heavy work; after breaking up a section, he took the pickaxe and prised up the jagged lumps he'd raised; then he resumed his blows. The noise echoed in his ears but he was making progress. Once the surface had been broken, he would still have to dig, but that could be done comparatively silently, even after the old girl came home. He must finish tonight.

Time passed. Alan had no sense of how long he had been working as the chunks of concrete mounted at the side of his excavated plot. He used a spade to dig down in the area where he was sure the gun lay buried; the change of movement was welcome. Then he felt resistance, something solid. He crouched, groping with his hands, and touched the plastic covering the gun. He'd got there! As triumphant as any treasure hunter, Alan renewed his efforts, digging now more cautiously as he exposed the bundle.

He never heard the shed door open. All he saw was a sudden shaft of light from someone else's powerful torch; behind it stood a figure.

Alan's reaction was a reflex. Up came the spade.

She didn't stand a chance, though, unnervingly, she screamed before he hit her for the second time. Then he dropped the spade and grabbed the sledgehammer. He made quite sure that she was dead before he stopped his blows.

Now he had all the time in the world to complete his task.

23

AFTER TOM'S SON had gone, Steve had found money at Merrifields. Once, when he was at the house with Justin, he had seen the other boy go to a drawer in a desk in Richard's study and take out five pounds.

'Cat keeps a bit here for rainy days,' Justin had said. 'This is a rainy day,' and he laughed in what Steve thought was a weird way, though he laughed, too.

Justin had never robbed Cat before and now he did it only to impress Steve. Later, he'd replaced the money with a five-pound note he'd got from his mother, pretending that he needed it for a school trip. Cat would have known who'd been to the drawer, and the consequences could have been unpleasant, since he had power over all of them.

Today, there were thirty-five pounds in the drawer and Steve took the lot. Upstairs, there was jewellery. He stole it neatly, not turning the place upside down because what was the point of that? He'd got no quarrel with the Gardners. He found some silver spoons and forks, and after searching vainly for a holdall, took a pillow case from a bed and put them, with the slim video recorder, in that. You could always get money for a video. Then he took the mixer from the kitchen. He had to find a second pillow case to carry what would not go into the loaded first one, and, once again stumped by the limit on what he could carry, Steve left, walking home laden with his spoils. He would hide everything in his room and see if he couldn't sell the video himself without using Greg's brother as a middleman; he'd get more that way, and it was time he made his own connections.

He stuffed the pillow cases under some bushes in the front garden, hoping it wouldn't start to rain; damp would do the electrical things no good. He'd have to come down to collect them after everyone had gone to bed. Give Ivy her due, she didn't pry, so she wouldn't find them in his room, which he was expected to keep clean himself. He didn't mind that; it was a fair exchange for privacy.

Whistling, he entered the house, and Sharon, the baby in her arms, came out of the kitchen, intercepting him on his way upstairs.

'You're wanted in there,' she said, nodding towards the sitting-room. 'Trouble,' she added. 'Susan's here.'

Steve had noticed the blue Vauxhall in the road outside but had thought nothing of it as he stuffed his bundles underneath a prickly berberis. Susan came round to pay Ivy and sometimes to drop Mark off; perhaps he was stopping over tonight.

Ivy had heard their voices. She emerged from the front room and asked Steve to come inside. Her face was quite without expression and she walked back into the room ahead of him, seating herself beside Susan on the sofa. Between them was the decorated box which Steve had given her.

'I was very touched by this lovely present which you gave me, Steve,' she said. 'Where did you get it?'

'Oh – a shop in High Wycombe,' Steve replied. 'I went there with some mates.' He grinned at them, but at the same time he shifted his feet awkwardly.

'A box like this was stolen from Miss Darwin at The Willows on Thursday night when she was out,' said Ivy.

'Oh?' said Steve. 'How weird. Maybe she bought it at the same place.'

'She made hers. She does the decorating,' Ivy said. 'There's not another like it.'

As soon as Susan had made her accusation, Ivy had telephoned Miss Darwin to ask her to come round and identify the box, but there was no reply. Now that Steve was back, they must proceed without her.

'Some jewellery was stolen, too,' said Susan. 'And a radio, a toaster, and the video.'

'Well?' Steve shrugged, but his mind was racing round as he tried to see a route out of the trap.

'We've got a key to The Willows. You used it often enough to visit Tom,' said Ivy. 'There was no forced entry. You could have done it, Steve, and then there's this box, which you've only just given me.'

'Miss Darwin was visited by Mark one day,' said Susan. She wasn't going to reveal that he had acquired a key of his own and had entered the house uninvited. 'He told her about being friends with Mr Morton and she thought he might be the thief.'

Steve made a wry face.

'Not Mark,' he said. 'He'd not steal.'

'I hope you wouldn't either,' Ivy said. 'Steve, I want to go into your room now and look among your things in case there is any stolen property there.'

'Course there isn't,' Steve replied.

'Then you won't mind us looking, will you?' Ivy said. 'Susan will be a witness.' She stood up and left the room and Susan followed.

Steve thought about running off, but if he did, he would stand no chance, whereas if he faced it out, Ivy wouldn't shop him to the police. Miss Darwin could have her rotten jewellery back. He'd got that other stuff outside and it was worth a bit, but he'd have to shift it as soon as this little scene was over.

He'd come clean about The Willows, get it over, produce the tatty bits and bobs and let them crucify him with their tongues. He didn't want Ivy going through his things; there were one or two items he'd rather she didn't see – a few pills he'd bought but hadn't tried, and some books she wouldn't like, not to mention the condoms. She'd think he was too young for those. He hadn't used one yet; he didn't really want to, but the guys all talked about their scores and he might change his mind.

He put on a bold expression and opened the bottom drawer of his chest where, stuffed inside a sock, was Miss Darwin's jewellery. He gave the sock to Ivy.

'It's all there,' he said.

'What about the radio and the video recorder?' Susan asked. 'And the toaster?'

Steve shrugged again.

'They're gone,' he said. 'A man took them off me.' If he said he'd sold them to a mate, they'd want to know name, address, blood group, date of birth, everything. 'She'll get it off the insurance.'

'She wouldn't have got this.' Ivy felt cold with shock at the proof of his guilt. She balanced the sock in her hand while she tried to think how Joe would have dealt with him. It wouldn't have happened if he hadn't died; he'd have kept tabs on Steve, prevented this. Though she'd been anxious about the boy, she hadn't seen it shaping up. 'It's probably of sentimental value, like my ring your dad gave me,' she said.

He might have been caught trying to flog the jewellery; perhaps that was what he needed: a real fright. As it was, if Miss Darwin could be persuaded, this time he might be spared.

'Miss Darwin knows about the box,' Ivy told him. 'She wasn't able to be here tonight, otherwise she could have decided what to do about the rest of it. Whether to tell the police. I expect she'll have to. I'll go and see her tomorrow and ask what's to be done. You'll stay in your room now, Steve.'

She felt like Atlas bearing the burden of the world as she went downstairs with Susan.

'What will you do?' asked Susan, who felt extremely sorry for her.

'It won't be up to me, once Miss Darwin knows the truth,' said Ivy.

Susan resolved to postpone any drastic change in Mark's arrangements.

'Please don't let Mark go into town with Steve,' was her sole request.

Steve wondered if Ivy would lock him in his room. If so, he'd have to get out of the window to move the stuff from the garden. He must shift it off the premises, hide it somewhere else, even the grounds of one of the big houses in Wordsworth Road, like The Willows.

Alan had to hide the body. He could bury it in the hole from which he'd taken the gun. He'd need to dig a lot deeper, and it would take up far more space, but there was no hurry now.

Shooting would have been a cleaner way of doing it, if she'd come a little later, when the gun was ready, cleaned and loaded. He'd rolled her with his foot under the bench while he went on digging. Luckily his torch, which had fallen to the ground during the skirmish – not that she had put up much resistance – hadn't broken. She'd dropped hers and it had gone off. He'd find it when he'd got her out of the way.

He needn't test the gun here, in this poor light, where it was cold and damp. He could do it in comfort in the house. No one would come in upon him now while he made himself at home. He could even sleep there, as was his right, but he'd better not stay long in case someone came asking for the old bag.

He let himself out of the shed, then turned to take his jacket off the hook. He put it on; the night was cold, and he had sweated while he dug. Between the trees he saw lights shining from the house, a welcome beacon in the gloom. She must have returned from church and noticed his torch beam through the window of the shed, then come inquisitively down. Nosey old bitch, she deserved what she had got. He picked up the gun and the box of cartridges and strode back towards the house, swaggering with confidence, claiming what should have been his own.

He had no key. There'd be one on the body, obviously – she'd have it in her pocket or her bag. She must have dropped that when she fell. Alan did not bother to go back and hunt for it. The door might be open, if she'd gone into the house before noticing his light; if not, there'd be no problem now.

The front door was locked, so he went in by the back door, remembering how he'd seen the kid enter the other house only a short time earlier. Good luck to him if he could get away with it, thought Alan. He broke the glass in the same manner as the boy had done, then reached in and found the key. She'd left every light on in the place; when he'd returned earlier, he'd had to remind himself that she lived there on her own because, though the curtains had been drawn, there were slits of light showing behind them at almost all the windows.

Now, standing in the brightly lit kitchen, he saw that there was blood on his clothes, and his strong new shoes were covered in mud, not so much from his excavations, which had been comparatively dry, as from his wanderings. He was very dirty, sweaty as well as muddy.

He didn't like it. He could have a bath here, get himself cleaned up, but with no man in the house there'd be no change of clothing. There would be only women's stuff, and even if he found some things to fit, he wasn't going to start cross-dressing.

He took off his shoes, and, in his socks, he moved about, seeking comfort. The kitchen had been rearranged but there was still a large store cupboard leading from it; once, it had been a larder, and was cool. Inside, on a shelf facing the door, he found whisky, gin and sherry. He chose the whisky and drank some from the bottle before pouring more into a tumbler he saw face down on the drainer by the sink. He topped it up with water from the tap. Neat whisky fired him up but didn't quench his thirst. Then, nursing his glass, he went upstairs to take a look around.

The first room he entered was his own, and he was shocked. Instead of his posters and the dozens of books he hadn't looked at for years, even before he moved out when he was nineteen, there were clean walls painted primrose yellow, and, on the newly painted shelves a few books. He picked one up. It was *Coot Club*, and he saw his name inside, and the date, in his mother's writing. He hurled it across the floor into a corner. Against one wall there was a small desk, with some pencils and crayons in a box. There was a plain blue carpet, and new curtains printed with various plants were drawn across the window.

This was his room. How dare someone change everything?

Alan seized several coloured pencils and slashed them across the wall, breaking two of them, then threw them down to join *Coot Club* on the ground. He picked up the chair which stood before the desk and was about to fling it at the window when he remembered that the broken glass would cause a draught. He let it fall from his grasp, and it toppled over to lie on its side.

Damned old cow, he thought. She'd turned out all his stuff. His past had gone. Even so, he could live here till someone missed her. Maybe he could stave off queries, pretend to be her nephew – anything. People were so gullible. In prison he'd heard tales from men who had worked fiddles on the weakest of assumptions. But he must remember that the youth could give him away: the junior, apprentice thief, young Steve.

Alan had left the gun in the kitchen, and he went downstairs again to look at it, unwrapping its many layers of polythene, clicking the trigger. No rust was visible. He'd greased it well all those years ago and now he wiped it on a kitchen towel, then broke it open. An unloaded gun was useless. He peeled the protective coverings from the box of cartridges and took two out. They looked all right. Terrorists kept weapons concealed for years. He slid the cartridges into each barrel of the gun. Now, if a caller came, he was prepared.

After that, he began searching for food. In the refrigerator, covered in foil, there was a plate of sandwiches which tasted very fresh. He took them upstairs with him to his own room, where he had left his glass of whisky, and he sat down on the floor to eat them, rocking gently to and fro.

By the time Justin returned home that evening, everyone else was back at Merrifields. Terry was in their playroom, music on, the volume turned up very loud.

'They've been fighting again,' he said to Justin.

He looked very white. The rows between his mother and Richard frightened him, whereas they simply made Justin angry with their stepfather.

'Where are they?' Justin asked, turning the music down.

'Cat's gone to his workshop. I don't know where Mum is,' Terry answered.

Much to his surprise, he'd liked it round at that old lady's. Terry had known his mother was seething, ready to explode, but Cat was calm, and Miss Darwin seemed to have everything under control. Mum wouldn't flare up while they were there. The food that was set out was excellent; Mark seemed quite at home, and nothing went really wrong while they were in that house. Even Mark's mother had got quite chatty, trying to be nice to Mum, who wouldn't respond. Yet she could be lovely; why did she have to be so changeable? Was it because he, Terry, was sometimes naughty, like the night he ran away? But he didn't often do bad things. Justin was the one who hung around with boys who, Terry knew, had been taken home in police cars; he had seen it happen. Maybe they hadn't done much, but if you went in one of their cars, you'd caught their attention, just as he'd done, and he didn't want that to happen a second time.

'It's all Cat's fault,' said Justin. 'He gets up her nose. And mine,' he added, for good measure.

Terry knew this wasn't fair.

'He works hard. He pays for all of us,' he said.

'And he lets us know it,' Justin answered. 'I'll go and look for Mum.'

Terry thought she was best left till she'd had time to cool down, but it was no good telling Justin that. He turned the volume up again and lay back in his chair, rocking and gyrating to the beat.

Justin went all over the house looking for his mother, but she was not in her bedroom, nor her studio, nor the kitchen, nor her bathroom. He called her name in vain. She must have gone outside. He looked for her coat, the long loose black one with the hood which she often wore, and he could not see it. Was that what she'd had on today, going out to tea? He supposed so. Her bag was in the drawing-room. He opened it to look for money and found some coins and a five pound note in her purse; she never had a lot as she spent anything she could spare on drink. He took two pound coins; she wouldn't miss them. Where could she be? He'd go and see if Cat knew.

He didn't notice the broken glass by the French window, where Alan, after entering, had pulled the curtain across to close out the night. Alan and Steve had both left by the front door. Justin walked towards Richard's workshop.

'Cat – where's Mum?' he called, and had to repeat his question several times before his stepfather took any notice.

'I don't know,' was all he said, when at last he bothered to respond.

Justin went off, fuming. How dare he stay in there, locked in, all smug and toffee-nosed when Mum was miserable? Anyone could see that she was sad, the way she drank and flew into her tempers. She wouldn't do it if she was happy. He blamed Cat for everything.

He went back to the house and checked again that his mother was not there. Then he fetched an empty bottle from the box by the back door; there were always plenty of them around – his mother's gin and vodka bottles. He took it to the garage. There was petrol there. Cat kept a can in the boot of his car; he'd had one on the day he rescued Mum, though a flat tyre was the problem then.

He poured some petrol into the bottle and found a piece of rag which he stuffed in the top. He had to go back into the house to get some matches, but then he set off down the garden once again. With Cat gone, they'd be happy, him and Mum and Terry.

Justin's homemade bomb backfired on him, flaring as he lit it, catching petrol droplets which had fallen on his clothes, exploding into flames as he tried to throw it through the window of the workshop.

24

RICHARD PUT THE flames out, beating at Justin with his bare hands and rolling the boy on the ground. Justin's anorak was still damp despite its sojourn in Ivy's warm house, and its smouldering was soon extinguished, but his jeans, where petrol had dripped on to the denim, had scorched, and he was very badly burned. His screams had turned to whimpers when Richard, not daring to move him, covered him with his own jacket and hurried to the house to telephone for help.

'I'll be back in a few minutes, Justin,' he said. 'I've got to call an ambulance.'

Terry, his music turned up loud, had not heard the noise of the exploding bottle. Now he was vaguely aware of a door banging and disturbance in the house but he took no notice until Richard burst into the room.

'Turn that noise off and go and fetch your mother,' Richard, who had already telephoned, shouted at him, reaching out to Terry's music system, only to have Terry turn into a fiend, snatching at his hand. 'There's been an accident. Justin's badly burned. Find your mother, and when the ambulance comes, send them to the workshop. I'm going back to Justin. Come on, Terry,' he ordered. 'Get going. This is serious.' He rushed out of the room again, leaving Terry staring after him, horrified.

Richard, back beside the injured boy, did not know how to help him. He knelt beside him, stroking his damp hair and talking to him, assuring him that the ambulance would soon arrive. Justin was crying with shock as much as pain. To both of them, it seemed hours before they heard the siren and saw lights approaching over the garden.

As the paramedics bent over Justin, Richard rose.

'I don't know where his mother is. I'll go and find her,' he said. Had Terry even looked for her?

Walking back towards the house, he saw the boy, illuminated by the outside lights, standing in the garden. He looked small and shrunken, but Richard had no time for sympathy.

'Haven't you found your mother?' he called out. 'Where is she?'

'She's not in the house,' said Terry. He was coatless, arms clutched across him, teeth chattering in the cold. 'Is Justin dead?'

'No, of course not. He'll be all right,' said Richard. 'He must have been messing about with some petrol. It's very dangerous stuff. I'll find Verity. You get inside and keep warm.'

He went indoors and ran all over the house, into every room, calling Verity by name but, as Terry had said, she was not there. After she'd battered at the workshop door, she must have gone storming off into the night. Had she crossed the fence and gone over the fields, where the river was in flood? He knew that the boys had made themselves a crossing point and that she used it too. Stumbling over the flooded fields in darkness was foolhardy, but at the moment she must take her chance; he would have to go with Justin to the hospital.

He went back to the team working with Terry in the garden. They had him on a stretcher now and were ready to take him to the ambulance.

'We can't tell how bad he is until we get him into casualty,' said one of the crew. 'He's very shocked. How did it happen?'

'I'm not sure what he was doing but I think he'd got some petrol in a bottle.' Richard had scrunched his knee on broken glass when crouching by the boy. 'There was a bang – a flash – almost an explosion. I was in my workshop and came out at once.' He nodded at the shed.

'Lucky you were near,' was the comment. 'We'll get on, then.'

'I can't find his mother,' Richard said. 'She's out somewhere. I'll leave her a message and come with you.'

'Follow us in your car,' he was advised. 'There's the other boy to think of, isn't there? And you'll need to get back, later. I guess we'll be keeping Justin.' They had asked the boy's name and used it, talking to him reassuringly. 'Maybe you could get a neighbour in,' the paramedic added.

'All right.' Richard saw the sense of this. 'Tell Justin I'm on my way and that his mother will be coming.' If he could find her quickly, he could take her. Whatever she was up to, would she be fit to drive herself if she came later? She could take a taxi. He'd suggest it in his note.

When Justin had been taken away, he went into the house to write it. Terry was in the drawing-room.

'We've been robbed,' he said. 'Look – the window's broken and the video's gone.'

Richard almost didn't comprehend what Terry said: then he saw the broken window pane and the gap where the video recorder had slotted in on a shelf under the television set.

'Oh God,' he said. 'Well, it will have to wait. I can't deal with that now.

'Perhaps the burglar set Justin on fire,' said Terry.

'I don't think so,' Richard said. 'Where do you think your mother is? I'll have to go to the hospital.'

'Don't leave me here on my own,' said Terry, sniffing. 'The burglar might come back and get me.'

'He won't,' said Richard. 'He'll be busy hiding what he's taken, or selling it to someone.' There was no time to look around to see what else was missing. 'All right. Get a coat. I'm writing a note for your mother.'

Composing it, and writing down the number of the taxi firm, he grew calmer. Delay here would make no difference to Justin, who was in good hands. He stuck the Post-It note to the fridge door, where, in the days when communications had been easier, messages were left. Sooner or later, everyone went to the fridge. Then he remembered the ambulance attendant's suggestion about a neighbour. Miss Darwin might try ringing Verity at intervals, or might even come to the house and be there when she came home.

He dialled her number but got no reply. He glanced at his watch: it was nearly eight o'clock. So late! Verity must have been roaming round for more than two hours. Miss Darwin had said nothing, that afternoon, about going out later, but then, why should she? For all he knew, she had made a lot of friends and had a busy social life. He could try ringing her again from the hospital.

Before leaving, he decided to telephone the police. They must be told about the burglary, following so soon after The Willows had been robbed. The thief had not attacked Justin, however; Richard had a shrewd idea of what had really happened and the hatred it revealed horrified him.

It took a little time to get the information through, because Haverscot police station had closed for the night, but eventually a voice told Richard that an officer would find him at the hospital. He mentioned that his wife, the boy's mother, could not be found and agreed it was too soon to consider her a missing person.

Then he left the house, not locking up because Verity might not have a key and anyway, with a broken window, why bother? Despite his comforting words to Terry, Richard thought it possible for the thief to be lurking in the bushes, waiting to get in a second time and take what he had left behind earlier.

At the moment, Richard did not care. He stopped the car in the drive, however, and went back to lock up his workshop, with its array of tools, some of which could be used as lethal weapons.

Terry, strapped into the front passenger seat, leaned slightly towards his stepfather as they drove to Radbury Hospital. Every now and then he sniffed, and Richard managed not to tell him to blow his nose. When they reached the hospital and had found a parking slot, he reached into the car for a box of tissues and gave Terry a handful.

'Stick them in your pocket,' he said.

Terry did so, sniffing on.

Richard tried the telephone again, half an hour later. There was no reply from Merrifields, but this time The Willows' line was engaged. Richard now became seriously concerned about Verity. Wouldn't she have rung the hospital before driving over, if she ignored his advice about taking a taxi? Perhaps she had crashed her car. Various scenarios, all equally alarming, ran through his mind as he returned to Terry and decided that both of them needed food. After they'd tracked some down within the hospital, there might be firm news about Justin's condition and perhaps they would be allowed to see him. However, before that could happen, the police came. Richard described the sudden flash when he was in his workshop, and how he went outside to find Justin screaming on the ground. He explained about the burglary, which he and Terry had discovered only later.

It seemed that other officers had already gone to Merrifields; arson was a serious crime and there had been several incidents in the area, notably the recent burning of a barn where youths were suspected of having set it alight. Specialists would want to discover exactly what had happened outside Richard's workshop, and what Justin had planned to do.

They would succeed, too, Richard thought, but that was of academic importance at the moment.

The police officer said he would get on to his colleagues at Haverscot to see if Verity had returned. While he was talking to them in a quiet corner of the hospital, a nurse said that Richard and Terry could see Justin. His burns were serious, especially those on his legs and his hands, but he would survive.

Richard propelled Terry ahead of him into the cubicle where Justin, not yet allocated to a ward, lay. His face was scorched, and tufts of his hair were singed. He did not look at Richard.

'You'll feel better soon,' Richard said, encouragingly.

'It's all your fault.' Justin, sedated, spoke in a feeble growl.

Richard knew then that his suspicions were correct: Justin's fiery bomb had been meant for him, with serious intent, if not to kill. He felt a shaft like ice pierce him.

'Did the burglar do it?' Terry asked. 'Did you see him?'

Justin did not understand what he was saying. All he knew was that his body had become a mass of scorching pain and Richard, as always, was to blame.

'I want Mum,' he croaked.

'She'll be here soon,' said Richard.

At this point, a nurse told them they must go.

'Your dad can come and see you again soon, and he'll bring your mum,' she said.

'He's not my dad,' Richard heard Justin say in a sudden loud, clear voice, as he turned away. He did not look back, taking Terry with him, holding him by the sleeve of his jacket.

Outside, the police officer had no news of Verity, but there was evidence about what had caused Justin's injuries and Richard was needed back at Merrifields. There was no point in him and Terry staying any longer at the hospital; they had supplied all the necessary information, and could be telephoned if there was any change in Justin's condition. They drove home, with Terry very silent.

When they arrived, there was still no sign of Verity. Richard sent Terry off to have a bath and get ready for bed. Then he prepared to hear what the officers on the spot had to say.

They had found fragments of a bottle which had contained

petrol, and a box of matches. There were wisps of burnt rag. It was thought that there would be prints on some of the glass and on the matchbox,.

'The lad lit it himself, I'm afraid,' said the investigating Detective Inspector. At least the officers were not those who had come round after Terry's escapade, thought Richard wearily. Now that he knew Justin was out of danger, it was Verity about whom he was concerned. Where could she be?

He expressed his anxiety and mentioned the burglary.

'Ah yes — well, we've got some news for you about that,' said the inspector. 'We've caught your thief. While we were on our way here, we met a young lad with two pillow slips full of stuff whose possession he couldn't satisfactorily explain. He'd a video and some jewellery and silver. We picked him out in the headlights.' He smiled. 'It was quite pleasing,' he declared. 'He's a juvenile, so my colleagues are contacting his parents.'

'If they're ours, the postcode's on the video, in that invisible ink you recommend,' said Richard. 'And we've got photographs of most of the jewellery and silver.'

'I'm glad to hear it,' said the inspector. 'That'll make identification of the property much easier.

'But what about my wife?' pressed Richard. 'She was in a state. We'd had a row.' He took a deep breath. 'I'm thinking of the river. It's in flood. She might have fallen in and been swept away.' He paused, then continued, 'She came banging on my workshop door and I took no notice. I'm afraid I'd had it up to here,' he added, gesturing.

'We can't do much till daylight,' said the inspector. 'We'll use lights and dogs along the riverside, just in case. But she's probably gone round to a friend's, just to give you a fright, if you'd had words.' Poor guy, he thought; a row with the wife and a wild kid trying to torch his workshop.

'I'll come with you,' Richard said. Then he remembered Terry. 'Oh — I suppose I can't leave my other stepson on his own.' What could he do? Would Miss Darwin come round?

'We'll get a woman officer over to keep an eye on him,' said the inspector. 'You probably know the fields beside the river quite well — your local knowledge will be helpful to us.'

It looked like being quite a night.

25

A LAN WAS SITTING in his old room at The Willows. Before him was an open book: *Coot Club*, with his mother's inscription on the flyleaf.

It was his property. So was everything that had been in this room. Even if his father – Tom – had left him nothing in his will, surely all that had been in here, the books and furniture and his posters, rightfully belonged to him? They should have been restored, now that he was free.

Unseeingly, he turned the pages of the book. He had enjoyed the series when he was a boy, and his parents, anxious to occupy an only child, had sent him on a sailing course at a centre geared to youngsters, but he hadn't liked the cold and wet when his boat capsized. He'd never liked discomfort and he'd had more than enough of it in recent years. This house, compared with his rented flat, was luxurious: now that the old girl was dead, why shouldn't he move in until Mick got out?

He couldn't, without other clothes. He couldn't stay in these dirty bloodstained things. When he'd buried her, he'd have to get back to the flat and change. Sitting there on the floor, he was still consumed with rage: the woman who had bought this place had bundled up his stuff, got rid of everything, expunged his past, and he resented it. If he hadn't already killed her, he'd have certainly set up a plan to do it now.

From somewhere in the house, he heard the telephone start ringing. On and on it went, the sound shrilling in his ears. When at last it stopped, he crossed the landing to the main bedroom where there was an extension and, snatching at the handset, took it off the hook and let it dangle. Now, anyone ringing up the old woman would just think that she was chattering away. He didn't want people to come looking for her, but when he and Mick had robbed their bank and left the country, anyone could call.

He looked around the bedroom which had been his mother's: Tom's too, of course, but that didn't count. Though it contained different furniture and the curtains were now blue, printed with yellow flowers, instead of his mother's mushroom pink, patterned with daisies, there was a similarity to it, and he was unable to make himself do what he really wanted: tear the place apart, smash the mirrors, foul the bedlinen.

Mick might enjoy a few nights here; it would impress him if Alan laid it on; there'd be respect. He could sort things out in the morning – bury the body in daylight when he could see what he was doing, then go back to the flat and get some clothes.

But he ought to make the trip to Reading in darkness, so that no one could see the state that he was in.

Undecided, he went downstairs for some more whisky, filling the tumbler, splashing in only a little water. He took it back upstairs to the room where he had played music, made his models, sulked throughout his youth. He finished the sand-wiches, eyes still on the book which Mark had recently enjoyed. He did not hear the front door open, quietly.

After church, Marigold had gone round to see Susan Conway. She was sure that, by this time, Mark's mother would have had a significant conversation with Ivy; if the box and other items were to be returned, Marigold could tell the police her property had been brought back anonymously and the matter could rest there.

Susan hid her annoyance at Miss Darwin's appearance on her doorstep once again, adopting a professional air of welcome.

'I'm sure you want to get on – I know you're busy – but I wanted to ask if you'd had a discussion with – Ivy, is it?' said Marigold.

Couldn't she have telephoned, thought Susan, not realising that Marigold had, in any case, been out of the house and was passing the end of the road.

'Oh – Steve did do it,' Susan said. 'I think Ivy will be round to see you in the morning. The jewellery was in his room.'

'I see,' said Marigold.

'Come in, won't you?' Susan said, resigned. Tiresome though the interruption was, Miss Darwin had been very kind to Mark when she might have been extremely angry.

'I mustn't keep you,' said Marigold, but she took off her camel coat and let Susan hang it on a hook behind the front door, then went with her into the living-room.

'Mark's upstairs having his bath,' said Susan.

'Oh. Just as well, perhaps, that he shouldn't hear about this,' said Marigold. 'Though of course he'd caught on about the box.'

'Yes,' agreed Susan.

They sat facing one another on either side of the room.

'You're worried about leaving Mark with Ivy after this,' Marigold pronounced.

'Yes.'

'I can understand that. It's not her fault, however. You were satisfied with her when you made the original plan for Mark, after all.'

'Steve was quite young then, and his father was alive,' said Susan. 'He was more controllable. And Mark has a lot of freedom now. It's inevitable. I want him to be able to take care of himself.'

'He seems a most capable boy,' said Miss Darwin.

'Bad company can damage anyone,' said Susan.

'That's true. But Mark has other friends than Steve, hasn't he? Terry, for instance.'

'Oh yes,' said Susan. But Terry had been very silly, and she had met few others.

'I hope we can deal with this without the police pressing charges,' said Miss Darwin. 'Steve will have to be punished in some way. Perhaps he could help me in my garden – mow the lawn and cut down rubbish – unpaid for a while, and if he's a good worker I could offer him a regular job on Saturdays.'

'That's a good idea,' said Susan. 'I'm sure Ivy would be very grateful.'

'I don't want gratitude – just the return of my stolen property and a reformed junior criminal,' said Miss Darwin. 'He needs to be kept away from his dubious companions before it's too late. It would be a pity if he posed as either a hero or a martyr.'

'Yes.' Susan looked at the older woman. Her lips were set, her expression determined. Steve wouldn't be able to run rings round her. She smiled, and Miss Darwin's features relaxed too. She wished Susan smiled a genuine smile more often, not a superficial one which must be necessary in her job but was meaningless.

'I'll be happy to see Mark whenever he likes to call,' Miss Darwin said. 'And if you would like him to spend some time with me after school while you make up your mind about Ivy, he's most welcome. He can do his homework and be safe while you're at work, and I'll feed him, too. I like cooking,' she added truthfully. She had enjoyed preparing nourishing meals for her parents; now she rarely took much trouble for herself.

'That's very kind of you,' said Susan. 'If he could – just for a week or so – till I'm sure about things. On a business footing, of course.'

Marigold knew Susan would not accept what she would term as charity.

'Naturally,' she said. She could put what sums Susan

would insist on handing over into a fund for Mark. 'That's settled, then,' she added, suppressing her unfamiliar feeling of delight. 'I'll expect him after school tomorrow.' She rose to leave. 'You've done a good job with him and it can't be easy for you. I've known several widows and their sons have turned out very well, but it's sad to lack a father, and a boy is the better for a good one.' She moved towards the door. 'However, there are schoolmasters in boys' lives and the fathers of their friends, good male influences. Richard Gardner, for instance, is a very pleasant man.'

'Yes, he seems to be,' said Susan. 'That's not an easy situation, either. Being a stepfather, I mean.'

'No, it's not,' said Marigold, glad Susan had not taken her own remarks as implied criticism when they were intended as encouragement. 'But a lot of things that are worth doing are quite difficult.'

'I'm not a widow,' Susan said. 'I've never been married.'

'Nor have I,' said Marigold. 'Who cares?'

Nearing home, Marigold looked forward to her drink. Now and then she had an evening totally without one, just to prove she could, but since she had found that a few stiff ones coaxed her into a mood of cheerfulness, she sometimes even sang along to the radio. In London, this was never her way; she was always strictly sober and very solemn.

It had been a long day, full of tests. Now it was nearly over. Walking up the drive, she was glad to see the lights shining from her house, welcoming her home. She let herself in, still missing Sinbad's friendly greeting, and hung her coat in the cloakroom. She left her hat there, too, for it was rather damp; when it had dried off she'd take it upstairs. Then she went into the sitting-room and helped herself to a large gin and tonic, from the bottles and glasses kept in the corner fitment. She did not bother about ice or lemon, but after swallowing a mouthful she lit the fire and sat down on the sofa. In a few minutes she would fetch the sandwiches left from tea. Soon the gin took effect and her spirits lifted.

She was happy to be helping Mark, and was looking forward to his company, but she was not sanguine about Steve or Ivy, his unlucky stepmother. There would be a hard row to be hoed there, she thought, unless the boy could be given a fright about what the consequences of his crime might have been. Though nowadays, youngsters seemed to escape with a severe telling-off – a caution – for really serious offences. It seemed that they went after anything they wanted; young thieves did not respect other people or their property.

She topped up her glass before going to fetch the sandwiches, which would soon blot up the alcohol. Her father had always believed in a nip to keep out the cold; it had never caused him to lose control or behave badly. It made you shed your inhibitions; she knew that. Your true nature would be revealed – mawkish or maudlin, merry or bellicose; she had seen it often enough in other people but until she began trying it herself, after her return to Haverscot, she had not understood that she was, herself, one of the cheerful ones. She had never let herself go that far before.

Did poor Richard Gardner ever let go? He'd certainly been drinking when she saw him at The Red Lion, in the bar. He was an unhappy man, but his wife was miserable. What a bitter woman she seemed to be.

Carrying her second drink, she went out to the kitchen. When she opened the door, she felt a draught, and, more slowly than if she were completely sober, she realised that the glass in the back door was broken. She was already opening the fridge door when she saw earth on the floor and a large pair of men's shoes on the mat. She had just noticed a bottle of whisky, half-full, on the worktop by the sink when a moustached man with wild grey hair, dirty, and with blood on his face, burst into the room from the hall. He carried a shotgun, and, as she stared at him, transfixed, he halted by the door and fired two shots straight at her.

Alan thought he had seen a ghost. He couldn't have killed

the old cow after all, for here she was, as large as life and hideous, but she didn't fall after he had fired at her.

Marigold had been saved because the shelves in the fridge door, which had shielded her, had been stacked with bottles, tins and packs of juice whose fluid contents had stopped the shots, though some bits of metal flew about the room and one slightly grazed her hand. She had a brief advantage over her assailant because, although she was shocked and her ears rang with the sound of the explosions, she accepted what she saw, whereas he thought he beheld an apparition.

Milk, cream, mineral water, fruit juice and broken eggs cascaded on to the kitchen floor. As if it were a film unfolding before her, Marigold saw the man move, breaking the gun open as he did so, and he reached towards the box of cartridges which was standing near the bread bin. Marigold stretched out to grab the glass holding her drink which she had put down on the table. She picked it up and threw it at his head. It caught him on the ear and liquid splashed him but it barely put him off course. He was between her and the door: she might get to the back door before he reloaded the gun, but he could still hit her with it.

He was already shoving two new cartridges into the barrels when Marigold hit him over the head with the bottle of whisky from which Alan himself had drunk earlier. He sank to the floor in a most gratifying way, loosening his grip on the gun, and she snatched it from him.

He was only stunned. Marigold pushed the cartridges home and cocked it again, ready to fire. She pointed it at him as he began to struggle to his feet, ramming it against his chest. He was blinking at her, trying to clear his head which was fuddled with the whisky as well as the blow he had received. He was still sure that she must be a ghost come back to haunt him.

Marigold prodded him with the gun, then moved back, realising he might be able to seize it by the barrel and wrench it from her grasp.

'I can use this,' she said. 'Never doubt that.'

He didn't, but sick rage began to fill him now. He clung on to a cupboard top, managing to stand.

'You old bitch,' he said. 'You move into my house and take all my things away and think you're so great,' and then he broke into a string of obscenities.

What was he talking about? He was obviously mad, and also extremely dangerous and violent. Marigold knew she must be very careful and take no chances; he was much younger than she was and a great deal stronger. She held the gun pointing firmly at him and then discovered that he was a coward. Later, she realised that of course he must have been one, to have fired at her at all: armed as he was, an elderly woman posed no great challenge.

But, to Alan, she did: she looked intimidating, glowering at him from under her grim grey hair, her thick brows forming another serious line across her face. She was not wearing her glasses, but she did not need them for this encounter.

'Get in there,' she ordered, indicating the store room with the barrel of the gun. 'Go on.' She spoke firmly, like a general commanding his troops. 'On the count of three or I'll fire,' she warned. 'Open the door. I'm waiting.'

You naughty boy. Go up to your room at once or you'll be smacked, Alan heard his mother's voice. *I'm counting to three.* She had never had to carry out her threat.

Meekly, Alan went into the store-cupboard. There was no bolt on the outside of the door, but after she had banged it shut behind him – it opened outwards into the kitchen – Marigold pulled the table across in front of it and then, having dared to set the gun down, wedged that against the door with the fridge, which was very heavy, and difficult to move because of all the mess, but she did it. This barricade would not hold against a strong, determined man; she could not risk leaving it to telephone the police but must sit here, a sentry. In the morning when the milkman came, maybe she could shout for help. But that was hours away. It wasn't even midnight yet.

The floor was awash with the mess from the fridge. She sat clear of the worst of it, on a kitchen chair, holding the gun across her knees, ready to lift it if the cupboard door gave in to his battering as he rattled it, shouting and yelling. Maybe she should have shot him in the foot.

Then I'd have been charged with assault, she thought, resolving to hit his hands if they appeared.

Time passed, and after a while the man's cries diminished. Perhaps he had fallen asleep. Dare she risk leaving the room to telephone?

Just as she had decided to chance it, he resumed his cursing and swearing, and then he started throwing things around inside the cupboard. He must have found the light switch in there. She heard tins and bottles break, but the noise he made did not drown the sound of the front door-bell which, like angel music from the spheres, Marigold suddenly heard above the uproar. Surely whoever was there would hear the din and come to investigate? She'd add her yells to those of the intruder.

It was Richard at the door, and he did.

26

AT FIRST HE could not take in the spectacle before him.
As he opened the unlocked back door, noting the
broken pane of glass, he saw Miss Darwin rising from a
kitchen chair, holding a double-barrelled shotgun in a
business-like manner. The kitchen itself was in a chaotic
state, with smashed eggs, broken glass, milk and other
liquids all over the floor, and there was a loud background
sound of shouting, which he had heard as he came round
the side of the house when the front door-bell was not
answered.

'He's in there,' Marigold called above the noise. 'A
burglar.'

She had just realised that he must have been in the house
for some time before he appeared in the kitchen; he'd had
some whisky, and she'd seen, now, that the sandwiches she
was counting on for supper had vanished. They weren't
among the mess on the floor, nor left on a shelf inside the
fridge as other things had been.

Richard had been so intent upon the search for Verity that
he had almost forgotten about the break-in at Merrifields.
Unable to get Miss Darwin on the telephone, he had come
round to see if, by any freak chance, Verity had called at The
Willows. She might have done so, seeking sympathy; Miss
Darwin might have persuaded her to telephone her parents,

or even the Samaritans, thus accounting for the busy telephone line.

'Is Verity here?' he demanded, amazing Marigold by the irrelevance of the question.

'No.' She shook her head impatiently. 'Richard, please go and telephone the police. I daren't leave here in case he gets out. That door isn't secure.' She had already banged the intruder's knuckles once, extremely hard, and had been able to close the door again when he retreated, screaming.

'The police aren't far away.' said Richard. 'They're searching for Verity. She's disappeared.'

Marigold did not care if Verity had gone to the moon.

'Richard, there's a burglar in the store cupboard. Don't you understand? He came here with a gun and he shot at me. Please go and telephone, now.'

'Shot at you? Are you hurt?' Richard took a grip on himself.

'No. Richard, please,' she implored.

'Give me the gun. You go and phone. It'll be quicker than going to call them from outside.'

Outside? What did he mean? Marigold handed him the gun.

'Do you know how to use it?' she asked.

'Oh yes,' he said. There was no need to wonder if she did. 'You in there,' he called out loudly. 'Stop that racket. The police are on their way.'

Thus instructed, Alan, who had briefly quietened down when he heard sounds from beyond his prison, broke into a fresh burst of swearing. Marigold left them to it, hastening off to telephone. When she found she could get no dialling tone, it took her a few minutes to realise that the extension might be disconnected. Of course: the burglar had been up there while she drank her gin. The thought made her shudder. She hurried upstairs and made the call. The police seemed slow to understand what she was saying: an armed man breaking in, and now captive. She feared they thought her an insane woman making a hoax call.

Before returning to Richard, she went thankfully to the bathroom. For some time she had been fearing that her bladder would not last out the siege and such a possibility was mortifying.

While she was gone, Richard had been having a crazy conversation with her prisoner.

'So she's gone, then, has she? The ghost?' Alan had asked, after running out of breath with his curses.

'What ghost?' Richard asked.

'That old bat,' said Alan.

'If you mean the lady of the house,' said Richard pompously, 'she's no ghost. She's very real and she's fetching the police at this moment. They're not far away, in any case. They're looking for you,' he added, which was not the truth: not yet, for Steve, held at the police station and waiting for Ivy to arrive before he could be questioned, had not told the tale he had concocted in the time since his arrest. He was going to say that Alan Morton, escaped murderer, had stolen the articles found in his possession and forced him to carry them away and hide them. It was a good story, and he had decided it would get him off the hook.

Marigold, physically relieved, recalled, as she returned to the kitchen, what Richard had been saying about Verity. Wretched, hysterical woman: she was playing another of her silly tricks. Surely, after all the fuss when Terry ran away, she'd have more sense than cause such anxiety?

'I'll take over now, if you want to get back outside and resume your hunt,' she said, entering the kitchen.

'No,' he said. 'I'm not leaving you alone with our friend here.' He took a look at her. She was always pale, her complexion sallow, but now, in the bright strip lighting in the kitchen, she looked grey. 'You could use a drink. Have you got some brandy? Have a nip,' he suggested.

'I was having a second gin and tonic when this creature appeared,' said Marigold. 'I'd better not start mixing things.' She laughed, an odd, harsh, unamused sound. 'I threw it at him,' she continued. 'The glass, I mean. I scored a direct hit on his head. Then I used the whisky bottle. It was his fault it was handy — he'd left it out.'

'How untidy,' Richard answered calmly. What did she mean, she'd used it? Hit him with it? 'Well, then, what about some tea? Or coffee. I'd quite like a cup,' he added. 'Though I don't suppose the police will be more than a few minutes.'

'I expect they'd like some, too,' said Marigold. 'Isn't it what you're always supposed to give them, when they call?'

They went on chatting in this casual manner while Marigold, stepping carefully over the debris on the floor, filled the kettle and put it on.

'I'd better start clearing up the mess,' she said, reaching in a cupboard for some cups and saucers. Marigold was not equipped with mugs. Most of her best tea things were still in the dishwasher.

'The police may want to look at it,' said Richard. 'The mess, I mean. It's evidence.'

'Do you think so? Perhaps they'll want to see where the shots went,' said Marigold. She could still smell the explosive. 'The empty cartridge cases must be somewhere about. He'd unloaded them before I blipped him.'

Had she been sitting there holding an unloaded weapon? Richard mouthed the question at her.

'Oh, it's loaded all right,' she answered blithely. 'He was doing that but I interrupted him. Fancy shooting at a woman my age,' she went on. 'What a — what a—' the appropriate epithet eluded her.

Richard could think of several.

At this point in their dialogue, the kettle boiled and the police arrived. The kitchen seemed suddenly to be full of men in uniforms, but in fact at first there were only two, soon joined by others from the search party.

They extracted Alan from the cupboard and clapped handcuffs on him while they cautioned him. The whole scene seemed, to Marigold and Richard, quite surreal.

'Have you found my wife?' he asked them, but they had no news of Verity.

Alan, being led away, was shuddering.

'Don't let that – that thing near me,' he kept saying, peering sideways at Marigold. 'She's a ghost.'

'What can he mean?' asked Richard. 'He went on like that while you were telephoning.'

They didn't understand for quite some time. The search party seeking Verity were convinced, by now, that unless she had taken refuge with a friend, she must be in the river, and there was little more that could be done till daylight, but because of the summons to The Willows, where there was, allegedly, an armed man, they came into the grounds and played their powerful torches round the garden. They saw the muddy trail which Alan had made walking to and from the shed. They found Verity there, wrapped in her big coat, her tangled hair sticky with her own dried blood, her face unrecognisable.

It was a long night.

Eventually, Marigold went back for what remained of it to Merrifields with Richard. The policewoman left in the house had succeeded in getting Terry to bed and he was asleep, so he was not a problem for the moment. In the morning, Richard would have to tell him that his mother was dead – would have to say that she had been murdered, because he would hear the truth in time. Perhaps Justin could be spared the news till he was stronger.

Richard had been questioned thoroughly, but there was no blood on his clothes, and the man, soon identified as Alan Morton, was smothered in it; there would be scientific proof that it was Verity's. Separately, Richard and Marigold gave their statements. All this was done at The Willows. Alan, swiftly removed to Radbury police station, had left plenty of evidence, enough to lead, months later, to his second conviction for murder. The spade and the sledgehammer in the shed were stained with Verity's blood, to which adhered strands of her dyed hair. When the police realised who Alan was, his actions became easier to deduce. The gun used to shoot at Marigold might well prove to be the same weapon that had killed his wife so long ago.

'He kept calling me a ghost,' said Marigold. 'He must have thought he'd killed me, not someone he had never heard of. Poor Verity. I wonder what she was doing here.'

'Just wandering about, I expect,' said Richard. 'Perhaps she came to see you at the house, and then heard something from the shed and walked on down there.'

'We shall never really know,' said Marigold.

'If I hadn't ignored her when she came banging at my workshop door, she wouldn't have run off,' said Richard. He had described their row to Marigold as they sat by the revived fire in the drawing-room at Merrifields.

'You weren't to know that she'd meet a murderer in my garden shed,' said Marigold. 'If I'd been in, she wouldn't have gone down there.'

'She couldn't be happy,' Richard sighed. 'I couldn't make her happy, anyway.'

'It's not your fault,' said Marigold. 'Some people just don't have it in them. They can't learn to count their blessings. I'm sure you did everything you could for all of them.'

Richard had told her about Justin's part in causing his own injuries.

'He hates me so much,' he said. 'At least Verity never knew that he'd been burned.'

What was he going to do about those boys? Would he have to face a future of caring for two disaffected stepsons, at least one of whom loathed him? Poor man, thought Marigold.

'Where's their own father?' she asked. 'Will he come to the fore now?'

'I've no idea,' said Richard. 'Her parents might tell him about this, I suppose. They may know where he is. Perhaps they'll help in some way. The boys are fond of them. What a shock it's going to be for them.'

'Well, when it's a reasonable enough hour, you can tell them, Richard,' said Marigold. She was suffering, now, from a physical reaction to the night's events and had begun to tremble, only slightly but uncontrollably, her jaw shaking. She hoped he wouldn't notice.

He did, however.

'You're frozen. You must go to bed,' he said.

'It's too late,' she said. 'Or do I mean too early? I'd like a bath, though. That would warm me up. And what about you?'

'I'd like one too,' said Richard. 'We can both be satisfied, for as you know, there are several bathrooms here now. What if I make up the fire, we both have baths, then come down again and tuck ourselves up with rugs, and put some music on? That will pass the time till the rest of the world wakes up.'

Less than an hour later, they were both ensconced, Marigold on the sofa, Richard in the largest armchair with his legs resting on the second, rugs over them, and Elgar's violin concerto playing softly in the background. Richard fell asleep quite quickly; Marigold took much longer, and she woke first, hearing a gentle snore.

She smiled. Now she had, for the first time in her life, slept with a man.

He rang Caroline early in the morning, telling her that there had been an accident and that his wife was dead.

'Oh dear! I'm sorry.' Caroline sounded genuinely distressed. She hesitated. 'Are you coping? Shall I come down?'

He could not believe his ears. She was offering to help: this woman who might be carrying his child but did not mean to let him know the truth.

'No. It's all right. Someone very kind is helping me,' he said. 'A neighbour.' He asked Caroline to let it be known that he would not be in the office today and possibly not tomorrow either.

At that moment, Marigold was giving Terry his breakfast in the kitchen. He had been told a sanitised version of the facts: his mother had gone out walking in the night; there had been a burglar, and tragically the two had met, with fatal consequences. It was close enough to the truth for now. Neither Marigold nor Richard yet knew about Steve's role in the Merrifields robbery.

Terry was chastened, almost stunned, but then he cried. Amidst his tears, his brother's name was uttered several times and Richard assured him that Justin would recover. They would go and see him later.

'I don't have to go to school?'

'Not today.'

'Oh.' There were more tears, but then Richard said that Terry's grandparents were coming to stay for a while. This cheered him up and he began telling Marigold about their house in Devon, which was near the sea, and about their small sailing boat. Richard had told Marigold that the grandmother was a friendly, easy person, though the grandfather was less predictable.

'Verity was like him in some ways,' he said.

Oh dear, thought Marigold, who was hoping the couple would take the children on: surely Richard could not be expected, now, to raise them? Perhaps there were aunts and uncles, even godparents.

'Before they get here, we must ring up the hospital and find out how Justin is this morning,' Richard told Terry. 'Then we must go round to Miss Darwin's house and clean it up. She was very brave last night. She captured the man – the villain. He was a very wicked man.'

'The man who killed Mum?' Terry could say it, even if Richard could not bring himself to do so.

'Richard helped me,' said Marigold. Let the poor man win some respect from these difficult children. 'Is that a good idea?' she asked.

'Yes,' said Richard firmly. 'We need occupying and we can't do much here. I'll get some glass and fix the broken windows – yours and mine. And you can't clear all that mess up yourself.'

Marigold's resolution to have stronger locks fitted could be carried out later. Whatever his fate, Steve had had a fright and wouldn't be coming round again; at least, not yet.

'Very well,' she said. 'Thank you both.'

She was determined not to cancel her arrangement with Mark; he was due that afternoon and he would need something to eat. Maybe, while they cleaned the kitchen up, Terry could suggest a menu likely to appeal to him.

Two police officers arrived at Merrifields just as they were ready to set out for The Willows, and Richard asked if they had finished their work in Miss Darwin's kitchen.

'Oh yes,' one of them said, and added, 'You'll need a new fridge, Miss Darwin. It's damaged beyond repair and it's a prime exhibit in the case.'

Marigold knew that it had proved strong enough to save her life.

'I expect the insurance company will pay,' she said, and she laughed. Two claims within so few days must be a record.

The cleaning operation was under way when Ivy Burton arrived at The Willows, pushing Adam, wrapped cocoon-like in his padded stroller. With her, on a set of reins, was the toddler she was minding for the morning. She had brought back Miss Darwin's stolen jewellery.

'Oh, what a mess! What's happened?' Ivy said, seeing what was going on.

'There was some trouble here last night,' said Miss Darwin. 'Mr Gardner and Terry are very kindly clearing up.' She bustled Ivy into the sitting-room, with the toddler, closing the door. Adam, who was asleep, they left parked in the hall.

'I'm sorry I had to bring them with me,' Ivy said. She was almost in tears. 'Sharon's at her job, you see – that's my daughter. Adam's my grandson – in the pushchair,' she explained. 'This one, William, I'm looking after for a few hours. I'd no one to leave them with.'

'I understand,' said Miss Darwin. It was a bit tough on Mrs Burton to have a thieving stepson on her hands as well as her own children, and be expected to bring up her grandson, too.

'I'll keep him tethered,' Ivy said. 'You've such nice things. He's into everything, is William.'

'Mrs Burton, I must tell you quickly that Mr Gardner's wife was killed last night, and the other boy, Justin, has been badly burned in an accident,' said Miss Darwin swiftly, before Ivy could launch into an apology for Steve's misdeeds. With Richard and Terry so close at hand, she must be warned.

'Oh my God!' Ivy stared at her.

'You hadn't heard?' Marigold thought the news might have arrived by grapevine already.

Ivy shook her blonde curls. Despite her difficult and chequered life, she was very well preserved, thought Marigold.

'What happened? Was it in the car?' she asked.

'No – nothing like that,' said Miss Darwin. 'There was an intruder here – that's why the kitchen's in that state. He broke in, but he'd already met poor Mrs Gardner. He's been arrested for her murder.'

'Alan Morton,' Ivy said, exhaling.

'Yes. How did you know that?' asked Miss Darwin.

William, by now, was getting bored and making fretty noises. Ivy found some sweets in her pocket and unwrapped one, popping it into his mouth without turning her attention away from the conversation.

'He met Steve yesterday at the Gardners' place,' said Ivy. 'Steve's still at Radbury police station. The police found him carrying things he'd stolen from Merrifields – he'd got it all in pillow slips. Can you credit it? Walking along with them, he was, after I thought he was safely locked up in his room.'

'But how did he meet Alan Morton?' Marigold was mystified.

'Steve broke into Merrifields and Alan Morton saw him

and went in after him. When the police picked Steve up, he said Alan had done the job and had threatened Steve and made him carry off the stuff for him. Of course that part's not true,' said Ivy. 'Steve admitted it to me when I was let see him on our own last night. Seems Alan Morton saw him snooping round here again, yesterday afternoon, and then Steve realised with all the Gardners here that he could get into their place and help himself.' She sighed heavily. 'It's a fine thing if you can't go out and leave your house unoccupied without some young tearaway breaking in and thieving. My house is empty now. I hope none of his friends is in there while my back's turned. He's got into bad company since his dad died, I'm afraid.' Ivy paused, and then said soberly, 'What you're really saying is that Alan met poor Mrs Gardner and went for her.'

'Something like that,' said Miss Darwin.

'I came here to apologise to you,' said Ivy. 'But now you've told me this – oh dear! I don't know what to say. He came in here and threatened you, I suppose? Alan, I mean.'

'Yes, he did, but as you can see, I'm all right and the police soon came and took him away,' said Miss Darwin.

'But the boy? You said he was burned?'

'That was a separate incident. He was playing about with petrol and set himself alight, by accident.'

Ivy remembered Steve's petrol-smelling jeans. She knew he sometimes saw young Justin around town; better not to mention it just now.

'Oh dear,' she said again. 'Will he be all right?'

'I think so,' said Miss Darwin. Richard had telephoned the hospital before they left the house, and had learned that Justin was in a stable condition. They told one so little, she had reflected.

Ivy's mind had returned to Steve.

'If Mr Gardner gets his things back – he will – the police got everything – maybe he won't press charges,' she said, hopefully. 'What about you, Miss Darwin? I was going to ask you to let him off.'

'I'd be willing to,' said Miss Darwin. 'But in view of last night's events, it may not be within my power. And the same may apply to Mr Gardner.'

'But Steve had nothing to do with — with Mrs Gardner's death,' Ivy protested.

'No, but you've just told me that he's blaming Alan Morton for the burglary at Merrifields. He'll involve himself if he sticks to that story,' said Marigold.

Ivy looked at her, unable to reply.

'He'd better talk to a solicitor and take whatever advice he's given,' said Marigold. 'My own advice would be to tell the truth.'

'He needn't say anything,' said Ivy. 'That's the law. He's only told me, so far.'

'And it's the law that let Alan Morton out of prison after just a few years, when he had been given a life sentence for killing his wife,' said Marigold. 'If that sentence had been implemented literally he would not have been released and Mrs Gardner would still be alive.'

Ivy, searching Steve's drawers for further stolen property, had found, among other articles which had given her reason for concern, the newspaper cuttings he had hidden, with the report of Alan's trial.

'He came over to The Willows last November. Alan did,' she said. 'I don't know if he'd escaped or if he was on one of them shopping trips they let them out for. That's how Steve knew who he was, last night. Steve and Mark were here. Of course neither of them said a word to me, and nor did Mr Morton, but that's when he went downhill. He died soon after. Steve told me last night, at the police station.'

'We all have secrets,' said Marigold, who had very few.

'Poor Mr Gardner, though, with them two boys. How will he manage? It's funny, you never think of that, when you take on someone else's kids. When you get married, I mean. You don't think of them dying and leaving you with their kids. I never thought Steve would be a problem. He was a lovely little lad. My mother died when I was eight and my dad married a lovely woman. They had two more kids and we all got on a treat.'

At this point, William had had enough and let out a bellow.

'I'd best take him off,' said Ivy. 'I'm ever so sorry, Miss Darwin. About everything.'

'Yes,' said Marigold. 'So am I.'

Two weeks later, Justin was discharged from hospital and soon afterwards was taken, with his brother, down to Devonshire. Verity's mother had spent the intervening time at Merrifields, with one excursion home to make some preparations, as she did not altogether trust her husband. The boys were going to live there for the present.

That evening, Richard took Miss Darwin out to dinner at The Red Lion.

'It's not a celebration, but I'm glad they've gone,' he said to her, across the table. 'They represent my failure.'

When he picked her up, Marigold was just seeing off Susan Conway, who had come to collect Mark after his few hours spent at The Willows. It was too much to expect that anything could be sparked off between them, but Marigold hoped to contrive occasional meetings as the days grew longer. She had learned that Mark knew nothing whatsoever about his father.

'We've all failed at some things,' Marigold declared. 'What about your daughter? When's she coming home?'

'Oh – not yet. I'm not sure when she's due for leave,' he answered.

'She knows what's happened?'

'I haven't told her yet,' said Richard. 'Her mother may have done so, if she saw it in the paper.'

There had been a brief report, but because Alan had so swiftly been charged, the case was *sub judice* and not a subject for lurid journalism. Luckily the incident involving Justin had not attracted any attention.

After an inquest into Verity's death had been opened and

adjourned, her funeral had taken place. Richard and Miss Darwin had gone together: tentatively, she had said that she would like to be there, and he had welcomed her support at what was, for him, a bizarre ordeal. Justin, still with a scarred face, bandaged hands, and, beneath his dark school trousers, dressings on his legs, had been there with Terry and their grandparents. Richard and Marigold had sat together on the other side of the aisle in the crematorium chapel. Terry had wept throughout, but Justin had been dry-eyed and he had never once glanced at Richard. A tall, broad-shouldered man with a bushy grey beard had been among the small group of mourners: the boys' father. Later, at The Red Lion, where he was staying, he and Richard had had an illuminating talk. His present wife was tired of living overseas and wanted to return. He wondered if it would be possible to come back into the boys' lives. So far, they'd scarcely spoken; he wasn't sure they even knew who he was.

'I'm sure they do,' said Richard. 'They missed you. After all, you are their father.' He hesitated. 'They are a bit confused,' he felt it fair to warn. 'But they never really took to me. Especially Justin.'

'What happened? Some accident, I heard.'

'Yes. I shouldn't be too curious,' Richard suggested. 'Let him tell you himself, if he wants to.'

He'd gone home feeling shriven. A huge load had been lifted from his shoulders.

Tonight, he'd picked a good claret from The Red Lion's list, and it went well with the steak they had both chosen.

'I'm thinking of leaving my job,' he told Miss Darwin, as they tried the cheeses. 'Of course, I'll have to be here for the resumed inquest, and, I suppose, the trial, but I've more or less decided on early retirement. I've only got myself to pay for now.'

He was planning to settle some money on the two boys, if only to salve his conscience, but their grandparents were not penniless, and their father seemed willing to take on some responsibility for them. 'I might start up my own business,' he went on. 'Perhaps in France.'

'I see.' Marigold was dismayed at the prospect of losing such a friend, the best one that she had ever had. 'I'm going to have the shed pulled down,' she told him. 'As soon as the police say it can be dismantled. I'll put up another one in a different part of the garden. I thought I'd plant some roses on the site.'

'That's a nice idea,' he said. 'She didn't like them, though. Said they were too pretty-pretty.'

'Well, I like them, and I'm the one who'll be looking at them,' was the answer, and Marigold finished up her wine.

'Let me fill your glass again,' said Richard.

He thought of telling her about Caroline and the baby, but decided not to burden her any more. Through no fault of her own, she had been drawn into his personal tragedy, and she had been a stalwart source of comfort.

She'd make her life here gently, calmly, without him. She'd got the choral society now, and that nice little boy Mark who had the pleasant, rather pretty, most efficient mother.

'What about Steve Burton? Do we know if he'll be prosecuted?' Richard asked her.

'Not yet. I think it's all still being decided,' said Marigold. 'I can't think locking him up will achieve anything.'

'Let's hope Morton gets a really long sentence this time,' Richard said.

'He'll get life. It's mandatory, but he'll qualify for release again unless the judge lays down a specific length of time for him to be in prison.'

'Then he'll kill someone else,' Richard said. 'If he's thwarted.'

'Yes,' agreed Marigold. 'Perhaps another stranger.'

A Question of Belief

1

HE'D LEFT HER everything: the house, and the mortgage, even the car, because that would be found where he had abandoned it near the river. She'd think he'd jumped in, and after a while his death would be presumed and she'd get probate. Did that take seven years? There might be complications but she would be able to carry on a normal life. He didn't think she'd hurry to report him missing. She wouldn't want him back. By the time she took action, or the car was found, he'd be far away.

He'd made no plans. He had no goal. He was a broken, defeated man and he did not know what else to do. At least she would be free of him, free from the shame.

At first, when he was released on bail before the trial, he had planned to kill himself, but that would have been too easy. It would have been a confession of guilt, but then she and everyone else he cared about believed he'd done it.

Andrew, his student son, had said, 'Surely there are other ways, Dad,' almost with pity, but contempt had been there, too. The boy had been mocked by his friends, and so had Jackie, his daughter, who was still at school. It had been worse for her, because they had always been so close.

'I can't expect you to understand, only to believe in me,' he'd said, and had made a move to hug her, but she had drawn back from him in revulsion. That was what had killed his final hope of support.

Lesley, his wife, had at first accepted what he told her had happened, but when he was dismissed from Lavery's, the large store where he was a departmental manager, she had changed her mind.

He'd been given no opportunity to defend himself before it went to court. There was no internal enquiry, and at that stage taking legal action would have meant risking a huge financial loss if he failed. He had consulted a solicitor who had pointed out the hazards.

'It seems you've got no proof,' he said. 'It's her word against yours. You'd need witnesses to testify on your behalf.'

He had tried to find them, but none of his colleagues was prepared to be involved, though one or two showed sympathy, and even regret.

'You'd have been safe if you'd gone along with it,' said Bob, from soft furnishings. 'That's what I did, and after a bit she let me go.' He'd grinned, sheepishly. 'It was all right,' he said. 'An experience.

Taught me to be more careful in the future.'

'What if Polly'd found out?' he'd asked, horrified. Polly was Bob's wife.

'She didn't,' Bob had answered. 'And if you tell her,' he'd added, suddenly menacing, 'I'll say you made it up to get yourself off the hook.'

But then she'd gone to the police, made it public.

Disappearing now, he'd got some money – not a lot, because if he took any out of the bank account, suicide would be discounted. He had almost a hundred pounds, saved from his social security payment; his watch, which he could sell; and he took the radio from the car because that was what car thieves went for and it would look as if the abandoned vehicle had been pillaged. He left it unlocked, with the keys in the ignition.

It was to be a long time before the thought of revenge occurred to him.

Autumn seemed to be lasting for ever. Frances Dixon could not remember when the trees had displayed such brilliant shades of gold and russet, and for so long. Throughout October the leaves hung upon the branches, reluctant to give up their hold, and sunlight shafted down among them for days on end. She savoured it. Such moments were for treasuring.

She spent many hours working in her garden, planting still more bulbs, though in the years since she had lived at Badger's End she had naturalised hundreds under the apple trees. It was partly because of its name and partly because of its garden that she had bought the house nearly ten years ago, in an act of defiance. It was a square Edwardian stone house with a slate roof: not beautiful, but sound.

'It seems solid enough,' her daughter Hazel had grudgingly admitted, when brought on a voyage of inspection, permitted by her mother only after the contract had been signed. Frances had sold her house in Hertfordshire quite easily and at a good price; she had lived there for a long time, and she moved before the recession sent prices down.

Hazel had thought her mother, who was sixty-two years old at the time, mad to move so far away, at her age.

'What will you do if you're ill?' she had demanded.

'Call the doctor,' Frances replied. 'As I should here, if I were bad enough.'

'Your friends,' her daughter had said. 'It's hard to make new ones at your age.'

'What friends?' her mother had asked, with asperity.

In recent years, many houses in the neighbour-hood had changed hands and were occupied by younger families. People Frances had known had moved away or died, but Hazel had grown used to having her mother close at hand, a captive baby-sitter on whom her own successful career in public relations had depended. If any of Hazel's three children were ill, or the au pair proved unsatisfactory, Hazel enrolled her mother to hold the fort, never even saying that she didn't know how she would manage without Frances's support.

But when I was raising you, I had to do it, Frances longed to scream at her, forced by her daughter to abandon a planned theatre visit, or a supper party for those few of her friends remaining in the area, because one of Hazel's children had to be collected from the station, or because Hazel's sister, Arabella, a physicist married to another physicist living in Cambridge, had a rush of work or a domestic crisis and sent an appeal. Frances loved her grandchildren, but there were so many of them – Hazel's three, Arabella's five (and who knew if there might not be more) and three stepchildren from her husband's previous marriage. In school holidays, the daughters never seemed to think their own mother needed a break too as they made plans for her to look after their families. When she retired, and wanted time to learn to paint or follow interests of her own, she was completely at their mercy and it had all become too much.

If I'm not near, they can't send for me, Frances had decided one day after she fell and broke her wrist. The pain was intense, and she felt weepy. I'm tired of being brave, she recognised, while managing to be stoical on the way to hospital.

Luckily it was her left wrist. Frances was right-handed. She had plenty of time to reflect as she patiently endured the weeks in plaster waiting for it to heal.

Frances had been widowed when she was forty, and she had brought up her two daughters on her own. It had not been easy, and now she felt she was rearing her grandchildren as well. She had deeply loved her husband, who was a freelance travel writer, and when he died suddenly of a heart attack while caught up in a riot in South America, he left her little in the way of insurance: only enough to clear the mortgage. At the time, though, that was a considerable boon; rising and falling interest rates had not affected her. She had already returned to part-time teaching, for he was often away and, apart from the increased income, working occupied her mind. She was thankful that her own career left her free in the school holidays; if either of her own girls were ill in term-time, there was a woman she could call upon to help and who would look after them when Frances went out in the evenings, which wasn't very often.

Hazel and Arabella seemed unable to find such people. Perhaps they no longer existed, or perhaps neither of them understood how to treat those who worked for them. Certainly, au pairs turned over at a rapid rate in both households. Hazel's was orderly, running to strict timetables with everything minutely planned, while Arabella lived in academic chaos, even squalor. Since both had had the same upbringing – a sort of halfway house between the two – Frances had decided that environment was not the most important factor in development, though it must be an influence. Genes were responsible for many aspects of an individual's disposition. Her husband had been volatile, often disorganised, intensely sensitive; she was more pragmatic, less prone to sudden whims and enthusiasms. She sometimes wondered how their marriage, cut short so suddenly, would have endured; it had been a passionate and fulfilling partnership, and she still missed him, thinking of him every day of her life. Would their natures have polarised through the years? Would they have irritated one another, or would they, as she liked to think, have drawn closer, become more like each other, less extreme?

She would never discover.

Life in Chingbury was very different from what she had known before. Badger's End was on the outskirts of the village, which, when she moved in, was still small, but as the years passed it had expanded. There were now some small clusters of modern houses where people lived who worked as far away as Swindon.

Frances had spent the first years taming the garden, learning as she went. She had always enjoyed keeping the small plot behind the Hertfordshire house in order; it had a lawn, where the girls had played badminton, and there were small borders where she put bedding plants and grew roses; there was never time for more. Now, the fresh air and the freedom — even the rain, and the occasional snowfall — were a benison to her. For at least a year she revelled in the knowledge that if she wanted to make the trip to Bristol to the theatre, or to the nearer cinema, she could go, without having to change her plans at the last minute. She did not miss her family at all. She'd really only seen them, she concluded, when they needed her: the sudden trips she'd had to make to Hazel's house, and the late drive home or early morning departure ready for her own work had been very taxing as the years had gone by.

Soon after breaking her wrist, while she was staying with Hazel – not because of her own injury but because Hazel had a product launch – she had heard Hazel say to a friend, who had come to show her some fabric samples for proposed new curtains, that she didn't know how they'd cope when Frances went gaga.

'How will you know when she has flipped?' asked the friend, who was an interior designer.

'Oh, she'll start losing things and she won't know the name of the prime minister,' said Hazel. 'There are tests.'

Ice-cold fury filled Frances as she overheard these words. She walked straight out of the house and stormed round the streets muttering angrily beneath her breath, and did not return for two hours, then had to apologise to Hazel for alarming her by her unexplained absence. She had not stayed long enough to hear Hazel's friend reprove her for her heartlessness and tell her she was lucky to have a mother; her own had died and was much missed.

'My father died when I was eight,' said Hazel, but she didn't win that round because her friend then reminded her that Frances had brought her up alone when there was very little help for single mothers, even widows, whereas now it almost paid a woman not to marry.

The two women made up their tiff over some wine. Hazel, after all, was single now, though her ex-husband paid proper maintenance for the children.

It might do them good to spend more time with him, Frances had sometimes thought, stifling guilt lest she seem to be abandoning them. But they were all now in their teens, the two elder ones at university.

She'd always rather liked her son-in-law; she'd found him more congenial than Arabella's physicist. He was a systems analyst, and he had taken off with a secretary from his office.

The friend had gone when Frances returned after going to a pub for a whisky. As soon as she went back to Hertfordshire she had telephoned the estate agent, any earlier doubts about the wisdom of her plan dismissed.

She had never once regretted what she had done. She made friends, slowly, over time; they were not like old friends, who knew one's history and to whom long spells without contact made no difference because threads were picked up and links renewed as if the last meeting had been only days before. She had had to make an effort, joining a painting class, a gardening club and going to local fine arts lectures. Gradually, over the years, she had dropped out of these activities, spending more and more time in her garden, by now knowledgeable herself. She visited other gardens, too: notable ones within a day's driving distance, and once every year she went on holiday which took her to gardens overseas not normally open to the public. Like-minded travellers made up each group, mostly women, but there were a few men too. Some of the women were themselves garden designers; what a fine career, Frances thought, and wondered if Charlotte, the granddaughter she thought needed her the most, would ever consider doing that. Perhaps she would like to go with her grandmother on the next garden holiday? But perhaps not: perhaps she sought young company and a sunny beach.

Frances was spending some of these glorious October weeks paying late visits to gardens which she went to every year. Soon they would close down until the spring.

This Saturday, she was setting off for Singleton, a manor house some thirty miles away. She'd have her lunch there, in the Orangery.

Denis Smith sat in the back of the Ford Transit van. He felt quite excited, setting off for a day in the country, and being paid for going. The van had been driven out of London by Orlando, but at the service station where Tessa had met them, she had taken over. It was clear that she was now the boss. She was quite a looker, Denis thought, with her red curly hair and pale skin, and blue eyes like he imagined the sea must be. He'd never seen the sea.

Denis had come along with Biff, whom he'd met while they were both doing community service — Denis for theft, Biff for trying to set fire to a pet shop.

'Them little animals, all cooped up. It ain't right,' he'd said to Denis. Biff was broad and strong, with dark curly hair worn rather long, a snake tattooed on one arm, and *Save the Apes* with a representation of St Francis on the other. As they painted a community hall together, he told Denis about St Francis talking to the animals and how harmless beasts were used in animal experimentation and were hunted for pleasure. 'It ain't right,' he repeated. 'Them as does it are like animals.'

Denis said, rashly, 'But you want to save animals.'

'Yeah. Stands to reason, they can't save themselves,' said Biff. 'Besides, sometimes you get paid,' he added, irrelevantly, as it seemed.

'Paid? What for?' asked Denis.

'For helping them out. Making a noise. Throwing smoke bombs. Letting the dogs out,' said Biff. 'It depends. It's a laugh, anyway.'

When Denis agreed to go on Biff's next excursion, he learned that they were to receive fifty pounds each for the day's activities, and meals. For Biff and Denis, neither of whom had ever had a steady job nor tried very hard to get one, this was novel. Denis hadn't thought too much about their destination, or the ethics of their cause. It was something to do, and Biff, now, was his mate. This was good, because Biff kept others off his back. Denis was not good at fending for himself, and when he begged, his takings were sometimes stolen by other, brasher beggars. His flat, when the social found him one, had been invaded, too, by squatters, and it was Denis who, in the end, had moved out because they were into drugs and fighting. At the moment he was sleeping in a shed at the back of an empty shop in a derelict area where the recession had hit hard. Biff spent a night there now and then, when he had nowhere better to go. Denis didn't know where he was at other times. It was better not to ask people about their movements.

Biff said that their next project — he called it that — was to free animals kept caged and used to test drugs. He didn't know the location. Tessa and Orlando always kept the targets secret until they were on their way, in case the news leaked out.

When they reached the service area where Tessa joined them, she was waiting in a black VW Golf. She got out and opened the back, and Orlando helped her transfer several bags and packages which they stowed in the transit, having told the others to form a screen to hide their actions from onlookers. As well as Biff and Denis, there were Steve and Jet, who were already in the van when Orlando collected Denis and Biff from a roadside in Hammersmith, where they'd gone by Tube. Biff had paid, saying he'd get their fares back from Orlando.

Denis wondered what was in the bags and bundles. He saw something dark and shiny, like the barrel of a shotgun, but it was stowed away in an instant and he hoped he was mistaken. He hadn't reckoned on getting mixed up with anything violent. Letting rabbits out of cages wasn't even criminal damage, was it, if you did it peacefully? He was unaware that the holdalls contained empty bottles, tins of lighter fuel, and dry rags, and that there was a crowbar.

Biff had brought a rucksack which held cans of beer. He seemed to know all the others well, telling Denis he'd been on several trips with them and reminiscing about how they'd freed some sheep who were going to be sent to market, and how they'd set fire to a factory where drugs tested on animals were packed.

Steve and Jet held hands in the back of the van and seemed more intent on one another than the present cause. Denis didn't take much notice of them, and Biff concentrated on Tessa and Orlando, talking loudly, discussing the passing traffic, until Tessa told him to keep quiet and let her concentrate. Orlando, who wore shabby jeans and a drab khaki jacket, seemed ordinary enough but he talked a bit posh, and so did Tessa, though she said very little at first. She drove fast, aggressively.

Orlando was not his real name. He'd been christened Roland like his father but had turned it around when he created a new identity for himself after his mother failed to return from a holiday in

Greece; she had decided to stay there with a man called Spiros who ran a car rental business. Roland senior had consoled himself with a series of affairs with much younger women, but had not remarried, devoting most of his energies to increasing his already considerable income. In due time he had launched his son on a career as a banker. By day, Orlando wore a dark suit and sleeked back his fair hair with gel. At weekends, his spare hours were, when she agreed, spent with Tessa, or working on her behalf as she hunted down those who, in her view, oppressed dumb animals.

Sitting behind Orlando in the van, Denis felt that he was on the brink of a whole new existence, all thanks to Biff.

Denis was eighteen, and had been in care for most of his life, moving between various children's homes and several sets of foster parents until, after his sixteenth birthday, he was deemed independent and expected to fend for himself. This was when he was placed in a council flat, a boy alone, to be eventually forced out of it by other boys. Rootless and quite frightened, he had drifted round amusement arcades and cheap cafés, meeting other youngsters like himself, none with effective parents or a secure adult in the background. They hid their fears beneath a brash bravado. Some were into drugs and Denis had tried that, but beyond the odd smoke, he wasn't interested. Besides, it cost money and he had none. He'd had a job for a while, sweeping up at the back of a pub, but it was only part-time and after a few days he was sacked because he had put the rubbish in the wrong bin.

'Can't you read?' the exasperated landlord had demanded, when for the third time Denis had mixed dust, grime and general detritus with tins, and had, accidentally, caused some waste paper to catch light.

Denis couldn't, not properly, just a few words here and there.

'Anyway, where's your sense?' the landlord had added, not waiting for an answer. 'Can't you see what's what?'

After that, Denis had started begging, and had done quite well in subways and in shopping centres, though you had to watch out for the police. He was sleeping rough when he was arrested, with another youth, for breaking into a newsagent's. Denis had kept watch while his companion robbed the till. He'd admitted, then, to other thefts, things he'd sold for cash, but he didn't mention the coat he was wearing at the time of his arrest. He needed it. He was listed as being of no fixed address, and he almost hoped to be sent to a young offenders' prison. If so, he would be housed, fed and clothed and told what to do. His friend, who had a history of past crimes and was older, did go down, but Denis, still under eighteen at the time, was spared.

'Lucky for you,' said Biff, when he heard this story, minus the bit about not being able to read. Denis, small and fair-haired, with blue eyes and scarcely any growth of beard, might have had a bad time inside.

Protecting Denis made Biff feel good, and when he met Tessa and Orlando at a demonstration, his life acquired a purpose.

Biff had gone to the demonstration with no convinced opinions; he'd seen the protestors gathering, with their banners, and attached himself to their ranks. It was all about sheep, sending them abroad for slaughtering. Cruel, people said, and how would you like to be cramped up in a truck without food and water? Biff had found himself marching along near Tessa; her red hair was tucked up under a woollen cap and he saw it only later, when they were all drinking beer outside a pub. Orlando – her bloke, as Biff thought of him then – had bought it for them and included Biff and some others in the round. He'd eagerly agreed to go on more demonstrations with them when he discovered that Tessa and Orlando went on small private expeditions and wanted back-up, for which they were prepared to pay a fee, and later he decided that he must introduce young Denis to the team. Orlando seemed to run it, and Biff took Denis to meet him one evening. It meant going up West, and meeting at a pub. Denis enjoyed himself. He said very little, sipping his beer and nodding when Orlando asked if he was available at weekends and at short notice.

Orlando thought he seemed a pleasant enough youth, and he was small and slight, which could be useful for wriggling under wire and taking risks which neither Orlando nor Tessa was prepared to run. Tessa maintained, on some occasions, that they needed extra bodies, to provide a diversion from their main attack. Jet and Steve, whom Orlando had recruited earlier, were convinced animal rights defenders; these two, Biff and Denis, were more opportunist, but this made them no less useful. Tessa would be pleased with Denis, he decided.

Biff was the go-between. He telephoned Orlando, who had a mobile phone, to make arrangements.

Parting from them, Orlando gave each of them ten pounds for their evening's expenses, and went back to his flat. He would spend the evening sketching posters for Tessa's crusade against the drug barons. She said they still did dreadful things to mice and rabbits, testing out their theories.

You had to, didn't you, before you tried them out on humans? That was what Orlando thought, but Tessa meant more to him than just her theories, and if going along with them earned him her favour, he was prepared to do it. Besides, there was a lot to be said for using more natural remedies, like herbs and flowers, as in ancient times.

Their next trip, Denis's first outing with them, was to thwart the efforts of a team financed by a major drug company which was engaged in some long-term research into, among other things, the causes of nervous diseases. Some of their experiments, it was alleged, were cruel and unnecessary.

Orlando had organised his part in the expedition with meticulous care. The van was hired from a garage he had not used before and he arrived on foot, having travelled there by public transport. Once or twice there had been violence on these trips and it was wise to leave no trail.

They were travelling west. Denis, sitting behind Orlando, could see some traffic ahead of them but very little more. The doors at the back of the van were solid. He hoped they'd soon arrive. This was boring.

After a while, they turned off and began to travel along narrower single carriageway roads. Orlando had a map out and was consulting it. He and Tessa seemed to be in some disagreement about the route they should be taking, and Biff and Denis heard her say, quite sharply, 'This is the way we're going, Orlando. This is my campaign.'

'That's Tessa for you,' Biff said airily, to Denis, who, free from any responsibility for himself, just nodded.

Soon they turned off again, and now they were in what was just a lane. Staring past Orlando's head, Denis saw a lot of green bushes, like in parks, and there were trees with leaves on, brown and a sort of orange. Nice. They were travelling quite fast when suddenly towards them came a car, a small blue one. They'd had it, Denis thought: there was going to be a smash. But Tessa had jammed on the brakes and started blasting on the horn.

There were no seat-belts in the back. All four of

them were catapulted forward, but unhurt. Tessa paid no heed, revving the engine while the blue car reversed away. What if it hit something coming up behind, Orlando thought, and called out, 'God, Tessa, look where you're going, can't you?'

But Tessa was advancing on the retreating car, blasting her horn and flashing her lights as she did so.

'It's only some old bat,' she said. 'She can bloody well get out of my way,' and she continued to move forward until the blue car reached a passing spot where the road widened. It drew in, and Tessa accelerated, roaring past Frances Dixon with a final loud blast on the horn.

'She's as much right on the road as we have,' Orlando growled, lowering his head to avoid recognition by the other driver in case she filed a complaint.

'Don't be so wet, Orlando,' Tessa said.

She always chose confrontation; negotiation was a weakness, in her view. He found this strange and disconcerting, but it made her more exciting.

Now that they had survived the encounter, Denis felt elated. This was better than hanging round street corners waiting for something to happen.

Something was happening.

Of those in the back, only Denis and Biff really saw the other car.

2

WHAT SHOULD HE call himself?
Walking away from his car, giving it a final
pat because it had served all the family well for
years, Philip Winter contemplated being reborn
under another name. He could be Tom Harris, he
thought: that was a straightforward sort of name,
and, indeed, he remembered that the science master
at his school had been named Harris. He was a
genial man who wore hand-knitted cardigans and
had a pretty daughter. But was adopting a false
identity an offence? And what about social security:
he would not be able to obtain it without proof of
identity. He could say he had lost his papers – had
them stolen. You read about fraud all the time, and
while he was at Lavery's, he'd witnessed some of it.
Maybe he would be able to manage without state
aid or documents. He could try.

He felt a huge sense of loss as he set off, leaving
his past behind, and he was afraid, but the fear was

no worse than the horror which had preceded it, and now he had shed his responsibilities. He had no problems except his own survival, and he didn't care a great deal about that.

He turned away from the river, intending to go to the nearest station and catch the first train out of it that travelled north. It was a beautiful October afternoon, warm enough for summer. After a prolonged wet and chilly spell, the weather had turned glorious and the bronze leaves still clung to the trees he passed as he walked towards the centre of the town. He had never been here before, which had seemed a good enough reason for visiting it now.

Unless someone stole his car, the police would notice it and make enquiries. They'd start looking for him here, maybe in the river. How would Lesley feel then? Would she be sad, or relieved. When they didn't find his body, would she be anxious? He couldn't imagine her reaction, and at the moment, he simply didn't care. Walking on, he came to a long distance bus station. A coach was about to leave, and he saw that it was heading west. On impulse, he boarded it.

'All the way,' he said extravagantly, offering a twenty-pound note. Some change would come in handy.

He took a seat near the back, a man of forty-two, dark-haired, wearing a trench-coat and dark trousers: no one special. He spoke to no one, gazing out of the window as they bowled along, and when they stopped in Salisbury, he got off, though the coach was going on to Bournemouth. It was dark now, and he had nowhere to spend the night. Should he spend money on a bed and breakfast place? He walked around the town, trying to decide, but it would use up precious funds. He could spend most of the evening in a pub if he nursed a drink, and he did this, making half a pint last for two hours, then going out into the street again. Eventually, he found a bench seat and stretched out on it for the remainder of the chilly night. His spirits fell as the temperature dropped and he thought how much one took for granted: even when the world had turned against him, until now food and shelter had not disappeared. He did not sleep.

When daylight came, he started moving once again, trying to restore his circulation. He must have a cup of tea and something to eat. That needn't cost a lot. Then he'd resume his plan of heading north, and he'd spend no more money on his travel. He would hitch a lift.

Walking round the streets, he couldn't find an open café, so he headed towards the outskirts, hoping at a major road junction to pick up a ride. The weather was still fine, but, so early, it was cold, and cars whizzed past him as he walked on, thumb extended when a vehicle passed by. At last a man in a pick-up, with a dog in the back, took him to a main crossroads, and there he waited for a long time before a tanker driver stopped for him, saying he liked a bit of company. You met all sorts of folks on the road, he said, but he never gave lifts to girls. They meant trouble – they could be running away from home, or on the game, or looking for prey.

'What do you mean by that?' asked Philip.

'You may be trying to persuade them to go home,' said the driver. 'But they'll still cry rape and land you in a lot of strife.'

'I believe you,' Philip answered, fervently.

The driver wanted to know where he was going and why he chose to hitch. It was surprisingly easy to invent a reason, Philip found. He said his car had been stolen, with all his money which was in his jacket. He'd gone to the toilet at a service area, he said, and had locked the car but that hadn't stopped two lads from taking it away.

'Didn't the police offer to run you home?' the driver asked.

'I haven't told them yet,' said Philip. 'I'll do it when I get home. My wife's away,' he added. 'Otherwise I'd have rung her.'

What an unlikely tale, thought the driver.

'It'll probably be on video, at the service area,' he pointed out. 'I hope you get it sorted.' He thought his passenger might have walked away from some serious problem, even a police court. Obviously he'd slept rough last night; you'd only got to look at him, with his crumpled trench-coat and his bristly chin. Still, he seemed harmless enough, and the driver, who had seen his share of life's difficulties, probed no further. It wasn't his business. If the police were after the guy, as seemed most likely, they'd soon find him. He put a fresh tape in his stereo and they drove on to the accompaniment of a country and western medley. After a while, Philip fell asleep.

The tanker was heading north. Philip woke when the driver stopped for petrol.

'Got to have a rest now, mate,' he said. 'You can hang on if you want, but you might like to find yourself another ride.'

He'd had enough of this passenger, who had proved to be poor company, and he didn't want to see him on a wanted poster and feel obliged to mention they had met. The man had a car radio in his raincoat pocket; the driver had noticed it when he slumped over to slumber in a more comfortable position than his original upright pose. Maybe it was stolen.

'It's all right. I need a bite to eat,' said Philip, who had woken feeling rather faint. He'd had no food since breakfast the previous morning; just the beer last night, and a packet of crisps he'd bought to go with it. 'Thanks anyway,' he added.

He'd slept heavily as they drove along: he'd no idea where they were or how far they had travelled. For months now, ever since it happened, he'd been sleeping badly. Perhaps, as he had severed his connections with the past, he'd be able to sleep properly again.

Before eating, he went to the men's toilet, where he washed his face and hands. That made him feel better. Food here was expensive, but a good meal should last him all day, so he bought egg, chips and sausages, with baked beans, and had a pot of tea. The place was very busy and he had to queue. He hoped he wouldn't see the driver in the cafeteria; he ought to spread himself around, obtain another lift from someone else.

He supposed you could live here if you had nowhere else to go. These places stayed open round the clock; there were food and shelter, and cloakroom facilities, though no showers. Philip smiled at the idea. It wasn't so way out. Why shouldn't he spend the day here, and even the night; then leave? He'd wait, anyway, until the driver who had brought him had moved on. Money was going to be the problem. He had been receiving unemployment benefit since losing his job. Perhaps he could go on getting it elsewhere; didn't those New Age travellers who camped at Stonehenge and such spots go on drawing it, with special arrangements made to give it to them, regardless of where they were? They couldn't be actively seeking work: it was a weird system.

He'd been able to find no other job because each employer wanted to know why he had left his last one, and required a reference, which Lavery's were not prepared to supply.

Maybe he could find work where he would be paid in cash. He could do gardening, but the season was about to end. He could decorate – he was a dab hand at paper-hanging. He wasn't much of a carpenter – simple shelving fixed on brackets and fitting hooks were about his level.

Musing, he drank his tea. Who were all these people round him? Where were they going, and why? He wondered about them, idly watching the shuffling customers with their trays. What an anonymous sort of place. He couldn't sit here all day long; he'd have to walk around, and at least buy a paper.

Philip rose and went out to the shop, where he bought *The Times* which was selling at a lower price than most tabloids; there was a lot to read in that, though much of it, he thought wryly, would be very dull.

He found a seat near the video games installed for recreation, but before long the noise wore him down, so he went back into the restaurant area and sat at a table. No one challenged him; he did not need to buy another cup of tea. Eventually, however, he grew restless and decided he must move on. He'd try to get to a town, where he could sell the radio, which was a nuisance in his pocket; he felt he must conceal its bulk, and that made him look guilty. If anyone became suspicious and asked him where he'd got it, a truthful answer might not be believed: he could find himself accused of stealing his own car radio.

He trudged along the exit route, still carrying *The Times*. He'd take the first lift he was offered and see how far the driver was going; it would be difficult for him to be dropped except when the vehicle was either turning off or stopping. He was in the hands of fate.

It was better than being at the mercy of an unjust justice system.

He had to wait for some time, but at last a man in a plumber's van stopped for him. He was leaving the motorway at the next junction.

Philip did not stay with him to the end of his journey: at the roundabout after the slip road he alighted, uttered his thanks, and headed off in a westerly direction while the plumber turned the other way.

He could walk along this road, unlike the motorway. The exercise was good, and he stepped out, often forgetting to turn and display his upturned thumb to passing motorists. No one stopped for him. People in cars didn't like giving lifts. The setting sun was brilliant in the autumn sky, a ball of fire sending streaks of light across the hills. On the fringe of the Lake District, this was a beautiful part of England and one he had driven through but never visited. He hadn't really meant to come here: he'd been aiming in a general way at the north, perhaps Liverpool or Leeds – nowhere precise – but chance had carried him to this point. There must be a town or village soon, he thought, plodding on, and feeling thirsty. His left heel was sore; his shoes were comfortable, but they were not meant for walking long distances. He could have dressed more appropriately for this enterprise, but when he left home, he had no plan except to get away. Now, he was determined to leave no trail, to disappear.

After Philip had walked for three or four miles, with traffic passing him regardless, he heard another vehicle coming up behind him and saw it was a bus. His economic resolution vanished and he hailed it. To his relief, it stopped, and he took a ticket to the town advertised above its windscreen. By the time it dropped him in the centre, it was dark. He pulled his trench-coat collar up and set off to explore. He had to find a bed for tonight. Tomorrow he'd sell the radio. How soft he was, he thought; only a few hours ago he'd been fantasising about spending the night in that service station, and now here he was, longing for a shower and a clean bed. He wondered how easy it would be to pick up some casual work. While he was waiting for his trial he had done the whole house over, painting every room, and had spruced the garden up so that not a weed survived and all the plants and shrubs were staked and trimmed. Lesley would not have to give it a thought until the spring; he'd even laid the mower up. He might try job-hunting in the morning; there would be notices in shop windows in a place like this. He rubbed a hand across his chin, rasping the stubble. He ought to get a razor; no one would employ him with several days' growth adorning his chin. He could, however, grow a beard: that would save trouble, and act as a disguise in case he was reported missing and his photograph was displayed. Lesley would have an old one somewhere, from a holiday, or there was his pass-port. They'd been to Corsica last year, all four of them; this year, there had been no trip abroad because he was a man condemned before his case was heard.

How would Lesley manage, with the mortgage to pay? She could get a better job; she was capable of it. If he were reported missing, she might get help towards it; you read of bankrupt men in mansions whose mortgages were paid and who were granted legal aid. The houses were in their wives' names, no doubt. She could find a lodger, a student or a teacher; she'd think of something. She'd survive.

His own indifference shocked him, and, seeing a café open, he went in and ordered tea and a toasted cheese sandwich. That would do him for the evening. After that, he'd look for a room. Would anyone take him, with no luggage? He'd even left *The Times* on the bus.

The first place he tried turned him down. The woman who opened the door looked him over thoroughly and then decided she had no vacancies and had forgotten to move the card from her window. He thanked her and moved on. One advantage of this area was that there was no shortage of boarding houses. He tried another in a different street, and this time was accepted.

'My car was stolen, with my case inside,' he said here. 'That's why I look rather untidy, I'm afraid. Luckily I had my wallet on me,' and he displayed a twenty-pound note. 'I'm sure you insist on payment in advance.'

He was well spoken and his clothes were good,

but that was no testament to honesty and he had already told her a false tale; however, the woman welcomed him, lent him a pair of her husband's pyjamas and found him a new toothbrush. Philip was amazed. How gullible some people were: tell your lie confidently and it would be believed. He must remember that. It was what had made him a victim: that woman had lied and had been believed, and he, telling the truth, had been pilloried.

His room was small but spotless. He had a hot bath in which he luxuriated, and he washed his socks, shirt and boxer shorts in the basin, using the toilet soap. He squeezed the excess water out of them in his towel, something he remembered seeing his mother do, and then hung them up in his room. There was no radiator but there was a coin-operated electric heater. He fed it a pound and hoped that would provide enough heat to dry them overnight.

He was tired, but was too wound up to sleep. He lay under the covers with the events of the past two days running through his mind like a film. It seemed an incredible dream, but then everything that had happened since he was first accused had had an unreal quality; he had felt that none of it could really be happening to him. After a while he dropped off, only to wake at four o'clock in the morning. He got out of bed to test the moistness of his laundry and found that his socks were still damp, so he put another pound in the meter. The money was disappearing, but he couldn't go on in wet socks. He'd better buy another pair. Some things were essential. Then he went back to bed where again sleep eluded him. There was a pile of tattered magazines on a table so, giving up, he selected an old *Reader's Digest* and began reading it. Concentration was difficult, as he had discovered during the preceding months. His eyes traversed the pages but his brain absorbed only random sentences. His mind kept returning to what had brought him to this moment.

How could she do it? How could she tell such lies so brazenly and watch the destruction of him and his family? What harm had he ever done her? He knew he had not convinced the jury of his innocence, but they did not believe beyond reasonable doubt in his guilt. He might have gone to prison: at least he had been spared that, but perhaps it would have been better if he had been convicted; there would have been an appeal, possibly a further investigation. Someone who, like Bob, knew the truth might have had enough courage to speak up for him. Over and over again he recalled his own actions, trying to remember a word or gesture that she could, in all fairness, have misconstrued, but he failed. As for raping her, he had not touched her; it was she who had seized hold of him.

He couldn't even picture her face now; his imagination refused to yield it to the eye of memory, but he would never forget his own daughter's horrified stare.

'Dad, you didn't,' she said, when at last she

understood the accusation against him.

'No, I didn't,' he had told her, but he had not convinced her. If she lost her trust, who else would believe the woman had lied? Certainly Lesley did not.

'You made a pass, at least,' she had said, and had looked at him with contempt. 'Why choose her?' she'd added, and in vain he had said that his was not the choice; it was the other way round.

'I've never heard anything so pathetic,' Lesley, bitterly hurt herself, had said.

They'd met, he and Lesley, when he was doing business studies at a polytechnic. Lesley was taking A levels; she wanted to be a teacher but this had never happened because they married before she could go to training college, and then Andrew was born. She took a secretarial course when Jackie was seven, and since then had had various office jobs. At the time of his arrest she had been, for some years, personal assistant to the director of a lighting centre. She'd kept her job; her boss had been sympathetic about the difficult situation she was in and he would not add to her problems by making things hard for her at work – not that he could have dismissed her because of her husband's failings. Some of the staff, though, had made snide remarks.

His accuser was a Lavery's customer, one who had had an account for years and spent large sums there every month. He'd admired her; he was prepared to admit that. She was chic and confident, and she knew what she wanted, or seemed to, at first. She'd buy items of glass or ceramics, then return a few days later to say that they were not suitable and she wanted to change them. Philip never noticed that Bob disappeared when she came into the department; in any case, Bob's station was across the floor; he managed soft furnishings. She always asked for Philip to serve her, and indeed, one of the assistants used to tease him about it.

'Your girlfriend's here,' he'd say, when he was in the office. 'Wants your special services,' and he would wink and leer. How ironic that reaction turned out to be.

Philip took no more trouble over Mrs Sandra White than any other customer; all were entitled to receive his full attention. She was known to the sales staff: a well-dressed woman in her forties. She wore expensive scent, which Philip noticed when she stood close to him inspecting some object she contemplated buying, but so did many women shoppers. Philip knew nothing about her private life; she paid with her Lavery's account card and once their transactions were concluded, he never gave another thought to her. There were other customers he found more attractive, but beyond a mild occasional lustful urge, soon suppressed, he did not fantasise about them. He was married and he had no wish to stray; he did not even flirt.

So he was out of his depth when the accusation came.

How could she do it?

It was all because he'd turned her down, his

solicitor, who believed him, had explained. Ulti-
mately the jury had given him the benefit of the
doubt, apart from two of them, who had found him
guilty, and so he had escaped imprisonment. After
he was dismissed from Lavery's, when her complaint was made, there was a murmur among the
staff that he had been unlucky, and one of them,
Betty, spoke up for him in court. She was called as
a defence witness and was questioned about his
manner with female customers. She had declared
that he was always courteous, never familiar, and
that she had noticed nothing untoward, but none of
the men came forward. Philip suspected that some,
like Bob, might know more about Mrs White than
they cared to disclose. His solicitor found it
interesting that it was a woman who had testified
for him.

Mrs White had not called the police until a week
after Philip had, she alleged, raped her. By then it
was too late to prove scientifically that he had had
sexual intercourse with her, but a hair from his head
had been found on her clothing, and she had
marked him. Colleagues had observed the scratches
on his face, and Mrs White maintained that they
were made by her in her struggle to escape him.

It was he who had fought her off, not the other
way around, and it was he who had been a
simpleton when he found her purse left on the
counter after she had finished shopping on that fatal
day. Her account and credit cards were inside; there
was no mistaking whose it was. They'd paged her,

but with no result; she had already left the store. Instead of handing the purse in, Philip, thinking she would be anxious about its loss, had telephoned her himself, and she had been so grateful, almost tearful, as she thanked him and asked him to be good enough to bring it to her himself, on his way home.

Foolishly, he had agreed. It would help her, and was not much out of his way for she lived only a few bus stops from the store. He missed his usual train home, which Lesley remembered; she also remembered the scratches on his face, which he said he'd got when he walked into a sharp protrusion in the storeroom. But Lesley gave no evidence: a wife is not obliged to testify against her husband.

Mrs White had opened the door of her flat – the main door to the street worked in response to an entryphone – and she had urged him to come in. Without giving it a thought, he had obeyed, the purse still in his hand. Then she had offered him a drink, and again, he had accepted, feeling that to refuse would seem ungracious. After all, he'd gone to some trouble on her behalf and naturally she wished to express her thanks. She'd poured him out a glass of wine, making him shed his coat, which she'd laid on a chair in the hall.

As they drank their wine, she had talked about the loneliness of marriage to a man whose work often took him overseas. They'd divorced, she said: it was hurtful to admit he'd found a younger second wife.

Philip had muttered a few sympathetic words and was about to leave when she made her proposition.

'You could visit me,' she said. 'I'll be here every Wednesday evening.'

'But why?' he'd asked, naively.

'What did you think she meant?' prosecuting counsel had enquired.

'I didn't know at first,' he said. 'Then she made it clear.'

'In what way?'

'She offered sex.' He had just managed to utter it. 'She said she wanted it.'

'And what did you say?'

'I tried to be polite. I thanked her but said that I was married.'

'What did she say then?'

In fact, she'd laughed loudly, opening her big mouth to show a lot of large white teeth, making him think of a shark. 'So what?' she'd said.

'She said it need not make a difference,' he told the court.

'I put it to you that you are inventing this. The truth is that you threw yourself upon the complainant, as she has described,' said prosecuting counsel.

'No,' he had almost shouted. 'I'm telling you the truth.'

Philip's own counsel, with agonising patience, had extracted his version of events from him. He had been sitting on the sofa holding his empty wine glass, preparing to move, when she leaned over, took the glass from him and set it down, then laid one hand on his thigh and thrust herself against him, pinning him among the soft pile of cushions at his back. In the same instant, her mouth was glued to his and she was trying to force her tongue between his lips. She almost succeeded, so great was his astonishment. He pushed her away, while still striving to be civil.

'You're making a mistake, Mrs White,' he had said. If he could only get to his feet and reach the door, he thought, his reactions those of many a woman in a similar predicament.

'But you like me,' she had said, still clinging to him, so that her cashmere sweater deposited shreds of wool on his suit jacket, as was later proved. He brushed it every night before he hung it up, but a few persistent fibres, not visible at a glance, had remained.

'Of course, Mrs White,' he agreed. 'But as a customer.'

'A very special one,' she had insisted. 'You've made that clear, by bringing me my purse.'

'You asked me to,' he said, fending her off, the muscles in his outstretched arms quivering under the strain. It was so silly and undignified. Why couldn't she just release him? Somehow, he managed to scramble up, and it was then that she sprang at him, scraping her nails down his cheek, trying to wind herself around him as he shrank back from her.

He was determined to escape, and he reached the

37

door, grabbing at his coat, while she was caught off balance. She picked the empty wine glass up and flung it at him, and as he ducked it hit the wall and shattered. Later, she said that this had happened as she attempted to defend herself.

Counsel for the defence had suggested that she had left the purse behind deliberately, thus creating the opportunity for the scene that ensued.

The complainant had denied this vehemently.

'I couldn't know that Mr Winter would offer to return it himself,' she said.

'But the accused said that you asked him to,' was counsel's response.

'That's his story,' she replied.

No one had overheard his telephone conversation with her: there was no way to prove the truth of either account. It was a question of belief.

The judge, summing up, had been very fair, and some journalists said that it should never have come to court, but the case was no more fanciful than other incidents where accused men had been convicted on evidence which was just as slight.

Mud sticks, thought Philip; that was so true. Though acquitted, he could not get his job back; Lavery's believed the customer. Although he had been with them for twelve years, rising in a steady manner through the hierarchy, they would not even offer him a position in a provincial branch. To sue for wrongful dismissal would be to invite further publicity and cause more pain within the family, with no sure outcome. It could involve the loss of what little he had left, for it would be a civil case and it might go against him.

'You'll find another job,' his solicitor had consoled him.

But three months later he had not, except for a brief spell helping in a bar where very soon someone had recognised him and, despite the outcome of the case, the landlord had not appreciated the subsequent taunts and comments. The male customers' remarks were crude, but a number of professional women used the bar and they did not want their drinks served by someone with a tarnished reputation. So it had gone on, until now.

I ran away, he told himself, sitting up in the hard bed in his lodgings. I'm a coward. But his action would, in the long run, make things easier for Lesley and the children. Now they could stop watching every remark they made, and he no longer had to endure their guarded glances. Andrew's studies would cease to suffer; he would get his degree next year, and soon Jackie would follow him to college, unembarrassed by her father.

He tried the *Reader's Digest* again. Its jokes were often entertaining, and he managed to see the humour in a few of them as he leafed through the pages until he heard his landlady going downstairs.

Not shaving still seemed strange. He'd always been so spruce, going to the store, where beards were not encouraged, nor long hair. He'd had an almost pink and white complexion, with his greying hair slicked down, setting off his fair skin.

He'd been a handsome boy, tall and willowy, and had stayed slim. Now he was really thin; he had lost weight during the long waiting time before the trial, and had regained none of it.

He washed and put his clothes on. His socks were dry now, and warm. He had always dressed well: his appearance had been important in his job, where the staff were expected not only to be smart, but to have clean fingernails and unscuffed shoes. Now, he seemed to be going in reverse.

His landlady provided him with a splendid breakfast – bacon, two fried eggs, fried bread, a sausage and a tomato; he ate every crumb. This would have to be his pattern: one large meal a day, and an evening snack. His stomach would adjust. As he finished off with toast and marmalade, he realised that he had not eaten with such pleasure for months. So escape had done him good already.

While he ate, the landlady's husband consumed a similar feast, washed down with several cups of tea to Philip's one. Then he was ready to depart for his day's work. He was a builder, at present renovating a pub near Lancaster.

On impulse, Philip asked him for a lift.

'I'm going to Blackpool,' he invented – but why not go there? It was a large resort; there might be work, though perhaps not out of season.

The man agreed to take him on.

'You never had no car stolen, mate,' he said, when they were in his van, bowling back the way Philip had come the night before. 'You're on the road.

Maybe on the run. What have you done?'

'Left my wife,' said Philip bluntly.

The man laughed.

'Well, as long as you've not robbed a bank,' he said.

'I haven't,' Philip said. 'I'm nearly skint. I need to find a job.'

'I'd give you one, if I could,' said the builder. 'But there's not much going in my line just now. I've got this contract to help out a mate. What'll turn up next, I don't know.'

They parted near the town centre, and immediately Philip set out to sell the radio. It took him quite a while, but eventually a second-hand dealer gave him twelve pounds for it. It was a disappointingly small sum. He decided to keep his watch until another time. Then he went seeking notice boards advertising job vacancies. By evening, he'd found nothing, though he had just missed a position as a van driver and another as a storeman. Both openings had been filled when he arrived at the addresses. Once again, he spent the evening in a pub nursing a single beer, until it was closing time. Then he found a bus shelter where, after some youths who were in it had, at last, departed, he spent the rest of the night.

In the morning, although there might have been other opportunities in the town, he decided to move on. Cold and hungry, he resolved to accept the first lift that came along, regardless of the driver's final destination. He'd be warm in the cab of a lorry, and he would be going somewhere.

3

'WHERE ARE WE going today, then, Tessa?' Biff had dared to ask, when she had calmed down after nearly causing a collision with that blue Viva.

'We're going to harass a guy who makes blisters grow on mice and rabbits,' Tessa said. 'And we'll free the creatures, if we can.'

'Who'll feed them, then?' Denis asked. 'When they're let loose, like?'

'Give me strength. They're wild animals,' said Tessa. 'They'll live off the land.'

In one of the children's homes where Denis had spent time, they'd had some rabbits which had eaten dandelion leaves and lettuce. He supposed they'd have that sort of stuff round here. In the end, the rabbits had had babies, which were eaten by the mothers. Some of the children had found it quite a laugh but Denis had been sickened. Afterwards, he dreamt his own mother had eaten him.

When they parked to stretch their legs and hear Tessa's plans for their protest action, he saw dandelions among the grass at the roadside. She'd pulled off the road into a lay-by beside a group of trees, alongside a field in which there were some cattle. One of the beasts lowed loudly, and Denis, who had been planning to climb the gate and relieve himself in the shelter of the hedge, abruptly changed his mind.

'Won't hurt you, chum,' said Orlando, who had noticed his recruit's startled movement. 'Only a moo-cow.' He clambered over the gate himself and began shooing the young heifers away.

'For God's sake, Orlando, stop that,' called Tessa. 'We don't want some snotty farmer coming along to see who's upsetting his precious herd. We don't want to be noticed.'

Denis thought they'd been noticed already by the old dame they'd nearly driven off the road, but he kept quiet. Tessa's attitude was weird. She was so keen on saving animals, but she hadn't given a rap for the old woman, and she didn't seem too keen on this bunch of cows. He had no time to pursue this line of thought because Biff had begun unloading the cans of beer he'd brought and started to hand them round.

'No drinking,' ordered Tessa.

'Too late,' smirked Biff, who had already opened a can. This was a bit of all right. He was enjoying himself, and he could see that Denis was having the time of his young life. Biff, in the role of benefactor, felt good. He accepted the cans Steve and Jet were meekly handing him in obedience to Tessa's ban, finished his own, dropped the can where he stood, undid his fly and urinated proudly into the grass beyond his feet. After a short pause, Denis walked a short way along the road and turned his back modestly as he relieved himself. Steve followed him. Orlando had returned from the field and, when all the males were back in the van, Tessa and Jet climbed the gate, followed inquisitively by the heifers.

'Nice name, Jet,' said Biff, while they were absent.

'It's not her real name,' Steven said. 'She just likes it.'

Orlando felt it suited her. She had black hair and wore a lot of eyeliner, and a dark, almost black lipstick. She was very small and rather quiet, and she always dressed in black. He thought she had braved the field of heifers only because she did not want to seem afraid of them in front of Tessa. Tessa was the sort of person who inspired courage in her companions; he adored her.

Back in the van, Tessa addressed her troops.

'We're going to split up,' she said. 'Biff and I are going to spy out the land. We'll collect you four later, at a meeting place on the other side of that hill.' She gestured vaguely westwards. 'Orlando will be in charge of you.' She pulled a map from the pocket of the shabby waxed jacket she wore and showed it to Orlando, pointing out a route to him. 'I'll drop you at the start of the track you can follow which will bring you out near a crossroads where Biff and I will find you.'

Biff puffed out his chest. He'd been selected as her partner in a most important task. Great. He waited with impatience for the others to leave, so that he could sit in front beside her. He, not Steve, who was a student and had passed exams, was her choice.

While they drove off, Orlando, not pleased at the role allotted to him, led his little force up a rutted track. Jet's boots pinched and Steve complained of being out of breath as Orlando shepherded them along with bracing remarks about how it couldn't be much further, and when they reached the crossroads, there would be a garage with a shop where they could buy drinks and ice creams or Mars Bars. He felt like a teacher with a pack of awkward children as they spread out in single file. Only Denis did not complain; he was in paradise. He had never seen so much empty space before. There were low rolling hills, with clumps of trees here and there, and otherwise nothing but grassy downland, still green but with yellowing patches, and it seemed you were allowed to walk where you liked. There were no cows wandering around, but they met three people on horseback. He was quite alarmed as they cantered past. The only horses he had previously encountered were police horses deployed to keep order in a crowd. These riders, however, waved, and one called out, 'Hi, isn't it a lovely day?'

It was. There was a curious smell, and, sniffing it, Denis asked Orlando what it was.

Orlando laughed, but not unkindly.

'It's fresh air, you nit,' he said. 'Haven't you smelled it before?'

Denis hadn't; not like this. And he hadn't been called a nit before: dork, jerk, and much worse, but never a nit. Orlando was a weird guy, but he was all right.

'Not such a lot of it,' he answered.

He looked around. He could not see a single house. If he'd been alone, he thought he might not like it; he'd feel sort of naked. But with Orlando striding on in front, looking round now and then to see if the others were following, and Jet and Steve, hand in hand, behind him, he felt protected. They trudged on, and when they reached the summit of the hill, below them stretched a panoramic view. In the distance, on the skyline, were tall buildings which were part of some industrial area, but closer, beneath where they were walking, was a straggling village with many-coloured roofs and a church spire rising from among some trees. It was wild, thought Denis: this was his utmost term of approval.

Orlando, while they walked, was wondering what Tessa had in mind, choosing Biff as her companion. Why had she offloaded the rest of them? Couldn't they all have done whatever reconnoitring she had planned? It was true that she couldn't have left Biff and the other three to find their way over the downs, but was this walk really necessary?

He supposed it was doing them all good, in the sense that they were getting exercise, and Denis seemed entranced. Poor kid, he'd clearly never been to the country before, but though he seemed to like it, most townies, according to Tessa's father, wanted to introduce urban conditions into rural areas, banning cocks that crowed and braying donkeys. At least none of these three would get out of hand and behave badly, if they had to wait for Tessa when they reached the meeting place. Some of the demonstrations Orlando had been on with Tessa had developed into alarming events, when he had been afraid for his own and her safety, as bricks were thrown and obscenities yelled by sweating angry mobs who surely had lost sight of their original grievance. But the more timorous Orlando felt on these occasions, the better Tessa enjoyed it. She yelled with the rest, and grew excited. Sometimes, afterwards, she let him go to bed with her, and that reward made up for all his fears.

She'd never marry him. He asked her to, at intervals, but when she laughed and refused, he was just a mite relieved. She was like a mettlesome horse which was difficult to control; he couldn't do it: could anyone?

She rather wrecked your palate, though, for other flavours.

When Tessa dumped the others and swept Biff off

with her, he was sure she wanted sex. He didn't
believe her story of wanting to spy out the land. She
seemed to know her way about these confusing
lanes and narrow roads; the map had been needed
only for Orlando's sake. Biff had supposed that
Orlando was her lover. Perhaps he was, and she
wanted to make him jealous. He had seemed a bit
put out when they left, but not really angry, not like
Biff would be if anyone tried to cut him out with
a girl, but Biff would soon sort out a guy who tried
that on. He flexed his muscles under his grey
sweatshirt. Biff was a real man.

However, they were not driving off to a quiet spot
like where they'd parked before. Tessa was turning on
to a main road, and she drove fast towards some tall
buildings in the distance. Her gloveless hands, on the
wheel, were pale and slender; he'd noticed that she bit
her nails. She looked as if she couldn't iron a shirt,
much less drive a van which had a fault in its timing
which Biff longed to fix. He loved tinkering with
cars, and had a record of convictions for taking away
and driving without consent. In the end he'd been
sent on a course where lads like himself were taught
mechanics and rebuilt old heaps to discourage them
from re-offending. It had almost cured Biff of
stealing cars; he felt obliged to get his kicks from
other sources now; but he was still besotted with
engines. He'd often thought he'd like to work in a
garage, but he hadn't tried to find a job in one. Maybe,
when he got bored with this animal lark, he'd give it a
go.

Tessa had parked outside the gates of a large complex of buildings.

'That's where it all happens, Biff,' she said. 'In there, all sorts of terrible experiments go on. Animal genes are mixed with other genes to create monsters. Helpless rabbits are given dreadful diseases from which they die in agony.'

Apart from being clothes, Biff didn't know what genes were. Wasn't Jean a girl's name? His mum had had a friend called Jean. Biff hadn't seen his mum for years. When he thought about her, he remembered her with a pile of ironing, thumping away among clouds of steam. He looked at the high fencing, the gate with the security barrier and the manned guard room.

'We can't get in there to free them animals,' he said.

'No, I'm afraid we can't, not without a small army and a lot of weapons, and some master keys,' she said. 'I just wanted to have a look at the place. That's all. We're going to go for the man behind it, Biff. He's our target.'

She slid the van into gear and drove on towards the town which lay beyond the complex. On a Saturday afternoon there was a lot of traffic; she tapped her fingers on the wheel impatiently while they waited for some lights to change. Then she turned away from the main shopping area, driving down to a bridge over a river, which she crossed. She carried on up the hill on the further side, past a park and into a street of large, detached houses with trees and shrubs around them: a thieves' paradise, Biff thought, automatically eyeing the homes which were well sheltered from the passer-by. Tessa halted outside one of these.

'That's it,' she said. 'Hop out, Biff, and see if anyone's at home. I'm sure you can do it. Don't let them see you. They might be in the garden. I'll wait for you at the corner.'

Biff was out of the van in an instant, delighted at the importance of his role. Tessa watched him in the van's rear mirror. He'd disappeared almost at once. She wondered if any nosey neighbours were observing them. She had seen Neighbourhood Watch stickers on lamp posts and windows as they drove through the streets, but that scheme's efficiency depended on who was around at a given time. On a Saturday afternoon, people were often out: playing golf, shopping, visiting friends, taking children to theme parks or whatever families did.

She hoped Biff wouldn't get caught. If he didn't reappear in ten minutes, she'd abandon him.

But he did. He emerged from a gateway close to where she'd parked, having crossed intervening fences. He swaggered up the road towards her, grinning.

Tessa started the engine and drove off as he tumbled in beside her. She did not speak for several minutes, until they were back in the open countryside beyond the town. Then she stopped and faced him.

'Well?' she said.

'It's a great place,' said Biff. 'No one's in, but

there's some rabbits in a cage thing at the back. Pets, like. There was kids' washing on the line – small size stuff – you know.' He gestured with his hands. 'Lots of grass, too,' he added. 'Flowers, and that. And veg. Cabbages. There's a kind of office place, too, a hut. It's got stuff inside that I – that's worth a bit. Computers.' He'd been going to say, stuff that he could sell, but bit it back.

'An office, you said?' Tessa asked.

'Yeah. I suppose so.'

'Well done, Biff,' said Tessa. 'We'll go back there after dark.'

'There's a dog,' he volunteered. 'It barked at me. It's shut up in the house. There's an alarm,' he added.

'That's all right. We're not going inside,' said Tessa.

'I let the rabbits out,' said Biff. 'I thought that's what you wanted.'

'Did you, Biff? That wasn't really in the plan,' said Tessa.

'It was easy.' Biff was pleased with himself. 'They had such simple catches on their cages. They ran down the garden straight away. I expect they'll eat up all the cabbages.'

'I expect they will,' said Tessa, wondering if this display of initiative was going to thwart her scheme. It needn't, she decided. It might act as a diversion.

She looked at her watch. Orlando and his troop could not have reached the rendez-vous so soon;

she'd sent them on quite a trek. She drove up the road and through more residential streets until they had left the town behind and were in the country. Now they were travelling along a lane, one that was almost as narrow as where they had met the old woman in the Viva. Suddenly a cock pheasant ran into the road in front of them and Tessa swerved violently to miss it. She stopped and got out of the van to make sure that it had not been struck. There was no sign of it.

'What was that bird?' Biff asked. He'd followed her out of the van, and saw that she looked white and shaken.

'It's OK,' she said. 'I didn't hit it.'

'What was it?' Biff repeated. 'Was it a bantam?' He'd heard of them; they were sort of cockerels.

'No – no, it was a cock pheasant,' Tessa said. 'Beautiful, isn't he?'

'Certainly is,' said Biff, who had been impressed by the bird's size and his bright plumage.

'Imagine shooting him, for kicks,' said Tessa. 'That's what people do. Could you? Isn't it cruel?'

Biff had been on the point of making some crack about how, if they'd hit it, they could have roasted it over a camp fire, but he saw that Tessa would find such a remark out of order.

'Dunno,' he said, knowing that if he had a gun, he'd do it; no question about that. 'Suppose I could if I was starving,' he temporised.

'They're bred just to be killed,' said Tessa, now accelerating hard.

Biff grabbed the side of the van. He thought about offering to drive, but decided not to risk offending her.

So are cattle, bred to be killed, he thought; and sheep, and pigs. Would they exist, otherwise?

'You one of them vegetarians?' he asked. But he knew she wasn't. He'd seen her eat sausages and chips, after they'd been on that trip to Folkestone to blockade a ship that was exporting sheep.

'That's different,' Tessa said.

Biff couldn't see it, but he didn't argue, because now she had turned the van up a track like the one where they had left the others. This, though, led to a copse and was more secluded. She parked beneath a tree.

As she turned to face him, Biff understood that his first suspicions about why she had chosen him had, after all, been correct.

They moved into the back of the van, where there was more room. She was like a tiger, Biff thought, appreciating every move.

Afterwards, he remembered how upset she had been about the pheasant's narrow escape, and yet was unmoved by the earlier near collision with the Viva, when its driver, and even they, themselves, could have been hurt, and maybe killed.

Funny, really.

4

ORLANDO AND HIS band were waiting for them at the service station when they reached it just as dusk was falling. He'd bought drinks and snacks, as promised. Denis had noticed that he had a wad of notes in his wallet. They perched on a wall near the shop and pumps, eating Twix bars and drinking out of cans.

'We'll wait till dark. Then we'll move in,' said Tessa, and she drove them to the spot where she and Biff had parked half an hour earlier. She never looked at him as she ordered all of them out of the van and told them to light a fire.

'There's plenty of wood, and it's dry,' she said.

'Won't someone see us?' Denis whispered to Steve, as Jet and Orlando set to work with a cigarette lighter and some bits of paper from the van. They doused it with a very small amount of lighter fuel that had been loaded from Tessa's car, and it flared alarmingly, but some of the twigs caught, and, nurtured carefully, soon it was burning well.

'It's OK out here,' Steve reassured him. 'They'll think we're campers. Let's find some bigger sticks. Pity we haven't got some potatoes to bake,' he added. 'Still, I suppose they'd take too long. Tessa'll want to be off as soon as it's going well.'

'How can you cook potatoes on a fire like that?' asked Denis.

'Stick them in the embers,' Steve replied. 'They're great.'

Denis was amazed. This was, so far, the best day in his entire life, and the fire was brilliant. No wonder so many people wanted to live like this, go travelling around.

Steve was right about Tessa. The fire was blazing well, and they were all crouched round it, faces lit up by the flames, when she spoke.

'Right,' she said. 'We'll be off now. We can't free the animals, unfortunately, because the place they're in is so well guarded, but we can cause some grief. We're going to lob some petrol bombs over the wire. We'll get them ready now, so hold them carefully. We don't want an accident in the van. It's quite a short drive – you saw the place when you were walking over the hill.'

She made the preparations, putting fuel in three milk bottles, then stuffing rags into their openings. All of them except Denis had seen this done before, but only Tessa had ever thrown one. They were silent, driving towards the town, and on the outskirts Tessa parked beside the research complex, well away from the gate and the security control. There, she gave Jet, Steve and Denis cans of spray paint and told them to spray slogans on the boundary wall. Jet and Steve knew what to write: MURDERERS, SAVE WILD ANIMALS, WHAT PRICE KILL-ING MICE? Denis, illiterate, sprayed crosses and squirls, and, for fun, a swastika, but Steve blotted that one out. Meanwhile, Biff lit the petrol bombs and lobbed them over the wall. Tessa had told him he was the strongest, able to throw the furthest.

Like a javelin athlete, Biff did his best. Orlando could scarcely bear to watch: what if one exploded before it was thrown? But none did. They could not reach the buildings but the alarm went and the group piled back into the van. An approaching siren wailed as they sped off towards the town and the house where Tessa and Biff had been earlier.

'The man behind those experiments lives here,' Tessa told the others.

There were lights on now, in the house.

'You're not going to attack him, are you?' Orlando had to make his protest. If this was Tessa's plan, she was going too far. Tessa did not give him a direct answer.

'I think he'll come out,' she said. 'I think he'll hear about the attack we've just done at the research place and he'll go over there.' She drove down the road and stopped the engine.

'You take the wheel, Orlando,' she instructed. 'Be ready for a quick getaway when I come back.' Then she got out of the van, went round to the rear, rummaged in the bundles, and removed a shotgun. She thrust it under her coat and went walking back towards the house.

As Orlando slid behind the wheel, there was silence in the van.

'She going to kill the guy, then?' Biff asked nervously. Judging by the lights, the family had probably come home.

'Oh no,' said Orlando bracingly, but he could not be certain, with Tessa obviously on such a high.

They waited for what seemed like hours, but nothing happened, apart from several cars going by, and a woman with a dog. Then they heard two shots. All of them in the van held their breaths, waiting for uproar and for Tessa to come running back, but no windows were thrown open and there were no screams. Then they heard two more shots, and soon Tessa did appear, walking quietly towards them. She calmly put the gun back in the rear of the van, got in beside Orlando and told him to drive on. He already had the engine running and the noise masked the sound of the burglar alarm coming from the house she had just left.

She smelled of petrol and she was smiling in a way that alarmed the already scared Orlando. What had she done?

He knew that their best plan was to put distance between themselves and this area. He headed for the country once again. Denis was amazed at how quickly they left the busy streets behind. Soon they were driving along narrow lanes once more, with just the headlight beams piercing the darkness. When they'd put their camp fire out, he'd been startled by how dark it was around them: no street lights; no moon yet; and no stars.

They stopped in a quiet spot. Tessa wanted to take over the driving.

'Comfort interval,' she sang out, when Orlando had pulled in, drawing the van off the road into a gateway. She reached over and turned the lights off. 'Everyone back in five minutes,' she said.

Once again the night was black. Denis, tumbling out, blinked. He couldn't see a thing except the pale outline of the van. Jet bumped into him; then she and Steve, arms linked, went up the road together. Denis almost fell over his own feet, edging forward on the grass beside the road. His eyes began to adapt to the lack of light and he saw Orlando go round to the back of the van and open the door. He did something to the gun, wrapping it up, Denis thought.

He'd better have a pee, while he had a chance. He stepped forward, feeling with his outstretched toe for obstacles, not worrying now about concealment. Biff came up behind him.

'She shot something, Tessa did,' he said, 'Or someone.' His tone held admiration, only slightly tinged with disapproval. 'You heard them shots, Denis.'

'I thought it might be a car backfiring,' Denis said, but he hadn't, really.

'Let's hope that's what the neighbours thought,' said Biff.

What had she shot, though?

Orlando was asking her the same question. He was standing with her by the bonnet of the van.

'I haven't murdered anyone, you idiot,' Tessa said to him. 'I fixed his equipment. That's all. Broke some windows in his office and torched it. I don't care if it burns his whole house down. That'll stop him harming animals.'

Orlando didn't know whether to find her wonderful or terrifying. She was a bit of each, he knew.

'Hope no one saw you,' he said. Surely a neighbour had heard the shots?

'I don't think they did,' she said. 'And in case you're wondering, there was no one at home. The house lights must be on time switches.' She did not mention the security lights.

She'd seen the rabbits. They hadn't gone far. Two large brown ones were crouched among the vegetables; two more scampered over the garden when the lights came on. She'd shot both of them as they ran; the first pair were sitting targets. Then she'd set fire to the workshop shed. She'd kept back one of the cans of fuel used in their earlier attack, stuffing it in the large pocket of her waxed jacket. After breaking the window, she had poured its contents through the gap and dropped a lighted piece of paper into the room. The fluid had soon caught; the rest was left to chance. There were sure to be papers in there; a strong draught might fan the flames and she had broken every pane of glass. Then, as the alarm rang and the dog in the house started barking, she walked away. It would not do to be seen running.

'We'd better disappear,' said Orlando, who could not believe that no one had noticed the van parked in the street, if not Tessa and the rest of them. But it would be difficult to describe her accurately; her red hair was thrust up under a woollen cap, and coats like hers were universal.

'Yes,' she agreed. 'Get the others.'

She started the engine and switched on the lights, and the other four turned and ran towards her.

'They're afraid we'll abandon them,' she said, and began laughing. She was still laughing as she drove away.

When they reached the service area where she had left her VW, Orlando handed each of them a fifty-pound note.

'Keep quiet about where we've been today,' he told them, after Tessa, the gun and other gear returned to her car, had driven off. 'No one's been hurt.'

Criminal damage was the offence they had committed; that was all. Tessa was the arsonist.

He dropped the four of them outside Hammersmith Tube station. Then he returned the van. He'd paid in cash when he hired it, and he hadn't used his own name. Biff, some months ago, had obtained a stolen driving licence for him, a private deal between the two of them, and worth it, to Orlando, for protection.

Tessa still hadn't explained why she had fired the shots.

5

TESSA SLEPT LATE on Sunday morning.

She had not reached her parents' house in a Cotswold village until the small hours, having told them she was going to a party. It was true. After parting from Orlando and the others, she had been to a club where she had danced and drunk a lot of wine. She could never wind down after a raid or demonstration; on a high of excitement, she sought more thrills and ran more risks, eventually driving herself home fast, and dangerously. She met no police patrol car on her journey, nor another reckless driver.

Tessa was a solicitor with a city firm whose practice was mainly civil litigation. She enjoyed being overtly on the side of the law, and covertly defying it. So far, neither aspect of her life had intruded on the other; only Orlando had a place in both her worlds. They had met when her firm acted for a client of his bank; entranced, he had listened to her proselytising when he took her out to dinner. Tessa had admitted him to her private life because she needed an emotional prop. He was no threat; she could manipulate him as she chose, and he was eminently presentable: her parents were always pleased when she brought him down for a weekend. His presence in her life mollified them.

On Sunday morning Tessa's parents went to church while their daughter still slept on. Tessa's father, who was a judge, read the lesson, while her mother thought about Clive, their son, a barrister whose wife had left him for a sculptor, taking their two small children to live in Cornwall, where her lover had a studio. She'd hated life in London. Clive had accepted that, and had been willing to commute; they'd just found a house near Amersham and were about to move when she had fled. She'd met the sculptor on a family holiday, it seemed, and somehow, in spite of the distances involved, their romance had culminated in this crisis.

Had Clive been unkind to her, his mother wondered, having sung and appeared to pray; she stretched uncomfortably in her seat while the vicar spoke of tolerance. Surely not: Clive was a decent man, if unimaginative. Now, because they lived so far away, it would be difficult for him to see much of his two daughters, who were only four and six. As their grandmother, she would keep in touch, sending them postcards and presents, but they might as well be in Australia, she sometimes felt. If only Tessa would settle down: that would be some compensation. So often, in repose, her face wore a discontented expression and she was very tense. Millicent Graham knew very little about her daughter's private life but from time to time she had brought Orlando with her for a weekend. However, her interest in him was far from serious; Millicent knew he was only a passing fancy in Tessa's eyes. A woman with a job like hers, in a thriving firm, could combine motherhood with a profession. Millicent, who had never wanted to do the same, nor, as a young woman, been forced by circumstances to contribute to the family income, thought too much was demanded of today's mothers as they strove to juggle their various roles, and they expected a great deal from their husbands or partners, and from life itself. Millicent had expected to be loved and respected, and she had never doubted James's faithfulness. If she were to find out now that he had a mistress, she would be devastated. If he'd had one in the past, she didn't want to know. She thought briefly of his tubby body, his reddish, greying hair, his small but undeniable paunch, with amused affection. He was no Adonis, nor ever had been, but he had a first-class brain and his conversation still interested her. When they met again, after a separation of only the working day, she always felt a glow of pleasure: nothing sexual, simply comfort. He went to church because he saw it as his duty; she usually accompanied him, because she saw that as hers. Millicent had a degree in Modern Languages; she kept up her

French and German by reading, and now acted as a guide at a mansion owned by the National Trust, where this ability was useful when she escorted groups of foreign tourists round the building.

They walked back from church with a couple whose daughter was a research scientist.

'Someone chucked fire bombs at the laboratory last night,' Jenny's mother said. 'And there were a lot of slogans painted on the walls. Jenny went over there this morning, though there's no damage done. But her boss's house was attacked, too. He's got a study workshop in a shed; it was set on fire, and his children's pet rabbits were released and shot. Luckily the family were all out.'

'Oh no! Oh, how awful! Who was it?' Millicent asked.

'Animal rights activists, they say. The slogans were that sort of thing.'

'But to shoot the children's rabbits! That's hardly in accordance with their creed, is it?'

'No, but some of these groups have been infiltrated by anarchists,' said James Graham. 'The raids are used as an excuse to stir up trouble.'

'We all want to cure disease, and that's what they're trying to do in Jenny's lab. But these people seem more intent on causing harm. They don't mind injuring humans,' said Jenny's father.

'The suffragettes were militant,' said Millicent. 'Women might have been denied the vote for far longer if they had been less extreme. Such actions certainly attract attention.'

'Are you saying this effort last night was justified?' her husband asked her, knowing this was not her view but he liked to draw her out.

'Of course not, dear. There is an order of things in nature. Beatrix Potter has a lot to answer for,' said Millicent.

In their various ways, all were disturbed by the news. Jenny's parents feared she could be hurt in some future demonstration; the attack on Dr Frost's house was proof of that. The raiders could not have known in advance that no one was at home. The judge sighed over the impossibility of dealing effectively with those who might be arrested for such actions; they saw themselves as martyrs.

It was a beautiful day. His duty done, James Graham changed into shabby corduroy trousers and a worn sweater, and went out to give the lawn yet another final mow. Each autumn, he and the part-time gardener would decide when the grass had been cut for the final time, and annually James would squeeze in just one more trim on a dry autumn day.

Tessa's VW was parked outside the house. She'd arrived too late to bother with putting it in the garage. She had had it for three years; he imagined it was still in a reliable condition. He did not like to think of her driving around in a car that might let her down, though now, of course, she had a mobile phone. He might wash it for her after lunch. He had to break off from his mowing when Millicent called out that the meal was ready. Tessa was in good spirits after her long sleep and entertained them with an account of a meeting during the previous week at which she had out-manoeuvred a defaulting creditor and obtained substantial damages for her clients, though whether they would ever be paid was another matter.

After lunch, James resisted the temptation of a snooze with the Sunday papers. He was engaged on a case which required him to study some documents before going to court the next day, but he finished the mowing first, cleaned the machine, and reminded himself to lay it up for the winter the following weekend without fail. Then he went to ask Tessa for her car keys. He would have to move the Golf on to the concrete area near the tap before he could wash it.

'Don't worry, Dad,' she said, when he explained his plan. 'I know it's dirty. I'll put it through a machine when I pick up some petrol. Thanks, though.' She smiled at him, got up, and ruffled his faded red hair with a small hand as she passed. 'I'm leaving soon,' she added.

'Very well,' he said. 'I suppose you should get ahead of the traffic.' He had hoped she would stay for an early supper; they had so little chance to talk. He was sorry to be absolved from his beneficent act; he found washing cars soothing, and you saw results. Besides, he liked things to be clean and neat; the smooth lines on the long lawn gratified his eye now, as he took a last saunter down the garden.

Returning to the house, he went to his study and

picked up the papers relating to his current case, while listening with half an ear for sounds of Tessa's departure.

He heard her come down the stairs and followed her outside. She opened the passenger door of her car and put her bag – a soft holdall – in the back.

'Aren't you going to stow that out of sight?' he asked. 'Much safer, when you stop.'

'But I won't stop, except for petrol, and the carwash,' Tessa answered. 'I'll be with it at all times. Silly old His Honour fusspot.'

'I'm glad you didn't bring any work down this weekend,' he said. 'The rest will have done you good.' Like him, she sometimes had to study papers in times allegedly off duty.

'So am I,' she answered, and kissed his cheek.

She drove off, leaving her father unaware that her car contained, stowed out of sight, evidence, including a gun, of her participation in last night's raid.

She took Orlando home with her the next weekend.

The attack on the home of the research scientist and the deaths of the pet rabbits had attracted considerable coverage in the tabloid press. Well-wishers sent more rabbits for the children, who were pictured holding them. Guy Frost had pleaded for the media to go away in return for one photo call, hoping that another topic might soon divert their interest.

WHO ARE THESE PEOPLE? headlines asked, pointing out that the arson attack had to be connected with the fire bombs thrown ineffectually at the laboratory.

Though paint had been sprayed there, no cans were found at the site; Tessa had ordered her team to carry them away and dump them. She suspected that some of her recruits had pasts which could mean their fingerprints were on file. Not even Orlando saw her pocket one that Biff had handled.

Millicent mentioned the incident.

'What a cruel thing,' she said.

Orlando waited for Tessa to defend the actions of the animal protestors, though he knew her parents were unaware that she was one of them. She didn't.

'Talking of newspapers,' she said, 'had you seen that Philip Winter's disappeared? Isn't he the man who came up before you on a rape charge, Dad?'

James had seen an item in *The Times* about the discovery of the man's car beside a river, and the subsequent search by police frogmen for the body. It mentioned the missing man's recent acquittal on a rape charge.

'Yes,' the judge agreed. He remembered the case very clearly. In his opinion, it should not have come to trial; the evidence was weak and depended on the woman's accusation. Why should a hitherto respectable man suddenly act in such a fashion? The defence had not managed to blacken his accuser's reputation by allegations about her past, and the woman had walked away unscathed, but not appeased. At least the defendant had not been unjustly sentenced; juries often showed great good sense, though this one acquitted him more for reasons of doubt than certainty of the man's innocence.

Over dinner, they discussed the case, the rights and wrongs of anonymity for the accuser – the so-called victim.

'That man was a victim this time,' said James. 'How tragic it will be if he has committed suicide.'

'The woman who accused him has a lot to answer for,' said Millicent. 'I wonder if she knows about this?'

'She'll see it in the paper, as we've done,' said James.

'It seems most unfair that he was named and she wasn't,' said Millicent. 'And he lost his job, poor man.'

'Mrs Sandra White, of Belvoir Mansions,' Tessa said, and her father frowned at her.

'How did you learn who she was?' asked Orlando, amazed.

'Plenty of people knew her identity,' said Tessa dismissively. 'The man must be a prize wimp to get himself in such a mess.'

'I feel sorry for him,' said Orlando, who had read about the case. Sexual harassment was a lively topic of discussion in his office. Signals could so easily be misinterpreted. He was wondering if Tessa would make it clear as to whether he was to remain in the spare bedroom tonight or slip along the corridor to hers. He knew she enjoyed flouting the conventions beneath her parents' roof.

She'd certainly turned the conversation away from their lawless raid with great adroitness, he reflected wryly.

6

WHEN PHILIP HAD not returned home on the day he disappeared, his wife, Lesley, was only irritated. Why had he not told her that he planned to go away?

The last months had been a nightmare. On the evening of the alleged rape, he had come home two hours later than his usual time looking dishevelled, with his hair untidy and a large angry scratch, now crusted over, on his face. He said he had scraped it on a protrusion in the store room, but in all his years at Lavery's, such a thing had never happened before. She was sure he had been in some sort of fight.

'You've been drinking,' she declared. 'Were you mugged?'

He wasn't tough; he would have been easy prey for two or three determined youths – even for one. Like so many other commuters, he wore a trench-coat over his dark suit, and did not, at first glance, look particularly prosperous, merely clean and neat, an average businessman; but all such men were targets, for they carried money, credit cards and driving licences, items of value to any thief.

He told her no more, and the police did not come to see him until after Sandra White had lodged her complaint. Philip had maintained, at first, that their visit concerned some problem at the store, but then he was dismissed, and so she had to learn the truth.

He wasn't given time to state his case at Lavery's, and that was most unfair, but Lesley began to fear the complaint was justified. Perhaps he hadn't really tried to rape the customer – that did seem most unlikely – but he might have tried it on. Why go round to her flat if he didn't fancy her? He often served her personally, in the shop; that was confirmed at the trial by his colleagues, called as prosecution witnesses. She was surprised, though: Philip was not sexually voracious, nor was he prone to anger; petulance was more his line when things went wrong. The whole thing seemed incredible, but when police enquiries continued, and he was taken in for further questioning and tests, she began to wonder, for serial rapists, she had heard, were often mild-mannered men at home, with what were, on the surface, normal family lives.

But he wasn't a serial rapist: he was accused of raping one wealthy customer, whose name he had revealed to her.

She hadn't gone to the hearing: she couldn't, even

to show support for him; it was too painful. His solicitor was disappointed by her decision, implying it would not help his case if she failed to back him up. She was afraid that she would learn the truth in court, hear details of their intimate life discussed, and, in a sense, be tried herself. Afterwards, she could not accept that it was, in fact, the truth which had been established when he was acquitted. He'd been lucky. Everyone said that. The delay in reporting the assault was in his favour, and the absence of strong evidence; after all, he didn't deny that he had been to the woman's flat.

There was no celebration, no champagne and back-slapping. On the night of the verdict the evening meal was fish pie with green beans, followed by apricot fool, eaten in near silence, the only conversation being stilted exchanges between Andrew, who had come home from college to support his mother, and Jackie, as they discussed prospects for the next test match series. Andrew was keen on cricket and Jackie was fond enough of him to take an interest. Lesley ate in silence. When the washing up was done, Philip left the house to go for a walk. It was his habit, now, to do this every evening after supper. Lesley had no idea where he went, and in her worst moments she imagined he was stalking women.

The truth was that he could not bear to remain in the sitting-room with her, pretending to watch television, knowing what was in her thoughts and how she doubted him.

And now he seemed to have escaped more positively.

He'd taken his car, which they had agreed must be sold to bring in some money, and to save on its insurance and upkeep. She had her own small Fiat in which she went to work. Even after his acquittal he could not get a job, apart from odd spells of casual employment.

Then came the day when, while Lesley was at work, Jackie was at school, and Andrew was back at college, Philip went off in his car and, by nightfall, was still out.

'Where's Dad?' Jackie asked, at breakfast the next morning.

He was never late, appearing, wearing his white shirt and a tie as on any working day, but with a pullover. He did the tidying up and most of the housework now; it was the least he could do, since he was not earning, he had said, though in fairness Lesley did admit that he had always been helpful in the house.

'I don't know,' Lesley answered. It was pointless to pretend that he was sleeping in; if he'd gone away, Jackie would have to be told.

'Has he left us?' asked Jackie.

Her mother shrugged. He'd left no note, or if he had, she hadn't found it. Didn't departing husbands do that, except when they stormed out in a rage?

'Has he packed his stuff?' asked Jackie.

'I haven't looked,' said Lesley. 'I expect he'll be

back soon enough, or he'll ring up. You get off to school and don't worry.'

'I'm not worrying,' said Jackie. 'He'll do us all a favour if he's gone.'

Her bitter tone shocked Lesley, but she knew that Jackie had had to endure a lot of mockery at school after her father's arrest and trial.

'Has it stopped now, at school? That nasty talk?' she asked.

'Yes,' said Jackie, although it was not strictly true; to some she was a heroine because it was so awful for her to have a father accused of such a crime, but the general feeling was that he had been lucky to get off because he was, most likely, guilty.

Jackie, trying to be just, had said that the case had not been proved. She had gone to court, skiving off school to do so, watching from the gallery, seeing her father pale, tense, and diminished, being pitilessly cross-examined, yet standing firm, never contradicting himself. Despite the shame she felt, Jackie wanted to believe him, yet why should that woman lie about something so serious? Why get him into such a lot of trouble and make him lose his job? He must have done something wrong, if not what she said. After all, it couldn't have been much fun for her, having to talk about her divorce and being asked about her past lovers. She declared there had been none since she parted from her husband, and none had been discovered by the defence. Anyway, what difference did that make? Lots of people got married more than once, and had several boyfriends; making out a woman was a slag was what always happened in a rape case, Jackie knew. His arrest was the most dreadful thing that had happened in her life. If he was not an honest man, nothing was safe. Her heart told her he was innocent, but her cool and cynical head wanted to know why, if so, he had got himself into such a mess. Why was he in the woman's flat at all? Maybe he'd only tried to kiss her, but that, in itself, was disgusting.

He'd said he went there to return the purse. Why not just hand it over at the door, and leave?

She went off to school resolved not to wonder where he was; he'd spoiled enough of her life already and she would not let him wreck the rest. Lesley, having discovered that he had packed nothing, also decided, although anxiously, to forget about him for the moment.

It was Jackie who grew worried first, although she tried to hide it. Despite her angry, cruel words, she began to imagine fearful things and to feel guilty. Had her unforgiving attitude driven him away? Memories of happier times came, unbidden, came into her mind, and she wondered what had transformed him from the kind man who read stories to her when she was small, and made endless sandcastles when they went to Cornwall in the summer, into the ravening beast described in court.

He'd never been anything but kind to her.

Was he dead? Had her hostility driven him to

suicide? People didn't just vanish, did they? She knew that teenagers ran away from home after quarrelling with their parents – often over nothing – but it was the children who left, not the fathers. Fathers left because of marriage problems.

Well, there were marriage problems. Her mother hated him, just as Jackie thought she did. Both believed he had come on to that woman, even if it hadn't gone as far as she had alleged. It was gross. He didn't know what it had been like for her, having to hear the comments other youngsters made. It was the girls who were the worst; some of the boys had been quite cool about it, saying her father was unlucky, picking the wrong person if he wanted an affair. But he shouldn't have been after an affair. Her mother, for her age, was quite nice-looking; she hadn't let herself go. He didn't need to look around, or if he must, couldn't he do it in the normal way and get divorced? Not that Jackie would have liked that, either, but it wasn't criminal.

But he'd got off. He hadn't gone to gaol. It kept coming back to that. If only she could know the truth for certain. When, after two days, he still hadn't come home, nor been in touch, she asked her mother if he could be with his parents, who lived in Kent. Lesley agreed that he might have gone there; they, naturally, had been deeply upset about the trial, but were staunch believers in his innocence. His mother had been quite unwell as a result of her anxiety and distress; it was possible that he was with them. She telephoned them, approaching the reason for her call indirectly, saying she had rung to ask how they were. If Philip were there, they would assume she had rung to speak to him; she need not ask for him, outright.

But he wasn't there. Instead, they asked how he was, so Lesley reported that he was all right — out just now, or he would have spoken to them. If they thought that odd, it was too bad; she could do no more.

Where else could he be? She tried to think of friends whom he might visit, but there were few who were his exclusively. In the end she rang Betty, from Lavery's, who had given evidence for Philip. She had no news of him, nor, as far as she knew, had he been to the store since the hearing.

'Oh dear,' said Betty. 'Poor Philip. He didn't do it, you know, Lesley.' He'd told her all about it — described Sandra White's assault on him.

'Her tongue — ugh!' he'd said. 'It was like a persistent snake. Sometimes I think that I can taste it still.'

Betty had noticed that Mrs White never wanted a female assistant to look after her, but the younger men, though keen enough to attend to younger women customers, all avoided Mrs White. Philip, however, was a simple soul, and he became the fall guy. After Lesley's call she was worried. Philip's life had been destroyed by that woman's accusations; what if he had gone that step further and ended it?

The next morning Lesley told the police that he

had disappeared. A constable came to the house and took details about his car. It was rather soon to list him as a missing person, she was told, and even if he were found, all she would learn was that he was safe, not where he was.

'What if he's dead?' she asked, voicing it at last.

'Well, if his body turned up, we'd tell you then. You'd need to identify him,' was the blunt answer. 'We'll look out for his car. It'll probably be noticed, if we ask all forces to watch out for it.'

'He hasn't any money,' Lesley said. 'Well, he had his wallet on him, and he'd got a cash card.'

The officer took details of their bank account and later the same day was able to tell her that, to date, Philip had not withdrawn any money. At least he hadn't cleaned the account out and fled abroad. He hadn't got his passport with him, though; when he was remanded on bail, he had had to surrender it, but it had been returned and was in his desk.

The next day, his car, the keys still in it, was found beside the river, and a full-scale search was undertaken.

'We should have stood by him,' said Jackie, now in tears.

But Lesley saw it differently. To her, his flight was confirmation of his guilt.

7

WHAT DID YOU do when you had absolutely no money at all?

Philip could not apply for unemployment benefit without producing papers of some sort: doing that would reveal his identity and previous address. It was strange to be so rootless, and quite frightening. He wondered how soon Lesley would report him missing. Maybe she wouldn't bother, but if the car was found, she'd have to take some notice. The best solution would be if it were stolen; then she could claim on the insurance and they could all forget about him.

Since leaving the Lake District, he had followed a serpentine course, taking lifts, not caring where they were going. After several nights at Blackpool, on the front, he'd gone south again, and had spent one night in a men's hostel, something he hoped not to repeat. He was husbanding his money, using it in small amounts for food, and he had bought a spare pair of socks, and a pair of shorts. In Swindon, in a charity shop, he bought a second shirt, and these few belongings went with him everywhere in a plastic Safeway carrier. If he was going to sleep rough, he'd need a sleeping bag, and that would be expensive. Cardboard boxes, he thought, like those living on the streets in London: he'd seen such people daily in his working life. How could you carry a cardboard box around? Could you leave it somewhere, while you spent the day job-hunting or in the library? The library was warm and there were comfortable chairs, and plenty to read; you could doze there, quietly.

He had applied for several jobs. He could drive a van – he had his licence, which was clean. He could sweep up, could serve in a bar, could stack supermarket shelves. But no one took him on. Some were sorry, saying he had just missed a chance when an earlier applicant had been successful. They didn't take to him, Philip decided: was it his appearance? His beard was coming in quite grey; it made him look much older, and it was still sparse: he hadn't had to trim it yet. His shirt, rough dried, was always clean; didn't he look respectable?

Then he saw the report about his car. It had been found, and he was officially missing. He'd bought a tabloid newspaper, which he took into a café where he had soup and bread; that would be his hot meal for the day. He'd started filling up a small mineral water bottle with water from a public washroom, and carrying that around with him, and he looked for cut-price displays where he could buy cheap biscuits. Reading the tabloid, he saw a picture of himself dating from the trial, and a report that his wife and daughter were too upset to talk to newsmen. Frogmen were searching for his body, Philip read: he felt as though the news referred to a stranger, not himself. He acknowledged no remorse about his family's alleged distress: it was not him they cared about, simply themselves and this added notoriety.

If they'd stood by him, he wouldn't be in such a state now. What about trust, and duty: all those things that people thought were so important in relationships; where were they in his case? He would not let himself contemplate his parents' possible concern. He left the paper on the table, and walked off.

He wasn't wanted by the police. Anyone who thought they recognised him would not feel bound to report the sighting. If he let his beard grow longer, and his hair, he'd be extremely well disguised. Perhaps he'd pass as a poet, Philip thought, and then reflected that more likely, if he went on sleeping rough, he'd be taken for a down-and-out.

And he would be one.

Frances Dixon had heard about the attack on Guy Frost's house on the radio news the morning after it happened.

She was horrified. Nothing like this had occurred

in the area since she moved to Chingbury. Darsingford, where the Frosts lived, was where she went for shopping which could not be done in the village. It had been a market town and had now expanded to include some industry on its perimeter, with housing for those who worked there. There had been burglaries and muggings in the town, and car thefts, but very little violent crime, and this was different: this was terrorism, setting fire to the home of a man who was working to benefit mankind.

It seemed that the family had been out when the attack took place. Perhaps it would not have happened if they had been at home because the arsonists could have been discovered. Whatever the facts, it was wicked and cowardly, and Dr Frost had lost valuable disks and papers which were destroyed. The damage had been confined to his workshop in the garden shed.

But why kill the pet rabbits, when the protestors were proclaiming that they were defending animals?

The police seemed to think that this was strange.

Frances was not a churchgoer, and she met no one on that Sunday, which she spent working in the garden. It was one of the days on which she spoke to nobody. Since tucking herself away in this isolated spot, such days happened fairly frequently and sometimes she made a note of them, just for interest. Once a month she rang each daughter; sometimes they rang her. She sent each grandchild postcards now and then, all of them on the same day so that no one got forgotten. Now that they were growing up, they stayed with her less often, but sometimes one of Arabella's brood would come for several weeks in the summer. There was a tennis club in Chingbury, with two hard courts, where they could play, and at Friar's Court, where Dorothy and Hugo Ware lived, there was a pool, which the Wares let the youngsters use on visits. Friar's Court was an old stone house which had been part of an abbey; now, some of the outbuildings had been turned into units where people ran small businesses, among them a man who restored furniture, a potter, and a printer.

Frances had been offered the use of the pool, but she was a poor swimmer, and found that keeping her large garden orderly gave her enough exercise.

Earlier that summer, she had met the Frosts at a party the Wares held for their daughter, who had recently married a man who already had a small son and daughter from an earlier marriage. The Wares were wishing that she was not taking on this pair of stepchildren, who lived mainly with their mother but would spend some weekends with their father.

'It can work out,' Frances had consoled them, thinking of Arabella, who had made a success of her role as a stepmother but was, perhaps, less successful with her own children.

'It's so difficult in any case,' said Dorothy Ware, a large woman with wavy iron-grey hair. Her husband was a retired general who had been persuaded to write his memoirs. This kept him busy, and would be a useful historical record even if the result never reached a wide public.

Frances had met the Wares through their mutual interest in gardens. The Wares had seven acres of land surrounding their house; four of them formed a paddock, where from time to time a neighbour's two ponies grazed, and the rest was cultivated, some of it as a small arboretum. The general liked trees, had carefully selected those to plant, and had naturalised hundreds of bulbs beneath them. Snowdrops, daffodils, narcissi and bluebells flourished in their chosen areas; Frances loved to walk there.

She remembered the Frosts. They had struck her as a strong family: the craggy-featured father, a balding, thick-set, sturdy man, and the rather plain wife who wore glasses and had a sweet expression on her face as she kept an eye on the two young children, a girl and a boy, who played card games together on a rug on the grass and, when that bored them, chased each other round the garden.

Thank goodness only property and the rabbits had been hurt, but what an extraordinary thing to do: to shoot the pets.

For no particular reason, she remembered the near collision she had had in the lane the day of the attack: the white van which had come much too fast towards her and the aggressive driver who had almost pushed her backwards as she reversed away. Their encounter was at least twenty miles from the complex and the Frosts' house, and hours before either incident. They could not be connected.

What a pity the demonstrators did not use their energy to draw attention to human hardship, Frances thought, as, like Judge Graham forty miles away, she mowed her lawn.

Biff and Denis knew nothing about the shot rabbits. They never bothered with the paper, or any other form of news dissemination. There was no television in their world. They went on several other protests, not about animals but for causes which Biff had heard needed support. He got a buzz from the crowd's mood, the chanting and the movement as they massed together with the police walking along beside them, ready for a riot to break out. He'd seen policemen knocked to the ground and kicked. He wouldn't do that himself; the penalty if you were caught was much too high; but a sort of fury could get hold of you and make you want to hunt them down.

Denis was not so keen on the urban demonstrations, though they were something to do. He kept hoping for another trip to the country. Often, lying in his corner of the dingy hut where he slept, light entering through cracks in the boarded-up windows, he thought about the space and the darkness of the night. He would remember the field with the alarming cattle by the gate: their wet noses and their sweet breath puffing at him when at last he plucked up the nerve to go near them. They'd soon returned, after Orlando had scared them off.

Orlando hadn't minded them at all.

Biff had been in the country before. When he was quite young he'd been sent to a centre where he had cleared ditches and put up fences and climbed nearby hills. The food had been good, and they'd had some laughs, but he liked a bit of noise and people round him. Tessa and Orlando's raids were small stuff, in his view; he preferred being part of a large active crowd. The pay-offs, though, were better with Tessa, and he'd always go with her again. Besides, last time he'd had his bonus; that was what she'd called it, afterwards. He knew that if he told Denis what had happened, he wouldn't be believed.

Soon, the anti-hunting expeditions would be starting.

'That's real,' he told Denis. 'You chase them dogs and you chase the toffs on horses. It's great.'

Denis was ready to believe him.

Early in November, they went on such a demonstration, joining hunt saboteurs in a minibus where they sang anarchic songs on the way to a village where a targeted hunt was to meet. Biff and Denis had no major role to play; they were supporting actors in a cast which included people with canisters which they planned to spray around to confuse the hounds and lead them on a false trail.

The two were told not to be violent.

'But you can use your initiative,' they were advised.

Denis, sitting by a window in the minibus, tried

to understand the purpose of their protest. He knew that Tessa and Orlando thought it cruel to make mice and rabbits ill by dosing them with drugs or giving them diseases, all in the name of science. Now he had to accept that it was cruel to chase a fox with a pack of hounds which would tear it to shreds and eat it. But foxes ate chickens. Biff had told him that; he'd seen the results when he was sent to the country institution. Now, the people round him in the coach were talking about chasing the riders and the hounds. He heard a girl boast how, the previous season, her actions had caused a horse to take fright and stumble, throwing the rider who was taken to hospital. 'Stretchered, he was,' she said, with satisfaction. The horse had cut its leg and was led off bleeding. Hadn't that been cruel? Denis was puzzled.

People quietened down when they reached their destination. They were dropped outside the village, where they met some local demonstrators who, knowing the area, suggested how they should be deployed in groups. Some were sent to block a road down which the hunt would have to go to reach a wood where a fox might be found. Other demonstrators, favouring the hunt, stood peacefully about with placards proclaiming that banning hunting would throw hundreds out of work. WHAT ABOUT FISHING? said one sign.

This year, the police had new powers of arrest, so the saboteurs' strategy, now, meant avoiding the actual meet, where intruding could be trespass. No one wanted to end up in the back of a police van.

The two groups of demonstrators faced one another like troops before a battle, the protestors often dressed in black or combat gear, the supporters more conventionally in anoraks or waxed jackets, most of them country dwellers, some of whom earned their living from the land.

There came the distant sound of a horn and the crowd began to stir. The hunt had moved off from its meeting place and was approaching. Denis heard the clatter of horses' hooves on the tarmac of the road, and the murmur of voices, but none of it was loud, not until the group around him started chanting. Suddenly, sticks appeared in people's hands and Denis saw that Biff now held a cudgel. Where had that come from? The hunt supporters had fallen back on to the grass verges, allowing hounds and riders to pass, but the protestors formed a solid phalanx facing the oncoming hounds and the field behind them. Denis, bemused and rather frightened, saw two men in red coats riding enormous horses from whose nostrils plumed puffs of steamy breath. The men carried whips with long thongs which trailed beside them. One kept talking in encouraging tones to the sea of pale creamy hounds which billowed around his horse's hooves. An occasional yelp came from a hound, but they were mostly quiet. Behind, bobbing up and down in their saddles, was a mass of riders, men, women and children, most of them in black or navy coats, but there were a few splashes of scarlet here and there and some tweed. All of them wore dark hard hats. Denis felt panic. What if this huge army chose to charge at the protestors? They'd be bowled over, savaged by the hounds and trampled by the horses, as at a riot when the mounted police rode in. Denis had seen that happen, and it was scary. What if these riders used their whips on the demonstrators? He wanted to turn back, but he couldn't because of the press of people round him who were shouting now.

Suddenly the hunt turned aside, into a field where, miraculously, a gap in the fence had appeared. Tipped off in advance, two men had cut the wire and moved a couple of posts to let the field stream through before they reached the demonstrators.

Frustrated and furious as their quarry galloped away, the protestors set off in pursuit across the field, waving their sticks in the air and screaming. The weather had been dry for weeks, so the ground was not unduly wet, but where the horses had gone, it was churned up in places, and some of the demonstrators were inadequately shod for their chase. Denis, in his shabby trainers, stood back beside the hedge to let the protestors sweep past him, and he saw the hunt spread out, the hounds in front with the huntsman and the whipper-in, the other riders following in what looked to him an orderly manner. He caught his breath. It was a colourful and splendid sight, and the only cruelty he had seen so far was the expression on the faces of his companions.

Along the road, now, came a line of vehicles and cycles carrying the foot followers of the hunt. Meanwhile, the two original men, aided by two more, were swiftly repairing the gap they had made in the wire fence.

Biff was among the group of protestors who had surged into the field behind the horses; the rest regrouped to decide on their next tactic, which was to circumnavigate the wood so that they would be ready if a fox was flushed out on the further side. Denis sauntered after them, in no hurry.

The day was cold and crisp, the sky a brilliant blue. In London, unless it rained or was very windy, you scarcely noticed the weather; here it was so different. This was why he had come, he decided, inhaling deeply. On either side of the lane stretched fields, woodland, and this great, amazing space. Imagine living here, among all this emptiness! You'd soon get used to the quiet. It was quiet now; the cars following the hunt were all drawn up with their engines switched off. Denis walked slowly, letting the demonstrators round him overtake him; these were the local dedicated campaigners who plodded on with grim expressions, anxious lest the violent element among the imported saboteurs got out of hand, for to some of them the cause was immaterial; it was the chase that was the lure.

Denis found himself walking up a track towards a wood. He hesitated, then tagged along among the other stragglers. It was rather like the trail on which Orlando had led them on the day of that raid; then, they'd ended on the downs. They'd passed some downs on the way here today but Denis hadn't known where they were going; he couldn't read the road signs.

Now, from ahead, came excited yelps and deeper barks, then a great babble from the hounds. It was a bit like music, Denis thought.

'They've found a fox,' said a youth, brushing past him. Rushing on, he produced a horn from his own pocket and blew on it, unmelodiously but loudly. 'This'll call them off,' he promised, halting to blow the better.

Denis could not see the main pack of hounds but there were about forty riders waiting quietly at the edge of the wood, some of the horses fidgeting impatiently but most standing still, ears pricked, listening. The horn was blowing now – not the youth's, but the official one – as the cry of the hounds hit a crescendo. Denis thought he'd like to see them chasing after the fox. This wasn't like a night at the dogs; he'd been greyhound racing a few times and it was exciting, but this was different: this was real. There was more point to this than running round a track chasing a dummy hare.

Biff suddenly appeared beside him.

'Phew!' he exclaimed. 'This is great!'

Denis had forgotten about him. He was walking slowly now while ahead others were running, many of them yelling.

'I hit one of them,' Biff told him proudly. 'I hit one of them big horses.'

Denis stared at him. Hadn't he come on this trip to save foxes, not hurt horses? More figures were converging in the wood as those who had entered from other directions met. With various rallying calls and shouts, they formed themselves into a straggling line and set off after the hunt; the hounds, in full cry, were streaming across the country on the far side of the wood. Biff joined the pursuers, and Denis's slow walk grew even slower. The noises he heard now were not the hunt, but the yells of the demonstrators. He heard the youth blow his horn discordantly and hoped the hounds would take no notice. The protestors were upsetting it all. They were wrong. They were hunters too.

When at last he emerged from the wood into another field, he saw a drab crowd of people trailing towards a distant gate where a line of vans was drawn up. They began clambering into the vehicles, preparing to move to another position for a fresh assault; this was local transport they were using. Denis thought he saw Biff among them, but it was difficult, at such a distance, to distinguish individuals. Would Biff be going in a van when they had come by minibus? Denis did not know that this transport was provided by the local organisations, anxious to keep forces mobile. He did not care where they were going. He went back towards the wood, intending to make his way to the village where the minibus had dropped them. Presumably it would return there later to collect them for the homeward trip. He did not hurry. Time had never had much importance for Denis, and today it mattered even less. He was alone in the wood now. The paths and rides had been churned up as much by the protestors as the horses, few of which had come this way since most had been outside the wood in sight of where the fox broke cover. A hen pheasant ran in front of him. What a big wild bird, thought Denis. Then he saw a grey squirrel race up a tree trunk. It crouched above him, watching him over its front paws, its whiskers twitching, not at all afraid. Denis had seen squirrels in a park, but never as close as this.

The wood was settling back to normal. On another day, Denis might have come across beaters and obstructed a shooting party, but not now. With the departure of the hunt and its followers, peace returned, and with it came that strange quiet he had noted before. It was broken only by the soft sound of his own footsteps as he moved on. He had been rather fearful of the silence on the expedition with Orlando and the rest; now, it did not worry him. No one was going to drag him into a scrap or a brawl, and there was no traffic to dodge. What would it be like to live here? The wood didn't seem to belong to anyone. Couldn't he build a hut? There were plenty of trees and bushes around; it should be simple to use branches and make a den. Long ago, with some other boys, he'd played on a patch of waste ground near the foster home he was in at the time; they'd had a hide-out there. He'd almost forgotten about it. That had been one of the better times. The foster mother had read stories to them. He'd cried when he left to go back to a children's home. He thought he'd been moved on because he'd been naughty, not realising that it had only ever been a stop-gap placement. After that, he had often behaved badly on purpose, seeing that being good made no difference.

What could you eat, if you lived in a wood? It would be cold at night, but he could light a fire. He'd slept out often enough; that wouldn't bother him, though here there would be no warm grating to give out heat, and he had no big cardboard box. Once, when an old dosser had died, he'd taken the man's sleeping bag and had used it until someone stole it from him when he'd gone off to the toilet. Even the toilet wouldn't be a problem in a wood.

People came round to those sleeping on the streets with soup and sandwiches, if you were lucky. Sometimes they brought blankets. That wouldn't happen here. Denis wondered if he could catch rabbits, or some of those big birds, and cook them. How did you get the feathers off, and the fur? Would they sit quietly enough for you to pounce on them? He'd got a knife. He could use that to kill them. He thought about it, walking back towards the village. Then he saw the fox. It took him a moment to realise what it was – the rather muddy animal, bigger than a cat, which slunk across the road ahead of him and went into the field. He watched it lope towards the wood from which it had been driven earlier in the day.

That was good, then. It had escaped the hunt. In fact, this wily fox had crossed a stream and the hounds had lost its scent as it doubled back, surviving to be pursued another time. The hunt, meanwhile, had moved to a different covert where it found a second fox, losing many of the saboteurs this time as the chase moved fast and in a direction they had not anticipated. Hanging about in exposed fields with no action bored the maverick brigade, denied the chance to disrupt the sport and hurl abuse. The more conventional objectors tended to go home when they had made their point.

Biff had forgotten about Denis, for he had fallen in with some new friends. He had already met some of this mob when he went on a march protesting against a recent government bill some people found objectionable. Biff had no idea what it was about. Unfortunately, out here in the wilds, there were no handy snack bars or chip shops to get a bite. Tessa and Orlando, on their trips, always organised the feeding of the troops – that was what they called it. On these bigger demonstrations you had to think about yourself.

As the day wore on, he grew hungry, and at last one of their group called up their minibus by mobile phone. When they were all aboard, it was agreed that they would stop for refreshments at the first possible opportunity. Denis was only one of several stragglers who missed their transport home.

'They should have kept with us. That was the instruction,' said one of the organisers, a woman in a waxed jacket and wellingtons, wearing a green hood. 'They must get back as best they can. They can hitch a lift.'

Biff hoped Denis would not get lost. The kid was useless on his own. Still, he had to learn. He'd turn up. Biff moved up in the bus to sit beside a long-haired girl he'd noticed earlier. He might try his luck there.

He didn't get very far with her on the journey, but he discovered where she lived. He could always find her, if he had the time.

8

NO TRACE OF Philip Winter had been found.
Lesley tried to carry on as usual, but each day she expected to hear that his body had been discovered. Jackie, too, could not stop thinking about her father, at one minute blaming herself for driving him away from home, the next furious with him for what she saw as his betrayal. In that angry mood, she shared her mother's belief that he must have done something to the woman, even if it wasn't total rape.

But Jackie knew that people sometimes made up stories, often only just for fun, though often to shock or impress their listeners. At school, a girl had alleged that a master had put his hand on her leg in class. It hadn't happened; she'd done it for a joke, telling her parents who had instantly complained. The incident soon spiralled out of control; the master was suspended, and the girl, frightened now, stuck to her story. None of her friends wanted to get her into trouble by exposing the lie, yet it seemed unfair to the master, who taught history and was not particularly unpopular; he wore pebble glasses and rode a bicycle to school, and, had he been one of the children, might have been a target for bullying. The girl had picked him rather than one of his less vulnerable colleagues. In the end, she had, in tears, retracted her allegations, but only after some other pupils had threatened her with dire consequences if she did not. It could so easily have ended the master's career; as it was, he lost his enthusiasm for teaching and some months later he left the school. No one knew what he was doing now.

If something like that had happened to her father, he was to be pitied, not punished. But had it? Why had he visited that flat? Had the woman really left her purse behind deliberately? Couldn't she find herself a man, if she wanted one? Round and round in Jackie's confused head churned the various possibilities, the doubts and fears.

And now, what if he were dead?

She ran through various scenarios, including his funeral with herself in black, down to the ground, weeping into a lace-edged handkerchief. People would pity the poor orphan. To lose a father's reputation and then, after his name had been cleared, the father himself, was surely tragic.

But had his name been truly cleared? Always, it came back to that, and how would she ever know the truth? People were vile and disgusting; she knew some awful things that would have shocked her mother if she had mentioned them. Jackie was beginning to find the world a frightening place, and you were alone in it. Who could help her now? Andrew was away, and since the trial had been home only briefly. He was afraid his girlfriend would dump him on account of his father's disgrace. He rang up sometimes, and Mum had told him about Dad going off. When he heard about the discovery of the car, he came home for a night, but Mum had sent him back to college. He couldn't help, she said; they must all carry on, and when some journalists wanted her to tell them how she felt, she said she didn't know.

'What if he's committed suicide?' they asked, and she refused to answer.

Lesley could not face the possibility that his despair had been so great that he could no longer face life, yet wouldn't he have left a note, if that was so? Most suicides did, didn't they, sowing guilt behind them as they did it, the sort of guilt that she felt now, the sense that she should have given him the benefit of the doubt.

But why should she do that? Why put the blame on her? It was Philip who had seen the woman and crossed swords with her.

When no body was found, the papers' interest soon died down. The car had been examined, and eventually the police said that Lesley could fetch it; the radio had gone, but as it had been left unlocked, thieves could have taken that with little effort.

Lesley could not face the trip. She said her son would go over for it when he next came home. They'd keep it for her, wouldn't they, meanwhile? Perhaps one of them would like to buy it.

This suggestion, thrown away, was taken seriously. It seemed that a new owner from the force might be found, after an appropriate interval.

The police officer who came to see her described how the river, now in flood, might yet yield up a body as the water fell. He spoke of tides, but not of gases which might bring it to the surface.

'Don't give up hope,' he added. 'Sometimes people go missing just to get away, when things get too difficult. Then they come back.'

'But with no money? No clothes?'

'He'll have had some money on him,' said the officer.

'Not much. He's been unemployed for months.'

He might still use his bank card. Lesley would not put a stop on it; there wasn't a great deal in the account, but he was entitled to some of it. The bank would let them know if money was withdrawn.

But he didn't use his card and first days, then weeks went by with no news. If he was found, the police would come and tell her personally; such information was not given in a telephone call. Lesley went to the office as usual, worrying about Jackie who wasn't eating properly and whose school work was suffering. How could he do this to them, after what he'd done already, Lesley thought, in anger. She went to see Jackie's teacher to explain the situation, though everyone must know all the details from the press.

If he were to walk in now, Lesley was not sure how she would react, nor could she predict Jackie's response.

At least we'd know, she thought: the uncertainty would end.

Mrs Sandra White had also read that Philip had disappeared.

How feeble, was her first reflection. The fact that she had wrecked his life and reputation did not worry her. Though she sought sexual satisfaction from men, she despised most of them, living comfortably on generous alimony. Her husband had had to make it worth her while to let him go.

Sandra had planned to find another husband, but if she did, she stood to lose her handsome income. So far, she had failed to attract a man as rich; those who might be detachable from existing spouses wanted young, fresh flesh; one had told her so. Sandra White was forty-six.

In her mail, one morning a few days after Philip's car had been found, she received a letter in a plain manila envelope. It contained a newspaper cutting reporting her victim's disappearance and hinting at the possibility of his suicide. Across the cutting, printed in the same bold black felt pen as the address, were the words: YOU ARE RESPONSIBLE FOR THIS.

Sandra stared at it, bewildered. Then her anger rose as she understood that whoever had sent her the cutting believed she had provoked the stupid man to kill himself.

What nonsense! He'd been let off, which he didn't deserve because he had insulted her and a term in prison would have done him good. Why should she now be blamed for what he chose to do afterwards?

But who could have sent this to her? Not Philip, if he was dead. Some friends of his? That woman from Lavery's who had spoken up for him?

It had a South London postmark.

Next day she received another, reporting the same tale but in more sensational terms, cut from a different paper. After that there was a brief lull.

Philip's former colleagues at Lavery's had been concerned when they learned about his disappearance and the discovery of his abandoned car. Betty, the defence witness, went to see Lesley, taking flowers from several of the staff, offering sympathy and wanting to know if there was any further news. She lived in quite another district and had made a special journey after work.

Lesley had to ask her in, accept the flowers and thank her for them. How kind she was. Lesley's eyes filled with tears and Betty misinterpreted the reason. She put an arm round Lesley's shoulders, in a sympathetic gesture.

'It's awful that that woman could get away with it,' she said. 'In spite of what the papers said, I know you believed him, but so many people didn't. And everyone knows who Philip is but no one's been told about Mrs Sandra White. She'd tried it on before, I'm pretty certain,' Betty added. 'No one was going to admit it, though, because of wives and so on. Families could break up, if any of the men had come forward.' Mrs White had been through most departments, Betty had heard, from hardware to men's outfitting. 'Are you going to make an appeal to him on television?'

'What's the good, if he's dead?' said Lesley.

'But he may not be. He may simply have run away,' said Betty. It would be in character. After all, according to Philip himself, he'd run away from the allegedly rapacious Mrs White.

'Well, if he just wants some time to himself, he'll run back again, no doubt,' said Lesley. Her tone was very bitter. Betty looked at her pale, unhappy face and felt her own heart harden. No wonder Philip had had to escape from home, one way or another.

'How's Jackie?' she asked. 'And Andrew?'

'All right. Jackie's upset,' said Lesley.

And you're not helping, Betty thought.

'I'm very sorry,' she said. 'We all liked Phil. Most of us think it's a terrible business. Cases like this make a mockery of the law – and all the time there are men out there really raping women, and getting away with it, who do it again and again and don't get put away because they make out the woman's a slut. No one asks about their sex lives.' Even Philip's sexual history had been left unexamined by the court.

She turned to go, refusing the cup of coffee which, belatedly, Lesley was offering. She'd be late getting home, but she'd warned her husband, who was older than she was and who had already retired. He'd have a hot meal waiting for her. She looked forward to it, and to the warm welcome she would receive.

She was one of the lucky ones.

It was your work which gave you your identity, thought Philip, on the road again. He'd bought himself a thick donkey jacket at a charity shop; it was only five pounds. Some dead person's garment, he supposed. Buying it made a big hole in his shrinking exchequer but the nights were getting cold and his trench-coat wasn't warm enough. It would do as a groundsheet, though, for sleeping out.

He'd been head of a department in a large branch of a well-known store. That had given him status – not as much as if he were a professional man – a doctor, say, or a solicitor – but you could command a high salary if you rose to manage a whole store. He wasn't capable of that; he'd reached his limit; but he had more rank than when he was a mere salesman. A road sweeper, even a refuse collector, had his role in life. Now, Philip had none. He was a bum, almost a beggar. He wasn't dead, however, and without a body, Lesley could not have a funeral.

He'd got a lift in a car with two young lads.

'Nice of you to pick me up,' he said, getting into

the back of their very shabby Allegro.

'We know what it's like, trying to get a ride,' said the driver. 'We're going to Plymouth to see our Mum. Want to come with us?'

'Thanks,' said Philip. Plymouth: why not? In another age he could have joined a ship there, no questions asked, and sailed the world as crew. Perhaps you could still do that.

The boys were brothers; they had been working as labourers on a building site, raising funds to go abroad. They were about Andrew's age, thought Philip, and, though not identical, were, they told him, twins. The one who drove pushed the old car on, and Philip thought it was making a rather nasty noise; a knocking sound was coming from the engine. Sure enough, after a while it began to falter, and the young man just managed to get it off the motorway at the next slip road and away from the roundabout at the top. All three of them then pushed it to a safer place, the driver leaning in to steer it through the window.

'I hoped it'd get us there,' said one twin.

'We had a bet on it, and I won,' said his brother, but he looked quite glum.

'It may not be anything much,' said Philip, though it had sounded bad. 'Look, I'll walk on and send you help. I'm sure to come to a telephone box or a place where I can use the phone before long.'

He left them, and after walking for a mile or more, he came to a small group of houses. He chose a bungalow, and rang its bell.

Footsteps approached the door. He sensed an eye was being applied to a peephole. He couldn't be a reassuring sight, dressed in his heavy jacket, with his new beard, not very clean. The door was opened, very cautiously, on a chain, and a pale blue eye looked round.

'I'm sorry to bother you,' he said.

'I never buy anything at the door,' said the owner of the eye, and banged the door before he could speak.

Philip tried the next house, where there was no answer, but at the third he found a woman working in the garden. She was digging the border over, and she held her fork protectively before her as he approached. However, she let him state the reason for his visit.

The young men had written down the number of their car, and the road reference. The woman said that she would telephone a local garage and get them rescued.

'They're nice young lads,' he told her. 'Not yobs. They were giving me a lift.'

'I see.' The woman looked him up and down. His anxious eyes peered at her above a pale face adorned by a moth-eaten moustache and beard. He wasn't your usual roadie, she thought. 'Would you like a cup of tea?' she asked.

'Please,' said Philip.

'I'll telephone, and then I'll bring you out one,' she volunteered, going off towards the house.

He watched her go. She wore jeans and a light

padded jacket that had seen better days, and boots, which she took off before entering the house. Philip picked up the fork and went on turning the soil over. It didn't do his shoes much good, but the ground was still quite dry. He'd always enjoyed gardening and last year had bought a greenhouse, quite a small one, big enough to grow tomatoes in and a few plants for the house.

The woman, bringing back his tea, was quite surprised.

'Would you like to finish it off?' she said. 'Then I can tidy up the roses and put in the wallflowers. I'll give you five pounds and something to eat. Oh, and I can find you a pair of boots to borrow.'

She brought him out a pair of wellingtons, a size too large and with a hole in the sole, and told him they'd been intended for a jumble sale.

Philip put the boots on, and continued digging. He asked her for some secateurs and cut down the withered herbaceous plants, carrying the dead cuttings to her bonfire spot.

'It's a lovely garden,' he said. 'Have you lived here long?'

'Ten years,' she answered.

She brought him some ham sandwiches for lunch, and another cup of tea. He enjoyed his meal sitting in the thin autumn sunlight.

He worked on after lunch, cutting dead wood out of an apple tree and neatening up the edges of the lawn. Then she said she had to fetch her children from school.

'Where were you going?' she asked him.

'To Plymouth, but I might as well go anywhere,' he said.

She frowned.

'Have you been in prison?' she asked.

'No.' He'd spent a night in a police station after he was charged, but the next day the police had allowed him bail.

'One has to be so careful,' she declared.

'I understand,' said Philip. 'I've got a wife and daughter,' he told her. 'And a son. We're separated,' he added, for good measure. After all, it was the truth.

The woman resolved she would take a chance.

'I'll take you to Darsingford,' she said. 'You can decide where to go from there. There are buses and trains.'

She dropped him at the edge of the town, then turned off for the school. She gave him ten pounds, too, and said he'd earned it.

So he had. He could afford a bed tonight.

9

WHEN DARKNESS FELL, Denis knew he wasn't
going home – if you could call it home – that
night. So what? He'd go when he felt like it. He
might lose his corner in the hut, and the blanket he
had hoarded since it was given to him by charity
workers, but he could always find Biff and the other
guys whom Biff counted as his mates; he knew
where they hung out and which pubs they used.
Denis wasn't so keen on pubs. They cost, because
you had to pay for other people's drinks, and he had
a weak head so that a couple of pints made him lose
his bottle. He knew himself to be a coward, though
he'd once tried to join the army, thinking that then
he'd get clothes and food, and have a roof over his
head, and be told what to do so that he didn't have
to make his own decisions. He'd failed the medical.
He had flat feet and a rattle in his chest which he'd
been told to take to his own doctor. Denis had no

doctor, but he had had asthma as a child. It seldom bothered him, these days.

He was hungry. He had a couple of pounds on him, enough to buy some chips and have plenty left for tomorrow. Surely there'd be a chippie in the place where the hunt had met? The minibus had dropped them outside the village; he walked on towards the cluster of houses.

But there was no chip shop, nor a café, only a pub which wasn't yet open. The short November day was ending; lights were on in windows and cars buzzed along the main road. As it was a Saturday, families were at home, but he saw two boys sparring in a friendly way near a telephone kiosk. Probably there were rough kids, even here, he thought, and, streetwise, he wondered if there were houses with unlatched windows, asking to be entered.

He wandered up a branching lane. It was narrow; cars must find it difficult to pass, he thought. He passed a block of cottages fronting the footpath and went round the back of them, looking for his opportunity, but a security light came on instantly and he shot back to the lane. On he went, now leaving the village, and he caught the smell of woodsmoke in the air. At first he didn't realise what it was, but then he saw, over a hedge, the sudden flare of a bonfire as it received a new forkful of dry withered stalks. In the light of the flames he made out a figure stoking the fire. Man or woman, he could not distinguish which, but he gave that no great thought. While this person was busy out of doors, the house might be unlocked.

He must be quick, but he knew this game.

Denis found the entrance gate, opened it carefully – it worked on a latch and did not squeak – and padded up the path towards the house. He was shielded by its bulk from the busy gardener's view. A dim light from within the house showed through the window panes, but no halogen glare sprang into action as he tested the front door, which was firmly locked. He moved round the building, hugging the wall, and came to another door, half glass, and this one was not locked. He slipped inside, closing the door behind him. It was warm in the house, and he breathed in deeply, unaware until then of how cold he had become.

He moved towards the lighted room. It was the kitchen, and what a snug, cosy place it was! There was a stove against one wall; he hadn't seen one like that before: it wasn't gas or electric. It had two silver circular slabs on top and he touched one. It was hot. There was a large table made of wood in the centre of the room, with chairs tucked round it. He must hurry: the person from the garden might come in at any minute and block his line of retreat. He'd grab some food and run.

But there was a purse on the table.

Denis opened it, took the bank notes from it, leaving the small change, and fled.

Frances Dixon, who had not realised quite how dark it had become while she was working in the garden, came in a little later. She put on the hall light, and noticed a trail of earth on the carpet leading from the side door to the kitchen, but attributed it to her own careless progress from the garden on the several journeys she had made to supervise her bonfire.

Denis had closed the gate carefully behind him, then he went back the way he had come. The darkness wasn't yet complete: the sky was grey against the blackness of the buildings and the trees, and he could see some stars. He ran for a bit, then slowed again to a walk. He had money now. There had been a wad of it in the purse.

By good luck, a bus came along as he reached the centre of the village. He couldn't read where it was going, but he simply said 'One single, please' to the driver who also gave out the tickets, and pulled out his own two pounds from his breast pocket.

'To town?' asked the driver.

'That's right,' said Denis.

The driver gave him back some change, and Denis settled down to enjoy the ride. His legs felt tired. He'd been on them, walking round, for hours.

There were very few other passengers, and they took no notice of him. Their journey carried them to another village, where a woman got off and two girls joined them. Denis gazed out of the window at the dark shapes of hedges, trees, and occasional buildings. There were no street lights, except by the clusters of houses, and not always then. When they reached the outskirts of the town, the bus did not stop until a woman who had been sitting at the back rang the bell, and it halted near a crossing to let her off. Denis decided to remain where he was, and the bus went on towards the town centre, where it stopped again and the driver said, 'All change,' getting out himself.

Denis alighted. There were some shops around him, mostly shut now, and a lot of traffic as people drove home or went out for the evening. He sauntered along the pavement looking at the goods displayed in the windows, and eventually came to a chip shop where he bought a large portion of chips and a sausage. Eating his meal from the wrappings, standing in the road, he saw a group of lads some fifty yards away; they were larking about together. He moved off the other way. He wasn't one of their gang and they might beat him up and take his money. A police patrol car drove past, not slowing down. No one took any notice of him.

He was tired. It had been a long, eventful day. He walked away from the centre of Darsingford, not realising that he had visited this town before, with Tessa and Orlando. He recognised no landmarks, and he was not in the area where Guy Frost and his family lived, but soon he was in a different residential neighbourhood. Here, it was quieter. Hardly a car went by, and the houses were dark, their curtains drawn against the night, with just a sliver of light showing here and there. In this part of town, most people had space to park inside their boundaries, even where they lacked garages, and very few cars were left beside the kerb.

Modern cars had effective alarm systems. Denis didn't try to risk opening any of those among the few left in the street. He looked for something older, where he could spend the night, and he found a Maestro parked well away from a street lamp, outside a semi-detached house where there was a glimmer of light at several windows.

It wasn't late. The owner might come out, he thought, to go to a club or pub.

Denis decided to take a chance. If he was found, he'd simply tell the truth – that his friends had dumped him and he'd nowhere to go. That was no crime. He wouldn't be taking the car; he'd simply be using it as a shelter.

It had a steering lock to deter thieves, but as he wasn't stealing it, that didn't matter. Denis opened the door fairly easily, as his pockets contained several useful bits and pieces. Then he lay down on the rear seat, pulling his anorak hood up round his head so that his face wouldn't show if anyone looked in. His feet, inside his trainers, felt quite dry; he didn't take his shoes off in case he had to run for it, but no one came to disturb him. Well fed, and only slightly chilly, Denis soon fell asleep.

Denis woke the next morning because he was cold in the back of the car. This saved him from discovery. At first, when he opened his eyes, he could not remember where he was; he was stiff and uncomfortable, and the only break in the darkness came from the street light along the road, for it was not yet dawn.

Slowly he recalled the events of the previous day, and now he did feel a sense of panic because he was so far from any familiar landmark. The spirit of adventure which had filled him earlier had departed, but he knew there were houses all around him. He could find his way back to London as soon as it got light. Someone would tell him the way to the main road where he could hitch a lift. Then he'd find Biff and resume his normal life. That was, if he wanted to.

He extracted himself from the car, unfolding his thin legs, and standing outside it, looked about. It must be very early. As he stood there, the headlights of an approaching car shone on him, so he turned to walk in the direction in which it was travelling, to hide his face. The car went past without stopping. Denis walked slowly on down the road. No one seemed to be stirring. Wouldn't people soon be setting off for work? Few of his acquaintances had ever had a steady job but those who were employed often left home early. It took him some time to realise that this was Sunday. By then he had reached the centre of the town, where all the shops were shut and everything seemed to be completely dead.

Buses would run, wouldn't they? And weren't there corner shops which opened at all hours? He could buy anything he liked, he thought happily, now he'd got all that money. That had been a bit of luck. He felt no guilt: it was a good snatch: the chance came and he took it. Biff would have approved, but Biff needn't know about it, for he'd want half the pickings.

Though Denis had grown used to having Biff around, thinking of things to do for both of them and generally taking charge, he was also accustomed to being uprooted, plucked away from people he knew and dumped amid strangers. When he left the final home for good, officially a school-leaver but usually a truant, and now responsible for himself with no one to control him, he had felt quite pleased. Free, he could do as he liked. It was later that the fear crept in, the sense of isolation though the streets were full of people. He had never had a constant figure in his life. Soon, though, he made friends with other youngsters without families or homes. You saw a guy for a few days, a few weeks, and then he went away. Someone else would always come along. Denis thought it would be nice if there was a person to come back to, someone who would notice if you went missing. No one would, if he did. Even Biff would think he'd just moved on.

Maybe he had, anyway, for now.

Squaring his shoulders, Denis walked towards whatever the new day had to offer. He wouldn't mind another look at those woods and fields. He might even explore the idea he'd had of building a den in a wild spot. If you did that on waste ground in town, you were flushed out, but here, no one would care, for who would find you, unless it was that pack of dogs? They might, of course. That wouldn't be too nice.

He could find his way back to that place where the hunt had met, couldn't he? But what had it been called? Could he locate the spot where he'd got off the bus, and catch one travelling the other way? This wasn't much of a town; if he returned to the chip shop, he'd see where the bus had dropped him last evening.

He could find that house again, where he'd got the money. It had been an easy place to do, and there'd be more stuff there, like radios and such. On the other hand, he'd need to find somewhere to sell it on: before, he'd known which pubs to go to and where there were shops who'd deal. There'd be buyers in this place, too, but he'd have to track them down.

Normally, the days of the week made little difference to Denis, but on Sundays things were quieter. In one of the foster homes where he'd been briefly, sometimes at weekends rows had broken out between the adults; and the various children, not at school, had scrapped and quarrelled and got into mischief. He hadn't liked the rows, because during the week his foster mother had been nice. The foster father had had a job; he worked on the railway.

Lights were on in a newsagent's shop and it was busy. Denis saw some youngsters and a few older people coming out with heavy bags of papers. One boy wheeled a bike away. He could pick up one of those bikes, thought Denis; you could bet the kid wouldn't chain it up outside every house, nor wheel it in where there was a driveway. He'd remember that, in case he needed wheels. It would be better to nick a car, though, to get back to London. He'd never done that himself, but he'd been with Biff when he fancied a run around and he knew how to hotwire a car. Hadn't he got into that Maestro last night? He could have driven it off this morning, just like that, if he'd broken the lock.

But as it was, he'd done no harm. He hadn't even broken the door, just undone it with a piece of wire. Biff said you should always carry wire, a small screwdriver, and a good penknife with various gadgets on it; you could use it to defend yourself, if you had to, though a knife was described as an offensive weapon and you could be charged for carrying one.

He'd do things right today, though; then he needn't be looking out for cops. He'd got money, so he had no need to steal. He'd have a look around, see what was on offer here. There might be an amusement arcade. That, in Denis's experience, was the place to go to while away the day.

But Darsingford did not run to such delights. It had a population of twenty thousand, a weekly market on Wednesdays, eight pubs, and one two-star hotel, five churches of differing denominations, two primary schools and a mixed comprehensive school which catered for a wide area around the town. There were industrial outcrops on the perimeter: furniture emporia, a do-it-yourself superstore, packing depots for health foods and cosmetics, and the scientific research complex where Guy Frost worked.

Denis did not get as far as these working outposts on that Sunday morning, though he had passed some of them on his bus ride into town. He found it hard to take in that the place was so small. Until his trips with Biff, his whole experience had been urban. He had never lived where the buildings ran out into empty landscape. If he kept going long enough on foot, he'd see fields and trees again. It was weird!

He could pick up a car and go driving down those little roads until it ran out of petrol. Even then, he had enough money to put more in the tank. He might do it for a laugh.

He wasn't bored yet. He went on and eventually he reached a river. Once again it was a lovely day, and Denis walked along the towpath till he reached a bench seat. There, he sat down to count his money. He could do that, well enough.

There was, he calculated, nearly two hundred pounds. Frances Dixon had just collected two weeks' pension from the post office, and she already had some money in her purse. Such an enormous sum spelled bliss to Denis. It would last him for a long time, though he'd rather like to buy a new pair of trainers. Maybe he could steal some.

Quite a lot was happening on the river. A skiff with two men rowing went past. They'd got up early, Denis thought: so had he, much earlier than was usual for him. Then two bigger boats slid by, with four oarsmen in each, and a cox. A jogger came along the path, panting and intent on his solitary progress. To look at him made Denis feel quite tired. He got up, and walked slowly on towards a bridge. He was very hungry, but he hadn't seen a single snack bar or café, though near the bridge there was one shuttered building which looked as though it might sell food. He could read the word SHUT on a sign on the door. Certain words, by usage, were familiar to him, and he could sign his name.

Reaching the bridge, he went up some steps and made his way back into the town. The main street was a little busier by this time; he found a supermarket which was open, and went in to buy something to eat.

It was a lovely shop, he thought: huge. At home he bought food from corner shops; though he sometimes walked round large stores, even nicking stuff from some of them, he was never an official customer. Now, he picked up a basket and went round the loaded shelves. What you could do with money! It would be good to have a regular supply but because Denis had no fixed address at present, he did not qualify for state aid.

He could get a fixed address here but he'd have to be in it for six months before he'd receive any money. At least, that was what he thought was the regulation. It'd be easy to find places for sleeping here, however, with all this space. Maybe there was a hostel, but he couldn't read any notice there might be which would tell him.

He bought a can of Coca-Cola, a Bounty Bar and some crisps, paying for them very circumspectly at the checkout. Then he went back to the river bank to eat his feast. He was sitting there when Philip Winter came along the towpath. He, too, had been shopping in the supermarket, and he had bought a date-expired pack of cheese sandwiches and a small bunch of bananas. He sat down at the other end of Denis's bench, and started on his meal, washing it down with water from his bottle.

Because the weather was good, Philip had decided not to spend his gardening money on a bed; he'd need that when the rain came, and the frost. He'd spent the night wrapped in his trench-coat, over his new warm jacket, on the towpath underneath the bridge. He'd looked around the town, after he arrived there, and passed the evening in a pub, choosing one which looked as though it might be quiet. Darsingford was still a country town, though the night life could include rowdiness and there had been the arson attack on the scientist, but on that Saturday night, Philip was able to avoid all fracas, and after midnight the river bank was quiet. Even the traffic crossing the bridge was minimal.

The shabby, grubby youth already on the bench looked up when Philip sat beside him. From his largesse, Denis offered the man, who he could see at a glance was down on his luck, a packet of crisps. Philip hesitated; then he accepted it.

'Thanks,' he said, and added, 'Have a sandwich.'

'You've only got the two,' said Denis. 'I've got plenty,' and he displayed the contents of his supermarket bag.

In his former life, Philip would no more have dreamed of speaking to a scruffy lad like this than he would have thought of flying to the moon. He was the sort of person to avoid for fear of being mugged. At best, he looked like one of the beggars in the London streets. Philip sometimes tossed coins into their caps or bowls; more often he walked past, deciding they had wished themselves into this condition. He'd done that: he'd run off, of his own free will, and now he was a destitute person. Here was, presumably, another.

'I've got some bananas, too,' said Philip. 'Have one of those, if you'd prefer it.'

'Ta,' said Denis.

They sat there munching in companionable silence. Two cabin cruisers chugged past, their occupants enjoying a last autumn weekend on the river.

'Must be great on one of them boats,' said Denis.

'Yes,' agreed Philip, who had once spent a holiday on the Norfolk Broads in such a vessel when the children were quite young.

'Come far?' asked Denis.

'Yes. A long way,' Philip said. He had come a great distance, not only in miles but in perceptions and experience. 'And you?'

'Yeah. From London,' Denis said. 'I don't know if

I'll stay, though. What's this place called? D'you know?'

'Darsingford,' said Philip.

'Oh.' Denis frowned. He'd heard that name before.

'How did you get here?' Philip asked, genuinely interested. Then he thought perhaps he should not have asked: there might well be some code among tramps and down-and-outs, a moratorium on curiosity.

But the lad did not seem to mind. He must be around Andrew's age, or somewhat younger, Philip thought, as Denis answered.

'I came with some mates. They went back and I didn't,' Denis told him.

'Oh.'

'We were in this wood,' said Denis, suddenly confidential. 'It was great.'

What was? The wood, or what went on there? Was he part of some cult?

'There were these dogs, see. They was going to catch a fox if they could find one. I suppose it's cruel, really,' he added, thoughtfully. 'But it didn't seem like that.'

He'd come with hunt saboteurs, Philip realised. He had no opinion in this dispute; an urban man, he lacked knowledge of country ways, but if hunting was banned, what about shooting and fishing? And what about all the associated jobs and businesses?

'Where did you spend the night?' he asked.

Denis told him about the car.

Two weeks ago, Philip would have been deeply shocked and disapproving. Now, he felt admiration for the boy's nerve.

'I've got some money, though,' Denis could not avoid boasting. 'I had a bit of luck,' he added.

Philip was not going to enquire into the nature of this piece of good fortune.

'That's good,' he said. 'Are you going back to London?'

'Not yet,' said Denis. 'I'd thought of camping in the wood, just for a bit. It's not far away. I came in on a bus.' He couldn't remember what the place was called, where he'd picked up the purse. CH something, it was, like chips. He could recognise that word.

'Got a tent?' asked Philip.

'No. I could make a hut, with branches,' Denis said.

'Be a bit chilly. The nights are cold now.'

'I could make a fire. Cook sausages and stuff.'

'People would see the smoke and come and shift you,' Philip said.

'People always mess things,' said Denis. 'Where did you spend the night, then?'

Philip told him.

'I had a wash in the public toilet,' he said. It hadn't been too wonderful. Some drunken citizens had left their marks there, all too noticeably.

'What are you going to do today, then?' Denis asked.

'I don't know,' said Philip. 'Everything's shut, or nearly everything. I want to get a job. I was going to look for advertisements in shop windows. Newsagents usually have them.' He'd seen some in the supermarket, too, but hadn't stopped to study them. 'I got some gardening yesterday,' he added proudly. 'Made ten pounds.'

Perhaps he shouldn't have said that. The lad might try to take it from him.

But Denis said, 'Great. That must be quite good. Gardening. It's in the space.'

What an odd remark, thought Philip.

'That's true,' he said. 'There's not a lot of it to do in winter, though. We're lucky that the weather's good at present.'

'Yeah. It is nice, isn't it?' said Denis. 'You don't see it in the city. The weather.'

'I suppose not.' Philip stood up. 'I'm moving on,' he said.

'Mind if I come with you to look at them adverts?' Denis asked. 'I might try for something, too.' This guy would read them out to him.

'Good idea,' said Philip. Then he smiled and held out his hand. 'I'm Phil,' he added. 'What's your name?'

Denis told him, as they both shook hands.

10

'NOT MUCH GOING on, is there?' Denis said, as they walked back into the town.

'Well, it's just a country town,' said Philip. 'It must have been built here because of a shallow place where you could cross the river easily. A ford. That's how it got it's name. There are other towns named like that – Oxford, for instance. Cross on foot, I mean,' he added, seeing Denis looking puzzled.

'Oh.'

There were more people about now and the traffic was increasing. The river was busier; a few boats were still available for hire and were being rowed downstream past them as they approached the bridge. There was a family group, the father, and the son, aged about twelve, manful at the oars, the mother steering and a small girl in the bow trailing her hands in water that must, Philip thought, be rather cold. Denis watched them, amazed. Lucky sods.

'Nice way to spend a fine Sunday,' said Philip.

'Suppose it costs a lot,' said Denis.

'I've no idea how much it is,' said Philip.

They went on, at length reaching the supermarket where a notice in the window said that shelf packers were required. Philip took a pencil and diary out of his pocket and wrote down the details, with the telephone number. Denis was staring at the notice, trying to make out the words that Philip had just read.

'Let's try the newsagent,' Philip said. 'There might be more to chose from, there.' There might be rooms to let, as well. He wondered if there was a Darsingford local paper; probably there was, and it would have details both of jobs and lodgings.

They made their way along the pavement where by now there were enough pedestrians to force them sometimes into single file. Philip caught sight of their reflection in the large plate-glass window of a shop selling furniture. He could barely recognise himself: the thick donkey jacket made him look almost sturdy. His hair seemed to have grown a lot and developed strong curls, and his beard was quite respectable. It needed neatening up, he thought: or should he let it flow, become like Edward Lear's? The disguise would be complete, but would a prospective employer be put off? Beside him was the scraggy figure of the youth: Denis's legs were spindle-thin in the tattered, faded jeans. His trainers were cracked and splitting; they must let in the wet. His anorak must once have been a warm beige colour but now it was stained and faded. He loped along, his face thin and pointed, fair wispy hair on end, his feeble stubble gleaming in the sun. How different he would look cleaned up and given fresh clothes, thought Philip, so used to inspecting junior staff.

The newsagent's was closed now. Its door was full of cards and the two stood looking at them, Denis baffled, Philip scanning them swiftly. One sounded dubious: French lessons given by genuine French-woman, ring after 5 p.m. Then he remembered that this was Darsingford; she might really be a teacher, not a prostitute. He pointed to a postcard.

'That looks possible, for me. Or for you,' Philip added generously. 'I expect you can drive.'

'Yeah,' said Denis, and added, 'But I haven't got a licence. Which one d'you mean?'

'That one.' Philip gestured at a card. It said that a van driver was required, clean licence. Otherwise, apart from a telephone number, there were no details.

Denis stared at where his finger pointed. He tried to spell the words out, then turned away quickly, lest Philip realise his inability to make it out.

'Yeah,' he said.

'There's one for you, if you'd got a car or motor-bike,' Philip said. 'Look.'

Once again, Denis concentrated on the card he indicated.

'I can't work out the writing,' he prevaricated.

'Pizza deliverer required. Own transport needed,'

Philip read aloud. The message was not typed, that was true; it was, however, very clearly printed. 'Good pay and mileage allowance,' he added. Denis watched the words as he read them, trying to take them in. Phil went too fast for him. He could pick out the D – his own name began with that. He looked for E, and the other letters in it and found them all. That made him smile.

Philip was watching him. The boy couldn't read, or not properly. You heard about adult illiteracy; here it was, right in front of him. Poor kid. He read out several other advertisements, slowly, a finger on each word as he repeated it. Cleaners were wanted; items were for sale. Philip wrote down the telephone number where the van driver was required.

'I'll try it in the morning,' he told Denis.

'Try it now,' said Denis.

'But it's Sunday. There'll be no one there.'

'You can't know that till you try,' said Denis, quoting a favourite phrase of Biff's.

'That's true. All right. I'll do it,' Philip said.

They walked on until they found a public telephone. It needed a phone card, but Philip had one in his wallet. He had always kept one for emergencies.

To his astonishment, the number answered, and he came away having arranged to be interviewed later in the day.

'The man needs a driver as he's lost his licence.' Philip was almost chuckling. 'He's desperate! I must clean myself up a bit, Denis. I need somewhere better than those public toilets near the bridge.'

'Try a pub,' said Denis. 'Best buy a drink, of course.'

'Good idea,' said Philip. 'You coming?'

'Sure,' said Denis.

Philip bought them each a lager from his tenner of the previous day. He drank half his, then went to the cloakroom, which wasn't wonderful but at least had hot and cold water, and some paper towels. He'd chosen, in the end, the public bar of the two-star hotel, adopting a bold demeanour as he entered, since they were a pair of down-market customers. They attracted some curious glances but the Sunday drinkers soon lost interest. Philip returned with slicked-down hair and a shining face, and wearing his clean underclothes and socks: amazing what it did for you.

'You could do with a wash too, Denis,' he told his companion.

Denis went meekly off. He needed the toilet, but hadn't thought of washing. He did, though, since it seemed to mean a lot to Phil.

While he was gone, Philip had thought of walking out and leaving him. How else was he to shed the youth? Then he remembered that Denis had offered him the crisps. He stayed.

The pub was warm and full of noise, the customers mostly couples in their thirties and forties, but some men on their own. Philip watched them while he waited. What about their Sunday lunch? Had they given up the habit, as so many people had? He and Lesley had maintained it; she was a good cook and it was a time when all of them met round the table and could talk. But had they communicated? These people in the pub were talking, but were they getting through to one another? If he and Lesley had really been in touch, would she have lost faith in him?

Denis was not gone long. He reappeared with a clean face and still grubby hands. The dirt in them seemed to be ingrained; his nails were bitten and he had a crooked finger on his left hand. He looked so pale, his pallor pocked with small outcrops of acne. The country air down here would do him good, thought Philip, as they left the hotel.

Philip's interview was at an address to the south of the town. He had tried to take in the directions he had been given on the telephone but was none too clear about where he had to go after he had crossed the river.

'I'll ask someone when I get near,' he told Denis. 'Right, then. Goodbye, Denis. Good luck.'

'Hope you get the job, mate,' Denis said.

Watching the older man walk away, he felt suddenly bereft. It had been good, the last few hours, going round with Phil. For an old bloke, he was all right. If he hung about, they might meet again later; Phil could do with a bit of help over finding a place to doss down in, if he didn't get the job.

After a while, Denis decided to follow him.

* * *

Crossing the bridge, Philip wondered if he should have changed into his trench-coat, then decided that a potential van driver should project a rugged image; his new beard and longer hair fitted in with this type-casting. For over twenty years he'd been a suited citizen; perhaps it was time for a change.

What would Denis do now? Would he stay in Darsingford, where there couldn't be much going on that would appeal to him, or would he decide to head back to London? He'd get a lift eventually: you did, if you waited long enough; Philip had learned that. What chance had the boy got? He had probably never had a job. He seemed taken with the great outdoors: in other circumstances and in an earlier generation he could have found employment on the land. Civilisation, with its so-called blessings and its labour-saving devices, had not contributed all that much to human happiness, Philip decided, marching stoutly onwards on the main road, which he had been told to follow until he met a roundabout where he must turn left. He followed these instructions, continuing along this lesser, residential road until he came to a park, and here he had to turn right. Fortunately, he remembered what he had been told about the route and soon he found himself in Wilton Road, where the advertiser lived in Number Twenty-Three.

He found the house, a thirties semi-detached set well back from the road behind a privet hedge.

Philip took a deep breath, walked up the path and rang the bell.

* * *

Denis kept Philip's tall, thin form in view. The bulky jacket gave him breadth, but he was not a powerful man. Denis did not wonder why he was on his own and sleeping rough; you met all sorts on the streets and it was better not to be too curious. Bad luck could hit anyone. He might have been inside; that was the most likely reason for him to be wandering about, without work. An educated man like Phil ought to be able to get a job if he really tried.

When he turned off the main road something struck Denis as familiar, but he couldn't have been here before, could he? He walked on, and saw the park, and Philip far ahead of him. Denis had been to so few places in his life that it wasn't difficult to eliminate possibilities as he ran them through his mind. Was this the town where he had come with Biff and Tessa, and Orlando? He hadn't recognised it yesterday, but then they had only driven to the house Tessa hit, and away again.

He saw Philip cross the road and turn right. Denis, hanging back, did the same. It was the place where Tessa had fired the shots. They'd waited for her here, by this junction, looking out towards the park. He was sure of it: it was weird.

Well, so what? Philip wasn't going into the same house; he'd already walked past the one where Tessa had carried out her mission.

Denis didn't, though. He walked right up to the front door and rang the bell. He'd say that it was

Sunday and had they been to church? Had they been saved? He had. Biff had tried this ruse several times, he'd told Denis, and had been rudely told to go away on two occasions, but once, it had worked well. He'd got into the house, asked for a glass of water, and while it was fetched, lifted some useful stuff. All you needed was a story to get you to the door. Another trick was to have a few bits and pieces for sale: tat picked up in a market. Proper pedlars had licences; a householder might ask to see one, but that didn't matter because the trick had served its purpose and you'd discovered that someone was at home. Those who asked were capable of ringing the police, so it was best to move on if that was your reception. If the house was empty, you could look for a way to enter.

When Denis rang the bell, he had his story ready. He adopted a meek expression, glad now that he had washed earlier, though you didn't have to be clean to be religious. There was some noise behind the door, and he heard a man's voice. It was too late to flee; he stood ready to brazen it out.

On the chain, the door was opened, and he faced Guy Frost, who had had a peephole fitted and unless the person on the step was recognised, insisted that the chain be used.

Denis saw a thickset, balding man. He wore spectacles with metal rims, and had very strongly marked eyebrows. Guy, in his turn, saw a grubby spindly youth who looked nervous.

Denis went immediately into his spiel about

Sunday but Guy cut him short.

'Go away at once or I'll telephone the police,' he said curtly, and banged the door shut.

Biff would have been angry at such a hostile response, and on his way out might have uprooted a plant or done some other minor damage, but Denis, made of frailer stuff, merely shrugged and went away.

Guy telephoned the police, however. The slightest suspicious incident must be reported. The young man had been alone, when most proselytisers came in twos and threes; he'd held no book nor pack of texts, and though he'd fastened an ingenuous gaze on Guy, he hadn't looked quite honest.

Denis didn't hang about; he knew when he'd been sussed. He hurried back the way he'd come, and went into the park. He was sitting on a bench there when a police car drove past. He hoped the fuzz wouldn't stop Philip and ask him questions; Denis didn't think he'd be very pleased.

He waited quite a while before returning to the centre of the town. He'd blown it, and he'd never know, now, if Phil had got the job.

11

ORLANDO **WAS VERY** worried by Tessa's action against the scientist, and he was afraid the police might trace them. That would be so dreadful. Quite apart from being arrested, tried, and even sent to prison, the disgrace would be a nightmare. He'd lose his job, and wouldn't Tessa be struck off, or whatever happened to law-breaking lawyers? And what about her father, an enlightened judge who tried, when not tied up by coils of legal string, to fit the sentence to the crime? How would he survive the notoriety of his daughter's trial?

Tessa was sure they wouldn't be caught. When they met, she refused to talk about it. They'd been on no more raids since then, not even demonstrations organised by recognised protestors. Orlando was thankful. It was wise to lie low for a while. This meant, however, that he saw much less of her because she didn't need him or the recruits he drummed up to add muscle to their exploits. Why did she want them, though? Biff, it was true, had gone with her to reconnoitre on that trip to Darsingford, but the two of them could have done it on their own: why Biff? Perhaps she knew that he, Orlando, would have tried to talk her out of the domestic part of the escapade, and it was true that several people spraying walls were more effective than only one or two. Tessa hadn't done any actual spraying and Biff had lobbed the petrol bombs over the wall. Maybe she was hedging her bets. None of the other four had any idea who Tessa really was; they knew only her first name. They had, however, seen her car.

He fretted about her. To take his mind off this preoccupation, Orlando had begun to persecute Mrs Sandra White, the unnamed false accuser of the unfortunate Philip Winter who had gone missing. The man's disappearance had sparked off this plan. Poor guy, it could have been the fate of any man who misread the signals. He wouldn't put it past Tessa, if she found her private space threatened, to do the same. But no; she would scorn such conduct. Tessa would never let such a situation develop. It would be a reckless man who tried anything on with Tessa without making sure his attentions were welcome. Orlando could never understand why she sometimes favoured him; maybe it was pity, because she knew he loved her so desperately. In her kinder moods, no one could be sweeter; she was much respected in her firm, and popular.

Though they'd met Biff together, on a demonstration at the docks, she'd never asked how Orlando had acquired the rest of the team. He'd discovered Jet one day when killing time in a bar in Covent Garden. He was going, on his own, to a concert. Orlando had a wide casual acquaintance among patrons of various bars in the area, but he was not part of any close, involved group. Standing alone, he saw a thin, dark girl, also alone, who was approached by a big blond man, a broker Orlando knew by sight. The man had begun talking to her, pinning her against a pillar. Jet had replied brusquely, turning her head away, but the man had been persistent, moving nearer, closing her line of retreat. Orlando had stepped forward. Physically, he was no match for the broker, who could have floored him with one blow, but in his own way, Orlando was a smooth operator.

'Ah – there you are, Jet,' he said, coming round behind the broker to Jet's side. He beamed at her. 'Sorry – I couldn't see you in this crowd. You must have wondered if I'd stood you up – as if I would! Have you got a drink?' She had. She was holding a glass which turned out to contain apple juice. 'Excuse me,' he addressed the broker. 'Do you mind?' and he elbowed the man aside.

The broker, scowling, moved away, and Orlando, pleased at his success, was also embarrassed, ready for tough talk from Jet, because some girls – like Tessa – wouldn't thank you for a rescue, saying they could handle the situation themselves. This one, though, had looked apprehensive, and she was so small.

And she was grateful.

'Thanks very much,' she said, and smiled. 'Why did you call me Jet?'

'Well, I was pretending we had a date, and I thought saying darling might seem presumptuous,' he said. 'Your hair's so gorgeous, just like jet,' he added, to explain. 'The name came to me in a flash.'

'Felicitous,' she suggested, and he agreed.

'I don't suppose it is your name,' he said.

'No, it's not,' she said. 'But you can use it.' She didn't tell him what her real name was. 'I am waiting for someone,' she went on. 'And he's late.'

'I'll stay with you until he arrives, then,' said Orlando. 'If that's all right?'

'I'd be glad,' she said.

He thought that she was pretty, and her thick, shining hair, cut to just below her ears, was beautiful. He hoped her expected date would fail to arrive. At that moment, Orlando was prepared to abandon his concert and risk inviting her to dinner, but then Steven appeared, a pale, thin lad looking just like many others you saw around. It seemed that they were students.

After that, returning to the bar once or twice a week, Orlando ran into them again and several times bought them dinner. Most students were hard-up, and these two displayed endearingly hearty appetites. When Tessa required extra recruits, he asked them what they felt about imperilled wildlife, and had no difficulty in transforming their vague views into firm belief in the justice of the cause. The chance of spending a day together at no cost, and, in fact, being paid, completed their conversion. Soon Jet developed real enthusiasm, shouting slogans and brandishing banners; Steven caught fire from her, yelling loudly and waving his fist. Orlando thought that these two had developed into the most dedicated of them all, not excepting Tessa, and they went on other demonstrations, ones not patronised by either Tessa or Orlando. He began to wonder if they were becoming excited by the event as much as by the cause. Reasons could be blurred. He, for instance, used any excuse to pursue Tessa.

Pestering Mrs Sandra White made an excellent diversion, and he was grateful that he had learned her identity so easily. He would have tracked her down, even if it meant telephoning every S. White in London – quite a task – but Tessa had simply handed him the information. He wrote her several letters, and delivered one in person to the block of flats. It was a good address; she must be comfortably off.

He'd asked Tessa what she thought about the case.

'The man couldn't have scored. She wouldn't have waited before complaining,' Tessa said. 'There'd have been definite evidence. She could have scratched his face when he turned her down, as he said had happened.'

'Doesn't a man also have the right to say no?' asked Orlando, and at that Tessa had laughed and, to his delighted astonishment, had kissed him.

'Do you want to say no now?' she'd asked.

'My God, no! I mean, no, I don't want to,' he'd replied, but even as he banished all his caution, he recognised that Tessa was capable of turning this situation around in a sudden change of mood and making it seem quite different. She was hardly a tranquil companion. Wherever had she got this wild side of her nature from?

He ordered a pizza for Mrs White, saying she would pay on delivery. He used a public call box, and watched the delivery arrive. In the end she paid, to get rid of the unpleasantness, coming down to the main front door to do so. He saw her then. He would recognise her now.

Sandra herself did not connect the false order with the newspaper cuttings and some anonymous letters she had received. It was only when further incidents occurred that she began to take the matter seriously.

Seeing her, putting a face to the woman who had been vicious enough to bring down a harmless, if ingenuous man, spurred Orlando on to further efforts. Devising them stopped him brooding about Tessa, or growing bored. The woman, seen in the lighting from a street lamp, was quite tall; she had dark hair, and was slim, in a black skirt and high-heeled shoes, and a black sweater. Orlando had waited not too far away, standing near a bus stop; he pretended to be looking at his evening paper.

He sent her some old, stale cod, wrapped in layers of clingfilm inside a padded bag. He posted it from a post office in the country, where he had gone to spend a weekend with a couple he had known since university. By the time it reached her, it was stinking, but she had to unwrap the outer covering to find that out. His next gambit was to telephone the electricity board, reporting a fault with the cooker, arranging for someone to come and mend it. He simply hoped she would be in when the fitter arrived; if not, at least she'd have the bother of his card to deal with, and his follow-up, assuming there would be one. He spent long periods of time trying to arrange new torments. He filled in advertisement coupons with her name and address so that brochures on every conceivable subject would arrive for her. Some of the products covered were of a nature to embarrass her. He chuckled, completing those.

His most ambitious scheme was sending her tickets to a city dinner which he was attending and at which, miraculously, Tessa had agreed to be his partner. He photocopied the invitation, deleting his own name, traced it on to a piece of heavy gilt-edged card which he bought at an art shop, then painstakingly inked it over. It was not embossed, but it might deceive her. He wrote her name on it – Mrs Sandra White and partner – in italic script.

He couldn't loiter at the entrance to the city hall where the dinner was taking place, though he would have liked to witness her reception, if she turned up, but he did hear later that a couple had arrived who were not on the guest list. Orlando did not know that Sandra White had hired her partner from an escort agency, and had had to pay him as well as suffer the embarrassment of being denied admittance.

After this, Sandra realised that she was the subject of a vendetta. Who could be doing this to her? Who was playing all these tricks? The fish wrappings had been thrown away — the smell seemed to cling to her hands for hours, no matter how often and how thoroughly she washed them — but she kept the letters.

Orlando had started to follow her — not frequently, for he had very little opportunity in the working week — but he began on a Saturday when he had nothing planned. He decided to wait outside her block of flats for half an hour or so, to see if she emerged. If she did, he'd pursue her.

He could hardly believe it when the big door opened and she came out. Now, in daylight, he could see her much more clearly. She wore a suede coat and had on high-heeled boots. He followed her as she stepped aboard a bus.

She left after only a few stops, and went into Lavery's, the very store where Philip Winter had worked. There, she sauntered through various sections, and, in the glass and china department, examined several bowls and vases. Orlando started looking at them too, and when she took a cut-glass bowl to the pay desk, he selected a small pottery vase that was not expensive, and lined up behind her. He'd use cash. He didn't want to leave a trail. The vase was nice enough to give someone for Christmas, which was not far off now; the store was very busy with people buying presents.

An assistant who knew nothing about her story served Mrs White. The next customer seemed to be chafing with impatience while his purchase was wrapped, but the salesman scarcely noticed his appearance.

Orlando caught up with Sandra as she wandered through soft furnishings; she eyed curtain fabric, studied bedspreads, and moved on to towels and bath accessories. He tried to think of a way to humiliate her in the store without discovery, but there would be surveillance cameras watching everyone, and the two of them were doubtless already captured on tape. Annoying someone anonymously was challenging. It was just as well, for the sake of the innocent. But she wasn't innocent; he was sure of it. Here was a woman who was in charge of her own life, confident and assured.

What if he got to know her? Suppose he somehow contrived to talk to her – pick her up – get friendly? Could he lead her on to make an approach to him and catch her out? That was entrapment, wasn't it? Sometimes it was a questionable ploy, but it could be justified. What could he do with the evidence, if he obtained it? He couldn't sue her; that would be too costly, but he'd have a defence if she accused him of rape.

He thought about it, following her out of the shop. She walked down the street, turned a corner, and went into a small new restaurant which was popular among the women with whom Sandra played bridge two afternoons a week. At weekends they were often busy with their families, and she had time to fill. She would go to the cinema, or to a theatre matinée, and occasionally to a gallery or on excursions to stately homes or gardens, always seeking company, but, too intense, she ran through so-called friends fast. They dropped her. Only the bridge club remained constant because she played well, and when it was her turn to be hostess, the refreshments she supplied were excellent.

These women knew nothing about her appearance in court. They wondered why she had no career. They were older than Sandra, with husbands near retirement, and all had interests outside their homes. If she did not need a salary, she had energy and time to work in some constructive way, maybe for a charity, they thought.

Apart from their bridge games, Sandra never met them, though she knew they saw each other. She had been drawn into the group when one member moved to Norfolk. Sandra had met another on a bridge weekend at a country hotel, and thus was asked to join.

She hoped she might run into an acquaintance at the restaurant. Sandra was very lonely.

She was bitter, too: her husband's abandonment of her in favour of a typist from his office had humiliated her. He had two children now and lived in Sussex. She'd made him pay in terms of cash, and as long as she was single and not earning, he would have to go on supporting her in considerable style. Such were the terms of her settlement.

Orlando knew none of this as he followed her into the restaurant, which was run by an Italian family but provided an eclectic menu. He wondered if she was meeting someone, but when he was shown to a table in a dark corner, he looked across the room and saw her sitting at another set for one. A half bottle of white wine appeared before her very swiftly, and he decided she was a regular customer; she was treated with some deference and he thought she must be a good tipper, but changed this opinion when she called the head waiter over and made some point about her first course. It looked like Parma ham; how could that be faulty? He decided she was an imperious person who could cause trouble if her every whim was not gratified.

Halfway through the main course she glanced at him, and, when he did not immediately look away, she held his gaze. Orlando felt a frisson, not of sexual excitement but of something more like his emotions when going on a raid with Tessa: half fear, half thrill. He let himself meet her glance a second time and then, with an insouciance he could never summon when he was with Tessa, he raised his glass in silent toast, expecting her to frown and turn away. To his astonishment, she responded, raising her glass and tossing her head almost flirtatiously.

Because he knew her history, he felt disgust: but wasn't this evidence that, like a spider, she was capable of luring the unfortunate Philip Winter into her web, ready for the kill?

She did not know that he, Orlando, was responsible for the recent irritations which had come her way. The knowledge gave him pleasure.

He finished his meal before she did, and left, not wanting her to think he would be easily ensnared. Next time, she would be the victim.

Orlando had not seen any of his team since the episode in Darsingford. He missed Jet and Steven. His means of communicating with them was imprecise; after each encounter they had either arranged to meet at a pub, or Jet had telephoned him. He knew their full names now, however, and their addresses in term-time. In return, he'd told them his, and truthfully, though this was contrary to Tessa's rules.

'If they don't know who we are, they can't cause us any future trouble,' she had said, but Orlando thought the young people risked more than he and Tessa; Biff and the new recruit, Denis, were likely to be known to the police, though probably Jet and Steven had blameless pasts.

Having fixed, with a different pizza company, for Mrs Sandra White to receive another order, Orlando sent a note to Jet, saying that in two days' time he would be in the bar where they had originally met at six o'clock, and hoped that she and Steve might be there too.

On the way, he met Biff who was begging in a subway. Orlando stopped. He couldn't walk right past.

'Hi there, Biff,' he said. 'How's everything?'

Biff, who was sitting cross-legged on the ground, looked up and shrugged. He indicated an upturned cap in which there were a few small coins.

'Not good, squire,' he said. He'd started calling Orlando 'squire' as a joke and the habit had stuck.

Orlando fumbled in his wallet and found a ten-pound note. Silently, he dropped it in the cap and, also silently, Biff palmed it and transferred it to his pocket.

'How's Denis?' asked Orlando.

'All right,' said Biff, lying, for he did not know. He'd worried a bit about Denis, when he wasn't in the minibus after the hunt saboteurs' expedition. Still, he'd thumb a ride back. After such a day, begging was dull, but as a rule he did quite well. His cheerful, if grubby, round face and large brown eyes appealed to passers by. Biff never intimidated them; that wasn't his tactic.

He'd been thinking of looking for Orlando. He knew his mobile phone telephone number, for Orlando had had to open up some line of communication and he could not rely on finding Biff.

Now, Biff got to his feet.

'Seen Tessa lately?' he asked. 'She got any plans for the weekend?'

'Not that I know of,' said Orlando.

'She's great,' said Biff, and his face took on a knowing expression. A smile curved his mouth under his scruffy unshaven upper lip, and the word lascivious came, unbidden, into Orlando's mind.

She wouldn't, he thought, genuinely shocked.

He remembered how he and the three others had been sent on a long walk while she and Biff went off alone. She could have, and she might: anything for a buzz.

'Yes, she is,' he agreed, in despair.

'We might do one of them farms,' said Biff. 'Where they take those little calves from, scarcely dry from their mother's innards. Cruel, it is.'

'I'll tell her you suggested it, when I see her,' said Orlando. 'Cheers,' and he walked on. Tessa carried out her wilder deeds for kicks; he went with her because he was in love with her. Biff came for the ride and the money pay-off; probably only Jet and Steve came from conviction, he reflected.

Why did he bother with Tessa, Orlando asked himself, standing on the escalator. There was no future in it; she'd toss him aside as easily as she had shot those rabbits. Yet she fascinated him, as a snake is fascinating. She was wonderful in bed and that was part of it; she even made him feel that he was special then, when he knew that he was a very ordinary man, competent at his job but no more, nothing much to write home about. If they were to marry, he would never know a moment's peace for fear of what she might be up to, but think of the delights that there would be!

Sitting in the train, he pictured children, dim figures flitting across the lawn of the judicial garden, with James and Millicent fond presences in the background, but where was his place in this idyllic scene? And where was Tessa?

She'd have no children; not his, not anyone's. He had a sudden intense feeling of impending doom, but dismissed it as caused by jealousy because he knew that Biff and Tessa had had it off together. His mind raced on. Did Biff do drugs? Orlando knew that he mixed with criminals. Needles, he thought: shared ones. Aids.

He shut his mind down on that possibility, stepping from the Tube. He'd think about Sandra White instead.

If he caught Aids from Tessa, could he pass it on to Sandra White? That would be a fine revenge, he thought. Perhaps he should try to pick her up, become overtly friendly with her, prepare the ground. She'd almost given him a signal in the restaurant, and if Philip Winter's story was true, she wouldn't need much wooing; she was a nymphomaniac.

Meanwhile, he'd made out an interesting advertisement for her, a business card he'd had done at one of those machines where they could be printed instantly.

Madame Sandra, it said, in Gothic script, and ran on to offer:

Interesting massage. All tastes, followed by her telephone number.

That was all: it was enigmatic. She'd get enough calls to be a serious nuisance. He'd stuck the cards in telephone booths and in various public lavatories, always taking care that no one saw him. He was not going to risk shop windows or newspapers, where they might question his identity. He sent them, also, to a number of men who advertised in Lonely Hearts columns. A few might bite.

Neither Steve nor Jet turned up at the bar. Disappointed, and lonely himself, Orlando went to the cinema, then home to bed. He dreamed, surprisingly, of Jet. She was screaming, pleading to be saved from some black horror that was threatening her. He woke without discovering what it was.

12

SANDRA WHITE WAS a very angry woman. Several unordered pizza deliveries had been made to her flat, and now she was receiving junk mail by the bundle. Brochures she had never sent for arrived daily; they advertised all sorts of goods from holidays to incontinence pads and contraception. She had written to the Mailing Preferences address, demanding that her name be withdrawn from any data base that could be providing it to companies, but still the brochures came, for Orlando filled in a new coupon almost daily.

Sandra tried to divert her mind from this nuisance by remembering the man she had seen in the restaurant. He had been quite nice-looking in an ordinary, mousey-haired, blue-eyed way, reasonably tall, and his casual dress was good. She knew that he had noticed her. Sandra wanted a lover, one she could control. She'd even thought of replying to some of the dating advertisements in a glossy paper, but so far an innate caution had prevented her. Besides, it would mean admitting that she had been unable to find a man another way. But how did you, these days? People did not ask her to parties, where she might meet an unattached male, and she shrank from going on holidays aimed at singles. She went to aerobics classes – all women – and had aroma-therapy, which was soothing, and there was her bridge. When nothing else offered, she read block-buster novels and wished that she was one of their successful women characters. She wanted power, and she had very little, except that she could make waiters, shop assistants and other inferior persons squirm.

Like that Philip Winter man. She had made him pay for his rejection of her. Now, it seemed, he'd drowned himself. Well, he was no great loss. She'd bought one of the tabloids when the story broke, and had read a sensationalised re-run of the trial. There were pictures of him and of the discontented-looking wife who had failed, it was implied, to offer him support. His family life was wrecked. So what, thought Sandra; he deserved it. She did not care if he were alive or dead: good riddance, for he had beaten her in court.

At first she hadn't meant to let it go so far, intending merely to get him into trouble at Lavery's, perhaps lose his job, because she did not want to see him there when she went shopping and she would not give up going to the store. Once started, however, the process had grown and grown, until she became elated at the lengths to which the man could be hounded down and, in the end, destroyed. The exhilaration of it had kept her going through the months before the case came to court.

They'd tried to dissuade her, of course: first the police and then her solicitor. They'd told her she'd be crucified. Well, they were wrong; it had not happened. It was Philip Winter who was pilloried, not her. She'd stood up to their questioning, implacable and cold. By paying Philip Winter out, she had avenged herself on other men who had failed her in her life, particularly her former husband.

It was some time before she began to wonder if Philip were still alive, and whether it was he who was subjecting her to all this harassment, and then she didn't think of this herself. She had notified the police after she had received more than thirty telephone calls which implied that she was a prostitute. The callers had even used her name.

'Have you any enemies?' she was asked. 'Someone with a grudge against you?'

But the police knew she had. They were the same officers who had investigated her rape charge. The problem was that it seemed her alleged attacker was now dead.

There were no clues to who was behind this present campaign. Sandra was able to name the last pizza firm, and the police said they would try to discover who had given the order, but were not optimistic. They'd be in touch, they said. Meanwhile, she should consider, if the trouble did not cease, changing her telephone number and going ex-directory.

Detective Sergeant Sykes, who had all along believed Philip Winter's story and had hoped the Crown Prosecution Service would decide not to pursue the case, was not too concerned about this new complaint. There was no proof that the woman was not orchestrating this herself in a plea for attention. She could have sent for the brochures, and she could be inventing her story about the telephone calls from punters. If her account were true, something would turn up; there would be further incidents, or more letters. She could have constructed those herself, and any future ones she might produce. With a suspect in mind, saliva on stamps could be tested. Philip Winter's DNA profile had not been needed, but it seemed unlikely that he had staged a disappearance simply in order to harass his accuser.

It could be the woman's former husband, of course, but why now, so long after they separated?

An officer went to see him in his large house in Sussex. When he heard the story, he laughed uproariously, even slapping his thigh with delight.

'Serve her right,' he said. He hadn't believed the rape allegation for a minute. Some poor guy had got across her and it was her revenge.

Orlando, ignorant of what she might be doing about his campaign, was sure that she would change her telephone number. He tried calling the old one and found it was not operating. That trick was one he wouldn't be able to repeat; he hoped it had caused her a great deal of irritation. No clients would have turned up on her doorstep; he hadn't given her address.

He went again to the restaurant where he had seen her eating on her own. Twice in the evening he failed to see her there, but the third time, on a Saturday at lunch-time, there she was. Perhaps she went there every week. She looked just as smart, and seemed just as poised, as on the previous occasion. He wasn't hurting her enough, he thought. She needed a more public humiliation. She'd utterly destroyed that unfortunate man, who was now lying dead somewhere, and what about his family? They'd lost their major earner. The daughter was still a schoolgirl and she'd been deprived of a father and of the father's good name.

Hunting Sandra White was more worthwhile than pursuing scientists and farmers, Orlando decided. How could he start talking to her?

But he didn't have to find a way, for she took the initiative, apparently recognising him when he was shown to a table near hers. For a wild moment, as she smiled at him, he wondered if she really was a tart, but surely that would have come out at the trial? Defence lawyers always tried to shred the rape victim's reputation. She might, he supposed, be a high-class hooker with a private clientele; she certainly seemed to have plenty of money.

She left the restaurant before he did, and, passing

near his table, dropped her purse.

Her purse! Wasn't that what she had left in the shop, for Philip Winter to retrieve? Had she done it on purpose then? He was sure it was intentional this time, for as he stopped to pick it up, though she was now by the door where the waiter was ready with her coat, she half turned, expectantly.

Orlando was already on his feet, bearing the purse before him, on his way to hand it back. It was an expensive one, made of tooled leather with her initials on it.

'Excuse me. I think this is yours,' he said.

'Oh – did I drop it? How very careless of me,' she said. 'Thank you so much,' and she smiled at him.

Close to, she looked older than he had first thought her. She wore a lot of eye make-up, and there was a small scar on one cheekbone. Did she get it in a fight? Orlando pulled himself together. This was his chance.

'Lucky it was here, not in the street,' he said, and tentatively smiled. He was, whilst pleased and excited, rather frightened. This was a terrifying woman who could eat your balls for breakfast, the sort he would never choose to tangle with in a thousand years. But he wasn't going to tangle with her: not like that, not intimately; only indirectly.

By now she was doing up her coat – a long black one with a velvet collar. He had none to collect, but he had to pay his bill. He paid cash, as he had done the last time; he did not want to leave a credit-card trail.

'No coat?' she asked, as the waiter, who had produced the check at a gesture, took his money.

'It's in my car,' he said.

'Oh? And where's that?'

'Just round the corner,' said Orlando. Then, riskily, he plunged. 'Are you going far? Can I help you on your way with a lift?'

'Oh, you are kind,' she said. 'I live about a mile away.'

He drove her, at her directions, to her door. Because it was a Saturday, there was space outside to park.

'Won't you come in?' she asked him, but he didn't dare. He might find himself in court before Tessa's father, on a charge of rape. Cravenly, he said he was going down to the country and must get on.

'Let me give you my card, then,' she said, and dipped into her handbag.

Sitting beside her, Orlando saw that its interior was extremely orderly. He thought of the handbags of other women he knew; most were too full and caused problems when they hunted for their keys. Hers was not the handbag of a woman who was careless with her purse. She withdrew a card from some section and gave it to him; then, confidently, she waited for him to get out of the driver's seat and open the passenger door for her. He did, of course.

He saw her long, slim legs emerge. She was quite sexy, he supposed, but she was frightening. Would he have thought that if he had not known her history?

She gave him a little wave before walking up the steps to the main door of her block and opening it. Orlando got back behind the wheel and glanced at the card. She'd crossed out her old telephone number and substituted the new one.

He couldn't use it to annoy her, though: she'd remember whom she'd told about the change. But she had given him some information on their short journey together. She'd said that she played bridge on Tuesday and Thursday afternoons, sometimes at home, sometimes with friends. If he followed her on one of these occasions, he would learn more of her habits and that could help him find a new way to inconvenience her.

He'd take time off to do it; he'd say he had to see his dentist.

Jet rang Orlando that evening.

She said she was sorry about not meeting him, but she and Steve had been to a rally and they were going on another demonstration the next day. Buses would take them to a port where lambs were loaded, live, for export. Would he like to join them?

He had nothing else to do. Tessa wouldn't ring him now, wanting to make a plan. He wondered how she was spending her weekend, and with whom. He agreed.

'What about Biff and Denis?' she asked him. 'Will they come? There's no money in it,' she added.

'If I can find them, I'll ask them,' Orlando said.

He'd take a turn around the streets where Biff often begged.

'Its awful, you know,' Jet said earnestly. 'They go for hours cooped up, with no food or water.'

'Yes, I know, Jet,' he agreed. 'I'll be there. I'll try and find the others.'

Looking for Biff would give him something to do. He'd go first to the subway where they'd met a few nights earlier, but he didn't know where Biff was living; he had a base somewhere, in a squat, Orlando thought, but no proper address. He might be hanging about hoping to touch the sympathies and pockets of club and theatre-goers. Orlando could ask other street characters if they'd seen him; many of them knew one another. He could suggest that if anyone saw Biff, they should ask him to call Orlando.

He saw no Biff, but he met a girl who knew him. She said she'd pass the message on. Orlando went back to his flat alone, opened a bottle of red wine and turned on the television while he drank it. There was nothing special on; he channel-hopped, and thought about the people in the streets. What a way to live! It was shameful that they had to; he understood that some of the young ones were trapped, with no means of support because they could not get either a job or state aid without an address. Some of them must have parents who were desperate to find them. Was it pride that stopped them going home? He knew there were charities which succeeded in helping many of them, but others fell through the net and took to prostitution, thieving, drugs. How did you subsist with absolutely no income whatsoever?

You begged, of course, and took what ever else came along.

On his fourth glass of wine, Orlando's thoughts turned towards himself. What was his aim? To be chairman of his or another firm? Not really. To marry Tessa? Not really that, either, because he knew it was impossible and would not work – yet if she were to suggest it, he would ecstatically agree. How could it be that in your head you could clearly know a certain course was the path to disaster, yet still follow it? Was it a sort of death wish?

His thoughts had reached this gloomy point when the telephone rang. It was Biff.

He agreed to come along the following day. He didn't know where Denis was just now, he added, so he'd bring a different friend, a girl, if she was free.

Well, now there was a plan for the next day.

Orlando, when the wine was finished, took himself off to bed.

What a pity I'm not power-mad at work, he thought; what a pity I lack drive and ambition, and, he feared, ability.

He might lose his job, because there were colleagues much abler than he was, and no one's post was safe. He might end up on the streets, like Biff.

Biff, unaccompanied despite his optimistic

declaration, had joined Jet at the meeting-place the next day by the time Orlando, in his drab demonstration garb, had arrived. Steven wasn't coming, Jet reported, giving no reason. They piled into the waiting coach and all sat together at the back, Jet in the corner by the window, Orlando next to her with Biff beside him. Orlando was missing Tessa. He had never been on a protest without her. Soon the bus filled up. There were a few students but some of the passengers were pale, angry-looking men and women, not particularly young, and they brought with them an atmosphere of hostility and almost, Orlando thought, aggression. He was sensitive to atmosphere and, in the office, caught mood swings by instinct. He felt uncomfortable in confrontational situations, favoured underdogs, but was no cavalier.

'How did you hear about this trip?' he asked Jet.

'At that rally I told you about,' she said. She glanced at him almost pleadingly. 'I thought it would be good,' she said.

'Well, it will be and it's a fine day,' he reassured her. 'We'll be at the seaside.'

'We won't see much of the sea,' said Jet. 'They're going to block the roads. Listen.'

The bus had moved off now, and a woman was explaining the plan. The battle plan, she called it. They would form a chain across the road to stop the lorries; several chosen operators would slash the lorry tyres, while others would crack windscreens. Local support would be out in force.

'But we're the commandos,' cried the leader.

Orlando knew that he should not be here. This wasn't his sort of scene at all, but nor could it be Jet's. He saw now that tears were rolling slowly down her cheeks.

'Why didn't Steve come?' he asked her.

'He decided not to,' she said. 'He didn't like that thing we did – you know, with Tessa.' She'd been unhappy about the attack at the house too, but, stubbornly, she had told Steve that sometimes harsh actions were necessary to get results.

'Oh dear,' Orlando said, inadequately. Obviously they'd quarrelled.

Jet went on crying for another mile or two, and Orlando produced a large and spotless handkerchief, which he passed to her. Jet, who had only a few crumpled tissues in her pocket, accepted it, wiped her eyes, and laughed.

'Just like in an old film,' she said, 'Thanks.'

She grew calmer then, while round them the other demonstrators got noisier.

'Don't worry, Jet,' said Orlando. 'We can always run away.'

He was becoming increasingly uneasy because of the mood developing inside the coach. A few individuals were, quite clearly, spoiling for a fight. This wouldn't be lawful protest; it was potential disaster. Biff was enjoying it, however. He'd brought some cans of beer; he'd had beer on the raid in Darsingford, Orlando remembered. Maybe including him wasn't such a brilliant idea after all.

Near the coast the weather deteriorated, and a fine rain began to fall. They left the coach in a side street in the town and were marshalled into a group to be addressed, through a loud hailer, by the woman who was so obviously their leader. Who had elected her, Orlando wondered: what organisation did she represent? She told them they would meet others in a few minutes. Lying down in the road to block the passage of the livestock was a passive way to protest. More active methods were up to the individual. They were to move off now, and join the rest of the protestors.

As they did so, carried along by the surge of those around them, Orlando saw that sticks and cudgels had appeared in various hands. His heart sank. Jet, however, had thrown off her earlier despair and was looking animated. She fell in beside a punk-like woman and a man with ringlets. They had begun shouting, and Jet joined in. Orlando heard cries of what sounded like 'Free God's creatures' but surely that couldn't be what they were yelling? He thought the mob was like the revolutionaries who shouted round the guillotine. The different contingents had now converged and there was a noisy crowd pressing towards the street leading to the docks. He saw Jet's woollen cap ahead of him and then she vanished. She was so small. Though height was not a common factor among the protestors, the human mass was great and Orlando felt alarm as the noise increased. He'd lost sight of Biff. With one of them on either side of her, Jet might have been protected, but it was too late for that. He pressed forward, elbowing people aside, trying to reach her bobbing dark green hat.

Suddenly the crowd halted and fanned across the street in a solid phalanx. Ahead, the first lorries were in sight and there was a rush towards them, but the police were there too, walking along beside the vehicles.

They did not stop the most determined demonstrators. Sticks and stones were thrown at windscreens; there were shouts, and more police appeared. They began dragging people away, and some protestors, triumphant at the chaos they had created, started lying down in the road. Others copied them as bleating sounds came from the trucks; through the sides of some of them, lambs could be seen, by now terrified.

Orlando, too, was afraid. The movement of the crowd was impossible to resist; unless you were on the fringe of it, you were carried along in a tide of bodies. Local residents had joined in; he saw elderly men and women lining the pavements. Soon they were swept along by the current of the crowd.

The lorries could no longer move. Resigned, the drivers switched off their engines as the police tried to clear a passage for them. More officers appeared and began bundling people off. Making themselves limp and heavy, the experienced protestors put on martyred looks and hoped their pictures would be in the papers.

No demonstration Orlando had gone to with

Tessa had ended in violence of this order. Sheer hate was manifest and it was not merely in defence of the livestock; this was hate for hatred's sake, hate for authority, defiance of the rule of law. Orlando did not approve of the sheep being transported, comfortless, for hours, and to a fate which ended in their death, but after all, they were bred for fodder; it was sentimental to think that but for this undertaking, they would have spent their lives gambolling about in verdant fields.

Then he saw Jet. Two policemen were carrying her away, and, impotent, Orlando saw her shut into a van.

Now, like the lambs, she was a prisoner, and he would have to rescue her.

But how? Should he get himself arrested, too? No, that was ridiculous. He'd go to the police station. Which one, though? She'd be entitled to a solicitor. He'd make sure she had one.

Tessa was a solicitor, but she wouldn't touch this.

Orlando turned aside from the sea of people. Once he'd managed to break through the barrier they formed, there was space and air, and the police did not pursue him because there were plenty of militant resisters to be dealt with.

A grey-haired woman was sitting on a doorstep nursing a cut knee. Orlando stopped beside her.

'Can I help?' he asked, solicitous, but Jet still had his once clean handkerchief. 'Shall I get an ambulance?'

'No – no. It's just a graze, and I'm a little shaken,' said the woman. 'Thank you, though.' She looked up at Orlando. 'What a dreadful day this is,' she said. 'I thought I was going to walk peaceably along, protesting at live exports, and it turned into a riot.'

'I thought much the same,' Orlando said. 'And the friend I came with has been arrested.'

'Oh dear!' The woman looked dismayed. 'Was he violent?'

'It's a girl,' Orlando said. 'And no, she couldn't have been. She's very small. I thought she might be trampled on. We got separated in the crowd. Were you alone?'

'No,' said the woman. 'My daughter's in there somewhere.'

'Perhaps she's been arrested too,' Orlando said. 'It's a bit indiscriminate. I suppose they're just dragging off whoever they can grab.' He looked at his new friend, who was now struggling to her feet. 'You ought to get that knee seen to,' he said.

'I'll wash it when I get home,' the woman answered. 'There's no need to bother a busy doctor with a trifle like this. You'd better go to the police station, if you want to find your friend.'

'But how will you get home?' Orlando asked.

'I came in my daughter's car,' the woman said. 'She left it in a multi-storey car park. Even if I could find it, I haven't got a key.'

'Is it far to where you live?'

'Two miles or so.'

'Maybe I could find a taxi for you,' said Orlando. 'Could you walk a little way, out of this area, to a place where we could phone for one?'

'But what about my daughter? She'll wonder where I am,' the woman said.

'Well, you'll be at home. She'll think of looking there eventually,' Orlando said. He was impatient to be rid of her, freed to go in search of Jet, but he couldn't just abandon her.

'I suppose you're right,' the woman said. 'Yes, I can walk, but not two miles. If you'd give me your arm.'

Limping, leaning on him, she guided him along the streets until they reached a wide square with a large church at one end and a hotel facing it.

'Let's go in there,' Orlando said. 'They'll ring for a cab.'

She looked at him.

'Have you any idea what you look like?' she said. 'They won't let you in. You're filthy.'

'Surely not?' Orlando had been clean and tidy when he started out, though it was true he had on what Tessa called his combat gear.

'They'll let you in,' he said. 'You're respectable, if wounded.' And she was; she wore a tweed coat, thick, though torn, ribbed tights, and sensible shoes with rubber soles.

'I'd rather try phoning for a taxi,' the woman said. 'There's a call box over there,' and she pointed.

Orlando's supply of phone cards, needed for the

harassment of Sandra White, was at home, with his wallet; he carried nothing on him which could reveal who he was, just some money in a pocket. This wasn't going to help Jet, if it came to bail, he realised. Then he saw a taxi, coming slowly up the road. He flagged it down. It had a passenger, but the driver stopped, and, on his radio, summoned another cab.

Orlando waited with her till it came, and she gave him a lift to the police station.

It was a long time before he was able to get Jet released. Because she was docile, weepy, and so small, they let her off without a charge, but she was cautioned.

They went back by train. Luckily Orlando had enough cash on him for their fare.

Jet told him that she thought she and Steve were finished now.

'But he was right,' she said. 'He said getting violent was wrong, and it is. Like today. And what Tessa did was awful.'

'No one got hurt then, though,' Orlando said, forgivingly.

'But they might have done. The rabbits died,' she said. 'They were shot.'

'I know. It was bad.' Orlando had to agree with her. He reminded himself that Jet knew nothing about Tessa apart from her first name, and he mustn't let slip any more information, in case Jet got an attack of conscience and went to the police.

Apart from Tessa herself, what about the judge? The tabloids would just love it.

'The animals suffered today, you know,' Jet said. 'The police were talking about it – I hadn't realised – they were going to be delayed so long, they'd be without food and water for an even longer time than if they'd gone straight through. I thought we were campaigning to ban cruelty to animals.'

'I think we were. You and I were,' said Orlando. 'And an old woman I met who'd got hurt in the scrimmage. But some other people weren't.'

What were they campaigning for, those others? Mob rule, or simply for the thrill of violent action?

When they returned to London, he put her in a taxi which would take her back to the flat she shared with other students.

'I hope you make it up with Steve,' he said. 'You must mind, or you wouldn't have cried.'

'I do mind,' Jet replied.

Things ended, though, he knew. Maybe they'd each reached the moment to let go.

He would with Tessa, one day; but he couldn't bear to think of it.

13

FRANCES DID NOT discover that she had been robbed until Monday morning. After clearing up Denis's muddy trail, and stoking her bonfire for the night, she had put her purse in her bag without opening it. He'd left the coins, and, never thinking, she did not notice it was slimmer than before. It still contained her credit cards and driving licence.

She had to go to Darsingford that morning, to the dentist. As she drove in, she thought about her daughter Arabella's various children, some of whom had stayed with her during the summer. They liked the order in her house. Meals were taken at set times, and the very few rules Frances imposed must be obeyed. She had bought two old bicycles which, if used, had to be maintained by their riders, who were obliged to say roughly where they were going, and approximately when they would be home. Games, such as Cheat, Rummy, Scrabble and Monopoly were played. At home, things ran to no particular schedule; everyone still at school could get there on foot or by local bus, and those who were hungry helped themselves to food. At weekends there were often brunch parties with other academic families, and some of the youngsters thrived on this, but Charlotte, Arabella's second daughter, who was rather shy, preferred routine. She had not visited her grandmother during this vacation, which was unusual, but she had been staying with a family in France.

After her session at the dentist's, Frances went into the supermarket, though Monday was not her normal day for shopping. It would save a trip later in the week. Chingbury no longer had a village shop; competition from the supermarkets, with their Sunday trading, had forced it to close, which was a sadness and a nuisance. The post office still clung on, selling minor items such as sweets and postcards, and hand-knitted goods made locally.

She wheeled her trolley round the shelves, stocking up today with cleaning items and other things she bought on a monthly basis. Then, when it was time to pay, she found there were no banknotes in her purse.

After her first instant's panic, she concluded that she must have left the money she had just cashed in a drawer, but she knew there had been other notes still in her purse; she wasn't down to nothing when she collected her two weeks' pension.

She hid her dismay. She had her bank card and her cheque book, so she could pay her bill, but as she left the shop, her mind squirrelled round the possibilities of what could have happened to her money. Sitting in the car, she checked her purse again. No, there was not a single note.

She'd have to go to the bank to get some more. Trying to keep calm, Frances put away her groceries, made sure her car was locked, then returned to the centre of the town. In the bank, she wrote a cheque and cashed it; luckily she had funds. Frances had a tight budget but she kept within it and had a nest-egg to fall back on in an emergency. After that, feeling slightly shaky, and with the injection the dentist had given her while he filled a tooth now wearing off, she went to Pandora's Box for a cup of coffee.

Drinking it, she ran over in her mind what her movements had been after visiting the post office. She'd come home and put her purse down on the table, then gone out to work in the garden. Normally, she cashed her pension on a Tuesday, but this week she had been to a lecture in Bristol and had left it, intending to postpone collecting it till the next week, but had run low in cash. As it happened, she had not needed any over the weekend. The travelling fishmonger had called on Friday night; that was before she'd got the money and anyway he was above suspicion; he had been coming regularly for years. She'd had no children in, washing the car; she'd had no one to the house at all. The purse, though, had lain on the kitchen table throughout Saturday and she had been in the garden for much of the day. The hunt had met in the village; someone following it might have walked in and helped himself. Or a saboteur. They'd been out in force, she'd heard from the Wares, whom she saw on Sunday. By then her purse was back inside her handbag.

She'd better report the theft to the police; other people might have been burgled, too.

She went to do it, before going home. They took down her statement, but were pessimistic about catching whoever was responsible, agreeing that it might have been a saboteur.

'Won't you come and test for fingerprints?' she asked.

They thought they could send someone round tomorrow or the next day, but there were other crimes to investigate: more important ones, was the inference.

'If he was a saboteur, he's miles away by now,' the desk sergeant told her, when she left.

She had to agree.

On Sunday afternoon she had been round to the Wares with some Michaelmas daisy roots she had divided the day before. She had promised to give them some varieties they had admired. When she arrived, she found Guy Frost's wife, Amanda, there. She had obviously been crying. Hugo bore Frances off, with the plants, to the garden, ostensibly to decide where to put them.

'Sorry – I've come at a bad time,' Frances said.

'You've rescued me,' said Hugo. 'I can't bear to

see a woman cry. Dorothy will calm her down.'

'What's the trouble?'

'It's that attack they had on Guy's workshed in the garden. Seems the children keep having nightmares imagining the new rabbits have been shot, and Amanda can't bear to look at the post in case there's a letter bomb.'

'Poor girl. It must be very difficult,' said Frances.

'Yes, I suppose it is,' the general allowed. 'The children, in particular, I can understand.'

'You're thinking she should pull herself together,' Frances deduced. 'People can't always manage it, Hugo. We're not all as brave as you.'

'I'm not brave,' the general said, but the decorations he had received proved otherwise. Courage, however, came in various forms and physical valour was his proven area. 'I'm a coward when it comes to problems,' he declared.

'What about Guy? They haven't come to grief over this, have they?' Frances asked.

'I don't think so, but a rough-looking lad came to the house this afternoon and Amanda took fright. Thought he was a vandal,' Hugo said. 'But he said he was some sort of evangelist. Guy didn't think he was genuine – he rang the police, but they couldn't find the fellow.'

'Oh dear!' said Frances.

'If he really was an evangelist, he'd have been calling at other doors,' said Hugo.

'You're right, of course, and Amanda knows that.'

'Yes. She's taken the children to her parents for a few days, but looking after them for more than a short time is too much for her mother, with her father failing.'

'Perhaps she'll bring them back after a little while on her own with Guy,' said Frances. 'They don't get much chance to be alone together.'

'I think she's more likely to move in with the parents too, from how the conversation was going,' Hugo said. 'I don't understand these things, but Dorothy does.'

'Leave it to her, then,' suggested Frances. 'How's the book coming on?'

'I'm stuck in Korea,' said the general, who had been there literally.

'Are you writing much about your brother?'

The general's brother had been taken prisoner after the fall of Singapore. He had survived, and rebuilt his health amazingly, but in his last years of life his war experiences had returned to haunt him with nightmares and he had wept over the fate of his lost comrades. Dorothy had told Frances that Hugo had recently had bad dreams about his battle campaigns. In those days there was no counselling; people just got on with it, without complaining.

'Yes, I am,' said the general. 'I'm amazed he made such a good physical recovery, but it was sad to see him experience it all again at the end.' He made no reference to his own reawakened memories.

Frances decided to keep him walking round the garden for as long as possible while Dorothy comforted Amanda, who was a friend of the Wares' daughter. Frances had grown very fond of the Wares, and, in turn, her self-sufficiency had impressed them. She was no clinger. The general had even said she would have made a good army wife, the highest form of praise he could bestow. Frances found him vulnerable and soft beneath his stern carapace. He had seen and experienced suffering. He knew the score.

'Guy can't give up,' she said. 'He mustn't let these people frighten him away.'

'They're cowards,' said the general fiercely, his thick grey eyebrows twitching. 'Attacking women and children.'

'They didn't fire the house, did they?' Frances pointed out. 'Just his workshop. Does – did he do much important work there?'

'I think he kept many of his records in the shed,' said the general. 'It meant he could do calculations and write reports at home. Of course the main tests, particularly those involving animals, have to be done at the centre. And it's heavily restricted. Nowadays no reputable scientist tests animals without good reason. It's all licensed and inspectors come around.'

'Life has become so precious, hasn't it?' said Frances. She bent to pick up a fallen chestnut leaf and inspected its faded tracery of veins. 'Death's the last enemy, which can't be defeated and must often be a welcome friend, seen from the patient's point of view.'

Hugo Ware did not want to accompany her down this avenue. Frances was a great one for dissection, but he thought some things were best left undisturbed.

'Guy built that workshop and worked there so that he could spend more time with Amanda and the children,' he said. 'Now it's rebounded on him.'

'Amanda can't want him to give up his post,' said Frances. 'That would mean surrendering to intimidation.'

'To be fair to them, some of the more reputable protest groups have denounced what happened,' Hugo said. 'This was some splinter movement, it seems. No one knows – or is saying – who they were. The youth who called on them today is probably up to no good, but not a terrorist. Guy was right to be suspicious, though. I suppose it was the last straw for Amanda.'

Now, a day later, discovering her burglary, Frances knew that it was illogical to connect the Frosts' visitor with either the hunt saboteurs or the theft at Badger's End, but someone had walked into her house and stolen from her. It could have happened at any time while she was busy in the garden.

It gave her a very nasty feeling. Here, in the country, she had felt safe, though it was true that a car had once been stolen from outside the only pub; vandalism and theft were rare in Chingbury.

She'd meant to have security lights fitted to the house; the Wares had got them and said that apart from the deterrent aspect, it was handy when you went out at night to have them come on automatically, though they were set off by passing cats.

After her coffee, she called at the electrical shop in the centre of the town to ask about them. She'd ring the electrician when she understood the choices available.

This research concluded, she went into the library. Though funding had been cut, it was still open every weekday.

A man sat at a table. He was going through advertisements in a newspaper. Frances noticed him only because he seemed so intent, and he was a stranger. She often ran into acquaintances here, and was always ready for a few minutes' conversation. It did not occur to her that she was lonely; she knew she was content and who could, or should, ask for more? The man had dark hair, greying round the edges; he'd taken off a donkey jacket which he had draped over the back of his chair, and the sweater he wore was a good, expensive one. Somehow it didn't go with the donkey jacket, although Frances wasn't really aware that this bothered her; it simply made her look at him more closely. As if he felt her stare, Philip looked up at her and she saw the short, new beard and soft moustache, but it was his haggard, exhausted face which really registered. She turned away, quite shaken. Whatever had gone wrong for him?

Reluctant to go home because her house had been invaded by a stranger, at last Frances could put it off no longer. Randomly choosing two biographies, she checked them out and left.

Philip had not got the driving job.

When he reached the advertiser's address, he discovered that there were two other applicants whom the man was already interviewing. One of them was known to him; Philip was not, and he could not offer a reference.

Walking away, he felt total despair. How was he going to earn money? He'd wasted the afternoon. He had lost Denis, though, and that was an advantage; alone, he might not be so good at surviving, but he stood more chance of getting a job than if he was followed by the shadow of the boy; after all, they were competing in the same narrow market, though Philip had the advantage of a clean driving licence.

He had nothing to do and nowhere to go, nothing even to read. No wonder layabout lads in cities got into trouble; he would be in trouble soon himself. As he had no address, he could not advertise his services. He'd been very lucky to earn that ten pounds, working in the woman's garden; Lesley would never employ a casual passer-by in that manner, or he hoped she would not do so.

He contemplated looking for a room for the night. It was still dry, but cooler; he had not heard a weather forecast and had no idea what to expect as darkness fell. The thought of a warm, dry bed, like the one in the Lake District, was as a dream of paradise, but he would not use money on that until he had a chance of earning more. He'd spend the evening in a pub, as he had done before; a beer would be nutritious, and he might run to a sandwich or some crisps. Something might turn up in the morning.

When the pub closed, Philip, who had exchanged no chat with other drinkers, staying in a corner reading a paper someone had left on a seat, remembered what Denis had done: spent the night in a car.

Philip wouldn't have the nerve to do it, even if he found a car that had been left unlocked. He was afraid of falling foul of the law. He knew what it could do to you although you had done nothing wrong. If he were to lie down in the entrance to a shop, the police might move him on, arrest him for vagrancy; wasn't that an offence? But he wasn't begging; he hadn't been reduced to that: not yet. He remembered what Denis had said about building a hut and living rough. It might be possible, but what about food, and washing? Philip had never been so much as a boy scout, let alone a commando: he would make a poor show at living off the land.

If he didn't find work tomorrow, he'd hitch to some much bigger town, where there would be cheap rooms and perhaps better opportunities. This place was too small.

Eventually he went back to the bridge where he had spent the previous night. It began to rain as he walked there, and at least he had some shelter, though the water trickled down the towpath in a rivulet towards him. His trench-coat, wrapped around him, soon grew sodden.

In the morning he drank some water from his plastic bottle and ate a banana. Then he went to the nearest public toilet, where, in cold water, he washed after a fashion and brushed his teeth.

When Frances saw him in the library, he had been there for some time. It was warm and dry in the large room with its chairs and tables. He even dozed a bit, before he scanned the job advertisements.

There were some possibilities. He left at last, to pursue them.

14

DENIS TRIED TO believe that he was glad to be rid of Phil. The guy had no idea of how to look after himself, and Denis had enough to do without taking him on, too, he told himself. He'd most likely got the job, so he'd be OK.

Though he had money now, Denis thought about looking for one himself, but with not being able to read the adverts, it was difficult. He could try asking, of course: he could ask if pubs wanted washing up done, or offer garden help. That mightn't be too bad. If he hadn't already blown it at the place where Tessa set the fire, he could have tried there. That garden was a mess, full of bushes. It wouldn't be too hard to sort it out, he thought; you'd need a chopper, a spade and a broom. The weather wasn't so nice today, however, and the idea he'd been playing with of building a hut in the woods had retreated from the forefront of his mind.

It was quite lonely without anyone to talk to.

Even old Phil had been better than nothing. Before, there'd always been someone else around, other folk his own age, and lately Biff, who'd taken charge. Not knowing what to do next was unsettling.

This was a terrible town for getting food. Nowhere was open, early in the morning. The chip shop hadn't opened the night before, and Darsingford didn't have the sort of cheap cafés he was used to; it was a place for toffs, he thought, though some of the passers-by weren't all that smart. A garage shop could have food; he remembered that from the expedition with Tessa and Orlando. He fancied a nice strong cup of tea, with lots of sugar, but he might not get that at a filling station. He was not only hungry; he was bored. There was nothing to do here. All the people he had seen so far this morning in the street were walking purposefully along. They were not even looking in shop windows. It was still early. He had spent the night in the same Maestro, reckoning that no one would have realised it had been unlocked. It was parked in the same spot; he waited until it was quite late before entering it. He'd had a meal in a Chinese restaurant he'd noticed earlier. Debonair, he'd enjoyed every course, paying for it in a lordly way. He'd learned from Biff how to put on an air of affluence, but it sat less comfortably on Denis. He didn't look the part, exactly; he knew that; but he'd been ready, if challenged, to produce his money, showing he could pay.

It was a great meal, and it went on for a long

time. He couldn't read the menu, so he'd said he'd lost his glasses and could the waiter recommend the best value choice; he'd had the cheapest all-in meal but there was a lot of it. He liked the fried rice. He hadn't had that before. Afterwards, he walked round the streets, avoiding the few groups of young people who were clustered here and there, though he was tempted to talk to some of them. Experienced in the ways of gangs, he did not risk it.

In the morning, it was not like Sunday. A milk float came along the road quite early, while it was still dark. Denis cowered in the Maestro, rolling on to the floor in case the milkman looked inside and saw him, but he didn't. When he had gone, Denis left the car. People would be going to work today and might soon be stirring in the street. He helped himself to a milk bottle from a step, pulled off the top and walked along drinking it; then he pitched the empty bottle across a hedge as he walked by. Soon the first cars set off, just a few passing down the streets; then he met the paper boys and girls out on their rounds. Again, the thought of snatching a bike occurred to him but it was too risky, with so few people about. He slouched on into the town and saw early buses in the streets. The traffic was increasing, and he watched it for a while, standing outside the chip shop, hoping it would open, but it didn't. Soon, though, a sweet warm smell wafted across to greet him; it came from a bakery. A small independent baker still flourished here and he went in. He bought three jam doughnuts, pointing to them because they looked so good and he had had one once.

Later that morning, leaving the library, Philip, too, found the bakery. It sold filled rolls, and he bought one before telephoning round for work. By then Denis had given up on Darsingford and was heading back to Chingbury. He'd got that money easily; the gardening person might need help and wouldn't know that he'd already been there, thieving. And if they wouldn't find him something to do, he might try the idea of sleeping in the wood. He'd light a fire, which would be cosy. He bought some matches and firelighters before setting out, not by bus but hitch-hiking: why waste the fare?

It took him quite a time to get a lift. Most cars, including, eventually, Frances in her Viva, drove straight past him.

After several abortive calls, Philip went directly to one of the factories on the outskirts of Darsingford, which had advertised for a driver. He might as well; walking there was cheaper than buying a new phone card. His was finished. There had been no more about him in the papers; interest in his disappearance had evaporated and now, with his beard, he looked so different; if there were any comment, he could say that it was an ordinary name, a coincidence.

The van driver's position had been filled, but, he was told, a temporary security guard was required as the regular man had had an accident over the weekend and was in hospital. They wanted references, but Philip had thought of this. He had gone into a large stationer's, which now housed the post office, and had bought a pad of Basildon Bond on which, in a neat italic hand, he had written out a reference signing it in the name of Robert Bruce: a total fiction, with an invented address. For this sort of job, it might just be enough; not everyone checked up on things. Denis's cheek in sleeping in the car had inspired Philip; he realised that he might need similar nerve.

Because the guard was urgently required, and because Philip's manner and speech were good, he got the job. Now he had only to last out the day and he would have shelter for the night.

The factory packed cosmetics; they had had a watchman only since the recent raid on a research laboratory nearby. The management feared further raids, and their products were not guaranteed as never tested on animals. The human guard could summon help more rapidly than alarms, and could activate sirens to scare off intruders. This was a short-term plan, he was told; more sophisticated measures were being contemplated.

Philip walked away on air. As soon as he was paid, he could rent a room. He'd need to sleep by day; he must not falter at his post. The short nap he'd had in the library had set him up enough for this expedition, but he had been wakeful for much of the night, cold and wet and wretched. Now he'd have a meal, a good hot one, in the bar at The Swan

Hotel, and if he could find a corner seat, perhaps they would leave him there to doze afterwards. The Swan was where he and Denis had washed and had a drink on Sunday. Philip went into the cloakroom where, again, he washed as thoroughly as he could. He took off his donkey jacket and, carrying it, his trench-coat and the plastic bag which contained his spare clothing and his bottle of water, he went into the bar where he ordered steak and kidney pudding and half a pint of bitter. In his good sweater, he did not look like the tramp he was.

The place was busy; it did a brisk lunch-time trade. Philip found a wing armchair in a corner, and a waitress brought his meal. Never had food tasted so good! He began to feel better as he ate the first mouthfuls and sipped his beer. You took so much for granted, he realised: home, food, warmth. That boy Denis had never really known the sort of security which Philip, though he worked hard for it, had never questioned. If he hadn't got this job, what would he have done? How much longer could he have held out without help? Eventually he would have had to go to the social services and plead for emergency aid; they might have shipped him to a hostel and perhaps provided funds. He wasn't sure what he would be entitled to if he used a false name or, at best, a false address. They might want proof of identity.

He wouldn't look too far ahead. He'd settle into the job, perform it well and conscientiously, and maybe by the time he was no longer needed in that capacity, another opening would appear. There were more factories around; he could try calling on their personnel managers. He'd have a reference from the packing firm by then. Life seemed a great deal brighter, now.

He'd got a paper, which he opened when his plate had been cleared away. It gave him an excuse to linger in the bar, which, with the new freedom in the licensing laws, stayed open all the afternoon. When the waitress saw him sleeping, tidy in his sweater, though she noticed, frowning, that his collar and shoes were not too clean, she left him undisturbed. He'd tipped her, after all. She went off duty soon. Philip slumbered undisturbed for nearly two hours. As no one wanted his seat, even the manager left him alone. Eventually, though, he started moving chairs and tables round noisily, to wake him up. He'd used their space quite long enough.

Philip went drowsily out into the street. Then he did some shopping. He'd been shown the small office where he would monitor the closed circuit television screens which had been installed. It had an electric kettle. The injured guard's mug and spoon were there in a cupboard. Philip bought packet soup, bread, cheese, and more bananas. He loved them, and Lesley had said they were full of potassium which was good for you.

He set out early for the factory, and, with enthusiasm, took up his post.

*   *   *

When Frances arrived home, she felt a moment's fear as she unlocked the back door to let herself in. She used that entrance because it was near the garage if her car was full of shopping which had to be unloaded – groceries, as now, and sometimes garden requirements, such as fertilizer; she grew most plants herself, in her greenhouse.

The thief had entered here, probably on Saturday afternoon while she was busy outside.

She did not touch the door frame, in case he had left a print. She hadn't dusted the hall since then, though she had vacuumed up the mud he had left. Would the police bother to come? They hadn't been too interested, but as she had been burgled, others might, too, and she decided to warn the Wares. Hugo and Dorothy left their back door unlocked when they were in the garden – of course they did: everybody did, even in towns. You went in and out.

She put her shopping away, then, locking up meticulously, walked down to Friar's Court, where she was easily persuaded to have a restorative glass of sherry and stay on for a bread and cheese lunch in the kitchen.

She and the Wares all shared a mild depression. She and Dorothy had tentatively touched on it, as summer wound down and the days shortened. It was something to do, Frances thought, with the much criticised plans for marking the passage of fifty years since the end of the Second World War. As a young officer, Hugo had taken part in the D-Day landings and he had not wanted to go back to the beaches to celebrate the event, but he had felt it his duty to be there. He had returned in low spirits. Dorothy had been in the ATS, and Frances was in the WAAF. Her husband had been a bomber pilot. All old now, the two women felt that their youthful sacrifices had been thrown away. Neither had been physically wounded, nor lost those close to them, so they were luckier than many, but they had often been in danger; this was worthwhile in the cause of freedom, but now one wasn't safe even in such spots as Darsingford, where Guy had come under siege, and here in Chingbury, Frances had been burgled. Only a few years ago, such a thing would have been impossible.

'It probably was one of the hunt saboteurs, or rather, one of the rag, tag and bobtail that attaches itself to the genuine protestors,' said Dorothy, who could not understand why drag hunting was not substituted for the live quarry. Surely that would end the argument, retain the sport, and protect those landowners who did not want the hunt running over their property?

'If you're right, that means he's long gone,' said Frances. 'I suppose he could have got in without my noticing. I was busy in the garden until it got dark.'

Badger's End was isolated, on the fringe of the village, offering more of an invitation to an opportunist thief than the grander Friar's Court, which sat amid its satellite buildings like a castle sheltered by walls and towers. Neither Ware mentioned this to their guest, who they could see had lost her usual calm.

'I'm sure it was a one-off,' said Dorothy reassuringly.

'I went into Brown's to look at security lights,' Frances said. The Wares had been urging her to instal them for more than a year. 'I've seen the varieties you can have. I'll ring up Jack when I get home and ask him to fix me up.' Jack was the local electrician who was employed by most people in the village to do their wiring and repairs.

Hugo was relieved to know she would have this in hand before the days got even shorter.

They went on to discuss the Frosts. Amanda's parents lived only ten miles away. Hugo, though sympathetic to her fears, thought she should back Guy up in his important work and return. Dorothy was more tolerant. When children are at risk, nothing else counts, she told her husband.

'She'll probably calm down quite soon,' said Frances. 'It's shock. The rough young man calling wouldn't be enough on its own.'

'She wanted to go to her parents straight away,' said Dorothy. 'They did, in fact, while the police examined the damage. All of them went. But they came back as soon as the house was cleared.'

Belatedly, Frances remembered that the police fingerprint man might come that afternoon, and so she went home. Meanwhile, Denis, who had decided not to seek employment, was on his way through the village once more, aiming for the woods. The sky had cleared, and again he felt the freedom in the air, the sense of space. In the wood, if he lit a fire, he wouldn't be too cold, and he'd see the stars.

Finding his way to a clearing in the wood at dusk was not quite the same as walking through it in daylight on a path marked by other feet. Denis tripped over undergrowth and caught his face on a bramble. It was wet, too; the rain that had fallen in the night had made the ground muddy, and water still dripped from boughs and the remaining leaves. As he left the village, lights had been coming on in houses, but his eyes had soon adjusted and he had not realised that it would seem darker among the trees. He began to repent of this enterprise, but he wasn't done for yet. He lit a firelighter, which flared and spurted, then he sought twigs and small branches to build his fire, but by now they were much too damp to catch. Some smoked a little, but he lacked the skill to build them into an ignitable shape and by the time he had used several fire-lighters, all he had achieved was a smouldering heap which would not catch alight.

This wasn't what he'd hoped for. He stayed there, nursing his smoking pyre, searching around him for drier material and bits of wood, but when he burrowed down, the buried leaves were damper still. He shivered. If he stayed here, he'd be frozen stiff. Briefly he thought fondly of a warm grating near a café where he had slept comfortably for several weeks last winter. The wood would be all right with the proper equipment, he decided; a little stove, for instance, and a tent and sleeping bag. Now, though, he'd go back to the village and look around; there might be a shed open. But, as Denis decided on this action, it began to rain quite hard. He'd get soaked if he left the wood in this. He moved in deeper, finding a thick bush and trying to crouch under it for shelter. There he stayed until, after more than an hour, the rain eased off, but by then it was pitch dark. He would never find his way out and over the fields. Faced with the limits imposed on him by the elements, Denis had to remain where he was. Though he felt very cold, the night was relatively mild for the time of year; however, fright and discomfort contributed to his sufferings. The rain, pattering through the trees, made an eerie sound, but after a while it stopped, though water still dripped around him. He hugged his parcel of food and crisps, and through the night ate much of what was in it. One after another, he lit the remaining firelighters, simply to break the darkness. He heard strange rustling sounds and squeaks; animals, he thought: rabbits and such, perhaps. Then a dog fox barked and startled Denis almost out of his wits. He had no idea what it was and imagined wolves. If only Biff were here; Biff would laugh off his fears, and he'd be able to get a fire going, too. Denis could look after himself in a town; there was always some corner where you could go. Out here was different.

He whimpered, clutching his bundle, legs drawn up against his body, a sad, lost boy, very frightened, weeping, but eventually, as children will, Denis cried himself to sleep.

When he woke, the air felt different, fresher somehow. It was still dark, and he still felt miserable, but it wasn't raining. It was much colder, though. He got up, and as the first streaks of the new day appeared, he began to struggle back the way he had come the previous evening. By the time he reached the edge of the wood, the sun was rising and, for the first time in his life, Denis watched it as day broke. A brilliant red globe appeared at the end of the field, above a ridge of trees. It was huge. He thought it must be a monster fireball as the sky around it became tinged with fiery red. Denis was spellbound, puzzled by what he was seeing, even frightened, but not in the terrified state he had known during the night. He was awed.

The sky changed all the time as he watched, and at last becoming capable of movement, he walked slowly over the field towards the gate. As it rose, the sun's vivid colour faded but the sky stayed red around it, growing paler only gradually. It was now much colder than the day before. A bright, fine day lay ahead.

Denis reached the road and started back towards the village. He had passed the house he had robbed and seen lights on, on his outward journey; now it was in darkness. Whoever lived there was still in bed, he thought, misjudging Frances who had also seen the brilliant sunrise, watching it from the conservatory at the back of the house.

She had had a shock, the previous day. When she returned from visiting the Wares, her grand-daughter, Charlotte, was sitting on the doorstep, with a rucksack, looking like a ghost.

'Why didn't you let yourself in, my dear?' asked Frances, when she'd kissed her warmly. 'You know where the spare key is. You must be frozen.'

'I didn't like to. You weren't expecting me,' said Charlotte.

'Silly girl,' said Frances. 'You know I'm always pleased to see you.'

This was true, but Charlotte was in trouble: Frances knew it, by the girl's expression.

15

ORLANDO HAD TELEPHONED Sandra White
on Sunday afternoon.

He was feeling depressed. The previous day's
demonstration had been a scary affair; he'd felt
endangered, and Jet had been at risk. There had
been a command from Tessa on his answerphone;
she sounded cross and had told him to ring her
when he got in, saying that it was important, but
when he obeyed she wasn't there. He left her an
affectionate message and said he would call the next
morning.

Who was she with, he wondered jealously; some
suave barrister, probably. Into his mind, unbidden,
came the image of Jet. What a sweet girl she was,
he thought, and probably she was as upset about
ending her affair with Steve as he was over his
unsatisfactory relationship with Tessa. You could
scarcely even give it that name: it was a coming
together in bed in a rapturous manner, very

infrequently, when for once he felt himself her equal, with between those occasions a rare summons to aid her in her crusade, and rarer invitations to partner her to some function. He was her fall-back man, no more. He would do better to pick up Jet's fragmented pieces and help her repair herself, he thought, sombrely drinking strong coffee. He had a lot going for him, after all: a lucrative career in which he was adequate, if not brilliant, with a salary that provided him with a good car – his BMW – and paid the mortgage on his flat, which was a spacious one in Pimlico. If he married Tessa, together they could buy a nice house in, possibly, Highgate. But he couldn't see himself coming back to a calm, married Tessa, though she might return to an insecure Orlando, busy preparing the dinner. He'd be the house-husband, but he wouldn't mind that, if Tessa were the wife.

Why couldn't he rid himself of this longing for her? It would bring him no enduring joy; he knew that, intellectually. Was he confusing lust with love? It had happened before, and to better men. She makes hungry where she most satisfies, he thought, like Cleopatra. What was it about some women, that they had this power? Could it ever work the other way?

Orlando rang up a friend to see if he felt like a game of squash, and persuaded the friend, who was reluctant, to consent. Afterwards, sweating and invigorated, he felt less gloomy, but the friend went home to his partner and Orlando was once more on his own. Tessa's answerphone again intercepted his call.

He decided to go and see Jet. She might still be shaken up by her arrest and he suspected her principles had taken a knock. He'd decided that he had none, himself. Even Biff professed an interest in animal welfare. We're a rootless generation, Orlando decided. Young men in earlier decades had fought wars, built empires, expanded overseas trade, explored tracts of land where no foot had fallen. You could still excavate unrevealed archaeological ruins and you could, perhaps, explore space, but there were few worlds left for the average man to conquer. Perhaps he should learn to fly, or buy a small boat and sail. Orlando sighed, parking his car outside Jet's flat. She might like to go for a drive.

But she was out. One girl was there, and Orlando asked her to say that he had called. He hoped she'd remember.

It was rotten, being alone at the weekend. He wondered if Biff was all right, and, by association, Denis. What hope was there for either of them, long term? They'd drift into petty crime, as Biff had done already. The demonstrations gave them an interest and some action. They ought to be apprenticed to some useful trade, as, a generation ago, might have been the case. What could be done about all these ill-educated young men, few of whom had hopes of a job and whose fathers might not have had one, either? No wonder they turned to crime, for a bit of excitement as well as for gain.

Thinking like this, Orlando's gloom returned, and so he had decided to take further steps to annoy Mrs White.

He rang her up and invited her to have dinner with him that night. She prevaricated a bit, but in the end she accepted. Now it was Orlando who was in a flutter of excitement, because he was taking a gamble and wondered if he could see it through.

He met her at the restaurant he had chosen, one where he had never been before. It was not far for her, in a taxi. He had not offered to pick her up; he was not going to risk physical proximity in his car, going home. She arrived five minutes late, and he was waiting for her, wearing a dark green velvet jacket which he thought she would like.

She did, commenting on it at once.

To Orlando's surprise, she was an easy guest and the evening went well. She chose expensive dishes, but he didn't mind that; avenging Philip Winter was a worthwhile investment. He asked her about her life and if she had done much travelling; he had found that most people, these days, had been somewhere abroad and often enjoyed recounting the ordeals of delayed flights, gales weathered on cruises, and half-built holiday hotels. She had been on a garden tour in Provence when it had rained every day and the hotel was indifferent. She had had to buy some weatherproof boots and had caught a cold.

'Did you go with a friend?' he asked, and she said no, but the other travellers were, on the whole, agreeable. She said there was usually someone who needed a helping hand, which she, Sandra, ever ready to aid a lonely soul, was always prepared to offer.

'There was this one elderly woman,' she said. 'She was so discourteous – refused to dine with me when I asked her. I thought it only polite, seeing her going off by herself. She said she liked speaking French.'

'And did she? Speak French, I mean?'

'Oh, she did,' Sandra allowed. 'She spoke excellent French.' And Sandra did not, and would have welcomed her own personal interpreter. 'I shan't go on a garden holiday again,' she said. 'It was an experiment. I prefer bridge vacations.'

She'd opened the subject herself. Orlando had been wondering how to work round to it. A few subtle questions here and there and he had managed to discover where she would be playing next week, and at what time.

He put her in a taxi and paid the driver more than enough to take her home.

'Thank you, Bobby,' she said. He had told her that was his name. 'It was a delightful evening. We'll do it again, shall we?' and her eyes held his.

He returned her gaze steadily, but he did not touch her, evading her outstretched hand and ignoring her expectant cheek.

The following day he ordered a male kissogram, in the guise of a police officer, to call on her at her bridge game. He had no trouble arranging it anonymously, paying in cash after telephoning to enquire the cost, posting instructions with the money through the agent's door. That should upset the apple cart, or rather the card table, very nicely, he thought.

It had to be Philip Winter. Who else would sink to such depths and seek to mortify her?

Sandra, after the arrival of the kissogram, was more than mortified; she was distraught. The resting actor who had arrived, garbed in police uniform, was used to provoking embarrassment, and the recipient of his attentions was not always gratified enough to be won round. Humiliation was often partly the object of his mission. This time, though, he had had his face soundly slapped and was shown the door quite smartly, once the assembled bridge players understood it was a set-up.

They let him in, of course: a policeman's disguise was the easiest way to gain admittance to a target's presence: gorilla-grams and such were harder, even where he was expected by the prankster, and much more uncomfortable to deliver, all hot and hairy in a synthetic fur suit.

'Sandra, the officer wants to speak to you,' the smart woman who had admitted him had said. Her Portuguese maid had whispered something to her first. He'd waved his driving licence under the maid's nose, making out it was his warrant card. People were so easy to con, and after all, as an actor, his job was to pretend to be other than what he was.

This was good practice. He hadn't reckoned on the swipe, however; it hurt, and she was aiming to follow it with another blow but the hostess intervened. She was dignified and calm, and older, and the unhappy actor did not persist. He'd done his job, though with no kiss, and none of those present confessed to having arranged his visit. Not everyone responded well when tricks like this were played.

The hostess, lips grimly pursed, showed him to the door.

'I believe impersonating a policeman is an offence,' she said. 'But I realise that this is someone's tasteless idea of a joke. The less said the better, in my view.'

She let him go while Sandra was submitting to the ministrations of the two other players and the hovering maid. Brandy was produced, and after a while the game resumed, with Sandra sighing heavily at intervals. That day, they finished early, and she left first.

The others, free to discuss the incident, were amazed that she should be the target for some prank. They all found her austere, with little conversation beyond the game. In the end they decided it must have been an act of spite by her ex-husband.

But Sandra knew it wasn't. It was not his style. Only one other person could harbour such malice towards her, and he, allegedly, was dead.

Of course he wasn't. He had gone into hiding to carry out his plan of vengeance, and he was following her. How else did he know where she would be this afternoon? He must have tapped her telephone or bugged her flat. Everyone knew you could buy tiny devices to carry out surveillance; he'd had plenty of time to find out about them and acquire whatever he needed. He'd had to fake his disappearance, so as to avoid suspicion, but she knew.

When she reached home, she called the police, and later that day a detective constable came round. She had expected at least Detective Sergeant Sykes himself, if not the Detective Inspector, and was affronted, but DC Proctor was a conscientious officer, aware of the ramifications of the case, and, being a woman, should be safe if Mrs White attempted any contact beyond what was formal.

After interviewing her, DC Proctor went to the house where the incident had taken place, and took a statement from the hostess. No one had thought to enquire where the kissogram messenger had come from, but there were not too many such concerns in operation now; their novelty had worn off, to some extent. It shouldn't be difficult to track down the source.

'But if it's the same person as ordered her the pizzas, he'll have managed it anonymously,' said Sykes, when DC Proctor reported back. 'Still, try to trace it,' he commanded. 'If Philip Winter is behind it all, we need to know. It'll mean he's not missing and we'll have to pick him up.'

As no sign of him had turned up, and no body

had been found, Winter was now on the missing persons list. If he was responsible for all this, he was doing rather well at upsetting Mrs White; still, such harassment was against the law and must be stopped, when the culprit could be traced.

Someone had better go and see the wife: make sure she'd had no news.

Lesley had received a lot of sympathy at first, but now her friends were finding other claims upon their time and their compassion; there was always someone needing attention and it wasn't as though anything could be done for her or the family; there was no corpse, no funeral.

'I wish we knew what had happened,' Jackie said one night. She was feeling guilty and inside her chest there was a great lump of pain. She did not recognise the agony of grief. 'Why didn't he leave a note? Even if— ' She meant, even if he had killed himself: it was not knowing that was so terrible.

Lesley had decided that he had wanted them to suffer. They hadn't fully believed his story, hadn't stood by him. All of them, Andrew included, had felt there must be some basis for the woman's allegations, that he'd tried something on, otherwise public money wouldn't have been wasted on prosecuting him. Andrew said it was to warn other people. On the other hand, girls blew hot and cold and you couldn't always gauge their moods correctly; he'd found that out. There could be some truth in his father's protestations of innocence, but a man of his age ought to have more sense than to get himself into such a situation.

Philip was having the male menopause, Lesley decided. He went sniffing after some rich female customer and lost his head. You read about such things in the tabloid press. Stupid fool. Now what was going to happen to her and to Jackie and Andrew? They were disgraced, and were left without his support. Her salary wasn't enough to pay the mortgage and maintain their style of living. And they couldn't claim on his insurance unless his body was discovered; not for seven years.

She wouldn't let herself think back as far as their first years together, their early happiness, the joy when Andrew was born. There had been good times; Philip was kind and took part in their family life, not disappearing off to golf or cricket or the pub, leaving her alone with the children, as some other husbands did. He'd worked hard and done well, if in an unspectacular fashion; he would never have made the board of Lavery's, but he had been, she would have sworn, reliable. Then this. Her illusions had been shattered, and she had realised how little they had really communicated in recent years. Everything had been at a superficial level because life was so busy, and she was very much tied up with the children. Even with Andrew away, she had got into a routine of work and chores which left scant time for talk. Philip had begun collecting old prints of London; he went round market stalls and boot sales looking for them, and he kept them in a drawer in the dining-room.

Were they really only prints of London? She'd never looked at them, shown no interest in them. She'd been much too busy.

Maybe they weren't prints at all, but pornographic pictures. She'd better check. If they were obscene, that would be proof of Philip's guilt.

The police had suggested he might simply want to disappear. People did, especially after some traumatic experience, and the trial had been that. Sometimes they had a loss of memory, in which case they could turn up again years later. Lesley had wanted to know how such people managed, without any money and no documents to prove identity.

'They do,' she was told. 'Sometimes they get new ones. The state is wonderful at looking after people.' And some of them soon learned to work the system. Philip Winter, if alive, would find a means of survival, or if he couldn't, he would reappear.

He'd done this to punish them, she decided, or to punish her, and he was succeeding. The uncertainty was wearing in the extreme. She could not mourn, nor could she embrace freedom. Did she want him to be dead? Going into the dining-room, determined to inspect his prints, she recalled, unbidden, their first meeting at a party which she'd gone to with another man, one she'd been seeing for some time. Philip had been there on his own. He'd seemed quiet and steady, ready to settle down, and he'd chased her, not hard but with persistence, giving her flowers and trying to find out the things that interested her. He'd been gentle in his court-ship, and that had been the tenor of their marriage: unexciting, but secure. Until now.

Someone had said, 'It's always the quiet ones,' as though he were a serial killer or some other deviant. But he'd been a good father and a reliable, if dull, companion. She'd wondered, rather often, if there could be more to life than this, but there was no discord, no quarrelling of any consequence. She'd never been unfaithful to him, nor had she cause to suppose that he had ever been anything but true to her. How stupid can you be, she thought, her hand on the drawer knob. He could have been sleeping around for years. But if he had, why try it on with a customer?

If he were dead, was she free to look around? To find someone else, someone more exciting, before it was too late?

She had just pulled out the prints, wrapped carefully in tissue, in a folder, and had seen one of St Paul's in the eighteenth century, when the doorbell rang.

She put the folder back. The top prints could be camouflage. She'd have to look more thoroughly some other time.

A police officer was at the door, a detective she had seen before. She let him in.

Later, when Lesley checked the prints again, all were as innocent as he had alleged: old prints of London.

16

LESLEY WINTER COULD not believe what Detective Sergeant Sykes had come to tell her.

Someone had been harassing Philip's accuser by sending her anonymous letters, and he was thought to be the only person bearing her a grudge. Sykes did not mention the other tricks that had been played on Sandra.

'He wouldn't do that,' said Lesley straight away. 'He wouldn't even think of it.' And anyway, wasn't he dead?

'Why not?' asked Detective Sergeant Sykes.

'He just wouldn't,' Lesley said. 'It's not in him.'

'Yet you thought attempted rape was?' he asked her.

She shrugged. How could she really know the truth?

'It wasn't proved,' she said.

'But you believed he'd at least done something stupid,' Sykes persisted.

'Why do you say that?'

'Because you didn't stand by him in public.'

'I don't know what to believe,' said Lesley. 'Anyway, if he's dead, he can't be writing letters to that woman.'

'If,' emphasised Sykes. 'You haven't heard from him? Not a word? Nor your son or daughter?'

Lesley shook her head.

'Who else has she accused?' she asked. 'Has she alleged rape before?'

'No,' said Sykes. 'Or not officially.'

'If Phil is alive, he'd better come forward,' Lesley said. 'At least he could clear his name over this.'

'I wish he would,' said Sykes, sighing. There were thieves and muggers out there, really dangerous criminals who ought to be locked up, and he was wasting his time over some poor stupid sod who'd got the wrong side of a vain woman with nothing to do but cause trouble.

He left, sure that Lesley herself was not responsible for the harassment; her hostility, and, he was sadly certain, her children's too, was reserved for Philip. She'd promised, however, to get in touch if she heard from him, even though it could mean his arrest. After the last prosecution, a mere hate campaign would be a minor matter.

Lesley said nothing to Andrew or Jackie about the police enquiry. Someone else could have it in for Sandra White if she made a habit of such accusations.

But why had Philip gone to see her? Lesley could

not accept that the purse had been left in Lavery's as bait. Could he still be alive? Did she want him to be?

She did not really know, shedding tears after Sykes left. It was lucky Jackie was out when the sergeant called. By the time Lesley had collected her from her friend Rachel's house, where she had spent the evening, her anger had returned.

How could Philip destroy them all in this manner?

After his first night's work, Philip walked back into Chingbury. He was very tired, but he had been able to wash himself all over in the cloakroom, and he had washed one set of underclothes and dried them on the radiator. The thought that he could do this every night was very comforting; it was strange how being grubby undermined your spirits. He'd had his bread and cheese, and packet soup, and he'd managed to stay awake and watch his screens, and to telephone in at the required intervals. He'd walked round the premises three times, as instructed, and he had been alert, eating a banana when the works manager called unexpectedly to make sure that he was not sleeping at his post.

It was only after this visit that he dared to spend time in the washroom. He'd have to vary it, he realised; these inspections might come nightly, and at staggered intervals. It was what he'd do, were he the man in charge.

Where could he go now? What he really needed

was a warm bed, but he would not be paid until the end of the week – he hoped he'd get his wages then – and after that he'd find a room. He'd stay in the job until another opportunity arose, or until, by demanding papers from him, his employers pushed him out. He was sure that giving his home address would mean a computer check revealing his detailed history. Why should this be so difficult for him when all the time one read of frauds success-fully contrived against the social services?

It was a fine, cold day. He must sleep somewhere. He couldn't go back to The Swan, not unless he hired a room, and there would be cheaper places.

He felt good. He'd worked, at last, and he was clean. Six hours sleep and he'd be better still. Life had been reduced to basics now.

When he left, the works had been sliding into gear, with early shifts clocking on and the regular door-keeper taking over. There had been smiles and nods, and 'Hi, there,' from one or two. Philip felt that life was possible. He needed food, however. By the time he reached the town centre, the super-market had opened and he went there, on the look-out again for sell-by-date reductions. The store was not yet busy; he bought some more bananas and a pack of sandwiches. Nearing the checkout, he heard shrieks and yells, and saw two small children among the cardboard boxes piled in a pen for customers to use. The children were screaming with delight, trampling on them, causing them to fall about and crushing some. Sharply, Philip remembered his mother cutting flaps for doors and windows in large boxes in which Andrew and Jackie had played happily for hours, when very young, using them as houses. Where was the children's mother? Practised at keeping an eye on customers in Lavery's, Philip glanced around and saw no woman who was obviously responsible for them. He frowned. Surely she'd come forward soon? The store should take some action, lift the children out of their enclosure and take them safely to an office, then broadcast for their mother. The bigger child was old enough to know his name. At the Five-Items-or-Fewer check-out, Philip, waiting for his turn to pay, glanced along the row of tills and saw the children suddenly submerged beneath a pile of boxes. One of them began to scream hysterically. Surely the mother would now appear? The shop, so early, was sparsely staffed: it did not pay to have it manned at full strength until later, Philip understood. Then he saw a scruffy young man approach the children. As Philip paid, the man lifted both of them out and set them on their feet beside the pen, bending to talk to them.

It was Denis, and in seconds Philip had taken him by the arm and led him forcibly away.

'Leave them,' he hissed, and Denis, bewildered, allowed himself to be removed.

The children had stopped yelling and were climbing back again among the cartons; meanwhile their mother was in Pandora's Box, having coffee with her lover who worked in a nearby office. They had so little time to meet and the kids were safe in the supermarket; she'd done this before. Then she took them on to nursery school before going to her own job in a dress shop which did not open until later.

'What's the panic?' Denis asked. Philip had dragged him out before he'd had a chance to buy anything. He'd entered the store and seen the kids enjoying themselves, and then the avalanche of boxes. The little girl had been buried underneath them. Denis didn't think about the mother; he was used to seeing kids running round on their own.

Philip bundled Denis away from the shop. If the surveillance cameras were working, the details would have been recorded – Denis had set both children on their feet; he'd not walked off with one of them. All the same, if the mother had approached, she – guilty because she had dumped them with the boxes while she shopped, presumably – could have made all sorts of accusations against the boy, and he could have had a very awkward time explaining himself. He'd probably already been in trouble; all his finesse with cars pointed to the likelihood. He was none too articulate, and even if you were, the law, once it had made up its mind that you were in the wrong, could make supposition look like the truth.

'It doesn't do to touch kids, even if they're lost,' said Philip. 'You could be accused of molesting them.'

'I never!' Denis was indignant. 'I'd not do that –

them as does is animals,' he said.

'Animals don't do that sort of thing,' said Philip. 'Animals behave, within their species.'

Phil did talk grand, thought Denis. Whatever did he mean? He didn't ask, however; the subject, now, had changed. Denis was extremely glad to see the older man: someone he knew; and, in an odd, resigned fashion, Philip, too, was pleased.

'I've had a sodding awful night,' said Denis.

'Have you? What happened?' Philip asked. By this time they were walking down the street.

Denis began describing his nocturnal adventures in the wood.

'If it hadn't rained, it'd have been brilliant,' he declared.

Denis had liked the wood when he went there with the hunt saboteurs. Philip remembered his description of it and he'd thought the boy had been excited by the action; now it seemed that the surroundings had impressed him. But it couldn't have been much fun overnight, with no protective clothing and no cover. It hadn't rained for long; Philip knew that from his own night's observation; but it had been cold. After all, it was November.

'You must be tired and hungry,' he suggested, suddenly reluctant to part from his companion but moved, too, by sympathy. Ahead, he saw the sign advertising Pandora's Box, which was open now and serving breakfast, a new venture in its weekly programme since coffee, light lunches and afternoon teas did not make enough profit. He could run to treating Denis to breakfast. Afterwards, the boy might be able to find them somewhere to sleep. He must be in as much need of that as Philip. 'Let's go in here and have some food,' he said.

Pandora's Box was not the sort of place Denis would have patronised alone, but he could see that old Phil had known better days. You met toffs on the streets, men who'd been in the army or in business, big earners whose marriages had ended and who had nowhere to live because they'd got no jobs. Their evident failure had disheartened Denis; what chance had he of finding work if educated guys like them could not? Some of them drank, which didn't help their chances, but they'd come off the booze if they could get a break. Or so they said.

Never one to pass up an opportunity, Denis fell in with Philip's plan. There was a vacant table in a corner and Philip, who wanted to be inconspicuous, made for it, with Denis following. The café was furnished with cane chairs and pale tables, and there were climbing plants adorning the walls. Its ambience was light and airy and most of the customers were female, though there were a few men in sharp suits here and there. Philip picked up the menu. Whatever hole it made in his budget, he'd have a good meal and see that Denis did, too. With the sandwiches he'd bought, that would do him for the day. He'd still got some packet soup to have at work.

Pandora offered an all-in cooked breakfast for two pounds forty-nine, including bacon, eggs, sausage and baked beans, with toast, roll and butter. Tea or coffee was included.

'How do you like that?' said Philip, showing Denis the menu and pointing to the small square of attached paper announcing this repast; at lunch-time, the dish for the day would be substituted. This system had begun to work quite well, the management was finding; at lunch-time they did salads and a vegetarian dish, and a three-course set menu. Shoppers liked it, and on market days they were very busy; though they were competing with the pubs and with The Swan, their clientele was different.

Denis stared at the small black symbols which had such significance if only you understood them.

'All right,' he said. 'Yeah. Same as you.'

Philip remembered, then, what he had suspected earlier. Denis was illiterate. He pointed with his finger and read out, quite slowly, every word. Denis went on gazing at the page and nodding wisely.

'Can you read at all, Denis?' he asked finally. 'Can you show me where it says "egg" for instance?' Surely that was easy enough.

Denis couldn't. Guessing wildly, his finger pointed to 'beans'.

Patiently, Philip read it out again, pointing to each syllable. The waitress arrived during this exercise and took their order, frowning slightly as she glanced at Denis, who let down the general tone because he was so grubby, but perhaps the father, as she designated Philip, had problems with the boy.

At least the older man was clean and nicely spoken.

'It don't matter,' Denis answered. 'I'm not bothered.'

'But you ought to be,' said Philip. 'How do you manage?'

Not well, was the obvious reply, but Denis did not give it.

'It's OK. I read books,' he said, and pulled a tattered comic from his pocket.

Philip glanced at it. There were pictures, but no words except for the occasional balloon coming out of someone's mouth and saying 'POW!' or 'ZAP!' or with only exclamation marks and stars enclosed. So that was reading.

'Put it away,' he said, as if to a child; this poor boy, as far as literary comprehension was concerned, was about equivalent to four or five, though he was capable enough of looking after himself in street conditions.

Philip had a ballpoint in his pocket, but this was not the place to give Denis a reading lesson. He'd try later, if they stayed together.

Their meal came quickly, and Denis fell upon his greedily, shovelling it into his mouth so that Philip felt constrained to say, 'No one's going to steal your food, Denis. You're in a nice place now. Watch it, can't you?'

Denis did not react with anger to this criticism, as many other youngsters might have done. Instead, he meekly watched how Philip ate and slowed down the process. Both drank several cups of tea.

'What are you going to do next?' Philip asked, pouring out the last few drops.

'Don't know. Get a bit of kip, maybe,' said Denis, who had been thinking of hitching back to town. He might try a bit of random thieving first, if he saw the chance, but not if old Phil was around. He'd not like it.

'Me too,' said Philip.

He wouldn't tell Denis about his job. Wary now, Philip thought the boy might demand to be taken on to the premises, to gain a roof over his head, if Philip had the run of the place. When it was time to go to work, he could lose Denis, even if they spent the day together.

'I passed some sheds, like,' Denis said. 'In gardens, you know. No one was around.'

'Where were they? Can you find them again?' Philip asked.

'Yeah. Course I can,' said Denis.

And he could. When Philip had paid the bill, Denis led him unerringly through the streets into a residential area where there were two acres of allotments with attendant sheds. A man was working on one plot; otherwise, the place was deserted.

'What's he doing?' Denis asked, seeing the lone man planting something.

Philip did not know what he could be putting in at this time of year. It might be broad beans, hoping they would germinate early in the spring. He suggested this as an answer and Denis did not query it. Cultivation of the soil was a mystery to him.

Now, he loped across the ground beyond the single working figure, testing shed doors and at the same time keeping a sharp eye on the bent man.

'Get behind them sheds, Phil,' he ordered, and Philip, obedient here to Denis's superior skills, took care to keep a shed's bulk between him and the potential for discovery.

Denis soon found a shed whose door he was able to force open causing minimal damage. It was well away from the man. Other gardeners might come out later, Philip knew, but you had to take a chance if you were out of luck. Maybe Denis had an instinct for choosing the shed least likely to be used that day. He slipped inside. It was empty, except for some paper sacks in a corner. They made good groundsheets, though they smelled of fertiliser. One at either side of the quite spacious shed, the two companions stretched out. Denis was very soon asleep. Philip spent a while pondering how short a time it had taken him to sink from comfort to this level. He'd rise above it. He'd improve his status. He'd show Lesley a thing or two, and as for Sandra White – well, one day he might find a way to avenge himself on her. She was the one who'd brought about his downfall. She was the one who needed to be brought down herself. But how?

Wondering if there was a way, he fell asleep.

The sound of hammering woke Philip, and he sat up abruptly, stiff and chilly, unable for some seconds to remember where he was. The noise was coming from somewhere close at hand, and he glanced across at Denis who was still asleep.

Grey chinks of light came filtering through gaps in the shed walls, though it was a fairly sturdy building. Denis had chosen well. Philip stood up and went to the door, opening it fractionally to peer out. He could not see anyone; the hammering came from somewhere behind the shed.

He could slip away now, leaving Denis. Perhaps that would be the best thing to do. Neither had an obligation to the other, but, left on his own, Philip would not have found so good a place to spend the day. He felt reluctant to abandon the boy, who might sleep for hours, but if he were to leave without waking him, no explanations would be needed. He would do so.

Philip slipped silently out of the shed and closed the door, then walked resolutely away. Once he'd put some distance between him and it, he felt safer. The hammering went on and, in the late afternoon light, he saw a man mending another shed not far from his recent shelter.

Denis did not follow Philip. He slept on.

17

THE POLICE CAME to see Frances at four o'clock on Tuesday afternoon. She and Charlotte were in the kitchen. The girl had gone out for a walk after breakfast, saying she had to think things through, and she still had not given any clue as to why she had so suddenly appeared.

She'd had a bath, and supper, and Frances had tucked her up in bed much as when she was still a child. Frances found her daughter Arabella, Charlotte's mother, easier than Hazel; she was vague and not unkind, but she was unheeding. Perhaps, if you had a flock of children to look after, some not your own, it was wise not to delve too deeply into what was worrying them. Problems unaired could resolve themselves without everyone concerned becoming upset.

The day was bright after the brilliant sunrise, belying the adage about the shepherd's warning. Frances spent the morning in the garden, trimming shrubs and tidying up the greenhouse where her cuttings were all potted up. Charlotte would tell her what was on her mind, in time, or else would leave, having sorted out her thoughts.

'We might go down to the pottery after lunch,' she suggested, when Charlotte returned, and, to Frances's relief, did justice to a plate of ham and salad. 'At least, I mean to,' she amended. 'I always get some Christmas presents there. You stay here, if you'd rather.'

'No, I'd like to come,' said Charlotte, who had witnessed, over the years, the Wares' transformation of their stables into the workshops now installed there. She had tried her hand at the potter's wheel, more than once. 'There's no future in it, is there?' she remarked, as they walked down the road.

'In what?'

'In rural crafts. In pottery,' said Charlotte.

'There may not be great riches in pottery, unless you become fashionable,' said Frances. 'But Jonathan makes a living and he's happy. He sells at shows and craft fairs and so on. I think he's doing quite well. The rent's not high, out here, and the surroundings are peaceful.'

'I suppose that's right,' said Charlotte, frowning. 'It's so difficult to know what is.'

'You mean what's right? Or what's right for you?'

'Both, I think,' said Charlotte.

'Truth and justice, law and order – those are right things,' said Frances. 'But we hear much too much

225

about individual rights, these days. The rights of various groups who consider themselves downtrodden and persecuted, and who, in making a fuss about what they consider are the wrongs they suffer, harm other people. We don't hear enough about the duties we have to one another.' Parents to children, for example. Frances thought; too much was said about parents' rights concerning children. In her opinion, parents had no such rights, nor the right even to have children. They were a consequence, a privilege, an expense, often a worry, as well as making sense of life, after a fashion. She said none of this, in case consequences of some grim kind were Charlotte's present problem.

'What do you think about testing drugs on animals?' asked Charlotte.

'Where necessary, it must be done before experimenting on people,' said her grandmother. 'It's very strictly controlled now.'

'Is it? How can you be sure?' asked Charlotte.

'It happens that I'm very sure,' said Frances. 'Recently some protestors carried out an attack on a scientist who lives in Darsingford. I've met him. His home workshop was burnt out and valuable computer files were destroyed. His children's pet rabbits were shot. If he'd been at home, or his family, any one of them could have been wounded, if not killed.'

'Oh,' said Charlotte, adding, 'I'd heard about that. I suppose something went wrong.'

'Wrong? The whole thing was wrong,' said

Frances firmly. 'I saw his wife yesterday at the Wares', as a matter of fact. She's been so unnerved that she's taken the children to stay with her parents.'

'I can't understand why the rabbits had to be shot,' Charlotte said, as they reached the pottery, where Jonathan was busy decorating some tulip-shaped vases, ready for the kiln. Charlotte had been coming here for years, and now he let her throw a pot, watching as she struggled with it, then found control and brought it up between her fingers, sending it outwards in a curve and elongating it again.

'You haven't lost your skills,' he said. 'Maybe you should take it up professionally.'

'I've thought about it,' Charlotte said. 'How's Brian?'

'Pretty good. He's had a cold,' said Jonathan. 'He's out earning the real money now.'

Jonathan's partner was an accountant. They had been together for a long time, Brian rescuing Jonathan from a failed career in advertising. They lived in an old stone house in Darsingford whence Brian set off to Swindon every day. Their garden, near the river, was, in June, a bower of roses.

'You're not doing so badly, Jonathan,' said Frances. She knew he had some orders from big stores for some of his figures and bowls. His designs and glazes were striking, improved after a holiday the two men had spent recently in Spain. Jonathan had come back with sketches and fresh ideas.

'Things have looked up lately,' he admitted. 'How long are you staying, Charlotte? What about coming to supper tomorrow night? Brian would hate to miss you.'

'I – er, I don't know how long I'll be here,' Charlotte said, with a sideways glance at her grandmother. 'But if gran will keep me that long, it sounds lovely.'

Frances, who liked to have her days planned well ahead, nodded.

'Thank you, Jonathan, we'd like that very much. Now, let me decide what I'm going to buy from you for Christmas.'

She liked to patronise him, but posting pottery was not a good idea. She chose a bowl for Hazel; if it could not be delivered until after Christmas, that was just too bad. She thought Hazel would be sure to like it, and she might mention Jonathan's work to some of her contacts, but asking her to do it would not be wise; she would have to seem to think of it herself.

Frances would be invited to one of her daughters' homes for Christmas. This happened every year, after they had worked it out between them – tossing for who lost, she sometimes thought. She'd gone in previous years because she wanted to maintain contact and to see her grandchildren; maybe she wouldn't, this time. Why not simply stay at home? She could ask Jonathan and Brian to dinner.

Walking back with Charlotte, they discussed

Jonathan's work and the peaceful atmosphere in his pottery. Even if he was working at full stretch, there was a calm ambience.

'He's happy, isn't he?' said Charlotte.

'Yes, I think he is,' Frances agreed. 'He and Brian are a very solid pair. Much more so than many heterosexual couples.'

'I suppose they aren't so often being tempted away, are they?' Charlotte said.

'Are married couples constantly tempted away from one another?' Frances asked her. 'And unmarried pairs? Surely not.'

'Sometimes. Sometimes they just get tired of one another,' Charlotte said. She wondered if that could possibly have happened to her grandmother and grandfather, had he not died so young, but she did not like to ask. However, Frances answered her unspoken question.

'I don't know if that would have happened to Dick and me,' she said. 'We were often apart and I had to make a life for myself and your mother and aunt. But we were always very happy when we met again.' Their reunions had been like honeymoons. There had never been anyone else she would consider marrying, though for years she had had a lover, a geologist, and married, whom she met in secret when it could be managed. She did not know his wife. Eventually he died, but their affair had petered out long before that, though occasionally they had met as friends. She might tell Charlotte about this one day, if the information could either interest her or help her with problems of her own.

They let themselves into the house and had just taken off their coats when the doorbell rang. Frances, on her way to put the kettle on, called out to Charlotte, asking her to see who was there.

A man stood on the step. He announced himself to be from the police and held out a card which Charlotte took to be some form of identification. He was not in uniform, but a white van stood outside.

'Oh!' gasped Charlotte, and banged the door in his face, then ran in to the kitchen.

'It's the police!' she cried, sat down at the kitchen table and laid her hands on it, then, bursting into tears, hid her face on her folded arms.

'Gracious me!' Frances was stunned. 'What is the matter, Charlotte? It's only about my stolen purse. They said they might come today, if they weren't too busy. What have you done with them?'

Not waiting for an answer, she went into the hall and opened the door, where the fingerprint officer was waiting patiently.

'I'm so sorry,' Frances said. 'My granddaughter should have let you in.'

'She looked as if she'd seen a ghost,' said the man. 'Perhaps I reminded her of someone she'd rather forget.'

'Perhaps,' said Frances, distractedly.

Or something, thought both of them.

Had she been in trouble with the police?

Charlotte had pulled herself together and found a teapot and some cups and saucers. She concentrated on making the tea, standing by the kettle while it came up to the boil, while Frances detained the fingerprint officer in the hall, explaining where there had been mud from the intruder's feet, and suggesting where he might have touched the door.

'But of course I've touched it since, and so has Charlotte,' she declared.

'I'll have to take your prints, and hers, for elimination,' said the officer.

'Yes, of course,' said Frances. 'I'm grateful that you've come. I haven't heard of any more break-ins in the village,' she added. 'Not that this was a break-in. I'm afraid it was all too easy for the thief to walk in while I was in the garden with the door unlocked.'

'Was your granddaughter here at the time?' asked the officer.

'No. No, she came yesterday afternoon, after I'd reported the theft,' said Frances, and walked through into the kitchen. 'I haven't told you, Charlotte. Someone got in here on Saturday and helped himself out of my purse, which was on the table.'

'Oh dear,' said Charlotte. 'That's awful. Did you lose a lot of money?'

'Enough,' said Frances. 'But he left my credit cards. Wasn't that strange? I believe you can sell them.'

'Perhaps he was an amateur,' said the fingerprint man, who had now unpacked his kit. 'Well, ladies, let's do you first and then I'll recognise a strange set.

Though I expect you've had other visitors.'

'Probably, but I may have dusted round,' said Frances, who did all her own housework. 'I could have dusted them off.'

'Shall we have some tea?' suggested Charlotte, whose colour had now come back. She ran a hand through her short dark hair. What it was to have a guilty conscience! 'I'm so sorry you've been burgled, gran.'

'I should have put the purse away,' said Frances.

'Or locked the door,' said the fingerprint man.

'Out here, in the wilds? When I was in and out all afternoon, working in the garden?' said Frances. 'I'm not going to start doing that.'

'The hunt sabs were out on Saturday. They were in Chingbury,' said the man, confirming that he shared her suspicions. 'They don't really go in for thieving, not the genuine protestors, but they bring all sorts of riff-raff with them. That may explain your visitor.'

'I hope it does,' said Frances. 'That'll mean he's gone again, even though he took my money.'

'They weren't too bad this time,' said the man. 'Though a horse was hurt and had to have its leg stitched.'

'Why hurt horses when you say your aim is saving foxes?' Frances asked.

'Why indeed?' said the man, proceeding with his task.

18

PHILIP WAS LOOKING forward to his next work session. He had his carrier bag, containing his packet soup and his date-expired sandwiches, with two bananas, and a book he had bought for ten pence at the charity shop; it was a tattered copy of, appropriately, *Hard Times*, the thickest volume on display and one he had never read. Somehow he'd never got into Dickens, though he'd enjoyed film adaptations on television. Reading on duty wasn't forbidden, as long as he remembered to watch his screens and carry out his inspections.

He wondered if they'd check his references. If he took on a security guard, he'd certainly check. Weren't ex-convicts sometimes employed as patrols? Who better, in a way, to know how to catch a thief?

Tonight, he'd wash and shave as the hour for release drew near. On his first duty spell, he couldn't wait to get cleaned up in comfort. Philip understood, now, how people ended up in hostels for the homeless – and they were the lucky ones. He'd be in another one himself if he lost this job, and if he could find one which would take him in, for sleeping out in winter would be too much for him. Though the one where he had stayed was not unduly squalid, he imagined stinking blankets, soiled pallet mattresses, and other horrors. He was too fastidious, he thought; years of comfort taken for granted by most citizens of the western world had made him soft. Maybe he'd always been weak; if he'd been a bolder, tougher man, would he have got himself into such a situation with the evil Sandra White? For she was evil: she had set him up in a manner which a more sophisticated man would have seen coming.

And Lesley had doubted him. What did that say about their years together, their whole marriage, the trust supposed to exist between them? He'd trusted her: he'd never questioned her fidelity, any more than he questioned her ability as a mother and as organiser of the household. He did his share of chores and was a fair cook, but she was the domestic boss, just as he took charge of their finances. He considered his prime duty was to be the provider but he wasn't providing for his family now; he couldn't even provide for himself.

It was time to do his rounds. He rose, took his torch, and set off.

The building, two storeys high and surrounded by a high wire fence, was made of concrete blocks, plastered over. It was not custom built for its purpose, having been adapted from its former use. Philip walked through the silent areas where, by day, the mostly female staff packed cosmetics first into jars and then into cartons. Everything was clinically very clean. He saw the different pots and bottles, into which were ladled cream and lotions for which the customer paid according to the package. The contents did no harm to anyone, and probably even benefited users, he supposed, though miracles were fables. Dream emulsions, he decided: those were what were being processed here.

He had dreams no longer. Even the aspirations he had had for Andrew and Jackie were in limbo now as he had no power to help them; they would have to achieve their own successes.

He went from section to section, shining his torch here and there, putting on lights and turning them off again. Then he returned to his surveillance screens and surveyed them all. There was nothing out of place. It was time for some refreshment. He went to boil his kettle: tonight his first soup packet was beef and tomato; he'd have the cream of asparagus and his sandwiches later, punctuating these meals with strong black instant coffee which helped to keep him awake.

At intervals during the night, Philip did exercises. Hands on hips, he swung his torso round, did press-ups and ran on the spot. He'd be stiff next day, he thought, but this was a way to pass the time and would make him fitter. He was so feeble, so flabby;

he needed to build up muscle. The hours wore on, and again he was subject to a sudden unheralded inspection. All was in order, however, and he had made the correct recorded notes about his inspection drills.

No one would really want to hit this place, surely: there was no money here except on Friday, pay day, and the cosmetics were of limited value to sell on: only packed jars would find a market and thieves would do much better going after goods in transit – lorry loads of cigarettes, designer clothes or spirits. Still, there had been that incident at the depot down the road and the arson attack on the far side of Darsingford, across the river; that had been a nasty business.

People grew obsessed, became fanatical, saw no other viewpoint as of merit but their own.

He'd never been fanatical about anything, not even the sales figures at Lavery's, nor his print collection. There wasn't much time for hobbies when you were married, with a garden to keep tidy, and the necessary household repairs and decoration to be done. He was a skilled paper-hanger and painter and could put up shelves and lay patio stones in competition with anyone, just as Lesley could make curtains and clothes for herself and Jackie – though Jackie, now, elected to buy her own and wore drab skirts or jeans when not in school uniform.

He wondered how Jackie was. He loved her, he admitted, and he minded bitterly that he had lost her respect. What if he returned to London and sought out Sandra White, loomed over her, bearded and gaunt as he now was, demanding that she retract her allegations? She'd simply call the police and have him arrested for threatening behaviour, if not assault, and he'd be in still more trouble, for, again, she would be believed, this time with some justification.

He could write to her, though: for the price of a stamp, he could frighten her with an intimidating letter. He could do it here, compose it on the typewriter in the front office. There'd be some paper in one of the cupboards.

There was, but it was headed with the company's name. He cut that off, and typed his message out.

YOU LIED, he wrote. It was enough.

He found a plain manila envelope and addressed the letter, then put it in his pocket. Leaving work early in the morning, now washed again and with his clean laundry in the plastic carrier, he set off to walk back into town. On the way, he saw a dry dog turd on the footpath. He'd send her a bit of that, next time: just that, no message. The turd would keep until tomorrow, or he would find another one; there was no shortage.

He felt happier, with this decided and the letter posted. He forgot about the postmark, and the fingerprints he had left on the sheet of paper, but when it arrived some days later, by second-class post, and was followed by the piece of hard dry excrement, the police officer who took the evidence from Sandra's flat did not. The matter, however, was not urgent.

When he had posted his letter, buying a book of stamps from a machine, Philip went to Pandora's Box for some good hot coffee and toast. He'd bought a paper, too, and scanned it briefly before settling down to do the crossword. He still had some cash in hand but he was afraid an emergency would force him to use it for his own subsistence. On Friday, he'd be paid; two hundred pounds would be put into his hand and he would be able to pay out forty for a week's rent for a room.

He could do it now. He had forty-five pounds left, and his watch, but he had to eat. If he had a room, he'd go back to it, get into bed and sleep like the dead. But he was managing. Once he'd got the room, he'd look for another job, maybe stacking shelves in the supermarket, if they had a vacancy. It was coming up to Christmas; they must be taking on extra staff and he wouldn't mind anti-social hours. But he'd need an address: he couldn't apply without one.

He'd given a false address to the cosmetic company, choosing the number of the Public Library, or what he assumed it to be – fifty-four, Church Road – as he'd seen number fifty-five to one side of it, a large pebble-dashed house behind a privet hedge and railings. Would they check him out? Not yet, he thought. He'd had to take a chance.

It was so easy to slip into lies and deceit; here he was, involved in both, though not a criminal, and Sandra White had set him on that course.

By the time he'd drunk his coffee and eaten every scrap of toast, the library would have opened. He went along there. He'd pretend to read and attempt to doze; if that didn't work, and he was expelled by one of the librarians, he'd seek the allotment shed again. Soon, with a periodical on his knee and his chair turned away from the librarians' working area with its computer terminal and shelves of reserved books and videos, he slept.

One of the two librarians on duty noticed him snoozing, but she did not disturb him. She did not recognise him as a regular reader, but he looked quite respectable. Perhaps he had a troubled life at home and needed to escape. You saw all sorts in libraries, and redundancies had produced more customers.

When Denis came in some time later, she noticed he was dirty and unkempt. He was entitled, as a member of the public, to be in there, but she'd keep an eye on him. He did not look to be a keen reader. She was quite surprised when, after being busy at the desk, she remembered to look out for him and saw him seated at a table with the older man, both their heads intently bent over whatever they were reading.

She was curious enough, when her duties permitted, to glance over their shoulders, and saw that it was a book about Little Bear. The older man seemed to be teaching the younger, grubby man to read.

Well, that was admirable. She left them undisturbed.

Denis, waking the day before to find Philip gone, had been quite hurt. Weren't they mates now? He'd thought so. Although Phil wasn't streetwise, knew nothing about finding a good spot to kip and wouldn't wear a simple bit of easy theft, he was a good bloke.

He'd been really scared, out all night in that wood, yet in a way he'd like to do it again. With Phil, it'd be OK. He'd probably know how to make a fire and build a shelter; old guys like him sometimes did. One of Denis's foster fathers had been good at outdoor things: he'd been a big man, much bigger than Phil, and he'd got the children playing games and making model aeroplanes. They'd respected him. After Denis was moved on, he'd never seen the man again. That was what happened; you were never settled. He'd once tried to explain that to his social worker but she hadn't seemed to understand. Funny how many of them were women; you'd expect them to be scared of some of the folk they had to deal with. Maybe they were. More guys should take it up, he thought: the kids might respect them more; most of them were dead scared of their fathers – those who had a father. He wondered if Phil had any kids.

He'd gone into the town and bought some chips.

There was nothing to do in this place; it was dead. Maybe he'd move on. He drifted into one of the pubs, where there were some fruit machines, and he played one for a bit, ending up by losing over four pounds. He'd bought a Coke, and stayed there for a while joshing with two lads who'd come in together and saw him lose his money. One of them took his place and soon cleaned up.

'Lucky bugger,' said his friend, and Denis agreed, moving on. He felt uneasy with them; if he upset them, there were two of them. If Biff were here, it'd be different. Biff always knew what to do or say to keep out of trouble, unless it was the sort of trouble he had asked for and could handle. Denis had seen plenty of fights and didn't want to get mixed up in one.

He'd drifted off, and had found a van to sleep in, a delivery van parked in a quiet road – someone's old jalopy with a strong lock on the steering wheel but an undefended door at the back. Denis opened it with ease, was able to shut himself inside, and was hidden from any passer-by. There were some old sacks in it. He wrapped them round him. They made good insulation and he slept well, only waking when the van's engine suddenly started and it was driven off.

He lay where he was, quiet as a mouse, not yet seen by the driver, who, in the dawn light, Denis saw had long hair in a pony-tail and wore a denim jacket. The van stopped at a petrol station and the man filled the tank. When he went into the shop to pay, Denis nipped out smartly and fled down the street. The driver, on his way to work on a building site, never saw him.

Denis, once he was sure he'd got away with it, chortled in triumph. What a breeze! He'd have liked Biff to see him handle that one. He strode on up the road in the direction from which he'd just come, returning to the safety of known territory.

It was chance that took him into the library. He recognised it when he looked through the windows. He'd been in libraries before; they were warm and dry, and there were books with pictures in, which he could look at. If he was quiet, no one would turn him out. They were for the public, weren't they? He went up the steps and through the door, and there, to his astonishment, sat Phil, dozing in a chair. He woke when Denis laid a hand on his knee, starting up, amazed to see him in these surroundings.

'Would you like a reading lesson?' were the first words spoken by Philip as means of diverting questions and accusations before they could be uttered, and Denis accepted eagerly.

As they pored over the Little Bear book, it was clear that Denis had a lot to learn if he were to be declared a competent reader. It was a task worth tackling, though, thought Philip, trying to bestir his drowsy brain. The boy might get a decent job if he could be rendered even slightly literate. After the lesson, he'd take him out and make him try to find one, even if it was only washing up or moving rubbish.

But who would employ such a hopeless-looking applicant, dirty and unshaven, and malodorous? And how could Philip get him cleaned up, with no spare clothing or facilities?

Denis wanted to keep the book when they left the library, and Philip gave him a stern lecture on theft.

'But it's public. It's for everyone, and free,' said Denis.

'You have to join,' said Philip. 'They wouldn't take us on as registered readers, not without someone to vouch for us or a proper address.' He couldn't invent another: the library would soon find out, if he tried. 'We can come back,' he said, rashly.

'Why don't we get a room?' said Denis. 'Then we'd have an address.'

'I haven't got enough money,' Philip said.

'I have,' said Denis, and he showed Philip what remained of Frances Dixon's pension.

Two hours later they were sitting in a small single room in a cheap lodging house in a down-market part of the town. While Denis kept out of the way, Philip had rented the room for a week, paying in advance.

As Denis had produced the funds, Philip had felt obliged to tell the boy about his job, which meant, said Denis, that they could take turns to use the bed, thus saving money as a double room cost more. Now, Philip declared that he must get some sleep before he went to work.

'I'll find us some food,' said Denis. He was

beaming. He was doing things to help old Phil, who was going to make a scholar of him.

Philip crashed out as soon as Denis left, too tired even to worry whether the boy meant to shop legitimately. He set the alarm on his watch for five o'clock. Then, warm and comfortable at last, though the bed was hard and the coarse sheets scratchy, he was soon sound asleep. Denis was not back when it was time for him to leave. Mistrustfully, and from habit, Philip took all his possessions with him. There was a bathroom on another landing at the lodgings, but it was not as clean and shining as the cloakroom at the works.

When Denis returned, he was as happy as a sandboy. He'd bought sandwiches and crisps at a newsagent's which sold snacks and sweets, and he'd stolen a Little Bear book which he saw on a stall in the market. He'd got there just as it was packing up and had bought some apples for ten pence from a trader wanting to clear his stock. He'd need more money soon. He'd get that while Phil was out. There'd be an unlocked door or window simply waiting for him, if he went seeking one.

Phil had let him take the keys. He could come and go as he chose, but he'd better be there to let the old guy in, next morning.

Phil said he'd refund the rent as soon as he was paid. He meant it, Denis guessed: he was a good old boy.

On his own, Denis felt restless. The room was on the top floor of a tall house high above the town, looking across to where Tessa had done her damage. He wondered if Biff had seen her again. Biff thought she was quite something. Denis briefly felt a pang; he missed Biff. Still, Phil would see him right now, for a bit, and Denis knew better than to think further ahead than the next few hours. He lay on his bed trying to puzzle out the words describing Little Bear's adventure. He could recognise *Bear* now; it was repeated often and there were drawings of Little Bear and either his mother or his father on almost every page.

Painstakingly, Denis tried to spell out each short word, but he could not concentrate for more than a few minutes. After a while he sat up, opened a packet of crisps, and ate them. Then he decided to go out. He walked down the steep stairs, which were uncarpeted. You'd make a noise, entering late, he thought, testing for sound as he tried to move quietly in his trainers. He'd look for a house to enter. He could always go back to that one in Chingbury. He'd already thought of that. There'd be money because the person he'd seen in the garden would soon get more. Who else lived there, wondered Denis: it was a huge place, by his standards. Maybe he'd just been lucky to find someone there alone. He might go over tomorrow; he'd have to find something to do while Phil was sleeping.

From a room on the ground floor came the sound of pop music, played quite softly, but otherwise there was silence. He thought about trying some of the doors in search of pickings but decided that was too chancy. Thieving was better done away from your own patch.

Denis, who had always been only an opportunist thief, had never broken into a house in darkness, though Biff had. His pickings had mostly come from shoplifting. He might try those houses in the area where he'd found the car to sleep in, Denis thought, setting out on a fine, dry night. He felt better when he was in the street. The quiet in the room, so different from the silence in the fields, had been unsettling. He was used to the noise of traffic, but what he heard now was much reduced in volume from the roar he was accustomed to hearing. Darsingford was not a very busy place at night.

The street lights lit his route as he walked through the town. Cars swished past and a bus was collecting passengers. He contemplated catching it, going off to wherever it would take him, which might be livelier than here. He tried to read the signboard above the windscreen and was just beginning to pick out and mouth S – W when it moved off. Good old Phil would teach him more tomorrow; maybe they'd have breakfast first, in that café, which was a really cool place. Denis had liked Pandora's Box with its cane seating and pretty decor, but he'd be scared to go in there alone; they might not want to serve him, and as he couldn't read the menu, ordering could be a problem, though he could always ask for sausage and chips. But the money was running low now. He wouldn't be able to afford too many more meals of that sort.

Once in the main street, he set off towards the road where he had slept in the car, but on the way, passing the bridge, he had a better idea. The area on the further side might offer more scope for his planned activities; the houses were much bigger and with larger gardens. There would be more cover where he could hide while assessing his prospects. If he had no luck, he could always move on to other streets.

He walked over the bridge and up the hill. He wouldn't go near the house Tessa'd done over and where he'd called on Sunday. Instead, he turned to the left by the park and went along a narrow road where the street lights seemed set further apart than in the busier part of the town. The road wound round, taking him back towards the river, and here the houses were older and, some of them, more cottage-like than those built when the town expanded. Here, in two renovated cottages transformed into a long, low house, lived Jonathan and Brian who were, this evening, entertaining Frances Dixon and her granddaughter.

Denis progressed methodically down the road, testing every parked car in case it had been left unlocked. He peered inside, for opening most of them posed no great problem if he saw a handbag or a brief case carelessly exposed, but he did not want to risk challenging an advanced alarm system. They made a lot of noise.

There could be alarms on the houses, too, he

realised; Biff had said that big places often had them and you needed to be careful, but when folk were in, they were often not set, and in any case you had a few minutes before anyone could arrive. In poorer areas, though, there were no alarms and less chance of capture, but also less chance of finding money: Denis, with no outlet here for radios and videos, or jewellery, was only interested in finding cash.

He crept up the short paths to several doorways and slid round the houses in darkness; not everyone had security lights, though he started back in alarm when one came on as he stepped out from behind some shrubs. You didn't find them in poor areas, either.

His eyes had grown accustomed to the darkness, and he began to play a game, testing himself by seeing how close he could get to a building before the light came on. Unable to see where they were positioned, he tried sidling along the wall of a low house with the dim shape of a white-painted conservatory at one side. Voices and laughter came from behind some curtains, beyond which he could see a glimmer of light. People were in there, having a party. He'd tried the door of a blue Viva parked in the road outside, but it was locked. There was no car in the driveway of the house. Brian rode a motor-cycle to his office; their shared estate car, used by Jonathan to get to Chingbury and to transport his pots, was in the garage.

Denis managed to reach the back of the house

without being exposed by a halogen beam. If he could get through an upstairs window, he might strike lucky.

Then a bright light shone and in a flash Denis was out of its range and hiding behind a bush. He saw a tabby cat walk delicately across the paved area at the back of the house, and smiled, safe from discovery. No one came to see what had made the light come on because nobody had noticed; the light was to deter as well as to reveal, and Denis drew nearer, able to look through a lighted window between slats in the blind. Beyond was a kitchen, large and scrupulously neat, with some plates on a drainer beside the sink but no debris of the meal Brian had just cooked; he cleared up as he went along and left only what would be stacked in the dishwasher. As Denis stared at what seemed to him the utmost in luxury, a man came in, carrying a tray laden with dishes. Denis shrank back but stood where he could still see in: the blind would screen him unless the man looked directly at him, and then he'd be off as fast as the cat, which had streaked away when he moved near it.

The man was old – quite as old as Phil – with neat grey hair and a calm face. He set the tray down on the table and began to unload the dishes from it. As he did so, another figure came into the kitchen, a girl. She held a glass and went over to the sink to fill it. Her grandmother had requested plain water as she had already enjoyed one glass of wine and would have no more because of driving home.

Denis, watching, saw the man lift a green bottle from the table and say something to the girl, but he barely registered their actions because he knew the girl.

It was Jet.

19

H E COULDN'T BELIEVE it.
  Denis forgot about being observed himself as
he stared through the glass at the small girl with
the short dark hair. If it wasn't her, it was her
double. He almost knocked on the window to
attract her attention but, just in time, thought
better of it. He'd no right to be out there, loitering
with intent – for that was what he was doing.

She left the kitchen, carrying the bottle, and soon
afterwards the man followed.

Did she live here? He thought she was a student in
London. Steve was her boyfriend and the two of them
were friends of Orlando's, just as Biff was – and Denis
himself, in a way. Gingerly, he tried the handle of the
back door and it yielded. Scarcely knowing what he
was doing, heart thumping, Denis opened it and
stood inside the room. He heard voices and laughter
coming from close by, and the chink of cutlery on
glass. They were eating somewhere else: you would,

in a place this size, he supposed, though the pine kitchen table was big enough to sit a family of ten around it, he decided wistfully.

Prudently, he retreated. If someone returned, it might be the man, not Jet. Was he her father? He looked the right age. Lucky girl to live here, with no worries about how to pay for the next meal, or the increasing cold. At this thought, Denis shivered and withdrew from his vantage point, out of range of the security light. He slipped round to the front of the house and hid behind a laurestinus, watching. When they'd all gone to bed, he might discover which was Jet's room and visit her. She wouldn't be scared – she'd know who he was straight away, Denis reasoned optimistically.

Brian had tried to prevent Charlotte from fetching the bottle of mineral water which, he said, should have been already on the table. Jonathan had forgotten it.

'The table's his job. The cooking's mine,' Brian had said, and had smiled affectionately at his friend who had murmured, '*Mea culpa.*'

Charlotte had visited the house before, with Frances. She knew that the two men had been together for about eight years. Brian, with his own good position, had given Jonathan the courage and security to start a new life as a potter, and he had done well enough to rent his own workshop in Chingbury. Until then he had used the garage at their house, but they had been refused planning permission to turn it into a proper studio, or to build one in the garden.

Charlotte, beset by her anxieties, had accepted a glass of wine before the meal and drank more during it. The effect was to give her a sense of being in a dream as she sat, rather quietly, in the long drawing-room with its beamed ceiling and pale walls adorned with original water colours which the two men collected. Vaguely she noticed how they dovetailed their activities, one taking her and Frances's coats, the other pouring drinks, never getting in one another's way. They were, she sensed, a team, and there was no aura of tension, as there often was at home between her parents, though she knew their marriage was a success. They sharpened their wits on one another and had spiky arguments which they found stimulating but which were often alarming to their offspring, who frequently, also, quarrelled among themselves.

Frances was dressed in a black wool skirt printed with tiny red flowers, and a red silk blouse. Charlotte had packed only jeans, leggings, and a change of underclothes. Frances had produced a peacock blue shirt which she had suggested, mildly, might be more appropriate for their evening out than Charlotte's bulky sweater. She wore it with black leggings, and she looked, thought her grandmother, rather like Peter Pan.

When she was out of the room with Brian, Jonathan quirked an eyebrow at Frances and asked, 'Trouble with Charlotte?'

Frances nodded.

'I don't know what it is,' she said. 'I may never be told.'

She always enjoyed her evenings with Brian and Jonathan. They often invited her on her own, and the three would discuss art, education, finance, and the state of the world – all subjects of interest to them – and sometimes, when they gave dinner parties, they asked her to make up the numbers. Among their friends were Guy and Amanda Frost. His research was of great importance, Frances knew, and it was dreadful that, misguidedly, his records had been destroyed.

It was she who raised the subject, over the pudding – a mousse containing apricots and almonds, gingered up with amaretto.

'How's Guy?' she asked. 'Have you heard from him?'

'I asked him round this evening,' Brian said. 'I knew that Amanda and the children have gone away. He said he's still too busy trying to retrieve his files.'

'I expect most of his stuff is duplicated at the lab,' said Jonathan.

'Guy Frost is a research scientist who lives up the hill,' Brian told Charlotte. 'He does – or did – a lot of work at home, in a glorified garden shed, but a pack of weirdos set it alight a few weeks ago and shot his children's pet rabbits.'

Some reaction from Charlotte was clearly expected.

'Gran told me,' she managed. She was suddenly unable to face the rest of her delicious, creamy pudding, and began pushing it around her plate while her hair fell forward in two half moons, partly obscuring her face. 'It's dreadful.'

'It could have been murder,' said Jonathan. 'If Guy or the family had been there. They might have been burned.'

'Or shot,' said Brian.

'It was murder of the rabbits, wasn't it?' said Charlotte, in a faint voice quite unlike her normal cool tone.

'Well – in a way, yes,' said Jonathan. 'You could say so, yes,' he added.

Why was he being so emphatic, wondered Frances, who was enjoying her meal. She never made exotic or romantic puddings. Even when people came to dinner, what they got was a flan, fruit salad or a fruit fool; sometimes summer pudding.

'It's wrong to torture animals,' said Charlotte.

'Yes, it is,' agreed Brian.

Frances waited. What was coming next?

'Wasn't that what it was about?' asked Charlotte. 'I mean, that man – your friend – he tortures animals, in his experiments.'

'He doesn't, Charlotte,' Jonathan answered gently. 'He has to use them for tests, yes, but they don't suffer.'

'How do you know?'

'For one thing, what he does is strictly controlled,

so that the rats, or whatever he uses, are sedated so as not to feel pain.' Jonathan felt certain that what he told her was the truth. 'And anyway, since Guy's experiments are to do with nervous diseases, I doubt if pain's involved.'

'But he must paralyse them. The rats. To reproduce the symptoms,' Charlotte argued, her voice rising, sounding angry.

'Maybe, but if humans can be cured as a result, isn't that worthwhile?'

'I didn't know you were a vegetarian, Charlotte,' Brian interposed. 'It was nice of you to eat the lamb, considering your scruples.'

'But I'm not,' said Charlotte. She picked up her fork and began prodding at her pudding once again.

'There are eggs in that,' Brian told her.

Frances was listening to this exchange. More was being said than seemed apparent on the surface.

'So?' Now Charlotte's tone was hostile.

'If you think rats shouldn't be used for medical research, you must be against eating meat, and that includes eggs, from which come chickens,' Brian said. He spoke calmly, looking at her across the table, and did not mention battery hens, but Charlotte couldn't meet his gaze.

'I'm sorry Guy couldn't come tonight. He could have explained things better than we can,' said Jonathan. 'He could have told you exactly what he's doing and what's involved. In fact, why don't we arrange that, Frances?' He turned to her. 'If Charlotte's staying on, I'm sure Guy would show her round the lab and she could see the situation for herself.'

'I – I won't be here long enough,' said Charlotte. 'I've got to get back to college.' She dabbed at her lips with the fine lawn napkin. 'I – er – I – would you excuse me, please?' she gasped, and got up from the table.

'You know where the bathroom is,' said Jonathan smoothly, ushering her from the room.

Brian looked at Frances.

'A confused young woman,' he said. 'Not unusual at her age. I hope our suggestion isn't going to drive her away.'

'She may be hiding here from a problem that she's got to face,' said Frances, as Jonathan returned.

'Love?' he asked. 'Or something?'

'Or something, I suspect,' said Frances.

Upstairs in the bathroom, Charlotte poured cold water into the basin and splashed her hot, angry face. She'd had several glasses of wine, otherwise she knew she would not have been so rude, whatever her convictions. Besides, she wasn't really convinced, only bewildered. One person's truth was another's terror, she could see. Steve, in abandoning the protests, had been right.

She opened the bathroom window and leaned out, inhaling the cool night air, casting a beam of light across the front garden. Suddenly a figure emerged from a large bush and as it crossed the sensor, the porch light came on.

'Jet! Hi, Jet!' came a shrill whisper. 'Down here. It's me – Denis. Can I come in and meet your folks?'

'God!' Charlotte, horrified, recognised him in the brilliance of the light – at least, it looked enough like Denis to make it seem probable that it was really him. 'What are you doing here?' she hissed, praying that her elders were busy talking round the dinner table.

'Came down with Biff, but he's gone,' said Denis. 'Are you going to let me in?' He spoke more loudly now.

'It's not my house,' she said. 'Meet you in the library tomorrow morning. Eleven o'clock,' she said, and closed the window.

What was he doing, skulking in the garden? Up to no good, she thought.

Charlotte took some deep breaths, dabbed at her grandmother's blouse, which she had splashed when trying to cool her face, and went downstairs again.

Both men rose as she entered. They had such good manners; it was rather sweet, thought Charlotte, used to more casual conduct from her siblings and her peers. Some of those old ways were really great.

'I'll make the coffee,' Jonathan said, and, as he passed her, gave her a gentle hug.

'Yes – let's go into the other room,' said Brian, and he shepherded them back into the drawing-room.

Her mind still in a daze, Charlotte allowed herself to be guided to a large armchair.

'I'm sorry – I think I was rude earlier,' she said, looking sheepish.

'No, dear. Just outspoken,' Brian said. 'I like that. I like a person to feel free to give her views.' He smiled at her and produced a box of Bendick's peppermint creams.

Charlotte, accepting one, had the feeling that they were treating her as if she were a penitent child, now forgiven. Perhaps that's what she was, she thought – penitent for her bad manners, and for any part she'd had in causing damage to that man's house and his children's rabbits.

'I think I'd like to meet Dr Frost and see his work, if you really meant it, and if Gran can keep me for another day or two,' she said.

Charlotte should be back at college. Did her parents know where she was? Weren't the authorities wondering why she wasn't at her classes? Had she no essays to deliver? And what was the subtext of her exchange with Brian and Jonathan about animals?

Such thoughts ran through Frances's head as she lay in bed that night.

She had parted from Charlotte on the landing, exchanging a light kiss on the cheek, then Frances had returned downstairs to check the doors and windows once again. She had yielded to the advice of the police fingerprint officer to call in his colleague who would recommend security measures she should take. It would mean special locks on the windows, and the loss of various freedoms which, out here in the country, Frances had taken for granted, even now, when mobile criminals could travel any distance very easily and be miles away in minutes.

Something like that must explain the escape of those who had attacked Guy Frost's house. How oddly Charlotte had reacted when the subject arose at dinner. It was most unlike her to be so abrupt, and it was not as though she had been dragged to the house as an unwilling guest; she liked the two men and had been eager to go, telling her grandmother that the pair gave out 'good vibes'.

'You feel everything's all right when they're there,' she had said. 'They seem strong.'

'They trust each other. They are sure of one another's affection,' Frances said.

Brian had told her of his great joy when he and Jonathan joined forces. Life had been lonely before, he said. He had not proclaimed his sexual orientation to the world: such things were private, he had felt: kiss and tell was never right and why make such a fuss? Meeting Jonathan had seemed, to both of them, a miracle, and neither sought outside excitement nor felt any need to proselytise.

'All this "outing",' Brian had said. 'So noisy and upsetting. Heterosexuals don't feel the need to boast about it; why should we?'

Some do, unfortunately, Frances thought, but let the subject drop. The business with Guy had been linked to public clamour, too. People needed interests, causes to pursue, but did they have to be so confrontational? Why was not more heard of the many good souls who turned their energies towards charitable work, helping the starving overseas, or even here at home? Because it wasn't news. Good news did not titillate; scandal and drama did.

As Charlotte was confused about the rights of animals, a trip to Guy's laboratory and a meeting with that dedicated man might be of benefit. Meanwhile, she was safe; if Arabella were anxious about her, she would telephone to see if she had been in touch with Frances. If the college was concerned, they would contact the parents, in due course. Frances decided to adopt a course of masterly inactivity.

She slept at last, and so did Charlotte, unaware that Denis had slipped into Brian and Jonathan's house while they were out in the road seeing the two women off. Hurrying from his cover behind a bush, Denis had nipped in through the unlocked kitchen door, run upstairs and into the first room at the top. It was a bedroom, and a wallet, Jonathan's, was on a tallboy where he had put it when he came home and hurried to do his share of the evening's preparations. Denis took the banknotes from it, replaced it, and ran back the way he had come just as the Viva drove away.

There'd been only twenty pounds in this one: not as lucky a hit as the other, in that village. Still, it was something.

* * *

Jonathan, like Frances, did not discover the theft for some time. In his case, it was the next morning when he stopped for petrol on the way to Chingbury and found the note section of his wallet empty. He paid with his credit card, but was unnerved. He knew there were two ten-pound notes left in it the previous evening after he had stopped on the way home to buy a bottle of whisky. Frances liked a nip, and they'd run out. He had paid with a twenty, and the change had all been in coins which had weighed down his pocket. He'd put them in a bowl he'd made, an early effort, somewhat flawed. The thief had not taken them: too bulky, perhaps. It had to be Charlotte who had stolen the money; she, alone, had spent time upstairs, after her little drama at the dinner table.

He didn't want to believe it, but what other explanation was there?

20

ORLANDO HAD NOT been able to observe the result of his venture with the kissogram, nor to check that it had been delivered, but he rang Sandra that Tuesday night to invite her out the following evening.

Would she accept? If she did, would she tell him about the kissogram?

He rang her from a public call box. She did not know his real name, nor his address, and he meant to preserve this anonymity until his game with her was over. How long would it last? He couldn't continue it indefinitely. It was expensive, for one thing, and so far, beyond irritating her, he had not accomplished the restoration of Philip Winter's reputation. In any case, the unfortunate man was almost certainly dead.

Sandra had been grievously humiliated by the advent of the kissogram policeman. It was the first of the unpleasant happenings which had been witnessed by others, and those who were present were women she was anxious to impress. At first she'd suspected that one of them could have been responsible: after all, who else knew where she would be that afternoon? But their reactions – though one of them, Meriel, had sniggered surreptitiously for several seconds – had disarmed her: they thought it shocking and in dreadful taste.

After she had gone, the other three decided that her grand manner had irritated someone.

'She's very insecure,' said the hostess. 'It's because her husband left her, I suppose.'

'Wounded pride, not wounded heart,' said Meriel. 'It was a hoot, though.' She laughed openly now, and the other two smiled.

They couldn't drop her from their four; her game was good, and she had time to play whenever they suggested. Besides, she was to partner Meriel in a major contest soon.

Because of this bad experience, Sandra felt an extra glow of pleasure when Orlando – 'Bobby' – telephoned her. Here was a genuine admirer. It did not matter that he was so much younger. Age differences did not signify these days. She wove a fantasy in which they went to bed, but sexual gratification was not her prime aim; she sought reassurance, proof of her desirability, and her power. By conferring her favours upon Bobby, she would demonstrate her generosity.

He must want her: otherwise, why would he seek her company? She'd quite forgotten telling him where her bridge game would be that afternoon, but even if she had remembered, she would never have imagined him to be the prankster.

When she agreed to meet him, he suggested a restaurant near Covent Garden and said he would be there at eight. So he wasn't going to pick her up in that nice car of his. What a pity. She wondered if he was married and did not want his wife to know where he was going. Somehow he didn't act like a married man, but then, which of them did, when out with another woman? Her husband had not advertised his married state, she was certain.

Just in case, she laid her bedroom out attractively, with a nightdress spread upon the turned-down sheets and a soft light burning. It had worked before, but no one ever came a second time.

He was waiting when she wafted into the restaurant on a cloud of Chanel, dressed in a narrow cream dress, high-heeled black shoes, handing her cream coat to the waiter as she entered.

Orlando did not touch her. He was never going to touch her. Ramrod stiff, yet smiling, he greeted her and saw her seated opposite him: no cosy banquette snuggling for him.

'How have you been?' he asked her, and wondered if she would tell him what had happened the afternoon before.

If he asked her about bridge, she might remember that he had known where she was going and begin to doubt him. He must be very careful.

How was this going to end? How could he

somehow bring her to submission, make her admit what she had done to that poor chap? Orlando had rather lost sight of this goal during his campaign of dirty tricks. As a boy, he'd never been one for practical jokes, but he was only too well aware of the pain of humiliation, for he suffered it often enough from Tessa. He had at last caught her in her office, where he was not supposed to ring her unless it was urgent, but she had left him so many messages to get in touch. He was to have a van ready on Friday evening: no troops this time, just himself and the transport, meeting at the usual place.

'Nine o'clock,' she'd said. 'And don't be late.'

What if he didn't go? He wasn't her slave, and he'd lost his enthusiasm for protecting animals.

But he would be there: he knew he would. He'd do her bidding, meekly, and he'd hope to find himself in bed with her afterwards. Even Tessa sometimes needed consolation, if that was what it was.

Meanwhile, here was Sandra, and though, when he asked her what she had been doing since their last meeting, she said she'd played bridge the day before, she mentioned nothing about the kissogram except to say they'd broken up earlier than usual because there had been a small disturbance.

'What sort of disturbance?' he had asked.

'It wasn't interesting,' she said, and would not enlarge.

At any rate, this indicated that it had happened: the kissogram had arrived.

He found a taxi after dinner, and she thought he would get in it with her, but he didn't. He gave the driver ten pounds and told him her address, then waved her away from the kerb.

Sandra found it most frustrating and, when she reached her flat, shed some bitter, angry tears.

Walking home, Orlando's mind turned to Jet, or Charlotte, which he knew was her real name. He hoped she was none the worse for her weekend's experience. She wasn't a trouble-maker, just a sweet girl whose principles had overcome her common sense. He was neither innocent nor sweet, and he had let himself be led along a violent path by Tessa. The episode in Darsingford had been inexcusable on any grounds. After this next venture, he would tell her she could count on him no longer.

He could say it, but would he stick to it?

He ought to talk it through with her, ask her why she was jeopardising her own career; if she were caught for what she'd done, she'd go to prison. It was arson, after all. And she'd shot those rabbits. What good had that done?

He knew she got a buzz from it: that was what she craved; the danger. She might as well take up bungee jumping.

He shouldn't even go with her this weekend. He should drop out now. But he wouldn't. He'd help her just one more time.

He went to yet another rental firm for the van, using his false name. What was Biff doing, he wondered, making the arrangements: Biff, the provider of the false driving licence.

Biff was, in fact, packing up after a night's begging not two streets from the restaurant where Orlando and Sandra had just dined.

Denis found it difficult to go to sleep. He wasn't used to being in a bed, with sheets, and was reluctant to take his clothes off, but old Phil had said he was to wash all over before dossing down.

He didn't go as far as that, but he scrubbed his hands and face, and then, seeing how grimed they were, and balancing on one leg at a time, his feet. After that, he put his singlet and his sweatshirt on again, but left his jeans off; they were filthy and they'd mark the sheets, which Phil would want to sleep in the next day. Then he lay down, pulling the bedclothes over him.

He was warm, and it was peaceful. The traffic had slackened outside and this was a strange sort of quiet: he felt the walls of the room were drawing close to him, pressing on him, and jumped out of bed to draw back the thin curtains, so that the street lights would shine into the room.

He'd liked the dark skies on that first trip with Orlando and Tessa; but he hadn't been alone then. In the woods the other night, the sounds of animals and then the storm had frightened him. Now, the enclosed feeling made him uncomfortable. He'd seldom been alone like this: really not since his sixteenth birthday when he was thrust, rudderless, into the world, and soon the shifting population of other young people had supplied him with company. Now, he wished for morning and old Phil's return.

Seeing Jet like that was a turn up. Denis's world was small, and once he'd recognised her, the surprise was not so great. It'd be good to see her in the morning. She might have news of Biff. He'd keep quiet about nipping into the house and taking that money; she wouldn't approve of him thieving from friends of hers, though she'd understand that he'd got to have some cash to live on. It was all right for her, with her student grant and that: she must be rich, visiting such a grand house. He'd had time to notice how different it was from any other house he'd been in. He hadn't seen much of the one where he'd found the purse, just the kitchen.

He allowed the idea of houses and those who occupied them to pass through his mind. What would it be like to spend all your life in the same one? Or even several years, with a mother and father there, while you were young? He'd never known that sort of life except for the brief spells in foster care, and he couldn't imagine experiencing it again.

He still remembered clearly the day of his abandonment. Until then, he'd lived high up in a tower block with his mother and a series of dads. She'd got another baby now, a girl, and the new dad had taken to bashing Denis, hitting him hard and once throwing him across the room. He was four.

There were rows between his mum and this dad, who even hit the baby. Then one day his mum had taken him on the bus to a shopping centre quite a long ride from where they lived. She'd led him into a shop, and then she'd disappeared. She'd given him a kiss, and gone.

He'd bawled, of course, though not at first. He was used to being left in shops, and in the flat alone, or with the baby. Years later, thinking about it, he guessed the baby had been left on her own that day.

His mother hadn't wanted him. She'd dumped him.

The kiss was strange, though.

He thought about it, lying on the sagging mattress, until sleep came. He was woken up by Phil returning. He'd arrived as another lodger left.

'We must get another key cut,' Philip said. This obvious solution to their admittance problem had struck him as he walked up the road, sure that Denis wouldn't be awake to let him in. He wasn't convinced the boy would be there at all.

'Oh!' Denis supposed it would be simple enough.

'I suppose there's somewhere in Darsingford where it can be done,' said Philip. He could ask at the library, or look in the Yellow Pages.

In spite of Denis's gestures with soap and water, the room smelt frowsty and of sweat. Philip flung the window open and in swirled chilly, damp, winter air.

'Ouch – it's cold,' said Denis, clutching the bedding round him.

'My turn for the bed,' said Philip. He wondered if any effort would be made to clean the room. He was the one who had better be there if it was attempted. Clean sheets would be most welcome; goodness knew what Denis had deposited in these, apart from any lurking parasites that might cling to his hair.

'Yeah – great,' said Denis, dragging his limbs out of their warm nest. His legs were painfully thin and scrawny, Philip noticed. 'Want some breakfast?' Denis added, waving towards the side table where a pack of sandwiches reposed.

He was a good-hearted lad, Philip thought. He shared what little he had, and it was he who had made the renting of the room possible.

'Thanks,' he said, and sat on the edge of the bed to eat a wedge of ham sandwich.

Denis ate the other one. A cup of hot tea would be nice, thought Philip, while Denis fancied a can of Coca-Cola.

'I'd best get out, then,' Denis said, though he spoke wistfully. 'You'll want to grab a bit of kip.'

'I'm dropping,' Philip said, with truth. 'Shall we meet during the afternoon, Denis? Or would you rather be free? You might pick up a job. You could ask at the supermarket.'

They had wanted shelf packers, but would they hire Denis, with his inability to read? How could he stack shelves when he could not tell what he was handling, except by the pictures on the tins or packets?

'I'll have a look around,' said Denis.

'We could have a meal before I go to work,' said Philip. 'I'll pay – I've got enough. Shall we meet at Pandora's Box, where we ate before, at about four?'

'OK,' said Denis. That was good. He didn't want to spend the day without seeing Phil.

Don't get into trouble, Philip wanted to say, as Denis pulled on his jeans and put on his trainers. He wore no socks, Philip noticed, and longed to go and buy him some, and some new trainers, for those he wore had cracks across the toes and the soles were very worn.

After Denis had gone, Philip took the sheets and blankets from the bed and shook them out of the window, then made it up again. Beggars can't be choosers, was his last thought, before he fell asleep.

21

AFTER BREAKFAST, CHARLOTTE told her grandmother that she wanted to go into Darsingford that morning.

She remembered her older sister saying that you needn't always give a reason for your actions: just do it, she would say, dying her hair blue and wearing a nose ring, and failing to provoke her mother into remonstration.

Charlotte had rarely expressed open rebellion at home; she liked to keep out of trouble and avoid the sharp arguments and bursts of temper indulged in by her siblings. Protesting on behalf of animals appealed to her because it was impersonal, and it protected her from having to take part in some other group activity which fellow students found attractive. Steve was a quiet, gentle creature who did not scare her and again her relationship with him protected her from other men. The incident in

Darsingford, however, followed by her own later arrest, had shaken her.

What if Tessa went on throwing firebombs and shooting children's pets? Had she tipped over into a form of madness? Charlotte did not know what her surname was, or even if Tessa was her real name, or where she lived. Orlando must know all these things, she thought: he had seemed on very familiar terms with her. The fact that she knew who was responsible for shooting the rabbits and the fire attack weighed heavily on Charlotte and she wondered what to do about it. Should she, for fear that Tessa might really hurt somebody on another raid, telephone the police anonymously, tip them off? Though what could she really tell them? She could say that Tessa drove a black VW Golf – she hadn't noticed even the registration initial – and had left it at that particular service station while the raid was carried out. That might be enough information to enable them to track her down. It would mean trouble for Orlando, though: what did he feel about it all?

She had fled to her grandmother's in order to have peace and space in which to think it out. When the police had arrived at Badger's End on Tuesday afternoon, she had instantly decided that they already knew what had happened and about her part in that night's activities.

She hadn't talked it over with her grandmother: Frances would tell her she must make up her own mind about what to do. Now it turned out that she knew the man whose house had been attacked, and Denis had appeared in the area. What was he doing here? He said he'd come with Biff. Why? Had they had another go at Dr Frost's house?

'You can take the car,' said Frances. She had got Charlotte through her driving test the year before, during a long summer visit. Arabella had not thought it important for her to learn; Frances did, and they had driven out together, practising, between the lessons Frances paid for. From gratitude, Charlotte had determined to pass first time, and she had done so, but she had few opportunities to gain experience.

'I haven't driven for ages,' Charlotte said.

'Take extra care, then,' Frances said, and did not ask why Charlotte wanted to go into town.

After she had gone, Frances walked down to the pottery to thank Jonathan for the pleasant evening.

She found him stacking up the kiln with a new batch of pots, and when he had finished this, he put the kettle on, making coffee for them both.

'It was such a good evening; I don't know what got into Charlotte,' she said. 'She's not usually so irritating. I don't know why she's come here. If she doesn't tell me soon, I may try to prise it out of her, but it's better if she does it on her own.'

'Is she short of money?' Jonathan asked.

'I don't think so – well, no more than any student. They're all hard up,' said Frances. 'Why?'

He shrugged. He couldn't tell her about his missing money.

'It's the usual thing, isn't it?' he said.

'Well – she might need it for a reason, like a sudden expense or having got seriously into debt, but I think she'd ask to borrow some, if that were the case,' said Frances.

'It sounded a bit as if she was into animal rights,' said Jonathan. 'Maybe she's got to pay a fine.'

'Oh dear! Oh, I don't think so,' said Frances. Yet it could be worse, more damaging. 'She's gone into Darsingford this morning. She didn't say why.'

Perhaps she had had an attack of conscience and gone to the bank. When he got home he might find twenty pounds pushed through the door, thought Jonathan, glad that he had not told Frances about the theft. Perhaps she need never know.

'Brian's going to ring Guy today and see about taking her round the lab,' he said. 'It'll make her think, at least. You're often full of doubts and uncertainties at her age, after all.'

'True.' Frances sighed. 'Things change so fast,' she said. 'If you think about it, in the lifetime of my own parents, the car was invented and men flew into space. In Charlotte's lifetime, who knows what other unimaginable feats will become common-place. Holidays on Mars, for instance.'

Jonathan shuddered.

'Not for me,' he said. 'I think about Napoleon. The Battle of Waterloo was not really so long ago, taking it by generations.'

'And America, so young and yet so powerful,' Frances said. 'Jonathan, I didn't tell you – I had a burglary the other day. It may have happened at the weekend. Someone came into the house and took the money from my purse. The police think it could have been one of the rent-a-mob rabble who came with the hunt saboteurs on Saturday. I didn't discover it till Monday, when I went into Darsingford.'

'Was Charlotte here then?' asked Jonathan.

'No. She came on Monday afternoon — she was here when I got back,' said Frances, puzzled by the apparent *non sequitur*. 'She was here when the police came to test for fingerprints. They had to eliminate hers and mine, and they did find another rather blurred one, on the door, not good enough for matching purposes. I'd been in and out a few times myself, you see, and covered it.'

Jonathan supposed he could tell the police about his own theft and let them test upstairs, but it was only twenty pounds, and he didn't want to discover that Charlotte was the culprit. Besides, depending on who called, the investigating officer might have an attitude about him and Brian: why court hostility?

'How very upsetting for you,' he said. 'I'm sorry.'

'Yes. I've ordered a security light,' said Frances. 'It seemed a good idea.'

'We're well alarmed here,' said Jonathan. 'Have to be, for the insurance. I've never fitted security lights, though. Doesn't seem necessary. We've got them at the house, of course. Scares people off, one hopes.' But doesn't prevent inside jobs, he thought.

It had to be Charlotte who had robbed him; no one else could have done it, and it was just coincidence that Frances had been burgled, too. Perhaps that was what had given Charlotte the idea: yes, that made sense.

He seemed a bit distracted, Frances thought, walking home. He and Brian couldn't have had a tiff after she and Charlotte had left, surely? But why not? Lovers did, and, often enough, made up. However, they were a pair who never seemed out of harmony and had certainly been playing as a team the previous evening.

Her thoughts returned to Charlotte when she reached Badger's End. Maybe she'd wanted to do some personal shopping in the town. It was the simplest explanation for her trip, and often the simple explanation was the right one.

Frances decided to make a cake for tea. Probably Charlotte would be back by then. She'd said she wasn't sure about lunch and not to cater for her.

Would he be there?

Charlotte had not decided what to say to Denis when she saw him. Why was he in the area, knowing what Tessa had done here? Of course she and Denis had had nothing to do with the arson attack but they had taken part in the raid at the research station, abortive though it had been. Stuck in the back of the van, she hadn't recognised the local roads, and the research complex was in a part of the town she did not know. Denis wouldn't have realised where they were. Tessa should be stopped from doing anything as serious again. Orlando might be able to prevent her; why hadn't she talked to him about it?

Because she hadn't been thinking straight herself, was the answer, and it was Brian and Jonathan last night, so kind and courteous when she, on the defensive, had behaved like a spoilt brat, who had made her see the light.

She parked in the yard behind the supermarket and walked down the street to the library. Denis was already there, sitting at a table, poring intently over a book, mouthing words out to himself. He didn't look up as she took the chair next to his, so intent was he. Charlotte wondered what was holding him so spellbound and saw it was a children's book, with large illustrations on each page. She was about to make a smart remark about what a kid he must be when some instinct made her bite back the words. He couldn't really read.

He had felt her presence.

'Jet — listen to this,' he said, and began to read a passage out to her. 'It's great,' he enthused. 'This kid — it's all a dream really. See?' and he showed her the book, *Alexander and the Magic Boat*. 'I read it all,' he said, proudly. 'Well, there was a word here and there I couldn't manage,' he added. 'The kid's name.' He pointed to it and tried to sound it out.

'It's a bit long, isn't it?' said Charlotte calmly. 'A good dodge is to break big words into smaller bits and work them out in stages. *Alex, and, er,*' she said, pointing to the sections. 'The Alex bit's the hardest, I suppose.' He might not know the name. Poor Denis. But it was great that he had cracked it.

'There's this guy, you see,' he said. 'Phil's his name. He's been teaching me, but it didn't take long. He's great, is Phil. Old, though. He's sleeping now.'

'Is he?' Charlotte wasn't really interested.

'Yes. He works nights,' said Denis. 'I'll tell you about it.'

'We'd better go somewhere else,' said Charlotte. 'It's not good to make too much noise in here. Had you better put the book back?'

'Oh – er, yes. But now me and Phil's got an address, maybe I can join,' said Denis with enthusiasm.

'I expect you can,' said Charlotte. 'But leave it now, eh?'

'Yeah – right,' said Denis.

He took the book back to the children's section, then couldn't see where to replace it.

'It'll be OK to leave it on the table,' Charlotte suggested, and so Denis put it on a low table where a pile of books lay, and a small girl instantly picked it up.

'It's really good,' Denis told her.

'Come on,' said Charlotte, taking his sleeve.

She led him away. His face seemed clean enough but his clothes were very grubby. He looked as if he'd been sleeping out, yet he said he'd got an address.

'Let's walk,' she said. 'Then you can tell me what you were doing last night.'

He wouldn't tell her about the money he had taken after she had gone.

'I was just having a look around,' he said, defensively. 'It's a nice place, that. Know them, do you? Those guys?'

'They're friends of my grandmother's,' said Charlotte. 'I'm spending a few days with her. She lives in a village a few miles away. When did you get here?'

'On Saturday. Biff took me to a hunt. It was great. I liked it. I don't see why they shouldn't enjoy theirselves.'

'He went back to London afterwards?' she asked.

'I suppose so. I decided to stay for a bit,' said Denis. 'Then I met this geezer, I told you. He's learning me to read.' He grinned at her, delighted with himself. 'Wait till I show him what I can do.' He pulled the Little Bear book out of his pocket. 'Listen,' he said, opening it at the first page. He had to stand still in order to concentrate, and Charlotte drew him against a shop front so that he was not blocking the pavement. He began to declaim the first page, slowly, hesitating, finding the word *Mother* difficult.

'Well done,' said Charlotte, and her eyes pricked with tears. Poor Denis, product of an education system that had failed him. He hadn't been with this Phil long, so he must have been on the brink of the breakthrough into comprehension which she remembered making, aged five or six, when the sounds for which she had learned the symbols stood suddenly fused. Her grandmother had spent a lot of time with her, she remembered, reading to her and encouraging her.

Denis was slowly deciphering the next page. It was hard work, but he persevered. Charlotte wondered if they would have to remain in the doorway till he finished the book, but he soon gave up, a little deflated because he was not fluent.

'You have to practise. It'll get easier,' she assured him. 'Come on, Denis, let's walk. It's cold standing about.'

Denis stuffed the book back in his pocket and they went on towards the crossroads leading to the bridge.

'You staying long?' he asked her.

'I don't know. No, I suppose I must go back to college,' she replied. 'Let's go to the river.'

They turned towards it, and were soon walking down the steps, as Philip had done when he found his sleeping spot under the bridge.

'Old Phil spent the night here,' Denis chuckled, waving a hand. 'Poor guy, he's not used to it. He's OK now, though, thanks to me.'

'Why you?'

'Oh – you know,' said Denis vaguely, deciding that it might not be wise to tell Jet how he had acquired funds. Last night's haul, after all, was from her friends.

Charlotte was picturing some ancient down-and-out, though Denis had said that this Phil had a job.

'Denis, you know that trip we went on, with Tessa, when she set that place on fire – it's here. In Darsingford, on the far side of the bridge. I didn't know that at the time, only later when it was in the paper.'

'Yeah – I didn't realise, not when I came here,' Denis said. 'I went up there, though, trying for some cash – you know, knocking on doors, looking starving.'

'Begging, you mean,' said Charlotte sternly. Wasn't it against the law? And so was arson.

'Sort of,' said Denis, not about to tell her that he was looking for a chance to steal. 'He came to the door – the man did. The one Tessa meant to shoot.'

'She didn't mean to shoot him. She knew he wasn't there,' said Charlotte.

But was that true? Scientists had received bomb threats and even bombs, by post, and sometimes they were opened by people who were not the intended targets.

Charlotte could not tell this ignorant, immature young man about her own battle with her conscience. He would have no better idea than she about what to do.

'It was wrong,' she said.

'Yeah – them rabbits,' said Denis. 'Poor little kids. I expect they was upset.'

'Let's do some reading, Denis,' Charlotte suggested. 'Get out your book and I'll help you.' It would give her time to think about how to inform on Tessa while protecting the rest of them: herself, Steve, Biff and Denis, and, of course, Orlando.

She worked hard at getting into Denis's head some of the sounds made by two consonants together: he had problems with CH, TH and SH, not to mention GH, the bane of foreigners learning English.

After a while it grew too cold for them.

'Let's go and have some lunch,' said Charlotte.

Where could she take him? He was too scruffy for Pandora's Box and there was no McDonald's in the town.

'You going to pay?' he asked her.

'Yes,' said Charlotte, only too anxious to do anything she could to help him. They could do some more reading, later. She'd get a notebook and some coloured pencils, and see if he was any good at writing.

'There's this place,' said Denis. 'I don't know what it's called. Me and Phil go there. I'll show you.'

He set off briskly, Charlotte struggling to keep up, and soon they were approaching the café.

'You've been in here with Phil?' she asked, astonished, as she realised where he was heading.

Charlotte supposed that, providing they could pay, they could not legally be turned away, just for being dirty and unkempt. She, after all, was not dressed in the height of chic, in her jeans, big sweater, velvet hat and padded jacket, but she and her clothes were clean.

'Yeah,' said Denis. 'What's it called, Jet?' and he began to sound out the letters. B and O were relatively easy but he was troubled by the X and said it meant a kiss. At last the matter was resolved, and they went in.

22

DENIS HAD GOT their keys.

Philip could not settle to a long, healing sleep. He woke after three hours, heart pounding, worrying. What if Denis disappeared? He, Philip, was the one who had rented the room; he could plead careless loss and pay for a new lock.

If he didn't sleep, he'd be useless tonight at work; he might drop off and be caught literally napping by his employers trying to surprise him; worse still, genuine malefactors might come along and get past his guard. But it was no good: in the end he had to get up, dress, and go out. Perhaps he could sleep again later. He'd go for a long walk; exercise might calm him down and tire his muscles.

He set off towards the river bank and walked for over half an hour along the path from the spot where he had first met Denis. For a while he thought about his future; what lay ahead of him from this point? Could he gradually improve his lot, get a better job, start again? People did. How did they do it? Did they need luck, cunning or guts? He did not think he had ever had much of any of these qualities. Hard work had raised him to a modest rung on the Lavery's ladder; luck and cunning might have moved him higher. He'd been lucky in his family, his calm, uneventful upbringing and his unadventurous marriage. Perhaps less good fortune early in his life would have developed his courage so that he could have been more venturesome as an adult.

He couldn't go on like this, working at night as a watchman, with no prospects, but if he moved to another town, somewhere larger, as he had already contemplated, would he stand a better chance? It could be more anonymous; soon, in Darsingford, he would become a recognisable figure, a bearded man who visited the library and Pandora's Box, and who lived in digs into which he took a scruffy youth.

But he'd done nothing wrong, unless renting a single room and letting Denis doss down there was a crime. He'd stolen nothing. But he'd supplied false references. Was that serious? He must give his employers his new address. He ought to do it tonight – leave a note in the office. That would remove one possible cause of difficulty, but there would be more. He needed forms. You couldn't live today without forms and documents. How easy would it be to go to the social security offices saying he had lost all his and wanted new ones? Could he use an assumed name, writing to himself and producing the envelope as proof of identity? If he gave his real name, wouldn't they put it into a computer and come up with his true particulars, thus revealing that he hadn't disappeared at all?

How did people who vanished for years manage? How did they acquire new driving licences? Maybe you could get by without one if you kept out of trouble on the road: after all, people were arrested all the time for driving without a licence. You needed it only if you were challenged, and perhaps if applying for a driving job.

He liked the idea of driving a van around. It was a pity he hadn't got that earlier position. Maybe there'd be more vacancies advertised in the new edition of the weekly paper. If he kept moving round from job to job, his documentation need never catch up with him as he would be a casual worker.

Eventually, he turned around and began to walk back to town. His head felt clearer and his rapidly beating heart had settled to a steady pace. He'd look for a day job. He'd pay for his own room, refund Denis and send the boy on his way. But where was his way? Illiterate, unkempt, with probably a history of petty crime behind him – though that, Philip acknowledged, was an unfair judgement, just because the boy was a drifter – what lay ahead for him?

Returning, Philip went to Pandora's Box. He'd have his meal, and make a cup of coffee last him until Denis arrived. He'd got his book; that would keep him company.

As he approached the doors of the café he saw a girl emerge, a young girl not much older than his own daughter, with a hat on, and a big loose jacket: with her was Denis.

He couldn't have picked her up.

She couldn't have picked him up, for his appearance was so unappealing.

But they were together. Seeing him, Denis's face lit up with a beaming smile.

'Here he is,' he said, grabbing the girl's sleeve. 'Here's Phil. I told you about him. This here's Jet,' he added, to Philip.

Charlotte did nothing to correct him about her proper name: to Denis she was Jet, and that was how it should remain.

'Hi,' she said, regarding Philip in surprise.

She saw a man, who, in appearance, was not unlike her father, with dark greying hair and sad eyes, and a grey beard, though this man's beard was wispy and her father's was luxuriant. It had not occurred to her until this moment that her father's eyes were sad. Why?

There was no time to follow up this thought.

'I'm going back with Jet to see where her gran lives,' Denis said. 'I'll see you, Phil.' Then he added, with shy pride, 'I've been reading, Phil. Jet helped me, too.'

'The key,' said Philip, coldly. 'May I have the key please, Denis?'

'Yeah – right.' Denis fumbled in his jacket and produced the two keys on their string. 'Right, Phil,' he said. 'How'll I get in, though, if you've gone before I'm back?'

How much did this girl know about their arrangements? What was she thinking?

Philip spoke directly to her.

'We need a second set of keys. Could you possibly wait while I get them cut? I saw a locksmith's place in a street near The Swan.'

'Oh yes – they'll do them in a tick,' said the girl blithely. 'All right – let's go there. Or, if you're going to eat, why don't we get them done and bring you the other set?' She held her hand out to receive them.

Philip could not argue. Silently, he handed them over, and she and Denis walked on down the road.

Now it was Charlotte who was pensive as she took Denis to the locksmith's, stood there with him while the keys were cut, then paid. Phil wore a thick donkey jacket and was shabby, but his voice was educated and he was clean. What had happened to reduce him to becoming a wanderer, as she thought he must be?

'What do you know about him?' she asked Denis as they walked back to the café with the keys.

'Not a lot. What is there to know?' asked Denis reasonably. 'He's a good bloke who's lost his wife and kids. That's all.'

'He's not gay? You're not— ?' She let the question hang. What did it matter, after all?

Denis laughed.

'I don't know about old Phil. I'm not interested,'

he said, and it was true. He'd had it off with a few girls but even that hadn't meant a lot; take it or leave it, that was his view. He wasn't bothered.

She waited outside the café while he took the keys in for Philip, who by now was just finishing his portion of the meal of the day: beef stew.

'See you later, Phil,' said Denis, not giving Philip time to ask how much the keys had cost. Jet had paid; why sting old Phil, unless she noticed? Her gran must be loaded, having friends like those two poofters where he'd been so lucky the night before.

Even so, when he discovered just where Jet's grandmother lived, Denis had a shock. Then he rallied. The old girl wouldn't know he was the one who'd ripped her off. Keep calm, look around, cadge some food and stuff: then she might even, out of charity, give him a donation.

Charlotte's motives in taking Denis to Chingbury were confused. She felt he was a danger to them — to her, to Orlando, Biff, Steve and himself. And Tessa. He might, however unintentionally, reveal what they had done, perhaps to Phil or to someone else. He'd admitted trying to beg at the Frosts' house. What she really wanted to do was to persuade him to leave the area, perhaps find him his fare to go back to London. If she decided to leave too, would he go with her?

She'd forget the matter of the raid. No one, after all, had been hurt; only the rabbits. If she went on no more demonstrations, she would be safe. Tessa must decide for herself what she wanted to do and take the consequences; the same went for Orlando. Denis on his own – she didn't count Phil as a restraint – was a loose cannon. She'd tell him that if he went back with her, she'd go on teaching him to read, or find him someone else who'd do it. She knew there were various schemes to aid illiterates; she'd find out about them, get him into one, at least see him started. And she'd return to her own studies, concentrate, do well. She'd go on no more protest marches or demonstrations. Not for ages, if ever.

When they arrived at Badger's End, Frances was out. Charlotte found the spare key which her grandmother kept in the greenhouse and let them into the house. There was a note on the kitchen table, saying that Frances had gone down to the Wares.

'Read it,' she said to Denis. Her grandmother's clear handwriting was not difficult to read; here was a test for him.

He tried hard – her name in full at the top, Charlotte – defeated him, and she told him to ignore that and try the next line.

I have he managed, but was stumped by *gone*, rhyming it with stone, and the connected letters added to his problems. He was discouraged, but Charlotte, enthused, told him to take off his jacket, wash his hands, and wait. Then she went to the room which her grandmother used as a study and fetched rough paper and some coloured pencils.

They were sitting together at the kitchen table

when Frances came home. Charlotte had drawn an apple; Denis had coloured it in. He had learned the sounds made by all the letters which it formed, and he had written it below. They'd done *bottle*, too, and *cat*; Charlotte was no great artist but she had not set herself a project that was beyond her powers.

Frances showed no surprise at seeing Denis there.

'It's Denis. I know him from London,' Charlotte introduced them. 'Mrs Dixon, Denis,' she added, and waited for him to make some response.

'Yeah – right,' said Denis.

While they worked, Charlotte had suggested he should return to Biff. She'd promised him some money. She'd buy his ticket, she insisted, and she'd give him twenty pounds if he would agree to go to the classes she would find for him.

It was easy for him to say yes. He could always change his mind. They'd leave on Saturday, she'd said.

Frances suggested he should stay to supper, and while she prepared it, he and Charlotte went on with their reading. Frances was pleased and touched as she noted their activities, while cooking mince and boiling spaghetti; she put in a lot of pasta, for Denis looked half starved.

'Where are you living, Denis?' she asked him, as they ate. He dangled the spaghetti above his mouth and sucked it in, while she and Charlotte twirled theirs round the forks with expertise.

'I'm staying with a friend in Darsingford,' said Denis, smoothly.

'Ah,' said Frances. Charlotte would have to take him back.

'I like the country,' Denis said. 'There's so much air and that.'

'Yes,' agreed his hostess. She wondered what his story was and how Charlotte and he had met; perhaps she was involved with some scheme for helping out of work young people. No doubt Charlotte would tell her later. It was surprising, though, to hear Denis call her 'Jet'. Before Frances could say so, Charlotte forestalled her by saying it was a nickname used by some of her friends. Frances accepted the explanation.

After they had gone, she saw the spare key on the kitchen sideboard. She must remember to replace it in the greenhouse.

Charlotte had given Denis some paper. She'd written several page headings for him to copy – his name, the words he'd learned. He must practise writing them, she said. He could do a bit more work before he went to bed.

She dropped him at the bridge. He said he'd make his own way to his room from there.

She hoped he would. She hoped he wouldn't get himself into any trouble. She'd given him no money, in case he spent it in a pub. She'd got to get him back to London.

Going back to Badger's End, she felt happier. She'd made a few decisions.

When she returned, Frances asked no questions. It was her way, though this time Charlotte wished that she would. She must give her an explanation, however sketchy.

'Denis has never had a proper job,' she said. 'As you could see, he can't really read, nor write properly. He'd soon learn though, if he'd stick at it.'

'I'm sure that's true,' said Frances, who had seen that the youth was keen to learn.

'He came down here with a friend of his,' she said.

'So I gathered,' said Frances, assuming that this was the one with whom Denis was staying.

'Sorry he was so dirty. He is a bit smelly,' Charlotte said. 'I thought of suggesting he had a bath, but he might have been insulted.'

'Yes, he might,' Frances agreed, wondering why he couldn't have one at his friend's.

'I've sorted out my mind,' Charlotte told her then. 'I just needed to get away. Soon I'll be going home for Christmas.'

'Yes, of course.' Frances waited, in case she would be told more, and when Charlotte did not add anything, she asked if she was all right for money.

'Yes, thanks, Gran – same as usual. I'm not in debt or anything. Just ordinary student poverty,' she said, smiling. Then light dawned. 'You thought I might be pregnant. I might need quite a bit of money, if I wanted an abortion,' she said.

'It had occurred to me to wonder,' Frances said. 'In my girlhood, an unwanted pregnancy, one outside marriage, was the ultimate disaster.'

'It wasn't that,' said Charlotte. 'I've broken up with Steven, you see – I was a bit confused about it all.'

'Not heartbroken?'

'No. Just a bit sad,' was the answer.

Frances had not met Steven.

'There'll be someone else,' she said. 'Best not be too serious too young.' Easy advice to give: harder to follow.

'I expect that's true,' said Charlotte. Then she said, 'I'll go back on Saturday, if that's all right. Denis is coming with me. I mean to get him into some sort of educational programme. I'm sure it will be possible.'

Frances thought so, too.

'It's worth doing. Or at least, trying to get him started,' Charlotte said. She'd told him to meet her at the station.

'Yes, it is.' Frances still had not learned how they had met.

While he was being discussed, Denis had found an open window at a house not far from the rented room. He'd picked up thirty pounds and a small portable radio. He was happy when he went to bed that night.

Philip had not expected to be paid until his Friday night shift was over. So he was surprised and pleased when, just as he went off duty on Friday morning, he was handed his pay packet, the amount in full because he had had no P45.

Now he could pay his debts, and he could move on; head north, as had been his original plan. But it would be better to amass more money first, do another week at the job. It was peaceful; no one bothered him, and last night no one had come to make sure he was not asleep. He had been undisturbed until his pay packet arrived. He had agreed to work every night, weekends included, for the present; the firm planned to engage a second man with the idea of the two of them working shifts, but this solved their immediate problem. It also meant better pay for Philip, and concealment. He'd seen no more about himself in the paper; Lesley couldn't be pressing the police to hunt for him and they wouldn't feel any sense of urgency, though he might be listed in some file or other.

He must offload Denis somehow: he could not go on sharing his room with an unwashed lad of uncertain habits, yet he felt a sense of responsibility towards the boy who, after all, had generously shared his food with Philip when they met, and who had paid for the room.

Denis was still asleep when he returned to the room. He lay sprawled, one hand flung above his head, his chest covered in a grey singlet, the rest of his clothes flung on the floor. He never washed a garment, but then he had no spares.

Philip saw the small radio on the night table. Beside it were some banknotes. His heart sank: where had Denis got hold of the money and the radio? That girl – Jet – had hardly bought him a radio. Where had he found her? In some pub? She was clearly local, for Denis had gone with her to see her grandmother.

Denis had not stirred at Philip's entrance, and, remembering how difficult it had been to sleep the day before, Philip decided not to wake him. He'd postpone a conversation which might lead to explanations he did not want to hear. He was in funds; he'd go out and have breakfast. If Denis still wasn't up when he returned, he'd rouse him then.

Philip tucked twenty-five pounds inside the Little Bear book which was also on the table, more than repaying his debt, and went out, locking the room so that the maid, if there was one, wouldn't walk in on Denis. So far their room had not been cleaned; it probably wasn't part of the service, but he'd have to ask about that and about clean sheets, when he paid for the week ahead.

He went off to Pandora's Box, which had just opened. It was good to have eggs and bacon and coffee, all hot and freshly prepared, and to be able to pay. He enjoyed it.

When he returned to the room, Denis had gone. So had the cash and the radio. And the Little Bear book.

23

WHEN SANDRA WHITE received the dog turd in the post, the police had to take her complaints of harassment more seriously. This was a nastier mail shot than those she had received before. Small and dry though it was, it was stinking and she said it had made her sick.

The offending specimen, with its wrapping paper, was removed, and quite soon Philip Winter's prints were detected on the inner paper which had surrounded it. None of his had been found on the anonymous letters she had received, but the assumption was that all must have come from him; possibly the reason for his disappearance was to leave him free to wage his war against her.

Detective Sergeant Sykes went to see Lesley.

'You'll be relieved to hear we've got proof your husband is alive,' he said. He did not tell her where they thought he was; postmarks could be misleading. The earlier mailings had come from London, but the pizzas could have been ordered by telephone from anywhere. Doubtless he was staying nowhere long.

Sykes explained to Lesley that Philip's finger-prints had been found on two communications sent to Sandra White. He did not reveal the malicious turn the harassment had taken. When he had gone, Lesley felt emotionally bewildered. She discovered that she was relieved he wasn't dead and some sense of her own guilt lifted with that realisation. But was he really capable of conducting a hate campaign by post? It was too bad of him to cause them all this extra misery. Her anger grew as she thought about his heartlessness.

Sandra and his plans for her downfall had been filed away at the back of Orlando's mind because now he had the more urgent problem of Tessa to confront.

She wanted to set off on this next – and his last, he had resolved – expedition on Friday night, which was unusual. Normally she campaigned on Satur-days, with Sunday for repose and restoration – and rewards, when he was lucky. His own office closed promptly on Fridays; city men with weekend cottages liked to head out to the country in good time. He'd decided to be very careful, wearing gloves throughout so that he left no trace in the hired van. He put on a baseball cap and his dark anorak, and when he collected the transport he wore tinted glasses.

Driving westwards, he contemplated asking for a

transfer to an overseas branch of the bank. Removing himself from Tessa might be the only way to overcome his addiction to her. She was like a drug, and cold turkey was the remedy. He wouldn't be going back with her to her parents' house tonight because he would have to return the van, but if she had nothing better to do, she might ask him down tomorrow.

The traffic was heavy, much heavier than on a Saturday, with all the weekend travellers speeding out of town. Tessa would be furious if he was late, but she must be driving through it too. What did she do with that shotgun, between raids, he wondered, and the other stuff she took with them?

This wasn't love, not really; what he felt for her was surely lust because she was so physically exciting. He'd had other sexual encounters, even thought himself in love before, but he had never known anything like Tessa's wild, abandoned passion. She was always the controller; she never used his name; he sometimes wondered if she knew who was with her in these moments. Any other man would have suited her as well as he, he thought, but he was safe. She trusted him.

But if he didn't love her, why did he do all this for her and put himself at risk, breaking the law? Perhaps it was a special sort of love, he told himself forlornly.

There were other girls: Jet – or Charlotte – for instance. But she was so young, so inexperienced, and maybe she'd get back with Steve eventually, or some other fellow student. He ought to look around for someone kind and sweet; someone to marry.

While Orlando was driving unhappily to meet her, Tessa was also on the road, having just concluded a successful piece of litigation. She'd gained huge compensation and costs for her client and now, elated, she was going to finish off some private business which had been her aim for months, even years. She'd learned last Sunday, from her parents, that Guy Frost's wife had left him, taking the children.

'It's only temporary, because of that awful business at their house,' Millicent had said. 'It must have terrified her.'

'But they weren't hurt. They weren't there,' said Tessa. 'Or so the papers said.'

'The rabbits were. That was sick,' said Millicent.

Was she sick?

Tessa asked herself that question as she drove along. She'd shot the rabbits on an impulse, wanting to cause misery to Guy and his family. All her work with the animal protest movement had been geared to that: to hurt Guy, by association, wreck his work and upset his domestic life. She didn't give a fig for animals, alive or dead, though she'd been fond of her pony and had liked the Jack Russell terrier her mother had when they first moved to the country. It had died and never been replaced.

When Guy, whom she had known at university, got married, she had thought that she would die of jealousy and pain. She identified her emotions even though she tried to think of them as grief. He had been her first lover, and she had never loved another, though she had been to bed with more than she could count.

How could he have preferred that milksop Amanda to her? It must be like drinking Ribena after tasting vintage claret.

Their ways had separated when she went to London and he to a research position in Edinburgh, but they had met at frequent intervals, Tessa becoming a regular on the shuttle flight. He'd travelled down less often, but they had gone on holiday together, always to exotic places like the Himalayas and Brazil. Guy's work had broadened; he was interested in parasitic diseases and viruses that attacked the nervous system. Tessa, bored by his dedication, constantly provoked quarrels and said he loved his bugs more than her.

Eventually he'd turned on her, accused her of having other lovers, which was true, and there was a blazing row which led to the end of their relationship. For over a year, Guy had wanted to finish it, but because they did not live together, he had let it drift, still revelling in its sexual aspect. Like Orlando later, when he was alone with her, he could think of nothing else, but her demands for more frequent meetings, and their constant quarrels, were exhausting; they'd separated mentally, and sex alone was not enough to bind them.

Then he met Amanda, and saw that there could

be a different sort of love – gentler, deeper, and worthwhile. Now he had a reason to break away from Tessa.

There had been a dreadful scene. She had screamed at him and pounded him with her fists. He'd gone to London intending to avoid being with her in a place where she could weaken his resolve by arousing him sexually. They'd had dinner in a restaurant where they had often been before – Tessa did not care for cooking – and she'd talked about her work, and her new flat, which she would show him later.

'You'll love it, Guy,' she'd said. 'It's got a view over the river.'

He was never going there. He had determined that in advance. He made some non-committal reply and, over coffee, had told her so.

'I'm not hearing this,' she said, putting down her coffee cup and staring at him in disbelief. She'd been expecting him to suggest they marry, and had been ready to discuss it, for of course they would when the right time came, but she was not prepared to go to Scotland. He would have to move south.

He made a little speech about their conflicting ambitions and opposing locations. They'd drifted apart, he said.

'Whose fault is that?' she demanded, accusing him of making excuses to postpone their meetings.

He'd pleaded work pressure, not mentioning Amanda until she asked him if there was someone else. Then he'd admitted it, repeating that he knew she was seeing other men. At this, she began hitting him, causing an uproar in the restaurant.

Two waiters caught her by each arm and marched her to the door, with Guy following. He flung money at one of the waiters, almost all he had in cash; there was no time for the credit-card routine. Then he rushed after her but she had vanished. A waiter said she had caught a passing taxi.

He telephoned her an hour later but there was no answer. He decided she was too angry to attempt to hurt herself, and fled back to Scotland without seeing her again.

When his project ended, he had obtained another post with a pharmaceutical company based in the south, nearer Amanda's parents. Her father was in poor health, his illness one that interested Guy, and his research could embrace its possible causes. Until the recent attack on them, things had run happily for Guy and his new family.

Tessa had kept tabs on his movements. While he and Amanda remained in Scotland, she had let them alone, trying to forget him, but when he moved, she tracked him down, parking in the road near their house, and watched the dull-looking woman, as Tessa thought of Amanda, taking the children off in her car. Once, she'd followed her to a supermarket and walked round the store behind her, hearing her talking to the boy and girl. The girl looked just like Guy.

Why should that goody-goody prig have Guy? He must be bored with her by now. Tessa had told herself that the marriage would not last; he'd tire of bland Amanda and domesticity and long for fireworks. He'd seek her out again.

It hadn't happened.

Some adversity would split them up, she had decided, and when none seemed to do so, she'd determined to provide a dose of it.

As her parents lived little more than an hour's drive from Darsingford, it had been easy enough to stalk Guy and make enquiries about his work. She did not plan to harm Amanda or the children, merely to drive a wedge between him and his wife and then she'd dry Guy's penitential tears. She'd wreck his work, so that his life and marriage would collapse. That whey-faced girl would be no comfort to him; he'd need Tessa.

She had become an animal rights activist in order to adopt their methods. They had attacked other scientists; she would attack Guy and bring terror to his life.

When she went to his house she had two plans, one to use if the children were there, and another if they were out. If they'd been there, she could not have done so much: petrol bombs in the garden would have been the limit. But Biff had found the place deserted, and so she did not care how much damage she did. When she saw the computer in his workshop she was delighted. Breaking that up would really hurt him. Owning the unlicensed gun gave her a sense of power and she shot the rabbits on an impulse. She was a good shot. One of her lovers, who farmed in Yorkshire, had taught her. She had gone potting vermin with him on his land. He'd wanted her to marry him, but after Guy, she found him very dull.

Orlando was a useful smokescreen. Tessa was fully aware of her charismatic hold on him; it had worked with every man she played with, and her powers had increased rather than diminished in her thirties. They'd work again with Guy if that woman could be removed, and now it had happened. What a spineless creature she had turned out to be: as if Tessa would be frightened off by a mere fire. Knowing nothing about Denis's visit to the Frosts' house, Tessa had admitted to herself that Amanda had lasted for a while after the attack, but imagined tears and tantrums had occupied the interval.

She had no suspicion of the heart-searchings that had compelled Amanda, in the end, to put the children's safety first, and, after leaving them on their own for two days with her parents, to join them.

Tessa's own parents had no idea that she had ever met Guy Frost; they knew only that she had had a boyfriend dating back to Cambridge who had gone to Scotland, and that after some years the romance had died.

'You're to follow me,' she told Orlando.

She had said he was to meet her in the cafeteria, and this surprised him because before his instructions always were to drive about until he found her car, then make the switch and load up as fast as possible. He was even more surprised when he saw that she was not in combat clothes but was wearing a long black skirt made of some woollen fabric, and a hip-length fleecy jacket, also black. Her hair stood out round her head like a brilliant halo, and her eyes were shining. She had never looked more beautiful, and even in these surroundings she attracted glances.

'What's this?' he asked, stooping to kiss her.

Tessa offered him a cool cheek, and he felt dismay at this chilly response.

'We've got a different plan tonight. I may need my own car,' she said. 'Come on. There's no time to lose.'

She walked briskly off, skirt swinging, feet in high-heeled shoes, but he knew she'd drive shoeless, or in pumps.

On the slip road back to the motorway she stopped the car and waited while he took from it the familiar holdall containing her equipment. To Orlando's relief, she did not hand him the shotgun, but there was a length of plastic piping and a long package wrapped in brown paper. Meekly, he stowed them in the van.

Soon she was back in her car and, instructing Orlando to follow her, she drove off. Orlando settled down behind her, wishing she would not go so fast, as the van was not as finely tuned as the Golf and lacked its acceleration. When she turned off for Darsingford, he was astonished. Surely she couldn't be returning to the scene of what he now thought of, quite spontaneously, as her crime?

She stopped not far from the research station, in a side road, and when he drew up close to her, berated him for not keeping on her tail.

Useless to protest. He waited for her next instruction.

'Come on,' she said, getting in beside him.

Orlando saw that she now had on a pair of flat-heeled shoes. He started up the engine, driving on to join the wider road where the research depot stood in its large plot, near some other factories and warehouses. She told him to stop outside a much smaller block whose name was painted on a board attached to the wire fencing by the gates.

'They pack cosmetics here,' she said, getting out of the van. 'Who knows what poor beasts they test them on. Bring the package and the tube.'

He obeyed, and she lifted out the holdall herself. Tessa gestured to him to unwrap the package and he did so, disclosing, to his astonishment, three large expensive firework rockets. Meanwhile Tessa had taken some wire cutters from the holdall and begun cutting the wire fence about a foot from the ground, opposite the building. He moved to help her, then drew back. He did not want to be involved with this.

Tessa slid the stick of one rocket into the pipe and poked it through the hole she had made, resting the end on the ground at a low angle.

'Light it,' she commanded. 'Then stand clear.'

The matches were in the holdall. Slowly, Orlando took them out. He had to remove his gloves to strike one. The first match flickered in the air and then went out, and Tessa, impatiently, told him to get a move on.

The first rocket went off with a whoosh, directly towards the shadowed building, and in seconds Tessa had placed another in the pipe. Orlando had already heard a crashing sound as the first one hit a window. The second went off, angled only slightly higher than the first.

'I'll do it,' he said, when Tessa loaded the last one, and he took the pipe from her, shoving it through the wire, resting it so that its trajectory would send the firework upwards. Tessa, packing up the wrappings, did not realise what he had done until it was too late and the rocket had exploded in the sky, sending out a shower of stars and small reports. Orlando had remained quite near it, wanting to conceal it from her, and he felt his face scorch as it soared away.

'What did you do that for?' Tessa said angrily. 'Come on, you idiot, let's get out of here.' She pulled something from the holdall and lobbed it over the fence. Then she thrust the bag and wrappings at him. 'Drive to the park where we stopped before, above the bridge,' she said. 'Wait there for me. I've got something else to do. Mind you wait, though. If I'm not back after an hour, then go back to London and get rid of the van.'

As she started up the Golf, he contemplated

abandoning her, leaving her to carry out alone whatever desperate scheme she had in mind, but he couldn't do it.

He bent to pick up the piece of piping which she had ignored. It would have his fingerprints on it. He put it in the van, then, with a heavy heart, he followed her into the town and across the bridge to the park, where he stopped.

Tessa had already reached Guy Frost's house.

24

DENIS HAD AGREED with Jet's plan to go back to London on Saturday because it was what she wanted to hear, and he liked keeping people happy. She'd said she'd pay his fare, but what a waste of money when you could travel free on the road. Waking on Friday morning, he looked round the room and saw Phil's plastic bag on the chair. So he'd been back after work. Denis yawned, stretched, and got out of bed. The old guy'd need to get his head down. He glanced at the night table, anxious about his money, but Phil wouldn't touch it: not old Phil, who was so keen on repaying Denis for the rent, as if it mattered between mates who shared what luck came their way, the good and the bad. His small pile of loot was safe, and then he saw the other money, stuck between the pages of the Little Bear book.

He could go, then. Denis wasn't one to turn his back on handouts and this was the repayment of a debt. Now he could leave old Phil to get on with it. He'd manage, as he'd found a job. It was all right for him; guys like Phil could get them, but the likes of Denis couldn't. He wasn't sure he wanted one, but he would like someone to look out for him, as Biff had done, yet he wasn't sure he wanted to go back to London. There was something about the space round here that still appealed to him, and yesterday with Jet had been just great.

He might go and look for Jet, try to spend the day out there, in that big house. Maybe the old girl would cook another meal. She was all right; she'd not been at all nosey.

Stuffing his few possessions into his pockets, Denis left his temporary lodgings. He kept his keys; he might decide to come back, and all trifles had their uses. He started walking out of Darsingford in the direction of Chingbury, passing the research establishment which Tessa had attacked. There were still signs of their slogans on the walls. Spraying paint was great; he'd liked that, but he hadn't written any words. Tessa had made them pick up all their paint tins afterwards. He'd laughed at that, as they'd shoved them into the bag she held. Biff had said something about litter, and Orlando had said they must keep Britain tidy. There'd be prints on those tins; his and Biff's prints were on file as they'd been nabbed by the police more than once so it was just as well she'd removed the evidence against them, not that they were likely to be connected with that affray. Was that what it was?

Had they caused an affray? Denis's grasp of legalese was limited.

Even so, Tessa had gone too far at that house. Fancy shooting little kids' rabbits! Denis had gone off her a bit after that but Biff had made excuses, said the animals might be being kept as pets as a cover for using them for secret experiments. Even so, why kill them?

He hadn't come this way with Jet; she'd driven in by another road. He mustn't get lost. Would he be able to read the road signs? Her gran's village was called Chingbury, that was CH, which Jet had said stood for CHOCOLATE, a long and difficult word, but she had broken it up into some small bits, just like an actual bar of *choc-o-late*, she'd said, and made him write it later. She was good, was Jet. A few more lessons and he'd read as well as she did.

Denis got a lift in a workman's van. The man was going to Swindon, but he dropped Denis on the main road, where he'd soon pick up another ride.

At first he was unlucky, trudging along, looking around him, still admiring the wide sky and the fields on either side, a light rain falling now. An old bus passed him, going the other way. It was travelling at some forty miles an hour, not capable of going faster, and the driver waved cheerily as Denis paused to look at it. Behind it came a camper van in rather better condition, but still shabby, with swirls of colour, faded now, ornamenting its once cream sides. Maybe he could get a van like that one day, take his house with him.

He walked on, and eventually was picked up by a student from a local college of technology who drove him the last few miles.

The rain was coming down harder. Denis thought some shelter would be nice. Jet's gran would welcome him, he decided. Soon he'd be in that big warm kitchen with a plate of something hot before him.

He rang the bell, but there was no answer. Walking round the house, he looked through the garage window and saw that it was empty. Since the burglary, Frances shut the garage when she went out, though before that she had never bothered. He tried the doors and windows. They wouldn't mind him waiting inside till they returned. Everything was tightly locked, however.

But not the greenhouse. He went over to it, opened the door, and stepped inside. It was not very warm but it was dry, and soon the rain began to slacken.

After a while, he remembered where Jet had found the key to let them into the house, the day before.

Frances was a volunteer worker in a hospital shop on alternate Fridays, and before she set off that morning, she asked Charlotte if she wanted to come along.

'I don't think so,' Charlotte answered. 'I'll do some work.'

Though she had left London in a hurry, she had brought some books and files with her. Now she was anxious to make up lost ground, and she should have handed in an essay this week. After Frances had gone, she settled down and concentrated for a while, then, restless, went out for a walk, ending up at the pottery when it began to rain.

Jonathan seemed preoccupied, not particularly pleased to see her, and she was put out. She'd always had a welcome before. Was he still annoyed with her because she'd been so rude on Wednesday evening?

'I'll sweep up, shall I?' she said, seeing that the studio floor was rather messy, with dried clay particles lying about and some dead leaves which must have blown in when the doors were opened.

'I don't want a lot of dust, Charlotte,' Jonathan answered curtly.

'Oh – right.' She felt at a loss. 'I'm going back tomorrow,' she told him.

'Oh?' He did not look at her, concentrating on the lump of clay he was turning into a tall urn-shaped vase.

Charlotte, who had always been fascinated by his skill, moved nearer.

'I should have gone today, really,' she said.

'Why didn't you?'

'What's another day?' she said lightly.

'A wasted opportunity,' he said.

'But I'm not wasting today. I've been working on my essay. Am I wasting your day by being here?' she asked sharply. 'Sorry, but you've never seemed to mind before.'

'Things were different. You were different,' Jonathan stated.

'It's because of the other night. You've gone off me,' Charlotte said.

'That's not the reason, though you weren't over civil,' he responded. 'But we welcome discussion at our table and you're entitled to your views. You didn't seem to have thought them out very clearly. That's all.'

'Well, if it isn't that, what is it?' she demanded.

'You went upstairs to cool down. What did you do besides?' he asked, pausing in his work to look at her. His pale wispy hair stood on end and he had a streak of clay down one cheek. She almost moved to wipe it away, but drew back.

'I washed my face and took in some fresh air through the bathroom window,' she replied. And saw Denis down below.

'You went into another room,' he charged her. 'My bedroom.'

'Oh Jonathan, I didn't! Why do you think I did?' she asked.

'You might have been curious about our arrangements,' he said. 'But now you know we don't share a room.'

'I don't. I didn't – oh!' She had turned quite pale. 'That's very private to you,' she said. 'How could you think so?'

'After you'd gone, twenty pounds were missing from my wallet,' he said. 'No one else went up there. Only you.'

'Oh Jonathan! As if I would!' she wailed. 'How could you think that of me?'

'I found it difficult,' he admitted. 'And I've said nothing to Brian. Nor Frances, naturally. I thought you might have an attack of conscience and take steps to put things right yourself.'

It was Denis. It had to be Denis, hanging about below and coming in either during the evening while they were eating, or later, perhaps while Brian and Jonathan were clearing up. And he could have burgled Frances: he and Biff had come with the hunt saboteurs. He'd told her so.

'But Frances was robbed too, before that,' she said. 'Before I came down. Couldn't it have been the same thief? It wasn't me, Jonathan. How could you think I'd do anything like that?'

'I found it very difficult to believe,' he repeated. Her dismay and shock were evident. 'If I'm wrong, I apologise, Charlotte,' he said, stiffly.

'I'll make it up. I'll give you twenty pounds,' she said. 'I'll have to get it from the bank.'

'Don't be silly. It's not the money – it's the principle,' he said. 'And it seemed the only explanation. The money was there when I got whisky on the way home and missing the next morning.'

'Nothing else went? Not your credit cards or driving licence?'

'No.'

'Only notes went from Frances's purse, too,' she said.

'That doesn't mean the same person took them.'

'No,' she agreed. 'Are you going to tell the police? Frances has.'

'I wasn't, because I blamed you,' he said. 'Now I'm not so sure.' He paused, then continued, 'No, I won't, because they'll enquire about the evening and they'll suspect you, too. It would mean too much trouble.'

'But the real thief will get away with it,' she said. Unless she did something about it: made Denis confess. But he'd have spent the money by this time, and would arresting him do any good? It would involve her, too. She'd tell him what she thought of him, however. If it was him. Fancy coming to Badger's End and being made welcome, fed, taught reading, and taken back to Darsingford after ripping off her grandmother and Jonathan.

'He'll get caught on some other job,' said Jonathan. 'I don't want to drag you into it, Charlotte. I'm sorry, my dear.' He put out a clay-covered hand and, with the back of it, lightly touched her cheek. 'Forgive me. I'm glad we got it sorted out. Like to make a pot or two?'

She couldn't refuse, and while Denis enjoyed the warmth of Badger's End, she stayed to lunch with Jonathan – bread and cheese – and spent the afternoon as his assistant, their amity restored.

25

PHILIP KNEW BETTER than to be convinced that Denis had left for good. He'd taken the money and his book, and the radio he must have liberated from its rightful owner, but had he really departed, moved on? Philip knew nothing about him. Curiosity had seemed out of place, and Philip was too concerned with his own problems to show much interest in Denis's past. In the strange, gipsy life he'd lived lately, the present was what mattered. People had secrets better not disclosed, and food and shelter became the most important items in a drop-out's life.

Philip did not like thinking of himself as a drop-out, but he'd become one, and if he hadn't met Denis, who was generous, his difficulties would have been much greater.

The money which had paid for this room had probably been stolen. Still, that was no affair of

Philip's, now that he had repaid Denis for his share, with interest.

Undisturbed, Philip slept soundly right through the day until it was time to prepare for another working shift.

He might move on. He could simply leave, after tonight.

When he reached the works, he did his rounds, going through the storerooms with their waiting packages, the vats of face cream, the jars and the conveyor belts, where the day workers supervised their filling and their final stacking in protective cartons. Two daytime shifts operated, which was why his hours were not longer; they covered the gap between the shifts, though he clocked on before the last shift left. He already felt quite settled in, even after so short a time, master of his video screens and his quiet empire of idle workrooms and stores. His previous existence – Lavery's, his home – seemed to belong to a different person, one always striving anxiously to please.

Philip thought about the scrap of dried-up dog dirt which he'd sent to Sandra White. That had been a silly, childish gesture, but it would have disgusted her. Anyone would have been nauseated at receiving that in the morning's mail. He'd do no more of that sort of thing. Now feeling rested, he'd given up on vengeance, though that woman was contemptible.

When all was quiet, he washed his clothes. He'd wash himself later on, nearer morning; that wasn't so important now that he could bath at the digs. The bathroom was far from inviting, but he cleaned the tub before he used it.

He was reading, drinking a cup of coffee, when the first rocket went off. He heard a crash as it struck an upstairs window, breaking the glass. Its impetus was halted but it exploded in the store-room above and sparks landed among piles of shredded paper waiting to be packed round pots of face cream in their cartons. Almost at once the smoke alarms sounded but there were no sprinklers in the building. Philip stared at his screens and saw where the trouble was. As he reached for the telephone, another rocket hit the building, then a third burst overhead. Philip heard the noise, like machine-gun fire, as the explosive shattered into stars.

There was no hot line or panic button in his office, though there was talk of having both installed. A major security firm had advised more precautions than were yet in force, and the insur-ance company also wanted them, but they were expensive. These allergen-free products were a new brand, launched recently, not yet breaking even financially. Balanced judgements of expenditure were important. No testing went on here, but demonstrations, like so much that was good or bad, had a knock-on effect and copy-cat protests could easily follow the earlier incident.

Having telephoned for the emergency services, Philip went to the area where the rocket had expired. Tessa could not have picked a better spot to start a conflagration; three or four small fires had already caught light. He snatched up a fire extinguisher from the outside corridor, and, after a short struggle, got it going, deploying it on the flames. As the fire caught hold, he sprayed foam round, moving to face each separate blaze as the last died down under his ministrations.

He was still up there, doing what he could, when the fire brigade arrived. As they wound out their hoses and their ladders, he knocked against a stack of boxes and they toppled over, sending him off balance so that he tripped and fell, and a sudden spurt of flame gushed out towards him.

When she left the house, Charlotte had taken the back door key with her. She put it in her pocket and, on her return, used it to let herself back into Badger's End.

Her grandmother had seen badgers in the garden snuffling round at night, large beasts, their sett in the spinney beyond her boundary, but Charlotte had never been there when they were seeking food so near to humans. She was thinking about that as she walked up the road from the pottery, a more comfortable line of reflection than her talk with Jonathan. Thank goodness they had sorted it out; obviously he and Brian were sensitive about their situation, possibly too quick to take offence, but how could he have thought that she would steal from anyone, much less him? They were friends.

Denis, in the kitchen, never saw her come up the path and did not hear her opening the door. He was listening for the car, the blue Viva which, though he did not realise it, Tessa had so nearly crashed into on that first raid.

Charlotte, in her rubber-soled boots, closed the door quietly and walked through into the hall. She heard a movement from the kitchen and the hairs on the back of her neck seemed to rise up on their own. It wasn't Frances; she would not be back until much later. Charlotte looked around for a weapon, and was on the point of opening the door so that she could run out again and save herself when she saw the umbrella stand in which, along with two umbrellas, was a walking stick. She grabbed it and advanced.

Denis had heard her now, and there was nowhere for him to flee to since she blocked the doorway. His mind worked slowly and he did not reason that the new arrival was one of the two women; he suspected another intruder, like himself, and grabbed the knife with which he'd been cutting bread. Charlotte stepped forward, thinking she could close the kitchen door on the burglar, though he might escape through the window. Very frightened, she advanced to stand on the threshold of the room and saw who was facing her, his back to the fridge, the knife wavering, looking more terrified than she was. It would be him, of course.

'Oh God, Denis! Put that knife down,' she said in a weary tone, walking in. 'What are you doing now?'

'Ah, it's you Jet,' said Denis, much relieved and smiling cheerfully. 'I thought it might be some thief.'

'How did you get in?' she asked, but she knew. If she'd taken the key from the greenhouse instead of the back door key, he could not have entered without breaking in, and even Denis might have had second thoughts about that. 'What have you stolen?' she added, angrily.

'Nothing. I was just having a bite,' said Denis. He picked up the hunk of bread he had hacked off a homemade loaf and laid butter on it, in chunks, because it had just come out of the fridge and was too cold to spread. He'd got the cheese out, too, she saw, and the piece of ham which they'd had hot for supper on Tuesday evening. He hadn't cut that yet.

Charlotte muttered under her breath. She went into the hall to replace the walking stick, then pulled off her coat. She still had on her velvet hat. Returning, she began packing away the food.

'Hey – Jet—' Denis objected. 'I'm just eating. Your gran wouldn't mind me having a snack. I'm starving.'

'Too bad,' said Charlotte. 'I think she'd mind a lot if she knew you'd stolen her pension and ripped off her friend in Darsingford, while we were having dinner there. You did it. Don't deny it.'

'It was only twenty quid,' Denis protested. 'Those poofters are loaded.'

'Those gentlemen—' she emphasised the word – 'might have given you some money if they'd seen you begging in the street. I'm sure they give to worthwhile charities that help people like you. My grandmother certainly does.'

'She shouldn't have left the place open,' Denis said. 'I was just passing. It was easy.'

'What have you taken this time?' Charlotte repeated her question.

'Nothing – only the food,' he said.

'Is that true?' she demanded. 'You haven't been upstairs and pinched her jewellery? She's got her purse with her today.'

'I haven't been upstairs,' he said. Not yet: he'd planned to poke about and see what he could find without trashing the place. He wouldn't do that to Jet's nice old gran, not after she'd fed him the other evening, but he'd not be above nicking a ring or pearls or something. You could sell those.

'Hm.' Charlotte wasn't sure if she could believe him. 'Take off your coat,' she ordered. 'Give it here,' and she held out her hand.

Meekly, he obeyed, and she searched his pockets, finding his wad of money, the small radio, and the Little Bear book.

'There. I told you,' he said, and pulled out the empty side pockets of his jeans.

'This is my grandmother's money,' she said. 'And Jonathan's.'

'What's left of it,' he said, and added, 'I paid for the room what me and Phil had, and our food.' He spoke proudly. 'Course, Phil's got a job now – nightwatchman at some factory near where we went

326

with Tess that night. He paid me back his share.'

Charlotte was wondering what to do. Justice demanded that she took his money and returned it to her grandmother and Jonathan, but that could end in difficult explanations and might lead to revelations about their part in the attack on Dr Frost. Charlotte had no illusions about what their fate would be if this was discovered: both of them would be locked up. She, now, was known to the police, marked down as a demonstrator and disturber of the peace; very likely Denis had a record, and there was Orlando to consider. And Steve.

No. Denis must be allowed to get away with it, this time, and to put miles between himself and Darsingford.

'You've got to go, Denis. Go, and don't come back. Get right away from here. If you were ever connected with what happened at that house that night, you'd go to prison for a long time.'

'Prison'd be OK, in the winter,' Denis said. 'Food and that. Things to do.'

'Don't you believe it,' Charlotte said. 'You get going now, Denis, and don't ever come back to this house or this district. I'll turn you in, next time.' She stood glowering at him. 'Take that bread you've got and go,' she repeated. 'If I don't get this cleared up before my grandmother comes back, I'll have some explaining to do. And where's that key?'

He gave it to her. It was in his hip pocket with two more.

'What are those?' she asked, and then she

recognised them. 'They're the keys to your lodgings, aren't they? Give them here. You're not to go back there and make things difficult for that poor man who was good to you.'

Denis handed them over without a word. Jet was all fired up. What a great little girl she was! He felt like saying so, but this was not the moment for any such sweet talk.

'I'll go,' he said.

'Go the other way,' she ordered. 'You're not to go to Darsingford. If I hear of any other burglaries, I'll drop you right in it.'

She wouldn't, of course, because it could rebound on her, but he might believe her threat.

'Cor – I'm terrified,' he said, laughing at her.

But he left, and she watched him walk down the path and along the road away from the village. Then she set about clearing up after him. He'd eaten so much that she thought she might have to tell her grandmother he'd been here and she'd fed him. What else ought she to reveal?

She'd suggest keeping the spare key in some new hiding place.

26

THE JUDGE AND his wife were discussing Christmas plans. Court had risen in time to let him get down to the country before it grew dark, and he had enjoyed a cup of tea by the fire in the drawing-room.

'Tessa hasn't mentioned anything. Perhaps she'll grace us with her presence,' said Millicent. 'It would be so nice if she'd plan ahead a little.'

'We could,' said the judge. 'We could close up the house and go on a cruise somewhere warm.'

They smiled at one another and Millicent rose to stir up the fire, a real one of logs in a wide hearth where the pile of accumulated ash glowed red.

'There's Clive,' she said. 'What's he going to do, I wonder? He might want to come here with the children, if he's allowed to have them for part of the time.'

'I suppose so,' James sighed. 'We always have to fit in with them, don't we? Shall we ever be permitted to please ourselves? It's what they do, after all.'

'It's what Tessa does,' said Tessa's mother. 'Clive is in a bit of a hole. Obviously if he brings the children here, it's easier at a time like Christmas. Space, and so on.' Clive was at present living in a small flat.

'True,' said the judge.

'Perhaps for the New Year? The cruise, I mean,' said Millicent. 'We could see what's available.'

'Or, at the last minute, flee to Sidmouth,' he said, and they both laughed.

'Flee from our children, you mean. Otherwise why not stay here, where it's warm and we've got our books and some good old films on tape,' said Millicent.

'They'll expect to be fed and housed, if it suits them,' said James. 'And they'll think they're doing us a favour by granting us the blessing of their company.'

'It would be nice to see the grandchildren,' Millicent said. 'They are so sweet.' She doted on them, and so, in his restrained way, did James. Both thought that stable grandparents in the background might reduce the damage of their parents' divorce.

'What will Orlando do? Poor fellow, his family seems to have cast him aside and he's got no future with Tessa. I'm afraid she's playing with him,' said the judge. Like a cat with a mouse, he thought. 'Milly, I'm worried about our Tessa.'

'In a new way?' asked Millicent. They had been

anxious for some time: proud of her successful career but aware that she was growing ever more brittle and dissatisfied.

'Yes – yes, in a new way,' the judge admitted. 'You know all that business with the arson attack in Darsingford, where Jenny works?'

'Yes.'

'Guy Frost, the scientist involved, whose rabbits were shot — ' he hesitated, fearful of putting into words his dread.

'Yes? What about him?'

'He was at Cambridge during Tessa's time there,' James said.

'So were hundreds of other men,' said Millicent. 'What are you trying to say?' Suddenly her whole inside seemed to lurch. 'James, if she knew him, she'd have said so after the raid.'

'Would she?' asked the judge. 'Can you be sure of that?'

She couldn't. Tessa had always been very secretive.

'I looked him up. He was in Scotland for quite a while. He moved to Darsingford two years ago,' he said.

'She was always going up there.' Millicent spoke slowly, then added, 'To Scotland. More than once a month, for years. To see friends, she used to say.'

'You thought it was one particular friend. A man. A lover, probably,' said James.

'I did,' Millicent remembered. 'I might have been wrong. Anyway, there's Orlando now.'

'He's a blind. A smokescreen. He's for show to hide what's really going on,' said James. 'I'm sure of it, Milly.'

'How can you know?' asked Millicent.

'Call it the result of a lifetime spent among the criminal classes,' said the judge. 'I can smell deception.'

'But you have to rely on evidence. And this is your daughter – a lawyer, too.'

'I have no evidence, only my instinct,' said James.

'Well – even if you're right, and she did know this Guy Frost years ago, that's when it was – years ago,' said Millicent.

'Yes.'

'Why is it worrying you, James?' asked Millicent.

'I don't know. That attack – so potentially lethal – there was something about it that didn't fit,' he said. 'Perhaps it was the rabbits. I'm being stupid. Tessa must have forgotten about the man long ago, if she ever knew him.'

'You can't really suspect her of being mixed up in that raid!' Millicent was aghast.

'Other people – even other judges – have problem children, Milly,' James replied sadly. 'What do we really know about her private life?'

'Not a lot,' his wife agreed. 'She doesn't seem to have many friends.' She used people, thought Millicent; she was using Orlando in some way.

'She's thirty-four years old, with a blossoming career, and she's highly intelligent. I'm telling

332

myself she wouldn't risk all that for some foolish gesture,' said James.

But she had come home very late the night of the incident, and had slept in the next day, when she had been in a happy, even elated mood; he had noticed that. He'd checked the dates to confirm that they tallied. As a child, and in her teens, moods of exhilaration had often followed wrongdoing which, when discovered, was bad enough to require punishment. Once she had locked her brother in the disused hayloft, taking away the ladder, and before he could be found, frightened in the darkness, he'd jumped to the ground, breaking his ankle. Tessa could be merciless; had she gone in for the bar, she would have been a powerful advocate. He did not remind his wife of her past misdemeanours.

'Why should she?' Millicent insisted. 'Oh James, I think you're letting your imagination run away with you.'

'Jealousy is a terrible, destructive thing,' he said. 'But no doubt you're right. I'm just anxious about her. We both are. And, as you've said, there is no evidence.' The gun, for instance; Tessa couldn't own one, could she?

Millicent rose and crossed the room to kiss his cheek, slightly bristly now at the end of the day.

'Do parents ever stop worrying about their children, even when they're so old that the children feel obliged to worry about them?' she asked.

'Probably not,' he said. 'Let's have a drink.'

He went on worrying.

* * *

Orlando waited in the van near the park gates, as instructed. He sat there for a few moments wondering what to do next, and, more to the point, what Tessa was doing.

She couldn't be going to attack that man again, and in normal dress, not combat gear. Or could she? He'd got the holdall; what had she kept in her car that he didn't know about? The shotgun?

He got slowly out of the vehicle and locked it, putting the key in his jacket pocket. Then he inhaled some deep breaths of still, damp, wintry night air. It was cold, but a long way off freezing. A car drove by, then another came towards him, but this was a quiet area, not on the way to anywhere. Sighing deeply, squaring his shoulders, he walked slowly towards Guy Frost's house.

On the way over, a fire engine and several police cars, all with lights flashing and sirens wailing, had torn past travelling in the opposite direction, no doubt going to the scene of Tessa's firework effort. What had she hoped to accomplish? And what had she lobbed over the fence as he left?

Tonight was the end. He didn't really know why he was not driving rapidly back to London, except that he couldn't bring himself to desert her, not in action, so to speak. It would be cowardly, but then he didn't think he was a brave person; someone brave would have stood up to her long ago and walked out of her life.

Someone brave wouldn't go around calling him-

334

self Orlando when his name was Roland.

Orlando wasn't sure which was Guy Frost's house, but then he decided it must be the one outside which Tessa's car was parked.

He tried the Golf's door. It was unlocked, and her keys were in the ignition. He took them out. Anyone could steal it, and then where would she be? Putting them in his pocket, with the van keys, he walked up the path towards the house, where bright lights shone out over the driveway.

Where was she? Was she skulking about in the shrubs which bordered the garden? He was now illumined for all to see. If challenged, he'd act the idiot and ask for directions to the rectory. That was a safe enough question anywhere, guaranteed to reduce suspicion. It would create a diversion, too, and give Tessa time for second thoughts.

He walked round to the rear garden, where, according to all the reports, Guy Frost had his workshop. How badly had the shed been damaged? Was it gutted?

It seemed not. He could see it now, quite clearly, lit by a bright security light on the exterior wall. There were lights inside, too.

Orlando advanced, and looked through the window. He saw Tessa there, with her back to him. She was holding her gun, tucked under her right arm, quite casually, but in a position from which she could soon raise it to her shoulder. He could not tell if it was cocked or not. She was talking, but he could not hear her clearly.

Oh God! She'd got the man, and possibly also his family in there! But he could see no one else, not even the scientist.

Orlando moved round, seeking the shed door and trying to think rationally. The children would, by rights, be in bed, of course, but what about their mother? Should he return to the house and, if she was there, get her to phone the police?

There might not be time.

Tessa couldn't intend to shoot this Guy Frost, could she? Why him and not some other scientist? What was this one doing that made him particularly detestable in her view? After the arson attack, the papers had said he was engaged in research into the relief of nervous disorders — not mental breakdown but illnesses which left the victim with impaired or total loss of movement: surely that was a more worthwhile occupation than thwarting such efforts?

If Tessa were to shoot him, that would be plain and unadulterated, violent, pointless murder.

Wavering outside, Orlando could hear the murmur of voices. He was reluctant to leave his vantage point but he must somehow try to stop Tessa, save the man and anyone else who might be in the shed.

He moved round the side of the shed to the door, which was shut. Guy Frost must have been inside, working, when Tessa entered, armed, yet dressed up to the nines. Why so smart when her intent was hostile?

He listened.

* * *

After the fire, the insurance company had insisted on an alarm being installed and Guy was supposed to set it when he was in his workshop, but he wanted Amanda to feel free to enter so he never did this, and although she was away now, he had not locked himself inside.

He did not hear the door open. The first thing he was aware of was a voice behind him saying 'Guy'.

He turned. Though he had not heard her voice for years, and it was only a single syllable, he knew at once who had spoken. There she stood, dressed all in black, her hair a brilliant splash of reddish gold, eyes blazing. At first he did not notice the gun she was holding, barrel pointing down, but cocked.

'Christ, Tessa! What on earth are you doing here?' he gasped.

'I've come to see you, of course,' said Tessa. 'So that milksop's left you. I've been waiting for you to get tired of her.'

'Oh God!' He was standing now, and he rubbed a hand across his forehead. 'Amanda hasn't left me. She's taken the children to stay with her parents. We had some trouble here,' he said.

'I know you did. Those poor rabbits,' Tessa said. 'What a shame. Were the children very sad?'

'Yes, they were.' But now Guy had seen what she was holding. He stared at her, incredulous. 'What are you doing here, Tessa?' he repeated. 'Why have you come?'

'I told you. I knew she'd go, and then you'd

realise just how foolish you'd been, if you hadn't already,' Tessa said.

'But I love Amanda,' Guy declared. 'Tessa, I love her. We have a happy life.'

'Where's the excitement, though?' she asked, her voice almost a hiss. 'I'll bet it's nothing like what we shared.'

'I don't want excitement, Tessa,' Guy insisted. 'You have to let the past go. It's over. It was over long ago.'

'Not for me,' she said. She took a step nearer him. 'Don't you want to kiss me, Guy?'

He didn't, but he could feel the old attraction, all the same, only this time it was tinged with fear.

'No,' he said. 'Go away, Tessa, and we'll forget this ever happened.'

'Forget what? My visit here today, or our love?'

'Everything,' he said.

She couldn't have been behind the raid. It wasn't possible. Or was it? She was quite ruthless: he knew that. Look at her now, marching about with a shotgun which he felt sure was loaded. She was not one for empty threats. Admitting that she could have been responsible, with sickening certainty he knew she was.

'We can't forget,' she said. 'It's our history.'

She must have been brooding about it all this time. Guy tried to think of a way to placate her, make her accept the truth, then leave.

'If you just go, quietly, I won't tell the police you've been, or that you set fire to the place and shot the rabbits,' he said, trying to speak calmly, concentrating on her, not taking his eyes from her. Would she deny it?

She didn't.

'Or Amanda?' she said, head on one side, almost coy. Tessa was never coy. 'You won't tell her?'

'Nor Amanda.' Most of all, not Amanda.

'And you'll entice her back?'

'She'll come willingly, when she's sure the threats to us have gone,' he said.

'Ah, but they won't have gone, will they, Guy?' she said. 'You'll never know when I might appear again, with flaming torches, or explosives.'

'You'll get caught, if you do,' he warned.

But who would suspect her? A judge's daughter: a successful lawyer. There'd be evidence, of course; that gun, for instance.

'I'm not going to let her have you,' Tessa said. 'If you won't send her packing, then it's the end,' and she slowly raised the gun, pointing it right at him.

'Put it down, Tessa,' Guy said. 'Don't do something you'll regret.'

'I won't regret it,' Tessa said. 'I want you, Guy. You've got one last chance.'

Could he bluff her, somehow? Make some conciliatory remark that would calm her down so that he could take the gun away from her? Should he suggest they go into the house?

No. He wasn't going to let Tessa invade Amanda's territory.

'Give me the gun, Tessa,' he said, and then he saw the door behind her open.

For an instant Guy's eyes left her, and Tessa noticed. Turning round, she saw Orlando in the doorway, raised the gun and, as she fired at him, Guy punched her hard in the back so that she stumbled. The sound of the shot was deafening, but both men moved towards her and Guy wrested the gun from her grasp. He pointed it at her. These things had two cartridges in them, didn't they?

Tessa had banged her elbow as she fell. She'd got those high-heeled shoes on, Orlando irrelevantly observed as he held his own arm, which felt as though it was on fire.

'Orlando!' she screamed his name. 'I told you to wait at the park,' she stormed. The pain in her elbow was, briefly, excruciating.

'Tessa, come away,' Orlando said. 'Let me take you out of here before someone gets hurt.' But he was already hurt. She'd shot him, not Guy; but of course the gun had gone off by accident.

'Have you been helping her?' Guy asked him, his voice deep, suspicious.

'Not to attack you, no,' said Orlando. 'I'm another victim, in a way. Come on, Tessa. Let me take you home.'

But could he, with his wounded arm? Was it a serious injury? He touched the painful area below his shoulder and his hand came away covered with blood.

For a moment Tessa looked appalled; Guy saw

the brief horrified expression on her face. Then, in a flash, it had gone. She'd fired on reflex, not with intent to hurt this man.

'Bloody fool, getting in the way,' she said.

'You'll go, Tessa,' said Guy. 'Let him take you, as he said.' But the man was hurt. Guy was a biochemist, not a doctor of medicine; nevertheless, he could not let a wounded man leave untreated. 'We'll have to fix your arm first,' he said, despairingly.

'It's all right. It's only a scratch,' said Orlando, who was sure he had received a serious injury.

Both men were intent on watching Tessa. She had retreated against the window, still rubbing her elbow, but it hurt less now. Hearing them discuss her fate was unendurable; she had to be the one in charge, but she'd lost her weapon. She'd retreat, but only to rethink her strategy.

'I'll drive myself,' she said. 'Let me pass.'

They did, Guy still holding the gun. She stalked past them, out into the darkness, and then Orlando remembered her car keys.

'I've got her keys. She'd left them in the car. I took them for some reason – thieves – anything,' he said.

'Let me have them,' said Guy. 'I'll give them to her. When she's gone I'll have a look at that arm.'

'All right,' said Orlando, who unlike a hero in a film did not feel up to running down the drive and throwing punches. He foraged in his pocket for the keys, handing them over without protest.

Guy put the gun down and went out of the studio, running after Tessa, who had reached her car and was sitting in the driver's seat thumping the steering wheel in frustrated rage. Guy opened the door.

'Tessa. Your keys,' he said, and she looked up, face blotched, mascara running down her cheeks, for once, but only briefly, broken. He dropped them in her lap, closed the door on her and turned away. As he hurried back to his workshop, he heard the car start up.

Orlando was sitting down, still looking dazed.

'She seems to have gone,' said Guy, who had found the sight of Tessa weeping quite unnerving. 'Come on – let's go into the house and see about you.'

While Guy was gone, Orlando had unloaded the gun. Other cartridges and weaponry were in the van. Would Tessa go to it and make a firebomb? She was quite capable of it. Well, he was past protecting her now. He allowed himself to be led into the house, where Guy helped him take off his jacket and inspected his injury. It was a flesh wound in his upper arm. Guy could see some shot there, and very gently, with small tweezers, he extracted several pieces. It was agony.

'You ought to go to hospital, of course,' he said.

'There'd be questions,' said Orlando.

Guy had poured him a large brandy, as an anaesthetic.

'Yes,' he agreed. 'Most of it missed you, I'd say,'

he added. Orlando's skin was badly burnt. 'A proper doctor ought to see it.'

'What are you going to do?' Orlando asked, ignoring his advice. 'Are you going to call the police?' She hadn't really meant to shoot him. Of course not. Why, this chap, Guy, was her real target.

'I don't think so. Not now,' said Guy. 'What do you think she'll do?'

Various possibilities ran through the minds of both men.

'I don't know,' said Orlando. 'It's the end for her, anyway.'

'She's done other things, hasn't she?' said Guy, dabbing away. 'You don't need stitches,' he went on. 'It's mostly scorching from the blast. But I'm not a medic. If it throbs, looks angry, if you get a temperature, you must see a doctor. You ought to anyway,' he repeated. 'Maybe you've got one who's a chum, or who you can string a line to.'

'I'll manage,' said Orlando. 'It was all a lie,' he added. 'All her concern for animals. She was after you all the time. You had an affair, didn't you?'

'Years ago,' said Guy. 'I've been married six years.'

'I don't understand it,' said Orlando, but in a way he did: he'd been obsessed with Tessa, as she was obsessed with Guy, but he had never wished to harm her, and didn't now.

'Where do you live?' asked Guy.

'In London,' said Orlando.

'I could put you on a train,' Guy said doubtfully.

'There's the van. I must deal with that,' said Orlando. 'Usually we leave Tessa's car and go on in the van. Tonight she brought her car. I suppose she thought she was going to make a night of it with you.' He'd have to get rid of all the stuff that was in the van: dump it somewhere. 'What about the gun?' he asked.

'I'll keep it for a bit. Just till we see what happens. It's evidence,' said Guy. She might accuse this poor chap of something, if she were caught.

'All right,' said Orlando, glad to share responsibility. 'I guess you haven't got a licence, though,' he said, and both men laughed.

'I'll be careful,' promised Guy.

'Don't let your wife see it,' said Orlando.

'I won't,' said Guy, who was worrying about Orlando driving, after the stiff brandy he had had, never mind his arm. 'What about a sandwich? Have you had anything to eat tonight?'

He hadn't.

Orlando felt much better after several ham sandwiches and some strong black coffee.

'I'm through with her too,' he said. 'I'd decided that, regardless. Tonight was the last time. I'd made up my mind.'

'Sensible,' said Guy. 'Takes a bit of doing, though.'

'Yes.' The two men, united by their curious link as Tessa's lovers, exchanged wry looks.

'She was quite a girl,' acknowledged Guy. 'Now,

344

come along. I'll walk you to your transport.'

Together, and in silence, they walked along the road to the park gates, where the van still stood.

'Will you be able to manage the gears?' asked Guy anxiously, as Orlando climbed in. His left arm was the injured one.

'Yes. It'll be all right.' Guy had dressed it very thoroughly. 'Thanks,' said Orlando. 'You could have turned me in,' he added.

'I don't know who you are, do I?' Guy replied. 'Good luck,' and he waited while Orlando started up the van and drove off.

Guy half expected Tessa to have returned when he went back to the house, but there was no sign of her.

27

LEAVING IN THE van, Orlando avoided the area near the factory which Tessa had selected for attack. He didn't think the rockets could have done serious damage; the fire brigade's response was probably automatic, resulting from some wired-in alarm. Maybe there were broken windows; the rockets had travelled fast, and the one that went up into the sky had been spectacular.

She'd planned it; it was her scheme, but he had been there and had helped her. He, in law, was also culpable. But they wouldn't be caught. They'd been quick. Even so, someone might have seen the stationary van, and her car. What would happen now?

What would Guy do? Would he eventually report Tessa? If he did, it would rake up the past, expose both Guy and Tessa to intense public scrutiny. The tabloid press would love such a story. It could kill Guy's marriage.

Orlando, driving steadily back to London, kept thinking of these possibilities and wondering what to do. He'd got all Tessa's gear except the gun. How should he dispose of it? He must stop drifting, must construct a plan.

His arm was hurting, but not badly; Guy had done a good job, telling him to take pain killers when he reached home, but not while he was driving: not on top of the brandy. The miles went by: no need, tonight, to call in at the service station as was their normal practice after such a trip. He wondered where Tessa was: she could be almost back in London by this time; he had spent at least an hour with Guy, being bandaged and revealing what Tessa had done on earlier raids. He'd said nothing about the attack on the cosmetic packing works earlier that night. The fewer people who knew about that, the better and the safer, though Guy would soon hear about it and realise they had been responsible.

He was feeling very tired. It would be wise to stop, but if he did, he'd never get going again. He opened the van window and let cool air blow in on him. That helped to wake him up. Traffic, on the motorway, was intermittent. It was late now and there wasn't a great deal; there were very few lorries. It was Friday, he remembered; usually the lawless trips took place on Saturdays and afterwards she always wanted sex. He knew that now, and if she didn't turn to him, then she found someone else.

Who would it be tonight?

He tried to think of other things: of Jet, so innocent and sweet, but soon his mind returned to Tessa. What she felt for Guy was not love: love did not seek to destroy its object. Perhaps, in truth, she hated him.

He did not want to destroy Tessa, and nor, he knew, did Guy, but how could she be protected, from herself, if not from justice?

Orlando was still meditating in this fashion when he arrived at the garage from which he had rented the van. He drove past, to the street where he had left his BMW. Even with his injured arm, it took him less than a minute to transfer the holdall, the pipe and the rocket wrappings from the van to the boot of his car. He glanced quickly round the van's interior: there was nothing else, no other trace of where they had been and what they had carried.

He'd forgotten his gloves. Where had he left them? He'd replaced them after lighting the rocket and had been wearing them when he followed Tessa to Guy Frost's house. He must have taken them off after he'd been hurt. They could incriminate him.

It was too late to think of that now.

Guy, however, had taken care of them. He had burnt them and dispersed the ashes in the garden.

Orlando left the van on the hard standing at the garage and, as arranged, put the keys through the door. Then he got into his car and started up the engine. He turned west, his mind already made up before he heard the radio news.

A man employed as a security guard had died in

a fire believed to have been started by animal rights activists at a cosmetic packing firm in Darsingford.

Orlando had to stop on this journey. He pulled up at the first service area he came to, used the washroom, splashing cold water on his face, and had a cup of coffee.

A man had died: an innocent man had perished after Tessa's rockets had started a fire, all because of her unforgiving bitterness towards Guy Frost.

And he, Orlando, had wasted two years of his life hanging around Tessa, fitting in with her moods and whims, and aiding and abetting her criminal activities.

It was nearly four o'clock in the morning when he turned in at the gate of Tessa's parents' house and parked on the gravel sweep opposite the front door. Lights came on as he walked towards it and pressed the bell. Would they hear it? Were they sound sleepers? Must he blow the horn of his car to arouse them? Orlando heard the bell shrilling inside the house as he kept his finger on the button. There was a big, heavy old iron knocker on the door; he banged that, too, and eventually a head poked out of an upstairs window and an irate voice called out, 'All right – all right. I'm coming. Who is that down there?'

'It's Orlando,' James Graham heard.

From the noise, he had been expecting to learn it was the police. James called to his wife as he started down the stairs, and she hurried to follow him, pulling on a dressing-gown as she went.

'What's happened? Has there been an accident?' asked James, opening the door and drawing Orlando into the house. He saw that the younger man was swaying as he stood, almost passing out. 'Where's Tessa?'

'I don't know. I thought she might be here,' said Orlando. 'She's all right – sort of. She was, anyway.'

'You'd better explain,' said James grimly, leading the way towards his study, just like a headmaster, thought Orlando inconsequentially, almost laughing at the notion. He felt a huge sense of relief at being swept along by other people, taken in charge for the second time that dreadful night.

'It's murder – it's murder,' he said, as James gestured to him to sit down.

'What's murder? For God's sake, Orlando, tell us what's happened,' Millicent implored.

So Orlando related the whole story. He described all their raids, mentioning the four other people who had been involved in the earlier exploits. At one point, Millicent went off to make some tea. Orlando was, she saw, severely shocked: tea would be better and more thirst-quenching than coffee. By now she had seen the bandage on his arm and knew that he had been hurt in a tussle over a gun.

James clarified some points in the story while they waited for Millicent's return. Neither had for an instant questioned the truth of his account, Orlando realised; neither had protested that their daughter could not have done such things.

While they were drinking their tea, the judge said, 'You say there is some evidence in your car. A bag of equipment.'

'Yes. And some wrappings and a tube.'

'I think it would be wise to bring that in,' said James Graham. 'And to put your car away, out of sight. May I have the keys?'

'They're in it,' said Orlando.

'I won't be long,' said James, and he went outside, still in his dressing-gown. He took everything out of the boot of the BMW and carried it into the house, then started up the car and drove it into the spare garage which Tessa often used.

While he was gone, Orlando said, 'He thinks she'll come here. That's why he wants to hide my car.'

'Yes,' agreed Millicent. 'Where else could she go?'

Orlando didn't know.

'I've shopped her,' he said sadly.

And yourself, thought Millicent.

'You had no choice,' she said. 'She must be stopped.'

When James returned, he told them he was going upstairs to put some clothes on.

'I'll hear the rest of what you have to say when I'm dressed,' he said.

He was using the time for thought as well, Millicent knew.

'How is your arm?' she asked. 'You ought to see a doctor.'

'It can wait,' Orlando said.

She had poured him out another cup of tea and he drank it gratefully.

'It was brave of you to come here,' she said.

'I'd decided before I heard the radio news,' Orlando replied. 'I was already on my way.'

'Well done,' she said, and wondered if this would earn him some clemency when, eventually, there was a trial, as there must be.

'Where's the gun?' asked James, when he returned, wearing a thick sweater and a pair of corduroy trousers.

'Guy said he'd get rid of it,' Orlando answered. 'I don't think he wants her charged.'

'But he didn't know about the security guard, when he said that,' said Tessa's father.

'I suppose there couldn't have been another incident. Perhaps that guard was at some different factory,' said Millicent.

'Unlikely. They reported it because of the previous attack in the same town,' said James.

They had listened to the news on the hour and heard the same short announcement that Orlando had described. He went on with his story, covering everything he could remember, even his and Jet's adventure the previous weekend.

'It would be a pity to drag those others into this,' he said.

'I agree,' said James. 'It may not be necessary. No one was hurt until today.'

'Except the rabbits,' said Orlando. 'It seems silly,

but it was such a pointless, awful thing to do. And the whole argument was about saving animals, yet she shot those pets.'

'She did it to hurt Guy,' said Millicent. She felt rather sick.

'This is awful for you,' said Orlando. 'This is your daughter we're talking about.'

'She can be very cruel,' said her father. Apart from persecuting her brother, there had been bad moments in her childhood: in one instance, she'd bullied another girl, physically tormenting her, setting the end of her plait on fire. Fire, even then, he thought. 'She wanted her own way all the time,' he added. And she got it, usually.

Eventually the tale was over. Orlando had revealed everything he knew.

'You must go to bed,' said Millicent. 'You've had no sleep. And you're in no state to go home,' she added.

'I won't run away,' he said.

But Tessa might. Would she? All of them were wondering that as Millicent took Orlando upstairs, found him a pair of her husband's pyjamas, and turned down the spare room bed.

'I'll go and fill you a hot bottle,' she said. 'Would you like a bath?'

He would, but he was much too tired. He said so.

He managed to undress while she was gone. His arm hurt, and he remembered about the pain killers which Guy had advised him to take. Millicent had thought of those, however, and she brought him some paracetamol with the hot water bottle.

'They're cosier than an electric blanket, I always think,' she said, putting it into his bed. Then she tucked him in. 'I'm so sorry, Orlando,' she added. 'You've been very badly wounded, and I'm not talking about your arm.'

'It was my own fault,' he answered. 'I walked into the line of fire. Each time.'

Downstairs, Millicent found her husband busy at his desk. He was writing down everything that Orlando had told him, while it was still fresh in his memory.

'What will happen to Orlando?' she asked.

'I don't know. We'll have to see,' said James. 'A great deal will depend on Tessa.'

'That poor man. The guard. I suppose he had a family,' she said. 'I wonder who he was.'

While she had been busy with Orlando, the judge had telephoned the chief constable, whom he knew well, saying he had heard about the incident at Darsingford. Was it true? Had the victim been identified?

A call came back some time later to say that an arson attack had involved a death, but the victim's identity had not been confirmed. He had been knocked over by falling boxes and was badly burnt.

'Tessa might get away with manslaughter,' said James. 'With a clever lawyer and some luck.'

'While of unsound mind,' said her mother. 'She must be mad, James.' It was a plea.

'What is madness?' he said. 'Was Hamlet mad?'

'Ophelia was,' said Millicent. 'Blighted in love, and so insane.' Like poor, unhappy Tessa.

'I'm going to ring Edward back,' said James. 'I just wanted to talk it over first with you, my dear. I think we must tell him what we know and let him take what steps he thinks appropriate. We'll try to leave the others out of it and do what we can to minimise Orlando's part in the whole sorry business. I'm afraid he loved not wisely, but too well.'

'It's tragic.'

'Yes. He's shown he has courage, coming here like this. He could have fled, kept quiet, tried to save himself.'

'I suppose so.'

'Self-preservation is a strong impulse,' said the judge.

'Do you think that's what's driving Tessa now?'

'We'll find out,' James replied. 'I think she'll turn up here and behave as if nothing's happened. She won't believe that Orlando, at the last, could grass her up, as the criminal fraternity would describe it.'

'What about Guy?'

'He let her go. She knows that. It shows she still has some power over him.'

'We'd better keep Orlando here,' said Millicent. 'It'll stop him doing something else heroic, like walking in to a police station.'

'Yes. We'll wait a while, and give Tessa time to calm down,' said James. 'The police can easily be brought to her. She may find Edward here, waiting for her, when she arrives.'

'That will flatter her,' said Millicent. 'To be arrested by the chief constable.' They looked at one another sadly.

'She may not know about the dead man. Not yet,' said James. 'She'll have had Wagner playing in the car, and when she reached the flat, if that's where she's gone.'

'We could telephone.'

James shook his head.

'Let's leave her for the moment. She won't do anything else just yet. Guy was her target, and he has the gun.'

'Without a licence.'

'Yes. Without a cartridge, though. Orlando unloaded it and put the second one in his pocket. I daresay there are others in the holdall,' said the judge. 'Maybe in Tessa's pockets, too.' He put his arms out and drew his wife towards him. 'Have courage, my dear. We're going to need it.'

Neither, even for an instant, contemplated trying to shield their daughter from the law.

It would mean the end of James's career. Millicent knew it; this wise, liberal judge would have to retire because the media would tear them all apart.

'I'm going up to shave, and put a tie on,' said James. 'Shall you get dressed, too?'

'Yes – oh yes. I must. One can deal with things better if one's properly clothed,' she said. 'We mustn't wake Orlando, though.'

They were having breakfast in the kitchen when she came. They heard the car: both were listening for it, and were waiting in the hall when she opened the front door.

She was wearing trousers and a reefer jacket. Her eyes were bright, her face beautifully made up.

'I've come to leave my car,' she said. 'I'm going skiing until after the new year. Piers is right behind me. We're taking his car.'

As she spoke, a young man entered the house. He was tall and fair, a younger version of Orlando, someone she had picked up in a club a few weeks before and met occasionally since then.

'Hullo, sir. Hullo,' the young man said, nodding in the direction of the elder pair. 'I've moved the bags into my car,' he added.

'Take them out again,' said James. 'And go away. Get going, if you don't want to end up in court.' He moved between Tessa and the front door. 'Go on, young man,' he said.

'For God's sake. His name's Piers, I told you,' Tessa said, 'Don't listen to him, Piers.'

Inevitably, he would have a name like that, thought James.

'The police will be coming here, Tessa. I'm sure you don't want to be embarrassed in front of – er – Piers, nor to involve him in your problems,' he said.

'What problems?' asked Tessa in an airy tone. 'I was with Piers throughout last night. Wasn't I, Piers?' She turned to her bewildered companion.

'Who has mentioned anything about last night?' said her father. 'But what you've just said is a lie.' He looked at Piers. 'Leave while you are free to do so,' he directed. 'If you swear to something you know to be untrue, you will commit perjury, a very serious offence, and this could be a matter of murder.'

'Murder?' Piers blenched.

'Perhaps my daughter has failed to tell you that I am a judge. Perhaps she has told you a false story about her recent nocturnal activities,' said James. 'I suggest you choose to believe me when I tell you that because of her, a man has died. I suggest you take my advice and go. No one need know that you were here at all.'

With a last desperate look at Tessa, Piers went.

Tessa made to follow, but her father stood in front of her, a burly man, with authority.

'You're going nowhere, Tessa,' he said, and now his voice was sad.

'Orlando hasn't died?' she asked, and added, defensively, 'He was all right. Anyway, it was his own fault.'

'Would you care if he was dead?' James spoke wearily. 'You went to Guy Frost's house with a gun. You went with intent.'

'I wouldn't have shot Guy,' said Tessa.

'Why was your gun loaded, then?'

She shrugged. The fire in her was dying down.

'You said someone was dead.'

'An unknown man. A security guard at the

factory you chose to attack first,' her father said.

'I didn't know there was a guard,' she answered, not denying, otherwise, his accusation. 'How do you know about this?' she demanded. 'I suppose Guy called the police. The shit.'

'There was a guard,' said James. He did not answer her last question.

'No one will know who did it. They'll think it was someone else. Someone with a record,' Tessa said.

'Why should they do that?'

'They might find something at the scene with prints on,' Tessa said, and now a smirk spread across her face. 'I thought of everything.'

'You didn't, Tessa,' said the judge, understanding that she'd planted something to incriminate another person: not Orlando, for he could not have a record, but one of the youngsters she'd taken on the earlier excursions. She'd needed them to form an admiring audience of courtiers, but also as diversions in case she was suspected. 'You forgot about honesty.'

'You've got to let me go, Dad,' said Tessa. 'I'll go away, keep my head down till it's sorted.'

'I will not,' said the judge. 'I will see justice done. I'm going now to telephone the police. They are expecting me to call,' he added. 'Go into the kitchen with your mother. You'd like some coffee, wouldn't you?'

He glanced across at Millicent, who, very pale, gestured to Tessa to precede her. Would she do so?

Both of them waited. Tessa might decide on flight and physically it would be difficult to restrain her. However, the fight had gone out of her, though she still maintained an air of defiance, walking, head held high, out of her father's presence. She allowed her mother to put a cup of coffee before her, and as she sipped it, Millicent wanted to take her in her arms and hug her, but when she moved towards her, Tessa rounded on her.

'Keep away,' she snapped. 'I'm your daughter. How could you do this to me?'

'We have to do what's best for you,' Millicent said. 'You're ill, my dear.'

Tessa did not answer. She sat there with a mulish look on her face until her father entered the room. He poured himself a cup of coffee and sat down to wait for the police.

'How did you know?' she asked again, her voice flat.

'Your car was seen near the factory,' her father said. It was not a lie. Orlando, for one, had seen it there. 'That's why you brought it here, isn't it? To hide it, while you ran away.'

If anyone had noticed it near the scene – and they could have done – it would have been traced to her, in London.

She did not contradict him. She started on her silence then, admitting nothing when the police arrived.

A bag containing lighter fuel, rags, and wrappings which later proved to have been in contact with fireworks, and some cans of spray paint, was found in her car. Oddly, the handle showed no prints: the judge had wiped it very thoroughly, when, after telephoning the police, he put it in the Golf.

He had also wiped a length of piping lying there: the forensic laboratory could find no prints on it, though it bore traces of explosive and they deduced it was used to fire the rockets. James had removed Tessa's waxed jacket. There were spare cartridges in its pocket, and if he had simply taken those away, they would have left traces. Much later, when the car had been taken away, like Guy, he had a bonfire. There was no evidence to connect Tessa with a firearm.

28

CHARLOTTE TOLD HER grandmother that Denis was the thief.

'I came back and found him here,' she said. 'He'd let himself in with the spare key.' She related the whole story, even confessing to her arrest.

'I've been so stupid,' she said.

'Not at all,' said Frances. 'You were right to be concerned about the animals.' She looked at Charlotte, young and passionate, at the beginning of her adult life. 'It's right to feel deeply,' she said. 'It's right to have the courage of your convictions. But it's also right and brave to admit that you may have been mistaken.'

She was concerned about this mysterious Tessa, whose true identity Charlotte did not know. The woman sounded dangerous and fanatical, but as far as Charlotte was concerned, their link was over. Charlotte would not go with her again.

'Concentrate on your degree,' she advised. 'Forget

all this. Tessa will probably do something else that's extreme and be arrested.'

'You don't think I should tell the police about her?'

'Not really.' Frances was thinking of Charlotte, who would be arrested too, if she informed on their leader. 'There are the others to consider.'

'I know,' Charlotte agreed.

She'd decided to go back to London in the morning, not staying for any proposed visit to Guy Frost's laboratory. It might be very interesting, but it could wait.

Poor Denis, Frances was thinking; he wasn't really wicked, just an opportunist thief who would probably be caught one day and locked up. She was content to let him keep what he had stolen from her.

'Put it down to experience,' she said. 'And be less gullible another time. Where do you think Denis has gone?'

'Back to where he came from. Some squat in London, I suppose,' Charlotte said.

But she was wrong.

Denis, leaving Chingbury, was annoyed with Jet. Why had he let her take his keys like that? Now he'd have trouble getting into the room tonight.

But he didn't want to hang about round here. He didn't want to be with Phil so much, getting told to wash and all that boring stuff, though the old geezer had been decent in his way. He'd planned to move on, and so he would. Soon, though, it would be getting dark. He didn't fancy another night in a wood, not with all those animals squeaking near him. He thought about going to demand the keys back from Jet, but if he did, she'd threatened to drop him in it over the money. Better not to risk it, he decided, walking on. If he hurried, he could get back to the room before Phil set off for work; he could be let in, sleep soft and comfortable once more, then leave in the morning.

Reaching the main road, he turned away from London, heading, contrary to Jet's instructions, towards Darsingford, hoping for a lift. Several cars had passed him, with no one slowing down, when a battered van drew up.

'Where you going, then?' a voice asked him.

A girl looked out of the passenger's window. She had long hair and wore a stud in her nose.

'Dunno,' Denis answered. 'Anywhere,' he added, grinning. 'Wherever you are.' After all, why not?

'We're going to save the trees,' the girl told him.

'What trees?' Denis asked, as the man driving leaned past the girl to take a look at him.

'The trees they're chopping down to make space for a road,' said the girl. 'We want to save them. There's crowds of people there already. More are on their way. You could come along.'

'Yeah,' said Denis. 'Good idea.' He liked trees. He'd be keen to save some.

'Get in the back, then,' said the girl, and Denis went to the rear of the van. Another girl was there already. She made room for him. Climbing in beside her, Denis felt a warm, familiar thrill. It was like being with Tessa and Orlando on their trips, but this time they were saving trees.

'It's in the country, then?' he asked. 'Where we're going?'

'Sure – course it is,' said the second girl. 'They just mean to chop them down to make their road. Spoiling the environment.'

Denis settled down to listen while she explained their reasons for protesting. They'd build houses in the trees, she said, so that no one could start sawing. Everything was organised; plenty of others were at the scene but the more there were, the better it would be. It was all about people power, and once they were there, in their tents and tree houses, or sleeping in their vehicles, the social would arrange their money, for they would have an address.

Denis had found a new family. He was happy, soon forgetting all about his former loose attachments.

He was far away when Philip died that night.

At the cosmetic packing factory, remnants of the rockets fired were found. Also discovered at the scene were two cans of spray paint. They were tested for prints but those on them were blurred: so much for Tessa's plans to protect herself by incriminating her former team. The tins had spent too long being tossed around in the holdall with her combat gear and other devices. House to house enquiries in the neighbourhood of the factory were undertaken in the hope — faint, because the area was mostly industrial — that someone would have noticed a parked vehicle or some other suspicious sign.

A police officer went round to Guy Frost's to make sure that he had not been subjected to another attack, since there had been an earlier one on the night his workshop was fired.

'No,' he responded. 'It's been quiet here. Nothing to report.'

When the officer had gone, Guy faced the truth, for Orlando had told him only part of it. As on the first occasion, there had been a diversionary attack before the real one, and this time a man had been found dead in the wreckage of the factory. Orlando would not have known that, however. Guy felt that as a good citizen he should have put the police straight on to Tessa, but he couldn't do it to her. And he couldn't drop the unfortunate Orlando in it, either. The police might trace her on their own. This time Tessa had surpassed herself. She should be apprehended, charged and punished, and prevented from committing further crimes. Was all this really because of him and his rejection of her? Surely there was more to it than that, some innate imbalance in her make-up? Guy did not want to feel responsible for pushing her over the edge, and he did not intend to bring about her downfall. She would do it for herself, or Orlando would act the role of nemesis.

Guy slept badly that night; memories of Tessa rose up in his mind and he felt guilt. He should have ended their relationship long before he did, but until he had the impetus of his deep feelings for Amanda, it was easier to let things drift. In the morning, he locked up carefully before setting off for work, and on the way he made a detour to an isolated spot beside the river. There, he threw the shotgun out into the water, as far from where he stood as possible.

He'd go and see Amanda and the children in the evening. Maybe by then there would be some news about the dead man and the hunt for who had caused his death. It wasn't murder; it was, at worst, manslaughter, because it must have been an accident that he was in the way.

Philip's personal papers were in the office where he had sat before his surveillance screens. His wallet was there, with his credit cards inside, and a cheque book. There was his driver's licence, too.

It took a little time to work out that he was the same Philip Winter who had disappeared. The factory management had not followed up his references because his employment would have been short term, as a regular security firm was soon to be engaged.

'So he'd have been for the chop,' said the investigating officer.

'Oh yes. Probably after next week,' was the answer. 'His hours were excessive but he wanted the job.'

Philip's possessions were all with him, in his

plastic bag. The address he had given soon proved to be the public library; he had never told his employers that it had changed. By the middle of the following morning his identity as Philip Winter, the missing alleged rapist, was determined, though official identification had yet to be established. His wife or some other relative or close associate would have to be brought down to view the body and confirm the findings.

Lesley had to do it.

She could not believe it. What had he been up to, sending poison-pen letters to that woman, and working as a watchman? Where had he been living?

It had better be got over and done with quickly, she decided. She'd soon lose her job if the police kept calling on her at work. She made a call to a friend, asking her to take care of Jackie after school, and left with the police officer who had come to see her, a detective from the force dealing with the case.

They drove in silence, Lesley sitting in the back of the comfortable car, unable to believe what was happening, but when she saw the body, she knew that the dead man was her husband, in spite of the beard he had grown. The fact that it was so grey was what made her cry, but the police officers decided it was grief.

And so it was, but not the sorrow of bereavement.

29

PHILIP WINTER'S FUNERAL took place a fortnight later, after an inquest had been opened
and adjourned. Lesley, all in black, with a wide-
brimmed hat, looked pale and tense; Jackie wept
throughout. Andrew stood expressionless beside his
mother. There was a scattering of mourners: a few
from Lavery's who had taken a day's leave, and some
neighbours. His frail parents stayed away, still
numb and bewildered by the events leading up to
his death, let alone the death itself, and unable to
face this further ordeal.

An unknown man was in the congregation at the
crematorium, a pale, thin man who looked
extremely sad: Orlando, Philip's avenger, who had
never met the dead man but had indirectly contributed to his death. He thought of speaking to the
widow afterwards, but decided not to.

Another man who was neither friend nor relative
was also there. Lesley recognised him as he stood

apart when she and the children were about to leave
in the undertaker's large black limousine. It was
Detective Sergeant Sykes. They stared at one
another, neither speaking.

Two nights previously, he had called on Lesley.

He'd offered his condolences, asking her to spare
him a few minutes, and she had been obliged to let
him in.

'I've got something I want you to listen to,' he
said. 'A tape recording.'

'What about?' she said, and then, 'It's all right,
Andrew and Jackie are at the cinema. It's to take
Jackie's mind off things, though it won't work.'

'It may, for a little while,' said Sykes.

He followed her into the comfortable sitting-
room, where a fire burned. The chairs and sofa were
deep and soft; the room was warm; and that poor
bugger had been living rough and in a cheap
boarding-house for the last weeks of his life, the
victim of a spiteful liar.

Sykes produced a small tape recorder and set it on
the coffee table. Then he spoke.

'The very day that Philip Winter died, that final
Friday, much about the time he went on duty at the
factory, I called on Mrs Sandra White,' he said. 'As
I'd told you, we knew he was alive because his
fingerprints were found on some anonymous communications that she had recently received.'

They hadn't been on all of them: only the last
two mailings, the letter saying 'YOU LIED' and the
offering of dog dirt; other prints were on the rest,

370

and that was baffling, yet who else could have sent them unless Philip had a friend who arranged to post them and who had not come forward? The junk mail and the pizzas, even the kissogram, had been easy to organise. Philip's movements, before he went to Darsingford had not been fully traced, but the librarian there had recognised him from a photograph and said he had been with a scruffy youth whom he was teaching to read. Sykes did not tell Lesley this; maybe the Darsingford police had done so, if she was curious about his final days. Sometimes people wanted every detail; often, they preferred not to know things that were distressing.

'I taped my interview with her,' he said. 'My visit was unofficial. I was so certain that the verdict was the right one, that Philip Winter was completely innocent. In my opinion, it should never have come to court. It was a waste of time and public money, and it destroyed him. I planned to prove it, and I did, but then he died, and in such a dreadful way. Making it public after that would have added to the media harassment.' There had been a lot of it, when his identity was revealed.

'Well?' Lesley waited, tapping her foot impatiently.

Sykes had rung Sandra's bell that Friday night, and when she opened the door to him, he had smiled, and said this was an informal call.

'Well, come in, then, Sergeant,' she invited, opening the door wide, making him think of a sly spider luring a fly into its web. But this fly had taken steps to protect himself.

She offered him a drink, and he accepted a glass of mineral water. Alcohol was not going to be admitted to this scene; not by him, at least. Sandra had poured herself some white wine. She sat down on the sofa, patting the space beside her, and Sykes took it. The voice-activated tape recorder would work best at close quarters.

He told her that they were still waiting for the results of tests on the offensive package she had received, though this was untrue. They knew that Philip Winter was the sender.

'You said you had no idea who could hold a grudge against you,' Sykes reminded her. 'But you had some unpleasantness with a man called Philip Winter, whom you alleged had tried to rape you.'

'Yes – it was horrible. But he's dead – the man who attacked me,' Sandra said. 'He killed himself. Guilt, you see,' she added.

'His body hasn't been found. He may have simply left home.'

'Why should he do that? He got off,' she said. 'Quite wrongly.'

'Suppose he felt that he was the one who'd been wronged, and went into hiding with the aim of harassing you,' suggested Sykes.

At this, Sandra White belied her name and blushed a deep and ugly red, almost purple. She shook her head.

Sykes pressed his advantage.

'If so, he's moved from annoying pranks to nastiness,' he said. 'Turds now. What next? It could be much worse, even dangerous.'

'Like what?' Sandra could scarcely get the words out.

'Oh – incendiary devices. Letter bombs,' said Sykes.

'Would he do that? He seemed so feeble,' Sandra said. The colour had now faded from her face, replaced by pallor and a sheen of sweat. To Sykes' relief, she moved away from him.

'He lost his job. He was unemployed,' he pointed out. 'His life was ruined.'

'He was acquitted,' Sandra said.

'But he was publicly disgraced. His wife didn't altogether believe in his innocence,' said Sykes.

'It all got a bit out of hand,' Sandra, now alarmed, reluctantly conceded.

'What did? You mean his attempt to have sex with you?'

'No. My complaint against him. I only meant to teach him a lesson.'

'Because he rejected you? Because, as he said on oath in court, you attempted intimacy and he would not cooperate?'

She shrugged. He wanted her to answer, so that her reaction would be recorded on the tape.

'Was that it?' he pressed her.

'Once it went ahead at the police station, I couldn't back down,' she said, defiantly and clearly.

'I should say he'd got a grievance, then,' said

Sykes. 'You seem to be telling me that he was completely blameless.'

'He was insolent,' she said.

'He returned your purse. Did you leave it in Lavery's on purpose?' Would she admit it? If so, he'd got her all sewn up.

'Yes.' Now her tone was that of a sulky child. 'I was unhappy and lonely,' she said. 'I've got no one here to take care of me. I'm so wretched,' and as she began to weep she moved towards Sykes again, but he rose swiftly to his feet.

'You did that to Philip Winter, didn't you? Moved towards him, and when he resisted, you scratched his face,' said Sykes. 'I'm surprised he stops at dog shit.'

'Why you – you— ' Now her face was filled with fury and she flew at him, long nails spread out like talons.

He backed out of range.

'I must warn you, Mrs White, that attacking a police officer is a serious offence,' he said.

She almost gibbered at him, quivering on the spot. Hardened as he was, Sykes found her an alarming sight. No wonder Winter had fled when she made a play for him. She'd got off rather lightly so far, with the kissogram and postal shocks.

'I want you to leave,' she said. 'Now go.'

'You committed perjury,' said Sykes, and spelled it out for her. 'You lied in court.'

'You can't prove it,' Sandra muttered. 'It was my word against his.'

'But the court were not convinced,' he pointed out. 'And now I have the evidence to clear his name and give him grounds for bringing a civil case against you. He'll get colossal damages.' As he spoke, Sykes withdrew the tape recorder from his pocket, praying it had worked. Even if he were to be disciplined for this, it was worth it. 'We'll trace Winter,' he told her. 'We know where he's been, but we may not find him before he carries out some other hoax or trick against you. You'd better think about how to stop him. Like making an official statement,' and he turned to go. 'I'll see myself out,' he said.

But that night, Philip Winter died.

Lesley listened in silence till the tape stopped.

'I don't know what to say,' she said.

'No,' said Sykes. 'I don't suppose you do.' He took the tape out of the machine. 'It's yours,' he said. 'You may care to play it to your children.'

He'd kept a copy, just in case Sandra White tried the same trick in future.

'His death was really an accident,' said Lesley.

'It will probably be recorded as manslaughter,' Sykes replied. 'It wasn't an accident that he was in that factory. It was because he had been disgraced – dishonoured.' That was the word.

'She's the true killer, then. That woman – Sandra White,' said Lesley.

'Is she?' Sykes asked, as he rose to leave. 'I'll see myself out,' he said.

*   *   *

Orlando had been named by no one as an accessory to Tessa's crimes. She invoked her right to silence, however that would be interpreted by the time the case came to court. Martyrdom was now to be her role: she admitted the attacks in Darsingford but revealed nothing about her past relationship with Guy and he, apprehensive, hoped that no one would expose the truth.

Her father had stated that an unknown man had told him Tessa was responsible for the death of Philip Winter.

'It's quite true,' he'd told Orlando. 'You've now said your real name's Roland. Just keep quiet, because if you don't, those others may be dragged down too.'

His arm had almost healed. Guy had done an expert job on what was not a very serious wound. Orlando maintained his belief that the gun had gone off by accident.

He had applied for a post in Singapore and, if he were appointed, would be leaving long before Tessa's trial. Once there, sending Sandra postal presents could be difficult, but he would try. Meanwhile, he'd arrange for more surprises: manure, he thought, a rich and steaming load to be delivered, and coal. He'd devise other teases in the time that remained.

He tried not to think of Tessa, who had been remanded to a psychiatric hospital, but she came to him in dreams, taunting, cruel, beautiful. And mad?

FIND ME A VILLAIN

Margaret Yorke

A chance encounter with a stranger, Priscilla Blunt, seems to offer Nina Crowther an escape from her problems. Middle-aged, struggling to recover from the shock of her husband divorcing her to marry a younger (and pregnant) woman, Nina happily falls in with Priscilla's idea to house-sit for her while she and her husband visit South Africa.

When the phone rings on her first night in the Blunts' Berkshire manor house she expects it to be one of her daughters, but when she lifts the receiver no-one speaks. All Nina hears is a shuddering sigh. As the calls persist Nina fears she has attracted an unwelcome suitor – or is it the man who is brutally murdering women in a nearby village? Or could it be one and the same person?

'*Find Me A Villain* is not simply about who committed a number of murders . . . Miss Yorke has used the detective form to write a sensitive novel about a woman coming to terms with her own life'
LITERARY REVIEW

THE SMOOTH FACE OF EVIL

Margaret Yorke

Alice Armitage is an elderly, and lonely, widow. An unwelcome guest in the large house she helped pay for, she endures the cold, vicious sniping of her son's ambitious wife, who makes it clear she'd rather Alice was conveniently tucked away in an old people's home.

So when the charming and obliging Terry Brett appears on the scene, Alice is happy to believe that she has found herself a new friend who will liven up her solitary existence.
For a while that seems to be the case, but Terry is a conman, and when he joins forces with Alice's scheming neighbour, Sue, their greed takes them further than they'd planned . . .

'A genuine slow-burner running efficiently on greed, lust and desolation'
OBSERVER

'As plausible as it is readable, which is saying a lot'
PUNCH

CRIME IN QUESTION

Margaret Yorke

Denis is living on the edge of society: neglected and unwanted, he scrapes by on his earnings as an odd-jobber. His is the sort of desperation that will tip into lawlessness at the drop of a monkey wrench.

A chance encounter with Len, inmate of the local open prison, enables Denis to prove himself as the accessory to a cunningly contrived crime . . . which ends in murder and has Denis running for his life.

'The author's talent for scratching below the placid surface of people and places to reveal anguish and wickedness is matchless'
THE TIMES

'Nobody does it better'
DAILY TELEGRAPH

ACT OF VIOLENCE

Margaret Yorke

The quiet market town of Mickleburgh knows very little serious crime, and local solicitor Oliver Foxton's days are occupied with wills, conveyancing, and the occasional drunk and disorderly. The outlying villages of Winbury, where he lives with wife Sarah, and Deerton, home of their friends the Stewarts, seem like rural havens.

So when four local schoolboys go on the rampage in Deerton and commit an astonishingly needless act of violence, the lives of the Foxtons and the Stewarts are shattered. Attempting to come to terms with what has happened to his friends, Oliver immerses himself in the renovation of an old doll's house belonging to his friend Prudence Wilmot, a local author, but finds that the doll inhabitants increasingly become a symbol of his own troubled marriage and the tensions the tragedy has sparked within it.

Meanwhile, the schoolboys who merely witnessed the violence come under pressure from their parents and the police to name the guilty party, and they must wrestle with both their misguided loyalty and a fear of reprisals, as gradually the police build their case. And all the time another hidden menace lurks in the background, as a released murderer, living nearby, is enthralled by the crime – and practising as a counsellor, stands poised to offer help . . .

Unblinkingly addressing the issues of today, Margaret Yorke has written a novel of chilling realism and once more proved herself the mistress of suspense.

'The mistress of the skilfully spun suspense novel . . . her quiet, unemphatic style of narrative makes the story a compelling read'
SUNDAY TELEGRAPH

FALSE PRETENCES

Margaret Yorke

When her goddaughter is arrested during an anti-roads protest in the West County, Isabel Vernon is startled to discover that the fair-haired child of her memory has become an overweight, shaven-headed environmentalist and that Isabel herself is now regarded as Emily Frost's next of kin.

Emily, released on bail to the Vernons at their home in the commuter village of Fordswick, meets a middle-aged drifter who encourages her to take up a job as home help to a local family. Emily forms an instant attachment to Rowena, the four-year-old girl in her charge and, missing her campaigning friends, is eager to make a success of her new position.

Emily's unconventional presence in the Vernons' house proves troubling, and is deepening the profound tensions within Isabel's marriage when the arrival of someone else in Fordswick threatens the safety of both Emily and the child, Rowena.

Dissecting the fragile state of ordinary lives with chilling clarity, FALSE PRETENCES reveals Margaret Yorke at her atmospheric, suspenseful best.

'Another contemporary masterpiece from Margaret Yorke'
THE LADY

'Yorke has an extraordinary feel for the passions that lurk beneath unremarkable façades'
SUNDAY TIMES